SO-ARJ-328

A True Story

Select Editions has an interesting history with nonfiction books. At the very beginning, back when we were called Condensed Books, it was not unusual to see the occasional nonfiction title in a volume. After all, we were the child of *Reader's Digest* magazine, with its long tradition of nonfiction selections. We mostly published fiction, but occasionally a true story would fit so well that we just had to use it. In fact, our very first volume, published in 1950, included *The Autobiography of Will Rogers*.

In the 1970s we launched our first nonfiction series, Today's Nonfiction Bestsellers, and followed it up in the '80s with Today's Best Nonfiction. With these series running, we were able to almost completely separate fiction and nonfiction for readers with a taste for only one or the other.

Now, with Select Editions, we are back to one series, and it is almost entirely fiction. But occasionally a nonfiction book comes along that has a great hero and a great story, and we're quite taken by it. **A Street Cat Named Bob** presents just such a hero—a feisty tabby—and just such a story, about redemption through caring for others. So for the first time in a while, we present a true story. We hope you'll like the way it fits in with its fictional partners in the volume. Enjoy!

Jim Menick
Executive Editor

SELECT EDITIONS

U.S. EDITORIAL

Executive Editor: James J. Menick

Senior Editor: Amy M. Reilly

Art Director: George McKeon

Managing Editor: Lorraine Burton

Production Assistant: Bryan Brandom

INTERNATIONAL EDITIONS

Managing Editor: Bonnie Grande

RIGHTS AND PERMISSIONS

Manager: Carol Weiss Staudter

Rights Associate: Arlene Pasciolla

The condensations in this volume have been created by The Reader's Digest Association, Inc., by special arrangement with the publishers, authors, or holders of copyrights.

With the exception of actual personages identified as such, the characters and incidents in the selections in this volume are entirely the products of the authors' imaginations and have no relation to any person or event in real life.

The credits that appear on page 576 are hereby made part of this copyright page.
© 2013 by The Reader's Digest Association, Inc.
Copyright © 2013 by The Reader's Digest Association (Canada) Ltd.

FIRST EDITION: Volume 330

All rights reserved. Unauthorized reproduction, in any manner, is prohibited.
Library of Congress Catalog Card Number: 98-640138
ISSN: 1541-0900
Printed in the United States of America

Reader's Digest is a registered trademark of
The Reader's Digest Association, Inc.

VOLUME 6 2013

SELECT EDITIONS

Selected and Edited by Reader's Digest

THE READER'S DIGEST ASSOCIATION, INC.
NEW YORK, NEW YORK · MONTREAL

Inside

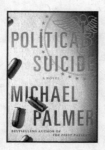

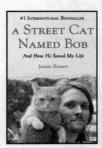

page 294

A STREET CAT NAMED BOB
James Bowen

A ginger tabby and a troubled young man both need a little help. They find that help in one another and form a loving, life-changing bond.

AFTER*WORDS*: *A Q. & A. with James Bowen.*

page 396

FLY AWAY
Kristin Hannah

Many people have suffered since Kate Ryan died four years ago. Can they find a way to heal before it's too late?

AFTER*WORDS*: *Second time around.*

#1 BESTSELLING AUTHOR OF THE GLASS CASTLE
and HALF BROKE HORSES

Jeannette Walls

THE
SILVER STAR

A NOVEL

CHAPTER ONE

MY SISTER saved my life when I was just a baby. Here's what happened. After a fight with her family, Mom decided to leave home in the middle of the night, taking us with her. I was only a few months old, so Mom put me in the infant carrier. She set it on the roof of the car while she stashed things in the trunk; then she settled Liz, who was three, in the backseat. Mom was going through a rough period at the time and had a lot on her mind.

Completely forgetting that she'd left me on the roof, Mom drove off.

Liz started shrieking my name and pointing up. At first Mom didn't understand what Liz was saying; then she realized what she'd done and slammed on the brakes. The carrier slid forward onto the hood, but since I was strapped in, I was all right. In fact, I wasn't even crying. In the years afterward, whenever Mom told the story, which she found hilarious and acted out in dramatic detail, she liked to say thank goodness Liz had her wits about her; otherwise, that carrier would have flown right off and I'd have been a goner.

Liz remembered the whole thing vividly, but she never thought it was funny. She had saved me. That was the kind of sister Liz was. And that was why, the night the whole mess started, I wasn't worried that Mom had been gone for four days. I was more worried about the chicken potpies.

I really hated it when the crust on our chicken potpies got burned, but the timer on the toaster oven was broken, and so that night, I was staring into the oven's glass window because, once those pies began turning brown, you had to watch them the entire time.

Liz was setting the table. Mom was off in Los Angeles at some recording studio auditioning for a role as a backup singer.

Mom had been going into the city a lot ever since we had moved to Lost Lake, a little town in the Colorado Desert of southern California. Usually she was gone for only a night or two, never this long. We didn't know exactly when she'd be back, and since the telephone had been turned off—Mom was arguing with the phone company about some long-distance calls she said she didn't make—she had no way of calling us.

Still, it didn't seem like a big deal. Mom's career had always taken up a sizable chunk of her time. Even when we were younger, she'd have a sitter or a friend watch us while she flew off to someplace like Nashville—so Liz and I were used to being on our own. Liz was in charge, since she was fifteen and I'd just turned twelve.

When Mom was away, all we ate were chicken potpies. I loved them. They were fun to eat. You each got your very own pie in the nifty little tinfoil pie plate. I liked to break up the crust and mush it together with the bits of carrots and peas and the yellow gunk. Liz thought mushing it all together made the crust soggy, and what she found so appealing about chicken potpies was the contrast between the crispy crust and the goopy filling. She preferred to leave the crust intact, cutting dainty wedges with each bite.

Once the pie crusts had turned that wonderful golden brown, I told Liz they were ready. She pulled them out of the toaster oven, and we sat down at the red Formica table. At dinnertime, when Mom was away, we liked to play games Liz made up. One game was called the Lying Game. One person gave two statements—one true, the second a lie—and the other person got to ask five questions about the statements, then had to guess which one was the lie. Liz usually won the Lying Game, but that night I was excited because I had what I thought was an unbelievable stumper: A frog's eyeballs go into its mouth when it's swallowing, or a frog's blood is green.

"That's easy," Liz said. "Green blood is the lie."

"I can't believe you guessed it right away!"

"We dissected frogs in biology."

I was still talking about how bizarre it was that a frog used its eyeballs to swallow, when Mom walked through the door carrying a white box tied with red string. "Key lime pie for my girls!" she announced. Her face was glowing, and she had a giddy smile. "It's a special occasion, because our lives are about to change."

As Mom cut the pie and passed the slices around, she told us that while she'd been at that recording studio, she'd met a man. He was a record producer named Mark Parker, and he'd told her that she had star quality. That night, he took her out to dinner and they talked about how to jump-start her career. "He's so smart and funny," Mom said. "You girls will adore him."

"Is he serious, or is he just a tire-kicker?" I asked.

"Watch it, Bean," Mom said.

BEAN'S not my real name, but that's what everyone calls me.

When I was born, Mom named me Jean, but the first time Liz laid eyes on me, she called me Jean the Bean because I was teeny like a bean and because it rhymed—Liz was always rhyming—and then simply Bean because it was shorter. But sometimes she would make it longer, calling me the Beaner, or Clean Bean when I'd taken a bath, Lean Bean because I was so skinny, Queen Bean just to make me feel good, or Mean Bean if I was in a bad mood.

Liz couldn't resist playing with words. That was why she loved the name of our new town, Lost Lake. "Let's go look for it," she'd say, or "I wonder who lost it," or "Maybe the lake should ask for directions."

We'd moved to Lost Lake from Pasadena four months ago, on New Year's Day of 1970, because Mom said a change of scenery would give us a fresh start for the new decade. Lost Lake was a pretty neat place, in my opinion. Most of the people who lived there were Mexicans who kept chickens and goats in their yards. Dogs and cats roamed the dusty streets, and irrigation canals at the edge of town carried water to the crop fields. No one looked sideways at you if you wore your big sister's hand-me-downs or your mom drove an old brown Dart. Our neighbors lived in little adobe houses, but we rented a cinder block bungalow. It was Mom's idea to paint the cinder blocks turquoise blue and the door and windowsills orange. "Let's not even pretend we want to blend in," she said.

Mom was a singer, songwriter, and actress. She'd never actually been in a movie or made a record, but she hated to be called "aspiring," and truth be told, she was a little older than the people described that way in the movie magazines she was always buying. Mom's thirty-sixth birthday was coming up, and she complained that the singers who were getting all the attention, like Janis Joplin and Joni Mitchell, were at least ten years younger than her.

Even so, Mom always said her big break was right around the corner. Sometimes she got callbacks after auditions, but she usually came home saying the guys at the studio were just tire-kickers who wanted a second look at her cleavage. Mom's career wasn't one that produced much in the way of income—yet. Mostly we lived on Mom's inheritance. It hadn't been a ton of money to begin with, and by the time we moved to Lost Lake, we were on a tight budget.

When Mom wasn't taking trips into L.A.—the drive was nearly

four hours in each direction—she tended to sleep late and spend the day writing songs, playing them on one of her guitars. Her favorite, a 1961 Zemaitis, cost about a year's rent. She also had a Gibson Southern Jumbo and a honey-colored Martin. If she wasn't practicing her songs, she was working on a musical play based on her life, about breaking away from her stifling Old South family, jettisoning her jerk of a husband, and discovering her true voice in music. She called the play *Finding the Magic.*

Mom always talked about how the secret to the creative process was finding the magic. That, she said, was what you needed to do in life as well. Find the magic. The three of us were magic, Mom liked to say. She assured us that no matter how famous she became, nothing would be more important to her than her two girls. We were a tribe of three, she said. The three of us were all we needed.

OVER the next few weeks, Mom kept talking about how Mark Parker had "discovered" her. She said it as a joke, but you could tell it actually had a sort of fairy-tale quality that appealed to her.

Mom began taking more trips to Los Angeles—sometimes for two or three days—and when she came back, she was gushy with Mark Parker stories. He was extraordinary, she said. He was working with her on the score for *Finding the Magic,* tightening the lyrics, polishing the arrangement. Mark ghosted a lot of lyrics, she told us. One day she brought home an album and pulled out the liner notes. Mark had circled the lyrics of a love song and had scrawled, "I wrote this about you before I met you."

MOM was still pretty for a mom. She had been homecoming queen at her high school in Virginia, and you could see why. She had large hazel eyes and sun-streaked blond hair that she kept in a ponytail when she was at home but teased up when she went to Los Angeles. She'd put on a few pounds since her high school days, she admitted, but she said the weight gave her a little extra cleavage, and a singer could never have too much in that department.

Mark liked her curves, Mom told us, and after she began seeing him, she started looking and acting younger. Her eyes were animated when she came home, describing how Mark had taken her sailing or made her poached scallops. Mom's name was Charlotte, and Mark had invented a cocktail for her with peach schnapps, bourbon, grenadine, and Tab that he called the Shakin' Charlotte.

Not everything about Mark was perfect, however. He was moody, Mom explained, and their collaboration had its stormy moments. Sometimes late at night Mom called Mark, and Liz and I could hear her yelling into the receiver, saying things like "That song needs to end on a chord, not a fade-out!" or "Mark, you expect too much of me!" Mom said that Mark was ready to produce a demo tape of her to play for the big labels, and it was natural for artistic types to have disagreements as a deadline approached.

I kept asking Mom when Liz and I were going to meet Mark Parker. Mom said that Mark was very busy, always jetting off to New York or London, and didn't have the time to come all the way out to Lost Lake. I suggested that we drive into Los Angeles some weekend to meet him, but Mom shook her head. "Bean, the truth of it is, he's jealous of you and Liz. He told me he thinks I talk about you girls too much. Mark can be a little possessive."

After Mom had been seeing Mark for a few months, she told us that, despite his hectic schedule, Mark had agreed to come to Lost Lake to meet Liz and me the following Wednesday after school. The three of us spent Tuesday evening furiously cleaning the bungalow, stuffing junk in the closet, scrubbing the rings of grime off the kitchen sink and the toilet, and moving Mom's purple butterfly chair to cover the spot where she'd spilled tea on the rug.

The next day, as soon as school was out, I hurried back to the bungalow. I was in sixth grade, in the elementary school, and Liz was a freshman in the high school, so I always got home first. Mom had told us Mark drove a yellow Triumph TR3, but the only car in front of the bungalow was our old brown Dart. When I got inside, I found Mom sitting on the floor, surrounded by a mess of books, records, and sheet music. She looked like she'd been crying.

"What happened?" I asked.

"He's gone," Mom said. "We got into a fight." To lure Mark to Lost Lake, Mom said, she had told him that Liz and I would be spending the night with friends. Once he'd arrived, she'd said there had been a change of plans and Liz and I were coming home after school. Mark exploded. He said he felt tricked, and he stormed out.

"What a jerk," I said.

"He's not a jerk. He's passionate. And he's obsessed with me."

"Then he'll be back."

"I don't know. He said he was leaving for his villa in Italy."

"Mark has a villa in Italy?"

"A movie-producer friend owns it, but he lets Mark use it."

"Wow," I said. Mom had always wanted to spend time in Italy, and here was a guy who could jet over there whenever he felt like it. Except for the fact that he didn't want to meet me and Liz, Mark Parker was everything Mom had ever wanted in a man. "I wish he liked us," I said, "because other than that, he's too good to be true."

"What's that supposed to mean?" Mom pulled up her shoulders and stared at me. "Do you think I'm making it all up?"

"Oh, not for a second," I said. "Making up a boyfriend would be too kooky." But as soon as the words came out of my mouth, it occurred to me that Mom was, in fact, making it all up. My face felt hot, like I was seeing Mom naked. Mom and I were looking at each other, and I realized she could tell that I knew she had made it up.

"Screw you!" Mom shouted. She was on her feet and started yelling about how much she'd sacrificed for me and Liz and what ungrateful parasites we were. I tried to calm Mom down, but that made her angrier. She never should have had kids, she went on, especially me. I was a mistake. She'd thrown away her life and her career for us, and we didn't even appreciate it.

"I can't stand being here!" she screamed. "I've got to get away."

Mom grabbed her handbag and stormed out. I heard her gun the Dart; then she drove away. The bungalow was silent.

I fed Fido, the little turtle Mom had bought me when she wouldn't let me get a dog. Then I curled up in Mom's butterfly chair, stroking Fido's head, waiting for Liz to get home.

Truth be told, Mom had a temper and was given to tantrums and meltdowns when things got overwhelming. The fits usually passed quickly, and then we all moved on as if nothing had happened. This one was different. Mom had said things that she'd never said before, like about me being a mistake. And the whole business about Mark Parker was weird. I needed Liz to help sort it all out.

Liz could make sense of anything. Her brain worked that way. She was talented, beautiful, funny, and most of all, incredibly smart. I'm not saying all that just because she was my sister. If you met her, you'd agree. She was tall and slender, with pale skin and long, wavy reddish gold hair.

Liz was one of those people who always made grown-ups, particularly teachers, use words like "prodigy" and "gifted." Liz knew things that other people didn't know, because she was always reading. She could do complicated math calculations without pencil and paper. She loved saying words backward—like calling Mark Parker "Kram Rekrap." She loved anagrams, where you rearranged the letters of words to make different words, turning "deliver" into "reviled" and "funeral" into "real fun." And she loved spoonerisms, like when you mean to say "dear old queen" but instead say "queer old dean," or when "bad money" comes out as "mad bunny" and "smart feller" turns into "fart smeller."

Liz's school let out only an hour after mine, but that afternoon it felt like forever. When she finally arrived at the bungalow, I didn't even let her set her books down before I started pouring out every detail of Mom's blowup.

"I just don't understand why she would make up all this Mark Parker stuff," I said.

Liz sighed. "Mom's always been a bit of a fibber," she said. Mom was all the time telling us things that Liz suspected weren't true, like how she used to go foxhunting with Jackie Kennedy in Virginia when they were both girls, or how she'd been the dancing banana in a cereal commercial. Mom had a red velvet jacket and liked to tell the story of how, when June Carter Cash had heard her play in a Nashville bar, she joined Mom on stage and they sang a duet together that brought the crowd to its feet. June had been wearing the red velvet jacket, and right there on stage she gave it to Mom.

"It didn't happen," Liz said. "I saw Mom buy that jacket at a church tag sale. She didn't know I was watching." Liz looked out the window. "Mark Parker is just another dancing banana."

"I really blew it, didn't I? I should have kept my big mouth shut."

"She knew you knew," Liz said, "and she couldn't handle it."

"Mom wasn't just making up a little story about some guy she met," I said. "There were the phone calls. And those liner notes."

"I know," Liz said. "It's kind of scary. I think she's gone through all of her money, and it's giving her some sort of a breakdown."

Liz said we should clean up the place so that when Mom came back, we could pretend the whole Mark Parker mess had never happened. We put the books back on the shelves, stacked the sheet music, and slid the records into their jackets.

WE EXPECTED Mom to come back that night or the next day, but by the weekend, we still hadn't heard from her. Whenever I started to fret, Liz told me not to worry. Then we got the letter.

Liz read it first, then handed it to me and went to sit in the butterfly chair at the picture window.

My Darling Liz and Sweet Bean,

It's 3 a.m. and I'm writing from a hotel in San Diego. I know I have not been at the top of my game recently, and to finish my songs—and be the mother I want to be—I need to make some time for myself. I need to find the magic again. You both should know that nothing is more important to me than my girls and that we will be together again soon!

The $200 I'm sending will keep you in chicken potpies until I get back. Chins up, and don't forget to floss!

Love,
Mom

I joined Liz at the window, and she squeezed my hand.

"Is she coming back?" I asked.

"Of course," Liz said.

"But when? She didn't say when."

"I don't think she knows."

TWO hundred dollars buys a lot of chicken potpies. We got them at Spinelli's grocery, an air-conditioned place with a big freezer in the back where the pies were stored. Mr. Spinelli, a dark-eyed man who was always flirting with Mom, sometimes put them on sale. When he did, we could get eight for a dollar, and we stocked up.

We ate our pies in the evening at the red Formica table. After dinner we cleaned up, did our homework, and went to bed. We'd looked after ourselves before when Mom was away, but thinking she might be away for days and days made us take our responsibilities seriously. We went to bed on time. We never left dirty dishes in the sink, and we flossed our teeth.

Liz had been doing some babysitting, but after Mom had been gone a week, she took on extra work and I got a job delivering *Grit,* a local newspaper. For the time being, money wasn't a problem. Still, we knew we couldn't live this way forever.

ONE day after Mom had been gone almost two weeks, I went to Spinelli's after school to stock up on chicken potpies. I thought I'd never get tired of chicken potpies, but I had to admit they were sort of wearing on me because we'd been eating them for breakfast, too.

Mr. Spinelli had a grill behind the counter, where he made hamburgers and hot dogs. They sure smelled good, but they were beyond our budget. I loaded up on more chicken potpies.

"Haven't seen your mom in a while, Miss Bean," Mr. Spinelli said. "What's she been up to?"

I froze up, then said, "She broke her leg."

"That's a shame," he said. "Tell you what. Get yourself an ice-cream sandwich. On me."

That night, Liz and I were doing our homework when there was a knock at the door. Liz opened it, and Mr. Spinelli stood outside, holding a brown paper bag with a loaf of bread sticking out the top.

"This is for your mother," he said. "How she's doing?"

"She's not here," Liz said. "She's in Los Angeles."

"Bean said she broke her leg."

Liz and Mr. Spinelli looked over at me, and I started glancing around, avoiding their eyes.

"She broke her leg in Los Angeles," Liz said smoothly. "But it's not serious. A friend's bringing her back in a few days."

"Good," Mr. Spinelli said. "I'll come see her then." He held out the groceries to Liz. "Here, you take these."

"WHAT are we going to do now?" I asked Liz once Mr. Spinelli had left. "Is he going to send the bandersnatches after us?"

"He might," Liz said.

"Bandersnatches" was the word Liz took from *Alice Through the Looking Glass*—her favorite book—for the do-gooding government busybodies who snooped around making sure that kids had the sort of families the busybodies thought they should have. Last year in Pasadena, a few months before we moved to Lost Lake, a bandersnatch had come around when the school principal got the idea that Mom was negligent in her parenting after I told a teacher our electricity got turned off because Mom forgot to pay the bill. Mom hit the ceiling. She said the principal was just a meddling do-gooder, and she warned us never to discuss our home life at school.

If the bandersnatches came after us, Liz said, they might put the two of us in a foster home. They might separate us. They might throw Mom in jail for abandoning her kids. Mom hadn't abandoned us; she just needed a little break. We could handle the situation fine.

"I have an idea," Liz said. "If we have to, we can go to Virginia."

Mom had come from a small town in Virginia called Byler, where her father had owned a cotton mill that made stuff like towels, socks, and underwear. Mom's brother, our uncle Tinsley, had sold the mill a few years ago, but he still lived in Byler with his wife, Martha, in a big old house called Mayfield. Mom had grown up in the house but had left twelve years ago, when she was twenty-three, driving off that night with me on the roof. She hadn't had much to do with her family since she left, not returning even when her parents died, but we knew Uncle Tinsley still lived at Mayfield, because from time to time, Mom complained it was unfair that he'd inherited it just because he was older and a guy. It would be hers if anything ever happened to Uncle Tinsley, and she'd sell it in a heartbeat, because the place had nothing but bad memories for her.

Since I was only a few months old when we left, I didn't remember Mayfield or Mom's family. Liz had some memories, and they weren't bad at all. In fact, they were sort of magical. She remembered a white house on a hill surrounded by trees, and Aunt Martha and Uncle Tinsley playing duets on a grand piano in a room with French doors that were opened to the sun. Uncle Tinsley was a tall, laughing man who held her hands while he swung her around and lifted her up to pick peaches from a tree.

"How are we going to get there?" I asked.

"We'll take the bus." Liz called the depot to find out the fares to Virginia. They weren't cheap, she said, but we had enough money for two cross-country tickets. "If it comes to that," she added.

THE next day, when I turned down the block on my way home from school, I saw a squad car parked outside the bungalow. A policeman in a blue uniform was peering through the picture window. That Mr. Spinelli had ratted us out after all. I turned around and headed back up the block.

I was waiting outside the high school when Liz came down the steps. "What are you so bug-eyed about?" she asked.

"Cops," I whispered. I told her about the policeman peering through the window.

"That's it," Liz said. "Beaner, we're going to Virginia."

Liz always carried our money under the lining in her shoe, so we went straight to the bus depot. Since the school year was almost over, none of our teachers would miss us. It was early June, picking season for strawberries, apricots, and peaches, and the teachers were used to migrant families coming and going at harvest time.

I stayed outside the depot while Liz bought the tickets. After a couple of minutes, Liz came back out. We'd been afraid that the clerk might raise questions about a kid buying tickets, but Liz said the woman had slid them across the counter without batting an eye.

The bus left at six forty-five the following morning. "Shouldn't we call Uncle Tinsley?" I asked.

"I think it's better if we just show up," Liz said. "That way, he can't say no."

THAT night, after finishing off our chicken potpies, Liz and I got out the suitcases left from what Mom called her deb days. They were a matching set in a tweedy tan, with brown crocodile trim.

"What should we take?" I asked.

"Clothes but no stuff," Liz said.

"What about Fido?"

"Leave him here," Liz said, "with extra food and water. He'll be fine until Mom comes back."

"What if Mom doesn't come back?"

"She'll be back. She's not abandoning us."

"And I don't want to abandon Fido."

Liz sighed and shook her head. Fido was coming to Virginia.

PACKING those suitcases got me to thinking about the other times we'd picked up and moved on short notice. That was what Mom did whenever she got fed up with things. Sometimes it was arguments with neighbors; sometimes it was boyfriends who took a powder. Sometimes the place we'd moved to didn't meet her expectations. Over the years, we'd moved to Venice Beach, Taos, Tucson, Seattle, and Pasadena, plus these smaller places, like Bisbee and Lost Lake.

While Liz and I had been on our own plenty of times, we'd never taken a trip without Mom. I wondered what to expect once we got to Virginia. Mom never had anything good to say about the place. She was always going on about the backward-thinking lintheads, who drove cars with duct-taped fenders, and about the mint-julep set who lived in the big old houses, selling off ancestor portraits to pay their taxes, reminiscing about the days when the coloreds knew their place. That was a long time ago, when Mom was growing up. Things had changed since then, and I figured Byler must have, too.

After turning off the lights, Liz and I lay side by side. I'd been sharing a bed with Liz for as long as I could remember. After we left Virginia when I was a baby, Mom found that putting me in with Liz made me stop crying. Later on we lived for long stretches in motels with only two beds. In Lost Lake we shared a bed so small we had to face the same direction, the person behind wrapping her arms around the person in front. Otherwise, we'd end up pulling the covers off each other. Some people might have thought sleeping with your sister was peculiar, but I loved it. You never felt lonely at night, and you always had someone to talk to.

"Do you think we'll like Virginia?" I asked.

"You'll like it, Bean."

"Mom hated it."

"Mom found something wrong with every place we ever lived."

I FELL asleep quickly, but even though it was still dark when my eyes popped open, I felt completely awake and charged up.

Liz was up, too. She turned on the light and sat down at the kitchen table. "We have to write Mom a letter," she said.

While I heated up our chicken potpies and poured out the last of the orange juice, Liz worked on the letter. She said she had to write it in a way that Mom would understand it but no one else would.

The letter was classic Liz.

Dear Queen of Hearts,

Due to the sudden presence of bandersnatches, we decided it was prudent to vacate the premises and pay a visit to the Mad Hatter, Tinsley, and Martha, the Dormouse. We'll be waiting for you on the other side of the Looking Glass in your old haunted haunts, that Land of the Lintheads, where Bean was born and the borogoves are mimsy.

Love,

Tweedledee and Tweedledum

We left the letter on the kitchen table, held down by the glazed iris-blue mug Mom had made when she was in her pottery phase.

CHAPTER TWO

Two people got off the bus when it pulled into the depot, so we were able to snag their primo seats up front, behind the driver. Liz let me have the window, and I held Fido in his Tupperware bowl with a little water on the bottom, an upside-down saucer for him to sit on, and holes punched in the lid so he could breathe.

As we pulled away, I looked out the window, hoping Mom had returned. But the street was empty.

The bus was crowded, and we played What's Their Story?—a game Liz had made up—trying to guess where the passengers were going, whether they were happy or scared, whether they were going on a visit or leaving their home forever. We guessed that the young military guy snoozing with his head on his duffel was on leave to visit his family in ranchland. A thin guy in a plaid jacket with lank hair pushed behind his jug ears was sitting across from us. As I looked at him, trying to figure out if he was an absentminded mathematical genius or just a schlub, he caught my eye and winked.

I quickly looked away, but when I glanced back at him later, he was still eyeballing me. He winked again. I had that uh-oh feeling, and sure enough, when Liz got up to go to the bathroom, the schlub came over and sat down next to me, draping his arm across the back of my seat. He pressed his finger down on Fido's Tupperware bowl.

"What you got in there?" he asked.

"My pet turtle."

"You got a ticket for him?" He looked at me intently, then gave another wink. "Just funning you," he said. "You girls going far?"

"Virginia," I said.

"All on your own?"

"We've got our mother's permission."

"I see," he said. "You're sisters." He leaned in on me. "You've got incredibly beautiful eyes, you know."

"Thank you," I said, and looked down. I felt very uncomfortable. Just then Liz came back from the bathroom. "You're in my seat."

"Simply getting to know your sister, miss." He rose up out of the seat. "She says you're going all the way to Virginia. Heck of a long journey for two pretty young gals to be making on their own."

"None of your business," Liz told him. She sat down. "A total perv," she whispered to me. "I can't believe you told that odiosity where we were going. That's such a Bean-headed thing to do."

The Perv took his seat but kept staring over at us, so Liz decided we needed to move. The only two free seats were at the very back, next to the bathroom. You could smell the chemicals and the other gross stuff in the toilet, and every time folks squeezed past us to use it, you could hear them doing number one or number two.

THE bus went only as far as New Orleans. Since we were sitting in the back, we were the last ones off. When we picked up our luggage, the Perv was gone. Our next bus didn't leave for two hours, so we put the luggage in a locker with Fido and went for a walk. Liz and I both had a serious case of what she called rigor buttis.

It was a hot, hazy day. People were wearing crazy clothes— tuxedo jackets but no shirts, top hats with feathers—or hardly anything. They were eating, drinking, laughing, and dancing to the music that street performers were playing on about every corner.

A trolley car came down the street, and we got on for a quick tour of the city. We took a seat in the middle. Just before the doors closed, a man shoved his hand between them, and they opened again. It was the Perv. He took the seat right behind us.

Liz grabbed my hand, and we moved up to a seat at the front. The Perv followed. We moved to the back. He followed. The other passengers were watching us, but no one said a thing. It was one of those situations where people knew something wasn't right, but at the same time, there was no law against a man changing seats.

At the next stop, Liz and I got off, still holding hands. So did the Perv. Liz led me into the crowd on the sidewalk, the Perv behind us. Then Liz quickly pulled me around, and we jumped back on the trolley. This time the doors closed before the Perv could get his hand in. The other passengers all started cheering and clapping, shouting things like "Dusted him!" As we pulled away, we could see the Perv through the window. He actually stomped his foot.

ONCE we were safely on the bus heading east we rehashed the way we tricked the Perv. It made me feel like we could handle just about anything. When it got dark, I fell asleep with my head on Liz's shoulder, but I woke up a short while later and could hear her quietly crying.

In Atlanta we changed for the bus to Richmond, and in Richmond we changed buses for the ride to Byler. For the first time since coming east, we left the freeway for smaller back roads. It was all so green. There were shiny green cornfields, dark green mountains, and golden-green hay fields lined with soft green trees.

We reached Byler late in the afternoon. It was a small town on a bending river with blue mountains rising up behind it. The bridge across the river clanked under the wheels of the bus. The streets of the town, lined with two-story buildings painted in fading colors, were quiet. The bus stopped at a depot with a black metal roof.

We were the only passengers who got off. As the bus pulled away, a middle-aged woman came through the door of the depot. She wore a red sweatshirt with a bulldog on it and was carrying a ring of keys. "You all waiting for someone?" she asked.

"Not really," Liz said. "You don't happen to know how to get to Tinsley Holladay's house, do you?"

The woman studied Liz with sudden interest. "Mayfield?" she asked. "The Holladay house? You all know Tinsley Holladay?"

"He's our uncle," I said.

"Well, knock me over with a feather. You are Charlotte's girls?"

"That's right," Liz said.

"Where's your momma?"

"We're visiting on our own," Liz said.

The woman locked the depot door. "It's quite a hike to Mayfield," she said. "I'll give you all a ride."

The woman obviously wasn't a perv, so we put the suitcases in the back of her pickup and climbed into the front. "Charlotte Holladay was a year ahead of me at Byler High," the woman said.

We drove out of the town and into the countryside. The woman kept fishing for details about Mom, but Liz was evasive, so the woman talked about Mayfield, how twenty years ago there was always something going on there—oyster roasts, cotillions, moonlight horseback rides, Civil War costume balls. "Everyone hankered for an invitation there," she said. "All us girls would have given our left arm to be Charlotte Holladay. She had everything."

A couple of miles outside town, we came to a small white church surrounded by tall trees and a group of old houses. We continued to a low stone wall with a set of wrought-iron gates held up by thick stone pillars. Carved into one of the pillars was MAYFIELD.

The woman stopped. "Charlotte Holladay," she said once more. "When you all see your momma, tell her Tammy Elbert says hello."

The gates were locked, so we climbed over the low stone wall and followed the driveway up a slope and around a stand of trees. At the top of the hill stood the house, three stories high, painted white, with what looked to be twenty chimneys sprouting all over the place. Six white columns held up the roof of the long front porch, and off to one side was a wing with a row of French doors.

"Oh, my gosh," I told Liz. "It's the house I've been dreaming about all my life."

Ever since I could remember, I'd been having this dream at least once a month about a big white house at the top of a knoll. In the dream, Liz and I run through the halls, exploring room after room after room of beautiful paintings and fine furniture. There are fireplaces and tall windows that let in long shafts of sunlight. I always thought it was just a dream, but this was the exact house.

As we got closer, we realized the house was in pretty sorry shape. The paint was peeling; the roof had rust stains. We climbed the wide steps to the porch, and a blackbird flew out of a broken window.

Liz rapped the brass knocker and then, after several seconds, rapped it again. At first I thought no one was home, but then we heard the scraping and sliding of bolts and the door opened. A man appeared holding a shotgun across his chest. He had rumpled graying hair, and he was wearing only a bathrobe and argyle socks.

"Get off my property," he said.

"Uncle Tinsley?" Liz asked.

"Who are you?"

"It's me. Liz."

He stared at her.

"And I'm Bean. Or Jean."

"We're Charlotte's daughters," Liz said.

"Charlotte's girls?" He stared at us. "What are you doing here?"

"We came for a visit," I said.

"Where's Charlotte?"

"We're not sure." Liz took a deep breath and started explaining how Mom had needed some time to herself and we were fine on our own until the police got snoopy. "So we decided to come visit you."

"You decided to come all the way from California to visit me?"

"That's right," Liz said.

"And I'm supposed to just take you in?"

"It's a visit," I said.

"You can't simply show up out of the blue." He wasn't expecting guests, he went on. The housekeeper hadn't been around in a while. He was in the midst of several important projects and had papers and research material spread throughout the house that couldn't be disturbed. "I can't just let you all in here," he said.

"We don't mind a mess," I said. I tried to peer behind Uncle Tinsley into the house, but he blocked the doorway.

"Where's Aunt Martha?" Liz asked.

Uncle Tinsley ignored the question. "It's not that it's a mess," he said to me. "It's all highly organized, and it can't be disturbed."

"Well, what are we supposed to do?" Liz asked.

Uncle Tinsley looked at the two of us for a long moment, then leaned the shotgun against the wall. "You can sleep in the barn."

He led us along a brick path that ran beneath towering trees with peeling white bark. It was twilight by then.

"Charlotte needed time by herself, so she just took off?" Uncle Tinsley asked.

"More or less," Liz said.

"She's going to come back," I said. "She wrote us a letter."

"So this is another one of Charlotte's debacles?" Uncle Tinsley shook his head in disgust. "Charlotte," he muttered. His sister was nothing but trouble, he went on. She was spoiled as a girl, and by the time she had grown up, she expected to get whatever she wanted. Not only that, whatever you did for her wasn't enough. Give her money and she thought she deserved more. When her life got difficult, she blamed Mother and Father for everything.

Uncle Tinsley was being pretty harsh about Mom, but this didn't seem like a good time to defend her. Liz seemed to feel the same way, because she didn't say anything, either.

The barn, which stood at the end of the tree line, was huge, with peeling white paint and a green metal roof. Inside was a black carriage with gilt trim. Next to it was a station wagon with real wooden sides. Uncle Tinsley led us up a narrow flight of stairs. At the top, there was this neat little room with a bed and table, a kitchenette, and a wood-burning stove.

"This used to be the groom's quarters," Uncle Tinsley said.

"Where is Aunt Martha?" Liz asked again.

"Charlotte didn't tell you?" Uncle Tinsley went over to the window and gazed at the fading light. "Martha passed away. Six years ago this September. Trucker ran a red light."

"Aunt Martha?" Liz said. "I can't believe she's gone."

Uncle Tinsley turned around and faced us. "You don't remember her. You were too small."

"I remember her really well," Liz said. She told Uncle Tinsley she remembered baking bread with her. And she remembered Aunt Martha and Uncle Tinsley playing the grand piano together with the French doors open to the sun. "I think about her a lot."

Uncle Tinsley nodded. "Me, too," he said. Then he paused, as if he was going to say something else, but he just shook his head and walked out the door, saying as he shut it, "You'll be fine in here."

We listened to him clambering down the steps. I noticed a small refrigerator next to the sink, and that was when I realized I was starving. I opened the refrigerator, but it was empty and unplugged. We decided it wasn't a good idea to pester Uncle Tinsley about food, but a few minutes later we heard footsteps on the stairs again. Uncle Tinsley appeared in the door, carrying a silver tray with a small pot, two bowls, a pitcher of water, and two wineglasses.

"Venison stew," he said. He unloaded the tray onto the table. "It's dark in here. You need some light." He flipped a switch on the wall, and an overhead bulb came on. "You all have a good night's sleep," he said, and closed the door again.

Liz filled the bowls, and we sat down at the table. I took a bite of the stew. "What's venison?" I asked.

"Deer."

"Oh." I took another bite. "It's pretty good," I said.

THE birds woke me early the next morning. I went to the window, and they were everywhere—in the trees outside, on the ground, swooping in and out of the barn like they owned the place.

Liz and I got dressed and walked to the house. When we knocked on the front door, there was no answer, so we went to the back. Through a window, we could see Uncle Tinsley in the kitchen. Liz rapped on the window. He opened the door but blocked it like he had the night before. He had shaved. He was wearing gray trousers and a light blue shirt with TMH monogrammed on the pocket.

"How did you girls sleep?" he asked.

"Just fine," Liz said. "Did Mom call, by any chance?"

"Afraid not."

"She does have the number, right?" I asked.

"It hasn't changed since we got it—two, four, six, eight," he said. "First phone number handed out in Byler, so we got to choose it. Speaking of choosing, how do you like your poached eggs?"

"Hard!" I said.

"Soft," Liz said.

"Have a seat." He pointed to some rusty cast-iron lawn furniture.

A few minutes later he came out carrying that same silver tray, loaded up with a stack of toast and three plates that each had a poached egg in the center. The plates had gold curlicues around the rim, but the edges were chipped. I picked up a corner of my egg and scooted a piece of toast under it, then stabbed the yolk with my fork, chopped up the white part of the egg, and mushed it together.

"Bean always mutilates her food," Liz told Uncle Tinsley.

"It tastes better mixed up," I said. "But that's not the only reason. You don't have to take as many bites, so it saves time. You don't have to work as hard chewing, because if it's all mushed up, it's sort of prechewed. Finally, food gets all mixed up in your stomach anyway, so that's obviously the way it was meant to be."

Uncle Tinsley chuckled and asked Liz, "Is she always like this?"

"Oh, yeah," Liz said. "She's the Beanhead."

We offered to wash the dishes, but Uncle Tinsley insisted it was easier if he did them himself, without a couple of kids underfoot. He told us to go off and do whatever girls our age did.

Liz and I walked around to the front of the house, where there were two big trees with big white flowers. On the far side of the lawn was a row of huge green bushes with a gap in the middle. We walked through the gap and found ourselves in an area where a few tough irises pushed up through the weeds in old overgrown flower beds. In the center was a round brick-edged pond. It was full of dead leaves, but in the water beneath, I saw a flash of orange.

"Fish!" I yelled. "Goldfish! There's goldfish in this pond!"

We knelt and studied the orange fish fluttering in and out of the shadows beneath the clumps of dead leaves. I decided this would be a great place for Fido to have a swim. The poor turtle had to be feeling cooped up after all that time in his box.

I ran back to the barn, but when I opened the Tupperware, Fido was floating in the water. He'd seemed fine when I fed him earlier. I set him down on the table, scooting him along with my finger, trying to jump-start him, even though I knew it was hopeless. Fido was dead, and it was my fault. I had thought I could protect and take care of him, but that bus trip had been too much for him.

I put Fido back in the Tupperware dish and carried him out to the pond. Liz put an arm around me and said we needed to ask Uncle Tinsley where to bury him.

Uncle Tinsley was puttering in the kitchen when we knocked.

"I thought the two of you were going to go off and play," he said.

"Fido died," I said.

Uncle Tinsley glanced at Liz.

"Bean's turtle," she said.

"We need to know where to bury him," I said.

Uncle Tinsley stepped out of the house and closed the door behind him. I handed him the Tupperware dish, and he looked down at Fido. "We bury all the family pets in the family cemetery," he said. He led us back to the barn, where he picked up a shovel with a long wooden handle; then we headed up the hill behind it.

"Fido's a peculiar name for a turtle," he said as we walked along.

"Bean really wanted a dog," Liz said, explaining how Mom had told us it was always the kids who wanted the pet but the mother who ended up taking care of it, and she had no interest in walking and cleaning up after a dog. So she'd bought me a turtle.

"Fido means 'I am faithful,'" I said. "Fido was a faithful turtle."

"I bet he was," Uncle Tinsley said.

Beyond the barn were a bunch of dilapidated buildings. Uncle Tinsley pointed out the smokehouse, the milking shed, the foaling shed, and the henhouse, explaining that Mayfield used to be a real working farm. He still had all two hundred and five acres, including a stretch of woods, as well as the big hayfield where the cemetery was. These days a farmer up the road, Mr. Muncie, hayed the field and gave Uncle Tinsley eggs and vegetables in return.

We passed through an orchard with apple and peach trees and out into a large pasture. At the top of the pasture, a cluster of trees shaded the family cemetery. It was weedy, and a number of the weathered old headstones had toppled over. Uncle Tinsley led us to one well-tended grave with a newish headstone. This was Martha's, he said, with a vacant spot next to it for him when the time came.

The pets, he explained, were buried near their owners. "Let's put Fido near Martha. She would have liked him," he said.

He dug a small hole, and I placed Fido in it. I found a nice piece of white quartz for a headstone. Uncle Tinsley gave a short eulogy. Fido had been a brave and faithful turtle, he said, who had made the long and perilous journey from California in order to serve as a guardian for his two sister-owners. Once he'd gotten them safely to Virginia, Fido's job was over, and he felt free to leave them for that secret island in the middle of the ocean that is turtle heaven.

The eulogy made me feel a lot better about both Fido and Uncle Tinsley. On the way back down the hill, I asked about the goldfish we'd found in the pond. "The fish are koi," Uncle Tinsley said. "That was Mother's garden. One of the finest private gardens in all of Virginia, back in the day. Mother won prizes for it."

We swung around the barn, and the white house came into view. I told Uncle Tinsley about my house dream and how, when we first arrived at Mayfield, I realized it was the actual house in the dream.

Uncle Tinsley became thoughtful. "I guess you'd better see the inside of the house, then," he said. "Just to make sure."

We followed Uncle Tinsley up the big porch steps. He took a deep breath and opened the door. The front hall was large and dark, with a lot of wooden cabinets that had glass doors. Newspapers, magazines, books, and mail were stacked high on the tables and the floor, alongside boxes of rocks and bottles filled with dirt and sand.

"It may look a tad cluttered," he said, "but that's because I'm in the middle of reorganizing everything."

"It's not so bad," Liz said. "It just needs a little tidying up."

"We can help," I said.

"Oh, no. Everything has its place. I know where everything is."

Uncle Tinsley showed us the parlor, the dining room, and the ballroom. Oil paintings hung crooked on the walls. The Persian carpets were worn and frayed; the silk curtains were faded and torn. A grand piano covered with a dark green velvet cloth stood in the ballroom with the French doors. There was all this stuff piled on every surface—more stacks of paper and notebooks, pendulum clocks, rolled-up maps, stacks of chipped china, ships in bottles, framed photographs, and all these little wooden boxes, one filled with coins, another with buttons, another with old medals. Everything was coated with dust.

"There sure is a ton of stuff in here," I said.

"Yes, but every single thing you see has value," Uncle Tinsley said. "If you have the brains to appreciate it."

He led us up a curving staircase and down a long hall, stopping in front of a pair of doors facing each other. Both had brass door knockers shaped like birds. "This is the bird wing," he said. "This is where you'll stay. Until your mother comes to pick you up."

"We're not sleeping in the barn anymore?" I asked.

"Not without Fido there to protect you."

Uncle Tinsley opened the doors. We each had our own room, he said. Both were wallpapered with bird motifs—common birds, like robins and cardinals, and exotic birds, like cockatiels and flamingos. The bird wing, he said, was designed for his twin aunts, who were little girls when the house was built. They had loved birds and kept a Victorian birdhouse of different kinds of finches.

"Where was Mom's room?" I asked.

"The whole bird wing was hers." He pointed through the door of one room. "When she brought you back from the hospital after you were born, she put you in that cradle in the corner there."

I looked at the cradle. It was small, white, and made of wicker, and I couldn't understand quite why, but it made me feel very safe.

THE next morning, over our poached eggs, Liz and I tried to talk Uncle Tinsley into letting us help him clean up the house just a little bit. But he insisted that nothing in the house could be thrown out or even moved. Everything, he said, was either a family treasure or part of his collections or necessary for his geological research.

We spent the morning following him around as he explained what all the stuff meant to him. He'd pick up an ivory-handled letter opener or a tricornered hat and explain where it came from, who had owned it, and why it had extraordinary significance.

"This place is like a museum," I said.

"And you're the curator," Liz told Uncle Tinsley.

"Well said," he replied. "But it's been a good while since I gave my last tour." We were standing in the ballroom. Uncle Tinsley looked around. "I admit the place is a tad cluttered. That was the phrase Martha liked to use. I've always loved to collect things, but when she was alive, she helped me keep the impulse in check."

Uncle Tinsley finally agreed to let us throw out some of the old newspapers and magazines and carry up to the attic and down to the basement boxes of mineral samples, spools of thread from the mill, and Confederate paper money. We washed windows, aired out rooms, scrubbed floors, and vacuumed the rugs and curtains with this Hoover from the 1950s that reminded me of a little spaceship.

By the end of the week, the house looked a lot better. Still, it didn't meet most people's definition of neat and tidy, and you had to accept the fact that you weren't living in a regular house but a place more like a junk shop crammed with all kinds of fascinating stuff—if you had the brains to see its value.

VENISON stew and eggs were the staples of Uncle Tinsley's diet. He explained that if he bagged two or three does during deer season, had the meat processed and double-wrapped, then stored it in the basement freezer, he had enough to last the entire year. So most nights we had venison stew with carrots, onions, tomatoes, and potatoes, with barley mixed in. The meat was a lot tougher than the chicken in potpies, and sometimes you really had to work your jaws before you could swallow it, but it was also spicier and tastier.

Thanks to Mr. Muncie, the eighty-seven-year-old neighbor who hayed the big pasture, Uncle Tinsley didn't have to buy eggs and vegetables. But he decided growing girls needed milk and cheese, so at the end of our first week, Uncle Tinsley declared it was time for a grocery run. We all climbed into the station wagon with the wood panels, which Uncle Tinsley called the Woody. We hadn't left Mayfield since the day we arrived, and I was itching to check out the area.

We drove past the church and the cluster of houses, then along farmland on the way to Byler. I was looking out the window as we passed a big fenced-in field, and I saw these two huge birdlike creatures. "Liz!" I shouted. "Look at those crazy birds!"

They reminded me of chickens, only they were the size of ponies, with long necks and legs and dark brown feathers. Their heads bobbed as they moved along with big careful steps.

"What the heck are they?" I asked.

Uncle Tinsley gave that little chuckle of his. "Scruggs's emus."

"Like ostriches, right?" Liz said.

"Near enough."

"Are they pets?" I asked.

"They weren't supposed to be. Scruggs thought he could make some money off them but never figured out how. So they're the world's ugliest lawn ornaments."

"They're not ugly," Liz said.

"Take a look at them up close sometime."

ONCE we got to Byler, Uncle Tinsley gave us what he called the nickel tour. The main street was Holladay Avenue. The buildings were old-fashioned, made of brick and stone. Some had pillars, and you got the feeling that Byler once was a bustling place, though it looked like nothing new had been built for years. Byler struck me as very sleepy. People moved slowly, and a lot of them were hardly moving at all, just sitting in chairs under store awnings, some of the men talking, whittling, or chewing tobacco and reading newspapers.

"What year are we in here?" Liz joked.

"The sixties never happened in this town," Uncle Tinsley said, "and people like it that way."

The mill stood at the end of Holladay Avenue, right on the river. It was made of dark redbrick, and it covered an entire block. The windows were two stories high, and smoke poured out of a pair of soaring chimneys. A sign in front said HOLLADAY TEXTILES.

"Charlotte tell you much family history?" Uncle Tinsley asked.

"It wasn't Mom's favorite subject," Liz said.

Before the Civil War, Uncle Tinsley explained, the Holladay family had owned a cotton plantation.

"A plantation?" I asked. "Our family had slaves?"

"We certainly did."

"I wish I didn't know that," Liz said.

"Those slaves were treated well," Uncle Tinsley said. "My great-great-grandfather Montgomery Holladay liked to say that if he was down to a final crust of bread, he would have shared it with them."

I glanced at Liz, who rolled her eyes.

If you went back far enough, Uncle Tinsley went on, just about all American families who could afford them owned slaves, not only Southerners. Ben Franklin owned slaves. Anyway, he said, the Yankees burned down the plantation during the war, but the family knew the cotton business. Once the war was over, Montgomery Holladay decided there was no point in shipping cotton to the factories up north to make the Yankees rich, so he sold the land and moved to Byler, where he used the money to build the mill.

The Holladays had owned the cotton mill—and pretty much the town itself—for generations. The mill was good to the Holladays, and the Holladays were good to the workers. The family built them houses with indoor plumbing. They gave out hams on Christmas and sponsored a baseball team called the Holladay Hitters. The mill workers never made much in terms of wages, but most of them had been dirt farmers, and factory work was a step up.

Things started to go downhill fast about ten years ago, Uncle Tinsley continued. Foreign mills began undercutting everybody's prices at the same time those Northern agitators started stirring up the workers to strike for higher wages. Southern mills started losing money, and as the years went by, more of them shut down.

By then, Uncle Tinsley said, his father had passed, and he was running Holladay Textiles himself. It, too, was in the red. Some Chicago investors agreed to buy the mill, but it didn't bring much—only enough for him and Charlotte to get by if they watched their pennies. The new owners laid off workers and squeezed every ounce of profit out of the place, not just doing away with the Christmas hams and the Holladay Hitters but cutting back bathroom breaks, turning off the air-conditioning, and using dirty cotton.

"Back in the day, Holladay Textiles made a quality product," Uncle Tinsley said. "Now they turn out towels so thin you can read a newspaper through them."

"Did you ever think of leaving Byler?" I asked. "Like Mom?"

"Leave Byler?" Uncle Tinsley asked. "Why would I leave Byler? I'm a Holladay. This is where I belong."

CHAPTER THREE

AT MAYFIELD we slept with the windows open, and you could hear the frogs croaking at night. I conked out as soon as my head hit the pillow, but those noisy birds woke me early every day. One morning in late June, after we'd been at Mayfield for almost two weeks, I woke up and reached out for Liz, then remembered that she was in the next room. Much as I had loved sharing a bed with Liz, I'd always thought it would be neat to have a room of my own. The truth was, it felt lonely.

I went into Liz's room to see if she was awake. She was sitting up in bed, reading a book called *Stranger in a Strange Land,* which she'd found while we were cleaning the house. I lay beside her.

"I wish Mom would hurry up and call," I said. "Uncle Tinsley's going to think we're a couple of moochers."

"I think he actually likes having us here," Liz said. She held up the book. "We're like friendly aliens visiting from another planet."

Truth be told, in the time we'd been there, Uncle Tinsley hadn't had a single other visitor. He spent his time in his library, writing to historical societies, requesting information on the Middleburg Holladays, and going through boxes of old letters, journals, and yellowed newspaper clippings that referred to the Holladay family in any way. And there was nothing he didn't know about the earth, its layers of rocks and soil and water. He studied geological charts, conducted tests on soil and rocks, and read scientific reports to cite in the articles he wrote and occasionally published.

While Liz liked to lie in bed and read after she woke up, I always wanted to get up and get cracking, and I went downstairs for breakfast. Uncle Tinsley was in the ballroom, nursing a cup of coffee and staring out the French doors. "I hadn't realized how tall the grass has gotten," he said. "I do believe it's time to mow."

After breakfast I went with Uncle Tinsley up to the equipment shed. Inside was an old-timey red tractor with FARMALL on the side and a little sidestep up to the seat. It fired right up. Uncle Tinsley backed it up to his pull-behind mower, a big green contraption. I helped him attach the mower to the rear of the tractor.

While Uncle Tinsley mowed, I cleared the leaves from the koi pond. I discovered overgrown brick paths between the old flower beds, and I pulled the weeds off them. By the end of the morning, I had cleared out the pond and most of the brick around it. The flower beds, however, still had a ways to go. Uncle Tinsley motioned me over. "Let's get us some peaches for lunch," he said.

He hoisted me up onto the tractor's little side step. With me hanging on for dear life, we drove up the hill to the orchard.

The apples and pears were too green, Uncle Tinsley said. But he had some early peaches that were ready to eat. They were bred centuries ago for the climate in this county, and they tasted nothing like the mealy Styrofoam that passed for fruit in the supermarkets.

Uncle Tinsley pulled a peach down from one of the trees and passed it to me. That peach was so juicy that when I bit into it, I felt like it almost burst in my mouth. I wolfed it down. "Dang," I said.

"Now, that's a peach," Uncle Tinsley said. "A Holladay peach."

WE BROUGHT back a paper bag full of peaches. They were so irresistible that Liz and I ate them all that afternoon, and the next morning, I went back up to the orchard for more.

The peach trees were behind the apples, and as I approached, I saw the branches of one swaying back and forth. When I got closer,

I realized that someone was behind the tree, a guy, and he was filling a bag with peaches just as fast as he could.

"Hey!" I shouted. "What are you doing?"

The guy, who was about my age, looked at me. He had longish brown hair, and eyes as dark as coffee. He was shirtless, and his sunbaked skin was streaked with sweat and grime. He held a peach in one hand, and I saw that part of a finger was missing.

"What are you doing?" I shouted again. "Those are our peaches."

The boy suddenly turned and ran, the bag in one hand.

"Stop!" I shouted. "Thief!"

I ran after him for a few steps, but he was fast, and I knew I couldn't catch him. I was so mad at that dirty kid for stealing our peaches that I picked one up and threw it after him. "Peach thief!"

I HEADED back to the house. Uncle Tinsley was in the library. I expected him to share my outrage over the scoundrel stealing our peaches. Instead, he smiled and started asking me questions. What did he look like? Did I notice if he was missing part of a finger?

"He sure was," I said. "Probably got it chopped off for stealing."

"That's Joe Wyatt," Uncle Tinsley said. "He's your father's family. His father was your father's brother. He's your cousin."

I was so stunned, I sat down on the floor.

"And I don't mind him taking a few peaches," he added.

Mom didn't talk much about either Liz's dad or my dad. All she'd told us was that she had met Liz's dad, Shelton Stewart, while in college in Richmond, and after a whirlwind romance, they got married in the most lavish wedding Byler had seen in a generation. Mom became pregnant almost immediately, and it didn't take long for her to discover that Shelton was a dishonest parasite. He'd come from an old South Carolina family, but their money was gone, and he expected Mom's family to support them while he spent his days playing golf and shooting grouse. Her father made it clear that wasn't going to happen, and so, shortly after Liz was born, Shelton Stewart walked out on Mom, and she and Liz never saw him again.

My dad, Mom had told us, was a Byler boy. He was a blast to be around, but she and he came from different worlds. He died in a mill accident before I was born. That was all she would say.

"You knew my dad?" I asked Uncle Tinsley.

"Of course I did."

That made me so nervous, I started rubbing my hands together. Mom's account of my dad had always left me hankering for more details, but she said she didn't want to talk about him. Mom didn't have a picture of him, and she wouldn't tell me his name. I'd always wondered what he had looked like. I didn't look like my mom. Did I look like my dad? Was he handsome? Funny? Smart?

"What was he like?" I asked.

"Charlie. Charlie Wyatt," Uncle Tinsley said. "He was a cocky fellow." He paused and looked at me. "He wanted to marry your mother, you know, but she never took him that seriously."

"How come?"

"Charlie was a fling, as far as she was concerned. Charlotte was pretty shaken up when Liz's father decided he didn't want to be a father after all. She went through a wild-divorcée period and got involved with a number of men whom Mother and Father disapproved of. Charlie was one of them. She never considered marrying him. To her he was just a linthead."

"What's that?" I'd heard Mom use the word, but I didn't know what it meant.

"A mill worker. They come off their shifts covered in lint."

I tried to take it in. All my life I had wanted to find out more about my dad and his family, and now, when I'd met someone who was related to him—and to me—I'd acted like a nut job, calling him names and throwing peaches at him. And he wasn't a thief. Since Uncle Tinsley didn't mind Joe Wyatt taking the peaches, he wasn't actually stealing. At least, that was one way of looking at it.

"I think I need to go apologize to Joe Wyatt," I said. "And maybe meet the other Wyatts."

"Not a bad idea," Uncle Tinsley said. "They're good people. The father's disabled and doesn't do too much these days. The mother works the night shift. She's the one holding the family together."

He scratched his chin. "I suppose I could drive you over there."

The way Uncle Tinsley said that made me realize he didn't want to do what he'd just volunteered to do. After all, he was a Holladay, the former owner of the mill. He'd be paying a visit to the mill-working family of the man who got his sister pregnant. It would be awkward for him to drop me off without coming in, but probably more awkward to sit down with the Wyatts and shoot the breeze.

"I'll go on my own," I said. "It will be a chance for me to see Byler up close on foot."

"Good plan," Uncle Tinsley said. "Better yet, Charlotte's old bicycle is around here someplace. You could ride it into town."

I went up to the bird wing to tell Liz about the Wyatts. She was sitting in a chair by a window, reading another book she'd found in Uncle Tinsley's library, this one by Edgar Allan Poe.

When I told her about the Wyatts, Liz jumped up and hugged me. "You're trembling," she said.

"I know, I know. I'm nervous," I said. "What if they're weirdos? What if they think I'm a weirdo?"

"It'll be fine. Do you want me to come?"

"Would you?"

"Of course, Beanstalker, you weirdo. We're in this together."

THE next morning, Uncle Tinsley found the bike Mom rode as a kid. It was in the equipment shed where he also found his old bike, but it needed a new tire, so Liz and I decided to ride double.

Mom's bike was a terrific Schwinn like they didn't make anymore, Uncle Tinsley said. It had a red frame, fat tires, and a chrome rack behind the seat. Uncle Tinsley wiped it down, pumped air in the tires, oiled the chain, and drew us a map of where the Wyatts lived, explaining that it was known as the mill hill. With Liz pedaling and me sitting behind her on the chrome rack, we set off.

The mill hill was in the north part of town, just past the mill, at the base of a wooded mountain. The houses were identical boxes, many of them with the original white paint now all faded, but some had been painted blue or yellow or pink. Chairs and couches lined porches, and auto parts were crammed into some of the little yards. But you could see that keeping up appearances was important to a lot of the folks on the hill. Some used whitewashed tires as planters for pansies or had colorful pinwheels spinning in the breeze.

The Wyatts' house was one that clearly showed pride of ownership. The sky-blue paint was fading, but the front yard was mowed, and the bushes around the foundation were evenly pruned.

Liz let me go first. I knocked on the door, and it was opened by a big woman with twinkling green eyes. Her dark hair, which had a streak of white, was gathered in a bun, and she was wearing an apron over a baggy dress. She smiled at me curiously.

"Mrs. Wyatt?" I asked.

"I reckon I am." She was drying her hands on a dish towel. They were big hands, like a man's. "You all selling something?"

"I'm Bean Holladay. Charlotte's daughter."

She let out a shriek of joy, dropped the dish towel, then wrapped her arms around me in a spine-crushing hug.

I introduced Liz, who held out her hand in greeting.

"This ain't a shaking family, it's a hugging family!" Mrs. Wyatt shouted as she enveloped Liz in another crushing hug. She pulled us into the house, hollering for Clarence to meet his nieces. "And don't you be Mrs. Wyatt–ing me," she told us. "I'm your aunt Al."

The front door led into the kitchen. A small boy sitting at the table stared at us with wide, unblinking eyes. There was a big coal cooking stove with two freshly baked pies on top of it. Plates, bowls, and pots were stacked on the shelves according to size, and ladles and stirring spoons hung on a rack above the stove.

I asked if Joe was there. "I met him yesterday, but I didn't know he was my cousin."

"Where'd you meet him?"

"In Uncle Tinsley's orchard."

"So you're the peach thrower?" Aunt Al let out a huge laugh. "I heard you got quite an arm on you." Joe was out and about, she said, and usually didn't come home until dinnertime, but he was surely going to be sorry he missed this. She had four children, she went on. Joe was thirteen, her middle boy. She introduced the kid at the table as her youngest, Earl. He was five, she said, and he was different, not much strength, and he'd never really learned to talk—so far, anyway. Her eldest, Truman, who was twenty, was serving his country overseas. Her daughter, Ruth, who was sixteen, had gone to North Carolina to help out Aunt Al's sister, who had three children to look after but had been taken down with meningitis.

A man came out of the back room, moving carefully, like he was hurt. Aunt Al introduced him as her husband, our uncle Clarence.

"Charlotte's daughters? You don't say." He was thin and slightly bent, his gaunt cheeks had deep lines, and his gray hair was crew-cut. He studied Liz. "You I remember," he said. Then he looked at me. "You I never laid eyes on. That momma of yours got you out of town before I had a chance to see my brother's only child."

"Well, now you got your chance," Aunt Al said. "Be sweet."

"Glad to meet you, Uncle Clarence," I said.

He looked at me suspiciously. "Where's your momma?"

"She stayed in California," I said. "We're just here for a visit."

"Decided not to come, did she? Now, why don't that surprise me?" Uncle Clarence started coughing.

"Don't be getting all cantankerous, Clarence," Aunt Al said. "Go sit down and catch your breath." He left the room, coughing.

"My husband can be a little crotchety," Aunt Al told us. "He's a good man, but his lot ain't been an easy one—what with his bad back and the white lung he got from working in the mill. He also worries hisself sick about Truman being over in Vietnam, but he ain't going to admit it. Anyways, how about some pie?" She cut us each a slice. "Best peaches in the county." She grinned.

"And you can't beat the price," I said.

Aunt Al burst into laughter. "You're going to fit right in, Bean."

We sat down at the kitchen table next to Earl and dug into the pie, which was unbelievably yummy.

"Did my dad look like Uncle Clarence?" I asked.

"Different as night and day, though you could still tell they was brothers. You never seen a picture of your poppa?"

I shook my head.

Aunt Al studied the dish towel that she seemed to carry everywhere. "I got something to show you." She left the room and came back with a thick scrapbook. Sitting next to me, she started paging through it, then pointed to a black-and-white photograph of a young man leaning in a doorway with his arms crossed and his hip cocked. "There he is," she said. "Charlie. Your daddy."

She slid the album toward me. I almost heard the blood rushing in my head. I bent down until my face was inches away from the picture. I wanted to take in every detail about my dad.

He was wearing a tight-fitting white T-shirt with a pack of cigarettes folded into a sleeve. He had wiry muscles and dark hair, just like mine, though it was slicked back. He had dark eyes, also like mine. What struck me most was his crooked grin, like he saw the world in his own special way and got a kick out of it.

"He sure was handsome," I said.

"Oh, he was a looker," Aunt Al said. "The ladies loved Charlie. It wasn't just his looks. It was mainly the way he lit up the room."

"What do you mean?"

"You don't know too much about your daddy, do you, sugar?"

I shook my head.

Charlie had been a loom fixer at the mill, Aunt Al said. He could repair anything. He never got much in the way of a formal education, but he was smart and always had to be doing something. And when he arrived at a party, that was when it started.

"You got his spark, I do believe," Aunt Al told me. But Charlie also had a wild streak, she went on, and that's what got him killed.

"I thought he died in a mill accident," Liz said. "That's what Mom told us."

Aunt Al looked like she was considering something. "No, hon," she finally said. "Your daddy was shot. Gunned down in cold blood by the brother of the man he'd killed."

"What?" I stared at Aunt Al.

"You're old enough," she said. "You ought to know."

After Liz's dad ran off, Aunt Al explained, Charlotte left Richmond and came home to Mayfield. She was feeling pretty mixed up about it all and dated around a bit. Then she and Charlie became sweet on each other. She ended up in a family way, and Charlie wanted to marry her—not just because it was the honorable thing to do but because he loved her. But Charlotte's father, Mercer Holladay, was of no mind to let his little girl marry one of the loom fixers from his very own mill. Charlotte also seemed to feel that, as much fun as he was, Charlie was beneath her station.

Charlie was still hoping to change her mind when one night at Gibson's pool hall a fellow named Ernie Mullens said something about Charlotte being a loose woman—to put it politely. When Ernie refused to apologize, Charlie took after him. Then Ernie pulled out a knife. Charlie whacked Ernie upside the head with his pool cue, and Ernie fell against the pool table, cracking his skull. It killed him dead. The jury decided it was self-defense. After the trial Ernie's brother, Bucky, swore he was going to kill Charlie. Two weeks later he shot Charlie Wyatt down on Holladay Avenue in broad daylight.

"Your daddy was murdered," Aunt Al said, "because he defended your momma's honor." Bucky was sent to the penitentiary, and when he got out, he left the state.

Aunt Al took the photograph of my dad out of the scrapbook and placed it in my hand. "This is for you."

"I FEEL like everything's changed," I said to Liz. We were walking back to Mayfield, pushing the Schwinn, because I wanted to talk. "Now I know who my dad was."

"And now you know who you are," Liz said. "You're Charlie Wyatt's girl."

"Yeah," I said. "I'm Charlie Wyatt's girl." We reached the bottom of the mill hill. "I feel like I've got a lot to ask Mom. So is she ever going to call?"

"She'll call."

WHEN we got home, Uncle Tinsley was sitting at the dining-room table working on his big genealogical chart of the Holladay family.

"How did it go, Bean?" he asked.

"Well, she found out how her dad died," Liz said.

"Did you know?" I asked.

"Of course," he said.

"Why didn't you tell me?"

"It wasn't my place," he said. "But all of Byler sure knew about it. Didn't talk about anything else for months. Or years, it seemed."

Mill workers drinking beer in pool halls were always getting in fights, he said. From time to time, they killed each other. However, this incident involved the daughter of the man practically everyone in town worked for. By the time Bucky Mullens came to stand trial, Charlotte was showing. Everyone knew she was carrying the child of the pool hall–brawling linthead Bucky had killed. It was quite the scandal. Mother and Father were mortified. So were he and Martha. They all felt that the Holladay name was soiled. Mother stopped going to the garden club; Father stayed off the golf course.

Mother and Father, Uncle Tinsley went on, couldn't help letting Charlotte know how they felt. She had come home when her marriage fell apart, and she expected to be supported. At the same time, she had declared that since she was an adult, she was going to do what she pleased. As a result, she brought shame on the family. Charlotte, for her part, felt the family had turned on her, and she hated Mother and Father, as well as him, for feeling the way they did.

"And so not long after you were born, Bean, she left Byler, vowing never to return," Uncle Tinsley said.

That night, I couldn't sleep. I was lying there chewing on everything I'd learned that day about Mom and my dad. In times like these, having your own room stunk, because there was no one to talk to. I got up and carried my pillow into Liz's room, crawling under the covers next to her. She wrapped an arm around me.

"I actually know something about my dad now," I said. "It really gives you a lot to think about. Maybe, when Mom gets here, you should talk to her about getting in touch with your dad."

"No," Liz said sharply. "After the way he walked out on Mom

and me, I will never have anything to do with him. Ever." She took a deep breath. "In a way, you're lucky. Your dad's dead. Mine left."

THE next morning, I was pulling weeds in the flower beds around the koi pond, still thinking about Charlie Wyatt. The sound of a woodpecker hammering in the sycamores made me look up, and I saw Joe Wyatt walking up the driveway, his burlap bag over his shoulder. I stood up. When he saw me, he headed my way.

"Hey," he said when he was a few feet away.

"Hey," I said.

"Ma said I should come over and say hello, seeing as how we're related and all."

I looked at him and realized he had the same dark eyes as my dad and me. "I guess we're cousins."

"Guess so."

"Sorry about calling you a thief."

He looked down, and I could see a grin spreading across his face. "Been called worse," he said. "Cuz, you particular to blackberries?"

Cuz. I liked that. "You bet I am."

"Well, then, let's go get us some."

I ran up to the barn to find my own sack.

It was the end of June, and the humidity had kept climbing. We crossed the pasture and came to a barbed-wire fence line separating the pasture from the woods. Walking the fence line, we came across huge clumps of thorny bushes thick with fat, dark berries.

We made our way up the hill, picking blackberries and eating as many as we kept. Joe told me that he spent much of the summer in the woods picking mulberries and blackberries, raiding orchards for peaches and apples, as well as now and then sneaking into someone's garden for a haul of tomatoes, cucumbers, and beans.

"Only if they've got more than enough," he said. "I never take what would be missed. That would be stealing."

"It's more like scavenging," I said. "Like what raccoons do."

"There you go, Cuz. Though I got to admit, not everyone looks on it kindly." From time to time, he said, farmers who spotted him in their orchards or cornfields took potshots at him. The worst that had ever happened was when someone's dog came after him and he lost part of a finger before making it over the fence. Joe grinned and held up his hand. "Wasn't a picking finger."

When our bags were full, we headed back to Mayfield. At the barn we stopped to drink from the faucet above the watering trough, sticking our heads under the spigot.

"Maybe we can do more scavenging, Cuz." Joe wiped his chin.

"Sure, Cuz," I said, wiping mine.

He walked down the drive, and I turned to the house. As I reached the front porch, Liz came out the door.

"Mom called," she said. "She'll be here in a couple of days."

THAT afternoon, Liz and I sat out by the koi pond talking about Mom's arrival. It had been five weeks and two days since she had the Mark Parker meltdown and took off. As much as I liked Byler and as thrilled as I was to know Uncle Tinsley and to have met my dad's family, I missed Mom. I had tons of things I wanted to discuss with her about my dad, and Liz and I also wanted to know if we would be going back to Lost Lake or somewhere else.

"Maybe we could stay here for a while," I told Liz.

"Maybe," she said. "It's sort of Mom's house, too."

TWO days after Mom called, we were still straightening Uncle Tinsley's stuff when we heard the Dart coming up the driveway.

Liz and I rushed through the door, across the big porch, and down the steps just as Mom got out of the car, which was pulling a little white-and-orange trailer. She had on her red velvet jacket, even though it was summer, and her hair was teased up the way she did it when she was going to an audition. We had a three-way hug in the middle of the driveway, laughing and whooping, with Mom going on about "my darlings," "my babies," and "my precious girls."

Uncle Tinsley came out of the house and leaned against one of the porch columns. "Nice of you to finally drop in, Char," he said.

"Nice to see you, too, Tin," Mom said.

Mom and Uncle Tinsley stood there looking at each other, so I started jabbering on about all the fun things we'd been doing, staying in her old rooms in the bird wing, clearing the koi pond, riding the Farmall, eating peaches, and gathering blackberries.

Uncle Tinsley cut me off. "Where have you been, Char?" he asked. "How could you go off and leave these kids alone?"

"Don't pass judgment on me," Mom told him.

"Now, please, no fighting," Liz said.

"Yes, let's be civil," Mom said.

We all went into the house, and Mom looked around at the clutter. "My God, Tin. What would Mother say?"

"What would she say about someone abandoning her children? But as you said, let's be civil."

Uncle Tinsley went into the kitchen to make a pot of tea. Mom started walking around the living room, picking up her mother's crystal vases and porcelain figurines, her father's old leather-covered binoculars, the family photos in their sterling frames.

Uncle Tinsley came in with the tea service on the silver tray.

"Being back here is all too dark and strange," Mom said. "I feel the old chill. Mother was always so cold and distant. She never truly loved me. And Father loved me for the wrong reasons."

"Charlotte, that's nonsense," Uncle Tinsley said. "This was always a warm house. You were Daddy's little girl—at least, until your divorce—and you loved it."

"That's what we had to pretend. We pretended it was perfect."

"Don't be ridiculous. You've always exaggerated everything."

Mom turned to us. "See what I mean, girls? See what happens around here when you try to speak the truth? You get attacked."

"Let's just have tea," Uncle Tinsley said.

We all sat down. Liz poured and passed the cups around.

Mom stared into her tea. "Everyone in this town lives in the past. All they ever talk about is the weather and the Bulldogs. Are they even aware that their president is a war criminal?"

"The weather's important if you live off what you grow," Uncle Tinsley said. "And some people think President Nixon's doing a pretty good job trying to wind up a war he didn't start." He stirred sugar into his tea. "What is the plan for you and the girls?"

"I don't like plans," Mom said. "I like options. We have several options, and we're going to consider them all."

"You could stay here," Uncle Tinsley said. "For a while."

"I don't consider that an option," Mom said.

"Char, you need to give these girls some stability."

"What do you know about looking after children?" Mom asked.

"I do know that if Martha and I had been blessed enough to have children, we never would have gone off and left them."

Mom slammed her teacup down and stood up. She was raising two daughters on her own, she said, and they were turning out darned well. He had no idea of the sacrifices she'd made. She wasn't going to be judged by her brother, a broken-down hermit still living in the house where he was born, in a dead-end mill town.

"Get your things, girls," she said. "We're going."

Liz and I glanced at each other, not sure what to say. I wanted to tell Mom how good Uncle Tinsley had been to us, but I was afraid she'd think I was taking his side, and that might make things worse.

"Didn't you hear me?" Mom asked.

We climbed the stairs to the bird wing.

"Jeez, they hate each other," I said.

"You'd think they'd at least be polite," Liz said.

"They're supposed to be the grown-ups," I said, and added, "I don't want to go. We just met the Wyatts, and I really like them."

"Me, too. But it's not up to us."

UNCLE Tinsley was sitting at a writing table, scribbling on a piece of paper, when we came downstairs carrying the two-tone deb-phase suitcases. He folded the paper and passed it to Liz.

"The telephone number," he said. "Call if you need me." He kissed us each on the cheek. "You two take care of yourselves."

"Thanks for letting me bury Fido near Aunt Martha," I said. "At first I thought you were grouchy, but now I think you're neat."

And then we walked out the door.

CHAPTER FOUR

MOM drove as if we were fleeing the scene of a crime. She was talking a mile a minute. Mayfield had really gone downhill, she said. It looked like Tinsley had become a complete recluse. Boy, seeing that place sure brought back memories—bad memories. Same thing with this entire hopeless loser of a town.

"I like Mayfield," I said. "I like Byler, too."

"Try growing up here," Mom said. She reached into her purse and took out a pack of cigarettes.

"You're smoking?" Liz asked.

"It's coming back to this place. It's made me a little tense."

Mom lit the cigarette with the car's push-in lighter. We turned up Holladay Avenue. The Fourth of July was a few days away, and workers were hanging flags from every lamppost.

We crossed the clanking iron bridge over the river. "I met the Wyatts," I said. "Aunt Al told me about my dad getting shot." I bit my lip. "You said he died in an accident."

Mom took a drag on her cigarette. "I told you that for your own good, Bean," she said. "You were too young to understand."

Getting out of Byler was another thing she had done for the good of her daughters, she said. There was no way she was going to let us grow up in a finger-wagging, narrow-minded town where everyone would whisper about me being the illegitimate child of a hotheaded loom fixer who killed someone and then got killed himself. "Not to mention that everyone saw Yours Truly as the slut who caused it all."

"But Mom," I said, "he was defending your honor."

"Maybe that's what he thought he was doing, but he made everything worse. By the time it was all over, Charlotte Holladay didn't have any honor left to defend." Mom took a long draw on her cigarette. "Charlotte the Harlot."

Anyway, she went on, she didn't want to talk about the past. The past didn't matter. What mattered was the future. "I've figured out the future for us," she said. "New York City!"

What had happened, she went on, was that she'd been in San Diego with friends for a little group support, then went to Baja to spend time alone looking for signs about what direction to take. She hadn't seen any signs, but then she got back to Lost Lake and found Liz's message about us going off to visit the Mad Hatter and the Dormouse. That, she realized, was the sign. She needed to put California behind her and follow her daughters to the East Coast. She'd rented the U-Haul and thrown most of the stuff from our bungalow inside.

"Don't you see, Liz?" Mom asked, sounding almost giddy. "When I read your note about the other side of the Looking Glass, it hit me. That's New York City! If you're a performer, New York and L.A.—they're the two sides of the Looking Glass."

Liz and I glanced at each other. We were all crowded in the front seat because Mom had boxes of sheet music in the back.

"Are we being realistic?" Liz asked.

"Realism, schmealism," Mom said. Was Gauguin being realistic when he set out for the South Pacific? Was that skinny kid with the raspy voice being realistic when he left Minneapolis for Greenwich Village after changing his name to Bob Dylan? "No one who dares to be great and reach for the stars worries about being realistic."

New York was where the real scene was, Mom said. She started going on about Greenwich Village, blues bars and folk clubs, violinists in subway stations. She became animated.

"What we're on now isn't just a car trip," she said. It was a holiday, a way of celebrating the forthcoming New York Adventures of the Tribe of Three. "I've got a surprise for you."

"What's the surprise?" Liz asked.

"I can't tell you, or it won't be a surprise," Mom said, and then she giggled. "But it's in Richmond."

WE REACHED Richmond late in the afternoon. Mom stopped the Dart with the orange-and-white trailer behind it in front of a building that looked like a palace. A man in a crimson coat with tails walked up and looked dubiously at the Dart and the U-Haul.

Mom turned to us. "This is the surprise. Mother and I used to stay here when we came into Richmond to shop."

She opened the car door and extended her hand to the doorman. After a pause he took her hand and helped her out of the car.

"Welcome to the Hotel Madison," he said.

"It's good to be back," Mom said.

We followed Mom out of the car. The doorman glanced down at my sneakers, which were caked with the orange mud of Byler. Mom led us into a cavernous lobby. Rows of marble columns lined both sides of the room. There were chandeliers, statues, overstuffed chairs, Persian rugs, and paintings. I'd never seen anything like it.

"Can we afford to stay here?" Liz asked.

"We can't afford not to stay here," Mom said. "After what we've been through, we not only deserve it, we need it."

Mom had been talking almost nonstop since we left Mayfield. Now she went on about the hotel's sweeping staircase that, she said, had been used in a scene from *Gone With the Wind*. When she and her mother stayed here, she told us, they'd shop for her wardrobe for the school year, and afterward they'd take tea and sandwiches in the tearoom, where ladies were required to wear white gloves.

At the check-in counter, Mom asked for two adjoining rooms. "Mom!" Liz whispered. "Two rooms?"

"We can't crowd up in a place like this," Mom said. "This is not some neon-lit fleabag motel. This is the Madison!"

A bellboy brought our two-toned suitcases up to the rooms on a trolley. Mom made a show of presenting him with a ten-dollar tip. "Let's freshen up, then go shopping," she said. "If we're going to eat in the main dining room, we'll need proper clothes."

Liz unlocked the door to our room. It was extravagantly furnished, with a fireplace. We lay down on the four-poster bed. The mattress was so soft that you sank into it.

"Mom's never been like this before," I said.

"Not this bad," Liz said.

"Maybe it's just a mood and it'll pass." I plumped up one of the oversized pillows and leaned against it.

After a while Mom knocked on our door. "Ladies," she called out, "time to hit the shops."

She was still wearing her red velvet jacket, but she had teased her hair even higher and had put on glossy lipstick and dark eyeliner.

After we rode the elevator down, Mom led us back through the lobby, which was now bustling with smartly dressed guests and waiters in tuxes hurrying along with silver trays of martinis. Liz and I were still wearing the cutoffs and T-shirts we had put on that morning at Mayfield, and I felt seriously out of place.

We followed Mom down a corridor lined with stores that sold everything from jewelry and perfumes to fancy carved pipes and imported cigars. Mom directed us into a dress shop. "My mother took me to this very store when I was your age," she said.

There were racks of clothes, tables of shoes and handbags, and headless mannequins wearing expensive-looking summer dresses.

The clerk came over, a slightly older woman. She smiled. "Is there anything in particular I can help you with?" she asked.

"We need ensembles for dinner," Mom said. "We checked in on impulse without bringing much in the way of clothes. We're looking for something a little formal but also *très* chic."

"I know precisely what you have in mind," the clerk said. She asked our sizes and started holding up dresses while Mom oohed and aahed. Soon there was a pile of possibilities draped over a rack.

Liz fingered one and looked at the price tag. "Mom, this costs eighty dollars," she said. "It's sort of out of our price range."

Mom glared at Liz. "That's not for you to say. I'm the mother."

The clerk looked between Mom and Liz as if she couldn't decide whom to believe and where this was headed.

"Do you have any bargain racks?" I asked.

"We're not that kind of establishment," the clerk said.

"Now, girls, you're not to worry about money," Mom said. She looked at the clerk. "They've been staying with their tightwad uncle and have picked up his penny-pinching habits."

"We can't afford this, Mom," Liz said. "You know that."

"We don't need to eat in the restaurant," I said. "We can order room service. Or takeout."

Mom looked at Liz and me. Her smile disappeared, and her face darkened. "How dare you? How dare you question my authority?"

She was trying to do something nice for us, Mom went on, something to lift our spirits, and this was the thanks she got? She had driven across the country to get us, and what did we do to show our gratitude? We publicly embarrassed her in a store where she'd been shopping since she was a girl. She'd had it with the two of us.

Knocking the dresses off the rack, Mom stormed out of the store.

"My goodness," the clerk said.

WE FOLLOWED Mom out to the corridor, but she had disappeared. "She must have gone back to her room," Liz said.

We crossed the lobby, rode the elevator up to our floor, and walked down the hushed carpeted hallway. We stopped at Mom's door, and Liz knocked. "Mom?" she called out. There was no answer. Liz knocked again. "Mom, we know you're in there."

"We're sorry," I said. "We'll be good."

There was still no answer.

Liz kept knocking.

"Go away!" Mom shouted.

"We love you, Mom," Liz said.

"You don't love me. You hate me! Go away!"

The door shook with a bang and the sound of shattering glass. Mom had thrown something. Then she started sobbing hysterically.

We headed back to the lobby. There was a line of people at the reception desk, but Liz went right to the front and I followed.

The clerk had polished black hair and was writing busily in a ledger. "The line starts back there," he said without looking up.

"We have a bit of an emergency," Liz told him.

The clerk looked up and raised his eyebrows.

"Our mom has locked herself in her room and won't come out," Liz said. "We need help."

WE TROOPED UP TO MOM'S room with the clerk and a security guard. She was still crying and refusing to open the door. The clerk went to a house phone and sent for a doctor. When the doctor arrived in his white jacket, the security guard took out a master key, opened the door, and led him into the room. Liz and I followed.

Mom was lying on the bed with a pillow over her head. The doctor, a small man with a mild Southern manner, stroked her shoulder. Mom took the pillow off her face and stared at the ceiling. Liz and I were standing by the wall, but Mom didn't look at us.

She let out a loud sigh. "No one understands how hard it is to be me," she told the doctor.

The doctor murmured in agreement. He told Mom he could give her a shot that would make her feel better, and after that she could probably use a few days of rest and observation at Commonwealth Medical. Mom closed her eyes and squeezed the doctor's hand.

The clerk ushered Liz and me out into the hall. "Now, what are we going to do with you two?" he asked.

"We have an uncle in Byler," Liz said.

"I think we'd better call him," the clerk said.

After talking to Uncle Tinsley, the clerk ordered us each a ginger ale that came with a plate of little sandwiches—turkey, shrimp salad, cucumber—with the crusts cut off, and we ate them at a tiny table in the lobby. An ambulance had arrived at the back entrance for Mom, the clerk told us, and the doctor had helped her into it. After we finished our sandwiches, we sat there waiting. The clerk kept coming over to see if we were all right. As the hours passed, the bustling lobby grew quieter, and by the time Uncle Tinsley showed up, just before midnight, it was deserted.

Uncle Tinsley's footsteps echoed off the high ceiling as he walked through the lobby toward us. "I was hoping to see you again," he said, "but I never imagined it would be this soon."

MOM had me worried, but to be honest, I was relieved to be back in Byler. I hadn't been looking forward to moving to New York.

After a couple of days, Mom called. She was feeling better. She'd had a bit of a meltdown, she admitted, but that was due to the stress of going back to Byler after all those years. She talked to Uncle Tinsley, and they decided that what made sense was for Liz and me to stay in Byler for the time being. Mom would go to New York by herself, and once she'd settled in, she would send for us.

"How long do you think it will take Mom to get settled in?" I asked Liz. We were getting ready for bed, brushing our teeth in the bird-wing bathroom.

"There's getting settled in, and then there's getting a grip on things." Liz rinsed and spit. "We might be here a while."

THE next morning, Liz told me that she'd been thinking about our situation. It was possible, she said, that Mom wouldn't send for us by the time summer was over. That would mean we'd go to school in Byler. We didn't want to be a burden to Uncle Tinsley. Although he lived in a grand house and his family used to run the town, the collars of his shirts were worn and he had holes in his socks. It was obvious his tight budget didn't include providing for two nieces.

"We need to get jobs," Liz said.

I thought that was a great idea. We could both babysit. We could mow lawns. Maybe we could even get store jobs bagging groceries.

At breakfast we told Uncle Tinsley about our plan. We thought he'd love the idea, but as soon as Liz started explaining, he said, "You girls are Holladays. You can't go around begging for work like a couple of hired hands. Mother would roll over in her grave."

"But we might still be here when school starts," Liz said.

"That's a distinct possibility," Uncle Tinsley said. "And I welcome it. We're all Holladays."

"We'll need school clothes," I added.

"We've got all the clothes you need," he said. "Follow me."

Uncle Tinsley led us upstairs to the maids' rooms on the third floor and opened musty trunks and cedar-lined closets stuffed with mothball-smelling clothes: polka-dotted dresses, tweed jackets, ruffled silk blouses, and knee-length pleated plaid skirts. "These are all hand-tailored, imported from England and France," he said.

"But Uncle Tinsley," I said, "they're kind of old-timey. People don't wear clothes like this anymore."

"That's the shame of it," he said. "It's all blue jeans and polyester. Never worn a pair of jeans in my life. Farmer clothes."

"But that's what everyone wears today," I said.

"And that's why we need to get jobs," Liz said. "To buy some."

"We need spending money," I said.

"If there's something you really need, we can talk about it," Uncle Tinsley said. "But you don't need clothes. We have clothes."

"Are you saying we're not allowed to get jobs?" Liz asked.

"If you don't need clothes, you don't need jobs." Uncle Tinsley's face softened. "You do need to get out of the house. Take the bikes, go into town, make friends. But don't forget, you're Holladays."

Liz and I walked up to the barn.

"Uncle Tinsley's wrong," Liz said. "We do need to get jobs. And not just for clothes. We need our own money."

"But Uncle Tinsley will get mad."

"I think Uncle Tinsley doesn't really mind us getting jobs," Liz said. "He just doesn't want to know about it. He wants to pretend we're all still living back in the day."

Uncle Tinsley had patched the flat tire on the bike he'd ridden as a kid. It was a Schwinn, like Mom's, only it was a guy's bike and it was blue. Liz and I got the bikes out of the garage and rode into town to look for work.

We had forgotten it was the Fourth of July. A parade was getting under way, and people were lined up along Holladay Avenue, waving enthusiastically as the Byler High School band marched along in red-and-white uniforms. It was followed by cheerleaders, a fire truck, and a float with waving women in worn sequined gowns. Finally, a group of older men in military uniforms turned up the avenue, looking serious and proud, holding big American flags. In the middle of the group was Uncle Clarence, dressed in a green uniform, moving stiffly but keeping pace. As the flags passed, most of the crowd stood up and saluted.

"Here come the patriots," Liz whispered in that sarcastic tone she'd picked up from Mom.

I kept quiet. Mom had been telling us for years about everything wrong with America—the war, the discrimination, the violence—but here were all these people, including Uncle Clarence, showing real pride in the flag and the country. Who was right? I usually had pretty strong opinions, but now I wasn't so sure.

When the parade passed, the people in the crowd started folding up their chairs and spilling onto Holladay Avenue. We walked along, pushing our bikes. Ahead we saw the Wyatts coming up the street. Joe was carrying Earl, who held a little American flag. Uncle Clarence had medals above the breast pocket of his green uniform.

"I do love Independence Day," Aunt Al said after giving us hugs. "Reminds you how lucky we are to be Americans. When Truman comes home, he'll be marching alongside Clarence in that parade."

"But he's thinking of reenlisting," Joe said.

"Why?" Liz asked. "We're losing the war."

"We're losing the war here at home with all these spoiled draft-dodging protesters," Uncle Clarence said. "We're not losing the war over there. Our boys are doing a hell of a fine job. Truman himself says so." He turned on his heel and stalked off.

"I didn't mean to upset him," Liz said. "Doesn't everyone know we're losing?"

"People have different views," Aunt Al said. "It's a touchy subject around here. There's a tradition of service in these parts."

"I'm enlisting when I graduate," Joe said.

"My Clarence was in Korea," Aunt Al went on. "So was your daddy, Bean. Got the Silver Star."

"What's that?"

"A medal," Aunt Al said. "Charlie was a hero. He ran out into enemy fire to save a wounded buddy."

"You're enlisting?" Liz asked Joe.

"That's what guys around here do," Joe said. "I want to fix helicopters and learn to fly them, like Truman."

Liz stared at him in disbelief, and I was afraid she was going to say something sarcastic, so I changed the subject. "We're going to go looking for jobs," I told Aunt Al.

"That's a tall order," she said. There was not a lot of work around Byler, she explained. The folks on the hill didn't have money to spare. She and Clarence couldn't even afford a car. On Davis Street and East Street, where the doctors and the lawyers lived, most people had coloreds who did the cooking and washing. However, there were retired folks around town who may have the odd job.

Liz and I spent the next couple of days knocking on doors all over Byler. Most of the folks on the hill apologetically explained that they couldn't afford to fork over cash to kids for jobs that they could do themselves. Our luck wasn't much better at the fancier houses on East Street and Davis Street. Black maids answered the doors, and some seemed surprised when they learned we were looking for the kind of work they were doing.

At the end of the second day, I rode over to the Wyatts' to tell Aunt Al that the job search wasn't going so well.

"Don't be discouraged," she said. "And wait right here. I got a surprise for you." She disappeared down the hall and came back with a ring box. I opened it, and hanging from a little red-white-and-blue ribbon was a star-shaped medal.

"Charlie Wyatt's Silver Star," she said.

I picked up the medal. The star was gold and had a small wreath in the middle surrounding a tiny second star that was silver. "A war hero," I said. "Did he have a lot of war stories?"

"Charlie was quite the talker, but he never did like to talk about how he got this Silver Star. He saved one buddy, but there were others he couldn't save, and it weighed on him. Uncle Clarence was keeping this in memory of his kid brother. But it's yours now."

"I don't want to take it if it's important to Uncle Clarence."

"No," Aunt Al said. "We talked, and Clarence thought about it and decided that Charlie would want his little girl to have it."

Charlie and Clarence had always been close, Aunt Al went on. Their parents were sharecroppers who had been killed in a tractor accident. At the time, Charlie was six and Clarence was eleven. None of their relatives could afford to feed both boys, and since Charlie was too young to earn his keep, no one wanted him. Clarence told the family taking him in that he would do the work of two hands if they took Charlie as well. The family agreed, and Clarence worked himself to the bone, dropping out of school to take on the responsibilities of a man. The brothers stayed together, but those years hardened Clarence, and when he went to work at the mill, most of the women thought he was downright mean.

"I saw the hurt orphan inside the bitter man," Aunt Al said. "Clarence just wasn't used to being cared for."

"I should thank him for the star," I said.

"He's out tending to his garden."

I walked out the back door. Uncle Clarence was kneeling in a few dirt rows of green beans, staked tomatoes, and cucumber vines, working a trowel around the base of the plants.

"Thank you for giving me my dad's Silver Star," I said.

Uncle Clarence didn't look up.

"Aunt Al said you two were close," I added.

He nodded. Then he put the trowel down. "Damned shame about your momma going crazy," he said, "but that woman should have the word 'trouble' tattooed on her forehead. Meeting your momma was the worst thing that ever happened to your daddy."

Liz and I continued our job hunt the next day. Most houses in Byler were old, but late in the afternoon we turned down a street that had newer ranches and split-levels. One house had a chain-link fence around the yard with a bunch of hubcaps hanging on it. A shiny black car was in the driveway, and a man had his head under the hood, fiddling with the engine, while a girl sat in the driver's seat.

The man shouted at the girl to turn the engine over, but she gave it too much gas, and when the engine roared, he jerked his head up, banging it on the hood. He started cussing loudly, yelling that the girl was trying to kill him, and then he turned around and saw us.

"Sorry, ladies. Didn't know you were there," he said. "I'm trying to fix this damned engine, and my girl here's not being much help."

He was a big man. Not fat, just big, like a bull.

"Maybe we can help," Liz said.

"We're looking for work," I said.

"That so? What kind of work?"

The man walked over to where we were standing. His walk was lumbering but also strangely light-footed, as though he could move very quickly if he needed to. His arms were thick as hams. He had short blond hair and small but very bright blue eyes.

"Any work," Liz said. "Yard work, babysitting, housecleaning."

He looked us up and down. "I haven't seen you two around."

"We've only been here a few weeks," I said.

"Your family move here?" he asked.

"We're just kind of visiting," Liz said.

"Kind of visiting," he said. "What's that mean?"

"We're staying with our uncle for a while," I said.

"Why are you doing that?"

"We were born here," I said. "But we haven't been back since we were little."

Liz gave me the look that said I was talking too much, but I didn't see how we were going to get jobs if we didn't answer the man's questions.

"Oh, really?" he said. "And who's your uncle?"

"Tinsley Holladay," I said.

"Oh, really?" he said again, leaning in like he was interested. He was so big that when he looked down on us, it felt like he was swallowing up the sky. "So you're Tinsley Holladay's nieces?" He smiled, as if the idea of that was amusing. "Do you have names?"

"I'm Liz, and this is my sister, Bean."

"Bean? What kind of name is that?"

"A nickname," I said. "It rhymes with my real name, Jean."

"Okay, Liz and Bean-rhymes-with-Jean, I'm Jerry Maddox. And that's my girl, Cindy." He motioned at her with his finger. "Cindy, come over here and meet Tinsley Holladay's nieces."

The girl got out of the car. She was a few years younger than me, thin, with blond hair like her dad's that came down to her shoulders.

Liz and I said hi, and I smiled at Cindy. She said hi, but she didn't smile back, just stared at us with the same blue eyes as her father's.

"I might have some work for Tinsley Holladay's nieces," Mr. Maddox said. "Either of you ever been behind the wheel of a car?"

"Mom has let me drive up and down the driveway," Liz said.

"That would be Tinsley Holladay's sister, Charlotte Holladay?"

"Yes," Liz said. "That's right."

"Do you know her?" I asked.

"Never met her, but I've heard of her." He smiled again.

Mr. Maddox had Liz get in the driver's seat. Liz had the privilege, he told us, of sitting behind the wheel of a Pontiac Le Mans, one of the classiest cars Detroit had ever turned out. He had Liz turn the engine on and off, then operate the turn signal and tap the brakes while he had me walk around the Le Mans, checking the lights. He told Liz to gun the engine. He adjusted the carburetor, tested the belts, and had me hold the funnel while he added oil.

Finally, he slammed down the hood. "All tuned up," he said. "You girls are good at taking orders." He pulled a wad of money out of his pants pocket, pulled out two fives, gave one to each of us. "I think we can work together. Come back Saturday after lunch."

"I TOLD you we'd get jobs," Liz said on the way home. She was practically crowing. "Didn't I say that, Bean?"

"Sure did. You're always right."

Halfway back to the house, we passed the field with the two emus. They were walking along the fence line, right by the road.

"Look," I said. "They want to meet us."

"Mom would call it a sign," Liz said.

We stopped to watch them. They moved slowly and deliberately, their long necks swaying from side to side. They had curling turquoise stripes on the sides of their heads, tiny stunted wings, and big, scaly feet with these sharp-taloned toes.

"They're so weird," I said. "They're too big to be birds. They have wings, but they can't fly. They look like they shouldn't exist."

"That's what makes them so special."

When we showed up at the Maddoxes' on Saturday, Cindy answered the door. She turned and called out, "They're here."

We followed Cindy into the house. The living room was filled with boxes and appliances, including a portable black-and-white TV on top of a console color TV. Both TVs were on and tuned to different stations, but the sound on the black-and-white TV was turned down. A pregnant woman with mousy blond hair sat on a black Naugahyde couch, nursing a large baby. She shouted, "Jerry."

Mr. Maddox came out of the back, introduced the woman as his wife, Doris, and gestured to us to follow him down the hall.

Mr. Maddox led us into a bedroom that had been converted into an office, with metal filing cabinets and a metal desk. He sat behind the desk and pointed at two folding chairs. "Take a seat, ladies," he said. "A lot of people work for me, and I always ask them about their backgrounds." He was a foreman at the mill, he explained, but he also had outside business dealings that involved sensitive matters. He needed to be able to trust the people who worked for him. "It's a two-way street, of course. Any questions about me?" He paused. "No? Well, tell me about yourselves."

Liz and I looked at each other. She started hesitantly explaining the part-time jobs we'd held, but Mr. Maddox also wanted to know about our schooling, Mom's rules, Mom herself. When Liz told him that some of the information was personal and irrelevant, he said that lots of jobs required background checks, and this was one of them. He would treat everything we told him with confidence.

It seemed impossible not to answer his questions. The funny thing was, nothing seemed to surprise him. He was sympathetic and understanding. He said Mom sounded like a talented and fascinating individual. He confided that his mom was a complicated woman herself—very smart, but boy, did she run hot and cold.

That really got us talking, and soon Mr. Maddox had wormed the whole story out of us—Mom taking off, the bandersnatches, the cross-country bus trip. He wanted to know exactly why Mom had left and why she'd had a meltdown, so I ended up telling him about Mark Parker, the boyfriend who kind of, sort of, didn't really exist.

I also told him how we'd dodged the odious Perv in New Orleans, thinking that the way Liz and I had handled it would impress him.

That was the very word he used. "I'm impressed. I like people who know how to deal with difficult situations. You're hired."

So that was how Liz and I began working for the Maddoxes.

CHAPTER FIVE

I worked mostly for Doris Maddox. She had light freckles and kept her mousy blond hair in a ponytail. She was a few years younger than Mom and was the sort of woman Mom would have said could be quite pretty if she'd just fix herself up a little, but she wore a faded cotton housedress and bedroom slippers.

In addition to her daughter, Cindy, Doris had two boys—a toddler, Jerry junior; and Randy, the baby. She was pregnant with her fourth child and spent most of her time on the couch, watching TV while smoking Salems, drinking RC Colas, and nursing Randy. When Mr. Maddox was in the room, Doris said little, but once he'd left, she complained about the morons on the game shows or the sluts in the soap operas. She also complained about Mr. Maddox, how he was always telling her what to do and staying out all hours.

Doris had me take care of Randy when she wasn't nursing him and also look after Jerry junior, who was three. My duties included changing their Pampers and heating Randy's jars of Gerber baby food and Jerry junior's SpaghettiOs, as well as running to the store for Doris's RCs and Salems. I also washed clothes, cleaned the bathroom, and mopped floors. Doris told me I was a hard worker.

Mr. Maddox was infatuated with the latest high-tech gadgets, and the house was full of trash compactors, vacuum cleaners, popcorn poppers, and hi-fi systems. Most of the boxes throughout the house contained appliances, though a lot had never been opened.

Mr. Maddox was always thinking about more efficient and improved ways of doing things. That was why he'd been hired at the mill, he told us—to increase efficiency.

Mr. Maddox was fascinated by the law. He clipped out newspaper articles about lawsuits, bankruptcies, swindles, and foreclosures. His side dealings included buying up and renting out old millhouses. He also had a business loaning money to mill workers who needed to get to the next paycheck, and from time to time, he said, he was forced to take legal action against people who owed him money or were trying to stiff him.

A lot of Mr. Maddox's business dealings required meetings. While I stayed at the house helping out Doris, Liz accompanied Mr. Maddox in the black Le Mans to collect rents and take meetings at bars, coffee shops, and offices, where he introduced her as his personal assistant, Liz Holladay of the Holladay family. Liz carried his briefcase, passed him documents when he asked for them, and took notes. Back at the house, she would file paperwork, call to set up his appointments, and answer Mr. Maddox's phone.

We never worked regular hours. Instead, Mr. Maddox would tell us when he'd need us next. And we never received regular pay. Mr. Maddox paid us what he thought we deserved, depending on how hard we'd worked that day.

Mr. Maddox also bought us clothes. We showed up for work one day, and he gave each of us a pale blue dress, saying they were a bonus. We didn't have to wear the dresses every day, only when Mr. Maddox told us to. I didn't particularly like the dress, which felt like a uniform, but Mr. Maddox said since I was working in his house and Liz was representing him in meetings with his business associates, we needed to dress in a way that he felt was appropriate. And, he added, the cost of the clothes was more than any cash bonus he would have given us, so we were coming out ahead.

Mr. Maddox always made it hard to argue with him.

WE HADN'T been working for the Maddoxes long when it dawned on me that Mr. Maddox and Doris had a fixation about germs and bacteria. They were always having me scrub down their walls, floors, and counters. They had more cleaning products than I knew existed.

Cindy was the only Maddox kid who was school age. Her parents homeschooled her because Doris was afraid she'd catch germs. Cindy hadn't done well on her last exam, so even though it was summer, she had schoolwork. Sometimes Doris had Liz or me read to Cindy. Cindy loved being read to. She also loved the way Liz would change the ending to a story if Cindy found it upsetting, having the little match girl survive instead of freezing to death.

Doris wanted me to tutor Cindy, who knew how to read but didn't seem to enjoy it. One day I had her read aloud from *The Yearling.* She made it through a chapter just fine, but when I asked her what she thought of it, she went blank. I realized she didn't understand a thing about what she'd read.

I was explaining to Cindy how words depended on other words for their meaning—how the bark of a dog is different from the bark of a tree—when I heard Mr. Maddox shout at Doris in the bedroom. He was going on about how she didn't need any new clothes. Who was she trying to impress? Was she trying to seduce someone?

Mr. Maddox came into the living room carrying a cardboard box, and he handed it to me. "Put this in the Le Mans," he said.

Inside the box were Doris's three faded housedresses and her one pair of shoes. Doris appeared in the hallway in her nightgown. "Those are my clothes," she said. "I don't have anything to wear."

"They're not your clothes," Mr. Maddox told her. "Who bought them? Jerry Maddox. Who worked his butt off to pay for them? Jerry Maddox. So who do they belong to?"

"Jerry Maddox," Doris said.

"That's correct. I just let you wear them when I want." He turned back to me. "Now go put that box in the car."

I felt like I was being drawn into the middle of the fight. Since I worked mainly for Doris, I glanced at her to see what she wanted me to do, half expecting her to tell me to give her the box. She was just standing there looking defeated, so I carried the box out to the breezeway and put it in the backseat of the Le Mans.

As I closed the car door, Mr. Maddox stepped outside. "You

think I was being hard on Doris, don't you?" he said. "She's a person who needs to be disciplined." Doris was fast when he first met her, Mr. Maddox went on. She wore too much makeup; her skirts were too short; she let men take advantage of her. "I had to protect her from herself. I still do. If I let her go out whenever she wants, she'll fall back into her old ways. Without clothes, she can't go out and get in trouble. I'm doing it for her own good. You see?"

He was looking at me with that direct fixed stare. I just nodded.

Mr. Maddox said he didn't need me the next couple of days, but he wanted Liz to come back, so the following morning I rode my bike to the Wyatts' to see if Joe was up to a little fruit scavenging.

Joe was finishing breakfast. Aunt Al made me a plate, too—gravy over biscuits and eggs fried in bacon fat. She poured Joe a cup of coffee, which he drank black, and asked if I wanted some.

"Ugh," I said. "Kids don't drink coffee."

" 'Round here they do," Joe said.

Aunt Al gave me a cup of milk, then added a little coffee and two heaping teaspoons of sugar. "Try this," she said.

I took a sip. The milk and sugar cut the bitterness of the coffee, making it like a soda-fountain drink with a tiny kick.

"Did you all ever find yourselves any work?" Aunt Al asked.

"Sure did," I said. "Your boss at the mill, Mr. Maddox. He's our boss, too, now. He hired me and Liz to work around his house."

"Is that a fact?" Aunt Al set down her coffee. "Jerry Maddox can ride people hard. Sure does at the mill, where they all hate him. My Ruthie used to work for that family, but she just finally couldn't take it anymore. And she gets along with everyone."

"Mr. Maddox hasn't been too hard on us, but he does boss his wife around something awful."

"That man would boss the calf out of the cow. Your uncle Tinsley don't mind you working for him?"

"We haven't exactly told Uncle Tinsley," I said, and took a glug of my milk-with-coffee. "He didn't want us to get jobs. He said Holladays don't work for other people. But we need the money."

"I hear you there," she said. "But you ought to know about the history between Mr. Maddox and your uncle."

Aunt Al explained that the new mill owners had brought in Mr. Maddox to run the place. Uncle Tinsley had worked out an arrangement to stay on as a consultant. But in no time he and Mr. Maddox butted heads. Mr. Maddox's job was running the shop floor, and the new owners had told him to cut costs and raise production. He followed people around with a stopwatch, pushing them to work faster, hollering at them for taking bathroom breaks. He announced that, every month, he was going to fire the five slowest workers until he'd cut the number of employees by half.

It was at Mr. Maddox's recommendation that the owners did away with the baseball team and the free hams at Christmas. He got them to sell off the houses that the mill rented to the workers, buying up a lot of them himself on the cheap and raising the rent.

The mill had never been an easy place, Aunt Al said, but for the most part, all the workers got along. But after Mr. Maddox started firing people, former friends turned on one another, ratting on their coworkers so they could keep their jobs and feed their families.

Mr. Holladay insisted that a lot of Mr. Maddox's changes were doing more harm than good. He felt that Mr. Maddox was making the workers miserable, which was making them less motivated. He and Mr. Maddox kept arguing about the best way to run the mill. Mr. Holladay took his complaints to the new owners, but they sided with Mr. Maddox and forced Mr. Holladay out.

"The mill with his name on it," Aunt Al said. "The mill his family had founded, owned, and operated for the better part of a century. After that, people in Byler started avoiding your uncle."

"But he didn't do anything wrong," I said.

"True enough. But Mr. Maddox won the fight."

"I guess that's why Uncle Tinsley sort of keeps to himself."

"He lost his parents, his wife, and his mill all in the space of a few short years. The poor man's just had too much taken from him."

I finished the last of my eggs and biscuits. "Maybe we should tell Uncle Tinsley we're working for Mr. Maddox," I said. "I feel bad.

He's been good to us, and we're sneaking around behind his back."

"I'm none too big on giving advice," Aunt Al said. "Most times when folks ask for advice, they already know what they should do. They just want to hear it from someone else."

"Enough jawboning," Joe said. "Let's go get some apples, Cuz."

IN THE bird wing that night, I told Liz what Aunt Al had said about the bad blood between Mr. Maddox and Uncle Tinsley. "It doesn't feel right working for someone Uncle Tinsley hates."

"We need the money."

"Still, he's letting us stay here, and we're lying to him."

"We're not lying; we're just not telling him everything," Liz said. If Uncle Tinsley would be realistic, she went on, admit that we needed money for clothes and school supplies, that would be one thing. But as long as he was pretending we could wear debutante clothes from the forties and didn't need to worry about buying schoolbooks and cafeteria lunches, then we had to do what we had to do. "Keeping something to yourself is not the same as lying."

Liz had a point, but I still felt funny about it.

THE next afternoon, when Liz came back from work, she said she'd asked Mr. Maddox about his clash with Uncle Tinsley. Mr. Maddox had told her that he and Uncle Tinsley had indeed disagreed how the mill should be run. Uncle Tinsley lost the argument, Mr. Maddox said. He hadn't mentioned it before because he didn't want to sound like he was bad-mouthing our uncle. But he'd be happy to give us the real story if we wanted to hear it.

"I think we should take him up on his offer," Liz said.

I WAS glad Mr. Maddox was willing to give his side of the story. It made me feel like he cared what we thought of him.

Sometimes Mr. Maddox worked the day shift at the mill, but sometimes he worked nights and weekends. This particular week, he was working afternoons but had his mornings free, so the next day after breakfast, Liz and I biked to Mr. Maddox's house.

Mr. Maddox was in his office at his desk, feeding sheets of paper into a machine that shredded them into spaghetti-thin strips.

"Never just wad papers up and throw them out," Mr. Maddox said. "Your enemies will go through your trash to find anything they can use against you. You have to protect yourself."

Mr. Maddox shredded the last sheet of paper. "So you want to hear what happened between me and your uncle? I'd be happy to tell you, but you tell me something first." He took the two folding chairs out of the closet and had us sit down. "Does your uncle Tinsley know you're working for me?"

Liz and I exchanged glances. "Not exactly," she said.

"We wanted to tell him," I said, "but . . ."

"But he probably wouldn't be too happy," Mr. Maddox said.

"We love Uncle Tinsley—" Liz began.

"But sometimes Uncle Tinsley doesn't see things the way they really are," Mr. Maddox said.

"Exactly," Liz said.

"So I think it's a good idea that you don't tell him," Mr. Maddox said. He smiled. "Let's keep it between ourselves."

"But other people already know," Liz said. "You keep introducing me as Tinsley Holladay's niece."

"Also, I told my Aunt Al—Al Wyatt," I said. "Joe Wyatt, too."

"The Wyatts," Mr. Maddox said. "Wife works the late shift. Husband's a shirker who claims he's got white lung. That girl of theirs used to babysit for us, but things started going missing, so we told her to hit the road." He leaned back. "Anyway, just because a few people know you're working for me doesn't mean your uncle will find out. He doesn't get around much these days. And if he does find out, we'll handle the matter when it comes up."

Mr. Maddox explained that the Chicago company brought him in because the mill was losing money. The new owners said there were two choices: Cut costs by thirty percent and try to eke out a profit, or shut down the mill for good, disassemble the entire operation, and sell it—looms and all—to a factory in Asia.

"People at the mill hated me for firing their friends," Mr. Maddox said. "The fact is, they should have been down on their hands and knees, thanking me for saving some of their jobs. The slope heads in Asia are willing to work for twenty cents an hour. Meanwhile, I have your uncle moaning about keeping the baseball team going and how the quality of the bath towels isn't what it used to be. As if people care about quality these days. All they care about is price. So Uncle Tinsley had to go. The news that he was getting the boot spun him around like a top." Mr. Maddox pointed his forefinger in the air and made a circling motion. "Don't get me wrong, I think your uncle's a great guy, but you have to admit his judgment some-times sucks." He looked at the two of us. "Well, don't you?"

I shifted in my seat. Liz studied her fingernails. There wasn't a whole lot to say.

MOM called once a week and talked to Liz, then to me. Life in New York was exciting, she said, but challenging. The only afford-able apartment she could find was in a rough neighborhood with a crummy school. Lots of kids in New York went to private schools, but they were way beyond our budget. Liz and I belonged in a spe-cial public school for gifted students, she explained, but it was too late to apply this year, so what we needed to do was start the school year in Byler—Uncle Tinsley had said he'd be happy to have us stay on—then, once she'd found a cheap apartment in a neighborhood with a good school, she'd bring us to New York.

That was fine by me. Frankly, Mom had begun to get on my nerves. By now it was early August, and whenever I felt like talking to a grown-up, I'd go see Aunt Al. She told me stories about my dad, like the time he built an entire car out of junkyard parts and the time he gave Aunt Al a ride on his motorcycle.

Uncle Clarence was a certifiable curmudgeon, and I suppose Aunt Al was right that it was on account of his hard life. But it seemed to me that Aunt Al also had it tough—working the late shift at what Mom would call a dead-end job, coming home to make her family breakfast, grabbing a few hours' sleep, and getting up to make them dinner. Her grouchy husband was disabled, one son was off at war, her youngest wasn't quite right, but she never complained. Instead, she talked about how blessed she was and how many wonderful things Jesus had brought into her life, what with people like me showing up out of the blue. But her greatest blessings were her kids—Truman, the proud serviceman; Joe, who could do anything he set his mind to; Ruthie, who had spent the summer nursing Aunt Al's sister and was going to get herself a good office job; and her little special Earl. She loved them all.

One day shortly after Mom told me we should start school in Byler, I biked over to the Wyatts'. When I walked into the kitchen, Aunt Al was reading a letter. It was from Ruth, she said. Aunt Al's sister had recovered from meningitis. Ruth would be home in a few days, and she was looking forward to meeting Liz and me.

"I've got news, too," I said. "It looks like Liz and I are going to Byler High this fall."

"Honey!" Aunt Al gave me one of her big hugs. "I'm so glad you're staying with us instead of going off to the big city."

"Mom said life in New York was more challenging than she'd expected."

"That's one word for it." Aunt Al laughed. "Speaking of challenges, you're in for quite a time. This is the year that, like it or not, we're integrating."

Back in the fifties, she went on, the Supreme Court had ruled that black kids were allowed to attend white schools. In almost all Southern towns, however, black kids kept going to the black school, and white kids kept going to the white school.

As Aunt Al was talking, Uncle Clarence came in from the garden. Pulling off his straw hat and wiping his forehead, he filled a water glass at the sink and took a gulp. "Everyone was free to attend whatever school they wanted, and people chose to go to school with their own kind," he said. "That's natural. It's called freedom of choice. What's more American than that?"

"The Supreme Court disagreed," Aunt Al said. Last year the court ordered the forced integration of all Southern schools. So the Byler superintendent was closing down Nelson High, which had been the black school for fifty years. Beginning this year the kids from Nelson would be going to Byler High.

"It's the doing of those damned Harvards," Uncle Clarence said. "They started this war, told our boys to fight it; then they changed their minds about the war and went around spitting on our boys for serving their country. And now the Harvards want to tell us how to run our schools." He coughed. "Now I'm all riled up, so I best get back to my tomatoes." He picked up his hat and went out.

LATER that week, on a morning when Mr. Maddox didn't have any work for us, Liz and I rode over to the mill hill. While we were parking our bikes in the Wyatts' front yard, a tall young woman around Liz's age came running out the door. She had a wide smile just like Aunt Al's and long dark hair held back by barrettes, and she wore those plastic cat's-eye glasses that you saw on old ladies.

"You must be Liz and Bean," she cried, giving us both a bone-crushing Wyatt hug. "I'm Ruth, and I been dying to meet you."

Ruth led us into the house, explaining that the harvest season was under way and she and her mom were in the middle of canning. The kitchen table was piled with red, green, orange, and yellow tomatoes. Earl was lining up rows of mason jars on the counter, while Aunt Al stirred a big steaming pot.

"Uncle Clarence grew all these tomatoes?" I asked.

"Everything Daddy grows, we eat fresh," Ruth said.

"With all these mouths to feed, it don't go far," Aunt Al said. "Joe brings me my canning tomatoes. Some people may wag their finger at what my boy does, but the food he brings home helps keep this family fed, and those farmers grow more than they can sell, anyway."

"Ma told me you all will be going to Byler High this fall," Ruth said. "A lot of the white folks are making a fuss about integration."

"I don't get it," I said. "What's the big deal? There were always Mexican kids in the schools in California, and they were just like everyone else, except they had darker skin and ate spicier food."

"It's a little more complicated in these parts," Aunt Al said.

"A few people in Byler are saying integration could actually be good," Ruth went on. The Byler High football team would get those big, strong, fast black boys from Nelson, she explained, and they might take us to state. White players would have to be cut from the team to make room for the blacks. The Byler High cheerleaders, who all had boyfriends on the team, were saying that they'd quit the squad if their boyfriends were cut, because they didn't want to cheer for a bunch of coloreds who stole their boyfriends' positions.

The cheerleaders all came from well-to-do families, Ruth said. Mill hill boys sometimes made it onto the football team, but no girl from the hill had ever become a cheerleader. A cheerleader had to be a certain type, and that type just wasn't found on the hill. All the girls on the hill knew this, so they never even tried out.

"Until now," Ruth said. "Because if some of the cheerleaders who are the right type quit, other girls will have a chance to make the squad." She started screwing lids on the jars Aunt Al had filled. "So I'm planning to try out for the cheerleading squad. I don't have any problem cheering for the colored boys."

A bunch of the other hill girls were going to try out as well, and they were all meeting in a little while to practice. "Why don't you all come practice with us?" Ruth asked.

"You bet," I said.

"Sure," Liz said in that voice she used when her heart wasn't really in something.

"Well, okay, then," Ruth said. "But we'll need to fix your hair."

"You all go on," Aunt Al said. "I'll finish up here."

Ruth led us to her tiny bedroom. She said she wanted to show us her hope chest. She pulled a small trunk from under the bed and opened it. Inside were dish towels, bath towels, and a blanket. She said that she wasn't counting entirely on marriage. She was a top student in the secretarial track at Byler High. She had no intention of working at the mill—not to disparage her ma, of course. It was her ma who encouraged her to get herself a good office job.

"I've been doing some office work for Mr. Maddox," Liz said.

"I heard," Ruth said. "I worked for that family for a while. Watch yourself around him."

"What for?" I asked.

"Just watch yourself."

I looked at Liz to see if she was going to say anything about Mr. Maddox telling us he had to fire Ruth. Liz gave me an almost unnoticeable shake of the head, and then she said, "So what is this we're supposed to do with our hair?"

"You can't have it flopping all over the place if you're going to be a cheerleader," Ruth said, and opened a jewelry box full of barrettes and ponytail holders. She found a pair of baubles and barrettes that matched the blue shirt I was wearing, then a set that matched Liz's yellow shorts. She brushed my hair back, pulling it into a tight ponytail. Then she turned to Liz, whose reddish blond hair was thick and wavy and fell halfway down her back.

She pulled back Liz's hair into a tight ponytail and used barrettes to pin the stray ringlets in place. Without all of her flowing hair, Liz's face looked smaller and a little forlorn. She studied herself in the mirror inside the jewelry box lid. "I'm not sure this is me."

"You look real cute," Ruth said. "All nice and tidied up."

A LITTLE later eight girls showed up at the Wyatts'. Ruth had us form a line on the street in front of the house. She took off her cat's-eye glasses and set them on the front steps, saying she cheered without them even though she could barely see, because there was no way on God's green earth she'd make the squad wearing glasses that everyone knew came from the state's free clinic. Without those ugly glasses, Ruth's dark eyes were large and beautiful.

Ruth knew all the chants and the moves and the names for the moves. She showed us the eagle, the Russian jump, the candlestick, and the pike. I had always been a little uncoordinated, but I gave it my best shot, and it was actually fun. Liz, however, started out halfheartedly, and the little enthusiasm she had steadily dwindled until she gave up altogether and went to sit on the Wyatts' steps.

After cheerleading practice, the other girls wandered up the street, and Ruth went inside to help Aunt Al finish up the canning. Liz and I got on our bikes.

"So you're going to become a cheerleader now?" she asked.

"Maybe. What's wrong with that?"

"All that rah-rah stuff. It's excruciating."

WHEN we showed up for work one day shortly after that cheerleading practice, Mr. Maddox ushered us into his office. He handed each of us a thin little booklet with a blue leatherlike cover and fancy gold lettering that said BYLER NATIONAL BANK.

"I opened up a savings account for each of you," he said. "These are your very own passbooks."

I turned to the first page of mine. JEAN HOLLADAY was typed on the first line, along with JEROME T. MADDOX. There were columns marked "Deposits," "Withdrawals," "Interest," and "Balance." The deposit column had "$20.00" typed in, and so did the balance column.

Now, Mr. Maddox explained, he could deposit our pay directly into our accounts from one of his accounts. It would be simpler and more efficient, not to mention safer, because there was no chance that the deposited money could be lost or stolen. It would allow us not only to save money but to earn interest, accumulating wealth rather than squandering our earnings on soda pops and records.

Liz was examining her book. "It all looks very official," she said.

"It's a rite of passage," Mr. Maddox said. "Like getting your driver's license. Since neither of you girls has a dad—and Tinsley Holladay, whatever his virtues, ain't much help in that department—I'm stepping up to show you the way things work."

"If it's my passbook, why is your name on it?" I asked.

"They're joint accounts," Mr. Maddox said. He needed to be able to make direct deposits. He didn't expect us to know all this, because we'd never had savings accounts, but that was banking. "This is my way of helping you move along to becoming an adult, understanding the way the system works."

"But I like getting money," I said. It was fun fingering the worn bills that had passed through hundreds of other people's hands. "If your money's locked away in some bank, you can't look at it and feel it and count it. I like cash."

"Cash is just sitting in your pocket, tempting you to piss it away."

"Maybe so. But I still like getting cash."

"You'll be earning interest, Bean," Liz said.

"Someone's using her brain," he said.

"I don't care. I just want the money."

"Your choice. But it's the loser's choice. Typical Holladay."

I DIDN'T make the cheerleading squad.

Tryouts were held a couple of weeks before school began, and I could tell from the moment I got to the gym just how seriously the other girls took cheerleading. They were wearing the red-and-white Byler colors, and they had their hair held back with little baubles in the shape of bulldogs. The black girls were in one group and the whites in another. The JV coach barely looked my way when it came my turn, as if she already knew which girls she would pick.

Afterward I sat in the bleachers to watch the varsity tryouts. Three of the girls who'd been on the squad had followed through with their threat to quit, which meant there would be three open slots for girls from the mill hill and Nelson High.

Ruth took her turn, and I thought she nailed it. Then the black girls took their turns. They acted sassy, swinging their hips and shaking their heads, almost like they were dancing.

The results were posted a few days later, and Ruth made the team. So did two black girls. When I went over to the Wyatts' to congratulate Ruth, she gave me a big hug. Folks on the hill, Aunt Al told me, were over the moon that one of their own had finally made the squad. The cheerleading coach's selections had also created a lot of grumbling. Some whites in Byler had been willing to accept a single black cheerleader but thought that two was too many. At the same time, the Nelson students felt they should have had three cheerleading slots, since they were half the school now. A black girl and a white girl had gotten into a catfight over it.

"Don't know what this bodes for the school year," Aunt Al said.

She was mixing up a bowl of pimento cheese for sandwiches when Uncle Clarence came through the front door clutching a bottle in a paper bag, a huge grin on his face. He kissed Aunt Al and his kids and hugged me, talking all the while in the tones of a preacher man, asking how everybody was doing on this glorious day, going on about his beautiful daughter and how the mill hill finally got itself a cheerleader. "That there's reason for a celebration. Let's have some music. Somebody get me my guitar!"

Joe came back with an ancient guitar. Uncle Clarence took a long slug from the bottle, then picked up the guitar and started to play it like nobody I'd ever heard. He was plucking and strumming away, almost like he was in a trance, the music flowing up out of him.

I was stunned. This crazy dancing guitar player wasn't the Uncle Clarence I knew.

"There's mean drunks and there's sad drunks," Aunt Al said. "When my Clarence drinks, he's a dancing drunk."

The rest of the Wyatts started clapping and shouting and jigging, and I joined in. We all circled around Uncle Clarence, who was playing so fast that his hands were a blur. Then he threw his head back and began to howl.

Doris's pregnancy was getting along. One day in late August, Mr. Maddox told me she had a doctor's appointment. He wanted Liz to stay at the house to answer the phone, but I needed to come with them to take care of the baby while the doctor saw Doris.

Mr. Maddox had given Doris her clothes back a few days after he had me put them in his car, and she was wearing one of her housedresses. He told her to get in the back of the Le Mans with the baby, and he had me sit up front next to him. He gunned the car, and it shot out of the driveway. We were just going to a routine checkup, and we weren't even late, but he drove like a demon.

About halfway to the hospital, Mr. Maddox pulled into the parking lot of a convenience store. "I'm getting chips and sodas for everyone," he announced. "What do you want?"

"You decide, honey," Doris said.

"I want an orange soda," I said. "Nehi, Orange Crush, or Fanta. And Cheetos. Not the puffy ones but the crunchy fried ones."

"Sit tight," Mr. Maddox said, and climbed out of the car.

A couple of minutes later he returned carrying a brown paper bag. He got into the car, reached into the bag, and handed me an RC Cola and a little cardboard cylinder.

"What's this?" I asked.

"Chips and soda." He passed Doris the same.

"I asked for orange soda and Cheetos," I said.

"That's RC, which is the best cola on the market, and those are Pringles. They're just out, and they're better than Cheetos."

"But that's not what I wanted."

"I asked what you wanted, but I didn't tell you that I was going to get you what you wanted," he said.

I pulled back the tab on the lid of the Pringles container. Inside was a perfect stack of chips. I ate one. "This tastes funny," I said.

"What are you talking about?" Mr. Maddox asked. "Pringles taste better than Cheetos. They're superior in every way." Pringles were uniform in shape, he said, and they didn't break, because they were stacked neatly inside the cylinder. You didn't have to deal with burned spots that you sometimes found on regular potato chips. "What's more, you don't get that orange crap on your fingers."

"I like that orange crap," I said. "It goes with the orange soda that I also asked for but didn't get." And, I continued, Cheetos were in fact better than Pringles—in my opinion, anyway. They came in a variety of sizes, so you could choose big or little, depending on your mood. And they came in all sorts of different shapes, so you could have fun trying to figure out what each one looked like.

Mr. Maddox was gripping the steering wheel, and I could see a vein on his temple pulsing, as if his head were going to explode.

"That's the stupidest thing I've ever heard." He pointed a finger at my face. "I'm telling you, Pringles are better than Cheetos."

"He's right," Doris piped in. "Jerry knows what he's talking about. You'd best listen to him rather than trying to argue."

Mr. Maddox nodded. "You made a bad choice about the Cheetos, so I overruled it. That's what I have to do when the people around me make bad choices. So shut up and eat your damned Pringles."

THAT AFTERNOON, I TOLD LIZ about the Cheetos and Pringles debate. "I don't see why he got so bent out of shape," I said. "If he thinks Pringles are better than Cheetos, that's his opinion, but if I like Cheetos, that's my opinion. If I have a fact wrong, that's one thing. But an opinion isn't a fact. He can't tell me my opinion is wrong."

"Bean, you're getting all worked up over a bunch of snacks," Liz said. "It's not important."

"He can't tell me what to think."

"He sure can, especially if you're working for him—but that doesn't mean you have to think it. At the same time, you don't have to tell him you disagree. You don't have to argue."

"In other words, I should shut up and eat the damned Pringles?"

"Choose your battles," she said. "It's like with Mom. Sometimes it's better to go along with what they say."

That was what she did with Mr. Maddox, Liz said. He had strong opinions on just about everything, and what worked best was simply to listen. Mr. Maddox had told Liz he knew he could be a hothead, and one of the reasons he liked her was that she didn't get upset when he got a little out of control. She knew how to handle herself. He also trusted and respected her, and that was why he let her see confidential legal papers about the lawsuits he was involved in.

CHAPTER SIX

BY THE end of summer, Liz and I had saved up enough money for new clothes. Mr. Maddox had been paying me in cash, as I wanted, and I had been keeping it in a cigar box in the little white cradle, along with the photograph of my dad and his Silver Star. Liz withdrew some money from her savings account, and one afternoon we went down to Kresge on Holladay Avenue. Liz insisted that in addition to jeans and T-shirts, we needed to invest in one really striking outfit. She kept saying it was important to make a good first impression at a new school. Liz picked out a bright orange-and-purple skirt and a shiny purple shirt for herself. For me she found a pair of lime-green pants and a lime-green vest.

On the first day of school, we put on our really striking outfits, and even though there was a bus stop within walking distance of Mayfield, Uncle Tinsley drove us to Byler High in the Woody.

The school was a big brick building, three stories high. Hundreds of students were under the huge poplar trees in front of the school, the black kids in one group and the white kids in another. As soon as we pulled up, I realized that all of the white kids were wearing faded jeans, sneakers, and T-shirts, while all of the black kids had on flashy bright clothes, like the ones Liz and I were wearing.

"We're dressed like the black kids!" I blurted out.

Uncle Tinsley chuckled. "Well, I do believe you are," he said.

"Everyone will stare," I said. "We need to go home and change."

"It's too late," Liz said. "Anyway, like Mom is always saying, who wants to blend in when you can stand out?"

We certainly stood out. The other kids, both black and white, were eyeing me, giggling and doing double takes as I walked from class to class. "Hey, Day-Glo Girl!" some white boy shouted.

That night, I hung the lime-green pants in the closet. Tomorrow I'd put on jeans and a T-shirt. Liz said she would do the same, but I knew that even if I never wore those pants again, from here on out I would be known as Day-Glo Girl.

BYLER High was one old building. It had stairways and high ceilings and was noisy, with lockers slamming and bells ringing between periods and students yelling in the crowded halls. It became clear that kids who'd known each other all their lives had no interest in meeting a new girl. Even if I gave them my friendliest smile, they looked away. Maybe it was because of integration, but there was also a lot of pushing and shoving in the halls. You could tell that Byler High was filled with riled-up kids itching for a fight.

When I was in sixth grade, I'd thought junior high would be hard, with thick books and mysterious subjects like algebra. But despite the intimidating names, such as literature and comprehension, social studies, and home economics, the courses were no big deal. Literature and comprehension was just reading. Social studies was just news with a little history thrown in. And the first thing we learned in home economics—required for seventh-grade girls—was how to set a table. Knife on the right side of the plate, spoon next to that, forks on the left, lined up in the order they were to be used.

Our teacher, Mrs. Thompson, said she was teaching us "survival skills" that every woman needed to know. The seventh-grade guys got to take shop and learn useful things, like how to fix a flat tire and how to build a bookcase. We weren't even learning practical stuff, like how to keep a budget. It was all about being proper, knowing where the water glass stood in relation to the juice glass.

I learned that you could get out of home ec one day a week if you joined the pep squad. So without really knowing what the pep squad was, I decided to volunteer. Our job was to help the cheerleaders rev up the crowds during pregame pep rallies on Fridays, the day of the football games, and then at the games that evening. We also made the spirit stick—a painted broomstick gussied up with Bulldog doohickeys—which was awarded to the class that showed the most spirit during rallies, and we painted the posters that went up in the hallways before each game.

Byler's first game that year was against the Big Creek Owls. When we met in the gym, Terri Pruitt, the senior who was the leader of the squad, said we needed to come up with owl-themed posters. When I told Liz about it, she rattled off a string of really neat owl puns and rhymes we could use—"Disembowel the Owls," "Pluck the Owls," "Befoul the Owls," "Owls Are Foul Fowls," and best of all, "Bulldogs Growl, Owls Howl."

"Why don't you join the pep squad?" I told Liz. "You'd be great."

"I don't think so," she said. "The whole thing's too tribal."

At the next meeting of the pep squad, I read out Liz's list of slogans. Terri loved "Bulldogs Growl, Owls Howl." She said we could make a big banner by spray-painting the words on an old sheet and hanging it in the gym for Friday's pep rally. She turned to Vanessa

Johnson, the one black girl on the pep squad, who was in my English class. "Vanessa, you can help Bean," Terri said.

"So I'm the help?" Vanessa asked. She was taller than most of the girls, with long athletic arms and legs. She stared at Terri.

"We're all helping each other, okay?"

Terri found the sheet and spray paint and had us take them outside. As we walked down the hall, I started telling Vanessa that we should outline the words in pencil first, to make sure we got them centered and they didn't scrunch up at the end.

"Who put you in charge?" she asked.

"That's not fair," I said. "It was just an idea."

Vanessa put her hands on her hips. "Fair? You want to talk about what's fair and what's not fair? What's not fair is having your own school closed down and being forced to go to the cracker school."

"What do you mean? I thought the black kids wanted to go to the white schools."

"Why would we want to go to the white school when we had our own school?" At Nelson they had their own football team, Vanessa said; their own cheerleading squad, their own school colors. But now the Nelson kids had to give up those colors. They knew none of them would ever be elected class president at Byler or named homecoming king or queen or be declared "Most Likely to Succeed." Byler would never be their school.

"If that's how you feel, why did you join the pep squad?"

"I didn't make JV cheerleader, even though I was better than the white girls who did," she said. "That doesn't mean I'm going to sit in the bleachers." Her sister, Leticia, she explained, was one of the two Nelson cheerleaders chosen for the Byler squad. Vanessa said she would be at every game, cheering on Leticia and rooting for the Nelson boys on the Byler team. Then she looked me in the eye. "And I ain't giving up. I'm making cheerleader myself next year."

I held up the sheet. "Then I guess we should get cracking on this banner."

"The cracker wants to get cracking," she said, and for the first time she smiled.

THE FOLLOWING SATURDAY, I was in the basement of the Maddoxes' house, folding laundry, when Mr. Maddox appeared at the top of the stairs. He clambered down the steps and came over, moving in that strangely light-footed way he had for such a large man. "Keeping busy," he said. "I like that. You work for me, you keep busy."

"Thanks. I folded the big stuff. Now I'm matching socks," I said.

Mr. Maddox stretched his arm out, propping himself against the basement wall. He towered over me, and I felt a little boxed in. I wasn't used to being so close to a grown man. His smell made me think of sweat and work, muscle and meat. It was a little unsettling.

"Another thing I like about you," he said, "is that you're not scared of me. I'm a big guy, and I know some people get nervous when I'm standing next to them like this."

"Nope," I said. "Not me."

"No," he said. "You're not afraid." He reached over and put his hand on my shoulder. It was a hot September day, and I was wearing a sleeveless shirt. His enormous hand was so calloused that I thought I could feel the individual ridges of his fingerprints.

"You take your responsibilities seriously," he went on, "and you don't make a big deal out of little things. Unlike Doris. You've got a good sense of humor; you're fun to be around. You've got spunk, and you're mature for your age. How old are you again?"

"Twelve."

"Twelve? That's all? You look and act much older than that." Mr. Maddox suddenly slipped his thick thumb into my armpit and stroked it. "And you've already got your peach fuzz coming in."

I jerked back. "Cut it out!"

Mr. Maddox held my shoulder with his thumb still in my armpit for just a moment longer, then dropped his hand and laughed. "Now don't go getting all stupid on me. I didn't do anything wrong. I was just commenting on your coming-of-age. I grew up with sisters, and I know all about women and when they start developing. If we're going to have a working relationship, we need to be able to talk about things like this. Maybe someday you won't be able to come to work for me because you started your cycle and got cramps, and you'll need to tell me that. Happens all the time at the mill."

I looked down at the pile of socks. I couldn't think of anything to say. I didn't want to get all stupid and blow it out of proportion. Even though Mr. Maddox sticking his thumb in my armpit felt completely wrong, I couldn't disagree with a single thing he said.

Mr. Maddox reached over and pushed my chin up. "You're not mad at me, are you? If you're mad, you should say something. You can call me a name." He paused. "Or you can hit me." He spread out his arms. "Right here in the stomach. Hard as you can."

"No, thanks."

"Don't want to hit me? Why not?" He paused again. "I know you're not scared of me, so I guess you're not mad at me. Good." He took out his roll of bills and pulled off a twenty. "Here's for your day's work," he said, and headed back up the stairs.

Twenty dollars was way more than Mr. Maddox usually paid me for a day's work. The whole thing had been creepy, and by taking the money, I felt I was letting him buy me off. But twenty dollars was a lot of money. Mr. Maddox knew I needed it, and he knew I'd take it. I put the money in my pocket, finished matching the socks, and left without saying good-bye to anyone.

I had planned to tell Liz what had happened with Mr. Maddox, but it was embarrassing. Also, he hadn't actually done anything wrong, and if he had, he'd more or less apologized. I kept telling myself that I didn't want to make a bigger deal out of it than it was. I just had to figure out how to handle him. Like Liz did.

USUALLY Mom called once a week, but every now and then she called a few days late. When that happened, she'd apologize, saying she meant to call, but you know how crazy the music world can get.

The time wasn't right for Liz and me to come to New York, Mom told us. Besides, it was good for us to be exposed to life in Byler. It would help us understand why she made the decision to leave.

When I told Mom I joined the pep squad, she sighed. "Why would you want to do that?" she asked. She'd been a cheerleader herself, she said, and she shuddered to remember it. Football was barbaric. And cheerleading was a way of brainwashing women into thinking that the men were the stars and the most women could expect out of life was to stand on the sidelines and cheer them on.

"Don't be someone else's little cheerleader," Mom said. "Be the star of your own show. Even if there's no audience."

I knew Mom had a point. Still, I liked being on the pep squad. It was fun, and I'd made some friends. What was wrong with that?

Liz, however, took Mom's advice to heart. She'd been leaning in that direction anyway, and was glad to have Mom's perspective to support her views. I'd been trying my best to make things work out at Byler, but Liz was constantly making comments about quaint local customs and correcting other kids' grammar. After the first day of school, Liz and I had worn jeans, but after a couple of weeks, she'd gone back to outfits that made her stand out, including the orange-and-purple skirt, a beret, and even some of Mom's old clothes. While I was in the habit of thinking of Liz as brilliant, beautiful, and all-around perfect, it was clear the kids at Byler thought she acted peculiar and put on airs.

IN CALIFORNIA we'd never paid much attention to school sports. The only people who really cared were the kids on the teams. But in Byler the entire town was obsessed with the Bulldogs. Signs cheering on the team appeared in the storefronts along Holladay Avenue. Teachers interrupted class to talk about the upcoming game. And everyone treated the members of the team like gods.

On the day of a game, you were supposed to wear red and white to school. I put on a red-and-white T-shirt the day the Bulldogs were scheduled to play the Owls in the season opener. Liz made a point of wearing her orange-and-purple skirt, saying that she was a nonconformist, like Mom.

Everyone at Byler was required to attend the pep rally, held the day of the game. I got out of home ec to decorate the gym. Each class sat together, and they all competed to cheer the loudest, with the noisiest class winning the spirit stick and the privilege of waving it around at the game that night. When it was the seventh-graders' turn, Vanessa and I stood in front of the class, pumping our fists in the air. One kid shouted, "You go, Day-Glo Girl!" I just grinned and pumped my fists even harder, and I'll admit I was downright proud when we won that spirit stick.

The game started in the early evening. The floodlights had been turned on, and a hot wind blew across the football field.

The Wyatt family showed up early to get seats down front so they could cheer Ruth on. Liz didn't come, but Uncle Tinsley showed up, wearing a gray felt hat and an old red-and-white varsity jacket with a big B on it. He walked over to where I was standing with the pep squad. "Class of '48," he said. "We swept the division." He winked. "Go get 'em, Bulldogs."

The bleachers filled up quickly, and just like in the school cafeteria, the blacks and the whites sat separately. After the band came out, the Bulldogs were introduced one by one, each running onto the field when his name was called. The white fans cheered for the white Byler players, but they stayed pretty quiet for the black players who'd been at Nelson. At the same time, the blacks in the bleachers cheered for the black players but not the white ones.

When the Owls took the field, their fans cheered for the entire team, but the Owls had only one black player. One of the things people had been talking about before the game was that the Owls had always been a weak team, but Big Creek was a tiny town up in the mountains, and hardly any blacks lived there, so the team hadn't had the integration issues Byler was going through.

At the start of the game, the crowd was cheering every time the Bulldogs completed a pass or made a tackle. The cheerleaders were along the sidelines, jumping around and shaking their pom-poms, while the pep squad ran back and forth in front of the bleachers, pumping the crowd, yelling, "Bulldogs growl, Owls howl!"

Everyone was having a blast. However, by the second quarter the Bulldogs had fallen behind by two touchdowns, and the mood of the crowd turned sour. I didn't know much about football, so I asked Ruth what was going on. Dale Scarberry, the white quarterback, was passing only to the white receivers, she explained, and the new black players weren't blocking for their white teammates. If that kept up, the Bulldogs would be massacred.

When Dale Scarberry threw a pass that was picked off by one of the Owls, I was surprised to hear the Byler fans—both the students and the adults—start booing their own team. They kept it up every time another Bulldog made a mistake, shouting things like "You're stinking up the field!" "Idiot!" "Bench him!" and "You suck!"

The Owls scored again, and that was when things got really ugly. We pep squadders were still jumping and pumping, trying to get the crowd back on our side, when someone threw a paper bag of garbage on the field. I dashed out to pick it up, and when I got back to the sideline, I saw a white man in the bleachers stand and hurl a hamburger at Vanessa's sister, Leticia, as she was raising her pompoms over her head with a big grin. The hamburger hit her in the chest, leaving a greasy mark on her pretty red-and-white uniform.

Leticia ignored it—she even went on smiling—and the cheerleaders continued their routine. Then a white man threw a big cup filled with ice and cola. When it hit Leticia on the shoulder, the lid flew off, drenching her uniform. Leticia kept kicking and cheering as vigorously as before, though she had stopped smiling.

Aunt Al turned to face the two white men. "Hey, now, that ain't right!" she shouted.

At that point, a black man standing on the bleacher steps hurled a soda cup at Ruth. The drink splattered down her uniform.

That was too much for Joe. He sprang up and charged toward the black man, but other blacks knocked him down before he got there. A bunch of white fans jumped across the bleacher seats to defend Joe, and then all hell broke loose, people throwing drinks and food, shouting, trading punches, women cursing and pulling hair, babies crying, and kids screaming. The ruckus went on until the police rushed into the bleachers with their nightsticks out and broke it up.

We lost the game 36 to 6.

IN SCHOOL on Monday, all anyone could talk about was the game. Some white students were outraged about the brawl, but they blamed it on integration, saying this was what was going to happen when you mixed black and white. Some black kids were just as disgusted, although they said the ruckus wasn't their fault. They'd just been defending themselves. Most students were less upset about the brawl than about the shellacking the Bulldogs had taken at the hands of the Big Creek Owls, whom they usually creamed.

The principal, at the end of his morning announcements over the P.A. system, mentioned the need for "mutual respect and school unity." But it wasn't until English class, after lunch, that any of my teachers directly raised the subject.

My English teacher, Miss Jarvis, a thin-lipped young woman who got very excited about the readings she assigned, told us that she thought we ought to discuss what had happened at the game.

"The whites started it," said Vanessa Johnson. "Throwing that Coke at my sister."

"Stuff always gets thrown at games," said Tinky Brewster, a kid from the hill. "It's just like you all to make it a racial thing."

"We're not simply going to trade accusations here," Miss Jarvis said. "But I'd like people's views on what we can do to make integration a success here at Byler High."

White kids said the problem was that blacks were always carrying on about slavery, even though blacks were freed a hundred years ago. Anyway, a bunch of the white kids from the hill said, none of their families had owned slaves. In fact, most of their great-great-grandparents had been indentured servants, but you never heard people complaining about the Irish being enslaved.

Slavery ended a hundred years ago, the black kids replied, but until recently they couldn't eat in the Bulldog Diner, and today they got glared at when they did. They started getting hired at Holladay Textiles only a few years ago, and they were still given the worst jobs. They said whites wanted blacks to shut up and go back to cleaning toilets and cooking food for white people.

"Well, we're not going to resolve this issue in a day," Miss Jarvis said. Instead, she wanted us to read a book about racial conflict in a small Southern town. It was called *To Kill a Mockingbird*.

I LIKED *TO KILL A MOCKINGBIRD,* but I didn't think it was the most amazing book ever written, the way Miss Jarvis did. The best part, I thought, wasn't the stuff about race but the way Scout and the two boys snooped around the big haunted house where the scary recluse lived. That really reminded me of being a kid.

A lot of kids in the class had problems with the book. The white ones said they knew blacks shouldn't be lynched, and they didn't need a book preaching to them about it. The black kids wondered why the hero had to be a noble white guy trying to save a helpless black guy. They also didn't like that all the good blacks knew their place and made their children stand when the noble white guy walked by. It was all that Stepin-Fetchit-yass-suh-no-suh stuff.

"This discussion isn't going the way I'd anticipated," Miss Jarvis said. What she wanted us to do, she went on, was to put our thoughts down on paper.

WHEN Uncle Tinsley heard about the assignment, his eyes lit up. "*To Kill a Mockingbird* is a fine book in its own way," he said. "But if you really want to understand Southern race relations, you need to read the great historian C. Vann Woodward."

Uncle Tinsley was sitting at his desk in the library. He pulled out a book from the floor-to-ceiling bookcase behind him and passed it to me. The title was *The Strange Career of Jim Crow.*

I started reading, but the writing was so complicated that I got bogged down on the very first page. Uncle Tinsley grabbed the book back and eagerly explained the ideas while I took notes.

Because blacks and whites in the South had lived together under slavery, Uncle Tinsley said, they got along better after the Civil War than blacks and whites up north, where the races hadn't mixed nearly as much. Legal segregation started first in the North. In fact, the Jim Crow laws began in the South only at the turn of the century. Around that time, outsiders started using what C. Vann Woodward called "negrophobia" to turn poor whites against poor blacks, when the two groups should have been natural allies.

Uncle Tinsley helped me write the paper—basically dictating

chunks of it—and had me read it to him. A ways in, he cut me off. I needed to throw myself into the presentation, he said. He'd been in the drama club at Washington and Lee, and he showed me how to gesture for emphasis and use what he called pregnant pauses.

The next day, when it was my turn to read my essay to the class, I didn't know if the other kids would be interested in what Uncle Tinsley had helped me write, and that made me nervous. It didn't help that he had me throw in fancy words and phrases like "white man's burden" and "negrophobia." I tried to use the gestures he had shown me, but I forgot the pregnant pauses. Instead, I rushed through the essay. When I finished, I looked up. Most kids seemed bewildered.

Tinky Brewster raised his hand. "What's 'negrophobia'?"

"You don't have to know what it means to know it's a highfalutin word for people who don't like black folks," Vanessa piped up from the back of the class. "Bean, you one crazy white girl."

The entire class cracked up.

Liz and I were scrounging around in the attic one afternoon when we came across an old guitar. Liz toyed with the tuning pegs and declared that the sound wasn't half bad. When we brought it downstairs, Uncle Tinsley told us it was Mom's first guitar, from when she was about Liz's age. Liz took the guitar into the music shop in town, where the clerk put on new strings and tuned it. Liz started spending afternoons in the bird wing, strumming on it.

Mom had tried to teach us both to play the guitar. I was hopeless. Tone-deaf, Mom said. Liz showed real potential, but she couldn't take criticism, and Mom was always telling her what she was doing wrong. Liz finally said, "I've had it."

Now, since Mom wasn't around looking over her shoulder, Liz could have fun picking out notes and chords, following songs on the radio, and figuring out what worked and what didn't.

After a while Liz decided she needed a better guitar. The music store in Byler had a used Silvertone for a hundred and ten dollars, and Liz decided to buy it with the money in her passbook savings account. Since the peach-fuzz business, I had wanted to avoid Mr. Maddox, so

I hadn't been working much, but Liz was still helping in his office, and she had socked away nearly two hundred dollars in her account.

One Monday afternoon in November, Liz biked into town with plans to go to the bank, withdraw the money, and bring back the guitar. It had a strap, and she was going to bike home with it slung upside down across her back. She was pretty excited.

By the time the light started fading, it was chilly enough to see your breath. I was in front of the house raking leaves when Liz came pedaling up the driveway. She didn't have the guitar.

"What happened?" I asked. "Did someone else already buy it?"

"My money isn't in the bank. Mr. Maddox took it out," Liz said.

She parked the bike, and we sat on the front steps. After going to the bank, she'd gone over to the Maddoxes to find out what had happened to her money. Mr. Maddox told her that he'd moved the money out of her account and invested it in T-bills, which had a higher rate of interest but couldn't be liquidated for one year. He said if he hadn't been so busy, he would have explained it to her before. When Liz told him she wanted the money to buy a guitar, he said she was a fool to waste her money on a passing fancy.

"I can't believe it," Liz said. "That's my money. Mr. Maddox can't tell me what to do with it."

The very moment Liz uttered those words, Uncle Tinsley came out of the house carrying a ladle. Dinner was ready. "Mr. Maddox?" he asked. "Jerry Maddox? What about Jerry Maddox?"

Liz and I looked at each other. It was one thing to avoid telling Uncle Tinsley what we'd been up to. It was another thing to outright lie now that he'd asked point-blank.

"Mr. Maddox won't give me my money," Liz said again.

"What do you mean?" Uncle Tinsley asked.

"We've been working for him."

Uncle Tinsley looked at the two of us without saying anything. Then he sat down next to us, put the ladle on the step, and pressed his fingers against his temples. I couldn't tell if he was upset, angry, disgusted, or worried. Maybe he was feeling all those things at once.

"We needed money for clothes," Liz said.

Uncle Tinsley took a deep breath. "Holladays working for Maddoxes," he said. "I never thought it would come to that." He looked over at us. "And you kept it from me."

"We just didn't want to upset you," I said.

"Well, now I know, and now I'm about as upset as I could be," he said. "So you might as well tell me the whole story."

Liz and I explained it all: how we hadn't wanted to be a burden, so we'd gone looking for jobs and Mr. Maddox was the only one who'd give us work; how he'd set up the passbook savings accounts but now, when Liz went to get her money to buy the guitar, Mr. Maddox had invested it in these T-bills and so she couldn't have it.

Uncle Tinsley took another deep breath and let the air out with a sigh. "If you'd come to me in the first place, I could have told you something like this would happen with Maddox. He's a vile snake." He stood. "I don't want you to have anything to do with him."

"What about my money?" Liz asked.

"Forget the money," he said. "Write it off to experience."

I'D BEEN sharing Liz's room ever since the day I'd found out about my dad. That night, when Liz turned out the lights in the bird wing, we lay side by side in bed, staring up at the ceiling.

"I'm going to get my money," Liz suddenly said.

"How?" I asked. "Uncle Tinsley told us not to have anything to do with Mr. Maddox."

"I don't care," she said. "That money's mine. I worked for it. I need it. I earned it. I'm going to get it."

CHAPTER SEVEN

AFTER school on Tuesday, Liz got on the blue Schwinn and rode into town see Mr. Maddox. By dinnertime she hadn't returned. I went into the kitchen, where Uncle Tinsley was opening a can of tomatoes to stretch out the stew. He dumped it into the pot. "Where's Liz?"

"She had some stuff to do. She should be back soon."

"I see," Uncle Tinsley said. He ladled out the stew.

I carried the bowls to the table. After he'd said his usual blessing and eaten a few bites, Uncle Tinsley asked, "You said Liz had stuff to do. What stuff?" He eyed me intently.

I looked at my spoon. "You know, stuff. Errands and things."

"Bean, you're a terrible liar. Your eyes are darting around all over the place. Now look at me square and tell me where Liz is."

I raised my eyes and felt my lower lip quivering.

"I guess you don't need to tell me. There are only two things I've asked both of you not to do since you got here. One was not to get jobs, and you went out and got them. The other was to forget the money, and the very next day, Liz goes to get it."

"Please don't be mad at us, Uncle Tinsley. Liz just wanted to get her money. It was hers. And please don't kick us out."

"I'm not going to kick you out, Bean," Uncle Tinsley said. Through the rest of dinner, he kept glancing at his watch. "She shouldn't be out this late," he said at one point. A few minutes later he said, "I'm going to ground that girl until her hair turns white."

WE WERE rinsing out the bowls at the kitchen sink when we heard a knock at the door. I ran to see who it was, turning on the porch light. When I opened the door, a strange man stood there with his arm around Liz. She was crying. She had bruises on her cheek and chin, and her shirt was torn. She was looking down, holding a soft-drink cup with both hands and sucking on the straw, but the drink was all gone and the ice cubes were rattling around.

"Liz?" I said. She didn't look up, and when I tried to hug her, she turned away.

Uncle Tinsley had come up behind me. "What happened here?"

"Mr. Holladay, I didn't know she was your niece," the man said. He was skinny, with black hair and a mustache, and he wore a blue mechanic's jacket with the name WAYNE stitched on the pocket. "What happened wasn't right, Mr. Holladay."

"What did happen?"

Wayne explained that he worked at a garage but also ran a one-man car service part-time. Jerry Maddox occasionally hired him because, although Mr. Maddox had that fancy Le Mans, he got a charge out of being driven to business meetings, like he was a big shot with a chauffeur. "Mr. Maddox said it enhances the aura."

"Get to the point, Wayne."

Wayne had been at the garage late that afternoon when Mr. Maddox drove up with this young woman. He said the carburetor on the Le Mans was acting up, but he had some meetings he needed to attend, and he wanted Wayne to drive him and the girl around. As they were getting in the car, Wayne said, Mr. Maddox pulled him aside and said the girl was a hooker and he might be getting a little backseat action between meetings.

"Sweet Jesus," Uncle Tinsley said.

They drove around town, Wayne continued, stopping at various places with him and the girl waiting in the car while Mr. Maddox went inside. As evening came on, the girl complained to Mr. Maddox, saying things like, "It's my money. I earned it." Mr. Maddox told her she'd get the money, but first she needed to do what he wanted. Wayne figured it was just a hooker and a john haggling over the fee. Their argument grew heated. Then, in the rearview mirror, Wayne saw Mr. Maddox backhand her. She started crying. Mr. Maddox caught Wayne's glance. "Keep your eyes on the road," he said. "I don't pay you to watch; I pay you to drive."

By then it was dark. As Wayne drove through town, he heard the two of them struggling, the girl begging Mr. Maddox to stop and him backhanding her a couple more times. Then they came to a red light. The girl suddenly jumped out of the car. Mr. Maddox jumped out after her, but the girl ran around the car and jumped back in next to Wayne, locking the door. "Go!" she screamed.

Wayne took off, leaving Mr. Maddox at the street corner. The girl was sobbing. Her shirt was half torn off. Wayne said he mentioned, by way of showing some sympathy, that whoring could be a rough line of work, but the girl said Tinsley Holladay was her uncle and she wanted Wayne to take her to Mayfield. That, Wayne said, was when he realized she wasn't a hooker after all.

"She was awful upset, Mr. Holladay," Wayne said. "But I was in 'Nam and I know how to deal with people losing it. So I stopped at the Park 'N Eat and got her a Coke. I think that helped calm her."

"Thank you," Uncle Tinsley said. "You did the right thing."

"Mr. Maddox has got to be pretty pissed with me, but I don't care. What he did was wrong—and I'll testify to that."

I tried to hug Liz again. This time she didn't turn away, but her body was completely rigid. She let her cup drop, the ice scattering across the floor, and collapsed in my arms.

"Thank you for all you've done, Wayne," Uncle Tinsley said. "You're a good man." He was usually tight with money, but he took a twenty-dollar bill from his wallet and offered it to Wayne.

"I couldn't accept," Wayne said. "I didn't do it for the money."

"I insist. After what happened, Maddox isn't going to pay you."

"Well, then, thank you very much."

"We can handle it from here," Uncle Tinsley said.

He opened the door, and Wayne walked out.

I squeezed Liz again. "Liz, are you okay?"

She shook her head.

"What are we going to do?" I asked Uncle Tinsley.

"Let's get Liz cleaned up and into bed," he said.

"Shouldn't we call the police first?"

"I don't know if that's such a good idea," Uncle Tinsley said.

"We've got to do something." I gave Liz a gentle shake. "Don't you think?" I asked her.

"I don't know," Liz said. "I just don't know."

"Don't you want to press charges?" I asked. I kept thinking about Wayne saying he'd testify.

"I don't know," she said again.

"What's done is done," Uncle Tinsley said. "You can't undo it by pressing charges. It'll only create more trouble—and scandal."

"What do you want to do, Liz?"

"I just want to take a bath."

I RAN LIZ A BATH. I WORRIED I might be destroying evidence or something, but Liz really wanted that bath. She also wanted the water as hot as it could be, and she asked me to stay.

"What happened, Liz? Did he actually—"

"He tried to. But I don't want to talk about it."

"Shouldn't we go to the hospital?"

"I don't want anyone examining me."

"Are you worried about getting pregnant?"

"No. He didn't . . . I said I don't want to talk about it."

When Liz climbed into the tub, she kept on her underwear.

"You were smart, Liz," I said. "You got away from Maddox just like we got away from that perv in New Orleans."

"I'm not smart," she said. "I never should have gotten in the car."

After the bath, Liz got into bed and pulled the covers up over her head, saying she wanted to be alone. I went back downstairs. Uncle Tinsley was in the living room. I tried calling Mom to ask what we should do about pressing charges, but there was no answer.

"We should go to the police," I said. "Or at least talk to a lawyer. It's worse than Wayne said. Liz said Maddox tried to rape her."

"That poor girl," Uncle Tinsley said. "Still, nothing you can do will undo the damage. It'll only make things worse."

"But Maddox can't get away with this."

"You don't know Maddox," Uncle Tinsley said. We may have been working for Maddox, he continued, but we didn't understand what kind of man he really was. Maddox loved nothing better than a fight, and he did a lot of his fighting in the courthouse. He sued neighbors over boundary disputes. He sued doctors for malpractice. He sued dry cleaners, claiming they shrank his clothes. While most people saw the court as a place to seek justice, Maddox saw it as a place to take down anyone who happened to get on his wrong side.

Years ago, Uncle Tinsley said, when Maddox was living in a boardinghouse in Rhode Island, he stole some jewelry from his landlady. The police searched his room and found the jewelry, and Maddox was convicted. Then along came a civil-rights lawyer who argued that the police didn't have the right to search Maddox's room without his permission. The case went all the way to the Rhode Island Supreme Court. Maddox won, although everyone knew he was guilty. And that was when Maddox realized that guilt and innocence were incidental, that people who understood the law could also figure out how to bend the law.

"He brags about winning that case," Uncle Tinsley said. "He fights dirty. That's why you don't want to tangle with Maddox."

I WENT back up to the bird wing. Uncle Tinsley wanting to pretend nothing happened made me wonder if maybe what Mom had said about her family was true—they were all experts at pretending.

Liz still had the covers over her head. I took my dad's photo and his Silver Star from the cigar box that I kept in the white cradle and brought them into the bathroom to study them in the light.

I ran my finger over the tiny silver star that was inside the bigger gold star, and I wondered what advice my dad would give me if he were around. I looked at his crooked grin and the cocky way his arms were crossed as he leaned against the door frame, and I knew Charlie Wyatt would never pretend nothing happened.

THE next morning, I woke before Liz and went downstairs to make her a cup of tea. Uncle Tinsley was in the kitchen. He started talking about what a hard frost we'd had during the night.

It was clear that Uncle Tinsley wasn't going to make any reference to what had happened with Maddox, in the hope that we would put it all behind us. I had decided during the night that Liz and I should at least see a lawyer. I didn't know much about the law, but I did know that everyone got a lawyer, even the poor black guy in *To Kill a Mockingbird*. I had a classmate, Billy Corbin, whose father was a lawyer. I could look him up in the phone book.

When I brought the cup of tea up to Liz, she was awake, lying in bed. Her face was even more swollen and bruised than the night before. "There's no way I'm going to school," she said.

"You don't have to," I said. I passed her the cup of tea and explained my plan for the two of us to go see Billy Corbin's dad.

"Whatever you think," Liz said, sounding like she was in a daze.

Before leaving the house, I tried calling Mom again. I was certain she would want us to press charges, since she was always going on about women standing up for their rights. I let the phone ring a long time, but there was still no answer.

Instead of taking the bus to school, Liz and I walked into town. The sun was out, and it was melting the frost. When we got to Holladay Avenue, I found a phone booth. I looked up Mr. Corbin's address in the phone book dangling from a chain. His office was over a shoe store, up a rickety flight of stairs, and his door had a glass pane etched with WILLIAM T. CORBIN, ESQ., ATTORNEY AT LAW. We knocked, but there was no answer. The door was locked.

"We'll just wait," I said. We sat down at the top of the stairs. After a while a man came climbing up, carrying two big briefcases. He looked tired, and his suit was rumpled.

"Mr. Corbin?" I asked.

"The one and only. Who wants to know?"

"I'm Bean Holladay. This is my sister, Liz. We need to talk to you. About a legal matter."

He smiled. "Let me guess. Your mother grounded you."

"It's serious," I said.

He took out a key and unlocked the door. "I suspect it is." He looked at Liz. "What happened to you?"

"That's what we're here to talk about," I said.

Mr. Corbin's office was a mess, with legal papers stacked everywhere. I took that as a good sign. Any lawyer who couldn't afford a secretary to keep his office neat must be honest.

Mr. Corbin had us sit in cracked leather chairs facing his desk. "Now, tell me what happened," he said.

I cleared my throat. "It's kind of complicated," I said.

"And awful," Liz added. It was the first thing she'd said since we'd got to town.

"You probably can't tell me anything I haven't heard before," he said. "And if a lawyer can't keep his mouth shut about things his clients tell him, he shouldn't be a lawyer."

"What do you charge?" I asked.

"Let's not worry about that. Let's just hear what the problem is."

"It involves Jerry Maddox," I said.

He raised his eyebrows. "Then I imagine it is complicated."

After that, the whole story came spilling out. Mr. Corbin listened quietly, his clasped hands propping up his chin.

"Wayne told us he'll testify," I said.

"What a mess," Mr. Corbin said, almost to himself. "So you didn't go to the hospital or to the police?"

"I wanted to talk to a lawyer first."

"Why isn't your uncle here with you?"

"He wants us to forget the whole thing ever happened."

"And you don't want to forget it? You want to file charges?"

"What I want is for my uncle to blow Mr. Maddox's brains out with his shotgun," I said.

"I'm going to pretend I didn't hear that."

"That isn't going to happen, so we came to find out what we're supposed to do, legal-wise."

"It's not really a question of what you're supposed to do. It's more a question of what you want to do." We had two options, Mr. Corbin went on. One, we could press charges, which would create a nasty trial with a lot of awful publicity but might result in Mr. Maddox being punished for what he allegedly did. On the other hand, there was no guarantee of that. Two, we could decide it was an incident that involved bad judgment on the part of both parties—since Liz did voluntarily get into the back of the car with Mr. Maddox—and didn't need to be rehashed in a public courtroom.

"What's the right thing to do?" I asked.

"I can't decide that for you," he said. "You two have to decide that. And unfortunately, you don't have a choice between a good option and a bad option. Each option is bad in its own way."

"We can't just do nothing," I said. "What Maddox did was wrong. He'll be walking around laughing about how he got away with it. And he might do it again."

"Possibly."

"I just don't want it to happen again," Liz said. "I'm scared of him doing it again. I'm scared of even running into him."

"You could always leave town," Mr. Corbin said. "Can't you go stay with your mother?"

"We tried that last summer," I said. "It didn't work out so well. Anyway, Maddox attacked my sister, and we're supposed to go into hiding? That's not right."

"No, it's not. It's an option, nonetheless."

"I don't know what to do," Liz said. "My thoughts keep jumbling up. Bean, what do you think?"

"The thing is," I said, "if we don't at least file charges, it will be like nothing ever happened."

"Legally speaking, that's true," Mr. Corbin said. "If you do file charges, you can always drop them later, but bear in mind that these things sometimes develop a momentum of their own."

"Well, if we don't want to pretend it never happened and we don't want to leave town, we have no choice. We have to file charges."

Mr. Corbin asked, "Bean, how old are you?"

"Twelve. I'll be thirteen in April."

"You're a little young to be making this decision on your own. Should you decide to proceed, you'll need your uncle with you."

"He's going to be mad," I said.

"I'll call him." Mr. Corbin picked up the phone and dialed. "Tinsley," he said. "Bill Corbin here." He explained that Liz and I were in his office and that we'd decided to file charges against Maddox. He stopped and listened. "No, sir. It's not my advice. I outlined their options, and they made the decision." He listened again. Then he handed the phone to me. "He wants to talk to you."

"What the hell are you doing?" Uncle Tinsley asked.

"We're going to file charges," I said.

"I thought you were going to drop the whole matter."

"He'll think he can try it again. And what if he does? Do we just let him? Hide from him? We can't. So we're filing charges."

There was a long pause.

"I'll meet you at the sheriff's office."

MR. CORBIN CALLED THE sheriff's department and told them we were coming over. When I asked him how much we owed him, Mr. Corbin said he considered it pro bono. That meant free, Liz said.

"So you'll be our lawyer?" I asked. "Pro bono?"

"If you press charges, the state's prosecutor becomes your lawyer," Mr. Corbin said. "You won't need me."

"Oh," I said.

The sheriff's department was in a low brick building. The deputy at the desk didn't seem particularly happy to see us. He had me wait in the lobby while he took Liz into the back to take her statement.

A few minutes later Uncle Tinsley came through the door. He sat down next to me in the row of orange plastic chairs. We didn't say anything. After a bit he reached over and ruffled my hair.

Liz wasn't in the back for long.

"How'd it go?" I asked when she came out.

"They took some pictures, asked questions, and I answered them, okay?" she said. "Let's go home."

BY THE time we got back to Mayfield, the school day was half over. Uncle Tinsley said we might as well just stay home and unwind. A few hours later we heard a car roar up the driveway. I went to the window and saw Maddox's black Le Mans screech to a stop. Doris Maddox got out, more pregnant than ever, and slammed the door behind her. Liz was up in the bird wing, but Uncle Tinsley and I went out to meet Doris.

For a moment I genuinely believed Doris had come to apologize. She was constantly complaining about what a scoundrel her husband was. I thought she was going to say something like, "Look, what my husband did was wrong, but he does provide for me and my kids, and if you go ahead with this, it will hurt my family."

But as soon as I saw Doris's face, I realized she had not come to make amends. Her mouth was tight, and her eyes were all fired up.

"What the hell do you think you're doing?" she shouted. "How dare you? How dare you, after all we've done for you?"

The deputies, she said, had come to her house and arrested her husband, taking him down to the jail. His lawyer was arranging bail even as she spoke, and Jerry would be out by the end of the day.

We didn't know what we were up against, Doris said. Her husband knew the law inside and out. We would regret the day we started this. "No jury's going to believe you lying sluts."

At first I was stunned, but when Doris accused us of lying, I got pretty steamed myself. "Don't you get all high and mighty," I said. "We have an eyewitness. He'll testify to what happened. Your husband hurt Liz, and now you're pretending he's a saint?"

"Your sister's a whore!" Doris shouted. "My husband hired her as his secretary. He trusted her, and he treated her like a queen. We know the two of you were stealing from us. Your sister was drinking yesterday, and she put the moves on Jerry in the backseat of that car. When he turned her down, she made up this story. She was out to get him because he had your worthless uncle fired. You think you've got your evidence? Well, we've got our evidence. A vodka bottle with y'all's fingerprints all over it as proof."

I had no idea what she was talking about, since I'd never had a drink of vodka in my life and I was pretty sure Liz hadn't, either. "You can try to twist the facts as much as you want," I said. "But you know your husband did this. The truth will come out."

"When the truth about you two comes out," Doris said, "you won't be able to show your skanky faces in this town. Mark my words. My husband will destroy you!"

Doris climbed back into the Le Mans, slammed the door, jerked the car into reverse, then gunned it down the driveway.

THAT evening, Liz announced there was absolutely no way she was going to school the next day. Neither Uncle Tinsley nor I tried to talk her into it.

The next morning, as soon as I got to the bus stop, I could tell that everyone knew. Word spread quickly in a small town like Byler. The other kids were clearly discussing it, and when they saw me, they started shushing each other, saying things like, "Here she comes," "Dummy up," and "Where's the other one?"

When I got to school, there was time before first period to go to the library, which had a copy of the *Byler Daily News*. I expected Maddox's arrest to be a front-page story because the paper usually played up anything local, no matter how small—a horse getting stuck in a pond or a farmer growing a five-pound tomato. The story wasn't on the front page. I found it at the back, in a section called Police Blotter. The headline was MILL BOSS CHARGED.

> Jerry Maddox, 43, a foreman at Holladay Textiles, has been charged with the alleged assault of a local girl, 15, whose name is being withheld because of her age. He has been released on bail. No trial date has been set.

I was shocked. I thought the story was a big deal. Sure, people were gossiping about it, but they didn't know the real story. I'd been counting on the town reading in official detail exactly what had happened. I thought that was one way to punish Maddox.

The article didn't even say "attempted rape," as if the editors were afraid of spelling it out. "Assault." What did that mean? Maddox might as well have shoved some girl who sassed him in a parking-lot argument over a fender bender.

The rest of the day was awful. In the halls kids stared at me. Girls giggled and pointed. Guys smirked and, in mocking, cheeping voices, said things like, "Help! I'm being molested!"

On my way to class, I ran into Vanessa. She saw me and shook her head. "Going to the law," she said. "Such a white thing to do."

"What would you do?" I asked.

"I wouldn't get into no car with Mr. Maddox in the first place," she said. "You climb in the backseat with the boss man, you got to expect something's going to happen. That's just the way it is."

LIZ decided she wasn't going back to school the next day, either. She said she was not leaving the house until the bruises on her face had gone away. It was Friday, and things in the halls at school went from bad to worse. Kids snickered behind my back, throwing wadded-up paper at my head and tripping me.

The football game that night was against the Orange Hornets. I hadn't been much help to the pep squad. Still, the posters got made, and on Friday the school gathered in the gym for the pep rally.

When it came time for me and Vanessa to rile up the seventh-graders to win the spirit stick, we walked onto the gym floor and pumped our fists in the air. We got no reaction. Most kids were just staring, as if they couldn't believe I had the nerve to be out there. I kept trying to rev them up, but then there was a boo, then a few more boos. Then the trash started coming—spit wads, Corn Nuts, pennies. Vanessa was pushing right through it, wearing the same steely expression I'd seen on her sister's face after she got hit with the soda cup during the football game. I tried to follow Vanessa's example, but it got louder. I walked off, leaving Vanessa to shake the spirit stick on her own.

The pep-squad adviser, Terri Pruitt, was standing by the door. "Are you all right, Bean?" she asked.

I nodded. "But I think I'm quitting the pep squad."

She squeezed my shoulder. "It's probably for the best," she said.

Liz hadn't set foot out of the house since going to the cops four days earlier. She kept obsessing about whether filing the charges had been the right thing to do and whether the whole mess was all her fault because she'd been stupid enough to think she could get her money back if she got in the car with Mr. Maddox.

"Don't think like that," I said.

"I can't help it," she said. "I can't control my thoughts." The argument going on inside her head was so heated, she said, that she felt like different voices were making the cases for and against her. One voice kept talking about Alice in Wonderland's "Eat Me" cake, saying a slice of it would make her grow so tall that people would be scared of her. Another voice recommended Alice's "Drink Me" bottle—a sip would make her so small, no one would notice her.

Liz and her voices had me worried. I'd kept trying to call Mom without any luck, but I figured she'd say Liz needed to get out of the house, breathe some fresh air, and clear her head. On Saturday morning I insisted that she come with me to the Wyatts'.

"I don't feel like it," Liz said. "And my face is still a mess."

"I don't care," I said. "You've got to get out."

Liz was sitting in bed in her pajamas. I started pulling her clothes out of the chest of drawers, throwing them at her, and snapping my fingers to speed her up.

Uncle Tinsley was glad to see Liz up and dressed. To celebrate, he opened a can of Vienna sausages to go with our poached eggs. After breakfast we rode the Schwinns over to the hill. Aunt Al was in the kitchen. She had a pot of grits going and was grating cheese into it. As soon as she saw us, she gave us great big hugs, then offered us some grits. Liz said we'd already eaten and she was full.

"I've still got some room left," I said.

Aunt Al laughed and passed me a bowl.

"I hope you know, I believe every word of your story," she said to Liz. The town was divided over the charges, she continued. "A lot of folks don't believe you, but there's a lot who do." Thing was, she went on, most of them that believed Liz wouldn't come out and say so. They were good people, Aunt Al said, but they were scared. They had jobs they couldn't afford to lose, and they didn't want to take sides against Jerry Maddox. But they were happy to see someone else stand up to him. "You're one gutsy girl."

"Or crazy," Liz said.

"It's not crazy," I said. "What would be crazy would be to pretend nothing happened."

Aunt Al patted my arm. "You got more than a lick of your dad in you, child."

CHAPTER EIGHT

BY MONDAY, Liz's face was looking a lot better, and although she didn't want to do it, Uncle Tinsley and I decided it was time for her to go back to school.

Liz took forever getting dressed. We missed the bus, and since Uncle Tinsley hated wasting gas, we walked to school. Classes had started by the time we arrived, and we got tardies—our first.

I hadn't told Liz about the way I'd been teased since she filed the charges. When we walked down the hall, girls who had ignored her now went out of their way to whisper loud enough for her to hear, saying things like, "Here she comes!" and "Crazy Lizzie!"

That night, Liz joked that she felt like Moses parting the Red Sea, but it was horrible. She started to hate coming to school. The other girls openly taunted her and tripped her when she walked by, but then the judge set a date in March for the trial, and it became clear to everyone that the case wasn't going away. That was when we realized we had more to worry about than the kids at Byler High.

Piles of garbage started appearing on the lawn and driveway at Mayfield. We'd get up in the morning, and it would be strewn all over the place—used Pampers, empty bottles of RC and cans of SpaghettiOs, shredded paper, and those cylindrical Pringles containers. All that stuff practically had Maddox's name on it.

One day, on our way to the bus stop, Maddox's Le Mans appeared out of nowhere with Maddox behind the wheel. He gunned the car toward us, swerving so close that we jumped into the ditch to keep from getting hit. As the Le Mans passed, I picked up a rock and hurled it, but the car sped off and the rock missed.

After that it seemed like Maddox cruised around looking for us almost every day, trying to run us off the road. I started carrying around a pocketful of rocks. I did give the car one good dent, but most of the time Maddox got away too quickly for me to score a hit.

We didn't tell Uncle Tinsley. We never seriously considered going to the police, either, since we wouldn't be able to prove anything. But Maddox's campaign was having an effect on Liz. She was terrified and didn't want to leave the house. She also started talking more and more about the voices and how they were warning her that Maddox was hiding behind every bush and tree.

I kept telling Liz that the voices would go away once Maddox got convicted and sent to prison. It was now December, with the trial three months away, and I was worried sick that Liz might fall apart by then. I wondered if we should drop the case. But if we pulled out, Maddox would know he had terrorized us into giving up. He would haunt Liz, and that might make the voices get worse.

I decided there was only one thing to do. I couldn't wait for the trial. I had to kill Jerry Maddox.

I DIDN'T have a car to mow Maddox down, so I had to strategize. There was a ridge behind his house with a lot of boulders. I'd noticed one in particular when I was working for the Maddoxes, and I'd thought at the time that if it ever rolled down, it might do some damage, or even kill someone. So I decided to roll it down myself.

I would hide on the ridge until Maddox came out to the back porch, which he did every day to check the thermometer and put the stuff from his paper shredder into the trash cans, and then I'd send that rock barreling down the hill and crush him like a bug.

After school the next day, I rode the red Schwinn into Byler, left it at the library bike stand, and cut through the yard of one of Maddox's neighbors to the ridge behind his house. I scrambled up through the scrub pines to the rock, which was about as big as an armchair. I pushed on the rock to see how loose it was, and I discovered I couldn't budge the thing. It must have weighed a ton.

I needed a partner.

LIZ wasn't cut out for this type of assignment. The only person I could turn to was Joe Wyatt. I'd already told him all about Maddox's harassment campaign, and so at school the next day, I explained my plan and asked if he'd be willing to help out.

"When do we do it, Cuz?" he asked.

I told him how big and heavy the rock was. Joe didn't make such good grades in school, but he was smart when it came to doing things, and he told me what we needed to do was lever the rock into motion. His dad, he said, had a tamping bar that would do the job.

The next day, Joe met me at the library, carrying the heavy iron bar. We circled up into the woods behind Maddox's house, and I showed Joe the rock. He worked the tamping bar under it, but it wouldn't budge, so he got a smaller rock that he used as a fulcrum, and with both of us pulling down on the long end of the bar, we worked the big rock forward.

"This'll do it," Joe said.

"Maddox is a goner," I said.

We sat down on the pine needles and waited.

After about an hour the back door opened. We jumped up and grabbed the handle of the tamping bar. But instead of Maddox coming out the door, it was Doris. She had just given birth and was carrying her newborn in one arm and a bag of trash in the other.

I felt my body sag. As much as I hated Doris for siding with her husband, I wasn't about to kill her—and certainly not the new baby. I realized I really didn't want to kill anyone, not even Maddox.

"Maybe this isn't such a good idea after all," I said.

"I was thinking the same thing," Joe said.

We watched Doris take the lid off the can, drop the bag in, and replace the lid. Then she went back inside. Joe pulled the tamping bar from under the rock. We headed across the hill, away from the house.

"Does this mean we're wimps?" I asked.

"Nah," Joe said. He kicked at a pinecone in his path. "You know, we could get Maddox where it really hurts."

"What do you mean?"

"The Le Mans."

JOE and I talked about smashing the windshield, but we worried that the noise might bring Maddox running out of the house. Then he suggested keying the car, but we also nixed that idea, because it would only do cosmetic damage, and Maddox could still cruise around, trying to mow us down. We decided that the best course of action would be to immobilize the Le Mans by slashing the tires. Maddox could buy new ones, but we'd have made a real statement.

We waited until the weekend, when Maddox would be home. We needed the cover of darkness, so Joe told me to meet him at the library at dusk. He always carried his jackknife on him, he said, so I didn't need to worry about weapons.

When I rode up at the appointed time on Saturday, Joe was waiting at the library bike stand. He got on the Schwinn, and with me sitting on the rack behind, we pedaled over to Maddox's neighborhood. When we got to his street, we could see the Le Mans parked in the breezeway down the block. Joe had me hide with the Schwinn behind a bush at the corner. My job was to be the lookout, and if anyone approached, I was supposed to hoot like an owl. By then the sun had gone down. While I waited, Joe casually walked down the street. When the coast was clear, he ducked behind a rhododendron a few houses from the Maddoxes.

Joe scurried from bush to bush, stopping at each one to suss out the situation. When he reached the bush closest to Maddox's house, he dropped down on his stomach and shimmied to the Le Mans.

Joe was out of my sight when a porch light flicked on at the house across the street from Maddox's. The front door opened, and an older lady let out a little dog. I started hooting like crazy. The dog began to bark. Suddenly Joe came running as fast as he could toward me. I had the bike ready to roll when he reached me.

"Got two tires," he said breathlessly as he jumped on. I clambered aboard and pushed off with both feet while Joe stood up on the pedals, working them as fast as he could.

We circled around town instead of going through it, and fifteen minutes later we got to the bottom of the mill hill. Joe was about to get off and walk the rest of the way home, and I was going to peel off for Mayfield, when the squad car pulled up alongside us. The cop pointed to the side of the road. Joe stopped the bike, and the cop parked behind us and got out.

"What seems to be the hurry here?" he asked.

"Got to get home for dinner," Joe said.

"We had a report of some slashed tires over on Willow Lane," the cop said. "Know anything about it?"

"No, sir," Joe said.

"You're saying you didn't do it?"

"Yes, sir."

"We're just bike riding," I said.

"I'm not talking to you," the cop said. He turned back to Joe. "Son, empty your pockets onto the hood of the car."

Joe sighed. He climbed off the bike and started taking stuff out of his pockets: keys, change, string, a chestnut, and the jackknife.

The cop picked up the knife. "This is a concealed weapon."

"It's my whittling knife," Joe said.

"It's a concealed lethal weapon," the cop said. "Follow me." He opened the back door of the squad car. "Get in."

Joe climbed into the backseat. I straddled the Schwinn as the cop car pulled away. I wanted to wave to Joe, but he didn't look back.

I PEDALED through the darkness back to Mayfield. While Joe and I were planning the operation, slashing Maddox's tires seemed not only justifiable but something I had to do to defend myself and Liz and to strike back against someone trying to kill us. But it occurred to me that if I tried to explain the tire-slashing operation to anyone, it would sound stupid, the kind of boneheaded crime that landed kids in juvie. On top of it all, I had gotten Joe into trouble. I kept thinking of him staring straight ahead as the squad car drove off.

I couldn't tell Uncle Tinsley or Liz about any of it, so I went to bed saying nothing. First thing next morning, I rode the Schwinn over to the Wyatts' house to find out what had happened to Joe. I never knocked anymore—Aunt Al insisted I come on in, seeing as I was family—and when I stepped inside, Joe was sitting at the kitchen table with Earl while Aunt Al fried eggs in bacon fat. I wanted to hug Joe, but he was acting all nonchalant and offhand. The cops, he said, had confiscated his knife, but they didn't have any evidence that he'd done anything wrong, so they let him go.

"I swear, you'd think those deputies would have better ways to spend their time than bringing in mill hill boys for carrying around whittling knives," Aunt Al said. "Bean, you want an egg?"

"Sure do," I said. I sat down next to Joe. I felt giddy that we'd gotten away with the operation, though we couldn't say anything in front of Aunt Al. Joe poured me a cup of milk-with-coffee, and we just sat there grinning like a couple of crocodiles. Then Aunt Al passed me a crispy, glistening fat-fried egg.

We had finished breakfast when there was a knock on the door.

Joe went to answer it. Maddox was standing on the front step. He wore a hooded black sweatshirt with the hood pushed back. He shoved his finger in Joe's face. "I know it was you," he said.

"You know what was me?"

"Don't act all innocent with me, you little s.o.b."

"Please, none of that language in my house," Aunt Al said. "What's this all about?"

Maddox pushed past Joe, entered the house, and looked over at me. "Why am I not surprised to see you here?" he asked.

"She's family," Aunt Al said. "Now, please, what's this all about?"

"I'll tell you what this is about. Your boy slashed my tires."

"Did not," Joe said.

"I know it was you," Maddox said. "At first I couldn't figure out who did it, but this morning a buddy on the force mentioned that the Wyatt boy had been picked up for carrying a knife and that he'd been in the company of one of the Holladay sisters at the time, and that's when the light went on. It was you."

"He says he didn't do it," Aunt Al said. "If you had any proof, you'd charge him."

"Just because I don't have proof doesn't mean he didn't do it, and doesn't mean he won't get what's coming to him."

Maddox's voice brought Uncle Clarence into the kitchen. "What's going on here?"

"Your boy needs a beating," Maddox said. "Firstly, for slashing my tires. Secondly, for lying about it."

"Is that true, son?" Uncle Clarence asked.

"He didn't do it," I said. "He was with me last night."

"You were probably in on it," Maddox said. He pointed at Aunt Al. "You work for the mill." He turned to Uncle Clarence. "And you take the mill's disability checks. People who work for the mill and take the mill's money do what I say. And I say that boy needs a beating."

Maddox and Uncle Clarence looked at each other for a long moment. Then Uncle Clarence walked out of the room. He came back carrying a leather belt.

"Oh, Clarence," Aunt Al said. But she didn't try to stop him.

"Outside," Maddox said.

He led Joe and Uncle Clarence into the backyard. Joe was staring straight ahead saying nothing, like he'd done in the squad car. Aunt Al and I followed them. In the garden the dead vines of Uncle Clarence's tomatoes were still tied to their stakes. Aunt Al clutched my arm when Uncle Clarence told Joe to bend over and grab his ankles, and with Maddox standing by, Uncle Clarence began whaling Joe's butt with the belt.

I felt the urge to rush over and grab Uncle Clarence's arm. Aunt Al seemed to sense this, because she clutched me even tighter. When Uncle Clarence finally stopped, Joe stood. He didn't look at anyone or say anything. Instead, he walked off into the woods.

Maddox clapped Uncle Clarence on the back. "Just to show there's no hard feelings," he said, "let's go have a beer."

Uncle Clarence didn't feel like having a beer with Maddox, so Maddox left. Uncle Clarence had a fit of coughing; then he headed off to the veterans hall. I sat with Aunt Al and Earl in the kitchen.

No one said anything for a minute, and then Aunt Al spoke up. "What in tarnation did you two think you were doing?"

So she knew.

"It was all my fault," I said. I explained how Maddox had been throwing garbage on our yard and trying to mow us down with his car and Liz was hearing voices, so I felt we had to do something to fight back, and Joe was the only one who could help me.

"Honey, I understand the urge to get even," she said, "but you all was throwing rocks at an angry bull."

I asked Aunt Al about Liz's voices. Aunt Al said that she sometimes heard God talking to her and other times the devil, so maybe it was nothing more than that.

Then Ruth came home from teaching Sunday school. "Why all the long faces?" she asked.

"Your pa had to give Joe a hiding," Aunt Al said.

"Maddox made him do it," I added.

"Dad beat Joe because Mr. Maddox told him to?"

"Right out back," I said.

"Mr. Maddox was here?" Ruth asked. She sat down at the table.

I explained what had happened. When I finished, Ruth looked down and ran her fingers through her hair, like her head hurt.

"You know, I never told anyone why I stopped working for Maddox," she said.

Aunt Al gave Ruth a startled look.

"He put the moves on me," Ruth said. "He didn't do what he did to Liz, but he cornered me and started pawing like crazy. I got away, but I sure was scared."

"Honey," Aunt Al said, "I asked you if anything had happened, and you told me no."

Ruth took off her glasses. "I never wanted anyone to know."

BY THEN it was clear that Mom had pulled another one of her disappearing acts. Ever since we'd filed the charges, I'd been calling her, but the phone just rang and rang. Finally, after four weeks, Mom called. She'd been at a retreat in the Catskills, she explained. She'd tried to call before she left, but she couldn't get through, and since the Buddhists had no telephone, she hadn't been able to call.

"It was all so good for my head," she said. "I feel very balanced." She started going on about how the Buddhists had taught her about her chi and how to center it, but I cut her off.

"Mom, this man attacked Liz. There's going to be a trial."

Mom let out a shriek. As I filled her in, she kept yelling, "How dare he?" and "I'll kill him!" She was leaving immediately, she said, and would drive all night to get to Mayfield in the morning.

Mom didn't reach Byler by the time we left for school the next day, but she had arrived when we returned. Mom hugged Liz. She didn't want to let go, so Mom kept hugging her and saying, "Everything's going to be all right, baby. Momma's here."

Then Mom turned to hug me. I was surprised by how angry I

felt at her. *Where have you been all this time?* I wanted to say. But I said nothing and hugged her back. Mom rubbed her face against my shoulder. I felt a little wetness, and I realized she was crying. I wondered if Mom was really going to help us get through all this or if she was going to be one more person who needed reassurance.

When Liz told Mom how the other kids at school were treating her, Mom said Liz didn't have to go anymore, at least until the trial was over. Mom would homeschool her.

She offered to homeschool me, too, but I took a pass. Most of the kids had stopped giving me a hard time, and the last thing I wanted to do was sit around Mayfield all day, brooding about Maddox, listening to Mom explain the world as she saw it, and reading a bunch of depressing poetry by Edgar Allan Poe, who had replaced Lewis Carroll as Liz's favorite writer. I needed to be out and about.

Since Liz and I had gone back to sharing a bedroom, Mom moved into the other room in the bird wing. When she told the Byler High authorities that she would take over Liz's education for the time being, they were happy to oblige, since the upcoming trial had caused nothing but tension at school. Mom spent the days with Liz, the two of them composing poetry and talking about survival, transcendence, and life energy, all the subjects Mom had explored during her spiritual retreat. Mom had brought her two favorite guitars with her—the Zemaitis and the honey-colored Martin—and she gave the Martin to Liz, promising she would never criticize her playing, no matter what rules Liz broke.

I had been ticked off at Mom when she first showed up, but she was rising to the occasion. Liz told her about the voices she kept hearing. Mom said Liz shouldn't fear the voices. That was how the mind and the soul talked to each other, she said. Mom said Liz should listen to the voices, channel them, and turn them into art, poetry, and music. "Don't be afraid of your dark places," Mom told her. "If you can shine a light on them, you'll find treasure there."

Mom had never made a big deal out of Christmas. Uncle Tinsley had ignored it ever since Martha died, but when school let out for Christmas break, he told us that because this was the first family gathering at Mayfield in years, we should do something to acknowledge the holiday. Uncle Tinsley and I found a small, perfectly shaped cedar in the hedgerow along the upper pasture. We chopped it down, dragged it back to the house, and decorated it with the Holladay family collection of fragile antique ornaments.

We avoided talking about the trial, and on Christmas Day, instead of giving each other presents, Mom decided we should all put on performances. She sang several numbers from her play *Finding the Magic*. Liz recited Poe's poem "The Bells," which wasn't very Christmasy and, in fact, was really dark. I read my negrophobia essay, this time remembering to use Uncle Tinsley's pregnant pauses. That prompted Mom to joke that Uncle Tinsley should dig out the old Confederate sword that the Holladays had been handing down for generations and give it to me because I was really getting in touch with my Southern roots.

"Hey, Uncle Tinsley," I said, "maybe for your performance you can play the piano."

He shook his head. "Martha and I used to play together. But I don't play anymore." He stood up. "My performance will be in the kitchen." For dinner he was going to make squash casserole and roast loin of venison with mushrooms, onions, turnips, and apples.

It was dark by the time dinner was ready. While Liz and I set the table, Mom found a bottle of wine in the basement. She poured glasses for herself and Uncle Tinsley.

Uncle Tinsley said his short prayer, thanking God for the bountiful feast before us, then raised his glass. "To the Holladays."

Mom gave her little smile, and I thought she was going to say something sarcastic, but then her face softened. She raised her glass. "To the four of us," she said. "We're all that's left."

Liz stayed home all winter with Mom, who took her job as a teacher seriously. Uncle Tinsley was working on his geology paper and genealogical charts, as well as making the occasional hunting trip, coming home a couple of times with a dead doe strapped to the hood of the Woody. He also pitched in on Liz's schooling, giving her lectures about calculus, the geology of the Culpeper Basin, and the composition of Virginia's orange clay.

Maddox kept trying to mow me down with the Le Mans, but since Liz was never with me, I stopped worrying about him as much and started to enjoy school a little more. Miss Jarvis, who was the yearbook adviser as well as my English teacher, talked me into joining the yearbook staff, which was more fun than the pep squad.

Meanwhile, the kids were getting used to the idea of integration. The football team had a terrible year, but the basketball team was doing better, thanks to a couple of really tall black players. One guy was so big that he was called Tyrone "The Tower" Perry, or sometimes just Tower. The cheerleaders were also looking more like a team, the black girls doing a little less dancing and the white girls doing a little more. Vanessa's mother, who owned a beauty parlor for black women and sold Avon cosmetics, had a powder-blue Cadillac, and she started driving a group of black and white cheerleaders, including Ruth, to the away games.

I ended up spending a lot of time at the Wyatts' house. That beating had really changed Joe. He pulled into himself and talked even less than before. But then Dog came along.

Joe had always wanted a dog. Uncle Clarence thought a dog that didn't hunt or herd sheep and just sat around scarfing down dog food was a waste of money. After the beating, however, Aunt Al talked him into letting her get one for Joe. We all went to the pound, where Joe picked out a black-and-white dog that was a mix of breeds. Joe called him a purebred mutt and named him Dog.

Dog was a smart, saucy little guy who followed Joe everywhere. He went with Joe to the bus stop every morning, and when Joe got off the bus in the afternoon, Dog was sitting there waiting for him, regardless of the weather. That mutt really lifted Joe's spirits.

It actually snowed a couple of times that winter, and Joe and I got into some fierce snowball fights with the other mill hill kids, the gang of us interrupting the fight to pelt passing cars, and everyone, including Dog, running for the woods when the drivers got out to try and chase us down, shouting, "Come back here, you lintheads!"

When all was said and done, except for the Maddox mess, I was having a great time in Byler.

CHAPTER NINE

I HAD a good feeling about the trial. We met a few times with Dickey Bryson, the prosecuting attorney. He was a bulky man, and he smiled a lot. The case was pretty simple, he told us. At the trial, he'd start with the deputy who took Liz's statement and the photos; then he'd put me and Uncle Tinsley on the stand to testify about Liz's beat-up condition when she came home; then he'd put Wayne on to testify to what he'd witnessed when he drove Liz and Maddox around. Finally, he'd put Liz on to give her version of events.

It seemed to me like a slam-dunk case. Maddox did what he did. We had an eyewitness. How could we not win? I kept repeating this to Liz, but as the trial got nearer, she became a nervous wreck.

The morning of the trial, the sky was clear, but it was wickedly cold. Liz, Mom, and I were getting dressed in the bird wing when Liz put her hand to her mouth and rushed into the bathroom. Her stomach was empty, but I could hear her retching and heaving over the toilet. When Liz came out, Mom handed her a box of mints. "Most performers have anxiety at showtime," she said.

I put on the lime-green pants I hadn't worn since the first day of school, and Liz got out her orange-and-purple skirt. We wanted to look respectable, and these were the only dressy clothes we had. We'd burned the clothes Maddox had bought us. I was afraid Mom was going to wear one of her hippie dresses, but instead, she pulled out a pair of black pants and her red velvet jacket.

"Mom, you sure that's the right thing to wear?" I asked.

"You two can dress for the judge if you want," she said. "I'm dressing for the jury."

Uncle Tinsley waited for us at the foot of the stairs. He had on a pin-striped suit with a vest. No one felt like eating breakfast, so we piled into the Woody. During the drive, we tried to buck Liz up.

"Don't let Maddox scare you," I said. "He's just a bully."

"You've got the facts and the law on your side," Uncle Tinsley said. "You'll do fine."

"Keep eye contact," Mom said, "and channel your chi."

"Just what I need—platitudes from the pep squad," Liz said.

That ended the bucking up. We rode along in silence; then Liz said, "I'm sorry. I know you're all trying to help."

The courthouse was a big stone building with turrets and tall windows. We pushed through the revolving brass door. Everyone involved in the whole mess was milling about in the lobby. Maddox was there, wearing a dark blue suit, and so were Doris and the Maddox kids. When Maddox saw us, he glared. I glared right back.

Dickey Bryson was talking to another man in a suit. The man turned around and started talking to Maddox while Dickey Bryson came over to us carrying an accordion file under one arm. He told us that the man talking to Maddox was his attorney, Leland Hayes.

Just before nine o'clock Joe and Aunt Al pushed through the revolving glass doors, followed by Wayne. The bailiff opened the doors to the courtroom and ushered us in.

The courtroom had a high ceiling, and the tall windows let in the pale March light. It all had a solemn feel.

"All rise," the bailiff called, and the noise we made standing in unison reminded me of church. The judge came in, an unsmiling man whose black reading glasses matched his black robe. He took a seat at his big elevated desk and looked through the papers on it.

"Judge Bradley," Uncle Tinsley whispered. "He was at Washington and Lee when I was there."

So far, so good, I thought. The trial seemed like it was going to be a serious and official proceeding. I took that as a positive sign.

"Mr. Maddox," the judge said, "stand and be arraigned."

Maddox stood up and straightened his shoulders. A woman at a small desk in front of the judge also stood and read the charges against him: attempted rape, aggravated sexual assault, and assault and battery.

"What is your plea?" the judge asked after each charge.

"Not guilty!" Maddox said loudly each time.

"You may be seated."

Maddox sat back down. He and his lawyer were at a table on the far side of the gallery. At the table next to them, Dickey Bryson was busily scribbling on a yellow legal pad.

A uniformed deputy ushered in a group of men and women who sat on one side of the courtroom. "Jury pool," Uncle Tinsley whispered. One of them was Tammy Elbert, the woman who'd driven us to Mayfield when we first arrived in Byler, who said she'd have given anything in high school to be Charlotte Holladay.

The judge talked for a few minutes about the duties of jurors and the responsibilities of citizens. Then he asked the witnesses to come up to the front. After we came forward, he asked the people in the jury pool if any of them knew any of us or any of the attorneys.

One man in a plaid jacket stood up. "I know just about everybody here," he said. "Reckon we all do."

"I reckon you do," the judge said. "Would that prevent any of you from delivering an impartial verdict?"

They looked at one another and shook their heads.

"Let the record show that no juror believes he cannot be impartial."

The two lawyers stood and read off names from their legal pads. The people who were called climbed into the jury box. Tammy Elbert was one of them. Within ten minutes the jury box was filled, and the rest of the pool left the courtroom. The judge asked the witnesses to step outside, so we all followed the deputy through the doors, leaving Mom sitting on the bench next to Joe and Aunt Al.

Wayne lit a cigarette and headed down the hall toward the ashtray while the deputy led the rest of us into a small room. In half an hour the deputy came back, beckoning Uncle Tinsley to follow him. Twenty minutes later the deputy came back and beckoned me.

The clerk swore me in, and I sat in the witness chair. Maddox had his arms crossed, as if challenging me to pull this off. In the gallery behind him, Uncle Tinsley had taken a seat next to Mom. The jurors were studying me like I was some sort of curiosity.

Sitting in the witness chair, with all those people staring at me, made my mouth dry and my throat tight. When Dickey Bryson asked me to state my name, my voice came out in a squeak. Yikes, I thought.

"Take your time," Dickey Bryson said.

In answer to his questions, I explained how Liz and I had started working for the Maddoxes, how I mostly did stuff for Mrs. Maddox, how Liz was more like Mr. Maddox's personal assistant, and how he had set up the passbook savings accounts. Dickey Bryson then asked what happened the night Liz came back with Wayne, and I told the jury everything I could remember. The more I talked, the more comfortable I felt, and by the time Dickey Bryson said, "No further questions," I thought I had done a fairly good job.

Leland Hayes stood up and buttoned his coat. He had short graying hair and a long sunburned nose. When he smiled, crow's-feet formed at the corners of his slate-colored eyes.

"Good morning, young lady," he began. "So you worked for Jerry Maddox here?" Leland Hayes pointed at him.

"Yes, sir." Dickey Bryson had told me to keep my answers short.

"It was mighty generous of him to give you a job, wasn't it?"

"I suppose. But we worked for our money. It wasn't charity."

"Just answer yes or no. Now, why did you go to work for him?"

"We needed the money."

"Didn't your parents provide for you?"

"Lots of kids work," I said.

"Answer the question, please. Do your parents provide for you?"

"I only have one. My mom. My dad died."

"My sympathies. That must be tough, growing up without a dad. How did he die?"

Dickey Bryson stood up. "Objection," he said. "Irrelevant."

"Sustained," the judge said.

I looked over at the jury. Tammy Elbert had a tiny smile. She knew how my dad had been killed. They all did.

"Now you're living with your uncle, isn't that correct?"

"Yes, sir."

"Why is that? Is it because your momma can't take care of you?"

"Objection," Dickey Bryson said again. "Irrelevant."

"I'll proffer that it is relevant, Your Honor," Leland Hayes said. "It goes to the question of motive and character."

"I'll allow it," the judge said.

"So why aren't you living with your momma?"

I looked over at Mom. She was sitting very erect, with her lips pressed together. "It's sort of complicated," I said.

"You strike me as a very smart young lady. I'm sure you can explain to the jury something that's sort of complicated."

"Mom had some stuff she needed to do, so we decided to visit Uncle Tinsley."

"Stuff? What stuff? Can you be more specific?"

I glanced at Mom again. She looked like she was about to explode. I turned to the judge. "Do I have to answer that?" I asked.

"I'm afraid so," the judge said.

"Well, Mom had sort of a meltdown, and she needed some time to herself, so we decided to come visit Uncle Tinsley."

"So you two girls came to Virginia on your own. All the way from California. Has your momma left you on your own before?"

"Just for short periods. And she always made sure there were plenty of chicken potpies for us to eat."

"Well, that was real responsible of her." Leland Hayes glanced at the jury. Tammy Elbert was looking at Mom, whose face was almost as red as her velvet jacket. "So your mother is a performer?"

"A singer and a songwriter."

"And performance is a form of make-believe, right?"

"I guess."

"Does your mother engage in a lot of make-believe? Has she ever, say, made up a boyfriend who didn't really exist?"

"Objection!" Dickey Bryson shouted. "Irrelevant."

"I'll withdraw the question." Leland Hayes cleared his throat. "When your mother had her meltdown, she left you to survive on your own. That's tough. It meant you had to do whatever it took to get by. Even tell lies if you felt you had to."

"Objection. Argumentative."

"Sustained."

"I'll rephrase. Have you ever needed to lie to get by?"

"Nope," I said emphatically.

"Did you or did you not lie to your Uncle Tinsley about working for Mr. Maddox?"

"That wasn't exactly a lie. We just decided not to mention it."

"So you didn't lie to your uncle, who had let you into his house and was feeding you and taking care of you. You just misled him?"

"I guess."

"You like your Uncle Tinsley, don't you?"

"He's great."

"He's looking after you because your mother wasn't. So you want to make him happy. When you're not misleading him. Has your uncle ever told you that he dislikes Mr. Maddox?"

"He had a good reason to."

"Because Mr. Maddox recommended that the Holladay Textiles owners terminate your uncle's relationship with the mill?"

"Uncle Tinsley also thought he treated the workers bad—"

The judge cut me off. "Just answer yes or no."

"So would you ever lie about Mr. Maddox if you thought it would make your uncle happy?"

"Objection!" Dickey Bryson shouted.

"Sustained," the judge said.

Hayes looked at his legal pad again. "Did you eat food from the Maddoxes' refrigerator without their permission?"

"If I was making the kids sandwiches, I'd sometimes make myself one, too."

"So you did eat the Maddoxes' food without their permission. Did you also drink Mr. Maddox's vodka without his permission, which was one reason he had to fire you?"

"What?"

"Yes or no."

"No!" I shouted.

"Did you steal money from his dresser drawer, which was the other reason he had to fire you?"

"No!"

"Do you have a vendetta against Mr. Maddox?"

"No."

"Is Joe Wyatt your cousin?"

"Yes."

"Did you and Joe Wyatt slash the tires of Mr. Maddox's car?"

I looked down at my hands. "I didn't do it," I said.

"So Joe Wyatt did it?"

I shrugged. "How would I know?"

"Maybe because you were there. Remember that you're under oath. Did you help Joe Wyatt plan or carry out this crime?"

"It's because Maddox was trying to kill us!" I shouted. "He was trying to run us over with that Le Mans. It was self-defense—"

"I think we get the picture," Leland Hayes said. "A nasty little feud. No further questions."

"But you're not giving me a chance to explain!"

"Young lady, that will be all," the judge said.

Once Leland Hayes sat down, Dickey Bryson stood up. He asked me to tell the jury what I'd meant by saying Maddox tried to run us down, and I told them how, when we were walking to the bus stop, he'd come barreling down the road in his Le Mans and swerve at us and we had to jump into the ditch to get out of his way.

Then Leland Hayes had another turn. "Did you ever report these alleged incidents to the police?" he asked.

"No," I said.

"So there's no record of these alleged incidents taking place."

"But they did."

"The jury can decide that. What you are admitting is that you and Mr. Maddox were feuding?"

"I guess you could call it that. But it all started because he—"

"No further questions."

The judge told me to step down, but I could hardly move. I had just betrayed Mom. I had ratted out Joe. And I had admitted lying to Uncle Tinsley. How did that happen? All I wanted to do was get up and tell the truth about what Maddox did to Liz, and I ended up looking like a lying, stealing, feuding tire-slitter.

I finally stepped down from the witness stand. Dickey Bryson told me that since I'd finished testifying, I could sit in the gallery.

I took a seat between Mom and Uncle Tinsley. He patted my arm, but Mom just sat there, rigid as stone.

DICKEY Bryson asked the bailiff to bring in Wayne Clemmons. He was wearing a gray windbreaker, and he hadn't bothered to shave. After he swore his oath and took a seat, he mumbled his name, keeping his head down like he was studying his work boots.

Dickey Bryson asked him to describe what he had witnessed on the night in question.

"Nothing much," Wayne said. "All's I know is Maddox and the girl was in the back of my car, arguing about money. She wanted money from him. But I didn't really witness nothing."

Bryson looked up, startled. "Are you certain?"

"I was driving the car. My eyes was on the road."

Bryson riffled through his accordion file and held up a piece of paper. "Mr. Clemmons, did you or did you not give a statement to the police saying that you had observed Jerry Maddox physically and sexually assaulting Liz Holladay in the back of your taxi?"

"I don't recollect what I told the police," Wayne said. "My memory's been shot to hell since I came back from 'Nam. I forget things that did happen and remember things that didn't happen."

"Mr. Clemmons, let me remind you that you're under oath here."

"Like I said, my eyes was on the road. How was I supposed to know what was going on in the backseat of the car?"

Before I even realized what I was doing, I was on my feet. "That's a pack of lies!" I shouted.

The judge banged his gavel down. "I'll have order in this court."

"But he can't sit there and lie—"

The judge banged his gavel again and roared, "Order!"

Then he motioned to the bailiff, whispered in his ear, and the bailiff beckoned me with his finger. I stood up, and the bailiff led me out of the courtroom, and after he closed the door, he said, "Judge don't want you back inside for the duration."

Then the door to the courtroom opened, and Wayne walked out.

"Why'd you lie?" I blurted out.

"Enough, young lady," the bailiff said.

Wayne just shook his head and walked out the revolving door.

"Don't go back into the witness room," the bailiff said, "and no talking to the other witnesses."

I sat on a bench in the hall. After a few minutes the bailiff came back out and opened the witness-room door. "You're up, miss," he said. Liz walked out and followed him into the courtroom.

IT WAS past one o'clock by the time the doors to the courtroom opened and everyone filed out. Liz came through the doors, flanked by Mom and Uncle Tinsley. She had her head down.

"How did it go?" I asked Liz, but she walked right past me without saying anything.

"Just hunky-dory," Mom said.

"That attorney was pretty hard on her," Uncle Tinsley said. "Then Maddox took the stand. He basically said he fired you for stealing, and the two of you made this all up to get back at him."

"Dirtbag liar!" I said. "They couldn't possibly believe that."

"I think they don't know what to believe," Uncle Tinsley said.

WE ATE lunch at the Bulldog Diner. Afterward we went back to the courthouse and sat on the uncomfortable benches in the hallway as the jury began deliberating. I figured they'd be there for the long haul, but in less than an hour, the bailiff called everyone back into the courtroom. He told me that, since the jury had reached a verdict, the judge was allowing me to return to the courtroom.

The jurors filed in. When I looked at Tammy Elbert, she kept her eyes on the judge. The clerk passed the judge a piece of paper. He unfolded it and read it. "The verdict is not guilty on all charges."

Aunt Al gasped, and Mom shouted, "No!"

The judge banged his gavel. "Court dismissed."

Maddox slapped Leland Hayes on the back and went over and started shaking the jurors' hands. Liz and I sat there in silence. I felt completely confused, like the world had turned upside down and we were living in a place where the guilty were innocent and the innocent were guilty. I didn't know what to do.

Dickey Bryson came over to where we were sitting. "These he-said-she-said cases are tough to prove," he said.

"But we had a witness," I said.

"Not today you didn't."

WE GOT into the Woody. Uncle Tinsley headed down Holladay Avenue saying nothing. Mom was so agitated that she could hardly contain herself. That defense attorney was a monster, she told us. All those outrageous things he had said about her. And the way he had behaved toward her girls was hideous. He had treated Liz even worse than he had me, she went on. He had taken Liz's imagination and creativity and used them against her. He accused her of making things up. He said Liz's banged-up face in the police photos could have been caused by Tinsley smacking her for coming home late. He asked Liz about the perv we'd ditched in New Orleans, then told the jury that this was evidence she called men "perverts" without any proof and that she considered outsmarting them a game. He declared that Liz was essentially a habitual liar with an overactive imagination and an obsession with the idea of perverts.

Mom went on about how much she hated Byler. The town was small-minded, mean-spirited, backward, and prejudiced. Sitting in that courtroom was the most humiliating experience of her life. We were really the ones on trial, not Maddox—put on trial for going out in the world and doing something creative with our lives instead of wasting away in this stifling, dying, claustrophobic mill town.

"Shut up, Charlotte," Uncle Tinsley said.

"That's the problem with this town," she said. "Everyone's supposed to just shut up and pretend nothing's wrong. Bean was the only one with the guts to stand up and say it was all a pack of lies."

"The jury thought what I said was all a pack of lies," Liz said in a quiet voice. "Nothing happened. You heard the verdict." I was sitting next to her in the back of the Woody. She looked out the window. "Was it a pack of lies," she said, "or a lack of pies? Plaque of eyes, arranged by size. Or black-eyed lies?" Liz was speaking in a distant monotone. "Plucked out eyes. Lucked-out lies. To no surprise, to our demise. All the liars told their lies. Who denies the lies? Who will scrutinize the lies? Who cries, who spies, who dies?"

"Please, stop it," I said.

"I can't."

THE day seemed to have gone on forever, but it was only mid-afternoon by the time we got back to the house. The sky had clouded over, and a drizzle had started. Liz said she was going to the bird wing to take a nap. Uncle Tinsley decided to build a fire in the living room and sent me out to fetch kindling from the wood-shed. I couldn't find any good kindling, so I chopped some from a couple of small logs, using the hatchet that hung on the wall.

When I had enough kindling, I carried it back to the house.

Uncle Tinsley was on his knees in front of the fireplace, wadding up newspaper. Mom was sitting in a wing chair next to the hearth.

"Bean, why don't you go see if Liz wants to come down," Mom said. "She could probably use a little primal heat."

I climbed the stairs to the second floor. When I opened the door to our room, I saw Liz lying on the bed with her clothes still on. I was going to turn around and let her sleep, but she suddenly made this groggy, gurgling noise that scared me.

"Liz?" I said. "Liz, are you okay?"

I sat down next to her, shaking her arm and calling her name, and when she looked up, her eyes were blurry and unfocused. She said a few words in a slurred voice, but I couldn't understand them. I ran back downstairs. "Something's wrong with Liz!" I screamed.

Mom jumped out of her chair, and Uncle Tinsley dropped the log he was holding. We all ran up the stairs. Uncle Tinsley shook Liz, and she responded with the same sort of incomprehensible noises.

"Did you take anything?" Uncle Tinsley shouted at her.

"Pills," she mumbled.

"Pills? What pills?"

"Mom's pills."

Uncle Tinsley looked at Mom. "What is she talking about?"

"She must mean the sleeping pills," Mom said.

"You've got sleeping pills? God, Charlotte. Go check the bottle."

Uncle Tinsley started slapping Liz's face and dragged her off the bed. Uncle Tinsley said that we needed to get Liz woken up.

Mom came back and said the bottle was empty but there had been only a few pills left, maybe eight at most. Uncle Tinsley half carried Liz into the bathroom while Mom followed, explaining that as the trial got near, she'd given Liz a pill from time to time to help with her nerves. At the sink, Uncle Tinsley forced Liz to drink several glasses of water and then kneel over the toilet while he stuck his fingers down her throat. She vomited all over his hand, but Uncle Tinsley kept at it until all he got from her was dry heaves. Then he pulled her into the bathtub, turned the shower on cold, and they stood there in their clothes, getting soaked. Liz flailed around, hitting Uncle Tinsley and asking Mom to make him stop.

"He's getting the poison out, honey," Mom said.

"Shouldn't we call an ambulance?" I asked.

Mom and Uncle Tinsley said no at exactly the same time. Uncle Tinsley said, "We've got it under control," and Mom said, "She'll be all right." After a moment Mom added, "We've had enough dealings with people in uniform for one day."

Once it seemed like the drugs were out of Liz's system, Uncle Tinsley brought her one of his big flannel shirts. Mom and I helped her into it, then wrapped her in a blanket and took her down to sit by the fire while Uncle Tinsley changed into dry clothes. Mom made Liz hot coffee, and I toweled and combed her hair.

"Did you try to kill yourself?" I asked Liz.

"I just wanted to go to sleep. I wanted everything to go away."

"That's really stupid," I said. I knew it wasn't a nice thing to say, but I couldn't help myself. "That's what Maddox has been doing—trying to kill us—and you're going to do it for him?"

"Leave me alone," Liz said. "I feel like crap."

"Bean's right," Mom said. "He'd love to hear you came home and OD'd. Don't give him that satisfaction."

Liz just sipped her coffee and stared at the fire.

Liz was still asleep when I woke up the next morning. I nudged her to see if she was okay, and she muttered that she was alive but wanted to be left alone. Since it was Saturday, I let her stay in bed.

I went down to the kitchen, where Uncle Tinsley was drinking coffee. I fixed myself a poached egg on toast and was sitting next to him eating it when Mom came in, carrying a book.

"I've got a terrific idea for a road trip," she said, and held up the book. It was a guide to the famous trees of Virginia—the bald cypress in the Nottoway River Swamp that was the biggest tree in the state, and the enormous live oak in Hampton, under which a Union soldier read the Emancipation Proclamation to a group of slaves, the first time it was read in the South. There were dozens, Mom went on, each of them fascinating, and what the three of us girls could do was drive around visiting the trees, communing with their spirits. "They'll inspire us. It's exactly what we need."

"A road trip?" Uncle Tinsley asked. "Seems a little half-baked."

"What about school?" I asked.

"I'll homeschool you," she said.

"We're just going to leave?" I asked.

"We can't stay here," Mom said. She looked at me strangely. "I mean, you're not saying you want to stay here, are you?"

I had been so overwhelmed by the trial and Liz taking those sleeping pills that I hadn't thought about what we were going to do next. "I don't know what I want," I said. "But we can't just leave."

"Why not?" Mom asked.

"Every time we run into a problem, we leave," I said. "But we run into a new problem in the new place, and then we have to leave there, too. Can't we just stay somewhere and solve the problem?"

"I agree," Uncle Tinsley said.

"You tried to solve a problem by bringing those charges against Maddox," Mom said, "and see where it got you?"

"What should we have done? Run away?" Suddenly I was furious. "You're pretty good at that, aren't you?"

"How dare you speak to me like that? I'm your mother."

"Then act like one, for a change. We wouldn't be in this whole mess if you had been acting like a mom all along."

I had never talked to Mom like that. As soon as I said it, I realized I had gone too far, but it was too late. Mom sat down at the table and sobbed. She tried to be a good mother, she said, but it was so hard. She didn't know what to do. We couldn't all fit into the crummy little one-room apartment she'd rented in New York, and she couldn't afford anything better. If we didn't want to go on the road trip, maybe we could find a house in the Catskills near her spiritual retreat, but there was no way she was staying in Byler.

Uncle Tinsley put his arm around Mom, and she leaned into his shoulder. "I'm not a bad person," she said.

"I know you're not," Uncle Tinsley said. "This has been difficult for all of us."

I almost apologized for what I'd said, but I stopped myself. I felt Mom needed to face facts. So I let Uncle Tinsley comfort her, poured a glass of orange juice for Liz, and went upstairs.

Liz was still asleep, but I kept nudging her until she finally rolled onto her back and looked up at the ceiling.

"How do you feel?" I asked.

"How do you think I feel?"

"Pretty awful," I said. "Here, drink this."

Liz sat up and took a sip of juice. I told her Mom's idea for the road trip and of moving to the Catskills near her spiritual retreat. Liz didn't say anything. I went on, saying that Mom said she had to leave Byler, so we had to decide what we were going to do.

"You're the older one, but here's how I see it," I said. I told her that I thought Mom's road-trip idea was as cockamamie as all her other ideas. And the Catskills plan was wacky. I didn't want to go off and live with a bunch of Buddhist monks. What if Mom took off when we got there? There were only three months of school left. We should at least finish out the school year in Byler. It wasn't such a bad place. We had Uncle Tinsley, and we had the Wyatts. Finally the business with Maddox was over. We might not like how it ended, but it had ended.

"I don't know," Liz said. "This all makes my brain hurt." She set her orange juice down on the nightstand. "I just want to sleep."

I went back downstairs. Uncle Tinsley was building another fire in the living room, and Mom was sitting in the wing chair. Her eyes were a little puffy from that crying jag. She seemed unusually calm but also sad, and I realized I was no longer angry. "Mom, I'm sorry about some of those things I said. I know it hurt."

"It wouldn't hurt if weren't all so true," Mom said.

"I can be a jerk sometimes," I said.

"Don't apologize for who you are," she said. "And don't ever be afraid to tell the truth."

CHAPTER TEN

LIZ stayed in bed all that day and slept through the night. The next morning, she still refused to get up. After breakfast Uncle Tinsley asked me to help him clean the gutters. We were walking back from the barn, each carrying one end of the aluminum extension ladder, when suddenly two emus came wandering up the driveway. The birds didn't seem afraid at all, cocking their heads and looking around with their enormous caramel-colored eyes.

"They must have gotten loose from Scruggs's field," Uncle Tinsley said. "Scruggs never did tend his fences."

We set the ladder on the ground, and I ran inside to get Liz, who pulled on a pair of jeans and rushed down the stairs. By then the emus were moseying toward the barn, taking long, deliberate steps. Their movements were somehow both awkward and graceful.

Uncle Tinsley decided he'd better get in touch with Scruggs, and he went inside to make the call. When he came back out, he said he'd spoken with Scruggs and the emus actually belonged to Scruggs's son-in-law, Tater, who was working a job over in the valley and wouldn't be back until the day after tomorrow. Tater was the only one who knew how to catch the birds, so Scruggs had asked if we could keep them until Tater returned.

"I reckon that's the neighborly thing to do," Uncle Tinsley said. "But we'll need to get them into the pasture."

The emus had meandered past the barn into the orchard. They were a few feet from the gate that led into the main pasture, which was surrounded by old three-board fencing. Walking slowly behind the emus, our arms stretched out, we were able to herd them the short distance to the open gate. Once they had gone through, Liz quickly shut the gate and latched it.

We brought Mom up to the field to show her the emus, but the size of their talons unnerved her, and she said she wanted nothing to do with them. Liz, however, found them captivating. While Uncle Tinsley and I cleaned the gutters, Liz spent the afternoon leaning on the fence, watching the emus. They seemed not of this world, she said, like aliens from another planet or maybe even angels. She decided that the bigger one was a male and the smaller was a female, and she named them Eugene and Eunice.

Not only did Liz love the emus, she also fell in love with the word "emu." She pronounced it "emyou" and also "emooo," drawing out the sound like a mooing cow. She pointed out that "emu" was "you-me" backward, and she came up with a whole list of neat words that rhymed with "emus," everything from "refuse" to "snooze" to "blues" to "choose" and "chews."

That night, she looked up emus in Uncle Tinsley's *Encyclopedia Britannica* and bombarded us with information—how they came from Australia, how they could run forty-five miles an hour, how the males sat on the nest, how they had these unique double feathers with two plumes growing from each quill.

"They're so weird and so beautiful," she said.

"Like you," I said.

I meant it as a joke, but Liz nodded. She felt that she was sort of like an emu herself, she said. Maybe that was why she'd had flying dreams ever since she was a little girl—at heart she was an emu. She was sure the emus also dreamed of flying. It was another thing they had in common. Both she and the emus wanted to fly—they just didn't have the wings they needed.

ON MONDAY morning I went back to school. The trial had been over for two days, but we still hadn't figured out what we were going to do next. Mom was set on clearing out of Byler. She kept talking about that harebrained road trip. Liz, meanwhile, kept refusing to go to school. When she wasn't watching the emus, she was obsessively writing emu poetry.

On Wednesday afternoon Tater and a couple of buddies arrived in a pickup with an empty cattle trailer attached to it. Tater was a small slope-shouldered guy with a tight, unsmiling mouth. He barely thanked us for keeping his emus, and complained about those stupid birds, what trouble they were. Some guy sold them to him as a breeding pair after convincing him that emu meat and emu eggs would be the next big thing, but this pair wouldn't breed or even lay eggs. He'd have barbecued them a long time ago, only he'd learned that the meat was gamier than hell.

With Uncle Tinsley directing, Tater backed the trailer up to the pasture gate. We all trooped into the field.

Liz had brought some bread along and tried luring the emus into the trailer, but when they peered into the dark interior, they scurried off. We spent over an hour hollering and trying to shoo the emus toward the trailer. It didn't work. Whenever we got them close, the emus screamed and flapped their stunted wings and dodged away. Once, Tater managed to get a hand on Eugene's neck, but he kicked with one of his huge taloned feet, and Tater had to jump back. "Damn birds," he said. "They're so stupid. I hate the ugly buggers."

"You hate them?" Liz asked. "I love them."

Tater looked at Liz. "You love them? You can have them."

"Oh, my God," Liz said. And she actually fell to her knees and held her arms out. "Thank you. Thank you so much."

Tater looked at Liz as if she were insane.

"Wait a minute," Uncle Tinsley said. "We can't just take these emus. Who's going to look after them?"

"Me," Liz said.

"I'll help," I said.

"We're talking about a serious long-term commitment here," Uncle Tinsley said.

"That's right," Mom said. "Anyway, we're not staying in Byler."

"We can't just leave these emus," Liz said.

Mom got a puzzled expression. "You want to stay in Byler because you fell in love with a couple of big, disgusting birds?"

"They need me. There's no one else to look after them."

"We don't belong here," Mom said.

"The emus don't belong here, either, but they're here."

Mom started to say something and then stopped.

"We'll keep the darn birds," Uncle Tinsley told Tater. Then he looked at Liz. "But only if you go back to school."

"All right," Liz said. "I'll go back to school."

"What about you, Mom?" I asked. "What are you going to do?"

Mom studied the sun setting behind the distant blue mountains.

"I can't stay here," she finally said. "I just can't."

THE next day, Liz went back to school and Mom packed to return to New York. Once there, she said that she would find a publisher for Liz's emu poetry. She was also going to find a rent-controlled apartment where we could all live real cheap, and then she would get us into one of those special public schools for gifted kids.

Everyone got up early the following morning. Mom put her suitcase in the trunk of the Dart and hugged us all. "The Tribe of Three," she said, "will be together again soon."

We watched as the Dart disappeared down the driveway.

WHEN LIZ RETURNED TO SCHOOL, it had been a week since the trial, and I hoped the other kids would stop teasing her and move on to something else. They didn't completely, but Liz developed a way of dealing with it. She drifted through the hallways in her own world, as if no one else existed. After school she played her guitar and worked on her emu poetry.

Despite Mom's talk about finding a publisher, Liz was terrified to show her poetry to anyone except family. I took it on myself to copy a bunch of the poems and slip them to Miss Jarvis, who sought out Liz and told her she had real talent. Liz started spending lunch hour in Miss Jarvis's classroom. A few of the other Byler High outsiders went there as well—Cecil Bailey, who sometimes got called a queer, and Kenneth Daniels, who wore a cape and also wrote poetry. No one at Miss Jarvis's lunch hour made fun of anyone else, and she encouraged them and praised their individuality. Liz had felt like such a scorned outsider at Byler that she hadn't realized the school had other outsiders as well. Discovering them was a real revelation.

I'D BEEN so busy with Liz and the emus that I hadn't seen much of the Wyatts since the trial, but one April afternoon shortly after I turned thirteen, Liz and I came home from school to find Uncle Tinsley and Aunt Al sitting on the front porch.

"Big goings-on down at the mill," Uncle Tinsley said.

"Your Mr. Maddox went and got hisself fired," Aunt Al said.

"What?" Liz said, like she couldn't believe what she was hearing.

"Al here was an eyewitness," Uncle Tinsley said.

Aunt Al said the verdict acquitting Maddox had really gone to his head. Wayne Clemmons had left the county the day after testifying, and people were saying Maddox had gotten to him one way or another—bribed him or threatened him.

Once the trial was over, Maddox became convinced he could get away with anything. He'd been pushy before the trial, Aunt Al said, but after he was acquitted, he went out of control on the mill floor, shoving the men and groping the women. He caught one girl eating a sandwich at her loom when it wasn't lunchtime, and he smashed the sandwich in her face. That was when the slowdowns started. The workers had had more than they could take from Maddox, and they were going to cause trouble for him. Thread got tangled. Looms started breaking. Lights went out. Toilets got clogged.

The mill owners expected the foremen to get results, and if one of them didn't, it was his fault. It started to get to Maddox, Aunt Al went on, and last night he plumb lost it. He got into an argument with Julius Johnson, a beefy black man who was Vanessa's uncle, over Julius taking a long bathroom break. Maddox started yelling at Julius, poking him in the chest. Julius grabbed his hand and told Maddox not to be poking him; he needed to show people a little respect. Maddox slapped Julius across the face, right in front of the whole shift, but before anyone could even say boo, Julius tackled Maddox, and those two big fellows ended up down on the shop floor trading punches until the security guard pulled them apart.

"Both Maddox and Julius was fired," Aunt Al said. Julius had become an instant hero among the black folk of Byler, and Samuel Morton of Morton Brothers Funeral Home, which serviced the coloreds, had already offered him a job.

Aunt Al reached over and tapped Liz on the arm. "If some skinny white girl was willing to stand up to Jerry Maddox," she said, "I reckon Julius Johnson figured he couldn't do any less."

WE FED the emus when we got home from school, with chicken feed. As soon as they saw us, they'd come running up to the fence.

I loved those ugly overgrown chickens, but not the way Liz did. She brought them treats, like cookies and broccoli. She followed them around the field. Eugene would let her get close enough to stroke him, and he even ate out of her hand, but Eunice was more skittish, so Liz left her food on the ground. The emus were her responsibility, she said, and she worried about them. A bobcat might attack them; they might get loose and end up as roadkill.

One afternoon a couple of weeks after Maddox got the boot, we went up to the pasture to find the gate open and the emus gone. We ran back to the house, and Uncle Tinsley told us that a crew from the power company had come through that morning trimming branches back from the wires and they must have forgotten to close the gate. Liz was so upset, she was shaking. We piled into the Woody and drove around, finally spotting the emus in a hayfield beside a country road a mile from Mayfield.

The hayfield, which was owned by Mr. Muncie, had barbed-wire fencing and an open gate. Liz got out and shut the gate, so the emus were safe for the moment, but none of us knew how to get them home. We'd herded the emus into the big pasture at Mayfield, but they'd been only a few feet from the gate. There was no way we could herd them along the road all the way back to Mayfield. Liz was practically hysterical.

"We need to rope those birds," Uncle Tinsley said.

That night, he called Bud Hawkins, a farrier down the road who owned a rodeo horse, to see if he could try lassoing the emus. Bud said he'd meet us at the field the next afternoon. Uncle Tinsley told us to recruit some friends as well. I told Joe, who said he'd bring a few buddies. Liz invited her new lunchtime friends.

When we pulled up to the hayfield in the Woody the next afternoon, Bud Hawkins was leading a bay horse off his trailer. The emus were on the other side of the field, watching suspiciously. While Bud saddled up his horse, a green Rambler drove up and Miss Jarvis got out with a few of the outsiders, including Kenneth Daniels in his black cape. Then Aunt Al arrived in a borrowed pickup with Earl beside her and Joe and his buddies in the bay. Then came the powder-blue Cadillac with Ruth, Vanessa, Leticia, and a couple of the black athletes, including Tower.

With everyone watching, Liz walked to Eugene, carrying a bowl of feed and a big, soft piece of rope with a loop in it. She placed the bowl on the ground, and when Eugene started pecking at the feed, she slipped the loop up past his head and around his neck.

Meanwhile, Bud trotted his horse toward Eunice. When she took off, he galloped after her, swinging the lariat over his head. Some of the kids were trying to help, Kenneth waving his black cape, Tower holding out his long arms, Ruth and Leticia rooting them on.

Eunice could really cover ground, darting to the side every time Bud threw the lariat. After an hour of chasing her, he trotted back to the fence. His shirt was soaked with sweat, and his horse's chest was covered with lather. "The good news is, the bird's starting to wear out," he said. "The bad news is, we're completely worn out."

Uncle Tinsley took charge, telling everyone to go into the field and gather behind Eunice, then form a long line, arms extended. Liz led Eugene through the gate and onto the road. With the kids in the line behind her touching fingertips, Eunice had nowhere to go but forward. She cautiously followed Eugene.

It was all going pretty well until we got to the corner of the hay-field, where the fence line stopped. Eunice panicked and hurled herself at the barbed-wire fence, trying to get back to the safety of the hayfield. She squeezed through but tore a bloody raw spot on her back. When Eugene realized that Eunice had taken off, he pan-icked as well, lurching and hissing so wildly that Liz pulled the rope off and he scrambled through the fence, too, skinning his back.

I felt like kicking a rock. After more than an hour of work, we were worse off than when we started. The birds were back in the same darned field, and they were all dinged up. The strange thing was, while Liz and I were really upset, everyone else was having the time of their lives. Uncle Tinsley was beaming and slapping people on the back, congratulating them on great teamwork, while the kids were hooting and doing elbow-flapping emu imitations as we all walked back to the cars in the late-afternoon light.

Now that the weather was warmer, I had gotten into the habit of biking over to the Wyatts' house on Saturdays to say hello and tuck into a plate of Aunt Al's fried eggs. Liz usually rode out to check on the emus, Mr. Muncie having said it was fine to keep them in his field until we figured out how to get them back. After the failed roundup, Liz decided we wouldn't be able to capture the emus—we couldn't outrun them or outsmart them. All we could do was try to win their trust, and that was what Liz had started working on.

One Saturday in early May, I walked into the Wyatts' kitchen to find Aunt Al sitting at the table next to Earl, writing Truman a letter. "How about some eggs?" she asked me.

As I was mopping up the drippings with toast, Joe came into the kitchen. "I'm going to the dump," he said to me. "Want to come?" All kinds of neat stuff got left at the dump, and Joe liked to see if he could fix things other people had thrown out.

The dump was on the far side of the river, and we walked across the clanking bridge, Dog trotting along behind us. It was a bright, windy spring day, the big flat-bottomed clouds sailing by overhead.

The dump was surrounded by a chain-link fence and sheets of corrugated tin, with clumps of wild daylilies flowering all happy and orange on the other side. People left appliances and machinery to the left of the gate, and we spent the afternoon examining eggbeaters, testing typewriters, and spinning the dials on old radios. Dog had a field day chewing on chicken bones and chasing rats. Joe found a wind-up clock he thought he could fix, and he brought it with him when we left at the end of the afternoon.

We walked back across the bridge and along Holladay Avenue, Dog at our heels. After passing the courthouse, we crossed the railroad tracks, then took a shortcut through an alley between the drugstore and the insurance agency. Behind the drugstore was a small parking area with a wooden staircase leading to the building's second floor. At the bottom of the stairs was Maddox's Le Mans.

I hadn't seen Maddox since the trial, but I knew I was going to run into him sooner or later, and I dreaded it. There was no sign of him, however, or of anyone else. As we came up to the Le Mans, Dog stopped, lifted his leg, and peed on one of the whitewall tires. It was almost like he knew who owned the car. Joe burst out laughing, and so did I. It was about the funniest thing I'd ever seen.

All of a sudden, the door at the top of the stairs flew open and Maddox came charging down, bellowing with rage about how dare that damn mutt take a piss on his car—it was vandalism, as bad as the tire-slashing we delinquents did, and this time he'd caught us red-handed. Maddox reached down and grabbed Dog by the scruff of the neck, popped the trunk of the Le Mans, and threw Dog in.

"Don't you hurt Dog," I said. "You hurt everything. You hurt my sister, and you know it."

"Jury didn't see it that way," he said. "Anyway, this dog's a menace, running around without a leash." He opened the door of the car. "You two get in the back. We're going to see your folks."

Joe and I looked at each other. I'll admit I was pretty scared, but we couldn't just let Maddox drive off with Dog. Joe threw the clock in the trash can, and we climbed into the car. No one said anything on the drive through town. I stared at the back of Maddox's thick neck and listened to Dog's muffled barking from inside the trunk.

Maddox stopped in front of the Wyatts' house. Dusk was approaching. He opened the glove compartment, pulled out a revolver, and shoved it in the pocket of his hooded black sweatshirt. Then he got out and popped the trunk, grabbed Dog by the scruff of the neck, and marched into the house without knocking. Joe and I followed. Aunt Al was at the kitchen table, trimming asparagus.

"Call your husband," Maddox said.

Aunt Al looked at Maddox and Dog and then at Joe and me. "What's going on?"

"I said call your husband."

Aunt Al stood up, moving slowly, like she was buying time while she decided what to do. Before she could say anything, Uncle Clarence appeared in the doorway.

"You got a gun, Clarence?" Maddox asked. "We need to put this dog down. He's a danger."

"Did he attack someone?" Aunt Al asked.

"All he did was pee on Mr. Maddox's car," I said. "On the tire."

"That's all?" Aunt Al said. "That's what dogs do."

"Damaged my personal property is what he did," Maddox said. "I'm not here to discuss it. I'm here to see this dog put down."

"You're not the boss anymore," Uncle Clarence said.

"But I can still kick your ass. You don't got a gun, Clarence, I got my revolver."

"I got a gun," Uncle Clarence said.

"Go get it," Maddox said. "Bring it out back."

Dog had been growling and squirming in Maddox's hand the whole time. Maddox barged out the back door into the yard between the house and the woods. Uncle Clarence disappeared and came back a moment later, carrying a rifle.

"Dad, you can't kill Dog," Joe said.

Uncle Clarence ignored him. "You all stay in here," he said, and went through the back door after Maddox.

We all stood there paralyzed. I was half in shock. I knew Uncle Clarence hadn't wanted Joe to get Dog, but I couldn't believe he'd shoot the little guy. I looked at Joe. His face was ash-colored.

We heard an incredibly loud shot that echoed up in the hills behind the house.

And then Dog started barking. We ran to the back door. In the fading light, we could see Uncle Clarence standing with the rifle in his hands. Maddox was lying faceup in Uncle Clarence's freshly planted vegetable garden. His leg was twisted awkwardly to the side, and I could tell he was dead.

"Good Lord, Clarence," Aunt Al said.

"Thought he was a bear," Uncle Clarence said. "Heard a noise out back and went to investigate. You all were inside. You didn't see nothing." He looked at his rifle. "Thought he was a bear."

AND that was what Uncle Clarence told the policemen who came to the house. Thought he was a bear. It was dark. Maddox was big as a bear and was wearing that black sweatshirt. When the police asked Uncle Clarence what Maddox had been doing in the backyard, Uncle Clarence said he didn't know, because he hadn't asked him because he thought he was a bear.

Aunt Al said we'd all been inside and hadn't seen anything. Joe and I nodded in agreement. No one mentioned the business about Dog. The police roped off the backyard, sent for an ambulance to pick up the body, and brought Uncle Clarence down to the station for questioning. Aunt Al called Uncle Tinsley to come and get me. When he arrived, she briefly told him the same story we told the police. Uncle Tinsley listened quietly. "I see," he said.

We were both silent most of the way home; then Uncle Tinsley finally said, "Thought he was a bear, did he?"

"Yep," I said.

Uncle Tinsley had his eyes on the road. "Well, that's an explanation people around here can live with. I know I can." We drove a little farther in silence, and then he looked over at me. "You seem to be holding up pretty well," he said. "You feeling okay?"

"Yep," I said.

I'd never seen a dead person before. I thought it might be upsetting, but it just wasn't. Maybe I was numb. What I did feel was extremely focused, like I was going through a tunnel and couldn't afford to look to either side but instead had to pay attention to what was in front of me and keep moving forward.

Uncle Tinsley rolled down his window and took a deep breath. "Smell that honeysuckle," he said.

BY THE time we got home, the moon was out. The porch lights were on, and Liz was standing at the top of the steps waiting for us.

"What happened?" she called out.

"Maddox is dead!" I shouted.

Uncle Tinsley and I climbed the steps. "It was getting dark, and Clarence Wyatt heard a noise behind the house," Uncle Tinsley said. "He says he thought it was a bear and shot it. Turned out to be Maddox."

Liz stared at us. "I feel dizzy. I feel sick. I need to lie down."

She ran into the house. I followed her up to the second floor and down the hall to the bird wing. She threw herself on the bed, but after a moment she sat up and started rocking back and forth.

"Uncle Clarence didn't think Maddox was a bear," Liz said. "What really happened?"

I started explaining, and Liz burst into tears. "It's okay," I said.

"No, it's not," Liz sobbed. "What about Doris and the kids?"

"He had money and all of those houses he rented out," I said. "She's better off without him."

"But those kids don't have a dad anymore."

"We don't have a dad," I said. "We got by."

"No, we didn't. Look at what's happened. And it's all my fault."

Liz's sobs got louder. She was gasping for air and going on about how she'd killed Maddox, killed the mad ox, willed it, killed it, she made the mad ox die, she made the bad bear lie, trapped in a dark box, the mad ox, the bad bear, the bad ox, the mad bear, the back-seat, the black car—it was all her fault, all her fault.

"It's not your fault," I said. "He started it all. But now it's over." I stroked her hair and repeated, "It's not your fault. It's over. It's all over," and after a while she stopped crying and nodded off.

TRUTH be told, I worried that it wasn't over. What if someone had seen us getting into Maddox's car in the alley? What if a neighbor on the hill had seen the three of us drive up? The police must wonder what Maddox was doing in the Wyatts' backyard.

The next day was Sunday. When I woke up, morning light filled the bedroom. Next to me Liz was sleeping, and I took that as a good sign. Downstairs Uncle Tinsley was dressed in a seersucker suit. He said he'd decided to go into town and, as he put it, show his face and take the pulse of the people. And the places to do that were the Baptist church and the Bulldog diner.

When Liz woke up, she seemed better, but she still looked pale and fragile. She spent the morning playing the guitar while I worked in the garden, weeding around the irises and thinking about my sister. Liz deserved a medal for what she'd gone through.

I put down the trowel and went up to the bird wing, where I took my dad's Silver Star out of the cigar box in the cradle. I had never actually put it on. I felt you had to earn the right to do that. Liz certainly had, not just for everything she'd gone through but for protecting her kid sister from their mother's wackiness until I was old enough to handle it. So had Uncle Clarence—not just for shooting Maddox but for taking on the work of a man when he was only a boy so that my dad would have a home. So had Aunt Al, for breathing in lint every night at the mill and then going home to care for her sick husband and her special little Earl. So had Uncle

Tinsley, for taking in his two wayward nieces, and Mom, for coming back to a place she hated, to be there for Liz.

I took the Silver Star downstairs. Liz was sitting on the piano bench with her guitar.

"This is for you." I held out the medal. "You deserve it."

Liz put down the guitar and took the medal. She looked at it. "I can't take this," she said. "It was your dad's." She handed it back. "But I'll never forget that you wanted to give it to me."

UNCLE Tinsley returned after lunch. We followed him into the living room, where he sat down in the brocade wing chair.

Everyone in Byler knew about the shooting, of course, he told us. What no one could figure out was what Maddox had been doing behind the Wyatt house. The police had talked to the Wyatts' neighbors, but people on the mill hill hated Maddox. So no one saw anything and no one heard anything—except the gunshot.

The town was full of speculation. Maddox couldn't have been up to any good. People suspected it had something to do with the feud. Was he spying on the family? Planning an ambush? But if that was what he was up to, why was his car parked out front? Still, he had that revolver on him. At the very least, he was trespassing, and a man had the right to protect his family and his property. That was why, after questioning Uncle Clarence, the police hadn't arrested him. His story was simple and made sense. People in these parts were always getting into hunting accidents.

And Maddox was a troublemaker even for the police, filing lawsuits and complaints, riding the men at the mill, and putting moves on women all over town. The cops knew that just about everyone in Byler except Doris was glad Maddox was gone, and so they were more than willing to shrug the whole thing off.

"Accidents happen." Uncle Tinsley held up his hands. " 'Thought he was a bear.' " He said, "I believe I'll play the piano."

He opened the French doors in the ballroom and took the green cover off the grand piano. He sat on the bench and started playing some classical stuff. It sounded pretty good, even to someone tone-deaf like me, and Liz and I listened for a little while. Then Liz said, "We need to go get the emus."

Uncle Tinsley was still playing when we left the house. We got ropes from the barn and walked to the hayfield. It was near feeding time, and the emus were standing at the gate waiting for us.

After three weeks of trying, Liz had gotten Eunice to eat out of the bowl while she held it. It had taken another week for Eunice to let Liz stroke her back while she was eating. That afternoon, as Eunice pecked away, Liz stroked her with the rope, getting her used to it, then slipped it around her neck. Eunice gave Liz a puzzled look, then went back to eating. I quickly put my rope over Eugene.

Liz and I both knew this whole emu-rescue business could turn out to be a big waste of time. Or worse. Now that we'd caught them, the emus might kick us with their talons or peck out our eyes or run into the road and cause a traffic accident. And once we got them back to Mayfield, those darned emus might escape again.

We led the emus out onto the road. They were a little frantic at first, but then they seemed to find something almost calming about the rope, like it was a relief to give up the fight. Eugene and I were in the lead. He was actually ahead of me, pulling on the rope as if he knew where we were going and wanted to get there. Every now and then a car passed, and the driver slowed, and the kids inside rolled down the windows and waved wildly at the sight of Liz and me bringing those big crazy birds back home.

Share Your Thoughts!

Communicate with us directly to chat about the stories and tell us what you liked or disliked. We want to keep giving you the kinds of books you want to read, and this is one way to make that happen. So let us know what you think. Share your thoughts with us at **SelectEditions@gmail.com**.

Mining Fact
for Fiction

The Silver Star is Jeannette Walls's third book, but it's her first truly fictitious story. Her first book, *The Glass Castle,* was a mega-hit memoir about her unique and sometimes terrifying childhood growing up with two brainy but dysfunctional parents. Her next book, *Half-Broke Horses,* was "fact-based fiction" and was essentially the story of her grandmother's unconventional life.

The Silver Star is all fiction, but Walls fans may recognize certain themes from previous books. "The sort of fiction I'm drawn to is close to real life; it's not orcs and hobbits and stuff," explains Walls. "My brain doesn't work that way. I'm an observer and a digger trying to cobble together a story that I hoped felt real and would make people ask questions about issues in the same way I hoped *The Glass Castle* would."

Some of the themes that arise in *The Silver Star* include bullying, good-hearted but troubled parents, integration, and prejudice. And the sisters in the book—supersmart Liz and plucky "Bean" Jean—strongly echo the relationship of Walls and her own older sister, Lori.

As anyone who has read *The Glass Castle* will know, Walls had a very unusual childhood. Her family moved around frequently, and she lived in dozens of different places, including Phoenix, Arizona, California, Nevada, and Welch, West Virginia. Her parents were unique, to put it mildly. Her father was brilliant but an alcoholic, and her mother was an artist who occasionally taught school to pay the bills. The family was extremely poor, and during her teenage years, Walls lived in a home without running water or electricity.

Walls left home at age 17 and moved to New York City to live with her older sister. She completed high school in New York and got a scholarship to Barnard College. She graduated in 1984 with honors and took a job at a Brooklyn newspaper called *The Phoenix,* which launched her early career in journalism. She worked at magazines and was a gossip columnist for many years before writing books full time.

Always a big reader, Walls says the most influential book in her life was *A Tree Grows in Brooklyn.* "I read it when I was ten years old and an outcast," she says. "Finding a friend like little Francie Nolan, who also was not very popular but loved reading and her no-account drunken daddy, was a revelation. I think it was the first time I experienced the incredible power of books." ■

Vital Stats

BORN: April 21, 1960; Phoenix, Arizona
RESIDENCE: Rural Virginia
EDUCATION: BA from Barnard College
FAMILY: Married to writer John Taylor; two sisters, one brother
FAVORITE AUTHORS: John Updike, John Steinbeck, Mona Simpson, Honoré de Balzac
FAVORITE NOVEL: *The End of the Affair* by Graham Greene

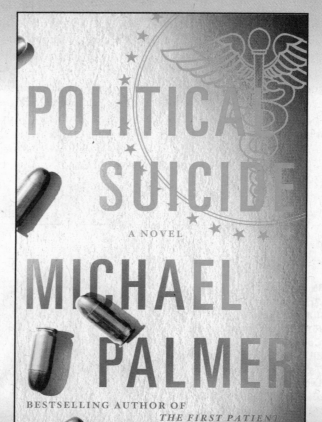

POLITICAL SUICIDE

A NOVEL

MICHAEL PALMER

BESTSELLING AUTHOR OF
THE FIRST PATIENT

May 3, 2003

THE three men, members of Mantis Company, slipped out the open hatch of the C-130 transport as it flew sixty-five thousand feet above the world. They had trained for this jump countless times. Their gear, ballistic helmets, oxygen masks, Aerox O_2 regulators, bailout bottles, all fastidiously maintained, assured them a successful landing. Altimeters marked their belly-to-earth rate of descent at one hundred fifteen miles per hour.

Minutes of free fall were spent in an effortless dive, with the men dropping in formation, still and straight. Automatic activation devices engaged the parachutes eight hundred feet before impact, the lowest altitude allowed for combat high altitude–low opening jumps.

They descended through the low cloud covering like missiles, emerging out of nothingness beneath a starless predawn sky. Their landings, each completed with a puma's grace, would have made their instructors back at Quantico proud. Perfection. Mantis demanded nothing less. In silence, the three changed into white cotton robes and the traditional head coverings of Taliban fighters.

Wearing their dusty garments, the men anticipated they would not immediately rouse any suspicion. Each of the three had a tanning-booth tan, as well as a closely trimmed mustache and a fully grown beard. The trio blended in with their surroundings—a mountainous, rocky region in southern Afghanistan.

"Miller, how many klicks to the target?"

Miller checked his handheld GPS. "Five kilometers, Sergeant."

"Gibson, ditch the gear."

Gibson hid their parachutes and other equipment behind a jagged boulder. By the time any Afghani stumbled upon the array of high-tech military paraphernalia, it hopefully would be too late.

They walked single file, moving silently across the rock-strewn terrain, with Miller and his GPS taking the lead. Dawn rose in streaks of brilliant pinks, yellows, and blues, beckoning the day. If anyone had checked the men's pulses, none would be above fifty.

Miller found the road, a rutted stretch of dirt that would carry them to the outskirts of Khewa, a town of twenty thousand that looked the same today as it did a century ago. Young women wearing chadors stopped farming the fields to give the trio a cursory glance. The disguises were good enough so that none of the women bothered with a closer inspection. The marines had estimated they could survive twelve hours or so before they were identified.

Way more than enough time.

The men of Mantis Company reached the crumbling clay brick

walls of Khewa's borders without incident. The town was defined by its absences—no cars, no electricity, no running water. Evidence of twenty years of war was seen everywhere. Bombed-out buildings were in greater number than habitable ones.

The smells of the market guided the men toward their destination. They wandered about casually through shabby stalls bunched together on each side of a single-lane dirt road. The central market was already bustling despite the newness of the day. In some stalls, slabs of fly-covered meat dangled like macabre wind chimes, while bloodstained butchers called out the day's prices in Pashto. Persian music blasted from cheap radios as the marines continued strolling.

"Don't look now," Gibson said, his voice hushed, "but it looks like we've been noticed."

An Afghani with a white beard descending to his chest, carrying a Kalashnikov assault rifle, approached the men the way he might a poisonous snake. The three marines turned their backs to the man and moved away from the women and children in the crowded market. To the extent they could control it, this operation was going to be soldiers only. When they stopped, the Afghani took two cautious steps toward them. His dark eyes narrowed. Then he began to shout and point frantically.

His shrill voice rose above the market's din, catching the attention of more men, each, it seemed, carrying a weapon different in make and age from the others. Racing up from all directions to surround the intruders, they were shouting in Pashto and pointing long, dirt-encrusted fingernails at the three men, now trapped inside the rapidly expanding circle.

"How do you like the show so far, Miller?" the sergeant asked, barely moving his lips.

"Just what you told us, Sarge," Miller said without a waver in his voice. "Provided they go and get Mr. Big."

The Taliban fighters were ten deep now, one hundred fifty of them at least, many with weapons leveled, pushing and shoving to get a closer look.

"Just keep your hands raised," the sergeant said to both his men, "and keep scanning the crowd for Al-Basheer. If our intelligence is correct, none of them will make a move until he gets here."

The closest men in the milling circle were a smothering five or six feet away. Miller spotted Al-Basheer first. His orange beard and bulbous nose were distinct giveaways.

"That's him, Sergeant," Miller said as the crowd parted to admit their leader, one of the most influential fighters in the region.

Al-Basheer strode through the ranks. The sergeant smiled and nodded, and immediately the three marines formed a tight triangle, facing outward with their shoulders touching.

"Whatever it takes," the sergeant said.

"Whatever it takes," Miller and Gibson echoed.

In a singular motion, the three men threw off their robes.

The crowd began screaming.

Strapped to each intruder's chest were bricks of explosive, with wires connected to a battery hinged to their waists.

"Whatever it takes," the sergeant said again.

The push of a button, a faint click, and in an instant, every man in the warrior circle was vaporized within a white hot ball of carefully concentrated light.

CHAPTER 1

Dr. Louis Francis Welcome could do a lot of things well, but doing nothing was not one of them. His desk at the Washington, D.C., Physician Wellness Office had never been so uncluttered. On a typical midafternoon, the voice mail light on Lou's telephone would be blinking red—a harbinger that one or more of his doctor clients needed advice and support in their recovery from mental illness, behavioral problems, or drug and alcohol abuse. At the moment, that light was dark, as it had been for much of the past several days.

Lou got paid to manage the cases of his assigned physicians, guiding them into recovery and eventually getting surrendered licenses reinstated. The holiday season inevitably brought an influx of new docs. But not recently.

So why was he not getting any new cases? There was only one explanation—Dr. Walter Filstrup, the director of the program.

Lou sauntered over to the reception desk, where Babs Peterbee seemed to be quite busy. "Hi there, Dr. Welcome," she said, her round, matronly face radiating a mix of caring and concern.

Lou said, "Any calls?"

"A man wanted to talk to you about the head of his department drinking too much. I referred him to Dr. Filstrup's voice mail."

"Did you get his name?"

Peterbee forced a smile. "Not my job."

"Is Walter in?" Lou asked. "His door's been closed since I got here."

"He's having a telephone meeting right now," Peterbee said, cocking her head to the door.

"Is this a real meeting or a Filstrup meeting?"

Peterbee strained to smile. "How's your daughter?" she asked.

"Emily's doing great, thank you," Lou said, shifting his six-foot frame from one foot to the other. "She's closing in on fourteen-going-on-thirty and is far more skilled than even our esteemed boss at skirting issues she doesn't want to deal with. So I'll ask again, is Walter *really* busy?"

Peterbee glanced down at her phone bank and shook her head. "Looks like he's off now."

Lou knocked once on Filstrup's door and opened it. The director's office was filled with neatly arranged medical textbooks and psychiatric journals, a reflection of the man's overriding need for order. Fit and trim, wearing a dark blue suit and white dress shirt, Filstrup shot to his feet, his face reddening by the nanosecond.

"Leave immediately, Welcome, then knock and wait."

"And you'll beckon me in?"

"No, I'll tell you I'm expecting an important call, and you should come back in an hour."

Lou pulled back the chair opposite Filstrup and sat. On the desk was a stack of client charts. "I haven't seen you this week, boss, so I thought I'd stop by and find out how business was." Lou gestured toward the stack. "Who's monitoring all these cases? Certainly not me."

"The board of trustees keeps renewing your contract," Filstrup said, "but they don't say how I'm supposed to use you."

"How about some work?" Lou asked. "I'm champing at the bit."

"You *have* cases to monitor," Filstrup said.

"What I have is a handful of doctors who are in solid recovery," Lou said. "I'm here to be helpful. I've never gone this long without getting a new case to monitor. What gives, Walter? Am I being punished because I'm not full-time?"

Lou had been part-time with the PWO for five years. Five years before that he was one of their clients, being monitored for amphetamine and alcohol dependence—the former used to cope with a killer moonlighting schedule and the latter to come down from the speed. It was Lou's belief that having battled his own addictions benefited the docs assigned to him. Filstrup, who was hired by the board well after Lou, would not concur.

"You're working almost full-time in the Eisenhower Memorial emergency room and twenty hours a week here," Filstrup said. "You've seemed stressed."

"Only by my reduced caseload," Lou said. "This wouldn't have anything to do with my not being a psychiatrist like yourself, would it?"

"Of course not," Filstrup replied, dismissing the statement with a wave.

Lou Welcome and Walter Filstrup had been at odds since day one, in large measure over their disagreement as to whether addiction was an illness or a moral issue. *Don't drink, go to meetings, and ask a higher power for help.* Lou knew that the terse, three-pronged instruction manual was all that the majority of addicts involved with AA ever needed. Psychotherapy had its place with some, but protracted, expensive treatment was often over the top.

The phone rang. Filstrup flashed an annoyed look and pushed the intercom button. "I told you to hold my calls, Mrs. Peterbee."

I thought you were expecting one, Lou mused.

"I'm sorry, Dr. Filstrup," the receptionist said. "Actually, this is for Dr. Welcome. I have the caller on hold."

Lou gave Filstrup a bewildered look. "Who is it, Mrs. P?" Lou asked.

"Our client Dr. Gary McHugh," she replied. "He said it's urgent."

Filstrup reflexively straightened up. "McHugh, the society doc? Put him through." Filstrup allowed the call to click over, then said in a cheery voice, "Gary, it's Walter Filstrup. How are you doing?"

The director's tone churned Lou's stomach, but it was not an unexpected reaction given who was on the line. Gary McHugh tended to the D.C. carriage trade and numbered among his patients a significant portion of all three branches of government. He was also one of Lou Welcome's closest friends, since their undergraduate days together at Georgetown. Several years before, McHugh had lost his driver's license for operating under the influence. The board of medicine's policy was to refer such physician offenders to the PWO, and Lou was placed in charge of his case.

Although McHugh adhered to the letter of his monitoring contract, he regarded the whole business as something of a joke. Lou never had much trust in the strength of McHugh's recovery—too much ego and too few AA meetings. Still, McHugh, a sportsman and pilot, had always been irrepressible, and Lou looked forward to their monthly progress meetings, as well as any other chance they had to get together.

"Am I on speakerphone?" McHugh barked.

"I was finishing a meeting with Lou Welcome," Filstrup said.

"Dr. Filstrup, I need to speak with him."

"I'm here," Lou said.

"Dr. Welcome, get me off speaker, please."

Lou stifled a grin at Filstrup's discomfort. With a shrug, he took the receiver and pressed it to his ear. "Hey, Gary, what gives?"

"Welcome, I'm in trouble—really big trouble. I need to see you right away. At my house. When can you get here?"

Lou checked his Mickey Mouse watch, a Father's Day gift from Emily. Nearly four—eight hours before he was due at the ER for the graveyard shift. McHugh lived in a tony neighborhood, midway between the Capitol and Annapolis. "About forty-five minutes."

"Get here in thirty," McHugh urged. "Before too much longer, the police are going to show up here to arrest me."

"For what?"

"For murder."

He hung up without saying good-bye.

MURDER.

The word reverberated through Lou's mind as he left the city and headed east. The December afternoon was already dark, and the wipers on Lou's ten-year-old Camry were working to keep up with a fine, windblown snow. He pulled off of Route 50 and onto a secondary road lined with McMansions, many already decorated for Christmas. White bulb country, Lou had once heard someone describe upscale neighborhoods such as this one—understated holiday decor, featuring small white lights on the front shrubs and electric candles in every window. Nice enough, but he was partial to the tangled strings of blinking colored bulbs outlining Dimitri's Pizza shop, just below his apartment in D.C.

Murder. *What in the hell was the man talking about?*

Lou cruised through the gated entrance of McHugh's elegant Tudor-style home. He observed only one car parked in the circular driveway—a Lexus, which belonged to Missy, McHugh's wife. McHugh prided himself on his high-end black Jaguar. Lou wondered if the car had somehow been involved in the man's current plight—a fatal accident of some sort, perhaps. Then he reminded himself that McHugh had very specifically said *murder*.

He braked his Toyota to a stop in front of the entranceway. McHugh—graying red hair, broad-shouldered—stood waiting. His face was distorted by a huge bruise between his left cheek and hairline. His left eye was swollen shut.

"Thanks for getting out here so quickly." McHugh said grimly.

"No problem. Gary, let's get inside. It's freezing out here."

Limping slightly, McHugh set Lou's coat on a hook in the foyer and shook his hand. His wrestler's grip had not been diminished by whatever had battered his face. His one open eye was bloodshot, and Lou smelled alcohol. Whatever had happened, booze was almost certainly part of it.

"What's going on, Gary?"

"Let's go in my study," McHugh said.

The cherry-paneled room was perhaps a third the size of Lou's entire apartment. A forty-inch plasma TV was tuned to CNN. The walls were decorated with pictures and souvenirs that defined the man—travels to exotic locales, black-tie parties featuring A-list notables, testimonials and letters of thanks, at least two from recent presidents. McHugh motioned Lou to one of two red leather armchairs, while he remained standing, glancing from time to time at the TV.

"Anytime now," he said, "CNN is going to report breaking news regarding the shooting death of Congressman Elias Colston in his garage." Despite the odor of alcohol, there was no evidence in Gary's speech or manner that he was intoxicated.

Lou stiffened. Colston, the chairman of the House Committee on Armed Services, was one of the more popular congressmen in the House. "How do you know?" he asked.

"I was there," McHugh said flatly, wincing as he sat down in the other chair. "I saw the body. At least two shots—one to the chest and one dead center in the forehead."

"When did this happen?"

"I got there at noon."

"And you had been drinking?"

There was an embarrassed silence, then, "Yes. Fairly heavily."

"Why hasn't the story broke by now?"

McHugh shrugged. "I guess because I'm the only one who saw him—besides the person who killed him, that is."

"And why didn't you call the police?"

"I . . . intended to find a phone booth and call them anonymously, rather than risk giving them my cell phone number. I knew if they caught up with me and I was found to be drinking, I could kiss my medical license good-bye."

"But before you could call anyone, you smashed up your car and did this to your face, yes?"

"You got it. I must have skidded off the road and hit a tree."

"You don't remember?"

"The first thing I remember after seeing Elias's body, I was being transferred from an ambulance stretcher to a bed in the ER."

Blackout from alcohol or concussion, Lou thought. *Most likely both.* "Are you okay now? I should check you over."

"They did everything—bloods, CAT scan. But all I wanted to do was get the hell out of the place. Missy came, and they let me go."

"Your alcohol level?"

"It was probably high. One of the nurses who knows me said a good lawyer could get me off any charges by saying I was head injured and couldn't authorize having my blood drawn. That may be the reason the police decided not to charge me on the spot."

"Why do you think they would charge you with Colston's murder?"

McHugh rose and began to pace. "Colston is a patient of mine. I've been to his house many times. There are security cameras."

"Then maybe one of them recorded the murder."

"Maybe, but it took place way in the back of the garage, by the stairs that go up to Colston's office. I don't remember any cameras there—just outside on the driveway. I'll bet the only thing those cameras recorded is me, driving up and driving away—maybe even with Elias's blood on me from when I checked him over."

"Gary, why would you be drinking in the morning and then go off to make a house call on one of your patients?"

"Because I wasn't making a house call, Lou. . . . I didn't go there to see Colston. I went there to see his wife, Jeannine." McHugh sighed. "We've been having an affair for more than two years."

"Oh, Gary," Lou groaned.

"That's not all," he said.

Before McHugh could explain, the news of Congressman Elias Colston's murder hit CNN like a wrecking ball. The report varied little from McHugh's account. Colston's body was discovered by his wife, Jeannine, after she returned from a meeting of a congressional spouses group in Washington. A spokeswoman for Jeannine Colston said only that their son and daughter had been notified at college and were on their way home, and that Jeannine had no other comment at that time. The feed of the crime scene around the Colstons' tasteful country home was bedlam.

Lou turned to his host. "Okay, Gary," he said. "What else is there you haven't told me?"

McHugh began pacing again. "I skidded off the road and hit a tree just after I had crossed the bridge."

"Bridge?"

"There's a stone bridge across a river about a mile down the road from the Colstons'. Unless they find it at the scene, the police are going to suspect that I stopped and tossed the murder weapon off the bridge and into the river, then kept going and went off the road."

Lou winced. "That's exactly what they're going to think," he said. Then he remembered something else—something that McHugh had been required to discuss the first day his PWO monitoring contract had begun. McHugh owned several pistols and some hunting rifles. The monitoring contract demanded that all guns be removed from the doctor's house, cataloged, and locked in a storage facility using a padlock provided by the PWO.

"The PWO has a record of the guns I turned in when I signed my contract," McHugh said as if reading Lou's thoughts. "They're all legally registered, so the police will learn about them."

Lou shrugged. *Not a big deal,* he was thinking. So why was McHugh being so dramatic about it, unless one of the guns was missing. No, there was something else. "Gary, why were you drinking at that hour of the morning?"

"Jeannine wanted to end it," McHugh said, staring at the screen.

"Did she say why?"

"Not really. She called me last night and said I shouldn't try and contact her. I tried to get her to explain what was going on. All she kept saying was that Elias needed her."

"Elias needed her. What did she mean by that?"

"I don't know. I love her, Lou. I really do."

McHugh gestured toward the screen, where CNN was now reporting that Maryland State Police had identified a person of interest in connection with the murder. Lou and McHugh both knew who that person of interest most likely was.

Means, motive, and opportunity—in the absence of absolute proof or an eyewitness, these were the three critical circumstantial components of a crime usually needed to convince a jury of guilt.

Means—an affinity for guns and a place, the river, where the murder weapon might have been disposed of.

Motive—an affair with the victim's wife.

Opportunity—security camera footage placing McHugh at the scene close to the time of the killing.

But there was even more. The suspect was operating in a blackout, incapable of providing anything useful toward his own defense.

Not good.

Lou wondered now if investigators would find blood, DNA, or other incriminating evidence in Gary's Jaguar or on his clothes.

Not good at all.

"Did you call your attorney?" Lou asked.

"I called him from the hospital. He was busy but promised he'd send one of his top associates over as soon as he could."

Before McHugh could expand on his answer, there was a soft knock on the office door and the petite Missy McHugh entered carrying a tray with a teapot, sugar bowl, and two blue china teacups.

"Here's the tea you asked for, darling."

Missy set the tray on their coffee table. She spoke the word *darling* as if it were a curse rather than a term of endearment. Her brown hair, streaked with silver, framed a pale, tired face. Lou had been an usher at their wedding, but the closeness between him and Gary had never carried over to her.

"Nice to see you, Lou," Missy said without a glance at the television. "I'm sorry it's under these unfortunate circumstances. Gary doesn't tell me very much, but I confess I wasn't all that surprised when he called me to get him away from the hospital and told me about the drinking and the accident. Now it appears he's going to lose his medical license."

Her baleful expression had Lou wondering how much she knew about her husband's life. The woman's iciness put a chill in the room.

"I'm going out for a while. The Whitmans' Christmas party is tonight. Gary, I assume you won't be coming."

McHugh ignored his wife and poured two cups of tea. Without another word, Missy turned and, a moment later, was out the door.

"I'm sorry you had to be here for that, Lou," McHugh said. "It's been years since we had much of a marriage. I guess I don't have to explain my relationship with Jeannine."

"I don't require explanations. You called and asked me here. We've been close friends for years, so here I am."

McHugh rubbed his face. "I didn't shoot Elias, Lou, but proving that isn't going to be easy. I called you because I'm going to need your help to check around about Elias—see if you can learn who might have wanted to kill him. Hire a detective if you need one."

"Gary, shouldn't that be a job for your lawyer or the police?"

"His *lawyer,* actually," said a woman. "But either would be correct."

Lou turned, expecting to see Missy McHugh again. The woman in the doorway couldn't have been more dissimilar. She was tall and slender—an athlete, Lou guessed, dressed in a gray pantsuit. Her straight ebony hair descended to just below her shoulders. She assessed him with intensely expressive brown eyes. There was something familiar about her, and Lou wondered if he was staring because of that or simply because he couldn't pull away.

"Lou, I'm assuming this is Sarah Cooper, my attorney."

"You assume correctly, Dr. McHugh." She turned to Lou. "Grayson Devlin, Dr. McHugh's usual attorney, is in court, so he sent me. Dr. McHugh, your wife let me in as she was leaving."

Sarah shook McHugh's hand, then Lou's. Her fingers were long and her grip confident. She wore a simple band on the fourth finger of her right hand but none on her left. Her eye-to-eye contact was so firm Lou felt thoroughly analyzed by the time she turned away.

"Thanks for getting over so quickly," McHugh said. "Grayson told me that you would take good care of me."

"Count on it," Sarah said.

"Lou, this woman was in charge of her firm's team in the Sandra Winkler trial. I assume you know about that case?"

Of course. That's where Lou had seen her before—on TV. She wasn't easy to forget. The case made news when a young mother from Bethesda was accused of strangling her eight-year-old daughter. Cooper earned her client an acquittal. Subsequently, a man accused of another, similar crime admitted to guilt in the case.

"Nice job," Lou said. "I'm afraid to admit it, but until the killer confessed, I was on the side of those who thought she was guilty."

"You were wrong," she said coolly. "And you would be?"

"Lou Welcome. I'm an ER doc at Eisenhower Memorial and a friend of Gary's."

"Can I ask why Dr. McHugh called you here now?" Sarah asked.

"You can ask, but I'm professionally constrained from telling you."

"Well, that certainly gets us off to a strong start."

McHugh cut in. "Lou is my monitor. I was required by the board to contract with Physician Wellness because of a DUI I once had."

"So if Dr. McHugh drinks, he loses his medical license," Sarah said. "Is that it?"

"Yes," McHugh said. "If I drink, I lose my license."

"And what's Dr. Welcome supposed to do for us here, Dr. McHugh? You may be facing some pretty serious charges. The fewer people you speak to about this, the better. I'd suggest you make that rule one."

"You can call me Gary. Lou is a friend of mine since college. He's going to help figure out who killed Elias Colston."

"No, he's not," Sarah said.

"Yes, he is," McHugh countered.

"Somehow, I think I must have a say in this," Lou cut in. "If Gary needs my help, I'm going to try to help him." Lou had actually not decided if there was anything he could do, but one sure way to get him to do something was to push in the opposite direction.

The attorney frowned. "His involvement could seriously compromise your case, Gary."

"He's going to help," McHugh said. "I didn't kill Colston."

"Gary," Sarah said, "this isn't *The People's Court* or *Judge Judy*. If you are charged with this crime, there are people whose livelihood will depend on seeing that you spend the rest of your life in prison, and the laws they will use are built around rules and technicalities. So what happens when this man does something amateurish that forces us to toss out evidence critical to your defense? We have plenty of highly trained investigators at our disposal."

"I don't care how good your investigators are," McHugh said. "I have a gut instinct about these things, and my gut is telling me I need him."

At that moment, the doorbell rang. McHugh wandered over to the window, peeled back the drapes, and peered out into the dark. Blue and red strobe lights illuminated his face.

"The police," he said. He looked first to Lou, next to Sarah. "Lou, I need you to go and speak with Jeannine. She knows you've been helping me with my recovery and is much more likely to speak with you than with any investigator. Now please, I'm counting on you both. Please don't let me down."

The doorbell rang again.

Lou and Sarah Cooper exchanged unspoken questions.

"I'll come with you, Gary," Sarah said finally, "but our discussion about this issue is not done. Dr. Welcome, here is my card. Please use it before you try to be of any help."

CHAPTER 2

STAFF Sergeants Bucky Townsend and Fenton Morales were the first pair in line to tackle the Big Hurt. To have gotten this far, Townsend, along with ninety-nine other members from Mantis

Company, had to pass a series of rigorous tests—physical and mental. The Big Hurt was their final exam to make the cut for Operation Talon.

A rolling fog, low enough to brush the frozen ground, spilled out from the woods surrounding the Mantis reservation, buried deep in West Virginia's Monongahela National Forest. In another hour, the temperature would be well below freezing.

Townsend, determined to keep moving, bounced to stay warm. He and the others had spent an hour in the chill of dawn, when the door to the large, rough-hewn cabin swung open and the legendary Major Charles Coon strode out onto the parade ground, his breath swirling out like a fighting bull's. Second in command to Colonel Wyatt Brody, he was solidly built, with eyes that glowed like the business end of an acetylene torch.

As one, a hundred eager marines snapped to attention—rows of wooden planks dressed in camo, eyes fixed forward, expressions blank as virgin slate. Coon slowly walked the line.

"You are the elite of the elite," he said, his voice a mix of gravel and thunder. "Out of seven hundred Mantis warriors, you are the final one hundred. Two-thirds of you will not be chosen for Operation Talon. Many of you will consider that a failure." Coon paused here but never turned his back on the men. They might not be his equal, but they had earned his respect. "You will not have failed. None of you. Just getting to this point means you have succeeded. The Big Hurt is reserved for Mantis only. It is the exclusive property of the best of the best, the bravest of the brave. You are Mantis!"

"Whatever it takes!" one hundred men shouted in perfect unison.

Whatever it takes, Townsend thought as he readied himself for the start.

Despite what Coon had proclaimed, failure was not an option. Townsend had almost no clue what Operation Talon entailed. He knew only that it was high priority, high profile, and high prestige—his kind of work. He had come a long way from being a dairy farmer's kid in Muskogee, Oklahoma.

Mantis—the most decorated unit in the United States military.

I'm proud to be an Okie from Muskogee. . . . The Merle Haggard song ran through his mind, as it did whenever he was keyed up.

"Team One, are you ready to commit?" Coon shouted at Townsend and Morales.

"Sir, we are ready to commit, sir!" they shouted in unison.

"Gentlemen, this is what you've been working toward. This moment. We are alone out here on this course, but believe me, whether they can see you or not, the country is watching you."

Coon fired his starter pistol, and the duo sprinted off, their heavy black combat boots crunching through the rime. A Mantis instructor indicated the first obstacle, labeled in crudely painted blue lettering on a board nailed to a tree: BELLY FLOP.

The Big Hurt was not designed to test a soldier's orienteering and navigation skills. It was about strength and grit—getting up, over, under, and through the toughest obstacles the military had to offer. Belly Flop was a fifty-yard crawl inches below barbed wire, through mud and frigid groundwater.

Twenty yards into the test, Townsend's muscles felt on fire as he clawed his way commando-style through thick, muddy clay. He raised up to negotiate a depression and tore his forearm through his sleeve on the teeth of an unforgiving strand of razor wire.

Whatever it takes, Townsend chanted to himself, grunting as he scrambled out of the mud. *I'm proud to be an Okie from Muskogee.*

Slightly dazed, he drove ahead.

"You're not a tourist!" the Mantis guide waiting at the end of the obstacle shouted at them. "Move it. Move it!"

Townsend followed another guide's outstretched arm, sprinting toward the next challenge. Glancing over his shoulder, he saw Morales coming up alongside him. "Let's go!" Townsend shouted.

UPSIE DAISY. The two men ascended and descended a twenty-foot wall and then sidestepped along G-STRING, a taut wire that crossed a dozen feet above a churning river with ice coating its banks.

"If you slip, you swim," the guide yelled after them.

A hundred-yard sprint along a twisting, uneven forest path, and there was another guide. "Get set for some climbing, ladies!"

Townsend rapidly negotiated the branches of a sixty-foot oak called SHISH-KA-BOB and then rappelled down.

"Not bad for an Okie," Morales said, panting to catch his breath.

"We're hot, baby," Townsend said, exuberant.

ORGAN GRINDER . . . TWIST AND SHOUT . . . GUT BLASTER. Cheering one another on, the two marines completed the rest of the obstacles.

"End of the line," a guide shouted. It appeared the Big Hurt had been beaten. Townsend's adrenaline rush dissipated. His arms grew heavy.

"Townsend . . . Morales."

Charles Coon strolled over to them.

Townsend noticed a gun rack just beyond the major that held M4A1 assault rifles. The marine knew the gun well. The selective fire weapon used 5.56mm rounds and had a telescoping stock.

"Gentleman, this is your final test," Coon said. "There are twenty-five weapons for you to choose from. The target will be over there." He motioned through a corridor in the woods to a crudely constructed wooden wall, twenty-five yards away.

Townsend had heard that the Rangers conducted a stress shoot as part of their training regimen, engaging targets after a grueling run. "Sir, what will we be firing at, sir?" he asked.

The major smiled thinly. "Soldier, you are the target," he said.

"Sir, yes, sir!" He bit back the urge to ask for clarification.

Coon continued. "We have loaded five of the guns in this rack with a live round. You do not know which gun has that live round. I do not know which guns have no cartridge. Do you understand?"

"Sir, yes, sir!" Townsend and Morales barked.

"You will each pick a gun, and I will fire that weapon at you. I will aim for the outside edge of your left chest wall. If you pick the gun carrying a live round, you will be shot through that spot. I assure you, I am a hell of a marksman. My shot will inflict minimal damage so long as you do not move. Understood?"

"Sir, yes, sir!"

"Morales, what is the percent probability that within the next minute you will be struck by a bullet?"

"Sir, twenty percent probability, sir!"

Coon nodded. "Gentlemen, pick a gun, set it in this holder beside me, and take up your position against the wall."

The men did as they were ordered. Townsend was muddy. His bones ached. He was blue with cold. He fought to keep from shivering. Twenty-five yards away, Coon got into firing position.

The officer gave no warning. Townsend kept his eyes fixed forward and watched as in what seemed like slow motion Coon pulled the trigger. The click was barely audible. Townsend glanced to his right and saw Morales still standing. Coon peered up from his scope and said, "Sergeant Morales, nicely done. You're dismissed."

Morales stepped away while the major switched guns.

Townsend kept his eyes fixed on the muzzle of the M4A1. Beyond it, he could see the commander press the gun barrel to his shoulder and peer into the scope. He saw the finger move. Then he saw the flash and at virtually the same instant heard a crack that reverberated off the trees. The searing pain in his side dropped him to his knees. Still, he resisted clutching the wound.

Townsend struggled to his feet without assistance as Charles Coon studied the tablet computer held by his chief medical officer.

"How did Morales do?" Coon asked.

"His vitals were normal," the medical officer said. "No elevation in heart rate, muscle tension within normal range, oxygen levels reflected a non-stress state."

"What about Townsend?" Coon asked.

"No different than Morales," the medical officer said. "Cool as a cucumber. Even after he got shot, his tracings look pure Mantis."

"Colonel Brody will be pleased to have these two," Coon said as the next pair of candidates approached.

EMILY Welcome, wearing lime green headgear, bobbed about the ring like a buoy in rough seas. Shuffling and dancing across from her, Lou went through the rudiments of defense and the basic punches. The kid was a natural.

No surprise. Lou had seen his daughter's athletic abilities evolve from her earliest days chasing butterflies. This was her first time in a boxing ring, and she was making it look easy.

Four days had passed since the arrest of Dr. Gary McHugh for the murder of Congressman Elias Colston. The murder weapon had not been recovered, but teams of divers continued to search the bottom of the icy Pensatuck River. Still, the authorities sounded quite certain they had their man. Apparently, the judge in his bail hearing felt the same way. Sarah Cooper's request for bail was denied.

Colston's funeral, certain to be a celebrity-studded event, was scheduled for later in the day. Without obtaining Sarah's blessing, Lou decided he would arrange a meeting with Colston's widow, Jeannine, sometime after the burial.

"Hey there, Papa, let's do some punching," Emily said, angling her mouth guard to make her words intelligible. "I'm liking this. I can't wait to see Kyle Smith's expression when I pop him in the nose. He's always bumping into me on purpose."

"You're not going to pop anyone in the nose. That's just Kyle's way of saying he likes you."

"I know. And a pop in the nose will be my way of saying that I like him back."

Lou stifled most of a grin. Emily had grown several inches in the past few months, and her shape was changing almost as rapidly. Growing up with her was going to be an adventure.

Her eyes were aflame with concentration as she circled him, keeping her hands up, precisely as he had told her. "Couldn't somebody call the cops on you for fighting me?" she asked.

"We're not supposed to hit each other," Lou reminded her. "This is just to practice your footwork."

"Then why am I wearing headgear and a mouth guard?"

"Because you're my daughter, and I'm pathologically overly protective. Plus I'm not exactly a kung fu master when it comes to stopping my punches an inch from your face."

"Makes sense," Emily said, sliding her mouth guard into place.

"Okay, let's do it again," Lou said. "Forward and back, then side-to-side, then shuffle, and last do the pivot. Ready?"

Emily ignored her father's instructions and instead lunged forward and, moving as quick as a firefly, caught Lou off guard with a solid right to his gut. He stepped back and dropped his mouthpiece into his glove.

"Do you know who Harry Houdini is . . . I mean *was?*" he asked.

"A famous magician?"

"Sort of. Before we step between these ropes again, I want you to be ready to tell me who he was and how he died."

Emily's eyes narrowed in her personalized teen-versus-parent way. "I have a feeling he got punched in the stomach," she said.

"The word is sucker punched."

"That's two words. Besides, I gave you warning when I dropped my shoulder. When you're in the ring, always be ready to be hit. That's what Cap told me."

"But he didn't tell you to sucker punch anyone—especially your old man," Cap's rich bass echoed from ringside.

Emily turned and broke into a smile. "Cap!" she cried, kneeling by the ropes, wrapping her arms around the tall, muscular Bahamian. Cap Duncan hugged her back, then climbed into the ring.

"Hey, doc, your kid has fast hands. But girl, around here, sucker punching anyone anywhere can get you suspended for a week."

"Sorry."

The apology, Lou knew, a rarity for his daughter, was a clear mark of the respect she had for the onetime street pug and AAU light-heavyweight champion. Hank Duncan earned the nickname Cap'n Crunch because of the sound noses reputedly made when he hit them. His promising pro career lasted just six fights—until he stood up to the mob and refused to take a dive against a fighter they were backing. A short while later, he flunked a drug test and was suspended, even though he had never used anything.

He ended up working for the very men who had destroyed him and turned to alcohol and narcotics to ease his humiliation. The path eventually took him to rehab and then a halfway house. Cap had become a counselor in the house when Lou Welcome checked in, fresh from his own nine-month stint in a treatment center. Two years later, Lou had gotten his medical license restored and Cap, his AA sponsor, was the owner of the Stick and Move Gym.

Cap had poured everything he owned into the Stick and Move— a converted warehouse a short walk from Lou's apartment. The gym was well equipped with a row of heavy bags, a half dozen speed bags, stationary bikes, and three regulation-size rings.

"Emily," Lou said, "why don't you practice your footwork in front of the mirror for a bit? I have to talk to the big guy, here."

"Sure thing, Pop."

Cap lifted the ropes and helped her from the ring. Lou waited until Emily was out of earshot, shadowboxing in front of the mirrors alongside four other fighters. It was impossible not to smile at the scene. Lou's ex, Renee, was not a fan of Emily staying in Lou's hardscrabble neighborhood and expressed more than a little displeasure at her desire to take up boxing. Lou's position was that as good as the school in Arlington was in terms of academics, it did little to expose students to the richness of multiculturalism. The more time Emily spent in his world, the more aware she seemed of the sheltered homogeneity in her own.

"Cap, have you read about the guy who got arrested for the murder of Congressman Colston? His name's Gary McHugh. He's a doc and has been a good friend of mine since college."

"Did he do it?"

"He says no, but he was in a blackout and doesn't remember much."

"I would wager that ninety percent of those in jail don't really remember what they did to get there."

"I believe he's innocent. But the court has a strong enough case to keep him without bail. Baltimore City Detention Center."

"Nasty place. Most jails are, even the newer ones. Less space, less protection, fewer guards than a prison. I would take a penitentiary over a jail anytime."

"Gary's having it tough there. Word is out that he's a doctor, and inmates want stuff from him. Is there anything we can do for him?"

"Let me check with the grapevine and see if anybody I know is doing time up there. If anyone is, I can ride up there with you during visitors hours and speak with him—see if we can get your pal a little protection."

Cap headed up the stairs to his office, perched on supports that suspended it out over the gym. Lou could see him through the plate glass window, making calls. Lou did a little footwork himself and was about to motion Emily back into the ring, when he saw Cap stand up from his desk, wave, and start back down the stairs.

"That was too easy, Doc. Two calls, and I've got a name. Seems like there's more brothers in the joint than out. That's sad, man, real sad. Rolando Booker's in Baltimore City right now for B and E. He's called Tiny. I suppose because he ain't. He and I used to run together after I was forced out of the ring. He's a good guy and a real artist with locks. Great at plannin', not so good at gettin' away with it. Everything I know about B and E—and that used to be quite a bit—Tiny taught me. So, we can make a road trip."

"Thanks. Gary means a lot to me, and he's scared stiff."

"It'll be good to reconnect with Tiny. He actually was a decent fighter at one time himself. Listen, I've got some pointers to give to the kid with the red trunks shadowboxing to Emily's right. He has some serious potential if he can just stay out of trouble."

"He's lucky to have you on his case."

Lou watched as his sponsor strode easily over to Emily, whispered something that made her grin, and sent her back to the ring. Then Cap turned to the boy. It was impossible to watch the man at work and not feel good. Lou knew that Cap was orphaned at a young age and had made this way through some seriously hard times.

You never know, Lou found himself thinking.

DETECTIVE Christopher Bryzinski, of the Maryland State Police, hated funerals. His father, a cop, was run down ten years ago on a Maryland highway, killed by a drunk driver on a gray and rainy day like this one. His mother, who, much like himself, was a revolving member of Weight Watchers, died soon after from a heart attack.

Bryzinski knew he needed to drop weight. He always needed to drop weight. His wife, Agnes, rode him about it mercilessly. But then, what would be the point of it all? If he gave up food and booze, Agnes might as well stuff him inside a wooden box.

Bryzinski shivered against the cold. He gazed at the guests who were shuffling across the depressing landscape of gravestones. His captain had sent him out here to take pictures and record notes about the attendees. The funeral for Elias Colston had been held in Bethesda, Maryland. Over a thousand were in attendance, including many of the military's top brass who had come to pay their last respects to the man who oversaw their funding as chairman of the House Armed Services Committee.

Only a fraction of the mob at the service had made the trip to Arlington. Jeannine Colston was making her way up the gentle slope, accompanied by her children. Bryzinski tried to imagine how she was handling the stories about her affair with her husband's killer. For a time, he wondered where Colston's son was buried. He had been killed in Afghanistan and had won an important medal. Father and son. Both marines, both dead.

The final groups of mourners made their way from their cars toward the burial site. Maybe a couple of unexpected faces would show up. That's what the captain was thinking. Still, no matter what, nothing would change the conclusion that Bryzinski had reached. Gary McHugh, the society doc in D.C., was the killer.

The wind kicked up in a sudden gust, spattering rain on beleaguered faces. The priest, his white robes flapping like sodden sails, was settled beneath a canvas canopy, preparing to read from the scriptures. Some people were openly weeping.

The chilly rain had peppered his face long enough for Bryzinski to declare his assignment a job well done. He eased away from the crowd and back down the hill. He had made it halfway to his Pontiac when a deep voice startled him from behind. Bryzinski whirled, and his eyes widened with recognition. Secretary of Defense Spencer Hogarth stood alone beneath a broad black umbrella.

"Detective Bryzinski?"

Bryzinski's throat tightened, and he found himself speechless in the presence of the square-jawed, silver-haired, leathery-skinned admiral, whom many pundits thought to be a potential nominee for the presidency. A champion of traditional American values, Hogarth had become a fixture in the news magazines.

"That's me," Bryzinski said, stunned more than flattered that Hogarth would know his name.

"Got a moment to talk?"

"Sure." Bryzinski wiped his face with the back of his hand.

"Detective Bryzinski, I could use your help. You are the lead investigator on the Elias Colston murder case, are you not?"

"I am," Bryzinski said, finding his mental footing now. "Do you have information about the congressman's murder, Mr. Secretary?"

"No," Hogarth said, grinning. "Flip it around."

Bryzinski appraised the man curiously. He felt riveted to Hogarth's eyes. "You mean if I have information about Colston's murder, you want me to share it?"

Hogarth's smile was engaging. "No wonder your reputation as a fine detective precedes you," he said.

Over his career, Bryzinski had not been above accepting the occasional inducement for a favor. Every cop did it. He sensed an offer coming from the secretary. But first, a feeling out on both sides.

"And exactly how will my sharing this information help in my investigation?"

"I have an interest in tracking this case," Hogarth said. "You keep me informed, and I see to it you know how grateful I am."

"I'm sorry, sir. With all due respect, that's not how we do business at the Maryland State Police. I hope you understand."

Hogarth placed his arm around Bryzinski's broad shoulders. Walking with slow, purposeful steps, he led the stunned detective toward the curbside row of parked cars.

"Let's make it short and sweet," Hogarth said. "Jamie Lambert. I assume that name means something to you."

"I don't—"

"Please, don't play games with me. Twelve years ago you shot Lambert during a shakedown you and your partner were running. You planted drugs on the kid and ended up getting off."

"I'm not going to admit to that. What, are you wearing a wire?"

"Lambert's not all I've learned about you. I know about your wife, Agnes. I know you don't have much money because you gamble too much. I know your parents are dead and that you're a reasonably well-respected police officer. What I don't know is if you're a smart man—smart enough to know I wouldn't approach you if I didn't have proof. Now, do we do business or not?"

Bryzinski's stomach lurched. At that instant, his foot sunk above his shoe in a nearly frozen puddle.

"The people who do what I ask, Chris," Hogarth said, "often find themselves with promotions or certain other rewards."

"And what is it you want in this case?"

"I want to know anything and everything pertaining to the murder investigation of Elias Colston. I want you to personally feed me all the information you get—every tip, every lead, every name."

"And if I don't do this," Bryzinski managed, "then would that make me not smart?"

"If you're not smart, Lambert will be just one of the things the world learns about you, starting with the detective's exam you didn't take yourself."

Bryzinski could only stare at the man. It had been years since the exam, and he was sure no one would ever find out. Now his job, his pension, everything was on the line for him. "I think you'll find that I'm a very smart man," he said.

Hogarth's smile this time was broader. "I'm sure that I will," he said. "I'm sure that I will."

CHAPTER 3

RENEE Welcome and Steve Gilbride shared a four-bedroom colonial in the upscale suburb of Arlington, Virginia. Renee sent Emily to the prestigious Carlisle School where she, herself, had gone.

Emily stayed alternate weekends with her father, as well as every other Thursday. By tradition, Lou always accompanied Emily into the house for the drop-off. This particular Sunday, Steve was in the city, and Renee, usually upbeat, seemed frazzled. Her wavy chestnut hair looked uncharacteristically unkempt. She was seated at the round kitchen table, which was littered with bills. She clattered her reading glasses down, picked up a bill from the stack, and fixed Emily with a hard stare.

"What's the meaning of this?" Renee said, holding up a phone bill. "There are three hundred dollars in text message charges here."

Emily examined the bill. "That's Katie. Isn't she in our Friends and Family network?" Katie Willard was one of Emily's closest friends from school.

"No, Katie is not in our Friends and Family network," said Renee.

Emily looked offended. "Well, Steve was supposed to add her."

"Don't bring Steve into this! What on earth could you possibly be texting so much about?" Renee asked.

"Stuff. I dunno, Mom. It's just how we communicate."

"Well, you'll need to come up with another way of communicating that doesn't cost three hundred dollars a month."

"Then, duh, just add Katie to our Friends and Family network."

"Don't you dare talk to me like that," Renee said. "You are thirteen years old, and you will show me some respect."

"Okay, time-out," Lou said, extending his arms. "Each of you, back off to a neutral corner and hold your breath for a minute." He looked from mother to daughter. The tension between the two of them seemed to lessen a tick.

"This is so unfair!" Emily said, slumping down onto the kitchen's wide-plank cherrywood floor. "I can't even have a pet."

"A pet?" Lou asked.

"Steve's son is allergic," Renee said.

"Why don't we compromise here?" Lou offered. "I'll get a pet." "Mom?"

"If a pet would make you happy, and you can't have one here," Renee said, "then it seems fair to have one at Dad's."

"What kind of pet?" Emily asked.

"How about a flea?"

"Very funny. How about a dog?"

"How about I have a job, and you're at my place only on the alternate weekends and one weekday?"

"Then what about a cat?" asked Emily, grinning now at what amounted to victory.

Lou's mind raced through alternatives from aardvark to zebra but came up with nothing. "Okay," he said. "We'll get a cat."

"Rescued from a shelter," Emily added. "And I've got to pick him out. And he's got to be neutered."

"But of course," Lou said.

Emily bounded over and kissed him on the cheek.

"I'm sooooo super excited! Bye! I love you." She made a delighted little squeal on her way upstairs to her bedroom.

"You're really going to have to go through with this cat thing, you know," Renee said.

"We had a cat at the halfway house. As I recall, it wasn't much of a problem."

Renee mumbled something that sounded like, "You wish."

Before Lou could ask her to repeat the remark, his cell phone rang. The caller ID was just the number. "Hello?"

"Dr. Lou Welcome?" a woman's voice asked.

"Yes."

"My name is Jeannine Colston. You wanted to speak with me?"

Lou had seen the hollowed-eye look many times before. Jeannine Colston was beaten down by exhaustion, loss, and the malicious snipings from family, friends, and the media. News of her affair with Gary McHugh, the man accused of brutally murdering her husband, had exploded in the press like a land mine.

"Thank you for seeing me, Mrs. Colston. I know it can't be an easy thing for you to do."

They faced one another across the front foyer of the Colstons' rambling colonial. Jeannine, whose striking patrician beauty was gray and tight-jawed, eyed him coolly. She hung Lou's coat in the closet and motioned him to a sofa in the living room.

"Given your friendship with Gary, I wasn't even going to return your call," she said.

"I understand. First let me extend my deepest condolences. I'm so sorry for your loss and everything that's been happening."

"Thank you, I appreciate that," she said. "I saw you at the funeral. A friend told me about you. After you left me those messages, I did some checking."

"I wasn't there to make trouble. I just wanted to get a better sense of your husband. I thought it might help me help Gary."

"I'm afraid Gary is beyond helping," she said. "I'm assuming you want to know what I think happened."

"If it's not too difficult." Lou forced himself not to avert his eyes.

"Well, I think Gary did it," Jeannine said matter-of-factly.

"I know the police are certain that's the case, but why are you?"

"Because I ended our . . . relationship. Because he was drinking and getting desperate. I can play you the messages he left on my mobile. I saved them after I shared them with the police."

"Do you feel like talking about why you ended things?" Lou asked.

"Is that why Gary sent you to see me? To find out why?"

"No," Lou said. "It's me who wants to know. Gary is steadfast that he didn't kill your husband. He knew I might be the only one who would believe him and asked if I'd look into things. So I'd like to understand the events leading up to your husband's murder."

Jeannine nodded. "Put simply, I had a change of heart. Elias came to me the evening before he . . . was killed. He took me in his arms and kissed me in a way he hadn't in years. I felt an electric charge shoot through my body. It was like our first kiss and the kiss on our wedding day rolled into one. I had been having misgivings about Gary. Guilt. Having my husband kiss me that way and tell me how much he loved me and needed me made up my mind." She began to sob.

Lou waited. "It's okay," he said finally.

"No, it's hardly okay. My surviving children despise me now. They blame me for their father's murder. If I wasn't having . . . having an affair—" Another gut-wrenching sob cut her words short.

Surviving children . . .

Lou had researched Mark Colston's heroic death in Afghanistan. The twenty-seven-year-old's platoon had come under attack by Taliban fighters. Five members of the platoon were wounded. From the accounts Lou had read, Mark Colston strode into the line of fire with the calmness of Gary Cooper in *High Noon*. He shot and killed all but one of the Taliban militiamen. The one he did not kill, he mortally wounded. However, before he died, that Taliban fighter tossed a grenade at the fallen U.S. soldiers. Mark immediately fell on the grenade, saving the lives of five men while sacrificing his own. He was posthumously awarded the Medal of Honor for bravery above and beyond the call of duty.

"I'm sure things will work out with your children," Lou said. "Nine years ago, my wife divorced me while I was in rehab. My daughter, Emily, was young then but not so young that she didn't understand I had done something very bad. But things change. Now she's thirteen, and the two of us are close. And I'm getting us a cat."

For the first time, Jeannine Colston managed a smile. "Good luck," she said. She paused, her expression wistful. "Now, then," she asked finally, "are there any other questions?"

"Congressman Colston's study is above the garage? Would you mind if I had a look around there?"

"As long as you don't need me to do it. I feel a migraine coming on, and the only thing that ever really works at this stage is a nap."

"No problem."

"The code is five twenty-nine eighty-two, our wedding date."

Lou repeated the number and thanked her. "I assume the police are done here," he said.

"From what I could tell, they were done almost as soon as they started. They knew they had their man, and so did I."

SARAH Joyce Cooper was on a partner track. She was known for her intellect and composure in the courtroom, but when Grayson

Devlin summoned her to a conference in his office, her nervousness was understandable.

When Sarah arrived, five of the partners were at the conference table. She took her seat and glanced at the papers in front of the lawyers. She could see they had been reviewing the McHugh case. She took a sip of lemon water against the raspiness in her throat.

Grayson Devlin spoke first. Tall and lean, with a love for designer suits, he could intimidate in the courtroom. "Sarah, I see that Dr. McHugh is still in jail. He's a good citizen. Can we get him out?"

"He was having an affair with the victim's wife, and he was on the scene intoxicated at around the time the murder took place."

"Point taken. How is your defense shaping up?"

Sarah took another drink of lemon water. "Until we turn something else up, we're going directly after the evidence," she said.

Heather Goddard, the only woman partner, made a disapproving sound. "That seems like a risky play to me," she said.

Sarah did not feel at all on the defensive by having Heather question the strategy. The partners of Devlin and Rodgers understood that in cases like McHugh's, their job was not to judge a client's guilt or innocence, but to cast enough reasonable doubt to win an acquittal. They functioned as a team to mount the best defense possible. If Heather had a concern, it was Sarah's job to address it.

"The evidence builds a circumstantial case at best. Without a murder weapon, I don't see any risk in attacking it," Sarah said. "But I share your concern, Heather. It's not my only strategy."

Sarah was pleased to see Heather smile. Since the death of Sarah's husband, David, Heather had become one of her closest confidantes. "What else do you have in mind?" Heather asked.

"Politicians make enemies. I've got an investigator checking around to see whose feathers he might have ruffled over the years."

Gordon Rodgers, the most senior partner after Devlin, appeared pleased. "Do you think a jury would buy that?" he asked.

"Without the murder weapon, anything is possible. The surveillance tape shows Dr. McHugh parking on the drive and leaving his car but not entering the garage. The next time we see him, he is stumbling back to his car. Then he drives away. The crime scene people fix the time of death between eleven and two. That window includes Dr. McHugh, but it leaves room for someone else as well."

"Someone else?"

"It's a bit of a long shot, but I think we have an opportunity to focus some attention on Jeannine Colston."

"I thought she had an alibi—some sort of meeting."

"It was a large meeting of congressional spouses. She hasn't produced any witness saying she was there when her husband was killed. The police were so sure of themselves with Dr. McHugh that they never asked if someone could support her alibi. All we have to do is create doubt. The longer we wait to ask her to produce an alibi witness, the less chance someone will be willing to swear under oath that Jeannine was at the meeting during the ME's window."

"So you're going to propose that Jeannine Colston shot and killed her husband before McHugh arrived at the property and then left for the meeting in the Capitol?"

"Or after. Try this: Dr. McHugh shows up intoxicated. Jeannine and he have a fight. Colston overhears the squabble and confronts his wife about the affair. Tempers flare, and Jeannine Colston gets a gun and kills him."

"Does Colston even own a gun?" Devlin asked.

"If you turn to page thirty-five in your brief," she said, "I have outlined our ballistics strategy."

The partners flipped to the page.

"The bullets recovered from Colston's body were fired from a .45 ACP," Sarah said. "Forensics showed the slugs had a six-groove left-hand twist rifling mark. The Colt company is the only major U.S. handgun manufacturer that consistently uses a left-hand twist. However, several foreign handgun manufacturers also use a left-hand twist, including Taurus. The Colstons have a registered Taurus PT1911. Reasonable doubt."

The inside of every gun barrel contained groove marks that helped a bullet spin and fly to where it was aimed. The "twist" referred to the inches of bore required for one complete rifling spiral.

"Did we test the Taurus?" Devlin asked.

"I plan to contract a three-fire test with one of our forensic experts," Sarah said. "I don't expect a match, but you never know."

Devlin smiled. "You never know" was a favorite adage of his.

"Of course," Heather said with a sly smile, "that doesn't mean the Colstons couldn't own another Taurus."

"Always possible," Sarah replied, "and a seed of doubt I will be happy to plant. Maybe the Colstons didn't register all their firearms. Remember, he was a military man—a marine. Maybe Jeannine used that unregistered gun to kill her husband, and then she hid the weapon somewhere. *Maybe*—one of our favorite words."

The partners murmured their approval. "Well done, Sarah," Devlin said. "But there's something else I want to discuss."

Uh-oh. "Anything," Sarah said.

"Do you think you should continue to head Gary McHugh's defense? I could rearrange my schedule and take over. He's a physician, and you're not completely comfortable defending doctors."

Sarah tried to appear unaffected by Devlin's remark. "I don't see that as a problem in the McHugh matter, Grayson." She pushed the image of David immobile in his hospital bed, dying a prolonged, needless death, out of her mind.

Devlin glanced at the notes in front of him. "You've recused yourself from three cases dealing with physicians," Devlin said.

Sarah bit the inside of her cheek to keep from responding too quickly. "I'm fine to handle this one," she said. She could be impartial. She could represent Gary McHugh—an arrogant doctor for sure—without being clouded by thoughts of David.

"I read your brief, and it looks as if another doctor is involved."

"That's true," Sarah said. "But I can handle it. McHugh has enlisted his help. Lou Welcome is a doctor in the ER at Eisenhower Memorial and a longtime friend of McHugh's. He also works part-time as an associate director of the Physician Wellness Office, helping alcoholic and chemically dependent physicians."

"And your position on this Welcome?"

"I've made it clear to Dr. Welcome that he is anything but welcome.

If he gets in our way or endangers our case, I will get him to back off."

The image of David was resurrected in her mind. Tubes snaked out of him in all directions, backed by the thrum of the machines that were keeping him alive.

"I hope you know that I would never do anything that would adversely affect this firm," Sarah said.

But if Welcome gets in my way or jeopardizes my chance to make partner here, I will cut him off at the knees.

ELIAS Colston had been shot to death in the center bay of a three-bay garage. The space was empty now. Lou ascended a carpeted stairway and opened the door at the top using the punch-code Jeannine had given him—the day she and Elias had married.

Elias's office occupied the entire second floor. It was paneled in dark wood. An expansive bookshelf filled one wall, with double-hung windows centered on the others. Carefully arranged in almost every available space were framed photos and testimonials, aligned so that Lou wondered if the police who had investigated the office had even touched them. Colston, a former marine, had apparently never lost his ingrained desire for neatness and order.

The desk, absent of clutter, was augmented by a workstation that held a printer, two phones, a file box, and a space for a computer, which he suspected had been dissected in some police lab.

The single row of photos on the top bookshelf was mirrored by one behind the desk chair. Wedding . . . children . . . military units . . . a football team . . . Marine Corps ribbons surrounding an obituary for Lance Corporal Mark Raymont Colston. Mark Colston was darkly handsome, with thick brows and gentle eyes.

Lou checked the drawers of the desk. To his astonishment, they had not been emptied. It felt so clear that the police investigating the case were simply going through the motions. Dr. Gary McHugh had shot his lover's husband to death. Case closed.

He swept together the papers and envelopes in the top drawer and set them on the desk. A few bills; letters of thanks from constituents. There was an envelope addressed to Mr. James Styles at a post office box in Bowie, Maryland. The return address read "Pine Forest Clinic, Shockley, Minnesota." The envelope was empty.

A trip to the Internet would help Lou see whether or not the Pine Forest Clinic or James Styles of Bowie, Maryland, was of any interest. For a time, Lou paced around the office. He wondered in passing what Elias Colston was doing in the garage when he was murdered. Getting set to leave? Waiting for someone?

At that instant, something caught Lou's attention. It was one of the framed photos on the top shelf of the bookcase, but this one was different from the others. This one was facing the wall. *Probably inspected and placed back carelessly,* he was thinking as he reached up for it. More likely, though, the photo had been carefully placed that way by Colston.

Lou reached up, brought the frame down, and turned it over.

The medal on display against a black velvet field was a gold five-pointed star suspended beneath a gold bar. The gold plaque beneath it read: MEDAL OF HONOR. MARK RAYMONT COLSTON.

For a minute, Lou gazed at the medal, trying to imagine the horrible circumstances surrounding it and wondering what had led the father of the recipient to turn it to the wall. It was then Lou felt a fullness beneath the felt backing.

Working on the desk, he released the eight catches holding the backing in place. It fell away, revealing a clear plastic sleeve.

And inside the sleeve was a CD.

LOU drove over the bridge where police theorized that Gary McHugh had disposed of the gun he had used to murder Elias. Their theory did not make sense to him as he rolled slowly over the span, looking from side to side at the partially ice-covered river and wondering how McHugh, in a virtual blackout after just shooting his friend to death, could have stopped, sized up the water to be sure the gun would not simply end up on the ice, and then tossed it over the waist-high stone railing.

Clearly the cops felt otherwise.

Immediately after the detectives arrived on the scene, Jeannine

Colston had informed them of her relationship with McHugh. According to her, they next examined the recording from the security cameras covering the front drive. McHugh coming and parking, leaving his car. McHugh returning and driving off. Word from the emergency room would have filled in some of the side pieces.

Motive, method, opportunity, alcohol.

In their haste to finish the investigation of what they considered a slam dunk, the police had missed an inexplicable finding—a framed medal for valor turned to the wall by . . . How could it not have been by Elias Colston? The congressman had carefully sequestered a recording of some sort and left a sign as unsubtle as Times Square on New Year's Eve indicating where it was located.

If harm comes to me, if you are inspecting my office, this is where you should look.

Lou fingered the CD resting on the passenger seat of his aging Toyota and began to scan the side roads for an isolated spot where he could listen in security. A dirt road caught his eye, cutting off to the left, overhung with ghostly winter branches. Lou pulled in thirty yards and stopped by a No Trespassing sign. He cut the engine. Dense silence engulfed him. He slipped in the CD.

There was a burst of static, then a recording of two men. Lou recognized Elias Colston's voice. The representative's funeral had featured the broadcast of a speech he had delivered some months before, pleading in the memory of his hero son for a decrease in military spending and a shift in priorities from defense to education. Wonderful rhetoric from the head of the House Armed Services Committee.

The other man was someone named Hector. He spoke with a Hispanic accent. It took Lou just a short while to become convinced that the conversation was being recorded by Colston and that Hector was unaware of it.

"Hector, I'm surprised to hear from you. How long has it been?"

"A couple of years, sir. Since just after . . . after Mark was . . ."

"It's okay, Hector, you can say it."

"Since Mark's funeral. I really miss him, sir. We all do. He was a real hero. The guys still talk about what he did."

"It's important to hear that, although I wish I didn't have to."

"You holding up okay?"

"Yes. Yes, I'm holding up as well as can be expected."

"And Mrs. Colston?"

"She has periods of great sadness, Hector, but she bounces back."

"That's understandable. I enjoyed the couple of times she had me over with Mark and that time for Thanksgiving. Give her my best."

"Where would you like to talk?"

"Mind if we go out to those tables? There's privacy."

"That'll be fine," Colston said.

There was a period of noise as the two men left wherever they were and settled in at one of the tables outside. Lou could not be certain, but it seemed as if Hector's speech was pressured and tense.

"So, sir," the marine said after a time, "let me explain why I asked to see you. It wasn't my idea. It was our commanding officer, Colonel Brody. He asked me to speak with you."

"Wyatt Brody? I met him at Mark's funeral."

"The colonel is one tough dude, sir. And that's something of an understatement. He's very upset about some of the things you've been doing in your committee—cutting expenses to Mantis."

"It hasn't been just Mantis, Hector. It's time to adjust our country's priorities in the direction of more and better education. Drugs, welfare, crime, overcrowded prisons. There is no solution to these social ills other than more teachers and better schools, and the money has to come from someplace. My proposals are a blueprint for hope. Hope for our cities. Hope for children everywhere."

"Pardon me for saying it, sir, but education ain't worth much if towel-headed terrorists can just walk in here and blow up our schools. So long as they got the oil, they got the power. And the only thing they'll ever listen to is somebody else's power that's bigger than what they got."

"I believe we have enough intelligence and firepower to prevent that, provided they are used in the right way."

"The colonel feels you should be showin' your son's unit more respect, especially given that you're a marine yourself. We're the number one best unit in the marines—hell, in the whole damn military. Our manpower and weaponry are being hacked away."

"Pushing for those cuts hasn't been easy for me, Hector."

"Mr. Colston, sir, you got to reconsider," Hector pleaded, his voice half an octave higher than it had been. "The colonel is hard like no one I ever dealt with. And he's got people around him."

"People?"

"Tough dudes, enlisted from the streets and put right in Mantis."

"What do you mean, Hector?"

There was a prolonged silence before Hector responded, this time in a strained whisper. "We call them the Palace Guards, and wherever the colonel is, they're not far away."

"Are they like a gang?"

"In a way, maybe. I really don't know."

"So, Hector, is this meeting a warning from Colonel Brody?"

Extended silence. Another harsh, whispered reply. "Mr. Colston, for Mark's sake, for your sake, you gotta take some of the pressure off of Mantis. Mark gave his life for the company and this country."

"You seem nervous, Hector. Has Colonel Brody threatened you?"

"It's Dr. Brody, sir. Did you know that?"

"Doctor? Like a medical doctor?"

"Not like any medical doctor you ever had, but yeah, he's a doctor of some kind. I tell you 'cause he is smart and tough and backed up by some of the hardest men this side of hell."

"Hector, you know I'm a pretty powerful man in Washington. I can bring some serious clout down on your Colonel Dr. Brody."

Lou heard some shuffling and imagined Hector pushing to his feet. "All I want is your word that you will lighten up on Mantis and replace some of the money you took away."

"The best I can do is to promise I'll think about my position."

"Please, do that, sir. Please."

"All right, Hector. One last thing. Do you know anything about Mantis soldiers killed at a place called Reddy Creek Armory?"

"Never heard about nothing like that. What is it?"

"I don't know. There was a blog written by a reporter in North

Carolina that mentioned it. When I tried learning more, the blog was gone, wiped off the Internet. I couldn't find any other mention of any killings anyplace. It's as if they never happened."

"No idea, sir."

"Okay. Thanks, Hector. Let me know if you hear anything."

"I will. Now please, do what I asked and help keep Mark's unit strong. He died for Mantis and our country."

The disc went silent. Eyes closed, Lou sat alone in the late afternoon chill. Suddenly, he realized he was soaked with sweat.

CHAPTER 4

THE American flag outside the state police barracks in College Park, Maryland, still flying at half-mast to honor Congressman Elias Colston, fluttered in a light breeze. Lou parked his Toyota and remained in his seat for a time, thinking about the violent deaths of Elias Colston and, before that, his son. He wanted to feel exhilarated about his discovery of the CD—a discovery that might ultimately connect the two—but the only emotion he could connect with was sadness.

Lou had listened to the recording twice and had made a copy for Sarah, which he buried beneath the socks in his bureau drawer. It was all there on that disc—everything the police would need to divert their attention away from Gary McHugh and onto Colonel Wyatt Brody, commander of the elite fighting force Mantis, under whom Mark Colston served until his death.

Before entering the police barracks, Lou tried, once again, to call Sarah. She was taking a deposition and would probably be out for the rest of the day. Her assistant turned him over to her voice mail. At least there was proof Lou had tried to get in touch with her.

The investigating and arresting officer, Detective Chris Bryzinski, sounded amiable on the phone, but he also sounded convinced of the guilt of Gary McHugh. Lou believed this detective would appreciate the significance of the remarkable conversation between Elias Colston and Colston's son's close friend. If things went the way Lou anticipated, Wyatt Brody would immediately become a person of interest in the murder of the congressman. Elias Colston had been spearheading the reduction of funds to Mantis. In addition, Brody appeared to have surrounded himself with some hand-picked toughs known to the rest of Mantis as the Palace Guards.

The compact one-story gray brick station was situated just off the Capital Beltway. Lou spoke to a uniformed officer through a Plexiglas shield and took a seat on a well-worn chair in the waiting area. He was right on time. Five minutes passed, then ten.

Lou fingered the disc in the pocket of his jacket. Finally the door to the inner sanctum of the station opened, and a bowling ball of a man motioned him in. He was five-six or -seven and seemed close to that wide across, huge-headed and balding. "Detective Bryzinski," he mumbled, not bothering with a handshake.

So much for impressions over the phone.

"Lou Welcome," Lou said. He followed the detective into his office, a cluttered space that reeked of stale coffee and possibly Bryzinski himself. Stacks of folders and loose papers covered every square inch of desk. Lou took the steel-armed institutional seat on the guest side of the desk. Bryzinski settled into his high-backed Staples standard.

"Sorry to keep you waiting," Bryzinski said. "We're short two men. I don't have a lot of time."

"Well, thanks for seeing me," Lou said.

Bryzinski pursed his lips. "So now," he said, "you told me who you were over the phone, and I checked you out. Let's cut to the chase. What's going on, and how does it affect my case?"

Lou put the CD on Bryzinski's desk. He reviewed his visit with Jeannine Colston and his inspection of Elias's office, avoiding any implication that Bryzinski and his cohorts had underdone their jobs. The detective seemed to be listening with one ear, not bothering to take any notes. It was not the least bit difficult for Lou to imagine the cop forming a conclusion before the investigation had actually begun and tailoring his inspection to support what facts he had.

"Did you bring the frame?" Bryzinski asked. Irritation replaced the ennui in the detective's voice. "It might have fingerprints."

Lou began to feel dumb. "I'm sure it's still in Colston's study."

"Look," Bryzinski said as if he were lecturing a third grader, "I bet you think you cracked the case wide open. You haven't." He patted a stack of papers. "These are from other people who think *they've* cracked the case wide open. Get what I'm saying?"

"I think this is more than just a random tip," Lou managed.

"I've got to go through each and every one of these. You know why? Because everybody wants in on the action when it's somebody big who gets killed. And you know what else? See these other piles? I got thirty-eight active cases, and I can't get a tip on any of 'em because they're nobodies, just regular people. So, I'll take this CD, since you're so insistent on dropping it off in person, and we'll put it through the sniff test. And even though I have better things to do, I'll drive back to the Colstons' place and get that frame."

"You're not going to listen to that disc right now?"

Bryzinski sighed. "I'm going to add your CD to the pile, and I'll listen to it. But I'm not going to do it this minute." He stood with some effort and lumbered to the door. Lou followed, giving one last forlorn look back at the CD.

"Should I call you?" Lou asked.

Bryzinski grinned. "Don't call us," he said. "We'll call you."

THE Baltimore City Detention Center loomed like a medieval castle, plunked down in a neighborhood advisable to keep away from after dark. The gray stone edifice held rows of grimy windows nearly obscured by rusty bars. *Impenetrable, imposing,* and *inescapable* were words that popped into Lou's head as he and Cap passed through the entrance.

Lou swallowed hard as he entered the brightly lit whitewashed lobby. This was the purgatory of the corrections system—lumping together guilty and innocent, each awaiting trial or transfer to long-term incarceration. These were men who could not make bail, or worse, who'd been denied bail. Gary McHugh fell into the latter category—alleged murderers almost never got bail.

Lou and Cap were ushered inside a metal door by an armed guard. Lou startled when the heavy door slammed behind them and the cannonlike sound echoed eerily down a long stretch of empty corridor. In a locker room, they were instructed to remove and lock up all personal effects—wallets, jewelry, pens, keys. They passed through the metal detector and followed the guard along a warren of corridors that brought them to the visitors center.

"I never get used to this," Cap said, "but it's a good reminder of where I could have ended up."

"Amen," Lou said.

Lou took his assigned seat on a long bench with partitions on either side of him. Cap got placed somewhere to Lou's right, five or six partitioned spaces away. Handprints marring the thick Plexiglas were the echoes of the desperate loved ones who had cried into the black phone Lou would soon use to speak with McHugh.

A loud buzzer pulled Lou's attention toward the door and Gary McHugh's entrance. The physician looked miserable in his orange prison jumpsuit. He slumped into his chair as he and Lou picked up the wall-mounted phones. "Thanks for coming, Lou," Gary said.

"How are you holding up?"

"I keep telling people I didn't do it, and nobody will believe me."

"You'll get your day in court," Lou said. "Stay strong."

"Not so easy here. Lou, this place is a nightmare. It's dirty and overcrowded. There's no decent exercise yard. You don't get a single second of privacy. And the gangs run the place. If I have any positive news, it's that after listening to one guy after another blame alcohol or drugs for the mess he's in, I've begun to realize that if I ever get the chance, I need to put more effort into my recovery."

McHugh's wife and children refused to visit him, and even his attorney had been acting somewhat distant and clinical. Lou debated trying to boost his friend's mood with an account of the recording he had found, but until Sarah had finished her deposition and listened to the CD herself, it did not seem like a wise idea.

"So, what have you learned, Lou?" McHugh asked. "What did Jeannine say? Does she think I did it?"

"She's hurt, Gary, rejected by her kids like you have been. At the moment, there isn't much doubt in her mind that you're guilty."

"Lou, I didn't kill him. You've got to keep searching. I don't care if I never get to practice medicine again, but if I get sent to prison—"

"Easy. Remember that 'day at a time' stuff? It's not just words."

McHugh wiped the sleeve of his orange jumpsuit across the sweat beading up on his brow. "Okay," he managed.

Cap came up behind Lou and whispered, "We're all set."

"Gary," Lou said into the receiver, "look down the row to your right. You see the large black guy? His name's Tiny Booker."

"I've seen him around. He's hard to miss."

"Tiny has got your back now. He's your protection. Don't lose faith, Gary. We're going to find proof that you're innocent."

The guard approached and motioned to his watch that the visit needed to end.

"Stay strong, pal. I'll be back soon."

Lou used the hours before his graveyard shift to nap and then hit an AA meeting. The discussion group dealt that day with Step One of the twelve steps—admitting one is powerless over his or her addiction and that their life had become unmanageable. Gary sounded as if he was inching toward that first step on the road to recovery.

When he finally left the ER, Lou headed down to the hospital caf for his first real meal in most of a day. Grapefruit juice, poached eggs on an English muffin, home fries, milk. He had just reached an empty table when his cell phone began vibrating.

It was Sarah Cooper. "Are you somewhere where you can pick me up?" she asked. She did not sound at all pleased.

Lou looked longingly at his breakfast. "I suppose so. I'm at Eisenhower Memorial. I just got off—"

"We need to go and speak to that detective you left me a message about. I just got off the phone with him. He's waiting at his office for us, but he says he's got to leave soon."

"Do you want to listen to the disc first?"

"Dr. Welcome, what part of 'he says he's got to leave soon' are you having trouble with?"

Lou picked at the edge of an English muffin. "Attorney Cooper, does being snide and nasty usually get you what you want?"

"I'll be just inside the street door to my office," Sarah said.

The line went dead.

Over the ten-minute drive to Sarah's office, Lou mustered the ten years of serenity that defined his recovery. From their initial meeting at McHugh's place, something hadn't been right between the two of them. But what?

Lou pulled to the curb, and she hurried out. There was no question that he found her attractive. It was hard not to. But if she wanted to push him away, she was doing a near perfect job.

"Drive!" Sarah ordered, slamming the door behind her and snapping her seat belt in place.

Lou slipped the car into the flow of traffic and headed west. "Do you mind telling me what's going on?" he asked. "Why the rush to go back to see Bryzinski?"

Sarah's look held all the warmth of concrete. "Do you think you went into medicine because you were arrogant, or did you become arrogant because you became a doctor?"

"I don't know what you mean."

"All right, let me try this another way: Do you think it would be right for me to stroll into the emergency ward and start sewing up patients?"

"No," he said. "That wouldn't be appropriate."

"So, do you think the rules we have for handling evidence in legal cases are any less crucial than the rules for treating patients?"

"I suppose not, but—"

"There is no 'but.' You may have messed up. You physicians screw up all the time because you just don't listen. The rules to follow are there, starting with: listen to the patient. But you decide when you're going to pay attention and when you just don't feel like it. Even if this Bryzinski has taken perfect care of that CD, there's potential for disaster, and all your good intentions fly out the window. When your patients tell you something, do you listen?"

"Of course I listen."

"And what about when I told you something back at Gary McHugh's house. Did you listen?"

Lou could not understand why she was so upset. He had made a thorough, even brilliant, search and had turned up a CD that was going to help his friend and her client. Then he had made a copy of the CD and had brought the original to the police. What was wrong with any of that? She should have been ecstatic about the discovery.

"Sarah, I found evidence that should at least infuse doubt into the case against Gary. I don't see why you're so upset."

She sighed deeply while Lou weaved his way through traffic. "You just don't understand how things work," she said.

"Why don't you explain to me how things work instead of getting so upset with me? I did try calling you. All that matters is the police have the evidence you'll need to help Gary."

Finally, Sarah turned to him. He immediately wished she hadn't.

"Do they?" she asked. "Just in case, did you make sure the copy you had made was a flawless reproduction?"

"No, but—"

"And did Jeannine Colston see you find the CD?"

"She was sleeping off a migraine and asked me not to wake her."

"So nobody knows that you found this evidence?"

"Well, Bryzinski does."

"You told me he didn't listen to the recording in front of you. Did Bryzinski know that nobody else had heard that recording?"

Lou nodded. "I understand what you're getting at."

"At last, light dawns. This isn't a child's game. A congressman has been murdered, Lou. Don't you get it?" Lou realized it was the first time she had called him by his given name. "This has nothing to do with evidence. Who looks bad if Gary McHugh isn't the killer? Whose butt is in a sling when the media starts reporting that the Keystone Cops bungled their way through yet another high-profile investigation? I'm not talking evidence. I'm talking the facts of life in the law—real and often very ugly facts."

Sarah Cooper had an edge like honed steel. It was humbling and not a little embarrassing to be spoken to the way she had spoken to him, but he could see her point. His enthusiasm and, yes, maybe his arrogance had overwhelmed his objectivity. And for whatever reason, Sarah was disinclined to cut him any slack at all.

The flag outside the low brick building was still at half-mast. The two of them were kept waiting only a short time before Chris Bryzinski lumbered into the waiting room.

Sarah introduced herself and shook hands with the man. "Thanks for making time for us," she said.

"No problem," Bryzinski replied. "It can't be long, though. We're swamped. Four accidents and one homicide."

Bryzinski asked the desk officer to buzz them through the door, then led them down the corridor to his office. Lou suppressed a grin watching Sarah's distaste as she breathed in the fetid air and surveyed the cluttered landscape.

"So?" Bryzinski asked, not inviting them to sit down.

"We won't take up much time," Lou said. "Attorney Cooper just wanted to talk with you about the CD I dropped off yesterday."

"In the interest of discovery," Sarah added, "I'd like to give a copy to the district attorney's office. Have you listened to it yet?"

"Actually, no. It's been really crazy here since the congressman's murder. Tips keep coming in. Despite the fact that we are confident we have our man, we still have to—"

"Could I see it, please?" Sarah asked.

"Detective Cartwright's in charge of managing everything that comes in on this case." He unclipped the radio from his belt. "Hey, Mike," he said, "it's me. What'd you do with that disc?"

Crackle and static spit back, making it hard to hear all the words, but Lou picked out the two most important ones: *what* and *disc*.

Bryzinski pushed the talk button on his radio. "The one in the brown cardboard jacket," he said.

More static. Lou heard Cartwright say, "Hang on."

The static and crackle returned.

"It's not there," Cartwright said.

"What do you mean, it's not there?"

"Not . . . in . . . pile," were the three audible words this time.

"All right. Keep looking," Bryzinski said. "When you find it, leave it on my desk." He replaced the radio. "Cartwright's having trouble locating it. That happens sometimes. But it's there. Nothing to worry about."

"I don't understand," Lou said, his voice up half an octave. "I dropped it off just yesterday morning."

Bryzinski did not back down. "Sorry, Doctor. If I wasn't so damn busy, and I had more time, I would go down to Cartwright's office and find it myself. I did sign for it, didn't I?"

"I don't think so," Lou said, feeling his cheeks flush.

"No big deal. Listen, tomorrow, if things slow down, I'll have it for you." He turned to Sarah. "I told the doc my department had too many tips to be rushing. We process things as they come in. Now, if you'll excuse me, I am falling further behind by the second."

Lou was about to say something when Sarah gripped his wrist.

"Thanks for your time, Detective," she said. "Here's my card. I'll be waiting for your call."

"My pleasure," Bryzinski replied, sliding the card into his pocket without even glancing at it. He then escorted them back to the waiting area for a perfunctory good-bye.

In the parking lot, Lou said, "I'm sorry. I still believe it's going to turn up, and I do have the copy. These are cops, not criminals."

"Drive me by your place. I want to get it now." She pulled her coat around her and entered the passenger side of the Toyota. "And no more grandstanding," she added. "We get this done, and you back off and let us handle things from here."

Lou studied her and finally climbed behind the wheel. "I won't cause you any trouble," he said.

For a time, they drove on in silence.

"So," Lou asked finally, "do you think Wyatt Brody's the one?"

"Let me hear what's on that CD before I decide anything. What I really want to know at this point is what Spencer Hogarth has to do with Detective Chris Bryzinski."

"Hogarth, the secretary of defense?"

"Bryzinski had what looked like a to-do list on top of that pigsty of a desk of his. Tops on that list was to update S. Hogarth."

"Curiouser and curiouser," Lou said.

Spencer Hogarth, the secretary of defense, had a love/hate relationship with the media, congress, and the public. To some, he was an incendiary with a frighteningly short fuse. To others, he was a crusader standing firm against terrorism in every form. For years, his prime adversary on Capitol Hill had been one Elias Colston.

"Hogarth and Colston were rivals over some pretty important stuff, and now his name shows up on the desk of the cop who's investigating Colston's murder. Coincidence?"

"I think not," Lou said in perfect unison with her.

They laughed, and for the first time, Sarah's expression softened.

"You know," she said, "it's hard for me to believe, but it appears you might actually have a sweet side to you. Sweet and idealistic. I'll bet you're even a half-decent doctor."

Lou glanced over at her. "Thanks," he said. "I've been thinking the same about you. You know, I always thought of Hogarth as being tough but never dirty. Maybe he's just anxious to keep on top of the case because of the history he and Colston had."

"I wish *I* could believe that everyone wanted to play by the rules. Your naïveté, at least until it wears thin, is sort of endearing."

"Bryzinski will turn up that disc," Lou averred.

Sarah's expression was strained. "Dr. Welcome," she said, "I don't know if I believe in UFOs or Big Foot, but I am a thousand percent sure of one thing."

"Yes?"

"Detective Christopher Bryzinski is up to something."

Lou could tell much about a person from their reaction to his neighborhood. The less they shrunk at the sight of graffiti and loitering bands of kids, the more likely it was that Lou would get along with them. Sarah seemed completely at ease, if not indifferent, to Lou's street. Perhaps they were destined to overcome their differences after all. Either that, or she was too absorbed in getting her hands on the copy of the Colston CD to notice the surroundings.

Lou parked in front of Dimitri's Pizza, which occupied the entire lower level of his building and featured, he would tell anyone who would listen, the tastiest, most lovingly prepared pies and calzones in the city.

"I'll wait here," Sarah said.

"It's fine for you to come up. You can meet Diversity, our cat."

"Our?"

"Mine and my daughter Emily's. She lives in Arlington but spends a lot of time here. She and I train at the Stick and Move boxing gym across the street."

"Sounds like my kind of gal. Most of the doctors I deal with live in places more like Dr. McHugh's."

"Living here helps keep me rightsized. Emily, too. The place and what's left over after every month's rent payment help fill in a hole I once dug for myself."

"I think I know something about that. And you feel safe here?"

"This is a great neighborhood with terrific people. We're careful enough not to leave our doors unlocked, but that's about it."

Sarah climbed out of the car. Lou picked up his mail and led Sarah up one flight. Then he saw his apartment door was slightly ajar.

Instantly, he was on red alert, every fiber tense. He turned, held a finger to his lips, and motioned toward the door. His senses crackled like a jumper cable as he mentally retraced his steps when he left for the hospital last evening. *We're careful enough not to leave our doors unlocked*. This was not carelessness. Something was wrong.

"Go out and call nine-one-one," he whispered. "I'm going in."

"Wait until I get back up here."

"All right, but hurry," said Lou.

As Sarah headed softly down the stairs, cell phone in hand, Lou knelt and made a careful study of the lock and the door itself. There were scuff marks along the base of the door. He held his breath and listened. Only silence. *Where was she?* His pulse was hammering.

Sarah opened the foyer door and started back up the stairs. Without waiting, Lou pushed against the door. He could feel Sarah behind him, her breathing rapid and uneven.

This was going to be bad.

An overturned end table by the couch was just the beginning. He pushed the door open more fully, swallowing back the bile that percolated into his throat. He took a step inside and then another, now not only assessing the carnage but also scanning the place for Diversity.

In the kitchen, he slid a knife from his butcher-block holder.

"Don't you want to wait for the police?" Sarah asked.

"They don't rush to these neighborhoods," he replied. "Besides, I don't think anyone's here."

The search, at least from what he could see in the kitchen and living room, was professionally thorough. The cushions of his couch had been slashed open, spilling out clumps of stuffing. Chairs were upended. End table drawers were pulled out. His laptop was gone. The kitchen was a total shambles.

The back door was closed, and he could see it was bolted. It looked as if the intruder had entered and exited through the front.

Still tense and brandishing the knife, Lou approached his bedroom. As he stepped through the doorway, Diversity dashed out and across Sarah's shoes. She cried out, lurching back against the wall.

"That's Diversity."

"I know" she said acidly. "Where did you put the CD?"

One look into his bedroom and Lou knew they were in trouble. The room had been taken apart. His bureau drawers had been pulled out and their contents dumped on the floor. Sarah, arms folded, watched as he searched through his clothes.

"It's gone, isn't it?" she said. "That's what they were after."

"It was hidden in that drawer under some papers. I . . . didn't think anyone would do this. They took my computer, too."

"Whoever did this knew exactly what they were after and how to find it. It would have been easier on you if you had just left it on the kitchen table."

"So now what?" Still holding the knife, he led Sarah to Emily's room. There was not a thing out of place.

"I guess that clinches what they were after," Sarah said. "Now we have two questions we need to answer: Who? And why?"

"I'm really sorry," Lou said.

"I know you are." They heard the siren of a police car. "No sense crying over spilled milk. You stay and take care of this business. I'll take a cab back to the office."

CHAPTER 5

IT TOOK most of two days for Lou to put his apartment back together—two days during which he had not heard a word from Sarah. No surprise. His next step would be to re-create as best he could the clandestinely recorded conversation between Elias Colston and Hector. Not exactly evidence Gary's attorney could use in court but the closest he could come to another apology.

First, though, it was Emily's weekend. Lou watched as the teen made a curious check of the apartment. He had done a decent job putting things back together. Crate and Barrel still carried white china, and a new Mac was no problem. For a time, he debated if he should even allow her to spend the weekend but finally decided that whoever ransacked their home had left with what they came for and weren't likely to return.

Gradually, it was back to business as usual. Emily played string games with Diversity, and she and Lou had a movie lined up for the evening. But now their day would feature lunch with Lou's father at the Wave Rider, virtually the only restaurant the three of them ever ate at together.

Dennis Welcome had four great loves in his life: his family, his red Chevy pickup with two hundred thousand miles on it, his carpenters union, and the Wave Rider's double bacon burger. Dennis lived in Virginia, and Lou shared a meal with him frequently, including Emily whenever possible. His father's lunch invitation offered a break from what had been an extremely stress-filled couple of days.

The Wave Rider, a surfer-themed sports bar that had rarely served an actual surfer, was pleasantly busy. Dennis, distinguishable by his salt-and-pepper crew cut, stood up from his booth and waved to Lou and Emily as they set foot inside. He wore faded blue jeans, dusty work boots, and a red flannel shirt.

"Grandpa!" Emily squealed as she sprinted into Dennis's arms.

"How are you, Dad?" Lou asked.

"Oh, great," Dennis said, tapping his knuckles on the top of Emily's head. "Okay, then, enough chitchat. I've got me a man-size craving."

"Rumor has it that the double bacon burger may be slightly less than healthy," Lou said.

"Blasphemy!" Dennis cried, looking to Emily for corroboration.

"Put Dad on trial for food treason," Emily said.

"Instead, I'd suggest you spend a little time researching arteriosclerosis," Lou said.

"And I'd suggest you spend a little time mending your shirt." She pointed to a one-inch tear just above his belt.

"Diversity," Lou groaned.

"What?" Dennis asked.

"Diversity is my new cat," Emily said without looking up from the menu. "He and Dad aren't exactly getting along."

"You got a cat? Who named him?"

Emily pointed at her chest. "In honor of multiculturalism."

For Emily, it was love at first purr. On the ride home from the ASPCA shelter, Diversity, a two-year-old orange and white tabby with amber eyes, nestled in her lap. Later he chased thread, batted a piece of paper, and clawed the carpet-fragment-on-a-pole Lou bought at the pet superstore.

However, when Lou returned home after dropping Emily back at the house in Arlington, Diversity had become a different cat. He hissed, hid under the bed, and made a flying tackle to dig his claws into Lou's legs every time he crossed the living room. But of course, whenever Emily was around the cat was an angel.

Dennis called the waitress over. Lou got a Cobb salad.

"So . . . you involved with the doc who killed Colston?" Dennis asked once their server had moved on.

"Dad, this isn't appropriate lunch conversation," Lou said.

Emily broke away from her texting. "I know that Congressman Colston was murdered by his wife's jealous lover," she said, holding up her smartphone. "We get all the news on these things. So, *are* you involved?"

"I heard that before he shot Colston," Dennis said, "McHugh was under monitoring with the PWO for a drinking problem."

"A PWO contract is confidential," Lou said. "It's not something we should be discussing."

"So, do you think he did it?" Dennis asked.

Lou threw up his hands. "Oh, for goodness' sake. Okay. I know Gary McHugh. He asked to see if I could come up with somebody other than him who might have wanted Elias Colston dead."

"And did you?" Emily asked.

"I'm working on it, but McHugh's lawyer, Sarah Cooper, wants me to stop interfering. She thinks I'm getting in her way."

"Sarah Cooper," Dennis exclaimed, "the one from the Sandra Winkler trial? She's peeved at you?"

"If by peeved you mean uncooperative and hostile, then yes."

"Do you know why she's so angry?" asked Emily.

"She was irritated with me from the moment we met."

"First the cat and now this lawyer," Dennis said. "Maybe you should change your deodorant."

Thankfully, their food arrived, sparing Lou from having to respond. Throughout most of their meal, Emily seemed preoccupied. She would eat, do something on her phone, and then eat some more. Suddenly, she cried out, "Oh, so that's her beef."

"Whose beef?" Lou asked.

"Sarah Cooper. Did you ever Google her?"

"Never occurred to me."

"It's all here. Her husband died, and she sued his doctor. She won, too. One of the articles says six million dollars."

Emily handed him her smartphone, open to an old article from the *Washington Post*. David Cooper, an attorney, had been complaining of headaches for months. The neurologist diagnosed migraines. The neurologist, whom Sarah referred to as "unbearably arrogant," refused to order an MRI. He also refused to involve an orthopedist or neurosurgeon but continued to prescribe anti-inflammatories and physical therapy. Then David awoke one morning, turned his head quickly, and partially severed his spinal cord, paralyzing himself from the neck down. After two miserable years on a ventilator, David Cooper died. The jury in the malpractice case concluded that more careful attention to his complaints would have enabled the neurologist to seek a lifesaving spinal fusion.

Stunned by the account, Lou handed Emily back her phone.

"She doesn't have a thing just against you, Dad," Emily said. "She's got a thing against doctors."

BUCKY Townsend and Fenton Morales clanked Bud bottles and toasted their good fortune. Tonight they had cause for celebration. Major Coon had given each the word that they were in for Operation Talon. Even though the two of them knew little of the objective of the mission, what mattered was its importance to the security of America. OT was priority number one at Mantis—the specifics of what the operation entailed were secondary.

"This is why we became marines," Morales said, taking a swig.

"Forget that, this is why we chose Mantis," Townsend countered.

"Yeah, though I still can't believe you made it. Heck, you're just an Okie from Muskogee."

"And a badass one at that."

"To OT and whatever our future holds."

"To OT," Townsend repeated.

They clanked their bottle necks again and raced to chug their beers. They ordered another round, then another. An hour later, Morales checked his watch. "We should get going," he said.

Townsend watched a couple of girls wearing dresses too short for the outside cold. "Why go?" he asked. "The night's still young." He exchanged smiles with a leggy young brunette.

Morales's look was admonishing. "You want Coon thinking you're more into booze and babes than you are into this mission?"

Townsend shared one last look with the brunette. Then, sighing loudly, he pushed back his stool and stood. "Whatever it takes," he said mournfully.

Morales put an arm around his friend and led him to the door.

"Whatever it takes," Morales repeated, chuckling softly.

Outside, the winter air slapped Townsend across the face. The gunshot wound to his side was healing rapidly, just as Coon had promised it would, but it still acted up in the cold.

"Glad you shut me off," Townsend said, exhaling a swirling tendril of mist into the dark night. "I was starting to feel it."

As they turned the corner, powerful high beams flashed on, blinding them. An engine revved up, followed by the angry whine of tires. Alcohol slowed their reaction time. The side door of a white cargo van slid open as the vehicle screeched to a stop beside them.

Four men, dressed in black, leapt out from the van, their faces obscured beneath head coverings that Townsend associated mostly with al-Qaeda. They tossed Townsend and Morales into the van like sacks of laundry. Two other men waiting inside the van shoved the muzzles of assault rifles up under the marines' chins. The van peeled away, momentum slamming the side door closed.

Townsend's world went black as duct tape was tightened across his mouth and a hood was pulled over his head. Next came plastic cuffs, which dug painfully into his wrists.

For perhaps half an hour, the van sped down a highway. Then it slowed and bounced along an uneven road, violently jostling Townsend about. He heard the men shouting at one another in Arabic.

Townsend breathed in and out slowly through his nose. He had no idea what was in store for him and Morales. What he did know was that regardless of whatever awaited them, he was not afraid.

WITH THE BAG STILL COVERING his head, Townsend was guided into a room cold enough to store meat. They snipped his manacles off, cut his shirt away, and shoved him down onto a chair. They lashed his ankles to the legs and his wrists to the armrests. Finally, the hood was removed.

Townsend and Morales were tied on identical chairs in a barren, windowless room, beneath a bare bulb. Three men crowded into the room with the two guards. Their heads were covered except for the opening in their bandannas displaying reptilian eyes. Their complexions were dark bronze. The fifth man, wearing a turban but no bandanna, had a hatchet face buried behind a dark beard. He appraised Townsend and Morales as if they were lambs destined for slaughter.

"What is Operation Talon?" he said in near perfect English.

"My name is Sergeant Bucky Townsend. I am a citizen of the United States of America."

Townsend had scored near perfect marks at SERE school—Survival, Evasion, Resistance, and Escape training. He knew how to respond during an interrogation. As long as it seemed there was a possibility they would talk, nothing would happen to them—nothing, that was, except some torture.

"What is Operation Talon?" the man asked again, this time addressing Morales specifically.

"My name is Sergeant Fenton Morales. I am a citizen of the United States of America."

The man nodded dully, assessing both marines with complete disinterest. He turned his back to the hostages, and when he faced them again he was wielding a pistol, a Glock 19. With his arm extended, the terrorist pointed the barrel of the gun at Morales's head.

"Last chance, Sergeant Morales," he said. "What is Operation Talon? When will it be taking place?"

"My name is Sergeant Fenton Morales, I am a—"

Morales's words were cut short by a loud pop, followed by a bright flash of light mixed with the acrid stench of gunpowder. Morales's head recoiled back violently as blood, bone, and brain splattered the wall behind him. Morales slumped forward in his chair, blood dripping from his forehead. Townsend stared wide-eyed at his friend.

Whatever it takes, he recited to himself. *Whatever it takes . . .*

Townsend felt sick, but he did not feel panicked. He would kill these men, or they would kill him, but they would not learn one word about Operation Talon. That just wasn't going to happen.

"Now, what is Operation Talon?"

Townsend stared straight ahead with unblinking eyes.

The terrorist leader slapped him viciously across the face, then motioned for Morales's corpse to be removed. Two guards cut him free. As they dragged him away, the heels of his boots left long rubber streaks across the gray linoleum floor.

The leader ushered the remaining guards out of the room and followed them, closing the door. When he returned, minutes later, he was wheeling a steel pushcart containing an array of instruments.

"What is Operation Talon?" the man said.

"My name is—"

The terrorist held up his hand, cutting Townsend's words short.

"Bucky," the man said, crouching down to get eye level with Townsend. "My name is Abdullah. I need information from you, information that I will hurt you to get. Do you understand?"

"Yes," Townsend said. "I understand. Hey, Abdullah, take these ropes off my wrists and give me your Glock. Just for a minute."

"I'm now going to blindfold you, Bucky. You will hear my footsteps walking around your chair. I'm going to be holding this." Abdullah picked up a ball-peen hammer. "I am going to strike you with this hammer. Maybe your knees, an elbow, your neck. You won't know when it's coming. You can avoid this unpleasantness if you answer my question. Exactly what is Operation Talon, and when will it be taking place?"

Townsend's nostrils flared as he fixed his gaze on the hammer gently tapping away against Abdullah's meaty palm.

"My name is Bucky Townsend—"

Townsend's world went dark again as Abdullah pulled a cloth blindfold across his eyes and tied it tightly in the back. Then, as promised, there were footsteps circling around him.

Breathe in . . . breathe out . . . in and out . . . whatever it takes . . .

The footsteps stopped, and Townsend waited for the pain. He waited . . . and waited. Nothing. Then the footsteps began again.

"You don't need to die like your friend Morales. You don't need the excruciating pain. Tell me about Talon, and you can go."

The footfalls continued, then came to another stop. Townsend felt the ball-peen hammer bouncing on his left knee, though not with any great force. He braced himself for the strike. All he could think of was dying with the bravery of Morales.

Townsend felt the blindfold being loosened. His eyes adjusted to the light, and he cried out. On the chair next to him, with an artfully done gunshot wound on his forehead, sat Fenton Morales, beaming.

"What the—"

"Nice going, pal," Morales said. "I knew you could do it."

The door opened, and Major Charles Coon entered the room, followed by a gangly man in his thirties wearing paint-stained fatigues. "Sergeant Townsend, meet Sergeant Brett Coughlin, the best makeup artist in the military. We use him and his special skills for jobs like this. That directed spray of blood and bone is a miracle."

Coughlin nodded toward Coon, then to Townsend. Then he set about peeling off the gunshot from Morales's forehead.

The tall man, who had identified himself as Abdullah, used a ten-inch razor-sharp bowie knife to slice through Townsend's restraints. Then he helped him to his feet.

"Orders are orders," the man said without emotion, peeling off his fake beard and revealing himself to be one of the Palace Guards.

Townsend understood. This was his final test for Operation Talon. Coon set a strong hand on his shoulder. "You did well."

He motioned a man into the room, whom Townsend recognized as Coon's chief medical officer. The CMO held an open laptop. "His vitals were below expected," he said. "He was basically at rest, almost in a sleep state. Heart rate, muscle tension, oxygen levels, everything. It's rather remarkable. I think we're there."

Coon nodded. "Sergeant Bucky Townsend, I'm pleased to inform you that you are now an official team member of Operation Talon."

"Sir, thank you, sir," Townsend said, snapping to attention. "You won't be disappointed."

"I'm sure that I won't be," Coon said. "I'd bet my career on it."

Lou picked up a pen and flipped to a blank page in his yellow legal pad. He was seated at his kitchen table with a steaming mug of cocoa. He started with the first few words he recollected from the conversation between Elias Colston and Hector.

Hi, Hector.

Or did Hector say hello first?

Lou tore off the sheet and started again, feeling more foolish by the minute. He simply had not listened to the recording enough for the conversation to take precise root anywhere in his memory.

For his fourth attempt, Lou tried an entirely different approach, jotting down words, phrases, and recollections in free association.

> *Colonel Brody requested the meeting . . .*
> *Colston wanted to cut funds for Mantis . . .*
> *The Palace Guards, toughs that are never far from the colonel . . .*
> *Ever heard of the Reddy Creek Armory?*

Something about a blog.

Lou set down his pen. This was hardly the detail Sarah had in mind. He hated giving her another reason to be disappointed in doctors, but this effort was fruitless. The best he could do was to bank on Detective Bryzinski coming up with the disc. He spied Diversity atop the refrigerator. The cat meowed, then hissed. "What do you think, pal?" he said. "Should I try to find this Hector?"

Diversity turned his head toward Lou's voice and meowed again.

"I'll take that as a yes."

Lou crossed to the phone by the couch. Jeannine Colston answered on the second ring. "I found something when I was looking through Elias's office," Lou said. "It was a CD recording of a conversation between Elias and a marine named Hector."

"Hector Rodriguez? Mark's friend?"

"I don't remember hearing his last name, but I believe that's who Elias was speaking with, yes."

"Why would Elias do such a thing?"

"Colonel Wyatt Brody, who heads up Mantis, asked Hector to arrange the meeting. I think that Elias wanted to have a record of the conversation because he knew what they were going to talk about."

"And what was that?" Jeannine asked.

"Your husband's position about cutting support to Mantis Company. He wanted to keep slashing funding, and Brody was using Mark's friend to get Elias to change his position."

"If Wyatt Brody thought he could change Elias, he did not know my husband." For the first time, there was a spark of energy in her voice. "He had his faults, but Elias was a rarity among politicians. He was never one to be influenced by lobbyists or his party. He thrived at the polls and on Capitol Hill by adhering to three principles—honesty, transparency, and doing the right thing."

"He was a good man," Lou said.

Jeannine went silent, regaining her composure. "So, what do you need now?"

"I need a way to contact Hector."

"I'll get it for you. Tell me, how did the police miss all of this?"

"I don't think they looked very hard. They had a theory of what happened, and they just looked for the evidence that fit that theory."

"And the recording might be connected to Elias's murder?"

"I'll be able to tell better after I speak with Hector."

Jeannine retrieved her address book and read off two numbers. "I don't know how easy he'll be to reach. I assume he's still with the marines. I can try to reach him to say you're going to call."

"If it's not too much trouble, that would be great."

"I want the same thing you do, Dr. Welcome—justice for my husband. Now that I think about it, there's another number you should have. His name is Steve Papavassiliou—Papa Steve, we call him. He's an ordnance specialist working with Mantis."

"Papa Steve?"

"He is . . . was Elias's closest friend and Mark's godfather. He and Elias served together in the marines. They were like brothers. If Elias spoke about Wyatt Brody with anybody, it would have been with Papa Steve." Jeannine gave Lou Papa Steve's number and promised to call Hector right away.

"One last thing," Lou said. "Did the congressman ever mention a place called the Pine Forest Clinic?"

"Not that I recall. What's that?"

"I guess from the logo that it's a clinic of some sort located in Shockley, Minnesota. I found an empty envelope in the top drawer of Elias's desk addressed to a James Styles at a PO box in Bowie."

"No idea."

After repeating her promise to try to contact Hector Rodriguez, Jeannine ended the call.

Lou left a message for Papa Steve. The man's gravelly voice mail greeting made him think of what Santa Claus might have sounded like if he carried a bazooka and a bag of C-4 explosives in his sleigh. He was on his way back to the kitchen table when Diversity attacked his leg from the couch. Lou shook free from his new nemesis, but the pain would endure considerably longer. Cursing, he rolled up his pant leg, blotted away the blood from three neat rows of gouges, and swathed the area with soapy water and Neosporin.

Twenty minutes later, the phone rang. "Dr. Welcome," said Lou, thinking it might be Papa Steve returning his call.

A youthful, somewhat anxious voice said, "My name is Hector Rodriguez. Mark Colston's mother called me. She said you wanted to speak with me about Congressman Colston's murder."

Lou explained his involvement with the case. "Elias Colston wrote down some notes regarding a conversation you had with him. Do you recall speaking with him? You talked about Mark Colston, Wyatt Brody, and a group you guys call the Palace Guards."

Lou thought about telling him the conversation had been recorded but did not want to risk spooking him even more.

"I don't know what you're talking about," the marine said.

"Hector, a good friend of mine is facing life in jail for a crime he might not have committed. I think your conversation with Colston could be the key to sorting things out. I'll come out there to speak with you. I won't need more than an hour of your time."

Lou held his breath.

"One hour," Hector said. "And not a minute more."

CHAPTER 6

TRAFFIC was reasonably light as Lou headed out of the city and toward the Monongahela Mountains, a segment of the Appalachian range straddling West Virginia and Virginia. Would Hector Rodriguez be able to remember enough details of his conversation to satisfy Sarah? Lou had his doubts.

It was just after sunset on a day that was hovering around freezing, when Lou rolled into Hayes, West Virginia. His plan was to spend some time before his rendezvous with Hector getting a feel for the place. Hector had provided detailed directions to their meeting spot, but Lou needed only to exit the highway to find the Wildwood Motel. Judging by the dearth of cars in the motel parking lot, he suspected it was not frequent that someone tacked up a NO before the word VACANCY.

Hayes was a military town—pretty much as expected but on a smaller scale. Lou quickly concluded that Main Street was where most of what passed for action took place. He made a stop at a bar called Ralphie's. He ordered a Diet Coke from the bartender— mid-forties, apron, tattoos, nicotine stains, five o'clock shadow.

"You ain't from around here," the bartender said with a twang.

"Name's Lou Welcome."

"Bell," the bartender said, extending his hand. "Ralphie Bell. You said Welcome?"

"Just like the mat."

"Like the wh— Oh, I get it." He chuckled.

"So, where is everybody?" Lou asked.

"Hayes stays quiet until eight or so. That's when the boys from the base are allowed to come into town, if they have the night off."

"Is the base far from here?"

"The entrance is 'bout a half mile away. Be careful you don't stumble onto their property. It includes some wild country, and not much of it is fenced in. Trespassin' and carryin' a weapon around here is really frowned on."

"Does Wyatt Brody ever come in here?"

Bell scoffed. "Once in a great while, but Colonel Brody don't really socialize with nobody that I know of. Soldiers say he's on some sort of mission from God."

Lou tried but could get no further insights on the man who might have murdered Elias Colston. It was going to be up to Hector Rodriguez to fill in some huge gaps.

Lou had no trouble finding his way back to the Wildwood, but he had a harder time locating the bonfire pit, where Hector insisted they meet. The path leading off from the rear of the motel was overgrown with brush, and the ground was crunchy with rime.

Using his cell phone as a flashlight, he emerged, after a hundred feet or so, into a wide clearing with a stone-rimmed pit. Beyond the pit, a sliver of moonlight escaping from clouds revealed the silhouette of a stocky man, standing more or less at attention.

"Dr. Welcome?" Hector's voice and accent were unmistakable.

"That's me. Thanks for doing this, Hector."

Lou approached him, prepared to shake hands, but Hector remained as he was. Even in his bulky military-issue parka, Lou could tell he was powerfully built, and through the evening gloom, he looked swarthy and handsome. A warrior.

"Tell me what you want to know." Hector's coolness matched the evening. Lou could tell Hector was breathing at half the rate he was. He suspected his pulse was a fraction of his.

"I didn't tell you the complete truth when we spoke by phone," Lou said. "Colston didn't take notes about your conversation. He recorded it and transferred the recording to a CD. I gave that CD to the police, and now it's gone missing."

Even from six feet away, Lou could see the younger man tense and go pale. Hector inhaled deeply and tilted his head skyward.

"Congressman Colston was my best friend's father," he said. "I said things I wouldn't want certain people to know about."

"I'm sorry, Hector, for misleading you in any way, but we've got to re-create that conversation. Every point you made. I have a tape recorder." Lou extracted a miniature instrument from his parka.

Hector's eyes flashed. "You don't get it, man," he said. "I told the congressman stuff that I shouldn't have told him. I loved that man. He was like a father to me. That's why I was trying to warn him to back off from Colonel Brody and Mantis. But if word gets out that I talked about the Palace Guards, then I'm a dead man walking. What in the hell could have happened to that disc? Who has it now?"

"I . . . I don't know. The police have it. I'm sure of that."

"Damn."

"As I recall, you didn't say much about the Palace Guards at all. Can you tell me about them now?"

"These guys—the Guards—they're bad, man." Hector looked about furtively. "They mark themselves with a tattoo of barbed wire wrapped around their wrist. That's how you can tell who's Guard. We all have one of a praying mantis on the bottom of our forearm. That's how you can tell who's Mantis."

"What's the connection between Brody and the Palace Guards?"

"If someone starts actin' up, the Guards pay them a visit, rough them up a little, remind them that they don't want to be on Colonel Brody's bad side, and that the next step is they're out of Mantis."

"Do you think Brody's desperate for money to fund Mantis? Your outfit has been hit by budget cuts initiated by Colston."

Hector shrugged. "Probably. Everyone's desperate for money."

"Do you think Brody could have murdered the congressman because he knew about the Palace Guards?"

"I doubt it. Either way, I hope that recording doesn't get back—"

The night exploded with a series of bright flashes and loud pops that came from somewhere down the path to the clearing. More gunshots . . . more flashes.

"Run!" Hector screamed. "Split up and run!"

The two men broke for the woods. Another shot rang out. Lou saw Hector stumble, then fall, clutching his leg. Lou stopped running and headed toward the marine, but a hail of bullets sprayed snow in front of him.

Hector lurched to his feet, still holding his leg. "I'm all right!" he cried out. "Get out of here! Run!"

Lou watched the marine vanish into the woods. Then he spotted an opening in the dense underbrush and plunged through it.

Lou stumbled as he reached the woods, but he managed to grab a tree trunk and keep from falling. The icy ground provided all the traction of a hockey rink. Branches lashed out like claws, gashing his face and hands. His foot caught a root and sent him sprawling. He landed heavily onto the hard-packed ground. He heard more gunfire, then something else—something that sent him scrambling on all fours, across the frozen snow and hard-packed dirt, until he regained his footing.

Voices.

It seemed like there were two men, and they definitely were after him. "I can see his tracks," a raspy voice called out from somewhere behind him. "Keep the flashlight steady."

Lou's only recourse was to keep running, but his hiking boots made every step feel leaden. In the icy night breathing became a problem, and a fearsome stitch developed in his left side.

"This way!" a man yelled out. "Over here."

Lou thought he had put some distance between himself and his pursuers, when the ground turned steeper. Before he could slow his stride, he was skidding downhill, tumbling at an awkward angle and landing heavily at the bottom of a small ravine. He touched his left temple and felt blood. His shoulder throbbed, and he wondered if his contused knee would hold weight.

Dazed, he hauled himself to his feet. The knee held. Then, from far up the steep slope, he saw two shafts of light dancing erratically off the trees and underbrush.

For most of a minute, he remained motionless and listened. From among the rustling winter branches, he heard the distinct sound of rushing water coming from his right—a stream. Ignoring the pain in his knee, he headed toward the running water. The stream was wider than he had expected—more a river lined with ice and snow, rippling across nearly submerged rocks and boulders. He stepped into the frigid water. In an instant, his boots filled. The numbness was sudden and utterly unpleasant. Rather than go directly across, he followed the flow, praying he could stay upright.

One step . . . then another . . . and another.

Gradually, he angled for the far side of the river. The longer he could stay in, the better chance he had. The water reached his knees. His jeans were soaked. At a bend, he risked a glance backward. The lights were there, still some distance away. How much of a trail had he left? How much more could he take? Standing in the middle of the river, Lou crouched behind a boulder and watched as the beams cut irregular paths through the darkness.

"I got tracks here," he heard one man say.

"He might have followed the river," said the other. "Let's separate. You head up the hill. I'll go this way."

Lou risked a relieved breath. Two against one were not odds he embraced, but one on one? He stood and kept working his way across the river. His knee ached and the water burned, but one step at a time, he was moving. He checked back again. Judging by the flashlight beam, maybe fifty yards separated him and his pursuer.

Without warning, his boot skidded off a mossy rock, and he pitched forward into the water, arms extended. His ankle twisted from the fall. Lou got back to his feet, now totally soaked and beginning to shiver. After a few hesitant attempts, he put decent weight on the foot. A sprain.

Once again, he was on the move. From behind, he heard splashing. *Keep moving . . . keep moving . . .*

The shivering had become ferocious now. Hypothermia was taking over. It probably wasn't going to help much, but he had to get out of the river. At that instant, there was a gunshot.

"You out there?" The raspy voice taunted him through the dark. "I'm gonna find you, an' I'm gonna kill you."

Two more pops. A branch to Lou's right splintered. He was ten feet or so from the bank. He forged forward, slipping with each step. Ahead, he could make out a broad clearing of some sort—a field? Then he realized that the blackness wasn't a field at all.

It was a lake.

Lou hauled himself onto the bank of the frigid river and stumbled across to the shore to what seemed like a nearly circular lake, frozen as far out as he could see. He tried to will himself to stop shaking. Was he better off with or without his freezing, water-soaked clothes?

To his right, twenty feet away, there was a dilapidated boathouse. Its roof had partially caved in. There was a rotting rowboat propped up against the side. A basketball-size boulder held it in place.

The odds on there being something in the house to wrap himself in were small, but it was worth checking. He had to move quickly, though. The boathouse was the first place the man heading downriver would check. The door was secured with a rusty bolt. Lou peered into a window. From what he could see, the place was empty.

At that moment, still some distance away, he heard branches cracking. Then he glanced over at the rotting boat, and the glimmer of an idea began to take shape. A feint—one of the moves Cap loved to use in the ring.

Silently, using all his strength, Lou set the huge rock aside and flipped the rowboat upright, cushioning the landing with his shoulder. The sorrowful craft remained intact. He shoved it to the lakeshore and slid it out onto the ice, which creaked but held firm.

Now for the feint.

Moving on his knees and pushing the boat ahead to keep his weight distributed, he eased across the ice. There was a restless cracking and a strained creak, but again, no give.

Five more yards onto the ice. Then another five. He was twenty yards from shore now. Lou turned the boat ninety degrees, removed his parka, and threw it on the ice. Then, crawling on his belly, he eased back to shore. He hauled the boulder to the far side of the shack.

Kneeling by the boathouse, Lou's adrenaline rush began to fade, and once again his teeth were chattering. He peered around the corner toward the woods. A dark shadow moved cautiously from the forest, a flashlight in one hand and a handgun in the other. Lou pulled back and flattened against the wall.

The ground crunched as the killer approached the wall where the boat had been. Lou saw the flashlight beam swing toward the lake and onto the rowboat. The light stopped on Lou's parka. "You ain't fooling me, bro," the man called out to the darkness. "I know you're behind that boat."

He fired two shots. Lou could sense him checking around his feet, following the tracks he had left. One cautious step at a time, the gunman moved onto the lake. A quarter of the way, Lou guessed. . . . Now maybe half.

Lou hoisted the boulder to his chest and moved forward. He could feel the adrenaline pounding in the muscles of his chest and arms. The gunman fired three more times.

Go ahead, big guy. Keep shooting . . . keep shooting.

Lou neared the lake's edge. The huge rock was on his shoulder now. In order to make an effective throw, he had to venture onto the ice again. But not too far.

"I hit you yet?" the man yelled.

Lou brought the rock over his head and heaved it with all the strength he had. The momentum sent him sprawling backward and landing heavily on the ice. He felt it crack beneath his weight.

The gunman was spinning toward the commotion behind him when the rock landed at his feet. The ice beneath him gave way instantly, and before he could raise his weapon to fire, he vanished. Lou heard the splash, but scrambling for the shore, there was nothing he could do to help the man. The killer cried out once. Then there was silence. Desperately cold, Lou reached the bank and began to stagger along the wooded shoreline.

He was alive but only long enough, he knew, to freeze to death. Gasping for air and shivering violently, Lou sank down on a fallen tree to check his injured ankle when he felt the muzzle of a gun press firmly against the back of his neck.

"Do not turn around," a youngish man's voice said. "Put your hands up and get facedown on the ground. Do it now, or I shoot!"

Shivering mercilessly, Lou did as instructed.

Strong hands wrenched his arms behind his back.

The last thing he felt before he lost consciousness were handcuffs being secured around his wrists.

Lou came to slowly, carried into awareness by a pounding head-ache. He was handcuffed to a stretcher in a van equipped as an ambulance. His sodden clothes had been replaced by military fatigues, and he was covered by a pile of blankets.

The van jounced over a rutted road. The young man sitting next to him wore a red cross armband. The driver had one that read MP. There was no reaction when Lou told them who he was and how he came to be in this situation.

"I'm telling you one of your own guys was shot," Lou said. "Hector Rodriguez. He could still be back there someplace. Don't you care?"

"Our orders are to bring you to the base," the driver said. "Whatever story you have to tell, you can tell it there."

Lou had little doubt that Brody had sent men to kill him and Hector—perhaps members of the Palace Guard Hector had spoken about. Somehow the contents of the missing CD had to have gotten back to him. No other explanation he could think of made sense. The ambulance slowed and came to a stop at a security checkpoint.

The MP and medic flashed their security clearance, and a razor-wire gate slid open. The van was on the move again. They traveled along some dirt streets. Off to the right there was a target range lit by powerful floodlights. They came to a stop at a dirt court-yard that housed three single-story buildings. The largest was up on short stilts with a porch across the length. A sign read: MANTIS COMPANY. WHATEVER IT TAKES.

"Just remember, I'm a civilian," Lou said as the men released him and guided him out of the van. "I've got rights."

"Not when you trespass on military land," the MP replied.

The men took hold of Lou's elbows and escorted him into the center building. They stopped in front of a wooden door, upon which, in black lettering, were the words: COL. WYATT BRODY, COMMANDER.

The fierce praying mantis painted beneath the lettering looked as if it could eat a cow. The MP knocked and waited until invited to enter. Then he set Lou's soggy wallet on the wooden desk. Wyatt Brody glanced at the wallet disdainfully. The office was rustic, with wooden bookcases filled with memorabilia and military tomes. The most impressive aspect of the office was two huge glass display cases covering the wall behind Brody's desk and the one opposite it. Inside the well-lit cases were polished handguns, mounted on green felt and labeled with brass placards.

"Impressive, isn't it, Dr. Welcome?" Brody said from his seat behind his desk. "Several of them are one of a kind."

Lou wasn't startled to hear his name. The MPs obviously searched his wallet and called ahead.

Brody nodded toward the door, and the two men left.

"One of your men has been shot," Lou said as soon as the door clicked shut. "He may be badly injured."

"I've already got a search party looking for him," Brody said. "Just as I had several looking for you."

Lou made a careful study of the man's expressionless face. Brody, dressed in a beige shirt and tie underneath an olive green jacket, was in his fifties, with closely cropped salt-and-pepper hair. He had a narrow face, aquiline nose, glacial blue eyes. His thin lips seemed to frown and grin simultaneously, as if he derived the same satisfaction from administering pleasure as inflicting pain.

"Take a seat," Brody said, motioning to a plain wooden chair.

"I prefer to stand," Lou said.

"It wasn't a request. I haven't arrested you for trespassing yet," Brody continued, "but all that could change with the push of a button. Now, take a seat."

Lou hesitated, then acquiesced.

Brody interlocked his fingers and studied Lou with his ice blue eyes. When he finally spoke, Lou could sense how Brody's dominating voice, stern yet without much inflection, could have a hypnotic effect on the men under his command.

"Why don't you tell me what you were doing on Mantis property?"

"Is running for my life a good reason? There were at least four guys trying to kill Hector Rodriguez and me. And I think I know who they were. Palace Guards. Rumor has it they work for you."

"Never heard of them," Brody said, his smile conveying many meanings.

"So, do you want to explain why your men tried to kill me and Hector?"

"My men? We don't hunt civilians. We go after the other side— the bad guys. If you were attacked it wasn't anybody directly connected to Mantis."

Brody's eyes never wavered from Lou's face, and Lou wasn't at all sure he would enjoy facing those eyes in the ring. "Well, why don't you tell me," he said, "why the Palace Guard, or whoever those men were, would want me dead?"

"I told you, Doctor, I don't know who this Palace Guard is. Maybe you were just in the wrong place at the wrong time."

"Could you explain why they would want to kill Hector?"

Brody continued to size Lou up. "If you have to know, Hector Rodriguez was not the most well-regarded soldier on this base. He was about to get kicked out of Mantis for performance reasons, and as retaliation he started spreading lies about me and about guys in his own platoon. So it wouldn't surprise me if Staff Sergeant Rodriguez stepped on the toes of the wrong person with the right connections. What were you doing talking with Hector Rodriguez in the first place?"

Lou thought of bobbing and weaving with the man but finally decided to hit him with a couple of straight-on body blows, just to see what he might jar loose. "I came here to speak with Mark Colston's best friend." There, he'd put it on the table—the first hint that his visit to Hayes had something to do with Elias Colston's murder. But there was no reaction from Brody.

"And why would you be doing that?" Brody asked.

"Well, some things have come to light, and I'm following them up as a favor for the guy accused of killing Congressman Colston."

"Tragic what's happened to that family," Brody said.

"Funny thing is," Lou continued, "the more digging I do to help out my friend, the more your name keeps coming up as a possible reason the congressman is dead."

"Me?" Brody's laugh was unrevealing. "I can only tell you what everyone knew—that Elias Colston and I were never the best of friends."

"Funny his son's death didn't bring you two closer together."

"Mark Colston was one of the bravest men I've ever had the privilege to lead," Brody said. "It's no secret I opposed the congressman. He wanted to cut our funding, and I wanted to expand it. We may have had our differences, but I don't go around killing people, if that's what you're insinuating."

"I confess the thought has been crossing my mind," Lou said.

Lou felt the room charging up, like the moment just before a thunderstorm. "You listen to me, Welcome," Brody said, his face now crimson. "I wasn't the one sleeping with Colston's wife. And I wasn't the one at their house drunk when he was killed." As quickly as it had arrived, the thunderstorm passed, and Wyatt Brody was ice once again. "I was at the Marine Day parade on the day Colston was killed. A thousand or so witnesses can attest to that."

"Arranging for someone to be murdered is no different than pulling the trigger yourself."

"I think we're done here," Brody said with a dismissive wave. "You're free to go."

"So are Tweedledum and Tweedledee driving me back to Hayes?"

"My men are busy searching for Sergeant Rodriguez," Brody said. "You're going to have to make it back to Hayes on your own."

"What? On foot?"

"You seem adept at traveling through the woods. Just watch your step. As you have learned, a lot of bad things can happen out there." Using the tip of one finger, he pushed Lou's wallet across at him.

"Thanks for the heads-up," Lou said.

"I want you to have time . . . to think."

Brody reached under his desk drawer and pressed a button. Two men entered. Palace Guards. One of them carried an extra parka.

"Men, escort this gentleman to the river trail and point him toward the town. Have a good morning, Dr. Welcome."

The Guards had moved to Lou when a man dressed in camouflage knocked on Brody's partially open door. He was tall, ruggedly handsome, and fit for any age, let alone the sixty or so years Lou guessed him to be. His light hair was cut short and level on the top.

"Sir, I'm sorry to interrupt, sir," the older man said. His leathery voice matched the weathered condition of his skin.

"What is it?" Brody snapped.

"In the hall?"

Brody sighed and followed the chiseled marine into the anteroom. The door was pushed nearly closed but remained ajar enough so that Lou managed to catch most of what was said.

"Sir, the police are here," the man said. "They rolled into the courtyard and asked me where they could find you. Apparently there's a new man at the gate, and he let them in."

"What do they want?" Brody said.

"There were gunshots fired behind the Wildwood Motel. The proprietor thought the men were wearing military camo. The police are checking out if it involved anybody on the base."

There was the sound of new arrivals. "Colonel Brody, I'm Sergeant Kendall. This is Corporal Walsh. Sorry to barge in, but we're investigating reports of gunshots behind the Wildwood Motel."

"Yes," Brody said. "We have a man who was caught wandering on base property. If you fellas want to take him in for questioning, that's fine with me. Just make sure he knows that the next time he trespasses on Mantis property, we may not be so charitable."

He reentered the office, and Lou stepped away from the two Guards. "Thanks for the chat, Colonel."

Brody stared at Lou, unblinking. Then the trace of a smile turned the sides of his mouth. "Lucky day for you," he said.

CHAPTER 7

LOU understood his obsessive nature could be a great asset one minute and an even greater shortcoming the next. Friends from college still talked about the day he studied twenty-four hours straight for an organic chemistry test. He ended up getting sick halfway through the exam and, were it not for being allowed a redo by an understanding professor, would have flunked. Now that intensity had been manifest in the need to learn everything he could about Colonel Wyatt Brody. Hours rolled past as Lou, hunched over his laptop, picked his way through the endless Wyatt Brody items.

Lou's eyes were burning from the connection with his monitor screen. He looked up only to scratch a note on his yellow legal pad and got up only for bathroom breaks and more coffee. Diversity lingered on the carpet nearby, surprisingly reluctant to resume his role as Lou's tormentor.

There was no startling information on Brody. Married once. Long ago divorced. U.S. Marine Corps since his graduation from the Naval Academy. It seemed the more Lou looked for answers, the fewer he found.

Mantis proved to be equally enigmatic. The outfit, formed in 2002 under the direction of Wyatt Brody, had the highest percentage of marines killed in action and the most number of medals bestowed for valor. It was a model unit. Members, it appeared, were all hand-selected by Wyatt Brody himself.

So why would a man so dedicated to his unit want to kill one of his own? Lou had been sick with worry for Hector. If he had been captured by Brody's Palace Guards, it seemed reasonable he would be tortured for whatever information they believed he possessed. Lou had filed a report with the Hayes Police Department, but it was obvious that jurisdiction presented a major obstacle to any investigation. The police could search the national forest and the woods behind the motel, but the base itself remained off-limits.

Lou was clicking through pages of Google images when something caught his eye. It was a photograph that had been uploaded to a Facebook page for Dr. Derek Vaughan, a retired professor. The picture showed a young Wyatt Brody, dressed in a cap and gown, receiving a plaque from a well-dressed man. The caption read:

> I present my favorite student, Wyatt Brody, graduating from the USU's MD/PhD program, the Dean's Medal for Research Excellence, 1985. His thesis: Studies on the Neurochemistry of Fear.

The Neurochemistry of Fear.

Lou sat motionless, staring at the screen. He knew the USU stood for Uniformed Services University of the Health Sciences, a university run by the federal government, with the mission of preparing graduates for service in the U.S. Medical Corps. He strained to put the pieces together. An MD/PhD does award-winning research into the neurochemistry of fear. Some years later, he founds Mantis, a company of marines with a remarkable record of bravery and the highest percentage of soldiers killed in action, coupled with the most medals of valor awarded.

Who are these marines? Lou wondered.

There was something unusual about Mantis Company, and Lou suspected the explanation had something to do with Wyatt Brody's thesis. He smiled grimly. This was the first step on the path toward unraveling the mystery. And he knew where to take the next one. He set his fingers on the keyboard. In seconds, he was connected to the website of the library of the Uniformed Services University.

THE NIMITZ LIBRARY, NAMED after Fleet Admiral Chester W. Nimitz, was a centerpiece of the campus of the U.S. Naval Academy in Annapolis. Lou approached the reference desk. The pert librarian, Adele Green, according to her nameplate, glanced up. "May I help you?" she asked.

"Yes, I called ahead," Lou said. "I'm the D.C. doc from—"

"Dr. Welcome," she said, smiling. "You wanted to read Wyatt Brody's thesis paper from 1985."

He returned her smile. She reached below her desk and removed a modestly thick eight-and-a-half-by-eleven leather-bound book.

"Funny," she said. "We have theses that don't get requested at all for decades. You're the second person who asked to see this one."

The statement instantly grabbed Lou's attention. "Oh? That's interesting. I wonder who else was researching Wyatt Brody."

"I have it right here," Green said, checking her screen. "Oh, my. The last borrower was our congressman, Elias Colston. It's awful what happened to him. Just terrible."

Adele Green's revelation hit Lou like a spear. Elias Colston was not only interested in Wyatt Brody, he had uncovered the unusual subject of the man's PhD thesis. *But why?*

Lou took the volume and settled in a carrel, then flipped open the bound thesis and read the title page: "Studies on the Neurochemistry of Fear: Clinical Experiments and a Review of the Literature."

The bulk of Brody's research, Lou quickly gleaned, focused on the centers in the midbrain known as the amygdala and the hypothalamus. Wyatt Brody had formed solid, fascinating hypotheses, and his laboratory work seemed to bear his theses out. Brody's experiments involved rats that were programmed with electrical shocks to fear specific benign stimuli, such as a pet toy or a specific food. Brody homed in on a number of structures that created the state of fear. Then he set out to identify the neurotransmitter chemicals produced and released by those structures and developed theories on how to block the fear reactions.

At the center of Brody's work on the neurochemical blockade of emotional arousal was a set of receptors located throughout the midbrain. This portion of Brody's thesis seemed to Lou to be less authoritative. It appeared that Brody had identified three or four transmitters, but his ability to block these transmitters with chemicals had not been clearly worked out.

Strange, Lou thought. It was as if Brody had lost interest in his work.

He read through the final portion of the thesis. The most promising antagonist versus the fear centers of the midbrain was methamphetamine. In its back-alley form, methamphetamine looked like rock candy and carried the name crystal meth. But if there was a practical application for the drug, the future creator of Mantis did not spell it out.

Bleary, Lou took some final notes and then prepared to return the thesis. Nearly four hours had passed. During those hours, some doors had been opened, but a myriad of questions remained. He flipped absently to the last page of the volume—the dedication.

Instantly, Lou experienced a midwinter chill.

Dedicated with deepest respect to my mentor, friend, and advisor, Admiral Spencer Hogarth.

LOU sat in the waiting room of Devlin and Rodgers's opulent law offices, nervously tapping out bongo riffs on his briefcase. He had not been in contact with Sarah since the break-in. He feared that what relationship existed between them had vanished along with Elias Colston's CD. But he had to admit, Sarah had made a strong impression on him both as an attorney and as a woman.

As a lawyer, she would want to be made aware of all the evidence, including what Lou had uncovered regarding Mantis and Wyatt Brody. He had been waiting for ten minutes when she emerged from behind a paneled door, dressed sharply in a gray business suit and crisp white linen shirt. Her expression, as usual, was stony.

"We'll go to my office," she said, not bothering with a greeting. Lou followed her down a lengthy corridor to an office decorated with tasteful, understated elegance. Light from a gray, overcast day filtered in through floor-to-ceiling windows. Her space featured a leather sofa with two chairs and built-in mahogany bookshelves filled with legal tomes. There was a photograph on display of a tall, well-conditioned man standing beside a kayak. Lou sensed that it was her late husband, David.

"So, did you come here to tell me that you found the CD?" Sarah said, settling in behind a desk roughly the size of a polo pitch.

"Look, Sarah," Lou said, "I've decided to issue one blanket apology that will cover all my wrongdoings, including not being more careful with the CD. You're going to have to forgive me if you want my help."

"Is that what you've been doing?" she scoffed. "Helping me?"

"I'm more helpful than you know . . . so far," Lou said.

Sarah set her elbows on the desk and leaned forward, her eyes mischievous. "Please, enlighten me," she said.

Lou began with his attempt at creating a transcript of the CD. "After I gave up," he continued, "I called Jeannine Colston." Lou detailed the conversation and his subsequent meeting with Hector. Color drained from Sarah's cheeks as he recounted the events in Hayes and the chase through the woods, which ended with the frigid death of the Palace Guard marine who was chasing him.

"Look me in the eyes and tell me you're not making this up."

"There's more," he said. "Much more."

Sarah listened, spellbound as Lou took her through the Mantis fortress, Brody, and his gun gallery. "He was preparing to send me back to town alone along a mile of trail," he said. "It's hard to believe there wouldn't have been some of the boys from the woods waiting out there for me. If the cops hadn't shown up and been brought to the office by one of the soldiers, I guarantee you I'd have been frozen toast."

Sarah rose from her chair, turned away from Lou, and gazed out the window. When she turned back, her arms were folded tightly across her chest. "Who is Wyatt Brody?" she asked.

"Funny you should ask," Lou said, unclasping his briefcase. He extracted a folder of notes and photocopies and set them on the desk. Then he went over his hours in the library.

Sarah scanned the notes. "You mention that Brody seemed to

stop writing analytically as he got near the end of the thesis. What do you make of that?"

Lou shrugged. "It stuck out, is all I can say."

"Do you think it means that his experiments were a failure?"

Lou met her gaze and could tell she knew exactly what he was thinking. "Or a success," he said.

"I'll read through this later. What next?"

Lou had been waiting for this moment. "Take a look at this." He slid the dedication page across to her.

Her reaction lit the room. "It's dedicated to Spencer Hogarth!"

"I couldn't believe it when I saw it."

"So, what do we do now?"

Lou grinned.

"What?" she said. "What's so funny?"

"You just said 'we.' That's all. You said, 'What do *we* do now?' "

"Okay, you got me. We're a 'we' on this thing starting right now. That said, I think I should start with an apology of my own—an apology for treating you the way I have."

"You can say what you want, but I believe I already know." Sarah's eyebrows rose. "Have you been researching me?"

"No," Lou said, "but my thirteen-year-old has. I told her you and I weren't getting along, and I didn't know why. She went online and learned about your . . . your husband's doctor."

"Fair enough. I'm dealing with it the best I can, but sometimes the whole thing just pops out. That's about the most I can say."

"That's more than enough. If you ever want to talk, I'm here."

"Thanks. So, what now? We can't use this thesis to go and get subpoenas. A decent judge would laugh me out of her chambers."

"No," Lou said, "but we can try to figure out if something on that missing CD cost Elias Colston his life."

"Like what?" Sarah asked, flipping through Lou's notes.

"Like Reddy Creek," Lou said. "Colston asked Hector if he knew anything about someplace called Reddy Creek, but he said he didn't. Colston read in some reporter's blog that two Mantis soldiers were killed there. I looked it up. No blog that I could find. It's a military armory in Raleigh, North Carolina. That's all I've learned so far. I can't find any mention of soldiers being killed there."

"Two dead marines at a U.S. armory . . . a blog written by a reporter . . . and no trace of either now. I smell a cover-up."

"Then I'll keep looking."

"No, let me take this one. We're a 'we,' remember. I'll start with my boss, Grayson. He knows everybody. If anybody can find this missing reporter from North Carolina, it's my boss."

"Terrific. I'll keep digging on Brody and Hogarth. Meanwhile, if there's anything you want me to convey to Gary, just let me know."

Sarah's eyes sparkled. "You did it, Doctor! You did it."

"What did I do? What?"

Her smile was to die for.

"Rather than charging off to meet with Gary, you asked."

ANOTHER graveyard shift came and ended. Buoyed by thoughts of his new connection with Sarah, Lou headed out of the hospital to the doctors parking lot. At the head of his to-do list was purchasing a ticket from Dulles International to Minneapolis and arranging for the rental car he would drive to the Pine Forest Clinic in Shockley. The medical director of the clinic, Dr. Gerald Sherwood, had agreed to give him a one-hour consultation, but to get even that, Lou had been forced to bend the purpose of his visit.

The clinic, according to a modest website, was an exclusive facility for the diagnosis and treatment of medical and neurological disorders. Payment had to be in cash or cashier's check at the time of the visit. Lou discarded the notion of mentioning James Styles of Bowie, Maryland, the name on the envelope he had found in Elias Colston's drawer.

As Lou wended his way between buildings to the doctors lot, he saw a uniformed cop slipping a ticket beneath his driver-side windshield wiper. His cruiser was parked a few feet away.

"Hey!" Lou shouted. "What's going on?"

The officer gave Lou a curious look. "You haven't got a sticker. That means you get a ticket."

"Nobody has a sticker—just look around."

The cop sheathed his ticket book like he was holstering a gun, climbed into the cruiser, and opened the window. "Have a great day," he said. "And make sure you look your ticket over carefully."

The patrol car turned into an open row and then drove away.

Lou slid the ticket out from beneath the wiper, brought it into the car, and turned on the interior light. One side looked like a standard orange ticket. On the other side was a note.

> Dr. Lou Welcome,
>
> You have to be careful, but you have to trust somebody. You can trust me. The police officer who gave you this ticket is a marine and a good friend of Elias Colston. We want to get to the truth about Elias's killer. Meet me Tuesday at the following coordinates: 38.84783,-76.73744. Nine p.m. sharp. Stay hidden beyond the wood line. You'll know when I arrive.
>
> Steve Papavassiliou (Mark Colston's Papa Steve)

You'll know when I arrive.

What had Papa Steve Papavassiliou meant by that? Judging from the way he had delivered his message and the use of map coordinates, the man was either an inveterate game player or paranoid, possibly both. Lou did not feel particularly trusting of Papavassiliou. Nevertheless, he had decided to play.

A website allowing him to input the GPS coordinates pinpointed the ninth hole of a public golf course in Midwood, Virginia, twenty-five miles outside the district. It was half past eight when Lou arrived. Sharpton Hills Golf Club was dark and deserted. He walked out onto the ninth fairway. The night was cloudless, the ground blanketed with a thin layer of snow. Lou took up a position inside the nearby wood line and shivered away the cold. The cloudless night and bright moonlight afforded him a good view. He wondered how Papa Steve would make his arrival known.

You have to be careful, but you have to trust somebody.

Lou and Sarah had discussed the note by phone and agreed it

would make sense to go through with the meeting, but cautiously. Later, they would decide how far Papavassiliou could be trusted.

Nine o'clock arrived. No Papavassiliou. As each minute passed, Lou became more and more suspicious of a setup. What was Papavassiliou's connection with Brody? Did he have evidence that would exonerate McHugh? Were the Palace Guards approaching from the trees behind him? Lou scanned the woods. Nothing.

At that moment, he heard a faint machinery thrum. Half a minute later, he saw the powerful lights of a chopper—like an alien spacecraft cruising low across the rolling landscape. The helicopter dropped down right in front of him.

You'll know when I arrive. Nicely put.

Lou shielded his eyes from the blizzard created by the rotor-generated winds. Quickly, the engine and lights were cut off, and the door to the cabin opened. A tall, broad-shouldered figure jumped down, and Lou recognized him instantly. All at once, the timely arrival of the police that night at the Mantis headquarters no longer seemed like a fortuitous coincidence. Steve Papavassiliou worked on the base, and it was he who had saved Lou from Wyatt Brody.

"Told ya' you'd know when I got here, Dr. Welcome." He shook hands with a grip that would have pressed garlic.

"Why the helicopter?" Lou asked.

"I've been flying whirlybirds for about as long as I been blowin' things up. Got friends in the business, so I borrowed one of their toys. The men close to Brody, his Palace Guards, are tough and willing to do most anything for him. No matter how cautious I was, the Guards could follow me, at least on the ground. But no way could they keep up with me in the air."

"Why is Brody following you at all? What's going on with him?"

"What's going on is I think Brody murdered Elias."

"You have proof?"

"Call it strong suspicion."

"Not one of the Palace Guards?"

"Possible, but I doubt Brody would give any of them control over him like that. He's all about keeping control to himself."

Lou peered through the darkness at the man. To this point at least, he liked what he saw. "What can I do?" he asked.

"Brody's taken a liking to me since I moved over to Mantis, but he doesn't let anyone get too close. If he did kill Elias, I want to nail him. Elias and I have been through a lot together. I miss him. You can help me because that would mean helping your friend Gary McHugh. It would also be payback for Hector."

"Payback?" Lou took a step back. He could feel his jaw tighten.

"Searchers found his body late yesterday on a wild part of the base," Papa Steve said. "Word is he fell off a cliff and broke his neck. Died instantly. Apparently, he'd been drinking. People think he was despondent about the rumor that he was going to get the boot from Mantis. Some people think he might have jumped."

"That's a lie," Lou snapped. "I was in the woods when guys he said were the Palace Guard tried to kill him and me. It's all a setup orchestrated by Wyatt Brody."

Papa Steve's eyes flashed. "I already know that," he said. "Let's have a seat in the cockpit and talk where it's warm."

The interior of the helicopter was an aviator's dream, compact and loaded with high-tech gadgetry.

"I saw you at Mantis," Lou said. "I think you saved my life."

"So do I. I saw the ambulance bring you in. Hector was my godson's closest friend in Mantis. He asked if I thought he should meet with you. I told him I didn't see why not. The cops showed up because of the gunshots. I just led them to Brody."

"So what are we doing here?" Lou asked. "Now it seems we've got two killers to catch, Colston's and Hector's."

"We're after Wyatt Brody. He's all that matters. He has been up to something for years. I promised Elias when I transferred to Mantis that I would find out what that something is."

"So you'd been helping Colston investigate Brody?"

"That's the reason I transferred," Papa Steve said. "Colston wanted to shut down Mantis, not because his son died, but because he felt, as did others in Congress, that Mantis is redundant. It could be integrated with the SEALs and other Special Forces outfits for better efficiency. You can guess that was not a popular idea with Wyatt Brody. He'd promised to ruin Colston any way he could."

"He doesn't know about your connection with Colston?"

"Can't tell. You know the old adage, keep your friends close and your enemies closer. That may be what he's doing."

"And you think what Elias was doing in Congress gave Brody enough motive to commit murder?"

"Anybody who threatens Mantis puts themselves in harm's way."

"Including you."

"And you," Papavassiliou said.

"So, what have you found out?" Lou asked.

"No matter how much funding Colston hacked from Mantis, Brody always found a way around it. But Elias started squeezing too hard, and Brody finally decided to take him out."

"Where does that leave us then?" Lou asked.

"I need something from you. I've been following Dr. McHugh's case. I wondered if you knew his attorney, Sarah Cooper."

"I know her," Lou said.

"Well, I need to see the ballistics report on the slugs that killed Elias. You saw Brody's gun collection, right? I'm willing to bet one of those weapons was used to kill my friend. I need that ballistics report to narrow down the choices."

The bullets. Maybe Papavassiliou was completely on the level, but maybe Brody wanted to know if he had anything to fear from the ballistics report and had asked Papa Steve to find out.

"I'll see what I can do," Lou said. "But you're not going to be able to prove that Brody had the opportunity to kill Colston. He told me he was at a Marine Day parade the day Colston was murdered. People saw him in the stadium. He couldn't have been the shooter."

Papa Steve appeared unfazed. "I've been keeping an eye on Brody. He leaves the base at the same time every Wednesday."

"Where does he go?" Lou asked.

Papa Steve shook his head. "I don't know. He's not easy to follow. The Palace Guards keep a close watch on him. But I do know he goes someplace every Wednesday for three or four hours."

"You were at the parade, weren't you?" Lou said.

Papa Steve smiled. "I wanted to see if Brody would disappear from the parade, too. He walked out like he was headed to the bathroom. I followed him, but the Palace Guards picked up my tail, so I had to back off. Brody was headed toward Elias Colston's house."

Lou quietly pondered the implications. "So he's a liar, but I already knew that. What now?"

"You get me the ballistics report, and we take it from there."

CHAPTER 8

SARAH eased her rental car to a stop in front of the office of the *Belmore Current*. EASTERN MAINE AT YOUR FINGERTIPS, the sign over the front door proclaimed.

Sarah pulled on the door handle before realizing that the interior lights were off and the place was locked. Then she noticed a handwritten note secured to the door: *Gone to Laundromat. Be back soon.*

She headed across the street and traded the chilly morning air for the heat of the Laundromat. She saw a woman who was pretty and petite, with shoulder-length curly dark hair. She was dressed in jeans, boots, and a bomber jacket.

You've got to be Edith.

Finding this woman had proved to be no simple feat. Sarah had concluded that the mystery blogger had to have been a reporter in Raleigh. Grayson Devlin had contacts at the area newspapers. After two days, he called Sarah into his office. "Her name is Edith Harmon," he said. "She used to work for the *News and Observer*."

Sarah's eyes brightened. "That's great. Where is she at now?"

"She's dropped the Edith Harmon name and goes by Cassie Wilkins," Devlin said, glancing down at his notes. "She runs a small newspaper in Belmore, Maine."

"Why did she change her name and leave the paper in Raleigh?"

"Don't know. That's the information I got from her editor."

Years ago, he told her, Devlin and Rodgers had won a major libel suit that could have bankrupted the North Carolina newspaper. Edith's new identity had been a closely guarded secret, and Devlin had given his promise that her confidentiality would be protected by Sarah.

"I'm expecting you to come back from Maine with something that's going to help us win the Gary McHugh case," he said.

"I'll do my best," she said. It took every ounce of willpower to keep from telling Devlin what she really thought—how the McHugh case might extend to the highest levels of government and a massive conspiracy that Edith Harmon might very well hold the key to unlocking. Until Sarah and Lou learned more, they agreed it would be best to keep the reveals to a minimum.

Sarah's excitement at the prospect of finding Edith Harmon was tempered by one painful nagging question. *Can I go back to coastal Maine? Can I really do it?* Returning to Maine and reliving those magic days with David would be emotional, but she was unwilling to disappoint a teammate. Lou was genuine and down-to-earth—a great mix of toughness and spirit. She felt determined not to let him down.

As she drove past the sign welcoming her to Belmore, thoughts of her last time in the state filled her mind. It was summertime then, and she and David were on their annual road trip. The drive through Maine proved especially poignant because it was the last one they ever took. Six months after the trip ended, David turned his head to say good morning to her and paralyzed himself.

"Hey, sweetie—" *Snap.* Did she actually hear the spinal cord snapping, or was that just in her mind?

"David!" She cried out his name. Her husband's only response had been to stare up at the ceiling, wide-eyed and absolutely still.

David . . .

Standing just inside the Laundromat, Sarah inhaled the detergent-laden air, then walked down the row of machines to the petite woman folding clothes. "Cassie Wilkins?" Sarah asked.

The woman turned. Wearing dark, oversized sunglasses, she was perhaps forty, strikingly pale but pretty and feminine.

"Yes?" the woman said, not smiling. "Can I help you?"

"My name is Sarah Cooper. I'm an attorney from Washington. I was hoping to speak with you. About Reddy Creek."

"I'm sorry, but I don't know what you're talking about."

"You're Edith Harmon," Sarah said in an urgent whisper. "Please. I promise I'll keep your secret safe. An innocent man's life is at stake. I just need to know what you can contribute that will help my case."

"You want to know what I can contribute?" the woman said. Angrily, she ripped off her glasses. Sarah reached her hand to her mouth and took a backward step. Edith Harmon's eyes were ringed by gruesome scars. Her milky gray eyes showed no iris or pupil.

"I think I've contributed enough," Edith said, unfolding a white cane resting beside her laundry basket. "I've contributed plenty."

Edith slipped on her sunglasses and went back to folding her laundry. Sarah stood several feet away, trying to figure her next move, when she noticed safety pins attached to various articles of clothing. One pin seemed to designate blue, two for green, and three for white.

"I'm not here to hurt you," Sarah said. "I'm not going to tell anybody your secret."

No response.

"Please, talk to me, Edith."

Still nothing. Edith continued meticulously about her business.

Sarah continued searching for an opening—any opening. "Do you use the pins to help you match your clothes?" she asked.

Edith turned around and faced Sarah. "Well now, attorney Cooper," she said, "you just earned yourself a point."

"I did? For what?"

"In all the time you've been standing here, you never once said I'm sorry, despite that it was clear when you came in you didn't know I was blind. I really detest pity."

Sarah laughed uncomfortably. "How could you tell?"

"I heard your feet scrape against the floor when I took off my glasses. You took a step backward, surprised by something unexpected."

"You're right, of course, but like it or not, I am sorry. And I want to know if your blindness is related to Reddy Creek. I want to know why you ran from North Carolina."

Edith folded a white blouse into four perfect creases. "I've been dreading someone would track me down. And if you found me, they can find me. Who was it? Who gave me up?"

"Can we go somewhere and talk?" Sarah asked.

Edith tucked her laundry basket under one arm and used her free hand to hold her cane. "Come to my office. I'll give you ten minutes. I'm not promising to answer your questions. But you'll answer mine. Got it?"

Once outside, Edith found the curb with several practiced taps of her cane, then walked unhurriedly across the street. She found the key to unlock the *Current*'s front door. Inside the office, Edith hung her jacket on the coat tree and motioned Sarah to do the same. Soon the two women were seated at a foldout table.

"What happened to your sight?" Sarah asked.

Edith held up a finger. "No, you first," she said. "How did you find me?"

Sarah told her about Grayson Devlin's contact at Edith's former paper. "We haven't told anybody else," she said.

Edith contemplated. "I have no place to go now," she said. "I'm not leaving Belmore. Even if they do come after me, they'll never find my son. He's the reason I ran. I knew they were capable of using my son to get at me. Nobody knows his real name or where he lives. His father took off before he was born."

"Who did this?" Sarah asked. "What happened to you?"

"I don't know exactly. I was working on an investigative piece on Reddy Creek Armory when a young soldier named Mike Fitz arranged a secret meeting with me, claiming no one would believe his story. According to him, two marines from Mantis Company—each had the tattoo of a mantis on his forearm above a ring of barbed wire—tried to rob the armory. Mike was on guard duty. There was a gunfight, and he shot and killed them both. His commanding officer took a report, and then everything disappeared. Somebody covered up the whole thing. The marines were reported as AWOL."

"Did this Mike know what they were trying to steal?"

"Weapons, naturally. Only the weapons they were after made little sense to him. There were better weapons to take—larger, more sophisticated ones. But they left those alone. Why? That was a big red flag for Mike. It seemed they knew what they were after from the get-go. They knew exactly what weapons to take. They were doing what marines are trained to do."

"And what's that?" Sarah asked.

"They were following orders. They were on a mission."

"How did they get inside the armory in the first place?"

"According to Mike, they couldn't have gotten in there without having access. Somebody arranged it."

"An inside job," Sarah said. "Who is this Mike?"

"Was," Edith corrected. "Mike Fitz is dead. He died when the car I was driving was forced off the road. He was in the passenger seat. His neck was broken. My face was so smashed that I lost my sight."

"You were forced off the road?"

"We were being followed," Edith said. "Whoever it was waited until we were on a winding stretch of road before sideswiping us and forcing my car off a cliff. It was night, and there were no witnesses. As far as the police were concerned, I lost control of my car. I had no way of proving otherwise."

Sarah shook her head in disbelief.

"My boss, Bruce, wouldn't run the story about Reddy Creek when I brought it to him. We didn't have a credible source."

"I don't get it," Sarah said. "You had Mike."

"Not exactly. After the cover-up at Reddy Creek, surprise, surprise, Mike was dishonorably discharged on a trumped-up drug charge. Bruce thought Mike was just out for revenge and didn't believe there was any cover-up."

"Your blog," Sarah said. "You wrote the blog because you couldn't get your article published."

Edith removed her dark glasses again, displaying the scarring. "Guess I found a way of convincing Bruce that Mike was legit."

"We can't let this go," Sarah said. "We've got to find out who did this to you and why."

"Let me ask you something," Edith said. "Why do you care so much?"

"Because Elias Colston, the congressman whom my client is in jail for allegedly murdering, was asking questions about Reddy Creek before he was killed. I suspect if we connect the dots, we'll find a link to whoever killed Mike and came close to killing you."

Edith stood quickly and turned her back to Sarah. "I'm afraid our ten minutes ended a while ago," she said softly.

Sarah stood as well. She came around and took hold of Edith's slender wrists. "An innocent man is going to be sentenced to death for a crime he didn't commit," she said. "Nothing can be done to take back what happened, but you can still fight. You can still hurt these people. You can still help me get to the truth."

"Why me? I'm just a blind reporter from a small-town paper. You have the power of a major Washington law firm."

Sarah took hold of Edith's hands. "No, I'd be blind if I thought I could do this without you. But if you feel you'd be putting your son at risk in any way, just tell me, and I'm out of here. I mean it."

"No, he's with cousins. He's the one who's kept me going when I started coming apart. He also encouraged me to find a way to protect myself." She reached in the pocket of her cardigan and extracted a small pistol—a derringer with piggybacked barrels and a jewel-inlaid handle. "Give me a noise, and I'll give you a hole. Wanna see?"

"No, thanks, Edith. I believe you."

Edith broke into an intense smile. "Ever since I was blinded, I've been waiting for two things to happen. First, for my boy to grow up to the point where he can go out in the world and live his life. Then, for my eyes to show up here in Maine so I can get revenge on the bastards who did this to me. Sarah, will you be my eyes?"

"You know I will," Sarah said.

"In that case, I have more to share with you."

IT WAS a Wednesday morning. From the moment Steve Papavassiliou lifted off the fairway of the Sharpton Hills Golf Club, Lou had been obsessed with finding out where Wyatt Brody had been going every Wednesday. If Papavassiliou's suspicions were right, two Wednesdays ago, during a military parade, Brody had veered off his usual destination and shot Elias Colston to death.

Today, Lou's problem would be to keep Brody in sight without ending up in Palace Guard handcuffs again. From what Papa Steve reported, the Guard returned to camp after an hour or so, leaving Brody to tend to his business alone.

Weather was no problem. Freezing or just above. Bright sky, scattered clouds. Patches of snow. Lou positioned himself down a cross street, not far from the entrance to the camp. The road from the Mantis base was two lanes wide and emptied into State Route 10. Traffic out of the base was light.

Lou checked his watch. Five minutes past ten. At that moment, a silver BMW sedan came barreling out from the access road and rocketed down Route 10. Behind the wheel, wearing aviator sunglasses, was Wyatt Brody. Lou put his Toyota in gear. The BMW was already accelerating south and in seconds would be out of sight. There was no sign of the Palace Guards. Five seconds more, Lou decided, glancing at the highway. Then a military Range Rover with two men in front rumbled out of the access road. Both men wore sunglasses similar to Brody's, and one of them was speaking into a two-way.

Lou waited until the Rover disappeared after Brody, then pulled out onto Route 10. Gradually, traffic increased, but the military SUV was easy to spot. He could do this.

Half an hour passed. Route 10 had expanded into four lanes. The Range Rover was a reasonable distance ahead, but Brody's silver BMW was nowhere. That was when Lou saw the blue strobes flashing in his rearview mirror. A Statie!

Thirty minutes on the road, and the game was already over.

Lou slowed, signaled right, and pulled over.

Officer, I was following the man I believe murdered Congressman Colston. I was going as fast as he was, but I'm the one who got caught.

Lou tried out the truth, rejected it, and was searching for a substitute when he was asked for the usual documents.

The trooper, an impressively buxom woman with a pretty enough face, looked sexy in her black tie, broad-brimmed hat, and stately olive of the West Virginia State Police. She spent a few minutes in her cruiser checking him out, then returned bearing papers. She said, "You're not in line to make the drivers' hall of fame, Doc. You changed lanes without signaling. We frown on that in West Virginia. What kind of doctor are you?"

"I'm an emergency doc in D.C. Eisenhower Memorial."

"Well, Doc, this is your lucky day. Believe it or not, but you might have saved my mother's life last year. Somebody in your ER did. She had a coronary while she was on a tour of D.C. Needed to get fibrillation. It saved her life."

"And she's doing okay now?"

"She's doing terrific. Nice of you to ask. And because you're a nice guy, I'm just giving you a warning."

"Thank you, Officer."

"Lemon. Judy Lemon. Here's my card in case you find yourself in these parts again." She fished one out from what seemed like a stack of fifty. "Also, you might want to slow down. You were five mph away from getting nailed for that."

"You got it, Officer Judy. Slow."

"No sense in speeding. There's a backup ahead. Construction."

Lou felt his pulse jump. A backup. His brain worked through the possibilities. At that moment, he glanced across the road in time to see the Mantis Range Rover approaching from the other direction, headed back toward Hayes. No silver BMW in sight.

Had the king separated from his Palace Guards?

Lou put himself into modest flirt mode. "Listen, Officer Judy, I really do appreciate just getting a warning."

"You're welcome."

"You were just doing your job."

"Sounds like there's something more you'd like to say." Her smile oozed pheromones.

"With that construction you told me about, getting stopped has made me hopelessly late for an appointment. How about a trade? If you could guide me past the holdup, I promise you dinner at the restaurant of your choice. Believe me, I'm good for it."

The trooper gave Lou's offer some thought. "You know what they say about scorning a woman with a gun," she said playfully.

"I don't know, actually, but I can guess. No scorning. Promise."

"I like steak."

"You got it. The biggest, juiciest one in the county."

"Deal. Follow me, cowboy."

Officer Lemon hurried back to her cruiser. Her strobes flashed on, and they cruised in the breakdown lane past a long, frustrated line of motorists. After half a mile, Lou spotted the silver Bimmer, pulled on his faded Redskins cap, and slouched down in his seat.

A quarter of a mile past the construction, Lou slowed, pulled off the road, and gave Officer Judy Lemon a thumbs-up and a good-bye wave. Minutes later, Wyatt Brody sped past, paying no attention to anything other than the road ahead.

Brody turned west toward Billingham, eventually coming to an industrialized section of town. Auto repair shops lined both sides of the road, tucked between a few fast-food joints and a number of warehouses, many of them corrugated steel. Lou watched the BMW glide into the parking lot of a self-storage facility.

Lou cruised down the access road, then shifted to Park and moved ahead on foot. He worked his way along the side of the last unit. The BMW stood idling beside an open storage door. A white, windowless panel truck backed out. Brody pulled the truck over and replaced it in the garage with his Bimmer. Then he used a pull-cord to lower the door and replaced the heavy padlock.

Lou raced back to the Toyota. He shifted into Drive, waited for a pickup to insert itself between him and the van, and followed.

THE RIDE SOUTH WOULD HAVE been quite beautiful had Lou taken more than a few seconds at a time to appreciate it. The Mononga-hela Mountains seemed to be constantly shifting against the pale early-afternoon sun. The road was winding, and he was forced to stay closer to Brody's van than he would have liked. Lou had been following Brody for almost two hours.

Lou's initial adrenaline rush was gone, replaced by the tension of losing the white van at any turn. Then he eased around a sharp bend and spotted Brody's brake lights. The van turned right. The road, if it could be called such, was an unmarked path cut into the woods—twin ruts that ran upward along the side of a foothill.

Violent jolts from rocks and holes snapped Lou's teeth together more than once. The Toyota skidded sideways in places. Then he saw the van brake and stop in something of a clearing, perhaps a hundred yards ahead. Cautiously, Lou backed up until the road flattened. There was enough room behind a huge boulder to pull his car over and conceal it. He opened his door and eased out into the chilly mountain air. From above, he could hear that Brody was keeping the truck idling.

Lou decided to chance the slope to his right. If he could get high enough, he would be looking down on the van. He pulled him-self up by icy tree trunks and rocks and crawled out onto a rocky bluff that featured enough brush for some concealment. He heard the rumble of an approaching vehicle. A second van, identical to Brody's, jounced down the hill and skidded to a stop almost nose to nose with Brody's van. The doors flew open, and two men stepped out. Moments later, the back of the truck creaked open, and three more men emerged. Latinos. Maybe Mexicans. Brody climbed out of his truck. One of the men saluted him.

"Manolo," Brody said, his voice carrying through the chilly air.

The other four arrivals circled to the back of Brody's panel truck and pulled the doors open. The moves were practiced. They'd done this many times before. Two of the men jumped into the back of the truck, while two others positioned themselves to receive the cargo. Brody stood silently beside the heavyset man named Manolo. Lou sensed what the crew was off-loading even before he saw one of the wooden cases pried open. Guns. And lots of them.

Brody stood a few paces away as Manolo inspected the cargo.

"These are good," he said to Brody, hefting one of the rifles. "Very good. Our people in Juárez will be pleased. All M4s?"

"Easier to get now that we've scaled back in Afghanistan."

Hello, Reddy Creek, Lou was thinking, mentally dropping one piece of the Brody puzzle into place. Brody ponies up weapons to a Juárez cartel in exchange for . . . for what?

One of Manolo's men opened the rear of the second panel truck and lugged out a huge cooler. Then another. As Lou watched from above, Manolo set one of the coolers on the ground at Brody's feet and opened the top. White vapor from dry ice billowed upward.

"This is the best batch we've cooked yet," Manolo said, extracting a plastic bag. "Seven hundred capsules per bag, Señor Colonel."

"I've told you," Brody growled, "don't screw with the formula."

Formula . . . Lou tensed.

"We make it better," Manolo said. He whistled loudly using two fingers, and a man, thin as the leafless branches overhead, approached.

"*Sí?*"

Lou could only ferret out a few words—one of them *Pedro.*

Brody brought a thermos from the passenger seat of his van and poured a clear red liquid into a small plastic cup.

"Why don't you tell me what that drink is?" Manolo asked.

"Do you tell your wife the name of your mistress?" Brody responded. "It is enough to know that what you make does not work without what my other source makes. It is better that way, *sí?*"

"I suppose so. My wife and my mistress. I like that one, señor."

The man, Pedro, took the cup of crimson liquid and swallowed it in one gulp along with a capsule.

"How long has this man been taking the formula?" Brody asked.

"A month, more or less. Every day."

Manolo went to the front seat of his truck and brought back what Lou thought might be a portable electrocardiogram machine.

Pedro unzipped his jacket and unbuttoned his shirt, baring his chest. Manolo pasted on several electrodes to Pedro's chest. Then Manolo gave Brody the cardiogram machine to hold.

Lou watched from above as Manolo pulled a revolver from the waistband of his pants. He chambered a round and showed Brody the weapon was loaded with a single bullet. He snapped his wrist and locked the cylinder back in place. Dramatically, he spun the cylinder fast enough to make the sound of a whirling roulette wheel.

Then he handed the gun to Pedro.

Lou did not need Spanish to interpret Manolo's instructions.

Pedro calmly slid the muzzle of the weapon into his mouth. Then he pulled the trigger.

Click. Empty chamber.

Smiling, Pedro handed the gun to Brody, who fired at a tree twice before a shot rang out and splintered wood. Then he handed the revolver to Manolo and studied the machine. "This reaction is spectacular," he said. "What did you guys do?"

"We made it better," Manolo said. "Better, purer ingredients."

"The meth?"

"New cook. New recipe."

Brody simply nodded.

The transfer continued in silence. The man, Pedro, who had cheated death, went right back to off-loading weapons. Brody returned the plastic bag to the dry ice and checked to be certain the coolers were secure in his van. Then, without another word, he climbed into the cab of his truck and headed down toward the highway. Manolo turned his truck around and headed back up the mountain.

Lou clambered down to the clearing and began following the van tracks uphill. Guns for drugs. Mantis and some sort of Mexican cartel. Was this the knowledge that had gotten Elias Colston killed?

About thirty minutes up the hill, the woods thickened. Lou trudged ahead, keeping a sharp eye out for guards. In a clearing up ahead a dilapidated structure drew his attention.

The ramshackle building, a drug cartel version of a still, Lou guessed, was made of corrugated steel and framed with rough wooden beams. White smoke with the pungent odor of ammonia wafted out from the smokestacks. The white truck was parked to the right of the building. Pedro and three others were taking guns from the back of the truck. Lou watched from behind a large pine.

Drugs for guns. Some sort of superamphetamine for M4s.

A classic barter. Manolo emerged from inside the still. Leashed to his wrist was a large German shepherd. The dog's keen ears were bent back. The animal's nostrils flared, and its head darted about.

Was the dog a coincidence, or did they suspect something?

Manolo started to walk down the road toward Lou. The shepherd's lips peeled back in an angry snarl. A growl, low and threatening as thunder, echoed off the trees. Then its growl turned into angry barking, and its jaws began snapping. Lou felt a wave of heat roll up his back. The animal was looking right where he was hiding.

"What's happening?" one of the gang asked.

"Matador's in a bad mood. Maybe he smells something—a rabbit or a rat. Pedro probably left the lid off the trash again."

Matador. The name meant bullfighter, but it also meant killer.

Lou's mouth went dry.

Manolo battled to keep the shepherd in line and began scanning the woods for the source of the animal's angst.

It would not be long before he discovered the answer.

Despite the chill surrounding him, Lou was sweating. Matador had downshifted to a low, rumbling growl. Lou desperately played through scenarios of escape and found none that had any promise. He kept his body rigid, trying to control his ragged breaths. *Breathe in through the nose . . . out through the mouth, like I'm in the ring.* The gospel according to Cap Duncan.

Manolo tied the snarling animal to a post and went back to the still. Lou backed up carefully and added ten yards to the distance between him and death. A couple of more moves and he would break for the Camry. He hunched over and took another precious ten yards. Then another. Manolo returned and again took Matador's leash. Lou seized the distraction and raced to another tree.

Manolo yanked on Matador's leash, trying to force the dog to heel.

Lou dropped to his butt and worked his way down the mountain. The rocks tore through his jeans and left painful scrapes on his legs. He could still hear excited barking but could not tell if the sounds were getting closer. Finally, he risked pulling himself to his feet.

Almost there.

Lou eased around the clearing where the guns-for-drugs exchange had taken place. Maybe seventy-five yards to go. The time for caution was over. He began to trot down toward the boulder where he had concealed the Toyota. From up the hill, he heard the sound of crunching ice and leaves, followed by an intense growl. Then Lou saw Matador streaking across the ridge, dragging his leash.

Lou broke into a sprint. His feet skidded on the icy slope, slowing his steps. He saw the front of his car poking out from behind the boulder. Behind him, no more than fifty feet away, the streaking brown missile headed down the embankment. His teeth were bared.

Then Lou tripped. He fell heavily, air exploding from his lungs. His face snapped against the ground, dazing him. Still, he managed to roll to his back. His hand wrapped around a dead branch.

He was scrambling to his feet when the blurred outline of Matador came into sharp focus—ten feet away and about to go airborne. Instinctively, Lou turned sideways and gripped the end of the branch with both hands. The shepherd's jaws were wide open. Lou tightened his grip on the branch, then swung. The impact was ferocious. Matador went down heavily, yelping plaintively.

Lou sprinted the remaining five yards to the car, climbed into the driver's seat, slammed the door, and fumbled his key into the ignition. Then he felt the weight of the car shift forward. Through the windshield, Matador stood on the hood, snarling, teeth bared. Lou turned the key and slammed the gearshift into reverse.

The shepherd jumped off the hood, landing on its feet. Lou backed down the road, turned onto the highway, and accelerated north.

CHAPTER 9

WYATT Brody strode into the dining hall. Seven hundred marines remained seated along spartan wooden benches. Set out on the table in front of each of them was a seven-ounce plastic tumbler, filled halfway with a clear crimson liquid. Next to each tumbler was a capsule, also crimson. The daily ritual had begun.

Major Charles Coon followed close behind Brody.

"Attention!" he called out as they reached their table.

The sound of benches scraping back echoed through the hall as the soldiers of Mantis rose to their feet, a forest of the bravest fighters the military had to offer. The men were waiting for Brody's selection for the morning presentation. The honor was not doled out lightly. Typically, one of the other officers led the men, but at times an enlisted man who strongly embodied the principles of Mantis would be selected for the privilege. The seven hundred waited for Brody's selection for the morning presentation.

"Staff Sergeant Bucky Townsend!" Brody called out.

"Sir! Staff Sergeant Bucky Townsend, present, sir!" he shouted.

"Staff Sergeant Townsend, come forward to present."

Townsend stood beside Brody and saluted, his arm at perfect angles. *He was Mantis.*

"My brothers," Townsend said, "glasses up."

Moving as a single entity, each man held a capsule in one hand and his drink in the other. "Crimson is the color of courage," they said in unison, "the color of blood spilled in battle, the color of valor. To justice. To country. To God. To Mantis. Whatever it takes!"

Then, as one with their commanding officers, each set the capsule on his tongue and drained the symbol of their collective strength and bravery. They were Mantis, a brotherhood bound by the power of the crimson liquid.

When breakfast ended, Brody once again addressed the men. He read twenty names from a clipboard—the tactical team of Operation Talon. "We will convene in the briefing room immediately."

"Sir, yes, sir," the twenty responded.

The briefing room was situated inside a crude wooden building. There were maps, projection machines, and several computers. Coon stood at the front, with Brody seated at a desk to his right.

"Gentlemen," Coon began, "you are the men who will be feet on the ground. The success of this mission rests in your hands."

"As this is the first time we're all together," Townsend said, "could you review the overall strategy of the mission?"

"Of course, Sergeant. We will take out ten high-value terrorist targets in a simultaneous, synchronized strike. The targets are in ten different geographic locations, five different countries."

"Will we be using drones in the attack?"

"Negative," Coon said. "We cannot use drones without risking high civilian casualties and significant global blowback. We need visual confirmation of our targets before making any kill."

"Are we still going to be deployed in ten teams of two?"

"Ten teams of two is correct," Coon said.

"What's the timing of this?"

"Deployment in five days or less. What else?"

"And after we locate our target?"

"Each team will infiltrate a suspect location, verify the validity of the target, and use a bomb to kill that target. Any team who does not make visual confirmation will wait for their target to show before detonation. We want ten dead in a twenty-four-hour period."

"Where will we procure the explosives?"

Coon turned to Brody, who stood and faced the men.

"You will be wearing them," he said.

Lou found a stretch of highway that offered reliable cell phone reception. His hands were still trembling as he keyed in Sarah's number. If Lou's suspicions were correct, then the murder of Elias Colston was part of a major conspiracy involving supremely powerful players who would stop at nothing to protect their secrets.

Sarah answered, and Lou felt his spirits lift at the sound of her voice. "I've been worried sick about you," she said. "Are you all right?"

"Well, considering I almost became a can of Alpo, I'm doing just fine." Lou recounted for her Wyatt Brody's guns-for-drugs exchange and his own close encounter with Matador.

"Why is Brody involved with Mexican drugs?" Sarah asked.

"The cartel's chemist is concocting the drug Brody created for his thesis—a drug that eliminates fear. Sarah, you should have seen how calmly this guy Pedro played Russian roulette. He was absolute ice. One of the ingredients of Brody's juice is methamphetamine, which isn't something easily obtained via a military purchase order. I'm certain he's using this concoction on Mantis soldiers."

"For what reason?"

"That I don't know," Lou said.

"So how does this connect to Reddy Creek?" Sarah asked.

"I've been thinking," Lou said. "Logic leads us to a conclusion that's irrefutable. We agree that Reddy Creek is Mantis, right?"

"According to Edith, the two marines who were killed raiding the armory had Mantis tattoos. So yes, Reddy Creek is Mantis."

"And we agree that Brody is Mantis. And Brody's thesis is dedicated to whom?"

"Spencer Hogarth," she said. "I got it."

"So if Hogarth is Brody and Brody is Mantis and Mantis is Reddy Creek then . . ."

"Then Hogarth is Reddy Creek," Sarah said.

"I think the whole business goes far beyond Reddy Creek. I can't imagine Brody hits the same supply depot each time he needs to feed the cartel. And I suspect Brody would need somebody high up to help him pull it off. Somebody with enough political capital to buy the information and cooperation to make this scheme work."

"Hogarth," Sarah said in a half whisper. "Would he know if Wyatt Brody killed Elias Colston to keep him quiet?"

"It's possible," Lou said. "Even if he doesn't know, we can help him find out. He's not going to want to be embroiled in any major scandal. Not with his political ambitions on the line. Either way, we get Gary McHugh off, which is our goal here."

"That's not our only goal," Sarah said. "I promised Edith I'd help her find the people responsible for blinding her and killing Mike Fitz. Now I know where to start."

"All roads lead to Hogarth," Lou said.

"I'll get a meeting with him. I'll make it happen."

"You've got to be careful."

"We'll keep our backs to the wall, don't worry. Meanwhile you need to hang low. Let Edith and me work on Hogarth. And remember, Brody may not know it was you there in the forest, but he's been alerted someone may be onto him, and you're on a very short list of people that might be."

"Consider me hung low," he said. Lou cringed at the notion he was holding back from Sarah but felt convinced his decision was the right one. Resting in his bureau drawer was a plane ticket for a flight tomorrow to Minneapolis.

THE Pine Forest Clinic was not for patients faint of wallet. The directions took Lou to a gated entryway with a uniformed guard who checked a guest list and passed him through to a sprawling mansion. A receptionist with a British accent gave him a clipboard of medical record forms. Lou felt certain he would not be kept waiting long, and he was not disappointed. The real question was how long he would last when the doctor learned the purpose of his visit.

The heavy mahogany door opened to Gerald Sherwood's office. The doctor was sixty or so with razor-cut graying hair and bright aquamarine eyes. From the instant of their meeting, Lou sensed for no particular reason that the man suspected the motive for this visit was something other than advertised.

As he walked to the chair across the desk from the doctor, Lou scanned the certificates on the walls. One of them caught his eye—

a diploma from the University of Virginia, Elias Colston's alma mater. It was hard to believe the connection was a coincidence.

"So, Mr. Welcome," Sherwood said in a rich, melodic voice, "it says here you have been having trouble with migraine headaches."

"Actually, Dr. Sherwood, I have never had a disabling headache in my life. I work in emergency medicine at Eisenhower Memorial in D.C." Lou remained focused on the man's eyes. "I need information about a patient of yours. James Styles of Bowie, Maryland." Lou passed across the envelope with Styles's name.

The spark in Sherwood's eyes was transient but revealing nonetheless. "You have made the long journey here for nothing. As a physician yourself, surely you know that even if this name meant something to me, I would never tell you. Confidentially is more than a word here. It is the way we attract patients and do business."

Lou slipped a photo of Elias Colston from his briefcase and set it next to the envelope. "Congressman Elias Colston was murdered two weeks ago in Maryland. I found this envelope in his desk while searching for clues as to who might have shot him." Lou waited for a reply, but there was none other than a shrug. "The man currently in jail for the murder, also a physician, is a friend of mine."

Nothing.

"I see you graduated from Virginia. Were you and Colston classmates? Did he come here for some medical problem?"

"Dr. Welcome," Sherwood said, "I will not answer any questions about any person. That's the way it is. Now, if you'll excuse me."

Lou stood and slipped the envelope into his briefcase, but he left the eight-by-ten head shot on the desk, facing his host.

"I'm a principled physician," Lou said before he turned to go, "but I am also capable of reasoning out ethical problems for myself. When push comes to shove, the most important voice I must listen to and answer to is the one inside my head that tells me what is right and what is wrong in any given situation. I believe my friend is innocent of murdering Elias Colston. At the moment, he is living in a cell in a Baltimore jail. You hold one of the clues that might help

252 | Michael Palmer

set him free—the clue as to whether the murder victim had any pre-existing medical conditions, and whether he came here under the assumed name of James Styles. If it is too difficult for you, you don't have to say anything. Just slide that picture back to me, and I will know."

Sherwood did not move. "Dr. Welcome, please don't force me to call security."

Leaving the photo, Lou turned and made his way back to where his car was parked. It was going to be a long trip home.

The Minneapolis–St. Paul airport was mobbed. He was wedged in line, shuffling toward the TSA screening equipment, when his cell phone began ringing.

"Dr. Welcome," he said.

The voice on the other end was a woman's with a British accent. "Dr. Welcome," she said, "you left a photo here today. The doctor says the answer to your question is yes."

LOU forced his eyes open. He was crammed on the living room sofa, a vicious kink in his neck. Diversity was nestled on his face. Consciousness returned grudgingly as he became fully awake.

"Hey, big fella," he said, gently setting the cat aside. Through the open blinds, dawn was just making an appearance. With no small effort, Lou stood and stretched.

Diversity meowed.

"How long has Wyatt Brody been hooked up with a Mexican drug cartel?" he asked the cat. "Is there any more information I could get from Dr. Sherwood?"

Diversity cocked his head.

"All you care about is tuna."

Lou noticed a brightly colored flyer lying beneath his front door. A restaurant menu. Lou retrieved the flyer, intending to move it to the trash. He'd never heard of a place called Al's All-American Grill. When Lou noted the address, his curiosity grew. The diner was located in Alexandria, Virginia, across the Potomac.

Lou flipped open the menu and saw a note in black marker.

Dear Doc,
  Come to the restaurant today between eight and noon.
  Your pal, Papa Steve

Two hours later, a small bell above the door announced Lou's entrance at Al's All-American Grill. About half of the diner's red leather booths were occupied. Lou strolled up and down searching for Papa Steve. No sign. Finally, he took a seat at a booth. A waitress with tousled dark hair took Lou's coffee order. She returned a moment later not only with coffee but also a plate of scrambled eggs and corn beef hash. "Our chef made it special for you."

Lou looked beyond the narrow passage between the counter and the kitchen and saw Papa Steve in a cook's apron waving at him with a spatula. "So, Doc, how do you like the hash?" he called out.

"You're a cook?" Lou said.

"Only once or twice a month, working for my buddy Alex." He gestured to the waitress. "She's been a friend for years."

Mark Colston's godfather removed his apron and announced that he was going on break. A moment later, he emerged through a set of swinging doors and took a seat in the booth across from Lou.

"Guess you got my message," said Lou. After calling Sarah from the highway, Lou had left a brief message for Papa Steve.

"It's not safe to talk by phone," Papa Steve said.

"Yeah, now I've seen firsthand how unsafe dealing with your commanding officer can be." Lou repeated the same story he had told Sarah. Papa Steve listened intently, his expression grim.

"So it's not just vitamins Brody's feeding us, eh?" he said.

"Is that what he told you it was? Vitamins?"

"Yup, a special blend. He's a doctor, you know. We were told the juice and capsules would boost our strength and immune systems."

"Now we know that somehow Brody is behind Elias's murder and why," Lou said. "We've just got to prove it."

"Well, my friend, you done good." Papa Steve moved closer. "Now it's time we nail the bastard. We're going to get the murder weapon in Wyatt Brody's gun case."

"What makes you think the murder weapon is there?"

"The ballistics report you faxed me," Papa Steve said. "The gun that killed Elias is a .45 ACP that fires slugs with a six left rifling mark. Brody has a few .45-caliber pistols but only one that fires a slug with that rifling mark. I took an inventory of Brody's .45-calibers and ran it by a friend of mine who knows guns. According to my source, the only match in Brody's collection is a Colt/U.S. Army 1911 .45 ACP five-inch barrel military pistol. Nice antique weapon. We get that gun, we run the ballistics test again, and we've got ourselves a murder weapon tied to the owner."

The notion of returning to the Mantis base held all the appeal of taking Matador for a walk. "I've been inside Brody's office, remember?" Lou said. "Assuming we can even sneak onto the base, his gun case probably has some seriously sophisticated locks."

"If push comes to shove, I can run a diversion and whip up a little something that will blow the office lock and then the display case. But it will reduce the operation to a snatch, grab, and run, and in addition to seven hundred soldiers, there are bound to be alarms."

"Well, I know someone," Lou said, "but I'm worried it's going to be too dangerous."

"If you want to help your doctor pal, we've got to take some risks. How good is your contact at B and E?"

"Cap is good at almost everything he does."

"Then bring him on board. It's great that Sarah is going after Hogarth. Power to her. But we can't trust that she'll get him to flip on Brody. We've got to have more evidence. So what do you say? Are you with me?"

Stealing a major piece of evidence was bound to sit poorly with Sarah and might trigger some sort of arcane courtroom battle. But not stealing it risked a different set of problems, including Wyatt Brody becoming wary of being a suspect in Elias Colston's murder and simply deep-sixing the gun in one of the base's lakes or bogs. And Cap would say yes in a heartbeat to doing his part with the locks despite the risk.

"I'm in," Lou said.

"We go on Tuesday. That gives us four days. Details to follow."

"Tell me something," Lou asked as he stood to go, "does the name James Styles mean anything to you?"

Papa Steve shook his head. "Nope. Why do you ask?"

"Oh, nothing," Lou said. "Just a name I came across while I was searching through Elias's desk."

LA CUCINA Dolce smelled of tomato sauce and Italian spices. Sarah took in the ambience of the elegant restaurant as the maître d' escorted her to a private dining room, unoccupied save for one corner table. Secretary of Defense Spencer Hogarth nodded in her direction as one of his three-man security detail helped her off with her coat. Another slid a wand from a black leather case and waved it around her body like a philharmonic maestro.

Recording devices. None found.

The maître d' escorted her to Hogarth's table. The secretary motioned her to a seat catty-cornered from him. "Would you care for anything to eat?" He gestured toward an antipasto appetizer. She had seen the man on television so many times that to see him in person crossed the threshold of surreal.

"We should keep this to business," she said.

"At least enjoy a glass of wine with me."

Hogarth filled the glass in front of Sarah from a half-empty bottle. She inspected the wine and took a sip. "Very nice," she said.

"It should be," Hogarth replied. "It's a Monfortino, 1997."

"Sounds expensive," Sarah said. "I sure hope that's not our tax dollars at work."

Hogarth responded with a tight, humorless smile.

"I'm the lawyer for Gary McHugh, in jail for murdering Elias Colston," Sarah began. "You may know that Dr. McHugh is innocent. I'm about to get the charges against him dropped, and one of those who will be moved up the list to chief suspect is you."

Hogarth's expression darkened. "I agreed to meet with you, Ms. Cooper, because Elias Colston was a friend of mine. I want to be of service to help bring his murderer to justice. I had no idea you were here to levy threats and allegations against me. If I had known that, I would have poured you a glass of less expensive wine."

"Secretary Hogarth, you can be of service if you tell me the truth. Did you kill Elias Colston?"

Hogarth huffed. "What motive could I have for killing an old friend? We've had our disagreements over military allocations, but we debate those differences, we don't start shooting over them."

"Does the name Reddy Creek mean anything to you?" Sarah gave Hogarth an enigmatic smile and took a swallow of wine.

"Reddy Creek is a town in North Carolina, I believe."

"It's also the name of one of your armories."

A spark of anger flared in Hogarth's eyes. "I do not enjoy having some lawyer show up at my restaurant, where I like to conduct my personal affairs, and fling unsubstantiated allegations at me."

Sarah was unruffled. "I can assure you, my allegations are anything but unsubstantiated."

"Enlighten me, then. Tell me what motive I would have for murdering my friend."

"The motive is that you've been feeding information to Wyatt Brody on gun shipments to armories along the East Coast. His men steal the weapons while someone on the inside covers up the thefts. The weapons are used to fund an illegal drug trade that benefits Mantis Company. How does that motive sound to you?"

"It sounds like something you could never prove," Hogarth said.

"Does proof really matter?" Sarah asked. "Your political ambitions are not exactly a closely guarded secret. I think one whiff of this scandal will be enough to derail your political career forever."

"What do you want, Ms. Cooper?"

"I want your help bringing down Wyatt Brody. That's what Elias Colston tried to do, and it cost him his life. I think Brody is the triggerman, and you're close enough to Brody to help us get him."

"You have nothing," Hogarth said, jabbing a finger at Sarah. "You think you can come in here and threaten me? Nobody threatens me, young lady, especially lawyers without any proof."

At that moment, the maître d' appeared in the doorway, escorting Edith Harmon. She was wearing dark glasses. The security team started after them, but Hogarth stopped them with a gesture.

"Over here," Sarah said.

Edith worked her way to the table using her folding cane. "Do you mind if I sit down?" she said to Hogarth.

"Who in the hell are you?" he demanded.

"This is my friend, Edith Harmon," Sarah said, studying Hogarth's expression for any glimmer of recognition. Not a flicker.

Edith took the seat next to Sarah. The two women had become friends, and Sarah felt emboldened by Edith. It was remarkably brave for her to confront the man who held some responsibility for her blindness.

"I have the invoices," Edith said flatly. "I don't know how you induced supply sergeants to cooperate, extortion or maybe just a little bribe. But I do know that we have the identity of at least one man behind the forged invoices."

"What is this woman talking about?" Hogarth said to Sarah.

She had defended enough criminals to know when one of her clients was lying, and Hogarth had just tipped his hand.

"She's talking about the invoices you had doctored," Sarah said. "The inventory at the armory needs to match the number of weapons shipped from the manufacturer. If there are fewer weapons than the invoices say should be on hand, questions will get asked by the auditors. But if the invoices are doctored, then Brody can divert a number of weapons, and nobody would even know to ask."

"This is ridiculous," Hogarth said.

"So one night," Edith said, "at Reddy Creek Armory there's a theft. Only there's a screwup. Maybe a guard gets sick. And a poor fellow named Mike Fitz gets caught in the middle and does his job, and two men with Mantis tattoos get killed, and he gets murdered."

"This is ludicrous," Hogarth snapped. "I don't need to take this sort of abuse from the likes of you."

"Are you referring to me?" Edith replied. "A blind woman? A woman whose life you helped to destroy? A woman who obtained the original invoices from the gun manufacturer who supplies

Reddy Creek? For all your power, Mr. Secretary, you don't know the half of what a woman like me can do to you."

A contemplative look washed across Hogarth's face. *Resigned,* Sarah thought. *He's going to cave.*

"What do you want me to do?" he asked finally.

"Mr. Secretary, if you want any hope of salvaging your political career, we need you to wear a wire and get Wyatt Brody to confess to Congressman Colston's murder." Sarah stood up from the table. "I'll give you twenty-four hours to make up your mind. If I don't hear from you by then, we go public with our information."

CHAPTER 10

FROM the moment Papa Steve first shared his plan to break into Mantis headquarters, Lou felt uneasy, but now he was more concerned than ever. Everything had been pushed up two days. To Cap's dismay, this meant less time to dust off his lock-picking skills.

Their meeting place, transmitted to Lou in another under-the-door menu, was twenty miles southeast of the Mantis base, near the town of Dudley. Following the plan, Lou left his car at a Dudley motel, and he and Cap walked half a mile out of town to the rendezvous point in the woods on the side of a dirt road. The bright sun did little to warm the chilly day. Even though Cap was wearing gloves, a jacket, and a fleece, he needed to dance his trademark boxing moves to keep warm.

Cap exhaled a weighty breath, sending up a cloud of vapor. "Welcome, I haven't had nerves like this since my last prizefight."

"If it makes you feel any better," Lou said, "I'm nervous, too."

Cap ruminated a moment. "Nah, that doesn't make me feel better at all." Then he smacked Lou playfully on the arm.

"Well," Lou said, "I've added a little contingency plan of my own just in case things come unglued."

Lou was about to explain when a green military truck appeared a quarter mile away. The canvas tarp covering the back shook and ruffled in the breeze. A minute later, it groaned to a stop. Papa Steve, wearing a fur-lined parka, hopped down from the cab. "Hiya, Cap," he said with a grin, taking Cap's hand. "It's a real honor. I was a big fan of yours back in the day."

"Thanks. Any friend of the doc's is a friend of mine."

"What happened?" Lou asked. "This wasn't supposed to go down so fast."

"Brody presented us with a situation too good to ignore," said Papa Steve.

"Can't we talk while we're driving?" Cap asked. "You must have some heat in the cab of that khaki junker."

"Actually, you boys won't be riding in the cab. You'll be under the chassis." Papa Steve knelt and pointed to a steel platform he had rigged to the undercarriage. "I've got a way to conceal the sides, but you've got to climb on the platform before I can secure it."

"You want us to ride under the truck for twenty miles?" Lou said.

"For a bit longer than that," said Papa Steve. "Until evening."

"That's hours from now!" Lou exclaimed.

"Can't we just ride in the back?" Cap asked.

Papa Steve shook his head. "The cargo in back is going to get inspected before I drive onto the base. It's too risky."

"What are you hauling?" Cap asked.

"Fireworks. Brody asked me to rig up a show. That's the reason I changed the plan. Only he's gonna get more than he bargained for."

"Talk to us," Lou said.

"It's the start of a mission. Operation Talon. Whatever it is, it must be important. Brody's got his crew selected, and he's ready to roll. There's a trio of Chinook helicopters that's going to take them to an airfield. Brody wants the Chinooks to fly out surrounded by the rocket's red glare. He's even recorded the music and wants me to match it with the fireworks."

"When do we know to break for Brody's office?" Lou asked.

"Wait until you hear the *1812 Overture*. You know that piece?"

"I know it," Cap said.

"Great. When you hear it, you'll rush for the office, break in without setting off any alarms, and do your thing. Believe me, no one will be watching. They're going to be having their own problems courtesy of *moi*. Are you guys ready to lock and load?"

"Not just yet," Lou said. "My contingency plan isn't here."

"Contingency plan? What the—"

At that instant, a state police car, headlights on, appeared in the distance and sped toward them. It stopped just behind the truck.

"Let me do the talking," Papa Steve said.

"Not to worry," Lou said. "I've got this one."

Judy Lemon approached with a swaggering sway of her hips that caught the attention of both Cap and Papa Steve. She came right up to Lou and took off her mirrored sunglasses. "I should arrest you for obstructing my steak dinner," she scolded.

"Doctor's honor I'm going to take you out for that," Lou said, holding up his hand as a sworn promise.

"Honor isn't what I'm looking for from you, Doc," Lemon said.

Lou swallowed hard at her come-hither smile. "Guys, this is Officer Judy Lemon, aka our backup."

Papa Steve flashed Lou an angry look. "I didn't say anything about needing a contingency plan! Lou, what have you told her?"

"Not much," Lou said. "Just, well—"

"Don't worry," Lemon said. "I've looked the other way for worse things than sneaking onto a military base and stealing a gun. Besides, Brody's been sticking it to the Staties so long now that I'd love to stick it right back at him."

Papa Steve did not appear at all satisfied. "There are a lot of big boys on that base with a lot of big guns. I don't see how the police are going to help out here. No offense."

"None taken, sweetheart," Lemon said. "And if Lou here doesn't want to take me out for dinner, you might do just fine as his replacement."

"Not that I don't trust this plan of yours, Papa Steve," Lou said. "But I've got a kid who needs a father."

Papa Steve set his hands on his hips. "Okay, so we've got backup. Now gear up. It's going to be cold riding under that truck."

"I'll be as close to the base as I can get," Lemon said.

Lou and Cap climbed under the truck and shimmied their way to the center of the cold steel platform, lying on their stomachs. Papa Steve secured the metal sides of the platform. Moments later, the engine rumbled, and the truck lurched forward.

Next stop, Mantis.

Lou could not say how long he and Cap rode under the vehicle. All he knew was that it came to an abrupt stop and did not move for some time. They had to be at the Mantis base guardhouse.

Lou's limbs were stiff, and his fingers and toes felt numb from the cold. Most of his thoughts, though, were with his boxing coach and AA sponsor, the gentle battering ram of a man huddled next to him.

"You okay?" Lou whispered.

"Been better, been worse," Cap said.

They heard footsteps crunching on the hard-packed ground outside. "Howdy, gentlemen," Papa Steve said to the Mantis guards.

"We're checking IDs today, Papa Steve. CO's orders. What's in the truck?"

"Fireworks for the big show tonight."

"We gotta search the back."

"Make it quick. I got a Mantis version of the big bang to set up."

Lou held his breath. From what he could hear, at least two men had climbed inches above where he and Cap lay and were conducting a thorough search of the cargo.

"You're all set, Papa Steve," one of the guards called out.

The truck slipped into gear. Minutes later, they stopped again. The driver-side door opened, then slammed closed. From outside, they heard Papa Steve whisper harshly. "Lou, Cap, you boys all right? Knock on the side. Once for yes, twice for no. It's safe."

Lou banged once against the side.

"Good. Now, hang tight. The show will feature some speeches, followed by a couple of marches. The *1812 Overture* will be last, with fireworks mixed in with enough of the real deal to get some serious attention. Soon as you hear the 1812 music, head for Brody's office. By the time things begin to blow up, you better be back at the truck. If things go right, we'll drive right off the base without too much trouble. Knock once if you've got all that."

Lou knocked.

"Hang tough, boys."

Lou guessed ten minutes had passed when they heard footsteps approaching. "Hey there, Papa Steve, how's it going?"

Brody!

"Getting ready to be off-loaded," Papa Steve said. "I think you'll be happy with my selection, Colonel. I've got aerial repeaters, shells, rockets, Thor missiles, display tubes. It'll be a spectacle."

"Good," Brody said. "These men are going on a very dangerous mission. They deserve a fitting send-off."

More footsteps. "Papa Steve, ready for the big show?"

"Major Coon," Papa Steve replied, "I'm ready to hook it all up."

Coon then said, "Excuse me, Commander, could I have a word?"

"Papa Steve," Brody said, "give us five minutes."

"Yes, sir."

Footsteps, probably Papa Steve leaving.

"Okay," Brody said finally, "what is it, Charlie?"

"I wanted you to know I've decided to handle the notification to the families myself. I think it's better that way, sir."

"I'll come with you to some of them. What's the story?"

"Just as we discussed. Helicopter crash after the assassinations were completed and the men had reassembled for the trip home. It's the most believable way for twenty soldiers to be killed at once."

"Makes sense," Lou heard Brody say. "This is a major milestone in the evolution of the new war, Charlie. Our technology has proven only that we have more money, not more resolve. But that is going to change with Operation Talon. Terrorists will soon be aware that Americans are willing and ready to replicate every tactic used against us, including those that involve a life for a life."

"You've done a good thing here, sir. This will change the course of the war. These parasites will not only learn to respect us but also to fear us. I just left the men. They're ready, sir. Also, we've moved the takeoff from the Langley airstrip to Dover, as you advised."

"Better Dover," Brody said. "I want as few people as possible to know anything about this. Let's get ready, my friend."

Footsteps . . . Brody and Coon walking away.

Lou's stomach had knotted up. He had learned enough to put together a truly frightening scenario. Operation Talon was a mass suicide mission. Twenty soldiers, primed by Brody's ruby drink, ready to die for their country. He might not know the target, but the intent of the mission was evident. Lying in the darkness, Lou recalled how easily the cartel man named Pedro had slipped the revolver into his mouth and pulled the trigger.

Now Mark Colston's heroism, surprising even to his father, made sense. Clearly it was only a matter of time before Elias Colston put all the pieces together. In megalomaniac Wyatt Brody's warped mind, the man had to die.

But now a new problem had arisen. Instead of trying to prove Brody killed Elias Colston, Lou had the responsibility of twenty brave, essentially innocent lives in his hands. The lives soon to be sacrificed on the altar of Operation Talon.

"Cap, that man's crazy," Lou said. "Drunk with power and his misguided theories of patriotism. Unless he's stopped, a lot of people are going to die."

The seconds dragged on. Papa Steve returned with a crew and unloaded the fireworks. The moment of action had to be close.

"Gentlemen," Brody's voice boomed from giant speakers. "Tonight we honor the men who will represent Mantis on its most important mission. From the beginning, Mantis has embodied the virtues of the true soldier. Please join me in affirming those virtues."

"Crimson is the color of courage," seven hundred voices barked out in perfect unison, "the color of blood spilled in battle, the color of valor. To justice. To country. To God. To Mantis. . . . Whatever it takes!"

Lou felt a tremendous surge of adrenaline. At all costs, the sacrifice of these men had to be averted.

"Alone we are powerful," Brody was saying. "Together we are unstoppable. Let us honor the men of Operation Talon. As I call your name, climb onto the trucks that will transport you to the heliport. Staff Sergeant Bucky Townsend, Muskogee, Oklahoma . . . Corporal Luis Sanchez, Vicksburg, Mississippi . . ."

The cheers became more rapturous after each name. When the list was completed, Sousa's "Stars and Stripes Forever" blared through the loudspeakers, accompanied by a barrage of fireworks and the rumbling of truck engines.

One more march, some more fireworks. Then, from the massive speakers, the *1812 Overture* began. *Music to die for,* Lou thought.

"Get ready, my friend," Lou said. "We're on."

LOU and Cap slid backward and dropped to the ground behind the truck. They were parked on the dirt courtyard housing Brody's headquarters and two smaller structures. Overhead, a variety of fireworks were turning the moonless sky into a fantasy garden. The explosions accompanying the display shook the earth.

Aside from the music, the core of the base was ghostly quiet and appeared completely deserted. If ever there was a time to penetrate Wyatt Brody's world, this was it.

Cap pulled out a compact knapsack he had wedged by his head. Small length of clothesline, powerful flashlight, leather pouch of tools, headlamp, stethoscope, hunting knife, and a pistol. Lou tapped Cap on the shoulder and pointed to the target building. The fighter nodded back and made a dash to Brody's building. He reached the perimeter and waved for Lou to join him. Keeping low, Lou shambled across the open area. He reached the stairs to the porch and flattened against a support next to Cap.

The *1812 Overture*'s first bridge, a series of chromatic runs that depicted anxious Russians anticipating battle, reverberated from the speakers, accompanied by the rumbling of some low-level fireworks. The music reflected Lou's growing sense of urgency.

Lou set his watch and started it. "We've got eleven minutes before the cannonade. Come on, buddy, it's time to do this thing."

They ascended the wooden staircase to the door. From the PA system, the strings were beginning battle with the horns. Cap turned on his headlight and took the lock-pick kit from his backpack. He removed a long silver wand with a little bend at the end.

"Where'd you get those?" Lou whispered.

"Online. Where does anyone get anything these days?"

The fireworks intensified as the horns began the powerful "La Marseillaise." The French counterattack was under way.

"We're in," Cap said, stepping back.

Lou turned the knob, and the door opened easily. The two friends moved quickly to Wyatt Brody's office. They went directly to the case behind Brody's desk. The polished antique Colt military pistol was at the center of the display, right where Papa Steve said it probably would be. It would leave a six left twist rifling mark on any bullet it fired.

Cap spent a few moments studying the situation. "The case is alarmed with glass-break sensors, but the actual lock wasn't a priority. It's a Yale. Tough but not killer tough."

Cap slid a long hooked tool into the lock. His muscular frame, the body that had battered dozens of fighters in the ring, seemed calm and totally at ease.

"The plug hole has beveled edges," Cap said, speaking more to himself than to Lou, "and the key pins are rounded off. I've got to do more scrubbing. Shouldn't be hard."

The music outside was intensifying—crashing cymbals, horns blaring. Lou guessed they had four minutes to get the case open, unhinge the gun, and make it back to the truck.

"I've got the pins set, but the lock isn't opening," Cap murmured.

"Two more minutes, and we've got to smash the case and take our chances with the alarm," Lou said.

He watched his friend work. Outside, the music was again building. The fireworks explosions were rattling the display cases. The finale was near. At the instant bells began chiming in the soundtrack, the lock popped with a satisfying click, and the case opened. Cap lifted the Colt and placed it in his knapsack along with his tools.

"We've got to move, Cap! Now!"

Lou shifted a pistol from the bottom row to fill in the space the Colt had occupied. Then he closed the case and followed Cap through the office to the porch. They reached the courtyard just as the speakers blared out the overture's dramatic climax. The lights of three helicopters rose slowly into the smoke-filled sky. The moment the choppers lifted off, the cannonade began. The finale.

Up ahead, Papa Steve was standing by the truck, motioning for them to hurry. He was holding a detonator up in his left hand.

Shoulder to shoulder, Lou and Cap had taken three steps toward Papa Steve when a Mantis guard stepped out from a building to their left. "Freeze right there, or I'll shoot!"

Lou dropped facedown on the hardened dirt. The overture climax continued, with cannon fire booming from the PA system as though the base were under siege.

And then, in an instant, it was.

Bright orange flames shot into the night. Trucks and jeeps thrown into the air landed with a bone-rattling crunch of metal. A pair of smaller explosions sprayed dirt and rocks into the air.

"I said stop!" the guard shouted.

A burst of machine-gun fire followed. Bullets slapped the ground by Lou's feet. Cap rolled over, then he had a pistol in his hand. One shot, and the soldier cried out and fell, clutching his shoulder.

"Nice shot!" Lou exclaimed.

"Nice shot, hell! I was aiming at his leg."

"Get to the truck!" Papa Steve was hollering.

Pistol drawn, he was providing them with cover fire. Small explosions continued to erupt throughout the woods. Lou and Cap were moving again, hunched over, weaving across the courtyard. More guards had materialized near the wounded soldier. Bullets whizzed past Lou's head. As he reached the truck, Lou heard the thud of bullets against rubber, followed by a loud hiss of air. The left rear tire deflated. Moments later, the right was flat as well.

They scrambled inside while Papa Steve fired one last burst and dove behind the wheel.

"You got the gun?" he asked as they lurched ahead.

Breathing heavily, Lou nodded. "How're we gonna get out of here with two flat tires?"

Papa Steve glanced over at him. "I thought you were the one with the blond bombshell contingency plan."

"Let's get to the guardhouse. I'll make the call on the way."

Lou had Judy Lemon's phone number on speed dial. The 1812 was over, and Papa Steve's explosions were on the wane. Soldiers emerged from the woods trying to determine whom to shoot.

"Dr. Lou? Is that you?" The voice of Judy Lemon, barely audible, crackled in Lou's ear.

"Judy, can you hear me?" Lou shouted. "Meet us at the gate!"

The truck was slowing down, its engine screeching. Up ahead, Lou caught sight of the guardhouse.

"Truck's dead," Papa Steve said. "We've got to run for the gate. Lou, where's that backup?"

As if on cue, blue and red strobes appeared. With Papa Steve's disruption, the front gate to the Mantis base was unguarded.

The driver-side window of Lemon's cruiser opened, and Lemon leaned out. "Hey, boys. Need a lift?"

The three clambered inside the cruiser. "Operation Talon," Lou said, breathing hard. "We've got to stop it."

"Why?" Papa Steve asked. "We've got the murder weapon."

"Talon is a suicide mission. Twenty guys are coming back in body bags unless we do something to stop it."

"Did you hear where they're going?" Papa Steve asked.

"Dover Air Force Base. I don't know their ultimate destination."

Papa Steve hesitated. The muscles in his face went taut, and he seemed to be having difficulty assimilating the new information. Then he shrugged and pointed to a dirt road. "That's the road to the heliport. Officer Judy, would you mind taking us there?"

The cruiser rocketed forward. A minute later, they were at the heliport. A guard stepped out from behind a utility shed.

"Down!" Lemon shouted.

The four of them ducked as a bullet struck the front windshield. Lemon hit the brake and skidded into a smoke-and-rubber-filled 360. She rolled out the door, rising to her feet with lightning quickness, her pistol trained on the Mantis guard's chest.

"Drop that weapon, solider," she said. "That's an order."

Papa Steve climbed out of the car. "Do as she says, son. We got no beef with you."

The standoff was short-lived. The baby-faced soldier lowered his weapon, and within moments, Lemon had his wrists handcuffed.

Papa Steve gestured toward a weathered army helicopter, one of two remaining on the helipad. "Gentlemen," he said. "If we want to stop Wyatt Brody, then we're going to need to go for a little ride. Follow me, and I'll teach you boys how to hot-wire a chopper."

CHAPTER 11

SARAH had grown fond of the remarkable woman she had come to regard as a friend. Edith had not visited Washington since before the so-called accident that blinded her, but she navigated the streets almost like a woman with sight. Once, on their way to Devlin and Rodgers's to make copies of the Reddy Creek invoices for safekeeping, Edith used her cane to keep Sarah from crossing a street in front of oncoming traffic.

"Open your ears," she had said with a smile.

When they arrived at Sarah's office, there was a surprise waiting. Bruce Patterson, Edith's former boss at the Raleigh *News and Observer,* had sent a box containing all the research Edith had compiled in her Reddy Creek investigation. She and Sarah spent the afternoon going through the material like archaeologists at a dig site.

It was late afternoon, and Hogarth still had not called to accept Sarah's offer. "Are you going to go public?" Edith asked.

"We can't back off," Sarah said. "Besides, thanks to you, we have a wealth of evidence here to establish a motive for Brody to commit murder. I'm confident a jury will have enough reasonable doubt to acquit McHugh, if the prosecutors go to trial at all."

The two women decided to go to Sarah's town house. Sarah locked arms with Edith, feeling warmed by the bond they had formed, and guided her toward the building.

"What's that?" Edith asked. "I heard something. A rustling."

Sarah went still, listening. Nothing. She took out her key and inserted it. At the instant the bolt turned, a hefty man looped around the shrubbery and came up behind them.

Detective Chris Bryzinski.

The College Park cop trained his gun on Sarah, barely giving Edith a glance. "Inside. Quickly. Not a word from either of you."

Sarah inched the door open and led Edith inside. Bryzinski grabbed Edith by the arm and swung her onto the living room rug. Sarah moved to help her, but the massive policeman called her off. She saw determination in his cold eyes, buried deep in fat—a man with a mission. Not good.

"Hogarth sent you, didn't he?" Sarah said.

"Shut up and sit in that chair."

"I'll scream."

Shoving Edith aside with his boot, Bryzinski rammed the barrel of his gun into Sarah's belly. She gasped and stumbled backward into a chair. Only then did she notice that the gun had a silencer.

Sarah had no doubt that within minutes she and Edith would be executed. Ten feet away, Edith had worked her way to her knees.

"Please," Sarah said, fixing on the detective's eyes. "You don't have to do this. I don't know what Hogarth is paying you, or what he has on you, but this is murder, plain and simple."

"Shut up!"

"You don't want our blood on your hands. Please, Chris, you swore an oath to protect and serve. Hogarth is a monster. He'd step on you like a bug if you were in his way. Don't give in."

"Shut up, dammit!"

A china figurine stood on the end table to her right, a wedding present from her parents. She could throw it at his face, relying on her quickness to overcome his massive bulk. "Is it money? Is that what this is all about?" Sarah inched her hand closer to the figurine.

"I'm afraid you've made a powerful enemy. There's nothing I can do."

Edith was on her knees. Sarah forced herself not to look at her. The figurine was only a couple of inches away.

"Tell me how much Hogarth's paying you. I have millions from the settlement of my husband's death. I'll give all of it to you—every cent. I mean it. Whatever Hogarth is paying, I can beat it."

Edith was up in a crouch, with one knee still on the rug.

"I wish it were money," Bryzinski said ruefully.

He raised his gun and aimed it dead center at Sarah's forehead.

"God forgive me," he muttered.

The muzzle of his gun was an ebony hole. Sarah grabbed the figurine and hurled it the instant she heard the gunshot. In the same motion, she threw herself over backward. Her head slammed against the floor. A brief burst of white light, and all went black.

A second? A minute? Ten? The first thing Sarah experienced when she came to was the ecstatic realization that she wasn't dead. She saw Chris Bryzinski, lying facedown, trying desperately to pull himself across the rug. And she heard Edith's voice. "I mean it! Move one more inch, and you're going to see how accurate I am with this thing."

"You bitch. You shot me."

"Keep talking," Edith said. "This derringer still has one shot." She waved the double-barreled weapon in his direction.

Shaking, Sarah scrambled to her feet and raced to Edith, pausing to pick up Bryzinski's pistol. "You okay?" Sarah asked.

"I'm glad he said that little prayer before he pulled the trigger," Edith said. "I wouldn't have gotten a bead on him otherwise."

Sarah left Bryzinski clutching his tree-trunk thigh and returned moments later with a white bedsheet and a kitchen knife. She cut the sheet, using one strip to gag the detective and several more to bandage his leg. Next, she found a pair of handcuffs in a fabric pouch latched to his belt and manacled his hands behind his back.

"What now?" Edith asked.

"We've got to go drop off this dirty laundry."

"So FAR, so good," Papa Steve said.

The twin-engine UH-1N Huey bucked against a strong headwind as it flew a northeastwardly course toward Dover.

"I need to call Sarah," Lou said from the copilot seat. "She's been working on Spencer Hogarth, trying to use him to get Brody to admit to Colston's murder. But we've also got to get him to stop Operation Talon."

"You can call using the Huey's sat phone," Papa Steve said.

Lou recited Sarah's number and heard ringing in his headset.

"Hello?" Sarah sounded unsure.

"Hey there, Sarah, it's Lou. I'm in a helicopter with Cap and Papa Steve, on our way to Dover Air Force Base. Are you okay?"

"Aside from having Detective Bryzinski try to kill us, we're fine. Edith and I are in the car. Bryzinski is in the trunk."

"Does he fit?"

"Just barely. We're certain Hogarth has something on him. He was about to do it, silencer and all, when Edith shot him in the leg."

"Edith?!"

"There's more to this woman than you think."

"I guess. So what are you going to do with him?"

"Use him for a bargaining chip with Hogarth."

"I have some information that might help." Talking over the noise of the chopper, Lou reviewed the events at Mantis Base. When he was done, he felt Sarah's pause.

"You have the murder weapon?" she asked finally.

"Your ballistics expert will tell us for sure, but yes, we probably do. My pal Cap has it in the backseat."

A hesitation. "I'll bet you think I'm furious," she said, "because you've gone rogue again when you promised me you wouldn't."

"The thought was crossing my mind."

"Well, let it pass. I feel like I owe you an apology for being so hard on you all this time. Edith and I nearly got ourselves killed by taking the same sort of risks you've taken."

"I can't believe it," Lou said. "I've been pardoned?"

"I'm done pushing you around."

"In that case, I'm done trying to stuff my feelings toward you. How's that?"

"I can handle it. See me when this is all over, Doc."

"So tell me, did Bryzinski confess that Hogarth hired him?"

"I think he needs a bit more time in the trunk to open up to us."

"I thought you might get Hogarth to stop Operation Talon, but since he tried to have you shot we're going to stop him ourselves."

"You'll get yourself killed. Listen, we can get to Hogarth. We'll give him a new deal. We'll offer to bury Reddy Creek if he stops Operation Talon."

"Great plan," Lou said. "Maybe this time he'll hire someone less incompetent to kill you."

"And you think going up against Brody is safer? Let us handle this. We can get to Hogarth. Believe me, he'll throw anyone or anything under the bus to save himself and his career. I want you to back off, Lou. Trust me on this. I've got a way."

"Fine, I trust you," Lou said. "But we're still going in. Maybe we can delay the mission launch until you get Hogarth to intervene. We need one another. We always did. Now, where are you?"

"If you think Hogarth is seeing the troops off at Dover, then that's where we're headed. I have his cell number. I can call him."

"Be careful, lady." Lou could not bring himself to say good-bye.

After the call ended, Cap tapped Lou on the shoulder. "You know, you two sound like an old married couple."

"I would say more like we're inching up to the discovery phase. Do you think one of you would fill in for me with Officer Lemon?"

"You bet," the two men called out in near unison.

The next forty-five minutes were spent with each man lost in his own thoughts.

"Hey, gentlemen," Papa Steve suddenly announced, "we're approaching Dover. Hold on tight."

Papa Steve lowered their altitude to seven hundred fifty feet. The radio began to crackle. Air traffic control announced that they were being monitored and needed to turn around. Papa Steve kept the copter flying slow and level. "It's a no-go on landing," he said. "The base is shut down to incoming traffic. Orders."

Lou said, "Tell them to relay this exact message to Colonel Wyatt Brody: Dr. Lou Welcome knows all about Manolo, and he's going to go public unless we get permission to land."

Papa Steve sent the message back to the tower. A stream of chatter ensued. After a tense few minutes of waiting and circling, the helicopter made a sudden and rapid course change.

"We're landing," Papa Steve said. "I guess your message worked. We'll touch down in a little over twenty minutes."

"Twenty minutes? Why so long?" Lou asked.

"I guess they have to prepare the welcome wagon for our arrival. Brace yourselves, boys."

It was time to find Hogarth.

Sarah called. Three rings, and she heard a satisfying click.

"Hello, who is this?"

"Secretary Hogarth, it's Sarah Cooper. We need to talk."

Did she hear him suck down a nervous breath? Sarah guessed that Spencer Hogarth for a moment believed he was conversing with a ghost.

"Sarah, are you calling to thank me for the wine?"

"Not the wine, Mr. Secretary. I have a new deal to make."

"Talk to me. You seem to have a way of getting my attention."

"No, this has to be done face-to-face. Meet me now, or I'm going to begin a hatchet job on your career. You know I can do it, too."

"Well, in that case, I'm at Dover air base. I'll meet you at the main gate."

Sarah ended the call. Then she said to Edith, "He's at Dover."

"Did he suspect anything?" Edith clutched her hands in her lap.

"No," Sarah said. "I'm sure he's calling Bryzinski right now."

"Will he hear him in the trunk?"

"Not the way we tied him down."

They arrived at the front gate to Dover air base, an impenetrable fortress of barbed wire and tall fencing. Armed guards with rifles stepped in front of Sarah's car as she stopped.

Please don't open my trunk, she was thinking.

Sarah lowered her window as one of the guards approached. "Ma'am," the guard said, "this is a restricted area."

"I've got a meeting with Spencer Hogarth."

"Secretary Hogarth? One minute, please."

The guard left, and two others took his place. Sarah took in a breath. Edith reached across and took her hand. "Hang in there," she said, her jaw set. "We're going to do this."

The first guard returned. "We need to check IDs first," he said.

Sarah exhaled a relieved breath.

A STRONG updraft wobbled the Huey, but Papa Steve, cool as ice on an igloo, brought the helicopter to a smooth touchdown. He then cut the engines. The three men looked out the windshield into total darkness. No lights. No movement of any kind.

"I've got a bad feeling about this, pal," Cap said.

"I can't see a soul out there," Papa Steve said. "My gut says trap."

Lou jumped out onto the tarmac. Cap and Papa Steve followed. The trio stood in a circle surveying the darkness. A row of weak blue lights, like gas flames, stretched down the runway, casting a glow on the massive transport aircraft parked there. The airplane's engines rumbled at low volume like the snore of a sleeping giant.

In the distance, tower lights barely reached that remote section of the air base where air traffic control had directed Papa Steve to land. A row of massive snowplows loomed like steel monsters.

Off to one side of the runway, Lou could see the three Chinook helicopters from Mantis, silent and dark. Maybe the men of Mantis Company were already aboard the transport aircraft.

"I'd like to up that bad feeling to a *really* bad feeling," Cap said.

As if on cue, blinding headlights from the snowplows all came on at once. Shadowy figures materialized from the night. Soldiers from

Mantis Company stood before them in a straight line, like a firing squad, rifles at the ready, locked on the three intruders.

A man emerged from between two of the soldiers. He wore a thick down parka and a camouflage cap. Brody. He was followed by an officer in identical dress, who Lou felt certain was Coon, second in command. The two men entered the beams of the snowplows' headlamps.

"Dr. Welcome, nice to see you," Brody said. "I guess you've come to say your good-byes to our troops. I know the traitor next to you who likes to blow things up, but this gentleman is new to me."

"It's over, Brody," Lou said. "We know what you've done, and soon these men will know, too. Operation Talon has to be stopped."

"Oh, I'm sorry," Brody said. "I didn't realize you were now in charge of national security. I'll just let these guys know that rather than fight, they should pack up and head home. Or better still, how about I have them shoot you and your friends for treason and for attempting to intervene with a military operation. Gentlemen, ready your weapons."

In an instant, twenty safety mechanisms were released. Lou raised his hands above his head. Cap and Papa Steve did the same.

"We're unarmed," Lou said. "I'm a doctor. Cap, here, is a fighter who teaches inner-city kids how to box. Papa Steve you know. Kill us, and you're killing Americans—killing what you all stand for."

"Enough!" Brody snapped. "Did you think mentioning Manolo's name would get you a free pass? I brought you in here so these men can see the forces trying to stop us. Men, Manolo is in charge of making the drink we all share every day. The composition of that drink is a complex one, but he does a rather good job, don't you think? We pay him in cash and sometimes, when necessary, in weapons. Does that knowledge make a difference to any of you?"

"It should make a difference," Lou said. "You're being manipulated by this man like guinea pigs, being asked to sacrifice your lives so that he can prove a point. I've read his research. I know."

The soldiers remained in position.

"Whatever it takes!" one of the men shouted.

The rest of Mantis Company echoed their battle cry.

"Whatever it takes!"

"No!" Lou pleaded. "Not whatever it takes. You are warriors. You do your best. You do what's right. You act with valor. But you don't take your own lives. This mission must be stopped."

"Fire!" Brody cried. "Take them out! These men are a threat to our national security."

Papa Steve stepped in front of Lou. "Don't do it! Stand down, guys. Don't shoot!"

Brody pulled a pistol from a holster hidden underneath his parka. He aimed the weapon at Papa Steve. "I will shoot them myself if you men don't follow this order. Now fire your weapons, dammit."

With feline grace and speed, Cap rushed Brody and, in virtually the same motion, landed a vicious right hook to the side of his nose, dropping the Mantis commander onto his butt. *Cap'n Crunch.*

Brody's pistol skidded away. Blood spurted from both his nostrils. His eyes glazed. Lou tensed himself for the hail of bullets.

One of the Mantis soldiers stepped forward with his weapon pointed not at the three intruders, but at Brody, who was shakily back on his feet, eyes still watering, clamping his bleeding nostrils shut with his cap.

"We're not afraid to die, sir," the soldier said. "None of us. But that doesn't mean we murder innocent Americans."

"Staff Sergeant Morales, you'd best point that weapon where it's supposed to be pointed," Brody rasped.

"Morales is right," another man said, stepping out of line to aim his weapon at Coon. "We're not stupid. We know what you felt the ruby drink was doing to us, but not many of us believed it or cared. We've always been ready to die for our country and commanders."

Papa Steve faced them. "Your commander is a murderer. He shot Elias Colston, Mark's father, in cold blood, because Colston knew the truth about Mantis. He didn't believe his son would have acted in battle the way he did unless he was under the influence of chemicals that altered his ability to experience fear."

"That's not so," Morales said.

"Ask Brody," Lou said. "Ask him if he thinks you men would

undertake this mission if not for the drug he fed you every day. You men are true soldiers. Maybe you'll be killed in the line of duty. That's a risk every soldier takes. But let it be a risk, not the goal."

Staff Sergeant Morales turned to Lou. "Doc, we appreciate what you're saying. But we are going on our mission. Like you said, we're soldiers, Mantis marines, and we're trained to follow orders."

Brody had staunched the bleeding from his nose. Lou caught the sliver of a smile creasing the corners of the commander's mouth. Fenton Morales lowered his gun, and the others did the same.

"Colonel Brody," Morales said, "I believe I am speaking for the group. Once these men have been taken into custody, we are prepared to board the transport and complete our mission as ordered."

Lou read Wyatt Brody's eyes: *You're dead, Welcome.*

"I'll radio for the MPs," Brody said. "You men can watch from the transport as these three are escorted away. Major Coon, supervise the securing of these men."

"Sir, yes, sir!" Coon said, saluting.

"Now, men, on that plane. You'll be airborne in fifteen minutes. Crimson is the color of courage, the color of blood spilled in battle, the color of valor. To justice. To country. To God. To Mantis."

"Whatever it takes!"

THE lights of an approaching sedan flashed several times. The car stopped, and Spencer Hogarth stepped out. He wore a long trench coat, and the silver of his hair shone like snow under a streetlight. He spoke to the guards, then he rapped twice on Sarah's roof.

She lowered her window and studied the secretary of defense's hard-bitten face. His worry lines seemed to have deepened, the bags under his eyes become fuller. She imagined what Hogarth was thinking, *How are you alive? What happened to Bryzinski?*

"Follow me," he said.

"Where are we going?"

"Someplace I know where it's safe to talk."

Or someplace where it's easy to have us killed, Sarah thought. She gripped Edith's loaded derringer in her pocket.

They followed Hogarth along empty streets. His Cadillac stopped in front of a closed hangar. Sarah parked, and the two women got out and moved toward where he was standing.

"Okay," Hogarth said. "What do you want from me?"

"Nothing has changed from the restaurant," Sarah said, her grip on the gun. "We have enough information to bury your career if it becomes public."

Hogarth eyed her coldly. "I thought you had a new deal to offer."

"I do," Sarah said. "We bury Reddy Creek, for good and forever, we'll sign papers, whatever you need to feel confident that Reddy Creek and the other armory robberies never come to the surface."

"In exchange for Brody's confession to murder? I thought you said we had a new deal. That's the old one."

"No, we got Brody dead to rights on murder one," Sarah said. "And we've got the weapon used to kill Elias Colston—a weapon that just happens to have come from Brody's gun collection."

Hogarth was surprised. "How did that come to be?"

"Doesn't matter," Sarah said. "What matters is we've got the weapon."

"So what do you want from me? Make your offer."

"Okay. You need to put a stop to Operation Talon."

"What?"

"We know all about Talon and your use of a psychotropic drug to block the soldiers' fear of death. These men are on nothing more than a mass-suicide mission. Our terrorists versus their terrorists."

"Nothing doing. Even if unsubstantiated word got out, the American people will stand behind our troops."

It was time for the final card. "We have Bryzinski," Sarah said.

"What?"

"The killer you hired made it as far as my condo. We shot him."

Sarah passed over a plastic bag with the cop's silencer in it.

"We have a recorded confession including who paid him. I've left instructions with my partners as to how they can find both him and the recording."

Hogarth digested the revelation. "I want proof he's alive."

"We're going to count down from five," Sarah said. "You agree to call Talon off, and we'll tell you where your pudgy buddy can be found. If I get to zero, we leave. Killing us won't do you any good now. By morning, the police and the media will have all they need to put you out of business and in prison."

"Wait a min—"

"Five," Edith said.

"This is . . . bigger than you realize," Hogarth stammered. "There are reasons for what we're doing."

"Four."

"I can't just stop it. Do you understand what you're doing? You're putting American lives at risk."

"Three."

Edith took Sarah by the arm and turned her toward their car.

"Okay! Okay! I'll stop it. Get back in your car and follow me."

Lou watched the processional of Mantis marines making their way up the staircase into the transport. He was desperate to stop them, but along with Cap and Papa Steve, his hands had been secured behind his back. The men of Operation Talon had waited until a call was placed to the MPs before boarding the plane.

"I didn't give Sarah enough time to deal with Hogarth," Lou said. "This is my fault."

"There's still time," Papa Steve said. "Take it from an old experienced geezer. So long as Brody doesn't just blow us away, anything can happen."

Lights from a pair of approaching vehicles appeared in the distance. *The MPs,* Lou thought.

The lead car began blaring its horn and flashing its lights. The vehicles were civilian, not military, the lead one a Mercedes. *Sarah!*

The second car, a black Cadillac, zoomed ahead and skidded to a stop in front of the transport's staircase. The driver-side door flew open, and Secretary Spencer Hogarth stumbled out shouting. "Brody! Where's Brody, dammit! Somebody find me Brody!"

Sarah's Mercedes came to a stop behind the Cadillac. A second later, she jumped out, followed by a woman wearing dark sunglasses and a fur-lined jacket, brandishing a folding cane. *Edith!* Sarah's eyes met Lou's immediately. He could see triumph in them.

"Unlock these men right now!" Sarah shouted to the Mantis marines standing guard.

"Sorry, ma'am, these men are to be detained by the MPs. Colonel Brody's orders."

"We'll see about that."

Above them, the men of Operation Talon's faces were pressed to the portholes.

"Where is Brody, Lou?" Sarah asked. "I told Hogarth that we had absolute proof Brody killed Elias Colston. We made a deal."

"I saw Brody board the plane," Cap said. "Maybe he decided to go on the mission, or maybe he was trying to do a repair job on the nose I busted."

"This mission isn't going on the mission," Sarah said. "Secretary Hogarth is about to see to that. Hang tight, guys. We'll get you out of those handcuffs. But we've got to find Brody first."

Several Talon marines had retraced their steps down the stairs to see what the commotion was about. Hogarth, meanwhile, continued to shout out Brody's name. His eyes were wild, his cheeks crimson.

"Wyatt Brody! Get out here, you murdering bastard."

Wyatt Brody emerged from the plane. His nose was swollen and discolored. A storm cloud had settled across his glowering face. "What's the meaning of this?" he shouted. "What are you doing, Spencer?"

"What am I doing? I'm trying to do damage control because you went off plan."

Lou watched as Brody charged down the staircase to confront his mentor. "What are you talking about, Spencer? This *is* the plan. With all due respect, you need to get a grip on your reality."

"If you didn't kill Elias Colston, none of this would have happened," Hogarth snapped.

"I don't know what in the hell you're talking about. I never—"

"Enough! They know, Wyatt. They know all about Talon and Mantis. They know about the armories. We have to shut it down and go into damage control mode, effective immediately."

"Spencer, this mission can't just be rescheduled. We have ten high-value targets that are going down. Operation Talon is a go."

Hogarth bellowed, "I'm in charge of this mission, and I'm pulling the plug. Civilians, Brody. Civilians know about what we're doing here. Do you grasp the ramifications?"

"I grasp that you are not sounding rational at the moment. You're threatening years of planning and hard work. My work! I don't know what this is all about, but I do know I'm not backing down."

"It's about you killing Elias Colston, you stupid ass!" Hogarth shouted. "And because of that we've got a massive security breach on our hands. Colston was not a threat. He wasn't going to blow the whistle on Mantis. You misread him, and it's cost us all. Now you stand down this instant. Mantis is over. Operation Talon is over."

"You're crazy! Nothing is over until I say it's over. Nothing!"

Lou and Sarah exchanged stunned looks.

Hogarth fell silent. But if anything, his eyes were even wilder. "That's it. I'm done with you," he said in a chillingly calm tone. "I'm relieving you of your command. Effective immediately."

"Under whose authority?"

"Under my authority. I'm the secretary of defense, and Operation Talon is my operation to run and to cancel." From his overcoat pocket, Hogarth drew a pistol and aimed it at Brody's midsection. "You have cost this country a great deal, Wyatt. A great deal indeed. Now tell your men this mission is over."

"I'll do no such thing," Brody said.

"Tell them it's over! Do it now!"

"No! Men, get back on that plane. Spencer, give me that gun!"

Fumbling for the pistol in his belt, Brody charged the older man. A pair of flashes burst from Hogarth's gun.

Brody staggered back, clutching his abdomen. Blood soaked through his shirt and oozed between his fingers. He stared down, then looked, eyes glazed, at Hogarth.

Brody raised his pistol. Blood dripped from his belly. He tried to level his gun, but his hand shook violently.

"You brought this on yourself," Hogarth said. He fired once more. Brody crumpled lifeless to the asphalt, blood pooling around his body. The secretary of defense lowered his weapon and turned to the Mantis marines. "He was going to kill me," he said with no remorse. "You're all witnesses. He was going to kill me."

SMOKE from Spencer Hogarth's gun vanished in the chilly breeze. Holding up his hands without holstering his weapon, Hogarth circled several times, pleading his case to dozens of witnesses. "You all saw that," he said. "Brody was going to kill me. I had no choice. Somebody call an ambulance. Now!"

Hogarth's gaze fell on Lou and the two others.

"Unlock these men," he ordered, as if testing whether or not his authority had survived.

For several moments, there was no response; then two marines cut away the manacles. Lou rubbed at his wrists.

"Who are you, and what are you doing here?" Hogarth asked Papa Steve, as if the man he had just shot to death wasn't there at all.

"Sir, Captain Steve Papavassiliou, of Mantis Company, sir! These are my companions, Dr. Lou Welcome and Cap Duncan. Admiral Hogarth, sir, please put away the gun."

Hogarth ignored the request. His attention turned to Lou. "So where is the murder weapon?" the secretary asked. "The one Brody used to kill Elias Colston."

"It's safe," Lou said, not at all surprised that Hogarth had pieced together his involvement. "That's all I can say."

"I see."

Hogarth continued to dangle his pistol loosely at his side. The Mantis marines and Major Coon were on the radio desperately calling for help.

"We have a very serious problem," Hogarth went on, keeping his gaze fixed on Lou, "that requires a great deal of discretion."

"No disrespect, pal" Cap said, taking a half step forward, "but you've got bigger issues than what we say or don't say."

Looking utterly shocked, Hogarth glared at Cap. "What you've seen here, what you know, cannot be made public. Not now, not ever. You have been exposed to highly classified information. This is a CIA military black op. Top secret. You are this far from being charged with treason."

Cap moved another inch forward. "When I said you've got bigger issues on your plate, I wasn't talking about the guy you killed lying over there by the staircase. Turn around, Mr. Secretary."

Hogarth spun around. Sarah and Edith were propping up a very wobbly Chris Bryzinski, hands tied behind his back. Blood had soaked through a makeshift tourniquet wrapped around his leg.

Hogarth stared at the detective, then at Sarah.

"We had a deal," he said. "Dammit, we had a deal."

Sarah spread her hands. "So sue me," she said.

Hogarth whirled frantically, searching for a way out.

"It's over," Lou said. "You've taken this as far as it can go."

For the first time, Hogarth seemed to realize that he was still holding his gun. From ten feet away, hand shaking, he pointed the weapon at Lou. "Back away," he said. "Let me out of here."

"To go where?" Lou asked. "You've contracted men to kill innocent civilians, you've stolen from our country, sanctioned suicidal missions. Where are you going to run?"

Hogarth swung his pistol from one person to the next.

"You think I did this for glory? For power?" he shouted, turning around. "I did this to win the war against terrorism. I did this to save lives! Our enemies do not fear death. They welcome it. We're at a disadvantage to them. Can't you see it? We need to fight fire with fire. That is our mission here. And we are doing it, too. Mantis is making our country stronger. Damn you, Cooper, we had a deal!"

Hogarth raised his gun and pointed it toward Sarah. Lou and Cap had seen enough. The sparring partners charged shoulder to shoulder and lunged at the man. But at the instant they reached him, Hogarth took a quick step back and jammed the gun barrel into his mouth, pulling the trigger in the same motion. The shot was surprisingly muffled but no less deadly. He crumpled to the ground, just a few feet from his protégé, his overcoat splayed open beneath him like the wings of a giant mantis, ready to take flight.

CHAPTER 12

BLINKING lights on the wings of the Boeing C-40 Clipper painted the night with a continuous flash of color. A cluster of grim Mantis men stood some distance from where Hogarth and Brody now lay as Lou finished giving an impassioned speech. He now looked to each man for confirmation. *Will you go along with this plan?*

Sarah stood by the Mercedes with Edith, Papa Steve, and Cap. Bryzinski was in the backseat. Lou could see the tension on each of their faces. At Lou's request, none of them had heard what he said to the men. Had he won them over? The answer came from the men. "Whatever it takes!"

Lou nodded. "Whatever it takes," he echoed.

As the first wave of help arrived, Lou told Papa Steve, "We laid the groundwork for everything that's going to follow. How about you and I take a walk?" He placed an arm around Papa Steve's burly shoulders as he led him to a secluded area behind a stack of empty pallets. "Coon will organize the response now that we've got our consensus. He's the ranking officer on the scene."

"And what consensus did we reach?" Papa Steve asked.

"The mission will remain a secret," Lou said. "Along with other things. As of this moment, Operation Talon doesn't exist. Neither does Manolo, the cartel, or the Mantis drink. It's all buried. Coon and the CIA will take care of Manolo. There can be no loose ends."

"I think that's really for the best. You did a hell of a job today, my friend. Cap, too. He's an amazing piece of work."

"That's an understatement."

"Thanks for speaking to the men. I watched their faces. I'm glad they took your advice. So what now?"

"Now we talk," Lou said. "Cap isn't the only piece of work around here. You're one yourself, and your friends are a testament to that. You have a lot of them. Very useful they are, too."

"What are you getting at, Lou?"

"Whenever you need help, one of your friends is there. The police officer that gave me a ticket, the guy who lent you a helicopter to meet me at the golf course. But one of those friends was even more impressive than the others—the one who knew so much about guns and ballistics."

Lou watched the man closely.

"A couple of days ago," Lou went on, "I flew out to Minnesota to see Dr. Sherwood, the director of the Pine Grove Clinic. Turns out, he and Elias were fraternity brothers at the University of Virginia. That's why Elias went to see him. Initially, Dr. Sherwood wouldn't tell me anything. But he had a change of heart and had his assistant call to tell me that Elias was a patient of his. Later, he called me himself with more information. Elias was dying from chronic myeloid leukemia. Six months, maybe a little more, with painful therapy. Does the name James Styles mean anything to you?"

"Should it?"

"It's the name Elias is known by at the clinic."

"You've learned an amazing amount," Papa Steve said.

"I don't think anyone knew Elias was dying—maybe not even Jeannine. No one, that is, except you."

"Lou, I don't—"

Lou reached out and gently placed his hands on Papa Steve's shoulders. "No more games, Steve," he said without rancor. "I understand what you did, and I understand why."

For a time, there was only silence. "I was hoping things would just pass," Papa Steve said finally. "How long have you known?"

"I began having suspicions when you told me you couldn't tail Brody because of the Palace Guards. You seemed too resourceful to be stopped by them. So I wondered why you wanted to protect the secret of where he was going. It was Mark Colston. You were protecting your godson. You never meant for me to find that CD."

"Of course not. The police were supposed to find it. I made it as easy as I could for them. It was the only picture in the whole damn office that was turned around. I did everything but hang an arrow from the ceiling pointing down to it. That buffoon Bryzinski should have found it, listened to it, and marched straight to Brody's door."

"The investigation of a murdered congressman would have been intense, and the pressure on Brody massive—especially with your ballistics friend on the job."

"Except Elias didn't know Jeannine was having an affair with your pal Gary," Papa Steve said, finishing Lou's thought. "Bryzinski had a prime suspect. The police did a half-baked job searching Elias's office because they already had their man in custody."

"Then I showed up," Lou said. "I became the police by proxy— the guy you fed enough information to keep on Brody's trail."

"All I wanted you to do was to get the police away from Gary and back on Brody. You did a lot more than I bargained for."

"By that, you mean I followed Brody and found out about the drugs and the Mantis juice."

"All I wanted you to do was get the murder weapon."

"Because you didn't want me to know the truth about Mantis."

"The motive for Elias's murder was supposed to be his knowledge of Reddy Creek," Papa Steve said. "Brody was stealing weapons because of budget cuts, and Elias was onto him. That's what the prosecutors would have said anyway, if the police had found the CD and had done their job by following the trail to its logical end."

"It's a weak case if you don't have the murder weapon, though."

"I couldn't have very well waltzed into a police station and said, 'Here, I think this is the gun used to kill Elias Colston.' I needed another way to get the gun into the right person's hands."

"It had to have been terrible for you."

"Shooting Elias? Killing my best friend? Yeah, Lou, it was worse than terrible. It was the hardest damn thing I've ever had to do.

I refused again and again, but Elias wouldn't let up." Papa Steve looked away and rubbed at his eyes with his hand.

"Eventually you caved in."

"Imagine if Cap asked you to kill him," Papa Steve said. "And you knew it was the right thing to do. You knew in your gut that it had to go down that way. Brody needed to be stopped."

"That's why you transferred to Mantis," Lou said.

"It was before Elias became ill. He had suspicions about Mantis and Brody. Mark's death, Brody's PhD thesis, the Reddy Creek incident, and the missing reporter's blog. But he didn't have proof."

"You got embedded with Mantis so you could follow Brody, and you found out about the Mantis drug. You knew all along."

"Mark and others died with incredible valor. Elias and I would never do anything to taint that. We had to eliminate Brody without having anyone learn about the chemicals the men were getting. Once you found that CD, all I wanted was your help getting the gun to the right people. End of story."

"Nobody was supposed to learn about Mantis," Lou said.

Papa Steve nodded. "That's what Elias wanted."

"With Brody gone, Mantis would be gone," Lou said.

"And so would its secret. We needed to take down Brody without leaving a black mark on those heroic young men. They would forever be associated with one of the most horrific examples of human experimentation since the Nazis. That would have been their legacy. For Mark, for the others, I did what had to be done."

"Whatever it takes," Lou said. "You picked the day because you knew Brody went to see Manolo each and every Wednesday. You knew he wouldn't have an alibi that would hold up."

"Elias must have said something to Jeannine," Papa Steve added. "She wouldn't have known it was his final good-bye. But I'm sure he spoke from the heart, because even though he didn't pay as much attention to her as he might have, he loved Jeannine to pieces."

"It was a kiss," Lou said, remembering. "A very special kiss."

"Well, whatever he said or did, I'm sure it made her realize the mistake she was making with Gary, so she ended the relationship."

"And Gary showed up at the Colstons' place, drunk and despondent. Wrong place, wrong time."

"He must have got there just after I left," Papa Steve said.

Silence.

"What happened out there with the men, Lou?" Papa Steve eventually asked. "What are we going to tell the world?"

"Wyatt Brody and Spencer Hogarth were involved in a weapons-theft scheme as a way to circumvent congressional budget cuts," Lou said. "Elias found out about Reddy Creek, and for that, Wyatt Brody killed him. We found the murder weapon in Brody's gun collection. We got it tested, and it came back a match. Brody was going to go public because the walls were closing in. Hogarth wouldn't stand for it, so he killed Brody. Once Hogarth realized he had no way out, he took his own life. End of story. That's what happened. And everybody from Mantis, Coon included, agrees."

"Anybody ever tell you that you're a piece of work?" Papa Steve asked.

IN THE third-floor courtroom of the circuit court for Baltimore County, Judge Sandra Griffey, a stern-looking black woman with a reputation for fairness and an unparalleled legal mind, looked over the motion Sarah filed for dismissal of the charges against Dr. Gary McHugh. Lou and Cap were among the dozen or so observers seated in the gallery.

To Lou's eyes, Gary looked gaunt. Thank goodness Cap had put Tiny on protective services duty, or Gary might have shown up to this hearing in far worse physical and emotional shape.

Judge Griffey slammed her gavel and brought the hearing to order. "The attorneys for the defendant have filed a motion for dismissal. Are the attorneys for the prosecution aware of this motion?"

The lead prosecutor rose from his seat. "The prosecution is aware, Your Honor."

"The defense may present the motion," Judge Griffey instructed.

Sarah stood, smoothing out the fabric of her pleated wool skirt, and cleared her throat. Lou focused on everything she did. He tugged on his crewneck sweater—a subconscious reaction that mimicked her movements. His finger got snagged on a small hole. Diversity's handiwork had followed him into court.

"Thank you, Your Honor," Sarah said. "New and important developments have emerged since my client's arrest that I have outlined in the motion. Forensic tests, corroborated by the prosecution's own ballistics expert, have confirmed that the weapon used to murder Elias Colston, an antique Colt pistol, was registered to the late Colonel Wyatt Brody. It is impossible for my client to have procured this weapon from the military base where Colonel Brody kept his collection under lock and key. Therefore, it is reasonable to conclude that Gary McHugh could not have fired the weapon that killed Elias Colston."

Lou was enraptured by Sarah's commanding performance. He could not have been more impressed with her poise and self-assurance. They'd been out for dinner once. At some point, he thought, he might arrange a dinner with her and Emily—but not yet.

Sarah went on to detail other highlights from her motion, including the motive Wyatt Brody had for committing murder as well as the opportunity. Her conclusions were impossible to refute.

"Does the prosecution have any objection to the motion to dismiss?" Judge Griffey asked.

"No, Your Honor. We accept the motion in full as presented."

"Very well," Judge Griffey said. "Dr. McHugh, please accept the court's sincere apology. This case is dismissed. You are free to go."

Gary beamed as he hugged Sarah. Then it was Lou's turn to give Gary a big embrace. "We did it, buddy!" Lou said.

"Thank you, Lou," Gary said. "I still can't believe it's over."

"Believe it. You're a free man. You heard the judge."

"I'm going to need to find a place to live."

Lou grimaced. Missy planned to file for divorce.

"I've actually given that some thought," Lou said.

"Yeah? What are you thinking? Four Seasons? Ritz?"

"More like the Hope House," Lou said. "It's a halfway house. I made a call and told them you might be coming to stay for a while.

They're saving you a room. I can provide you with an AA sponsor if you want." Lou thumbed behind him toward Cap. "But I've got to warn you—he's as strict as he is bald."

"That's pretty strict."

"This will be good for you, Gary."

"Okay. If it's what I need to do. Thanks, Lou. For everything."

"Whatever it takes," Lou said.

Gary eyed Lou with amused curiosity. "What does that mean?"

"It means from now on it's got to be a day at a time for you."

Sarah called out Gary's name. "There's paperwork to sign," she said. "Let's get this done."

"I've gotta run. I'll see you on the outside, buddy," Gary said.

Sarah waved at Lou in a way that said she would catch up with him later. Lou gave Sarah a thumbs-up.

Lou and Cap headed out of the courtroom together.

"Helluva show she put on in there," Cap said. "Helluva show."

"If you're ever in trouble, I know a great lawyer."

"So far, I've been able to settle all my disputes in the ring. I'm going to look after your buddy, Gary, just like I looked after you."

"Then I know he's going to be all right," Lou said.

Stepping outside, Lou shielded his eyes from the midday sun. It took him a moment to make out the West Virginia highway patrol car parked out front. Judy Lemon leaned up against her car, resplendent in her uniform. Papa Steve stood beside her, wearing jeans, a parka, and a broad-rimmed black leather cowboy hat.

"How'd it go in there?" Papa Steve asked.

"He's a free man," Lou said. "Case closed."

Hugs were exchanged. The four shared a closeness they would forever be reminded of anytime the *1812 Overture* played.

"Thanks for letting me know about the hearing," Papa Steve said. "I'm sorry I couldn't have gotten here sooner, but I'm glad for your friend, Gary. He'd still be in jail if it wasn't for you and Cap."

"And you and Officer Judy," Cap added.

"I thought you'd like to know that they've got confessions from the two Palace Guards who killed Hector," Papa Steve said. "He's going to be buried in Arlington Cemetery, and his family will receive the full military death benefit."

"That is great news," Lou said. "I've had a heavy heart about Hector. I'm glad to know Gary wasn't the only one for whom justice was served."

"I also came here to say good-bye," Papa Steve said, "at least for now. I've put in my papers, and I'm officially retiring from the corps. I figured I'd do a little bit of traveling before my bones get too creaky for the road."

Lou shot Papa Steve and Judy a questioning glance.

"So are you two . . .

"Happy, healthy, and headed out West," Judy said, preempting the need to supply any more details.

"What's with the hat?" Cap asked Papa Steve.

"We've got a reservation at a dude ranch in Arizona," Papa Steve said. "Saddle sores and hot tubs. I figured a fine Stetson hat will help me get into character."

"And don't tell me," Lou said. "You happen to have a friend who owns a fine hat store."

Papa Steve took Lou's right hand in both of his. "How'd you guess?" he said.

Share Your Thoughts!

Communicate with us directly to chat about the stories and tell us what you liked or disliked. We want to keep giving you the kinds of books you want to read, and this is one way to make that happen. So let us know what you think. Share your thoughts with us at **SelectEditions@gmail.com**.

How to Make
a Thriller Happen

WHEN Michael Palmer offers writing tips, he knows what he's talking about. Here are some from his website, MichaelPalmerBooks.com.

First, choose a *What If*. "Preparation for my books begins with a simple 'What if' question. I work hard at crafting it, and the reward is that I get to start on the long and harrowing road to a 400-page novel with clarity," he writes.

Then pick a protagonist. "Once I have 'What if?' straight, the next question is: 'Whose book is it?' What is this main character going to have at stake in the story?" According to Palmer, the elements of a good thriller are: 1) there is something that has been going on before the story starts; 2) the protagonist has been dealing with issues of her own before the story starts; and 3) the protagonist encounters the story because of who she is and what she does, setting a series of events in motion.

When it comes to the writing, there's the basic show, don't tell. "Writing 'He was a cruel and remorseless man' doesn't pack a whit of excitement or drama, but showing the character doing something cruel and remorseless certainly does. Characters must be defined by what they do, not by what you say they are," Palmer says.

Next, there's the concept of point of view. "Through whose eyes is this story—or this part of the story—being told? What is the character thinking and feeling? What does he know? How does she interpret what is going on?" Here's an idea to remember: "I have found it effective and quite frightening to describe scenes of murder from the point of view of the victim, often giving bits of background of the character to heighten sympathy."

And remember when your high school teachers told you to avoid adverbs? Palmer is right there with them. "The dialogue, if it's right, should obviate the need. Sometimes adverbs are needed when there is more than one way a sentence can be said, but mostly the contents should be their own adverb."

Palmer, when talking about what works and what doesn't, puts his finger on the most important thing: "Most people read a thriller thinking they are reading it to find out what happens at the end—the explanation for what is going on in the story. The truth is, whether readers are aware of it or not, most of the time they keep reading a book because they have been led to care about the characters and what happens to them." ■

Vital Stats

EDUCATION: Pre-med at Wesleyan University; Case Western Reserve University for med school; internal medicine training at Boston City and Mass General hospitals.
INSPIRATION FOR WRITING AFTER YEARS OF WORKING IN MEDICINE: "If Robin Cook can write a book and has the same education as I do, why can't I?"
PART-TIME JOB: Associate Director at Massachusetts Medical Society

#1 INTERNATIONAL BESTSELLER

A STREET CAT NAMED BOB

And How He Saved My Life

James Bowen

Chapter 1

FELLOW TRAVELERS

THERE'S a famous quote I read somewhere. It says we are all given second chances every day of our lives. They are there for the taking; it's just that we don't usually take them.

I spent a big chunk of my life proving that quote. I was given a lot of opportunities. For a long time I failed to take any of them. But then, in the early spring of 2007, that began to change. It was then that I befriended Bob. Looking back on it, something tells me it might have been his second chance, too.

I first encountered him on a gloomy Thursday evening in March. London hadn't quite shaken off the winter, and it was still bitingly cold on the streets, especially when the winds blew in off the Thames. There had even been a hint of frost in the air, which was why I'd arrived back at my new sheltered accommodation in Tottenham, north London, a little earlier than usual after a day busking around Covent Garden.

As normal, I had my black guitar case and rucksack slung over my shoulders, but on this evening I also had my closest friend, Belle, with me. We'd gone out together years ago but were just mates now. We were going to eat a cheap takeaway curry and watch a movie on the small television set I'd managed to find in a charity shop round the corner.

As usual, the lift in the apartment block wasn't working, so we headed for the stairs, resigned to making the long trudge up to the fifth floor. The strip lighting in the hallway was broken, and part of the ground floor was swathed in darkness, but as we made our way to the stairwell I couldn't help noticing a pair of glowing eyes in the gloom. When I heard a gentle, plaintive meowing, I realized what it was. Edging closer, in the half-light I could see a ginger cat curled up on a doormat outside one of the flats.

I'd grown up with cats and had always had a bit of a soft spot for them. I could tell he was a tom, a male. He wasn't in the slightest bit nervous—in fact, completely the opposite. He looked very much at home here, and judging by the way he was fixing me with a steady, intelligent stare, I was the one who was straying into his territory. It was as if he were saying, "So who are you, and what brings you here?"

I couldn't resist kneeling down and introducing myself. "Hello, mate. I've not seen you before. Do you live here?"

He looked at me with the same aloof expression, as if weighing me up.

I stroked his neck, partly to make friends but partly to see if he was wearing a collar or any identification. There was nothing, which suggested that he was a stray.

He seemed to enjoy the affection and began brushing himself lightly against me. As I petted him a little more, I could feel that his coat was in poor condition, with bald patches here and there. He was clearly in need of a good meal and a bit of TLC.

"Poor chap, I think he's a stray. He's really thin," I said, looking up at Belle, who was waiting patiently by the foot of the stairs.

She knew I had a weakness for cats. "No, James, you can't have him. He can't have just wandered in here and settled on this spot—he must belong to whoever lives there," she said, nodding toward the flat that the cat was sitting outside. "Probably waiting for them to come home and let him in."

Reluctantly, I agreed. I couldn't just pick up a cat and take him with me, even if all the signs pointed to the fact it was homeless. What if it did belong to the person living in that flat? They weren't going to take kindly to someone carrying off their pet, were they?

Besides, the last thing I needed right now was the extra responsibility of a cat. I was a failed musician and recovering drug addict living a hand-to-mouth existence in sheltered accommodation. I'd barely moved into this place myself and was still trying to sort out my flat. Taking responsibility for myself was hard enough.

THE following morning I headed downstairs and found the ginger tom still sitting there. Once again, I dropped down on one knee and stroked him. Once again, it was obvious that he loved it. He was purring away, appreciating the attention.

In daylight I could see that he was a gorgeous creature. He had a striking face with amazingly piercing green eyes. Looking closer, I could tell that he must have been in a fight or an accident because there were scratches on his face and legs. And his coat was in very poor condition with at least half a dozen bald patches where you could see the skin. I was genuinely concerned about him, but again, I told myself that I already had more than enough to worry about. So, reluctantly, I headed off to catch the bus to central London and Covent Garden where I was going to once more try to earn a few quid busking.

By the time I got back that night it was pretty late, almost ten o'clock. I immediately headed for the corridor, but there was no sign of the ginger tom. Part of me was disappointed. I'd taken a shine to him. But mostly I felt relieved. I assumed he must have been let in by his owner.

My HEART sank a bit when I went down again the next day and saw him back in the same position. He was slightly more vulnerable and disheveled than before, looked cold and hungry, and was shaking a little.

"Still here, then," I said, stroking him. "Not looking so good today."

I decided this had gone on for long enough. I knocked on the door of the flat. I had to say something. If this was their pet, it was no way to treat him. He needed something to eat and drink—and some medical attention.

A guy appeared at the door. He was unshaven, wearing a T-shirt and tracksuit bottoms and looked like he'd been sleeping even though it was the middle of the afternoon.

"Sorry to bother you, mate. Is this your cat?" I asked him.

For a second he looked at me as if I were mad. "What cat?" he said, before looking down and seeing the ginger tom curled up in a ball on the doormat. "Oh. No," he said with a disinterested shrug. "Nothing to do with me."

"He's been there for days," I said, again drawing a blank look.

"Has he? Well, as I say, nothing to do with me."

He then slammed the door shut.

I made my mind up. "Okay, you are coming with me," I said, digging into my rucksack for the box of biscuits I carried specifically to give treats to the cats and dogs that approached me when I was busking. I rattled it at him, and he was immediately up on all fours, following me.

I could see he was a bit uneasy on his feet and was carrying one of his back legs in an awkward manner, so we took our time climbing the five flights of stairs.

A few minutes later we were safely ensconced in my flat. It was threadbare, it's fair to say. Apart from the telly, all I had was a secondhand sofa bed, a mattress in the small bedroom, and in the kitchen area a half-working refrigerator, a microwave, a kettle, and a toaster. There was no cooker. The only other things in the flat were my books, videos, and knickknacks. I'm a bit of a magpie; I collect all sorts of stuff from the street. At that time I had a broken parking meter in one corner and a broken mannequin with a cowboy hat on its head in another. A friend once called my place "the old curiosity shop."

As he sussed out his new environment, the only thing the tom was curious about was the kitchen.

I fished out some milk from the fridge, poured it into a saucer, and mixed it with a bit of water. He lapped it up in seconds.

I had a bit of tuna, so I mixed it up with some mashed up biscuits and gave that to him as well. Again, he wolfed it down. *He must be absolutely starving,* I thought.

After the cold and dark of the corridor, the flat was five-star luxury as far as the tom was concerned. He seemed very pleased to be there and after being fed, headed for the living room where he curled up near the radiator.

As I sat and watched him, there was no doubt in my mind that there was something wrong with his leg. Sure enough, when I examined him, I found that he had a big abscess on the back of his rear right leg. The wound was the size of a large, caninelike tooth, which gave me a good idea how he'd got it. He'd probably been attacked by a dog or a fox that had stuck its teeth in and clung on as he'd tried to escape. He also had a lot of scratches, one on his face not far from his eye.

I sterilized the wound as best I could by putting him in the bath, then putting moisturizer around the wound and Vaseline on the wound itself. A lot of cats would have created havoc if I'd tried to treat them like that, but he was as good as gold.

He spent most of the day curled up on what was already his favorite spot, near the radiator. But he also roamed the flat every now and again, jumping up and scratching at whatever he could find. He found the mannequin in the corner a bit of a magnet. I didn't mind. I knew ginger toms could be lively, and I could tell he had a lot of pent-up energy. When I went to stroke him, he jumped up and started pawing at me. At one point he got quite animated, scratching furiously, almost cutting my hand.

"Okay, mate, calm down," I said, lifting him off me and putting him down on the floor. I couldn't be sure, but my guess was that he was still "complete" and well into puberty. It again underlined the nagging feeling that he must have come off the streets rather than from a home.

I spent the evening watching television, the tom curled up by the radiator, seemingly content to be there. He only moved when I went to bed, picking himself up and following me into the bedroom where he wrapped himself up into a ball at the edge of the bed. As I listened to his gentle purring in the dark, it felt good to have him there. He was company, I guess. I'd not had a lot of that lately.

On Sunday morning I got up early and decided to hit the streets to see if I could find his owner. I figured someone might have stuck up a "Lost Cat" poster. There was almost always a photocopied appeal for the return of a missing pet plastered on local lampposts.

Just in case I found the owner quickly, I took the cat with me, attached to a leash I'd made out of a shoelace. He was happy to walk by my side as we took the stairs to the ground floor.

Out of interest, I took the cat off his lead outside to see if he knew what direction to go in. But as we walked the streets, it was obvious he was completely lost. He looked at me as if to say, "I don't know where I am; I want to stay with you."

We were out for a few hours. At one point he scurried off into a bush to do his business, leaving me to ask any passing locals whether they recognized him. All I got were blank looks and shrugs.

As we wandered around, I couldn't help wondering about his story: where he'd come from and what sort of life he'd led before he'd come and sat on the mat downstairs. The fact that he wasn't house-trained was the main argument against him having been domesticated. But the more I got to know him, the more convinced I was that he had definitely been used to being around one person. He seemed to latch on to people who he thought would look after him. That's what he'd done with me.

The biggest clue about his background was his injury. He'd definitely picked that up in a fight. From the way it was leaking pus, the wound must have been a few days old, maybe even a week. That suggested another possibility: London has always had a large population of street cats, strays who wander the streets living off scraps and the comfort of strangers. These are the flotsam and jetsam of the city, fighting for survival on a daily basis. A lot of them were like this ginger tom, slightly battered, broken creatures.

Maybe he'd spotted a kindred spirit in me.

Chapter 2

ROAD TO RECOVERY

I'D BEEN around cats since I was a child. While I was growing up, my family had several Siamese and, at one stage, a beautiful tortoiseshell cat. My memories of the cats were generally fond, but the one that stuck most vividly in mind was the darkest.

I'd grown up in England and Australia, and for a while, we lived in a place called Craigie in western Australia. While we were there, we had a lovely white fluffy kitten. I can't remember where we got it from, but wherever it was, it was a terrible home. The poor little thing hadn't been checked out medically before being handed over to us and died within a couple of weeks of us getting it. I was five or six at the time and was devastated—as was my mother.

I'd thought about the kitten a lot this weekend as I'd spent time with the tom. I had an awful feeling that he would suffer the same fate. So that Sunday evening, I made a decision: I wasn't going to let that happen. I had to take him to a vet. I would get up early the next morning and take him to the nearest RSPCA center, down toward Finsbury Park.

My alarm woke me on Monday, and I got up to give the cat a bowl of mashed biscuits and tuna. It was another gray morning, but I couldn't use that as an excuse.

Given the state of his leg, I knew he wasn't going to be up to the ninety-minute walk, so I decided to carry him and placed him in a green recycling box. It wasn't ideal, but I couldn't find anything else. No sooner had we set off than it was clear that he didn't like it. He kept moving, sticking his paw over the top of the box and attempting to climb out. Eventually, I gave up.

"Come on, I'll carry you," I said, picking him up with my spare arm while carrying the recycling box in the other. He was soon scrambling up onto my shoulders, where he settled. I let him sit there while I carried the empty box with me all the way to the RSPCA center.

The center was packed with dogs and their owners, most of whom seemed to be teenage blokes with skinhead haircuts and aggressive tattoos. Seventy percent of the dogs were Staffordshire bull terriers that had almost certainly been injured in fights with other dogs, probably for people's amusement.

The cat sat on my lap or on my shoulder. I could tell he was nervous, and I couldn't blame him. He was getting snarled at by most of the dogs in the waiting room. One or two were being held tightly on their leashes as they strained to get closer.

One by one, the dogs were ushered into the treatment room. In the end it took us four and a half hours to be seen. The vet was middle-aged and had a kind of world-weary, seen-it-all expression.

"So what seems to be the problem?" he asked me.

I told him how I'd found the cat and pointed out the abscess.

"Okay, let's have a quick look at him," he said.

He could tell the cat was in pain and gave him a small dose of diazepam to help relieve it. He then explained that he was going to issue a prescription for a two-week course of cat-strength amoxicillin. "Come back and see me again if things haven't improved in a fortnight."

I thought I'd take the opportunity to ask about fleas.

He had a look around his coat but could find nothing. "However, it's probably worth you giving him some tablets for that. It can be a problem in young cats."

Again, I watched as he wrote a prescription. To his credit, he also checked to see if the tom was microchipped. He wasn't, which again suggested to me he was a street cat.

"You should get that done when you have a chance," he said. "I think he should also be neutered quite soon as well," he added, handing me a form and a brochure advertising a free neutering scheme for strays.

Leaving the vet's surgery, I went up to the counter at the dispensary and handed over the prescriptions. The white-coated lady punched in the details to the till and produced a bill. "That will be twenty-two pounds, please," she said.

My heart sank. "Twenty-two pounds! Really?" I asked. I had just over thirty pounds in the whole world at that point.

"Afraid so, love," the nurse said, looking sympathetic but implacable.

I handed over the thirty pounds in cash and took the change.

It was a lot of money for me. A day's wages. But I knew I had no option: I couldn't let my new friend down. "Looks like we're stuck with each other for the next fortnight," I said to the tom as we headed out of the door and walked back to the flat.

It was the truth. There was no way I was going to get rid of the cat until he'd completed his course of medicine. No one else was going to make sure he took his tablets, and I couldn't let him out on the streets in case he picked up an infection. I don't know why but having him to look after galvanized me. I felt like I had an extra purpose in my life, something positive to do for someone—or something—other than myself.

That afternoon I headed to a local pet store and got him a couple of weeks' worth of cat food. It cost me around nine pounds, which really was the last money I had.

That night I had to leave him on his own and head to Covent Garden with my guitar. I now had two mouths to feed.

OVER the course of the next few days, as I nursed him back to health, I got to know him better. By now I'd given him a name: Bob. I got the idea while watching a DVD of one of my old favorite TV series, *Twin Peaks*. There was a character in that called Killer Bob. He was actually schizophrenic, a kind of Jekyll and Hyde character. Part of the time he would be a normal, sane guy; the next he would be crazy and out of control. The tom was a bit like that. When he was happy, you couldn't have wished to see a calmer, kinder cat. But when the mood took him, he could be an absolute maniac.

It was pretty clear to me now that Bob must have lived outdoors. When it came to toilet time, he absolutely refused to go in the litter tray that I'd bought for him. Instead, I had to take him downstairs and let him do his business in the gardens that surrounded the flats.

There was no doubt that he was forming an affection for me. As, indeed, I was for him. As the days passed, he became more and more confident—and friendly.

Our life settled into a bit of a routine. I'd leave Bob in the flat in the morning and head to Covent Garden where I'd play until I got enough cash. When I got home, he'd be waiting for me at the door. He would then follow me to the sofa in the front room and watch telly with me.

I was beginning to realize what a smart cat he was. I could see that he understood everything I was saying to him. When I patted the sofa and invited him to come and sit next to me, he did. He also knew what I meant when I told him it was time for him to have his meds. He would look at me as if to say "Do I have to?" But he wouldn't struggle while I put tablets in his mouth and rubbed his throat gently until he swallowed them. Most cats would go mad if you tried to open their mouths. But he already trusted me.

It was around that point I began to realize there was something rather special about Bob. He wasn't perfect, by any means. He knew where the food lived and would regularly crash around the kitchen, knocking over pots and pans as he searched for it. But he listened if I said no. All I had to do was say, "No, get away from there, Bob," and he'd slink off. Again, it showed how intelligent he was.

I really enjoyed Bob's company, but I knew I had to be careful. I couldn't form too strong a friendship because, sooner or later, he would want to return to the streets. He wasn't the sort of cat that was going to enjoy being cooped up permanently. For the short term, however, I was his guardian and I was determined to fulfill that role to the best of my ability.

One morning I filled in the form the vet had given me for the neutering service. I stuck it in the post and, to my amazement, got a letter within a couple of days. It contained a certificate entitling us to a free neutering.

THE next morning I took Bob down to do his business outside again. He headed for his favorite spot in the bushes adjoining the neighboring houses. I suspected he was marking his territory. He had satisfied himself that everything was right when he suddenly froze and tensed up. I was about to go over to see what was bothering him when it became quite obvious what it was.

All of a sudden, Bob lunged forward at lightning speed. It really did all happen in a blur. Before I knew it, Bob had grabbed at something in the grass near the hedge. It was a gray mouse, no more than three inches long. The little fellow hadn't stood a chance. Bob had pounced with speed and precision and now had the creature clamped between his teeth. The mouse's legs were thrashing around, and Bob was carefully repositioning its body in his teeth so that he could finish it off. It wasn't long before the inevitable happened and the little creature gave up the fight. It was at that point that Bob released it and laid it on the ground.

I didn't want Bob to eat it. Mice were notorious breeding grounds for disease. So I knelt down and attempted to pick up his prey. He wasn't too happy about it and made a little noise that was part growl and part hiss. He then picked the mouse up again.

"Give it to me, Bob," I said, refusing to back down. "Give it to me."

He gave me a look as if to say, "Why should I?"

I fished around in my coat and found a nibble, offering him a trade. "Take this instead, Bob. It will be much better for you."

He still wasn't convinced, but after a few more moments, the standoff ended and he gave in. As soon as he stepped away from the mouse, I picked it up by its tail and disposed of it.

It was another reminder of one of the many fascinating things about cats: They are predators by nature. A lot of people don't like to think of their cute little kitty as a mass murderer, but that's what cats are, given half a chance. Bob had proved the point. His speed and his skill as a killer were amazing to behold.

It set me thinking again about the life he must have led. Had he relied on finding and eating prey like this every day? Had he always lived off the land? How had he become the cat he was today? I would love to have known. I was sure my street cat friend had a tale or two to tell.

In many ways, this was something else that Bob and I had in common. Ever since I'd ended up living rough on the streets, people had wondered about my past life. Some had a professional interest, of course. I'd spoken to social workers, psychologists, and even police officers who'd quizzed me about living on the streets. But a lot of ordinary people would ask me about it, too. I don't know why, but people are fascinated to learn how some members of society fall through the cracks. I think it's partly that feeling of "there but for the grace of God go I." But I think it also makes people feel better about their own lives. It makes them think, "Well, I may think my life is bad, but it could be worse. I could be that poor sod."

The answer to how people like me end up on the streets is always different, of course. But there are usually some similarities. Often drugs and alcohol play a big part in the story. In an awful lot of instances, the road that led them to living on the streets stretches all the way back to their childhood and their relationship with their family. That was certainly the way it was for me.

I lived quite a rootless childhood, traveling between the UK and Australia. I was born in Surrey, but when I was three my family moved to Melbourne. My mother and father had separated. While my father stayed in Surrey, my mother had got away from all the aggravation by landing a job selling for Rank Xerox, the photocopying company, in Melbourne. She was really good at it and was one of the company's top saleswomen.

My mother had itchy feet, however, and within about two years, we had moved from Melbourne to western Australia. We stayed there for about three or four years. Life in Australia was pretty good. We lived in a succession of large bungalows, each of which had a vast garden at the back. I had all the space a boy could want to play in, and I loved the Australian landscape. The trouble was that I didn't have any friends.

I found it very hard to fit in at school, mainly, I think, because we'd moved a lot. When I was nine, we moved back to the UK, to Sussex, near Horsham. I enjoyed being back in England and was just getting back into life in the northern hemisphere when we moved yet again—back to western Australia—when I was around twelve. This time we ended up in a place called Quinn's Rock. It was there that I think a lot of my problems really began. Because of all this traveling around, I never had a family home and never grew up in one place. There is no doubt in my mind that we moved home way too much, and it was not good for a growing child. It made it hard for me to become socially adept. I was always trying too hard to impress, which isn't good when you are a kid. It had the opposite result: I ended up being bullied at every school I went to. It was particularly bad in Quinn's Rock.

I probably stuck out with my British accent and my eager-to-please attitude. I was a sitting target, really. One day they decided to stone me. Literally. Quinn's Rock was called Quinn's Rock for a reason, and these kids took advantage of all the lumps of limestone that were lying around wherever you looked. I got a concussion after being bombarded on the way home from school.

We continued living this nomadic existence throughout my early teens. Moves were usually connected to my mother's many business ventures. At one point she started doing telemarketing training videos. That did quite well for a while. Then she set up a women's magazine, which didn't do so well. Sometimes we'd have plenty of money; other times we'd be strapped for cash. But that never lasted for long; she was a proper entrepreneur.

By the time I was in my midteens, I'd pretty much quit school. I left because I was just sick to death of the bullying. And I was very independent-minded. I became a wild kid who was always out late, always defying my mother, and generally thumbing his nose at authority, no matter what form it took.

I soon developed a knack for getting into trouble. Predictably, I got into drugs. I was set on the road to self-destruction.

My mother tried her hardest to get me off drugs. She did all the things mothers do. She went through my pockets and even locked me in my bedroom a few times. But I picked the locks easily with a bobby pin. I wasn't going to be hemmed in by her or anyone else. We argued even more then, and things went from bad to worse. Mum got me to go to a psychiatrist at one point. They diagnosed me with everything from schizophrenia to manic depression to attention-deficit hyperactivity disorder. Of course, I was a messed-up teenager who thought he knew better than everyone. With the benefit of hindsight, I can see that my mother must have felt power-less and terrified of what was going to happen to me. But I was oblivious to other people's feelings. I didn't care, and I didn't listen to anyone.

The situation got so bad between us that for a while I lived in Christian charity accommodation. I passed my time taking drugs and playing guitar.

Around my eighteenth birthday, I announced that I was going to move back to London to live with my half sister from my father's previous marriage. I'd be gone for six months or so. That was the plan. I would hang out with my half sister and pursue my grand dreams of making it as a musician. But things didn't exactly go to plan.

My brother-in-law hadn't taken too kindly to my arrival. I was a rebellious teenager who dressed like a Goth and was, probably, a complete pain in the arse, especially as I wasn't contributing to the household bills.

In Australia I'd worked in IT and sold mobile phones, but back in the UK I couldn't land a decent job. The first I'd been able to get had been working as a bartender. But my face hadn't fitted, and they'd sacked me after Christmas in 1997. As if that wasn't bad enough, they wrote the dole office a letter saying I'd quit the job, which meant I couldn't collect the benefits I was eligible for by virtue of having been born in England.

After that, I was even less welcome in my brother-in-law's house. Eventually, my half sister and he kicked me out. I had made contact with my dad and been to see him a couple of times, but it was clear we weren't going to get on. I started sleeping on friends' floors and sofas, leading a nomadic existence, carrying my sleeping bag with me to flats and squats around London. When I ran out of floors, I moved to the streets.

Things headed downward fast from there.

LIVING on the streets strips away your dignity, your identity— your everything, really. People treat you as a nonperson. They don't want anything to do with you. Soon you haven't got a real friend in the world. While I was sleeping rough, I managed to get a job as a kitchen porter, but they sacked me when they found out I was homeless. When you are homeless, you stand very little chance.

The one thing that might have saved me was going back to Australia. I had a return ticket but lost my passport two weeks before the flight. I didn't have the money to get a new one. Any hope I had of getting back to my family in Australia disappeared. And so, in a way, did I.

THE next phase of my life was a fog of drugs, drink, petty crime— and, well, hopelessness. Not helped by the fact that I developed a heroin habit.

I took it at first simply to help me get to sleep at night on the streets. It anesthetized me from the cold and the loneliness.

Unfortunately, it had taken a hold of my soul as well. By 1998 I was totally dependent on it. I probably came close to death a few times, although, to be honest, I was so out of it that I had no idea.

During that period, it didn't occur to me to contact anyone in my family. I had disappeared off the face of the earth, and I didn't really care. I was too wrapped up in surviving. Looking back now, I can only imagine that they must have been going through hell.

I got an inkling of the grief I was causing about a year after I had arrived in London and about nine months or so after I'd taken to the streets. It was around Christmastime, and I decided to give my father a call.

"Where the hell have you been? We've all been worried sick about you," he said.

I made some pathetic excuses, but he just shouted at me. He told me that my mother had been in contact with him, desperately trying to find out where I was. That was a measure of how worried she'd become. The two of them never spoke. He shouted and screamed at me for fully five minutes. I realize now it was a mixture of release and anger. He had probably thought I was dead, which, in a way, I had been.

That period of my life lasted a year or so. I was eventually picked up off the streets by a homeless charity and stayed in various shelters. I ended up on what's known as the "vulnerable housing" list, which qualified me as a priority for sheltered accommodation. The problem was that for the best part of the next decade I ended up living in horrendous hostels, B&Bs, and houses, sharing space with heroin and crack addicts who would steal anything that wasn't nailed down. Everything I had was stolen at some point. I had to sleep with my most important possessions tucked inside my clothes. Survival was all I could think about.

Inevitably, my drug dependency got worse. By the time I was in my late twenties, my habit had got so bad I was put on a drug rehabilitation program. For a while, the daily trip to the chemist and the fortnightly bus ride to my drug dependency unit in Camden became the focus of my life. I'd get out of bed and go and do one or the other on autopilot, as if in a daze, which, if I'm honest, I often was.

I did some counseling there as well. I talked endlessly about my habit, how it had started and how I was going to bring it to an end. It's easy to come up with excuses for drug addiction, but I'm certain I know the reason for mine. It was pure and simple loneliness. Heroin allowed me to anesthetize myself to my isolation, to the fact that I didn't have family or a huge circle of friends. I was on my own, and as strange and unfathomable as it will seem to most people, heroin was my friend.

Deep down, however, I knew it was killing me—literally. So over a period of a few years, I moved off heroin onto methadone, the synthetic opioid that is used as a substitute. By the spring of 2007, the plan was that I would eventually start weaning myself off that and get completely straight. The move to the flat in Tottenham was a key part of that process. It was an ordinary apartment block full of ordinary families.

To help pay the rent, I'd started busking. It wasn't much but it helped put food on the table and pay the gas and electricity. I knew it was my chance to turn the corner and put my life back on track. And I knew I had to take it this time. If I were a cat, this would have been my ninth life.

Chapter 3

The Snip

As we approached the end of Bob's second week of medication, he was looking a lot brighter. The wound at the back of his leg was healing, and the bald patches on his coat had begun to disappear. He also seemed happier—his eyes had a more lustrous glow to them.

He was on the road to recovery, and his boisterousness around the flat was the ultimate proof. He had been a whirling dervish since day one, flying around the place, but in the past week he'd become even more of a ball of energy. He would jump and run around like some kind of maniac, clawing furiously at everything and anything he could find, including me. There were scratches on every wooden surface in the flat. I even had scratches on the back of my hand and arm. I didn't mind. I knew it wasn't malicious and that he was only playing.

He had become such a menace in the kitchen, where he would claw at the cupboards and fridge door, that I'd had to buy a couple of cheap plastic child locks. I also had to be careful about leaving anything lying around that might become a plaything for him. A pair of shoes or item of clothing could be scratched to bits within minutes.

I'd been around enough cats in my life to recognize the signs: He was a young male with way too much testosterone flying around his body. He needed neutering. So a couple of days before his course of medicine finished, I decided to call the local vets, the Abbey Clinic on Dalston Lane. I rang the vets' surgery and spoke to a nurse. I explained my situation and asked whether Bob was eligible for a free operation. She said yes provided I had a certificate from a vet, which I did.

I explained that he was coming to the end of a course of antibiotics, but she said that shouldn't be a problem. She recommended that I book him in for an operation in two days' time. "If everything goes to plan, you'll be able to pick him up at the end of the day."

I got up nice and early on the day of the operation, knowing that I had to get him into the surgery by 10:00 a.m. It was the first time that we'd traveled any distance from the flat together since our visit to the RSPCA.

I stuck him in the same green plastic recycling box I'd used a fortnight earlier. The weather was miserable, so I took the lid and let it rest loosely on the box once we were out and about. He wasn't much more comfortable in it that day than he had been the first time. He kept sticking his head out.

We got to the Abbey Clinic in plenty of time and found the place packed with dogs tugging on their owners' leashes and growling at the cats inside their smart carriers. Bob stood out like a sore thumb in his improvised carrier, so he was immediately a target for their aggression.

Some cats would have bolted, I'm sure. But Bob wasn't fazed at all. He seemed to have placed his trust in me.

When my name was called out, a young nurse came out to meet us. She led me into a room where she asked me some standard questions.

"Once it's been carried out, the operation can't be reversed. So are you certain you don't want to breed from Bob at some future date?" she said.

I smiled. "Quite certain," I said, rubbing Bob on the head.

Her next question stumped me, however. "How old is Bob?"

"Ah. I really don't know," I said, before briefly explaining his story.

She explained that the fact that he hadn't been neutered was a good clue about his age. "Cats tend to become sexually mature at around six months of age. If they are left 'entire' after that they go through distinct physical changes. For instance, toms get fuller in the face. They also develop thicker skins and generally become quite big, certainly bigger than cats that have been neutered," she told me. "He's not that big, so I'd guess that he's maybe nine to ten months old."

As she passed me the release forms, she explained that there was a chance of complications but that it was tiny. "We will give him a thorough examination and run a blood test before we go ahead. If there's a problem, we will contact you. If everything goes okay, you can collect Bob in six hours," she said, looking down at her watch. "So at around four thirty. Is that okay?"

"Yeah, great." I nodded. "See you then."

After giving Bob a final cuddle, I headed back out into the overcast streets. There was rain brewing once more.

I didn't have time to head all the way into central London. By the time I'd set up and sung a few songs, it would be time to turn around again. So I decided to take my chances around the nearest railway station, Dalston Kingsland. It wasn't the greatest pitch in the world, but it provided me with a few quid and a place to while away the hours as I waited.

I tried to block Bob out of my thoughts as I played. I didn't want to think about him in the operating theater. I'd heard stories of cats and dogs going into vets' surgeries for minor procedures and never coming out again. I struggled to keep my darkest thoughts at bay. It didn't help that there were big black clouds glowering over me.

Time passed very, very slowly. Eventually, the clock reached 4:15 p.m. and I packed up. I almost ran the last few hundred yards to the clinic.

The nurse I'd seen earlier was at the reception desk talking to a colleague and greeted me with a smile. "He's fine, absolutely fine. Don't worry," she said. "Get your breath back, and I'll take you through."

It was weird, I hadn't felt this concerned about someone—or something—for years.

I went into the surgical area and saw Bob lying in a nice warm cage.

"Hello, Bob mate, how you doing?" I said.

He was still very dopey, so he didn't recognize me for a while, but when he did, he sat upright and started clawing at the doors of the cage as if to say, "Let me outta here."

The nurse got me to sign a discharge notice and then gave Bob a good once-over to make sure he was fit to leave.

She was really lovely and very helpful. She showed me where the incisions had been made. "It will stay swollen and sore around there for a couple of days, but that's normal. Just check every now and again to make sure there's no discharge. He probably won't want to eat much the day after, but his appetite will return. If he stays very sleepy and lethargic, give us a ring or bring him in."

I'd brought the recycling box along with me again and was just about to pick Bob up when she told me to wait.

"Hang on," she said. "I think we can do better than that."

She went away for a couple of minutes and then produced a lovely sky-blue carrying case. "Don't worry. We've got loads of spares. You can have this one. Just drop it back in when you're next passing."

"Really?" Maybe someone had left it behind. Or maybe someone had brought their cat in and returned to discover that the carrying case would not be needed anymore. I didn't want to dwell on it.

It was obvious that the op had taken a lot out of Bob. In the carrier on the way home he just lay there, half-asleep. The moment we got to the flat, he slowly padded over to his spot by the radiator and lay down. He slept there all night.

I took the day off work the next day to make sure he was okay. The advice from the vet was that he should be supervised for twenty-four to forty-eight hours. I could never have forgiven myself if something had gone wrong, so I stayed in the flat on twenty-four-hour Bob watch.

Fortunately, he was absolutely fine. The following morning, he was a bit perkier and ate a little bit of breakfast.

Over the next couple of days, he began becoming more like the old Bob. Within three days of the op, he was wolfing down his food just like before. I knew he'd still have the odd mad half hour, but I was glad I'd acted.

Chapter 4

CENTER OF ATTENTION

AS THE fortnight drew to a close, I realized that I had to think about getting Bob out of the flat and back onto the streets. That's where he had come from, and I assumed that's where he would want to return.

He'd continued to make really good progress and looked much healthier than when I'd first met him. He'd fattened up, too.

A day or two after I'd completed the course of medicine and he'd recovered fully, I took Bob downstairs, out through the hallway, and down the path toward the gate. Then I pointed him in the direction of the street.

He stood there, fixed to the spot, looking at me confused, as if to say, "What do you want me to do?"

"Go, go, go on," I said, making sweeping movements with my hands.

It had no effect whatsoever.

For a moment I just stood there, engaged in a staring competition with him. Then he turned on his heels and padded off, not in the direction of the street but toward the patch of ground where he liked to do his business. He then dug a hole, covered it all up, and strolled back toward me.

This time his expression said, "Okay, I did what you wanted. What now?"

It was then, for the first time, a thought began to crystallize in my head. "I think you want to hang around," I said quietly to him.

Part of me was pleased. I enjoyed his company, and he was certainly a character. But, being sensible, I knew I shouldn't let it happen. I was still struggling to look after myself. I was still on a drug dependency program and would be for the foreseeable future. How on earth was I going to look after a cat, even one as intelligent and self-sufficient as Bob?

With a heavy heart, I decided that I'd have to slowly start easing him out of the flat during the day. When I went to work in the morning, I'd take him out and leave him outside in the gardens. "Tough love," I told myself.

He didn't like it one bit. The first time I did it, he shot me a look that said, "Traitor." As I headed off with my guitar, he followed, quietly stalking me, zigzagging across the pavement like some spy trying to remain unseen. Except it was easy to spot his distinctive ginger fur bobbing and weaving around.

Each time I saw him, I'd stop and flamboyantly wave him back. He'd limp away reluctantly, throwing me a betrayed look as he went. Eventually he'd get the message and disappear.

When I got back six or so hours later, he would be waiting for me at the entrance to the flats. Part of me wanted to prevent him coming in. But that part was overwhelmed by the one that wanted to invite him up to the flat once more to curl up at my feet.

Over the next few days, the pair of us settled into a bit of a routine. Each day I'd leave him outside, and each night when I got back from busking, I'd find him waiting for me, either outside in an alleyway or sitting on the mat outside my flat if someone had let him in. He wasn't going away.

I decided I had to take the ultimate step and leave him out overnight. The first night I did it I saw him lurking in the area where the trash bins were kept. I tried to sneak in without him seeing me. It was a stupid move. He was a cat. He had more senses in one of his whiskers than I had in my entire body. No sooner had I opened the door to the building than he was there, squeezing his way in. I left him outside in the hallway that night, but he was on my doormat when I emerged again in the morning. For the next few days, we went through the same performance.

Eventually, he decided he'd won that particular battle. So I was soon dealing with another problem. He began following me down to the main road.

The first time he returned to the block when I shooed him away. The next time he tailed me for a hundred yards or so toward Tottenham High Road, where I got the bus to Covent Garden.

Part of me admired his tenacity and sheer perseverance.

Each day after that he went farther and farther, becoming bolder and bolder. Part of me wondered whether one day, after I left him, he'd actually keep going and find somewhere else to go. But each night I got home, there he was, waiting.

ONE day I headed out for work as usual. I had packed my large black acoustic guitar with its red trim, slung it over my shoulder along with my rucksack, and headed downstairs.

I saw Bob was sitting in an alleyway and said hello. When he started to follow me, I shooed him away. "Stay there. You can't come."

This time he seemed to get the message and slunk off. As I headed down the road, I looked back occasionally to see if he was there, but there was no sign of him.

To get to the bus stop that would take me to Covent Garden, I had to cross Tottenham High Road, one of the busiest and most dangerous roads in north London. This morning, as usual, cars, trucks, and motorbikes were carving their way through the clogged traffic. As I stood on the pavement trying to spot a gap so that I could run for the bus that was looming into view, I felt something rub against my leg. Instinctively, I looked down. I saw a familiar figure standing alongside me. To my horror, I could see that Bob was also looking for his opportunity to cross.

"What the hell are you doing here?"

He looked at me dismissively, as if I'd just asked a really stupid question. Then he focused once more on the road, edging himself nearer the edge of the curb as if getting ready to make a dash for it.

I couldn't let him risk it. It would almost certainly be suicide. So I swept him up and put him on my shoulder, where I knew he liked to sit. He sat there, snuggled up against the side of my head, as I wove my way through the traffic and across the road.

"All right, Bob, that's far enough," I said to him as I put him down on the pavement and shooed him away again.

He sidled off down the street into the throng. *Maybe now I've seen the last of him,* I thought to myself. He really was a long way from home.

Moments later, a red double-decker bus pulled up, the old-fashioned kind that you could jump on at the back. I went to sit down and was placing my guitar case in the storage space when I saw a sudden flash of ginger fur. Before I knew it, Bob had plonked himself on the seat next to me.

I was gobsmacked. I realized, finally, that I wasn't ever going to shake this cat off. Then I realized something else. I invited Bob to jump on my lap, which he did in the blink of an eye. A moment later, the conductor appeared. She smiled at Bob, then me. "Is he yours?" she said, stroking him.

"I guess he must be," I said.

I now had a deep-seated feeling that he was in my life to stay.

FOR the next forty-five minutes or so, Bob sat quietly next to me, his face pressed against the glass of the bus window, watching the world go by. He seemed to be fascinated by all the cars, cyclists, vans, and pedestrians whizzing past us; he wasn't fazed at all. The only time he pulled away from the window and looked to me for a little reassurance was when the blare of a police siren, a fire engine, or an ambulance got a bit too close for comfort.

"Nothing to worry about," I told him, giving him a friendly stroke. "This is what the middle of London sounds like, Bob. Better get used to it."

As my stop near Tottenham Court Road tube station loomed into view, I picked up my guitar, scooped up Bob, and headed for the exit. On the pavement, I fished around in my pocket and found the makeshift shoelace lead. I put it around his neck, then placed him down. I didn't want him wandering off. The junction of Tottenham Court Road and New Oxford Street was bustling with shoppers, tourists, and Londoners getting on with their day. He'd have been lost in a second or, even worse, crushed by one of the buses or black cabs whistling to and from Oxford Street.

Understandably, it was all a bit intimidating for Bob. As we picked our way along, I could tell from his uptight body language and the way he kept looking up at me that he was uneasy. So I decided to take one of my shortcuts through the backstreets to get to Covent Garden.

"Come on, Bob, let's get you out of the crowds."

Even then he wasn't one hundred percent happy. He kept shooting me looks as if to say he wasn't quite sure about this. After a few yards, I could tell that he wanted me to pick him up.

"All right, but don't make a habit of it," I said, gathering him up and placing him on my shoulders again. He'd soon settled into a comfortable spot, at a slight angle across my right shoulder blade, with his front paws placed on the top of my arm, looking out like the occupant of the bird's nest on some pirate ship. I couldn't help smiling. I must have looked like Long John Silver, except I had a puss rather than a parrot sailing along with me.

I could feel him purring lightly as we walked through the throng and into the smaller streets leading to Covent Garden. The crowds thinned out, and after a while, I began to forget Bob was there. Instead I started to immerse myself in the usual thoughts that went through my mind on the way to work. Was the weather going to be good enough for me to get a solid five hours' busking? What sort of crowd would there be? How long would it take me to make the twenty or thirty pounds I needed to get me and Bob through the next few days? It had taken the best part of five hours the previous day. Maybe it would be better today. That was the thing with busking, you never knew.

I was mulling all these things over when I was suddenly aware that almost every person we passed was looking at me. More to the point, they were looking at Bob.

I must have looked slightly incongruous, a tall, long-haired bloke walking along with a large ginger tom on his shoulders. Not something you see every day—even on the streets of London.

Most people, however, were reacting warmly. The moment they saw Bob, their faces broke into broad smiles.

"Ah, look at you two," said one well-dressed, middle-aged lady laden down with shopping bags. "He's gorgeous. Can I stroke him?"

"Of course," I said, thinking it would be a one-off event.

She plonked down her bags and placed her face right up to his. "What a lovely fellow you are," she said. "Isn't he good to sit there on your shoulders like that? He must really trust you."

I'd barely said good-bye to the lady when we were approached by two young girls, Swedish teenagers on holiday.

"What is his name? Can we take his picture?" they said, snapping away with their cameras the instant I nodded.

"His name's Bob," I said.

"Ah, Bob. Cool."

We chatted. One of them had a cat herself and produced a picture of it. I had to politely excuse myself after a couple of minutes, otherwise they'd have spent hours drooling over him.

We carried on but the going was slow. No sooner had the latest admirer gone away than the same thing was happening again—and again. I'd barely go three feet without being stopped by someone. It normally took me ten minutes to get from the bus stop to my pitch at Covent Garden. It had already taken me twice that because everyone had seemed to want to stop and talk to Bob.

I'D BEEN busking around Covent Garden for about a year and a half. I generally started at about two or three in the afternoon and carried on until around eight in the evening. On the weekends I would go earlier and do lunchtimes. On Thursday, Friday, and Saturday I'd carry on until quite late, trying to take advantage of the extra crowds hanging around at the end of the working week. My main pitch was on a patch of pavement directly outside Covent Garden tube station, on James Street. I'd work that until about 6:30 p.m., when the main evening rush hour was at its peak. Then, for the last couple of hours, I'd walk around all the pubs.

Busking at James Street was a bit of a gamble. Technically speaking, I wasn't supposed to be there. The Covent Garden area is divided up into areas when it comes to street people. It's regulated by officials from the local council, an officious bunch that were referred to as Covent Guardians.

My pitch should have been on the eastern side of Covent Garden, near the Royal Opera House. That's where the musicians were supposed to operate, according to the Covent Guardians. The other side of the piazza, the western side, was where the street performers were supposed to ply their trade. James Street, where I had begun playing, was meant to be the domain of the human statues. There were a few around—one guy dressed as Charlie Chaplin used to do quite well—but it was often clear, so I had made it my own little patch. I knew there was always the risk of getting moved along by the Covent Guardians, but I took my chances. The volume of people coming out of the tube station there was huge. If only one in a thousand of them made a "drop," then I could do okay.

It was just after 3:00 p.m. when I got to my pitch—finally.

I first checked to make sure the coast was clear. There was no sign of the Covent Guardians. There were a couple of people who worked at the tube station who sometimes gave me hassle because they knew I wasn't supposed to be there, but they weren't around either. So I put Bob down, unzipped my guitar case, took off my jacket, and got ready to tune up.

Ordinarily it would take me a good ten minutes to get tuned, start playing, and get people to pay me some attention.

Today, though, a couple of people slowed down in front of me and lobbed small denomination coins into my guitar case even before I'd played a note. *Generous of them,* I thought.

My back was turned to the crowd when I again heard the distinctive clinking of one coin hitting another. Behind me I heard a male voice. "Nice cat, mate."

I turned and saw an ordinary-looking guy in his midthirties giving me a thumbs-up and walking off with smile on his face.

I was taken aback. Bob had curled himself up in a comfortable ball in the empty guitar case. I knew he was a charmer. But this was something else.

I played pretty much the same stuff every day. It was what people liked, what the tourists wanted to hear. I would usually start with a song like "About a Girl" by Nirvana just to get the fingers going. That's what I did today, as Bob sat in front of me, watching the crowds walk out of the tube station.

I'd barely been playing for a few minutes when a group of kids stopped. They were wearing Brazilian football shirts and speaking Portuguese. One of them, a young girl, bent down and began stroking Bob. *"Ah, gato bonito,"* she said.

"She is saying you have a beautiful cat," one of the boys said helpfully.

Almost immediately other people stopped to see what the fuss was about. Half a dozen of the Brazilian kids and other passersby began fishing in their pockets and raining coins into the bag.

"Looks like you may not be such a bad companion after all, Bob. I'll invite you out for the day more often." I smiled at him.

As the late afternoon turned into the early evening and the crowds thickened, more and more people were slowing down and looking at Bob. There was clearly something about him.

As darkness was beginning to descend, one lady stopped for a chat. "How long have you had him?" she asked, bending down to stroke Bob.

"Oh, only a few weeks," I said. "We sort of found each other."

"Found each other? Sounds interesting."

I explained the story of how we'd met and how I'd spent a fortnight nursing him back to health.

"I had a ginger tom very much like this a few years ago," she said, looking emotional. For a moment I thought she was going to burst into tears. "You are lucky to have found him. They are just the best companions, so quiet and docile. You've found yourself a real friend there."

"I think you are right." I smiled.

She placed a fiver into the guitar case before leaving.

Bob was definitely a lady puller. Something like seventy percent of the people who had stopped so far had been female. After just over an hour, I had as much as I'd normally make in a good day, just over twenty pounds. As the passersby continued to make a fuss of him, I figured I might as well make the most of it. Make hay while the sun shines and all that.

Twenty pounds was enough to get me through a few days and to cover all the expenses of my flat. But that night, by the time I finished up at around 8:00 p.m., it was clear that I'd made a lot more than that. After packing up my guitar, it took me five minutes to count the coins that had piled up. There were a few notes scattered among them as well.

When I finally totted it all up, I shook my head quietly. I had made the princely sum of £63.77. I transferred all the coins into my rucksack and hauled it onto my shoulders. It was rattling like a giant piggy bank. It also weighed a ton! But I was ecstatic. That was the most I'd ever made in a day's work on the streets.

I picked up Bob, giving him a stroke on the back of the neck. "Well done, mate. That was what I call a good evening's work."

Bob was hungry, as was I. We needed to head home.

I walked back toward Tottenham Court Road bus stop with Bob once more on my shoulder.

"We'll have something nice to eat tonight, Bob," I said as we settled onto the bus for the trip back to Tottenham. Again, he pinned his nose up against the window, watching the bright lights and the traffic.

I got off the bus near a really nice Indian restaurant on Tottenham High Road. I'd walked past it many times, savoring the lengthy menu, but never had enough spare money to be able to afford anything.

I went in and ordered a chicken tikka masala with lemon rice, a peshwari naan, and a sag paneer to take away. The waiters threw me a few funny looks when they saw Bob on a lead beside me. So I said I'd pop back in twenty minutes and headed off with Bob to a supermarket across the road.

With the money we'd made, I treated Bob to a nice pouch of posh cat food, a couple of packs of his favorite nibbles, and some "cat milk." I treated myself to a couple of tins of lager.

"Let's push the boat out, Bob," I said. "It's been a day to remember."

After picking up our dinner, I almost ran home, I was so overwhelmed by the tempting smells coming out from the brown carrier bag. When we got inside, Bob and I wolfed down our food as if there were no tomorrow. I hadn't eaten so well in months—well, maybe years. I'm pretty sure he hadn't either.

We then curled up for a couple of hours, me watching television and him snuggled up in his favorite spot. We slept like logs that night.

Chapter 5

ONE MAN AND HIS CAT

THE next morning I was woken by a sudden, loud crash from the kitchen. I immediately guessed what it was. Once again Bob was trying to open the cupboards where I kept his food and had knocked something over.

I squinted at the clock. It was midmorning. I had let myself sleep in, but Bob had obviously decided he couldn't wait any longer. This was his way of saying, "Get up. I want my breakfast."

I hauled myself out of bed and stumbled into the kitchen. The small tin saucepan I used to boil milk was lying on the floor.

As soon as he saw me, Bob slid his way purposefully toward his bowl.

"Okay, mate, I get the picture," I said, unlocking the cupboards and reaching for a sachet of his favorite chicken dish. I spooned a couple of portions into the bowl and watched him devour it in seconds. He then gulped down the water in his bowl, licked his face and paws clean, and trotted off into the living room, looking very satisfied with himself.

If only all our lives were that simple, I thought to myself.

I'd considered not going to work but thought better of it. We may have had a lucky break, but that money wouldn't keep us going for long. The electricity and gas bills were due. It had also begun to dawn on me that I had an extra mouth to feed—a rather hungry one.

After wolfing down some breakfast of my own, I started getting my stuff together. I wasn't sure whether Bob would want to come out busking again today. I put some snacks in the bag just in case he did decide to follow me.

It was early afternoon as I headed off. It was obvious what I was doing; I had my rucksack and guitar lashed across my back. I took the chain off the front door, and as I was about to shut the door behind me, he bolted toward me and followed me out into the corridor.

When we got to the ground floor and out into the open air, he scurried off into the bushes. Afterward, rather than heading to me, he trotted off toward the area where the trash bins were kept.

I decided to head off without him. I knew he'd get back inside the building somehow, now that a lot of the neighbors knew him. One or two had started making a real fuss over him.

He would probably be waiting on the landing for me when I got home. *Fair enough,* I thought as I set off. Bob had done me a huge favor the previous day. I wasn't going to exploit our relationship by demanding he come along with me every day. He was my companion, not my employee!

The skies were gray, and there was a hint of rain in the air. If it was like this in central London, it was going to be a waste of time. Busking on a rainy day was never a good idea. If it was bucketing down in the center of town, I'd simply turn around and head back home. I would rather spend the day hanging out with Bob.

I was about two hundred yards down the road when I sensed something behind me. I turned and saw a familiar figure padding along the pavement.

"Ah, changed our mind, have we?" I said as he approached.

Bob tilted his head ever so slightly to one side and gave me one of those pitying looks, as if to say, "Well, why else would I be standing here?"

I still had the shoestring lead in my pocket. I put it on, and we started walking down the road together.

The streets of Tottenham are very different to those of Covent Garden, but just like the day before, people began staring at us. And, just like the day before, one or two looked at me disapprovingly. They clearly thought I was off my rocker, leading a ginger tom around on a piece of string.

"If this is going to become a regular thing, I really am going to have to get you a proper lead," I said quietly to Bob, feeling a bit self-conscious.

But for every person who gave me a dirty look, another half dozen smiled and nodded at me. One West Indian lady, weighed down with shopping bags, gave us a big, sunny grin. "Don't you two make a pretty picture!"

No one had engaged me in conversation on the streets around my flat in all the months I'd lived here. It was odd but also amazing. It was as if my Harry Potter invisibility cloak had slipped off my shoulders.

When we got to the crossing point at Tottenham High Road, Bob gave me a look as if to say, "Come on, you know what to do now," and I plonked him on my shoulders.

Soon we were on the bus, with Bob taking his favorite position, his head pressed against the glass. We were on the road again.

I'd been right about the weather. Soon rain was hammering down, forming intricate patterns on the window. Outside, you could just make out a sea of umbrellas. People were running, splashing through the streets to avoid the downpour.

Thankfully, the rain had eased off by the time we reached the center of town. Despite the weather, there were even bigger crowds in the center of town than there had been the previous day.

"We'll give it a go for a couple of hours," I said to Bob as I plonked him on my shoulders and headed off toward Covent Garden. "But if it starts to rain again, we'll head back. I promise."

In the space of ten minutes, half a dozen people had stopped us and at least half of them had asked to take a picture. I quickly learned that the key was to keep moving; otherwise you'd be surrounded before you knew it.

As we were reaching the end of Neal Street, something interesting happened. I suddenly felt Bob's paws readjusting themselves on my shoulder. Before I knew it, he was sliding off my shoulder and clambering down my arm. When I let him hop onto the pavement, he began walking ahead of me. I extended the lead to its full length and let him go. It was obvious that he recognized where we were and was going to take it from here. He was leading the way.

He marched ahead of me all the way to the pitch where we'd

been the previous night. He then stood there, waiting for me to take out my guitar and lay the guitar case down for him.

"There you go, Bob," I said.

He instantly sat down on the soft case as if it was where he belonged. He positioned himself so that he could watch the world walk by—which, this being Covent Garden, it was.

I'D TAUGHT myself to play the guitar when I was a teenager living in Australia. I'd had ambitions of making it as a musician, dreams of becoming the next Kurt Cobain. As naive and completely stupid as it sounds now, it had been part of my grand plan when I'd come back to England from Australia. That's what I'd told my mother and everyone else when I'd set off.

I'd had my moments, and for a brief time, I felt like I might actually get somewhere. Around 2002, when I'd got off the streets and into some sheltered accommodation in Dalston, one thing had led to another and I'd formed a four-piece guitar band called Hyper Fury with some guys I'd met. The name certainly summed me up. I was an angry young man. I really was hyper-furious, about life in general and about feeling that I'd not had a fair break. My music was an outlet for my anger and angst. We weren't very mainstream. Our songs were edgy and dark.

We actually put out two albums and did have some fans, so we managed to get gigs, mainly in north London. There was a big Goth scene going on, and we fitted in well with it. We looked and certainly sounded the part. We played wherever we were invited. The biggest gig we did was at the Dublin Castle, a famous music pub in north London, where we played a couple of times. Things were going so well at one point that I teamed up with a guy named Pete, and we started our own independent label, Corrupt Drive Records. But it didn't really work, or, to be more accurate, I didn't really work.

At the time, Belle and I were in a brief relationship. We got on great as friends. She is a really caring person and looked after me, but as a relationship, it was kind of doomed from the beginning. The problem was that she was on drugs as well. It really didn't help me—or her—as we struggled to kick our habits. When one of us was trying to get clean, the other one was using and vice versa. That's codependency.

It made it really difficult for me to break the cycle.

Looking back on it, if I'm honest, I wouldn't say I was trying hard. I think part of it was that I didn't really feel like the dream was ever going to become a reality. Mentally, at least, the band was something I put on the back burner. It was too easy to slip back into old habits—quite literally.

By 2005 I'd accepted that the band was a hobby, not a way of making a living. But I was struggling so badly with my habit that I fell by the wayside again. It became another one of those second chances that I let slip through my fingers. I guess I'll never know what might have been.

I never gave up on music, however. Even when the band broke up and it was clear that I wasn't going to get anywhere professionally, I'd spend most days playing guitar, improvising songs. It was a great outlet for me. God knows where I'd have been without it. And busking had certainly made a difference to my life in recent years. Without the money it generated, I dread to think what I would have ended up doing to earn cash.

That evening, as I settled into the session, the tourists were once more out in force. It was a repeat of the previous day. The moment I sat down—or, more precisely, the moment Bob sat down—people who would normally have rushed by began to slow down and interact with him. I was beginning to love the way that Bob seemed to be able to brighten up people's days.

He was a beautiful creature. But it wasn't just that. It was his personality that was attracting the attention. He had an unusual rapport with people—well, people who had his best interests at heart, at least. Now and again I'd see him bridle when he saw someone he didn't like.

A very smart, rich-looking Middle Eastern guy walked past once, arm in arm with an attractive blonde. She could easily have been a model.

"Oh, look. What a gorgeous cat," she said, suddenly stopping in her tracks and pulling on the guy's arm to slow him down. The guy looked distinctly unimpressed and flicked his hand dismissively, as if to say, "So what?"

The instant he did so, Bob arched his back ever so slightly and shifted his body position so that he was a few inches closer to me. It was subtle, but to me it was really telling. *I wonder whether this guy reminds Bob of someone from his past?* I thought to myself as the couple walked on. *Has he seen that look before?* I'd have given anything to know his story, discover what had led him to the hallway of my block of flats that evening. But that was something I was never going to know.

As I settled into my set, I was much more relaxed than twenty-four hours earlier. And as the coins started tinkling into the case at the same rate as the previous day, I thought to myself, *I'm enjoying this.*

It had been a long time since I'd said that.

BY THE time we headed home three hours later, my rucksack was once more jangling with the weight of coins. We'd collected well over sixty pounds again. This time I wasn't going to spend it on an expensive curry. I had more practical uses for the money. I needed to have better equipment for Bob. I couldn't walk around with him attached to a leash made out of a shoelace. Apart from anything else, it was dangerous.

The following day the weather was even worse, but Bob and I hopped on a bus headed in the direction of Archway. I knew the north London branch of the Cats Protection charity was there.

Bob seemed to sense immediately that this wasn't the same route we'd taken the previous days. Every now and again he would turn and look at me as if to say, "So where are you taking me today?"

The Cats Protection shop was a smart, modern place with all sorts of equipment, toys, and books about cats. There were loads of free pamphlets and brochures on every aspect of caring for a cat, from microchipping to toxoplasmosis and diet tips. I picked up a few for future reading.

There were only a couple of people working there, and the place was quiet, so they couldn't resist coming over for a chat as I took a look around with Bob sitting on my shoulder.

"He's a good-looking boy, isn't he?" one lady said, stroking Bob. He could tell he was in safe hands because he was leaning his body into her as she smoothed his coat and cooed over him.

We then fell into a conversation about how Bob and I had met. I then explained what had happened the previous two days.

Both women nodded. "A lot of cats like to go out for a walk with their owners," one told me. "They like to go for a walk in the park or for a short stroll down the street. But I have to say, Bob's a bit unusual, isn't he?"

"He is," her friend said. "I think you've got yourself a bit of a jewel there. He's obviously decided to attach himself to you."

It was nice to hear them confirming what, deep down, I knew already. Every now and again, I had a little pang of doubt about whether I was doing the right thing in keeping him in the flat with me. Their words were a real boost.

What I didn't know, however, was how best to manage Bob if he was going to be my constant companion on the streets of London. It wasn't the safest of environments, to put it mildly.

"The best thing you can do is to get a harness like this," one of the ladies said, unhooking a blue, woven nylon harness, collar, and matching lead.

She explained the pros and cons of it. "It's not a great idea just to fix a leash to a collar. The worst collars can harm your cat's neck, even choke him. And the problem with the better-quality collars is that they are made from elastic or are what they call 'breakaway' collars so that the cat can escape if the collar gets caught on something. There's a good chance that at some point you'll have an empty leash dangling in your hand," the lady explained. "I think you'd be much better off with a cat harness and a leash, especially given you are out all the time."

"Isn't it going to feel funny for him?" I asked.

"You'll need to ease him into it. It might take you a week or so.

Start him off wearing it for a few minutes a day before you are ready to go outside together. Then build it up from there." She could see me mulling it over. "Why not try it on him?"

"Why not?" I said.

Bob was sitting comfortably and didn't offer too much resistance, although I could tell that he was uncertain about what was happening.

"Just leave it on him and let him get used to the sensation of having it on his body," the lady said.

The harness, lead, and collar cost about thirteen pounds. It was one of the most expensive they had, but I figured he was worth it. If I'd been a businessman, chief executive of James & Bob Inc., I'd have been thinking you've got to look after your employees; you've got to invest in your human resources—except in this case it was my feline resources.

IT ONLY took me a couple of days to introduce Bob to the harness. At first he was a bit confused at having this extra-long, leather tail trailing behind him, but he soon got used to it.

It was during the third week of us busking together that he first decided he didn't want to join me. Ordinarily, the minute he saw me putting on my coat and packing my rucksack, he'd be up and moving toward me. But one day, as I went through the normal routine, he just shuffled off and lay down underneath the radiator, as if to say, "I'm having a day off."

I could tell he was tired.

"Don't fancy it today, Bob?" I said, stroking him.

He looked at me in that knowing way of his.

"No problem," I said, heading to the kitchen to put some snacks in a bowl to keep him going for the rest of the day until I got home that evening.

I'd read a report once that said leaving the TV on made pets feel less lonely when their owners are out. I didn't know whether that was true, but I switched the TV set on in any case. He immediately started staring at it.

GOING OUT THAT DAY REALLY brought home to me the difference Bob had made to my life. With him on my shoulder or walking on the lead in front of me, I turned heads everywhere. On my own I was invisible again. By now we were well known enough to the locals for a few people to express concern.

"Where's the cat today?" one stall owner said as he passed.

"He's having a day off," I said.

"Oh, good. I was worried something had happened to the little fella." He smiled, giving me the thumbs-up.

On the pavement at James Street, the sound of coins landing in the bag had become music to my ears. But without Bob, I wasn't making anywhere near as much money. It took me a few more hours to earn about half the cash I had made on a good day with him. It was back to the old days, but that was okay.

As I walked back that evening, something began to sink in. It wasn't all about making money. I wasn't going to starve. And my life was much richer for having Bob in it. It was a pleasure to have such a great companion. It felt like I'd been given a chance to get back on track.

It's not easy when you are working on the streets. People don't want to give you a chance. Before I had Bob, if I approached people in the pubs with my guitar strapped on, they would go "No change, sorry," before I'd even opened my mouth. People don't want to listen. All they see is someone they think is trying to get a free ride. They don't understand I'm working. Just because I'm not wearing a suit and a tie and carrying a briefcase, it doesn't mean that I am freeloading.

Having Bob there gave me a chance to interact with people. They would ask about him, and I would get a chance to explain my situation, how we got together and how we were making money to pay our bills. People would give me more of a fair hearing. They also began to see me in a different light. Seeing me with my cat softened me in their eyes. It humanized me. Especially after I'd been so dehumanized. In some ways it was giving me back my identity. I was becoming a person again.

Chapter 6

THE TWO MUSKETEERS

BOB wasn't just changing people's attitude toward me: he was changing my attitude toward others as well.

I'd never really had any responsibilities. I'd had the odd job here and there when I was younger in Australia, and I'd also been in a band, which required a bit of teamwork. But the truth was that, since I left home as a teenager, my main responsibility had always been to myself. I'd always had to look after number one, simply because there wasn't anyone else to do it. As a result, my life had become a very selfish one.

Bob's arrival had dramatically changed that. Another being's health and happiness was now down to me.

It had come as a bit of a shock, but I had begun to adapt to it. In fact, I enjoyed it. I knew it may sound silly, but for the first time I had an idea what it must be like looking after a child. Bob was my baby, and making sure he was warm, well fed, and safe was really rewarding. It was scary, too.

I worried about him constantly when I was out on the streets. My instincts were telling me that I had to watch out for him at every turn. The streets of London aren't all filled with kindhearted tourists and cat lovers. It happened less now that I had Bob, but I still got a volley of abuse every now and again, usually from drunken young blokes who felt the fact they were picking up a pay packet at the end of the week made them somehow superior to me.

I let their insults wash over me. I was used to them. It was a different matter when people turned their aggression on Bob. That's when my protective instincts really took over.

One Friday evening, quite soon after Bob and I had first come to Covent Garden together, I was playing at James Street when a bunch of young, very rowdy black lads came past. They had real attitude and were obviously on the lookout for trouble. A couple of them spotted Bob sitting on the pavement next to me and started making "woof" and "meow" noises, much to the amusement of their mates.

I could have coped with that. It was just stupid, puerile stuff. But then, for no reason whatsoever, one of them kicked the guitar case with Bob sitting in it. It wasn't a playful tap; it had real venom in it and sent the case—and Bob—sliding a foot or so along the pavement.

Bob was really distressed. He made a loud noise, almost like a scream, and jumped out of the case. Thankfully his lead was attached to the case; otherwise he would almost certainly have run off into the crowds. I might never have seen him again. Instead, restrained by the lead, he had no option but to hide behind my rucksack, which was standing nearby.

I got up immediately and confronted the guy. "What the hell did you do that for?" I said, standing toe-to-toe with him. I'm quite tall and towered over him, but it didn't seem to faze him.

"I just wanted to see if the cat was real," he said, laughing as if he'd cracked a brilliant joke.

I didn't see the funny side. "That's really clever, you bloody idiot," I said.

They all began circling me, and one of them began shoving into me with his chest and shoulders, but I stood my ground and shoved him back. For a second or two there was a standoff, but then I pointed to a CCTV camera that I knew was positioned near us. "Go on, then, do what you want. But just remember, you're on camera. See how far you get afterward."

They were street smart enough to know you couldn't get away with violence on camera. One of them gave me a look as if to say, "I'll get you for that." But they were soon moving on. I wasn't worried. In fact, I felt good about seeing them off. But I didn't hang around much longer that evening.

The incident proved a couple of things to me. First, it was always a good idea to be near a CCTV camera. That was the positive. The negative was that I'd been reminded that I really was on my own when trouble flared like this. There wasn't a policeman in sight. There wasn't a whiff of a Covent Guardian or any assistance from the staff in the tube station. Despite the fact that quite a lot of people were milling around when the gang confronted me, none of the passersby intervened. In fact, people did their best to melt into the background and shuffle off.

As we headed back to Tottenham that evening, Bob nuzzled up to me on the bus. "It's you and me against the world," I said. "We're the two Musketeers." He purred lightly in agreement.

The hard reality was that London was full of people we had to treat with caution. Ever since I'd started bringing Bob with me, I'd been wary of dogs, for instance. There were a lot of them, and it was no surprise that many took an instant interest in Bob. To be fair, in the vast majority of cases, people would notice if their dog was getting too close and give them a gentle tug on the lead. But others came too close for comfort.

Fortunately Bob just ignored them. If they came up to him, he would stare them out. Just how well he could handle himself I found out a week or so after the incident with the gang.

We were sitting in Neal Street in the late afternoon when a guy with a Staffordshire bull terrier loomed into view. He was shaven-headed, swigging extra-strength lager, and wearing a tatty tracksuit. From the way he was slaloming around the street, he was off his head already, even though it was barely 4:00 p.m.

They slowed down when they got to us purely because the Staff was straining at the leash as it tried to move in the direction of me and Bob.

As it happened, the dog wasn't threatening; he was just checking Bob out. Well, not even that; he was checking out the biscuits Bob had in front of him. He was inching his way toward the bowl, sniffing excitedly.

I couldn't believe what happened next.

I'd seen Bob around dogs a fair bit by now. His normal policy was to not give them the time of day. On this occasion, however, he must have felt action was necessary. As the Staffie leaned in toward the biscuits, Bob calmly looked up, raised himself, and then bopped the dog on the nose with his paw. It was so lightning fast it was a punch to do Muhammad Ali proud.

The dog couldn't believe it. He jumped back in shock and then carried on backtracking.

I was almost as shocked as the dog. I laughed out loud.

The owner looked at me and then down at his dog. I think he was so drunk he couldn't fully comprehend what had just happened, especially as it had occurred in the blink of an eye. He gave the dog a whack around the head, then tugged on its lead to move on. I think he was embarrassed that his fearsome-looking beast had been made to look stupid by a cat.

Bob watched quietly as the dog walked away. Within a few seconds he'd reverted back to his previous position, snoozing at my feet. It was as if it was a minor annoyance for him, like swatting a pesky fly. But for me it was a really revealing moment. It told me so much more about my companion and the life he had led before our fateful meeting at the bottom of the stairs. He wasn't afraid to defend himself. In fact, he knew how to look after himself rather well. He must have learned to do that somewhere, maybe in an environment where there were lots of dogs, and aggressive ones at that.

By now there was little doubt in my mind that he must have grown up on the streets. It wasn't just his street-fighter skills. He was a bit rough around the edges. Even now, after he'd been living with me for the best part of a month, he still didn't like using the litter trays I'd bought. He really hated those things and would scamper away whenever I put one down anywhere near him. Instead, he would hold on until he saw me going out the door and then do his business downstairs in the gardens.

I didn't want it to carry on like this. For a start, it wasn't much fun walking up and down five flights of stairs to take the cat out whenever he wanted to go to the toilet. So one day I said to myself that I would go twenty-four hours without letting him out so that he would have no alternative but to use the litter tray. But he won that contest hands down. He bottled everything up and waited—and waited and waited until I had to go out. Then he squeezed past me as I went out the door and bolted down the stairwell to get outside. Game, set, and match to Bob.

He also had a wild side to his personality. He was calmer than when he'd first arrived, thanks largely to the fact that he'd been neutered. But he could still be a complete maniac, frequently tearing around the flat.

The street instinct was also apparent when it came to food. Despite the fact I was feeding him on a regular basis, he still treated every meal as if it were his last. The moment I scooped some cat food into his bowl, he would stick his face in it and start guzzling as if there were no tomorrow. I figured he'd spent so long having to make the most of every eating opportunity that he hadn't adapted to being guaranteed a square meal twice a day. I knew how that felt. I couldn't really blame him.

Bob and I had so much in common. Maybe that was why the bond had formed so fast and was growing so deep.

THE single most irritating thing about him was the fact that his fur had begun coating every corner of the flat. It was perfectly natural, of course. Spring was here, and he was getting rid of his winter coat. To help the molting process, he was rubbing himself on anything and everything he could find, covering it in a thick film of fur. It was a real pain.

It was a good sign, though, that his coat and his body were returning to good health. The medication had helped with his bald patches, and the antibiotics had done the trick in healing his old wound, which had almost disappeared. All in all he looked in a lot better condition than he had done a month or so earlier.

Bob was one of the most meticulous cats I'd ever seen. Watching him methodically licking his paws fascinated me, especially the fact that it was linked so strongly to his ancient ancestors. Cats are stealth hunters, so they have to be as unobtrusive as possible. Smell is bad from a hunting point of view. Cat saliva contains a natural deodorant. It's been proven by zoologists that cats that lick the smell off themselves survive longer and have more successful offspring. It's also their way of hiding themselves from predators like large snakes, lizards, and other carnivorous mammals.

Of course, the most important reason that Bob and his ancestors had always licked themselves was to establish and maintain good health. Cats effectively self-medicate. Licking cuts down the number of parasites, such as lice, mites, and ticks, that can potentially damage the cat. It also stops infection in any open wounds, as cats' saliva also contains an antiseptic agent. As I watched him one day, it occurred to me that this was probably why Bob was licking himself so regularly. He knew his body had been in a bad way. This was his way of helping the healing process.

The other habit he'd developed was watching television. I first noticed that he watched things on screens one day when I was playing around on a computer in the local library. I often popped in there when I wasn't busking. I'd taken Bob along, and he had decided to sit on my lap and was staring at the screen with me. As I was moving the mouse around, he was trying to swat the cursor with his paw. So back at the flat, as an experiment one day, I put the TV on and left the room. I came back to find Bob ensconced on the sofa, watching.

Pretty soon, he became a bit of a telly addict. If something caught his eye, he was glued to the screen. I found it really funny watching him watching Channel Four racing. He really liked the horses. It wasn't something I watched, but I got a kick from seeing him sitting there fascinated by it.

Chapter 7

MAKING IT OFFICIAL

ONE Thursday morning, a few weeks after we had started our busking partnership in Covent Garden, I got up earlier than usual, made us both some breakfast, and headed out the door with Bob. Rather than heading for central London as usual, we got off the bus near Islington Green.

I'd made a decision. With him accompanying me almost every day on the streets now, I needed to do the responsible thing and get Bob microchipped.

Microchipping cats and dogs used to be a complicated business, but now it's simple. All it requires is a simple surgical procedure by which a vet injects a tiny chip into the cat's neck. The chip contains a serial number, which is then logged against the owner's details. That way, if a stray cat is found, people can scan the chip and find out where it belongs. Also, if worse came to worst and something happened to me, at least the records would show that Bob wasn't completely feral; he had once been in a loving home.

When I'd first begun researching the microchipping process in the library, I had quickly come to the conclusion that I couldn't afford it. Most vets were charging sixty to eighty pounds to insert a chip. I just didn't have that kind of money.

But then one day I got talking to a cat owner.

"You should go along to the Blue Cross van in Islington Green on a Thursday," she said. "They just charge for the cost of the chip. But make sure you get there early. There's always a big queue."

As predicted, we discovered a lengthy line of people when we got there. Luckily it was a bright, clear morning, so it wasn't a problem hanging around. After about an hour and a half, Bob and I reached the front of the line where we were greeted by a young veterinary nurse with bobbed hair.

"How much will it cost to get him microchipped?" I asked.

"It's fifteen pounds," she replied. "But you don't have to pay it all up front. You can pay it off over a few weeks. Say two pounds a week—how's that?"

"Cool," I said, pleasantly surprised. "I can do that."

She gave Bob a quick check to make sure he was in decent enough health, which he was. He was looking a lot better these days, especially now that he had fully shed his winter coat. He was lean and athletic.

She led us into the surgery where the vet was waiting.

"Morning," he said to me before turning to chat to the nurse. They had a quiet confab in the corner and then started preparing for the chipping procedure. The vet produced the syringe to inject the chip. The size of it took my breath away. It was a big old needle. But then I realized it had to be if it was going to insert the chip, which was the size of a large grain of rice, into the animal's skin.

Bob didn't like the look of it at all, and I couldn't really blame him. So the nurse and I got hold of him and tried to turn him away from the vet so that he couldn't see what he was doing.

Bob wasn't stupid, however, and knew something was up. He got quite agitated and tried to wriggle his way out of my grip.

"You'll be okay, mate," I said, stroking his tummy and hind legs while the vet closed in.

When the needle penetrated, Bob let out a loud squeal and began shaking in pain. The shaking soon dissipated and he calmed down. I gave him a little treat from my rucksack, then carefully scooped him up and headed back to the reception area.

"Well done, mate," I said.

The nurse asked me to go through a couple of complicated-looking forms. Fortunately the information she wanted was pretty straightforward.

"We need to fill in your details so they are in the database," she said. "We will need your name, address, phone number—all that kind of stuff."

It was only as I watched the nurse filling in the form that it struck me. "So, legally speaking, does that mean I am now registered as his owner?"

She looked up from the paperwork and smiled. "Yes. Is that okay?"

"Yeah, that's great," I said, slightly taken aback. "Really great."

By now Bob was settling down a little. I gave him a stroke on the front of the head. "Did you hear that, Bob?" I said. "Looks like we're officially a family."

I'm sure I drew even more looks than usual as we walked through Islington afterward. I was wearing a smile as wide as the Thames.

HAVING BOB WITH ME HAD already made a difference to the way I was living my life. He'd made me clean up my act in more ways than one. As well as giving me more routine and a sense of responsibility, he had also made me take a good look at myself. I didn't like what I saw.

I wasn't proud of the fact I was a recovering addict, and I certainly wasn't proud of the fact that I had to visit a clinic once a fortnight and collect medication from a pharmacy every day. So, unless it was absolutely necessary, I never took him with me on those trips. I know it may sound crazy, but I didn't want him seeing that side of my past. That was something else he'd helped me with: I really did see it as my past. I saw my future as being clean, living a normal life. I just had to complete the long journey that led to that point.

LIFE on the streets is never straightforward. You've always got to expect the unexpected. I learned that early on. Social workers always use the word "chaotic" when they talk about people like me. They call our lives chaotic because they don't conform to their idea of normality, but it is normality to us. So I wasn't surprised when, as that first summer with Bob drew to a close and autumn began, life started to get more complicated. I knew it couldn't stay the same. Nothing ever did.

Bob was still proving to be a crowd-pleaser, especially with tourists. Wherever they came from, they would stop and talk to him. By now I think I'd heard every language under the sun, from Afrikaans to Welsh, and learned the word for cat in all of them. I knew the Czech name, *kocka,* and the Russian, *koshka;* I knew the Turkish, *kedi,* and my favorite, the Chinese, *mao.* I was really surprised when I discovered their great leader had been a cat!

But no matter what weird or wonderful tongue was being spoken, the message was almost always the same. Everyone loved Bob.

However, I'd been getting a bit of hassle over at James Street from the Covent Guardians. I'd been continuing to play next to the tube station. On a couple of occasions a Guardian had come over and laid down the law, explaining that the area was for painted statues. The fact that there didn't seem to be any around at that moment didn't bother him. "You know the rules," he kept telling me. I did. But I also knew rules were there to be bent a little. Again, that was life on the streets. If we were the kind of people who stuck to the rules, we wouldn't have been there.

So each time the Guardian moved me on, I'd head off elsewhere for a few hours, then quietly slip back into James Street. It was a risk worth taking as far as I was concerned. I'd never heard of them calling in the police to deal with someone performing in the wrong place.

But the staff at the tube station were bothering me much more. They now also seemed to object to me busking outside their workplace. One really unpleasant inspector, a big, sweaty guy in uniform, came over to me one day and was quite threatening.

Bob was a great reader of people. He had spotted this guy the minute he started walking in our direction and squeezed himself closer to me.

"All right, mate?" I said.

"Not really. No. You had better piss off—or else," he said.

"Or else what?" I said, standing my ground.

"You'll see," he said, trying to intimidate me. "I'm warning you."

I knew he had no power outside the tube station and was just trying to spook me. But I decided that it might be smart to stay away for a while.

After a few days, rather than heading toward Covent Garden as usual, we climbed off the bus and headed through Soho, in the direction of Piccadilly Circus.

Of course, there were still rules and regulations. Piccadilly worked in a similar way to Covent Garden, with certain areas designated for buskers. This time I decided to stick to the rules. I knew that the area to the east of Piccadilly Circus, on the road leading to Leicester Square, was a good spot for buskers. So I headed there and picked a spot a few yards away from one of the entrances to Piccadilly Circus tube station, outside the Ripley's Believe It or Not exhibition.

It was a really busy late afternoon with hundreds of tourists on the street, heading to the West End's cinemas and theaters. I could tell Bob was nervous. It was probably the number of people and the fact that he was in unfamiliar surroundings.

Everything was fine until around six in the evening, when the crowds really thickened with the beginning of the rush hour. It was at that point that a promotions guy from Ripley's came out onto the street. He was wearing a big inflatable outfit that made him look three times his normal size and was making big arm gestures encouraging people to visit Ripley's.

I could tell immediately that Bob didn't like the look of him. I sensed him drawing in even closer to me. He was really unsure of the bloke and staring at him with a look of slight trepidation. He did look a bit freaky.

To my relief, after a while, Bob settled down and seemed to forget about the man. We just ignored him as he carried on trying to persuade people to step into Ripley's. I was singing a Johnny Cash song when, for no particular reason, the promotions guy suddenly approached us, pointing at Bob as if he wanted to come and stroke him. I didn't spot him until he was almost upon us, leaning down in his weird inflatable suit. By then it was too late.

Bob's reaction was instantaneous. He sprang up and bolted, running into the crowds with his new lead trailing behind him. Before I could even react, he'd disappeared, heading toward the entrance to the tube station.

Oh hell, I said to myself, my heart pumping. *He's gone. I've lost him.*

My instincts took over. I jumped up straightaway and ran after him. I just left the guitar. I was much more worried about Bob than an instrument. I could find one of those anywhere.

I immediately found myself in a sea of people heading toward the tube, all looking overwhelmed at finding themselves in the beating heart of London. I had to weave my way through them to get to the tube entrance.

It was impossible to see anything through the wall of people moving toward me, but as I finally got to the bottom of the steps inside the concourse, things began to thin out a little. I stopped and got down on my haunches to look around at floor level. One or two people gave me strange looks, but that didn't concern me.

"Bob, Bob, where are you, mate?" I shouted at one point, immediately realizing how futile that was with all the noise in there.

I had to make a guess and head in one direction. Should I go toward the barriers that led to the escalators and down to the trains or move toward the various other exits? Which way would Bob go? My hunch was that he wouldn't go down the tube. We'd never been down there together, and I had a feeling the moving escalators would frighten him.

So I moved toward the exits to the other side of Piccadilly Circus.

After a moment or two, I got a glimpse of something, just the faintest flash of ginger on one of the staircases. I then saw a lead trailing after it.

"Bob, Bob," I shouted again, squeezing myself through the crowds once more as I headed in that direction.

I was now within thirty feet of him, but I might as well have been a mile away, the crowds were so thick. There were streams of people coming down the staircase.

"Stop him, step on his lead," I shouted out, catching another glimpse of ginger in the evening light above me.

But no one was taking any notice.

Within moments the lead had disappeared and there was no sign of Bob. He must have reached the bottom of Regent Street and run off.

As I barged my way up the stairs and reached street level, I was in a real state. I was convinced that I'd never see him again.

I had to make a choice. Which way would he have headed on hitting the streets? He could have turned left toward Piccadilly or even headed into the giant Tower Records store there. Again, I trusted my instincts and guessed that he would have basically headed straight on—down the wider pavements of Regent Street.

Still in a complete panic, I began making my way down the street in the hope that someone had seen him. I knew I must have been looking crazed because people were looking at me askance.

Fortunately, not everyone reacted that way. After about thirty yards, I asked a young girl walking down the road if she'd seen a cat.

"Oh yeah," she said. "I saw a cat weaving along the street. Ginger. Had a lead hanging behind it. One bloke tried to stamp on the lead and catch it, but the cat was too quick for him."

My immediate reaction was joy. I could have kissed her. I just knew it was Bob. I carried on down Regent Street, sticking my head into every shop I passed.

After about half a dozen of them, my mood began to swing again, this time toward resignation. I was close to giving up.

A couple of hundred yards down Regent Street, there was a side street that led back down to Piccadilly. From there he could have headed in any one of a dozen directions, into Mayfair or even across the road down to St. James's and Haymarket. If he'd gone that far, then I knew he was lost.

I was about to give up and head down the side street when I stuck my head into a ladies' clothes shop. There were a couple of shop assistants there looking a bit perplexed and looking toward the back of the shop.

They turned to see me, and the moment I said the word "cat," their faces lit up.

"A ginger tom?" one of them said. He's round the back here." She gestured for me to come in.

"That's why we shut the door," the other one said. "We didn't want him to get run over."

"We figured someone was looking for him because of the lead."

They led me toward a row of open wardrobes filled with fancy-looking clothes. In the corner of one of them, curled up in a ball, was Bob.

I'd barely whispered softly, "Hey, Bob, it's me," before he jumped straight into my arms. All my fears evaporated as he purred deeply and rubbed himself against me.

"You gave me such a scare, mate," I said, stroking him. "I thought I'd lost you."

I looked up and saw that the two shopkeepers were standing nearby watching. One of them was dabbing her eyes, close to tears. "I'm so glad you found him," she said. "He looks like such a lovely cat. We were wondering what we'd do with him if no one showed up before closing time."

She came closer and stroked Bob as well. We then chatted for a couple of minutes as she and her colleague got ready to close the till and started preparing to shut up shop for the evening.

"Bye, Bob," the pair said as we headed off into the throng around Piccadilly Circus with Bob perched on my shoulder.

When I got back to Ripley's, I discovered, to my amazement, that my guitar was still there. Maybe the security guy at the door had kept an eye on it. Or one of the community support officers. I had no idea who the Good Samaritan was, but to be honest, I didn't care. I was just glad that Bob and I were reunited.

I wasted no time in gathering up my stuff and calling it a night. We'd not made enough money, but that wasn't my biggest concern. I stopped at a general store and, with most of the cash I had on me, bought myself a little belt clip that I attached first to me, then to Bob's lead. It would make sure that we remained connected. On the bus, rather than sitting on the seat next to me, as usual, he sat on my lap. He could be an inscrutable chap, but at other times I knew exactly what Bob was thinking. Tonight was one of those occasions. We were together, and neither of us wanted that to change.

Chapter 8

SANTA PAWS

AFTER the drama at Piccadilly, Bob and I clung to each other like two survivors hanging on to a life raft. We'd both been badly shaken by the incident.

As Christmas 2007 approached and our first calendar year together drew to a close, our life had settled into a routine. Each morning I'd get up to find him waiting patiently by his bowl in the kitchen. He'd guzzle down his breakfast, then give himself a good wash, licking his paws and face clean. I'd then get ready, pack up my rucksack, grab my guitar, and head into town.

With Christmas only days away, the crowds in Covent Garden were getting bigger. So, too, were the number of treats Bob was getting. From the very early days, people had got into the habit of giving him little presents.

The first came from a middle-aged lady who used to regularly stop and talk to us. She'd had a ginger tom herself many years earlier and Bob reminded her of him. She arrived one evening with a grin on her face and a bag from a fancy pet shop. "I hope you don't mind, but I bought Bob a little present. It's not much," she said, fishing out a stuffed toy mouse. "It's got a little catnip in it." She smiled. "Not a lot, don't worry."

There was a part of me that felt awkward about it. Catnip was, after all, addictive to cats. I'd read all sorts of stuff about how it can drive them crazy if they get hooked on it. It was bad enough with me trying desperately to straighten myself out. I didn't want Bob developing a habit as well. But she was too nice a lady to disappoint. She stayed for a little while, relishing the sight of Bob playing with the mouse.

As the weather took a turn for the worse, people began to give Bob more practical presents. One day, another lady, a striking-looking Russian, sidled up to us. "Hope you don't mind, but with the weather turning cold, I thought I'd knit Bob something to keep him warm," she said, producing a beautiful, light-blue knitted scarf from her shoulder bag.

"Wow," I said, genuinely taken aback. "That's great."

I immediately wrapped it around Bob's neck. It fitted perfectly and looked fantastic. The lady was over the moon. She reappeared a week or two later with a matching blue waistcoat. I was no fashion expert, as anyone who met me could tell, but even I could see that Bob looked amazing in it. People were soon queuing to take photographs.

After that, at least half a dozen more people had dropped off various items of knitted clothing for Bob. It struck me one day that he was becoming a fashion model. He was regularly modeling some new creation a kindly soul had made for him. It gave new meaning to the word "catwalk."

It also underlined what I'd realized already: I wasn't the only one forming a deep affection for Bob. He seemed to make friends with almost everyone he met. It was a gift I wished I had myself. I'd never found it that easy to bond with people.

No one had fallen more deeply in love with Bob than my ex-girlfriend Belle. We were still close friends, and she would pop round to the flat on a regular basis. It was partly to see me and hang out, but I was pretty sure that she was also coming over to see Bob. The two of them would play together for hours on the sofa. Bob thought the world of her; I could tell.

It was about three weeks before Christmas that she came round with a plastic bag in her hand and a big grin on her face.

"Bob, come here. I've got a surprise for you," Belle said, flopping onto the sofa with the bag. He padded over, curious to find out what was inside.

Belle pulled out a couple of small animal T-shirts. One just had a picture of a cute-looking kitten on it. The other was red with green trim. It had the words "Santa Paws" in large white letters with a big paw print underneath.

"Oh, that's really cool, Bob, isn't it?" I said. "The perfect thing to wear when we're in Covent Garden close to Christmas. It will really put a smile on people's faces."

It certainly did that. I don't know if it was the Christmas spirit or simply seeing him in his outfit, but the effect was amazing.

"Ah, look, it's Santa Paws," I'd hear people say almost every few minutes.

A lot of people would stop and drop a bit of silver into my guitar case; others, however, wanted to give Bob something.

On one occasion, a very well-heeled lady stopped and started cooing over Bob. "He's fabulous. What would he like for Christmas?"

"I don't know, madam," I replied. "He could do with a spare harness, I guess. Or something to keep him warm when the weather gets really cold. Or just get him some toys. Every boy likes toys at Christmas."

"Jolly good," she said, getting up and leaving.

I didn't think much more of it, but then, about an hour later, the lady reappeared with a smart-looking, hand-knitted stocking, with cat designs on the front. It was filled with goodies: food, toys, and stuff.

"You must promise me that you will keep it under your tree until Christmas morning."

I didn't have the heart to tell her I didn't have enough money for a Christmas tree. In the days after that, I made a decision. I should have a decent Christmas for once. I had something to celebrate. I had Bob. I suppose I'd become desensitized to Christmas because I hadn't had a decent one in years. I was one of those people who actively dreaded it. During the past decade, I'd spent most of them at places like Shelter, where they did a big Christmas lunch for homeless people. It was all very well meaning, and I'd had a laugh or two. But it just reminded me of what I didn't have: a normal life and a family. It just reminded me that I'd cocked up my life.

Once or twice I'd spent it on my own, trying to forget the fact that my family was on the other side of the world. Well, most of it. On a couple of occasions, I'd spent the day with my father. After going missing for a year when I first ended up on the streets, I'd stayed in contact, calling him very occasionally, and he'd invited me down to his house in south London. But it hadn't been the greatest of experiences, and we hadn't done it again. He didn't really think much of me. I couldn't really blame him. I wasn't exactly a son to be proud about.

This year was different, though. I invited Belle round on Christmas Eve for a drink. Then, for Christmas Day I splashed out on a ready-cooked turkey breast with all the trimmings. I got Bob some really nice treats, including his favorite chicken meal.

When Christmas Day arrived, we got up reasonably early and went out for a short walk. Back up at the flat, I gave Bob his stocking. There were treats, balls, and little soft things containing catnip. He absolutely loved it and was soon playing with his new toys like an excitable child on Christmas morning. It was pretty adorable.

I cooked our lunch early in the afternoon, then put a hat on each of us, had a can of beer, and watched television for the rest of the afternoon and evening. It was the best Christmas I'd had in years.

Chapter 9

MISTAKEN IDENTITY

BY THE spring and summer of 2008, being a busker on the streets of London was becoming more and more difficult.

There were a couple of reasons. The recession had already hit people in my position quite hard. The kindhearted folk who used to think nothing of dropping me and Bob a pound or two were now holding on to their money. One or two regulars even told me as much. They said they were worried about losing their jobs. As a result, I was working much longer hours often to make less money to feed me and Bob and keep us warm.

The bigger problem was that the authorities had started coming down hard on street performers who didn't work in the designated spots. I wasn't sure why they'd decided to do this, but I did know that it had begun to make my life a real headache. Even the Covent Guardians had started confiscating stuff if they felt you weren't taking what they said seriously.

There were also a few new faces among them. One of the more aggressive of the newcomers had threatened to take away my guitar a couple of times. I'd managed to dissuade him by promising to play in a designated area or move out of the neighborhood. I'd then sneaked around the corner for half an hour before returning to James Street.

It had become a constant game of hide-and-seek, but I was running out of places to hide. The new Guardians seemed to know where I was going to be. Most days now I'd be moved along or spoken to at some point. It was wearing me down. Deep down, I knew that my time as a busker was drawing to an end. The straw that broke the camel's back came one afternoon in May that year.

I'D HEADED into Covent Garden, as usual, with Bob. I had a friend staying with me at the time, a guy called Dylan, who I'd met way back when I was with the band. He'd been kicked out of his previous accommodation when he'd refused to pay an extortionate new rent. He needed a floor to sleep on for a couple of weeks. I'd been there myself, so I couldn't refuse him. He had begun sleeping on my sofa.

Bob hadn't taken too kindly to Dylan's arrival at first. I think he felt he was going to lose out in my affections. But as soon as he realized that Dylan was, in fact, another animal lover and that he was going to get more attention, he was fine. Bob thrived on attention.

This particular afternoon, Dylan decided he was going to come into London with us. It was a lovely sunny day, and he was playing with Bob as I set myself up on the corner of James Street. Looking back on it, I can't believe how fortunate it was that he was there.

I'd barely put the guitar strap over my shoulder when a British Transport Police van arrived at speed and pulled up alongside the pavement. Three officers jumped out and immediately started walking toward me.

"What's all this about?" Dylan said.

"Don't know. More of the usual stuff," I said, fully expecting to have to go through the usual tap dance of promising to move away.

I was wrong.

"Right you, you're coming with us," one of the officers said. "We're arresting you on suspicion of using threatening behavior."

"What? Threatening who? I don't know what the hell—"

Before I could finish my sentence, they had grabbed me. While one of them read me my rights, another one stuck me in handcuffs.

"We'll explain at the station. Get in the van before we make things even worse for you."

"What about my cat?" I said, gesturing at Bob.

"We've got some dog kennels at the station. We'll stick him in there," another of the officers said. "Unless you've got someone to take him."

My head was spinning. I had no idea what was happening. But then, out of the corner of my eye, I saw Dylan. "Will you look after Bob?" I said. "Take him back to the flat. The keys are in my rucksack."

He nodded, and I watched him scoop Bob up and reassure him. I could see the look on Bob's face: he was terrified by what was happening.

Through the mesh windows at the back of the van, I watched as the figures of Dylan and Bob disappeared from view.

We drove to the British Transport Police station, and within a few minutes I was standing in front of a desk clerk being asked to empty my pockets and to answer all sorts of questions. I was then led into a cell where I was told to wait. As I sat there, the walls gouged with graffiti and the floors smelling of stale urine, it brought awful memories flooding back. I'd had run-ins with the police before, mostly for petty theft.

When you are homeless or have a drug habit, you try to find easy options to make money. And, to be honest, few things are easier than shoplifting. The first time I did it to pay for my habit was in 2001, something like that. Before that, I'd been begging.

Anyhow, I got caught one day and was taken into police custody. At that time they gave me an on-the-spot fine of eight pounds. I was lucky to get away with that because it was my first time. Of course, it didn't stop me. I had a habit. I had to do what I had to do. You take the risk. You have to.

When you get arrested, it sucks. But you have got to bite the bullet. Obviously, you sit there feeling sorry for yourself, but you aren't going to fight the powers that be.

That was why busking had been so good for me. It was legal.

It kept me straight. But now, here I was back in jail. It felt like a real kick in the stomach. I'd been in the cell for about half an hour when the door opened suddenly and a white-shirted officer ushered me out. "Come on," he said.

"Where are you taking me now?" I asked.

"You'll see."

I was taken into a bare room with a few plastic chairs and a table. There were a couple of officers sitting opposite me. They looked disinterested, to be honest. But then one of them started questioning me.

"Where were you yesterday evening at around six thirty p.m.?"

"Um, I was busking in Covent Garden," I said.

"Where?"

"On the corner of James Street, opposite the entrance to the tube," I said.

"Did you go into the tube station at any time?" the copper asked.

"No, I never go in there," I said. "I travel by bus."

"Well, how come we've got two witnesses saying that you were in the station and that you verbally abused and spat at a female ticket attendant?"

"I've got absolutely no idea," I said, bemused.

"They saw you come up the escalator from the tube and try to go through the automatic barrier without a ticket."

"Well, as I say, that can't have been me."

"When you were challenged, you verbally abused a female member of staff."

I just sat there shaking my head. This was surreal.

"You were then led to the ticket booth and asked to buy a ticket," he went on. "When you did so, against your will, you spat at the window of the ticket booth."

That was it—I lost my cool. "Look," I said. "I told you I wasn't in the tube station last night. I'm never in there. And I never travel by tube. Me and my cat travel everywhere by bus."

They asked me if I wanted to make a statement, so I did, explaining that I'd been busking all night. I knew the CCTV footage would back this up. But, at the back of my mind, I was having all sorts of paranoid thoughts. What if this was all a setup? What if they had doctored the CCTV footage in the tube station? What if it went to court and it was my word against three or four London Underground officers? Worst of all, I found myself anxiously wondering what would happen to Bob. Who would look after him? Would he stay with them or head back onto the street? And what would happen to him there? Thinking about it did my head in.

They kept me in for about another two or three hours. I lost all track of time. There was no natural light in the room, so I had no idea whether it was day or night outside.

At one point, a lady police officer came in with a surly-looking male officer behind her. "I need to do a DNA test," she said as he took a position in the corner, where he stood with his arms folded, glaring at me.

"Okay," I said. I figured I had nothing to lose.

"Just sit there, and I'll take a swab of saliva from your mouth," she said.

She produced a little kit, with loads of swabs and test tubes. "Open wide."

Suddenly, I felt like I was at the dentist. She stuck a long cotton bud into my mouth, scraped around the inside of my cheek, and that was that.

Eventually, I was let out of the cell and taken back to the desk at the front of the station, where I signed for my stuff. I had to sign a form saying that I was released on bail and told that I had to return a couple of days later.

"When will I know if I am being formally charged?" I asked the duty officer, suspecting that he couldn't really tell me that. To my surprise he said that I'd probably know when I came back in a couple of days' time.

"Really?" I said.

"More than likely," he said.

That was good and bad, I decided immediately. Good in the sense that I'd not have to wait months to find out if I was going to be charged, and bad in the sense that if they were going to charge me, I could find myself spending time inside very soon.

AFTER being let free, I emerged into the streets in pitch darkness. There were already little groups of homeless people hunkering down for the night, hiding themselves away in alleyways. It was close to midnight, and the streets were full of drunks and people being kicked out of the pubs.

I breathed a huge sigh of relief when I got inside the flat. Dylan was watching television with Bob curled up in his usual spot. The minute I walked through the door, he jumped up and padded over to me, tilting his head and looking up at me.

"Hello, mate, you all right?" I said, dropping to my knees.

He immediately clambered up on my knee and started rubbing against my face.

Dylan had headed off into the kitchen but soon reappeared with a cold tin of lager from the fridge.

"That's a lifesaver, thanks," I said, ripping the ring off the tin and taking a slug of cold beer.

I sat up for a couple of hours with Dylan, trying to make sense of what had happened. I knew the ticket collectors at Covent Garden tube didn't like me, but I didn't think they'd go so far as to try and frame me for a crime I didn't commit.

"There's no way they can fix the DNA to match yours, mate," Dylan reassured me. I wished I could have been so certain.

I slept fitfully that night. I'd been really shaken by the experience. I couldn't erase the thought that my life could be about to take a terrible turn. I felt powerless, angry—and really scared.

I DECIDED to give Covent Garden a wide berth the next day. Bob and I played around one or two other places, but my heart wasn't in it. I was too worried about what was going to happen the following day. Again, I struggled to get much sleep.

I was due to report at the Transport Police station at midday and set off early to make sure I was on time. I didn't want to give them any excuses. I left Bob at home, just in case I was going to be kept there for hours again.

"Don't worry, mate, I'll be back before you know it," I reassured him as I left. If only I'd been as confident of that as I sounded.

It took me a while to find the station, which was hidden away on a backstreet off Tottenham Court Road. I then had to sit and hang around for twenty minutes. I was eventually called into a room where a couple of officers were waiting for me, one man and a younger woman. They had files in front of them, which looked ominous. I wondered what they'd dug up about my past.

The male officer was the first to speak. He told me that I wasn't going to be charged with the offense of threatening behavior. I guessed why. "The DNA didn't match the saliva on the ticket collector's booth, did it?" I said, feeling suddenly empowered.

He just looked at me with a tight-lipped smile. He couldn't say anything; I knew that. But he didn't need to. It seemed obvious to me that someone at the tube station had tried to set me up but had failed.

If that was the good news, the bad news wasn't long in following. The lady told me that I was being charged with illegally busking, or "touting for reward," to give it its formal title. They shoved a piece of paper toward me and told me I was to report to court in a week's time.

I left the station relieved. "Touting for reward" was a relatively minor offense, certainly compared to threatening behavior. If I was lucky, I'd get away with a small fine and a rap across the knuckles. Threatening behavior would have been a completely different matter. That would have left me open to a heavy punishment, maybe even imprisonment.

Part of me wanted to fight back at the injustice of what had happened. The description of the person who spat on the window bore no relation to my appearance. I held on to the paperwork and thought I could do them for wrongful arrest. But, to be honest, the main thought in my mind as I headed home was relief and a sense that I'd turned some sort of corner. I wasn't sure yet what it was.

I STILL HAD TO GET PAST THE court hearing. I went to the local Citizens Advice center and got a bit of legal advice. I should probably have done that earlier, but I'd been too messed up to think of it.

It turned out that because I was on a drug rehab program and living in sheltered accommodation, I was eligible for legal aid. But I didn't think I needed a solicitor representing me in court, so I simply got some advice about what to say. It was pretty straightforward. I needed to front up and admit that I was guilty of busking: plain and simple. I simply had to go along, plead accordingly, and hope the magistrate wasn't some kind of sadist with a hatred for street musicians.

When the day came, I put on a clean shirt and had a shave before heading to court. The waiting area was full of all sorts of people, from some really scary-looking guys with shaven heads and Eastern European accents to a couple of middle-aged guys in gray suits who were up on driving offenses.

"James Bowen. The court calls Mr. James Bowen," a plummy-sounding voice eventually announced. I took a deep breath and headed in.

The magistrates looked at me like I was a piece of dirt that had been blown in off the street. But, under the law, there wasn't too much they could do to me, especially as it was my first offense for busking. I got a three-month conditional discharge. I wasn't fined. But they made it clear that if I did reoffend, I could face a fine—and worse.

Belle and Bob were waiting for me outside the courthouse after the hearing. Bob immediately jumped off her lap and walked over to me. He didn't want to be too melodramatic about it all, but it was clear he was pleased to see me.

"How did it go?" Belle asked.

"Three-month conditional discharge, but if I get caught again, I'm for the high jump," I said.

"So what are you going to do?" she said.

I looked at her, then looked down at Bob. The answer must have been written all over my face. I had reached the end of the road.

I'd been busking on and off now for almost a decade. Times had changed, and my life had changed, certainly since Bob had come into it. It was becoming more and more clear to me that I couldn't carry on busking. It didn't make any sense on any level. There were times when it didn't earn me enough money to make ends meet. There were times when it put me—and more importantly, Bob—in dangerous situations. And now there was a real danger that if I was caught again, I could get banged up in prison. It just wasn't worth it.

Chapter 10

Number 683

Although I'd lost my livelihood, part of me had begun to see it might be a blessing in disguise.

Deep down, I knew I wasn't going to turn my life around singing Johnny Cash and Oasis songs on street corners. I wasn't going to build up the strength to get myself totally clean by relying on my guitar. It began to dawn on me that I was at a crossroads. I had an opportunity to put the past behind me, and for the first time in years, I felt like I was ready to take it.

That was all very well in theory, of course. I also knew the brutal truth: My options were pretty limited. How was I now going to earn money? No one was going to give me a job.

It wasn't because I was stupid. Thanks to the IT work I'd done when I was a teenager back in Australia, I was fairly knowledgeable when it came to computers. I spent as much time as I could on friends' laptops or on the computers at the local library and had taught myself a fair bit about the subject. But I didn't have any references or relevant experience in the UK to rely on, and when a prospective employer asked me where I'd spent the past ten years, I couldn't exactly say I'd been working for Google or Microsoft. So I had to forget that.

There wasn't even any point in me applying to do a training

course in computing because they wouldn't accept me. Officially I was still on a drug rehabilitation program and living in sheltered accommodation. They wouldn't touch me with a bargepole. I was a nonstarter when it came to getting a normal job.

I realized quickly that there was only one realistic alternative. So a couple of days after the court hearing, I set off with Bob for Covent Garden—for the first time in years without my guitar on my back. When I got to the piazza, I headed straight for the spot where I knew I'd probably find a girl called Sam, the area's *Big Issue* coordinator. The *Big Issue* is a street newspaper written by professional journalists and sold by people at risk.

I had tried selling the *Big Issue* before, back in 1998 and 1999 when I first ended up on the streets. It hadn't worked out. I'd lasted less than a year before I'd given it up. I could still remember how difficult it was and the grim, soul-destroying days I'd spent sitting on a wet and windy street-corner pitch trying to coax Londoners to part with their cash in return for a magazine.

So many people used to come up to me and snarl, "Get a job." That used to really upset me. They didn't realize that selling the *Big Issue* is a job. In fact, being a *Big Issue* seller effectively means you are running your own business. I had overheads. I had to buy copies to sell. So each day I turned up at the coordinator's stand, I had to have at least a few quid in order to buy copies of the magazine. The old saying is as true for *Big Issue* sellers as it is for anyone else: you have to have money to make money.

So many people think it's a charity job and that they give the magazines to the sellers for free. That's just not the case. If it were, people would be selling a lot more than they do. The *Big Issue* philosophy is that it is helping people to help themselves. But back then I wasn't really sure I wanted any help. I wasn't ready for it.

I wouldn't have even contemplated going back to selling the *Big Issue* if it hadn't been for Bob. The way he'd transformed my fortunes, and my spirits, had been amazing. If I could do as well selling the *Big Issue* as I'd done busking with Bob, then maybe I could take that big step forward.

I found Sam at the spot where the area's *Big Issue* sellers gathered to buy their magazines, on a side street off the main piazza. There were a few vendors there, all men. I recognized one or two. One of them was a guy called Steve, who I knew was a driver. I'd seen him around the place, delivering the magazines on Mondays when the new issue came out.

We'd registered each other's presence around Covent Garden a couple of times and were a bit wary of each other. I got the distinct impression he wasn't pleased to see me, but I didn't care. I hadn't come to see him; it was Sam I needed to talk to.

"Hello, you two not busking today?" she said, recognizing me and Bob.

"No, I'm going to have to knock that on the head," I said. "Bit of trouble with the cops. If I get caught doing it illegally again, I'm going to be in big trouble. Can't risk it now I've got Bob to look after. Can I, mate?"

"Okay," Sam said, her face signaling that she could see what was coming next.

"So," I said, rocking up and down on my heels. "I was wondering—"

Sam smiled and cut me off. "Well, it all depends on whether you meet the criteria," she said.

"I do," I said, knowing that, as a person in what was known as "vulnerable housing," I was eligible to sell the magazine.

"But you are going to have to go through all the red tape and go down to Vauxhall to sign up. You know where the offices are?" she said, reaching for a card.

"Not sure."

"Get a bus to Vauxhall and get off by the train station. It's across the road, not far from the river. Once you're badged up, just come back here and see me and we can get you going."

I took the card and headed home with Bob. "Better get ourselves organized, Bob," I said. "We're going for a job interview."

I needed to get some paperwork sorted before I could go to the *Big Issue* office, so the next day I went to see my housing worker. I explained my current situation and what had happened with the Transport Police. She happily gave me a letter saying that I was living in "vulnerable housing" and that selling the *Big Issue* would be a good way of helping me get my life back together again.

The day after that, I made myself look respectable, got my hair tied back, put on a decent shirt, and set off for Vauxhall. I took Bob with me. Part of my thinking was that Bob might help me sell magazines in the way that he'd helped me make money busking. He was going to be part of my team, so I wanted to get him registered as well, if that was at all possible.

The *Big Issue* offices are in an office block on the south side of the Thames, near Vauxhall Bridge. The first thing I noticed when I arrived in the reception area was a large sign saying "No Dogs Allowed." It didn't say anything about cats, however.

After filling in a few bits of paper, I was told to take a seat and wait. After a while, I was called in to an interview with a guy in one of the offices. He was a decent bloke, and we chatted for a while. He'd been on the streets himself years ago and had used the *Big Issue* as a stepping-stone to help get his life together. "I know what it's like out there, James, believe me."

It took just a few minutes before he gave me a thumbs-up and told me to go and get badged up in another office.

I had to have my photo taken and then wait to get a laminated badge with my vendor number on it. I asked the guy who was issuing the badges whether Bob could have an ID card as well.

"Sorry," he said, shaking his head. "Pets aren't allowed to have their own badges. We've had this before with dogs. Never with a cat, though."

"Well, what about if he is in the picture with me?" I asked.

He pulled a face, as if to say, "I'm not sure about that." But in the end he relented. "Go on, then," he said.

"Smile, Bob," I said as we sat in front of the camera. As he waited for the photo to be processed, the guy got on with the rest of the registration process. When you become a *Big Issue* seller, you get assigned a random number. They are not issued in sequence. If they did that, the numbers would now be running into the thousands because so many people have signed up, then just disappeared off the face of the earth. So when someone fails to show up on the records for a while, the number comes back into use.

After waiting about a quarter of an hour, the guy reappeared at the desk. "Here you go, Mr. Bowen," he said, handing me the laminated badge.

I couldn't help breaking into a big grin at the picture. Bob was on the left-hand side. We were a team. *Big Issue* Vendors Number 683.

IT WAS a long journey back to Tottenham, involving two buses. So I whiled away the hour and a half it took us by reading through the little booklet they'd given me. It began with the magazine's philosophy: "The *Big Issue* exists to offer homeless and vulnerably housed people the opportunity to earn a legitimate income by selling a magazine to the general public. We believe in offering 'a hand up, not a hand out' in enabling individuals to take control of their lives."

That's exactly what I want, I said to myself, *a hand up. And this time I'll accept it.*

The next bit stated that I had to undergo an "induction process and sign up to the code of conduct." I knew that meant that I'd have to work at a "trial pitch" where my performance would be assessed. If that went well, I'd be allocated a fixed pitch. I'd also get ten free copies of the magazine to get me started. It made it clear that it was then down to me: "Once they have sold these magazines, they can purchase further copies, which they buy for £1 and sell for £2, thereby making £1 per copy."

The rules went on to explain the simple economics of it. "We do not reimburse vendors for magazines that they fail to sell, hence each individual must manage their sales and finances carefully. These skills, along with the confidence and self-esteem they build through selling the magazine, are crucial in helping homeless people reintegrate into mainstream society."

But there was a lot more to it than that, as I would soon discover.

THE NEXT MORNING, I HEADED back down to Covent Garden to see Sam, the coordinator. I was keen to get on with my "induction."

"All go okay down at Vauxhall?" she said as Bob and I approached her.

"I guess it must have done. They gave me one of these." I grinned, producing my laminated badge from under my coat.

"Great," Sam said, smiling at the photo. "I'd better get you started, then."

She began by counting out my ten free copies of the magazine. "There you go," she said. "You know you'll have to buy them after this?"

"Yep, I understand," I said.

For a few minutes she studied a sheet of paper. "Just trying to work out where to put your trial pitch," she said apologetically.

A moment or two later I could see she'd made up her mind.

"Found somewhere?" I asked, feeling quite excited about it.

"Think so," Sam said. I couldn't believe what she said next. "Okay, we'll give you the training pitch just here," she said, pointing in the direction of Covent Garden tube station, a few yards farther up James Street.

I couldn't stop myself from bursting out laughing.

"Are you okay? Is that a problem?" she said, looking confused. "I can look to see if there's somewhere else."

"No, it's not a problem at all," I said. "It'll be great there. It'll be a real walk down memory lane. I'll get started right away."

I wasted no time and set up immediately. It was a few hours before I'd normally have set up busking, but there were lots of people milling around, mostly tourists. It was a bright, sunny morning, which, I knew from experience, always puts people in a more generous mood.

I was officially licensed to be there, so I placed myself as close to the station as possible. I got on with the job of trying to shift my ten copies.

I knew they'd given me this pitch because it was a nightmare. The entrance and exit of a tube station is not a place where people have the time to slow down and engage with someone trying to sell them something. A normal *Big Issue* seller would have done well to stop one in every thousand people that raced past.

I also knew that I wasn't a normal *Big Issue* seller. I had a secret weapon, one that had already cast his spell on Covent Garden. And he was soon weaving his magic.

I'D PUT Bob down on the pavement next to me where he was sitting contentedly, watching the world go by. Within moments of me setting up, a couple of young American tourists had pulled up to a halt and started pointing at Bob. "Aaaah," one of them said, reaching for her camera.

"Do you mind if we take a picture of your cat?" the other asked.

"Sure, why not?" I said, pleased that they'd had the decency to ask. "Would you like to buy a copy of the *Big Issue* while you're at it? It will help him and me get some dinner tonight."

"Oh sure," the second girl said, looking ashamed that she'd not thought of it.

"It's not compulsory," I added.

But before I could say anything else, she'd given me a five-pound note.

"Oh, I'm not sure I've got any change. I've literally just started," I said, feeling flustered. I know a lot of people think *Big Issue* sellers routinely say this, but I genuinely didn't have much in my pockets. When I counted it out, I had just under a pound in shrapnel and handed that over to her.

"That's fine," she said. "Keep the change and buy your cat something nice to eat."

As the American girls left, another group of tourists passed by, this time Germans. Again, they started cooing over Bob. They didn't buy a magazine, but it didn't matter. I knew already I'd have no trouble selling ten copies. In fact, I might even be heading back to Sam for more stock before the end of the day.

Sure enough, I sold six copies within the first hour. I already felt like I'd taken a big step in a new direction.

The icing on the cake came after I'd been there for about two and a half hours. I was down to my last two magazines. I was suddenly aware of a bit of a commotion inside the station. All of a sudden, a small group of London Underground staff appeared in the concourse in full view of me. They seemed to be deep in conversation about something, and one or two of them were on walkie-talkies. Then the large, sweaty figure of the ticket attendant spotted me and Bob outside the station. He immediately marched in our direction looking hassled and hot-tempered and as red as a beetroot. They say that revenge is a dish best eaten cold, so I decided to stay cool.

"What the hell are you doing here?" he said. "I thought you'd been locked up. You know you're not supposed to be here."

I didn't say anything at first. Instead, very slowly and deliberately, I flashed him my *Big Issue* badge. "I'm just doing my job, mate," I said, savoring the mixture of bewilderment and anger that immediately began spreading across his face. "I suggest you get on with yours."

I HADN'T got many decisions right in my life. Whenever I'd been given an opportunity in the past ten years, I'd screwed things up big-time. Within a couple of days of deciding to become a *Big Issue* seller, however, I was pretty sure that I'd taken a step in the right direction for once.

There is no sale or return with the *Big Issue,* so I learned quickly that if you miscalculated the amount of magazines, you could lose out quite badly. You can take a serious blow if you are stuck with fifty papers on Saturday night. Come Monday, you get no credit against the next purchase from the old magazines, so the old papers are pulp. At the same time, you didn't want to underbuy. Too few and you'd sell out too quickly and miss out on willing buyers. It was no different from running Marks and Spencer's—well, in theory.

It took a while to get the balance right.

While I was working out the best way to sell the *Big Issue,* I still lived from hand to mouth. What I earned between Monday and Saturday evening was generally gone by the next Monday morning.

Sometimes, at the start of the week, I'd turn up at the coordinator's stand with only a few quid. I'd ask Sam to do me a favor and buy ten papers for me on the understanding I'd pay her back as soon as I had some money. She would usually do this for vendors she knew she could trust. Then, when I had sold those copies, I'd go back and pay off what I owed and get some more papers. I'd build it up from there.

In real terms, I was actually making less money than I had been busking with Bob. But, as I settled down into this new routine, I decided it was a price worth paying. The fact that I was working legitimately made a huge difference.

The next couple of months flew by. With Bob at my side, I discovered that I could sell as many as thirty or even fifty papers on a good day. At £2 a paper, it could add up quite well, especially with the tips that some people gave me or, more usually, Bob.

After a few more weeks of trying out the spot at the tube station, I realized that far from being a "bad" pitch, the tube station was actually ideal for me and Bob. So I was disappointed when Sam told me that having finished my probation period I would be moving to another pitch.

It wasn't exactly a surprise. The thing about being a member of the *Big Issue* vendor community is that everyone can see how well the others are doing. When the vendors go to the coordinator, they can see who has been buying what quantities on a list that's there for everyone to see. So during that first fortnight, they would have seen that I was buying a lot of magazines. In that second week I noticed a subtle but definite change in the attitude toward me. I got the distinct feeling that the older hands had taken a dislike to me and hadn't taken too kindly to us doing so well out of what was supposed to be a bad pitch. For once, however, I buttoned my lip and accepted it. *Choose your battles, James,* I counseled myself.

It turned out to be good advice.

Chapter 11

UNDER THE WEATHER

IT WAS a cold and wet autumn that year. The trees were soon stripped of their foliage as the winds and heavy rains began to build. One particular morning, as Bob and I left the block of flats and set off for the bus stop, a fine drizzle was falling.

Bob wasn't a big fan of the rain, so at first I assumed that was to blame for the lethargic way in which he padded along the path. *Maybe he's got second thoughts about joining me today,* I said to myself. Or maybe it was true what they said about cats being able to sense bad weather in the air. As I cast an eye up to the sky, a giant bank of steely gray clouds was hovering over north London like some vast alien spaceship. *Maybe Bob was right and we should turn around,* I thought. But then I remembered the weekend was coming, and we didn't have enough money to get through it. *Beggars can't be choosers, even if they have been cleared of all charges,* I said to myself, trying to make light of the predicament.

Bob was still moving at a snail's pace, and it had taken us a couple of minutes to get a hundred yards down the road.

"Come on, mate, climb aboard," I said, turning around and ushering him up into his normal position. He draped himself on my shoulder, and we trudged off toward Tottenham High Road and the bus.

The ride was normally one of his favorite parts of the day. No matter how often we did it, Bob would never tire of pressing himself against the glass. But today he wasn't even bothered about taking the window seat, not that he'd have seen much through the condensation and streaks of rain that obscured our view. Instead, he curled up on my lap. He seemed drowsy, as if he was half-asleep. He was definitely not his normal, alert self.

It was when we got off at Tottenham Court Road that he took a distinct turn for the worse. Luckily the rain had eased off a bit, and I was able to splash my way through the backstreets in the direction of Covent Garden, sidestepping the bigger puddles and the giant umbrellas that flew at me every now and then.

Our new location wasn't a long way from the tube station, on the corner of Neal Street and Short's Gardens, outside a shoe shop. As we walked down Neal Street, I was suddenly aware that Bob was behaving oddly on my shoulder, twitching and rocking around.

"You all right there, mate?" I said, slowing down.

All of a sudden he began moving in a really agitated way, making weird retching noises as if he was choking. I placed him down on the street to see what was wrong. But before I could even kneel down, he began to vomit. It was just bile, but it kept coming. I could see his body convulsing as he retched and fought to expel whatever it was that was making him sick.

He must have been feeling sick during the bus journey, too, I could now see. I blamed myself for not spotting it sooner, and all sorts of crazy thoughts rushed through my mind. Had he simply eaten something that disagreed with him this morning? Had he swallowed something in the flat? Or was this something more serious? Was he going to drop dead in front of me? I'd heard stories about cats collapsing in front of their owners after drinking cleaning fluids or choking on bits of plastic. For a split second, an image of Bob dying flashed through my head. I managed to pull myself together before my imagination ran riot.

Come on, James, let's deal with this sensibly, I told myself.

I knew that all the retching meant that he was getting dehydrated. I decided that some water would be a good idea. So I scraped him up and held him in my arms as we walked on to Covent Garden and a general store I knew. I didn't have much cash on me, but I cobbled together enough to buy a liquidized chicken meal that Bob usually loved and some mineral water.

I placed him on the pavement near our normal pitch. I got out Bob's bowl and spooned the chicken into it. "Here we go, mate," I said, stroking him as I placed the bowl in front of him.

Ordinarily he would have guzzled it down, but not today. Instead he stood and looked at it for a while before he decided to tuck in. Even then he was very tentative. He only ate the jelly. He didn't touch a bit of the meat. Again, it set the alarm bells ringing. This wasn't the Bob I knew and loved. Something was definitely wrong.

I halfheartedly set myself up to start selling the magazine. We needed some money to get us through the next few days, especially if I was going to have to take Bob to a vet. But my heart wasn't in it. I was far more concerned with watching Bob than trying to capture the attention of passersby. He lay there, impassive. Unsurprisingly, not too many people stopped to make a donation. I cut the day short after less than two hours. Bob hadn't been sick again, but he definitely wasn't right. I had to get him home to the warmth and dryness of the flat.

As he lay on my lap on the bus returning to Tottenham, I felt the emotions welling up. It was all I could do to stop myself from bursting into tears. Bob was the best thing in my life. The thought of losing him was terrifying.

When we got home, Bob just headed straight for the radiator, where he curled up and went straight to sleep. He stayed there for hours. That night I didn't sleep much, worrying about him. I kept hauling myself out of bed to check on him. One time I was convinced he wasn't breathing and had to place my hand on his diaphragm to make sure it was moving. I couldn't believe how relieved I was when I found he was purring gently.

Money was so tight I simply had to go out again the following day. That presented me with a real dilemma. Should I leave Bob in the flat on his own? Or should I wrap him up warm and take him into central London with me so that I could keep an eagle eye on him?

Luckily the weather was a lot better today. The sun had decided to make an appearance. And when I wandered out of the kitchen with my cereal bowl in my hands, I saw Bob looking up at me. He looked a little perkier. And when I offered him a little food, he nibbled at it more enthusiastically.

I decided to take him with me. It was still early in the week, so I'd have to wait a few days before I could get him looked at by the vet at the Blue Cross van. In advance of that, I decided to do some research and headed for the local library where I logged on to a computer.

I'd forgotten what a bad idea it is to search through medical websites. They always give you the worst possible scenario. When I entered the main symptoms—lethargy, vomiting, appetite loss—a whole swathe of possible illnesses popped up. Just the *A*s in the list were bad enough. They included Addison's disease, acute kidney disease, and arsenic poisoning.

By the time I'd been reading for fifteen minutes, I was a nervous wreck.

I decided to switch tack and look at the best treatments for vomiting. That was more positive. The sites suggested plenty of water, rest, and supervision. So that was my plan for the next twenty-four to forty-eight hours. I'd keep an eye on him around the clock. If he started vomiting again, I'd head for the vet's immediately.

THE next day I decided to stay at home until late in the afternoon to give Bob a good chance to rest. He slept like a log. I wanted to keep an eye on him. But he seemed okay, so I decided to leave him for three or four hours and try to squeeze in some selling. I didn't have much option.

Trudging through the streets to Covent Garden, an idea struck me. I had come across a vet nurse called Rosemary. Her boyfriend, Steve, worked at a comic book shop near where we sometimes set up. Bob and I would pop in there every now and again, and we had become friends. Rosemary had been in there with Steve one day, and we'd struck up a conversation about Bob.

I decided to stick my head in there to see if either of them was around. Luckily Steve was there and gave me a phone number for Rosemary.

"She won't mind you ringing her," he said. "Especially as it's about Bob. She loves Bob."

When I spoke to Rosemary, she asked me a load of questions. "What does he eat? Does he ever eat anything else when he's out and about?"

"Well, he rummages around in the trash bins," I said.

It was a habit he had never shaken off. He was an absolute terror. I'd seen him tear the garbage bags to pieces in the kitchen. He was a street cat. You can take the cat off the street, but you can't take the street out of the cat.

"Hmmm," she said. "That might explain it."

She prescribed some probiotic medication, some antibiotics, and some special liquid to settle the stomach. "What's your address?" she said. "I'll get it biked over to you. Don't worry, it won't cost you anything. I'll just add it to another delivery in the area," she said. "This evening okay?"

"Yes, great," I said. I was overwhelmed. Such spontaneous acts of generosity hadn't exactly been a part of my life in the past few years. Random acts of violence, yes; kindness, no. It was one of the biggest changes that Bob had brought with him. Thanks to him, I'd rediscovered the good side of human nature. I had begun to place my trust—and faith—in people again.

Rosemary was as good as her word. The bike arrived early that evening, and I administered the first doses of the medicine straightaway.

Bob didn't like the taste of the probiotic. He screwed his face up and recoiled when I gave him his first spoonful of it.

"Tough luck, mate," I said. "If you didn't stick your face in rubbish bins, you wouldn't have to take this stuff."

The medicine had an almost immediate impact. That night he slept soundly and was a lot friskier the following morning. I had to hold his head in my hand to make sure he swallowed the probiotic.

By Thursday he was well on the road to recovery. But just as a precaution, I decided to pop along to the Blue Cross van on Islington Green.

The nurse on duty recognized him immediately and looked concerned when I told her Bob had been under the weather.

"Let's give him a quick checkup, shall we?"

She checked his weight and inside his mouth and had a good feel around his body. "All seems well," she said. "I think he's on the road to recovery."

We chatted for a couple of minutes before I headed off.

Seeing Bob sick had a profound effect on me. I'd never imagined him getting ill. It really shook me. It underlined a feeling that had been building inside me for a while now: It was time for me to get myself clean. I was fed up with my lifestyle. I was tired of the mind-numbing routine of having to go to the drug dependency unit every fortnight and the chemist every day. I was tired of feeling I could slip back into addiction at any time.

So the next time I went to see my counselor, I asked him about coming off methadone and taking the final step toward becoming clean. We'd talked about it before, but I don't think he'd ever taken me at my word. Now he could tell I was serious. "Won't be easy, James," he said.

"Yeah, I know that."

"You'll need to take a drug called Subutex. We can then slowly decrease the dosage of that so that you don't need to take anything," he said. "The transition can be hard, and you can have quite severe withdrawal symptoms," he said, leaning forward.

"That's my problem," I said. "But I want to do it. I want to do it for myself and for Bob."

"Okay, well, I will get things moving, and we will look at beginning the process in a few weeks' time."

For the first time in years, I felt like I could see the tiniest light at the end of a very dark tunnel.

EVENTUALLY, because of fierce competition among the sellers of the *Big Issue,* I had to make the decision to move away from Covent Garden. It would be a wrench. Bob and I had a loyal customer base there, and besides anything else, it was a fun place to work. The inescapable truth, however, was that Bob and I needed to move to a less competitive part of London, and somewhere I wasn't so well known. There was one obvious candidate: the Angel tube station in Islington where I once used to busk. It was a good area, less lucrative than Covent Garden but still worthwhile. So I decided the next day to visit the coordinator there, a great guy called Lee, who I knew a bit.

"What are the chances of me getting a good pitch here?" I asked him.

"Well, Camden Passage is pretty busy, as is the Green, but you could do outside the tube station if you like," he said. "No one fancies it much."

I had a feeling of déjà vu. It was Covent Garden all over again. For other *Big Issue* sellers in London, tube stations were reckoned to be a complete nightmare, the people are simply moving too fast, always in a hurry.

As I'd discovered at Covent Garden, however, Bob had the magical ability to slow them down. People would see him and suddenly they weren't in quite such a rush. It was as if he was providing them with a little bit of light relief, a little bit of warmth and friendliness in their otherwise frantic, impersonal lives. I'm sure a lot of people bought a *Big Issue* as a thank you for me giving them that little moment. So I was more than happy to take what was supposed to be a "difficult" pitch.

We started that same week. I left the Covent Garden vendors to it.

Almost immediately we began to get people slowing down to say hello to Bob. One or two people recognized us.

One evening, a well-dressed lady in a business suit stopped and did a sort of double take. "Don't you two work in Covent Garden?" she said.

"Not anymore, madam," I said with a smile, "not anymore."

The move to Angel definitely met with Bob's seal of approval; I only had to look at his body language each day as we headed to work. When we got off the bus, he wouldn't ask to climb on my shoulders in the way he tended to do when we'd been in central London. Instead, most mornings he would take the lead and march purposefully ahead of me, down Camden Passage, past all the antique stores, cafés, pubs, and restaurants, and toward the end of Islington High Street and the paved area around the tube station entrance.

When we eventually arrived at his favorite spot, facing the flower stall and the newspaper stand by the entrance to Angel tube, he watched me go through the arrival ritual, placing my bag down on the pavement and putting a copy of the *Big Issue* in front of it. Once this was done, he would sit himself down, lick himself clean, and get ready for the day.

After all the trouble I'd had at Covent Garden over the years, Islington seemed like a fresh start for us both. I felt like we were starting a new era and that this time it was going to last.

The Angel wasn't quite as busy as Covent Garden, but the tube station still saw a mass of humanity pouring in and out each day. It was a distinctively different type of person, though, more professional and, for want of a better word, more "upmarket." Each evening I'd notice hordes of people in business suits heading in and out. The bad news was that most of them barely even registered the fact that there was a ginger cat sitting outside the station. The good news was that a large proportion of those who did slow down and spot him took an instant shine. They were also really generous. I noticed immediately that the average purchase and tip at Islington was just that little bit bigger than in Covent Garden.

The Angel locals were also generous in a different kind of way: Almost as soon as we began selling the *Big Issue* there, people began giving Bob bits of food. On our third day, a smartly dressed lady stopped for a chat. She asked me whether we were going to be there every day from now on, which struck me as a bit suspicious. Was she going to make some sort of complaint? I was completely off the mark, however. The following day she appeared with a small bag containing some cat milk and a pouch of cat food. "There you go, Bob," she said happily, placing them on the pavement in front of him.

"He'll probably have that at home tonight if that's okay," I said, thanking her.

"Of course," she said. "As long as he enjoys it, that's the main thing."

After that, more and more locals started donating tidbits for him.

Our pitch was down the road from a large Sainsbury's supermarket. It soon became obvious that people were going in there to do their normal shopping and were picking up a little treat for Bob on their way round. They would then drop their presents off on their way back home.

One day, just a few weeks after we began at Angel, about half a dozen different people did this. By the end of the day, I couldn't fit all the tins of cat milk, pouches of food, and tins of tuna and other fish that had been piling up all day into my rucksack. I had to keep it all in a large Sainsbury's bag. When I got back to the flat, it filled up an entire shelf in one of the kitchen cupboards. It kept us going for almost a week.

The other thing that was a world apart from Covent Garden was the attitude of the staff at the tube station. At Covent Garden I was a hated figure almost. I could count on one hand the number of people with whom I'd forged a friendship in the years I'd been busking or selling the *Big Issue* there. In fact, I didn't even need that. I could think of two at most.

By contrast, the staff at Angel were really warm and generous toward Bob from the very beginning. One day, for instance, the sun had been blazingly hot. The mercury must have been up in the nineties. Everyone was walking around in shirtsleeves even though, technically, it was autumn. I was sweating like crazy in my black jeans and black T-shirt.

I deliberately placed Bob in the shade of the building behind us so that he didn't get too hot. I knew that heat was bad for cats. An hour or so after we'd set up our pitch, it became clear to me that I'd soon need to get some water for Bob. But before I was able to do something, a figure appeared from inside the tube station with a nice clean steel bowl brimming with clear water. I recognized the lady immediately. Her name was Davika, one of the ticket attendants. She'd stopped to talk to Bob on numerous occasions.

"Here you go, Bob," she said, stroking him on the back of the neck as she placed the bowl in front of him. "Don't want you getting dehydrated now, do we?" she said.

Bob had won the Islington crowd over in a matter of weeks. It was amazing really.

Chapter 12

FORTY-EIGHT HOURS

THE young doctor at the drug dependency unit scribbled his signature at the bottom of the prescription and handed it over to me with a stern expression on his face. "Remember, take this, then come back to me at least forty-eight hours later when you can feel the withdrawal symptoms have really kicked in," he said, holding my gaze. "It's going to be tough, but it will be a lot tougher if you don't stick to what I've said. Okay?"

"Okay, I understand." I nodded, picking myself up and heading out of his treatment room. "Just hope I can do it. See you in a couple of days."

It had been a couple of months since we'd first talked about coming off methadone. I thought I was ready for it, but my counselors and doctors obviously didn't share that opinion. Each time I'd come in, they had postponed it. I'd not got any kind of explanation as to why this was. Now, at last, they had decided it was time: I was going to make the final step toward being clean.

The prescription the counselor had just given me was for my last dose of methadone. Methadone had helped me kick my dependence on heroin, but I'd now tapered down my usage to such an extent that it was time to stop taking it for good. When I next visited the DDU in a couple of days' time, I would be given my first dose of a much milder medication, Subutex, which would ease me out of drug dependency completely. The counselor described the process as like landing an airplane, which I thought was a good analogy. In the following months he would slowly cut back my dosage until it was almost nonexistent. As he did so, he said I would slowly drop back down to earth, landing, hopefully, with a very gentle bump.

As I waited for the prescription to be made up, I didn't really dwell on the significance of it. My head was too busy with thoughts about what lay ahead during the next forty-eight hours.

The counselor had explained to me in graphic detail that coming off methadone wasn't easy. I'd experience "cold turkey," a series of unpleasant physical and mental withdrawal symptoms. I had to wait for those symptoms to become quite severe before I could go back to the clinic to get my first dose of Subutex. If I didn't, I risked having what's known as a precipitated withdrawal. This was basically a much worse withdrawal. It didn't bear thinking about.

I was confident at this point that I could do it. I just kept telling myself that I had to get over this last hurdle. Otherwise nothing was going to change. I'd been living this way for ten years. A lot of my life had just slipped away. When you are dependent on drugs, time becomes inconsequential; you only start worrying about it when you need your next fix. And that's when it becomes awful. Then all you can think about is making money to get some more. I'd made huge progress since I'd been in the depths of my addiction years earlier. The DDU had really put me back on track. But I was sick of the whole thing now. I felt like I had something to do with my life. I had Bob.

When I got home, he was pleased to see me, especially as I'd stopped off at the supermarket on the way home and had a bag full of goodies. Anyone who is trying to get rid of an addictive habit knows what it is like. The first forty-eight hours are the hardest. You are so used to getting your "fix" that you can't think of anything else. The trick is to think of something else. And that's what I hoped to do. And I was really grateful that I had Bob to help me achieve it.

That lunchtime we sat down in front of the television, had a snack together—and waited.

The withdrawal symptoms began to kick in twenty-four hours after I'd had my dose of methadone. Within eight hours of that I was sweating profusely and feeling very twitchy. By now it was the middle of the night, and I should have been asleep. I did nod off, but I felt like I was pretty much conscious all the time. It was a strange kind of sleep, full of dreams or, more accurately, hallucinations.

By the following morning I was experiencing really bad headaches, almost migraine-level pains. I found it hard to cope with any light or noise. I'd sit in the dark, but then I'd start dreaming or hallucinating and want to snap myself out of it. It was a vicious circle.

What I needed more than anything was something to take my mind off it all, which was where Bob proved my salvation. There were times when I wondered whether he and I had some kind of telepathic understanding. He could definitely read my mind sometimes and seemed to be doing so now. He knew that I needed him, so he was a constant presence, hanging around me, snuggling up close when I invited him but keeping his distance when I was having a bad time.

Sometimes I'd be nodding off, and he would come up to me and place his face close to me, as if to say, "You all right, mate? I'm here if you need me." At other times he would just sit with me, purring away, rubbing his tail on me and licking my face every now and again. As I slipped in and out of a weird hallucinatory universe, he was my sheet anchor to reality. He didn't seem to want to leave my side.

During the morning of the second day, I had a couple of hours where I felt much better. Bob and I played around. I did a bit of reading. It was hard, but it was a way to keep my mind occupied.

By the afternoon and early evening, however, the withdrawal symptoms were ramping up. I had been warned that you get what's called restless legs syndrome. Incredibly uncomfortable, nervous pulses run through your body, making it impossible to sit still. I started doing this. My legs would suddenly and involuntarily start kicking—it's not called kicking the habit for nothing. I think this freaked Bob out a bit. He gave me a couple of odd, sideways looks. But he didn't desert me.

That night was the worst of all. I couldn't watch television because the light and noise hurt my head. When I went into the dark, I just found my mind racing, filling up with all kinds of crazy, scary stuff. All the time my legs were kicking, and I was feeling extremes of hot and cold. One minute I was so hot I felt like I was inside a furnace. The next I'd feel ice-cold.

Every now and again, I'd have moments of lucidity. At one point, I remember thinking that I really understood why so many people find it so hard to kick their drug habit. It's a physical thing as well as a mental thing. That battle of wills that's going on in your brain is very one-sided. The addictive forces are definitely stronger than those that are trying to wean you off the drugs.

At another point, I was able to see the last decade and what my addiction had done to me. I saw—and sometimes smelled—the alleys and underpasses where I'd slept rough, the hostels where I'd feared for my life, the terrible things I'd done and considered doing just to score enough to get me through the next twelve hours. I saw with unbelievable clarity just how seriously addiction screws up your life.

That second night seemed to last forever. I'd look up at the clock, and it seemed at times as if it were moving backward. Outside it seemed as if the darkness were getting deeper and blacker rather than brightening up for morning. It was horrible.

But I had my secret weapon. At one stage, I was lying as still and quiet as possible, just trying to shut out the world. All of a sudden, I felt Bob clawing at my leg, digging into my skin quite painfully.

"Bob, what the hell are you doing?" I shouted at him a bit too aggressively, making him jump. Immediately I felt guilty.

I suspect he was worried that I was a little too still and quiet and was checking up to make sure I was alive.

Eventually, a thin, soupy gray light began to seep through the window, signaling that morning had arrived at last. I hauled myself out of bed and looked at the clock. It was almost eight o'clock. I knew the clinic would be open by nine. I couldn't wait any longer.

I splashed some cold water on my face. It felt absolutely awful on my clammy skin. In the mirror I could see that I looked drawn and my hair was a sweaty mess, but I wasn't going to worry about that at this point. Instead I threw on some clothes and headed for the bus stop.

Getting to Camden from Tottenham at that time of the day was always a trial. Today it seemed much worse. Every traffic light was on red, every road seemed to have a long backup of traffic. It was the journey from hell.

As I sat on the bus, I was still having temperature swings and my limbs were still twitching every now and again, although not as badly as during the night. People were looking at me as if I were some kind of nutcase. I probably looked unbelievably bad. At that point I didn't care. I just wanted to get to the DDU.

I arrived just after nine and found the waiting room half full already. One or two people looked as rough as I felt. I wondered whether they'd been through forty-eight hours as hellish as those I'd just been through.

"Hi, James, how are you feeling?" the counselor said as he came into the treatment room. He only needed to look at me to know the answer, of course, but I appreciated his concern.

"Not great," I said.

"Well, you've done well to get through the last two days. That's a huge step you've taken."

He checked me over and got me to give a urine sample. He then gave me a tablet of Subutex and scribbled out a new prescription.

"That should make you feel a lot better," he said. "Now let's start easing you off this, and out of this place completely."

I stayed there for a while to make sure the new medication didn't have any odd side effects. It didn't. Quite the opposite, in fact; it made me feel a thousand times better.

By the time I had got back to Tottenham, I felt completely transformed. It was a different feeling from what I'd experienced on methadone. The world seemed more vivid. I felt like I could see, hear, and smell more clearly. Colors were brighter. Sounds were crisper. It was weird. It may sound strange, but I felt more alive again.

I stopped on the way and bought Bob a couple of new flavor cat food pouches that had come onto the market. I also bought him a little squeezy mouse.

Back at the flat I made a huge fuss of him.

"We did it, mate," I said. "We did it."

The sense of achievement was incredible. Over the next few days, the transformation in my health and life in general was huge. It was as if someone had drawn back the curtains and shed some sunlight into my life.

Of course, in a way, someone had.

Chapter 13

HOMEWARD BOUND

I DIDN'T think Bob and I could have been closer, but the experience we'd just been through together tightened our bond even more. In the days that followed, he stuck to me like a limpet, watching over me in case I had a relapse.

There was no danger of that, however. I felt better than I had in years. The thought of returning to the dark dependencies of the past made me shiver. I had come too far now to turn back.

I decided to celebrate my breakthrough by doing up the flat a little bit. So Bob and I put in a few extra hours each day outside the tube station and then used the proceeds to buy some paint, a few cushions, and a couple of prints to put on the wall.

I then went to a good secondhand furniture shop and bought a sofa. It was covered in a burgundy red, heavy-duty fabric—with a bit of luck the sort of material that would be able to resist Bob's claws. The old one was knackered, partly due to natural wear and tear, but also because of Bob's habit of scratching at its legs and base. Bob was banned from scratching the new one.

As the weeks passed and the nights turned even darker and colder, we spent more and more time curled up on the new sofa. I was already looking forward to a nice Christmas for me and Bob, although, as it turned out, that was a little premature.

It wasn't often that I got mail apart from bills, so when I saw a letter in my mailbox one morning in early November 2008, I immediately noticed it. It was an airmail envelope and had a postmark—Tasmania, Australia. It was from my mother.

We'd not been in proper contact for years. However, despite the distance that had formed between us, the letter was very chatty and warm. She explained that she had moved to a new house in Tasmania. She seemed to be very happy there. And she was offering me an invitation. "If I was to pay your airfare to Australia and back, would you come and see me?" she asked. She explained that I could come over the Christmas holidays. She suggested I could also take in a trip to Melbourne to see my godparents, to whom I'd once been very close.

"Let me know," she said, signing off. "Love, Mum."

There would have been a time when I'd have thrown the letter straight into the trash. I'd have been defiant and stubborn and too proud to take a handout from my family. But I'd changed; my head was in a different place now. I had started to see life a lot more clearly, and I could almost feel some of the anger and paranoia that I'd felt in the past falling away.

It wasn't a straightforward decision, far from it. There were lots of pros and cons to take into consideration. The biggest pro, obviously, was that I'd get to see my mother again. No matter what ups and downs we'd had over the years, she was my mother and I missed her.

We'd been in contact a couple of times since I'd ended up on the streets, but I'd never been honest with her about what had really happened. We'd met once in the past ten years, when she'd come to England briefly. I'd spun her a story about having formed a band in London and said I wasn't going to come back to Australia while we were "trying to make it big." I hadn't felt great about telling her a pack of lies, but I didn't have the courage or the strength to tell her that I was sleeping rough, hooked on heroin, and wasting my life away.

I had no idea whether she believed me or not. At that point, I really didn't care. I was on my own and concerned only with my own survival. But now I'd changed. After all the years of neglect and deception, it would be a chance to make it up to her and to put the record straight. I felt like I needed to do that.

The other obvious positive was that I'd get to have a decent holiday in the sun, something that I had been deprived of for years. I still felt drained by the experience of switching to my new medication. A few weeks in a nice environment would do me the power of good. My mother told me she was living on a little farm way out in the middle of nowhere, near a river. It sounded idyllic. Australia, or more specifically, the Australian landscape, had always occupied a special place in my heart. Reconnecting with it would be good for my soul.

The list of pros was long. The list of cons, however, was even longer. And at the top of the list was my biggest concern of all: Bob. Who would look after him? How could I be sure he'd be there waiting for me when I got back? Did I want to be separated from my soul mate for weeks on end?

The answer to the first question presented itself almost immediately.

The moment I mentioned it, Belle volunteered to look after him at her flat. I knew she was trustworthy and would take care of him. But I still wondered what the effect would be on him.

The other big concern was money. My mother might have been offering to pay for my fare, but I still wouldn't be allowed into Australia without any money. I did some digging around and found that I'd need at least £500 in cash to gain admittance.

I spent a few days weighing up both sides of the argument but eventually decided I'd go. Why not? A change of scenery would do me good.

I had a lot to do. For a start I had to get a new passport, which wasn't easy given the way my life had disintegrated in recent years. A social worker gave me a hand and helped me organize the paperwork, including a birth certificate.

I then had to sort out the flights. The best deal by far was to fly with Air China to Beijing and then down to Melbourne, even though it was a much longer journey and involved a lengthy layover in Beijing. I sent my mother an e-mail with all the details, including my new passport number. A few days later I got a confirmation e-mail from the website through which my mother had booked the tickets. I was on my way. All I had to do now was raise £500. Easy.

The flight I'd found was heading to Australia in the first week of December. So for the next few weeks, I worked every hour of the day in all weather. Bob came with me most days, although I left him at home when it was raining heavily. I didn't want to risk him catching a chill or getting ill before I went away.

I was soon saving up a bit of cash, which I kept in a little tea caddy I'd found. Slowly but surely it began to fill up. As my departure date loomed into view, I had enough to make the trip.

I headed to Heathrow with a heavy heart. I'd said good-bye to Bob at Belle's flat. He'd not looked too concerned, but then he had no idea I was going to be away for the best part of six weeks. I knew he'd be safe with Belle, but it still didn't stop me fretting. I had become a paranoid parent.

After the long journey, seeing my mother was wonderful. She was waiting at the airport in Tasmania and gave me a couple of really long hugs. She was crying. She was pleased to see me alive, I think. I was really happy to see her, too.

The cottage was every bit as lovely as she'd described it in her letter. It was a big, airy bungalow with huge garden space at the back. It was surrounded by farmland with a river running by the bottom of her land. It was a very peaceful, picturesque place. Over the next month, I just hung out there, relaxing, recovering, and rebooting myself.

Within a couple of weeks, I felt like a different person. The anxieties of London were literally thousands of miles away. My mum's maternal instincts kicked in, and she made sure I was fed well. I could feel my strength returning. I could also sense that we were repairing our relationship.

At first we didn't talk in great depth, but in time, I began to open up. Then, one night as we sat on the veranda watching the sun go down, I had a couple of drinks and suddenly it all came out. It wasn't a big confession; there was no Hollywood drama. I just talked . . . and talked.

The emotional floodgates had been waiting to burst open for a while now. For years I had used drugs to escape my emotions—in fact, to make sure I didn't have any. Slowly but surely I'd changed that. And now my emotions were coming back.

As I explained some of the lows I'd been through over the last ten years, my mother looked horrified, as any parent would have done. "I guessed you weren't doing so great when I saw you, but I never guessed it was that bad," she said, close to tears.

At times she just sat there with her head in her hands muttering the word "why" every now and again. "Why didn't you tell me you'd lost your passport?" "Why didn't you call me and ask for help?" "Why didn't you contact your father?"

Inevitably, she blamed herself for it. She said she felt like she'd let me down, but I told her I didn't blame her. The reality was that I had left myself down. Ultimately, there was no one else to blame.

Once we'd broken the ice, so to speak, we talked much more easily. We talked a little about the past and my childhood in Australia and England. I felt comfortable being honest with her. I said that I'd felt she'd been a distant figure when I'd been younger and that being raised by nannies and moving around a lot had had an impact on me.

Naturally that upset her, but she argued that she'd been trying to provide an income for us, to keep a roof over our heads. I took her point, but I still wished she'd been there more for me.

We laughed a lot, too; it wasn't all dark conversation. We admitted how similar we were and chuckled at some of the arguments we used to have. "I'm a strong personality, and so are you," she said. "That's where you get it from."

But we spent most of the time talking about the present. She asked me all sorts of questions about the rehab process I'd been through and what I was hoping to achieve now that I was almost clean. I explained that it was still a case of taking one step at a time, but that, with luck, I'd be totally clean within a year or so. Sometimes she simply listened, which was something she hadn't always done. And so did I. I think we both learned a lot about each other.

During those long chats, I often talked about Bob. I'd brought a photo of him with me, which I showed to everyone and anyone who took an interest.

My mother smiled. "He looks a smart cookie."

"Oh, he is," I said, beaming with pride. "I don't know where I'd be now if it wasn't for Bob."

Spending time in Australia allowed me to clear my mind and take stock of where I wanted to go from here.

Part of me hankered to move back. I had family here. There was more of a support network than I had in London, certainly. But I kept thinking about Bob and the fact that he'd be as lost without me as I'd be without him. I didn't take the idea seriously for very long. By the time I'd started my sixth week in Australia, I was mentally already on the plane back to England.

My mother came to the airport with me and waved me off on my way to Melbourne, where I was going to spend some time with my godparents. They had been quite significant figures in my youth. They had owned what was then the biggest private telecom company in Australia and were the first to form a radio pager company in the country, so they had a lot of money at one point. As a boy, naturally, I used to love spending time at the mansion they'd built in Melbourne. I even lived with them for a while when me and my mother weren't getting on very well.

Their reaction to my story was the same as my mother's—they were shocked. They offered to help me out financially and even to find me work in Australia. But, again, I had to explain that I had responsibilities back in London.

The journey back was easy. I was so rested and revived by my time in Australia that I slept for most of the trip.

I was dying to see Bob again, though part of me worried he might have forgotten me. I needn't have had any concerns.

The minute I walked into Belle's flat, his tail popped up and he bounced off her sofa and ran up to me. I'd brought him back a few little presents, a couple of stuffed kangaroo toys. He was soon clawing away at one of them. As we headed home that evening, he immediately scampered up my arm to my shoulders. In an instant the emotional and physical journey I'd made to the other side of the world was forgotten. It was me and Bob against the world once more. It was as if I'd never been away.

BACK in London, I felt more sure of myself than I'd felt in years. Being reunited with Bob had lifted my spirits. Without him, a little part of me had been missing down in Tasmania. Now I felt whole again.

We were soon back into the old routine, sharing every aspect of our day-to-day life. Even now, after almost two years together, he remained a constant source of surprise to me.

Doing his business had always been a bit of a chore for Bob. He'd never taken to the litter trays that I'd bought him. I still had a few packs of them in the cupboard gathering dust. It was a real palaver for him to have to go all the way down five flights of stairs and out into the grounds, though. I'd noticed in the past few months, before I'd gone to Australia and again now that I was back, that he wasn't going to the toilet downstairs so often anymore. For a while I'd wondered whether it might be a medical problem, and I'd taken him to the Blue Cross truck to have him checked out. The vets found nothing untoward and suggested that it might just be a change in his metabolism.

The explanation was actually far less scientific—and a lot more funny—than that. One morning, soon after I'd got back from Australia, I woke up really early. My body clock was still all over the place. I hauled myself out of bed and stepped, bleary-eyed, toward the toilet. The door was half open, and I could hear a light tinkling sort of noise. *Weird,* I thought. When I gently nudged open the door, I was greeted by a sight that left me totally speechless: Bob was squatting on the toilet seat.

It was just like that scene in the movie *Meet the Parents* when Robert De Niro's cat, Mr. Jinx, does the same thing. Except in this case, it was absolutely real. Bob had obviously decided that going to the toilet downstairs was too much hassle. So, having seen me go to the toilet a few times in the past three years, he'd worked out what he needed to do and simply mimicked me.

When he saw me staring at him, Bob just fired me one of his withering looks, as if to say, "What are you looking at? I'm only going to the loo. What could be more normal than that?" He was right, of course. Why was I surprised at anything Bob did? He was capable of anything.

Our absence had definitely been noticed by a lot of the locals at the Angel. During our first week back on the pitch, a succession of people came up to us with big smiles, saying things like: "Ah, you're back" or "I thought you'd won the lottery." They were genuine, warmhearted welcomes.

One lady dropped off a card with "We Missed You" written on it. It felt great to be "home."

One day I was talking to Davika. She loved Bob and was chuckling at the way countless people were stopping and talking to him and taking his picture.

"He's putting Angel tube station on the map, isn't he?" she laughed.

"He is. You should put him on the staff, like that cat in Japan who is a stationmaster. He even wears a hat," I said.

"I'm not sure we've got any vacancies," she giggled.

"Well, you should at least give him an ID card or something," I joked.

She looked at me with a thoughtful look on her face and went away. I thought nothing more about it.

A couple of weeks later, Bob and I were sitting outside the station one evening when Davika appeared again. She had a big grin on her face.

I was immediately suspicious. "What's up?" I said.

"Nothing, I just wanted to give Bob this." She then produced a laminated travel card with Bob's photograph on it.

"That's fantastic," I said.

"I got the picture off the Internet," she said to my slight amazement. What the hell was Bob doing on the Internet?

"So what does it actually mean?" I said.

"It means he can travel free on the underground," she laughed.

"I thought that cats went free anyway?" I smiled.

"Well, it actually means we are all very fond of him. We think of him as part of the family."

It took a lot of willpower to stop myself from bursting into tears.

Chapter 14

BOB, THE *BIG ISSUE* CAT

IT WAS March 2009. As the sun disappeared and dusk descended over the Angel, the traffic was already thick on Islington High Street and the honking of horns was building into a cacophony of noise. The pavements were busy, too, with a stream of people flowing in and out of the station concourse.

I was checking that I had enough papers left to cope with the surge of activity I knew was about to arrive when I saw out of the corner of my eye that a group of kids had gathered around us. They were teenagers, three boys and a couple of girls. They looked South American, Spanish, or Portuguese, and they were animatedly pointing and talking about him.

"Ah, *sí* Bob," said one teenage girl, talking in what I guessed was Spanish.

"*Sí, sí.* Bob the Beeg Issew Cat," said another.

Weird, I thought to myself. *How do they know his name is Bob? He doesn't wear a name tag. And what do they mean by the* Big Issue *Cat?*

Curiosity soon got the better of me. "Sorry, I hope you don't mind me asking, but how do you know Bob?" I said, in the hope that one of them spoke decent English.

Fortunately one of them, a young boy, replied. "Oh, we see him on YouTube." He smiled. "Bob is very popular, yes?"

"Is he?" I said. "Someone told me he was on YouTube, but I've got no idea how many people watch it."

"Many people, I think." He smiled.

"Where are you from?"

"*España*. Spain."

"So Bob's popular in Spain?"

"*Sí, sí*," another one of the boys said when the boy translated back our conversation. "Bob *es una estrella en España*."

"Sorry, what did he say?" I asked the boy.

"He says that Bob is a star in Spain."

I was shocked. I knew that lots of people had taken photographs of Bob over the years. I'd jokingly wondered once whether he should be put forward for the *Guinness Book of Records:* the world's most photographed cat.

A couple of people had filmed him, too, some with their phones, others with proper video cameras. I started casting my mind back over those who had shot footage of him in recent months. Who could have shot a film that was now on YouTube? I made a note to check it out at the first opportunity.

The following morning I headed down to the local library with Bob and booked myself online. I punched in the search terms: Bob *Big Issue* Cat. Sure enough, there was a link to YouTube.

"Hey, Bob, look, he was right. You are a star on YouTube."

He hadn't been terribly interested until that point. It wasn't Channel Four racing, after all. But when I clicked on the first video and saw and heard myself talking, he jumped onto the keyboard and popped his face right up against the screen.

As I watched the first film, which was called "Bobcat and I," the memory came back to me. I'd been approached by a film student. He'd followed me around for a while when we were selling the *Big Issue* around Covent Garden. There was nice footage of us there and of us getting on the bus and walking the streets. Watching the film, it gave a pretty good summary of the day-to-day life of a *Big Issue* seller. There were clips of people fussing over Bob but also a sequence where I was confronted by some guys who didn't believe he was a "tame" cat.

The feeling that Bob was becoming some kind of celebrity had been building for a while. Every now and again someone would say, "Ah, is that Bob? I've heard about him." Or "Is this the famous Bobcat?" I'd always assumed it was through word of mouth. Then we'd been featured in a local newspaper. I'd even been approached by an American agent, who asked me whether I'd thought about writing a book about me and Bob!

As I headed toward the bus stop and absorbed what I had just discovered, I couldn't help smiling. On one of the films I had said that Bob had saved my life. When I first heard it, I thought it sounded a bit crass, a bit of an exaggeration, too. But as I walked along the road and put it all into perspective, it began to sink in: It was true; he really had.

In the two years since I'd found him sitting in that half-lit hallway, he had transformed my world. My trip to Australia had brought me and my mother back together. The wounds were being healed. I had the feeling we were going to become close again. My battle with drugs was drawing to a close. The day when I wouldn't have to take Subutex was looming into view on the horizon. I could finally see an end to my addiction. There had been times when I'd never have imagined that was possible.

Most of all, I'd finally laid down some roots. It might not have seemed much to most people, but my little flat in Tottenham had given me the kind of security and stability that I'd always secretly craved. I'd never lived for so long in the same place: I'd been there more than four years and would remain there even longer. There was no doubt in my mind that would not have happened if it hadn't been for Bob.

I was raised as a churchgoer but wasn't a practicing Christian. My view is that we should all take a bit from every religion and philosophy. I like Buddhist philosophies, in particular. They give you a structure you can build your life around. I definitely believe in karma, the idea that what goes around, comes around. I wondered whether Bob was my reward for having done something good, somewhere in my troubled life.

I also wondered sometimes whether Bob and I had known each other in a previous life. The way we bonded together, the instant connection that we made, was very unusual. Someone said to me once that we were the reincarnation of Dick Whittington and his cat. Except the roles had been reversed; Dick Whittington had come back as Bob—and I was his companion. I was happy to think of him in that way. Bob is my best mate and the one who has guided me toward a better way of life. He doesn't demand anything complicated in return. He just needs me to take care of him. And that's what I do.

I knew the road ahead wouldn't be smooth. We were sure to face our problems here and there—I was still working on the streets of London, after all. It was never going to be easy. But as long as we were together, I had a feeling it was going to be fine.

Everybody needs a break. Everybody deserves that second chance. Bob and I had taken ours. . . .

Share Your Thoughts!

Communicate with us directly to chat about the stories and tell us what you liked or disliked. We want to keep giving you the kinds of books you want to read, and this is one way to make that happen. So let us know what you think. Share your thoughts with us at **SelectEditions@gmail.com**.

A Q. & A. with James Bowen

We caught up with James right after his book was published in England.

SELECT EDITIONS: Has the book greatly changed your life?

JAMES BOWEN: It has meant that we don't have to go out busking or selling *The Big Issue* as much, which is great, obviously. It also means that Bob has got an even bigger wardrobe of hand-knitted scarves and mats to sit on when we're on the streets.

SE: Is Bob aware, do you think, of his new status as an internationally known celebrity?

JB: I definitely think he knows something is up. He's become very much more demanding. He can be a bit of a diva at times! Bob loves the attention. Whenever someone says hello, he rubs into their hand. He laps up the love, there's no question.

SE: Do you still go busking on the streets of Covent Garden?

JB: We only do so rarely at the moment. The big difference now is that whereas we used to be stopped occasionally, now it's every few seconds. But, as I say, Bob quite likes the attention, so it's not such a problem, really.

SE: How are the plans for the film progressing? And who would you most like to see play you?

JB: It's very early days, still at the talks stage, so far too soon to take it for granted. As for who would play me, I think Daniel Radcliffe would be a really interesting choice. He was stereotyped as Harry Potter but I've seen him in some other things, and he's got a lot to offer as an actor. I don't know if he likes cats . . .

SE: Which aspect of the story do you most hope the film makers get right?

JB: I hope it helps raise awareness about homelessness and what it's like to work on the streets. I hope it helps people to understand how invisible street people are and how charities like *The Big Issue* work and help people.

SE: What new challenges might follow for you and Bob?

JB: We'd like to create a new role for ourselves. I would like to be able to help with street charities and animal charities. They are the two areas where I think I can speak with some experience. It would mean a lot to me to be able to give something back to the people who have helped me and Bob so much, like the Blue Cross.

SE: If we asked Bob what kind of guy you are, what would he say?

JB: I would like to think I'm patient and loving. Loyal, too. He's still happy to come out with me on the streets and he sits calmly on my shoulders without making a fuss. So I think I'm doing okay. ∎

Vital Stats

BOB IN PRINT: The book has been published in 26 languages.

BOB ON FACEBOOK: James and Bob have their own page, James Bowen and Street Cat Bob, for fans to interact with them.

BOB AROUND THE WORLD: Fans post pictures of Bob in spots all across the globe at streetcatbob.blogspot.co.uk

MOST SURPRISING BOB APPEARANCE: On the cover of *Dogs Today Magazine*

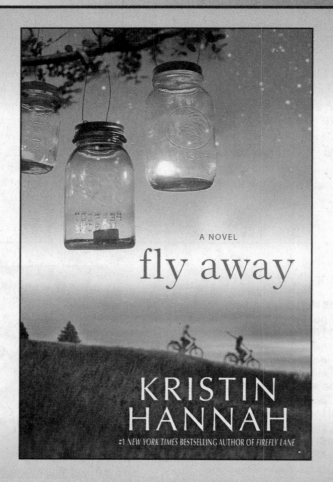

A NOVEL

fly away

KRISTIN
HANNAH

#1 *NEW YORK TIMES* BESTSELLING AUTHOR OF *FIREFLY LANE*

PROLOGUE

SHE *is in a restroom stall, slumped over, with tears drying on her cheeks, smearing the mascara she had applied so carefully only a few hours ago. You can see instantly that she doesn't belong here, and yet here she is.*

Grief is a sneaky thing, always coming and going like some guest you didn't invite and can't turn away. She wants this grief, although she'd never admit it. Lately it's the only thing that feels real. She finds herself thinking about her best friend on purpose even now, all this time later, because she wants to cry. She is like a child picking at a scab, unable to stop herself even though she knows it will hurt.

She has tried to go on alone. She is trying still, but sometimes one person can keep you standing, and without that single hand to hold, you can find yourself free-falling no matter how strong you used to be, no matter how hard you try to remain steady.

Once—a long time ago—she walked down a night-darkened road called Firefly Lane all alone, on the worst night of her life, and she found a kindred spirit.

That was our beginning. *More than thirty years ago.*

TullyandKate. You and me against the world. *Best friends forever. But stories end, don't they? You lose the people you love, and you have to find a way to go on.*

I need to let go. Say good-bye with a smile. *It won't be easy.*

She doesn't know yet what she has set in motion. In moments everything will change.

CHAPTER ONE

September 2, 2010, 10:14 p.m.

SHE felt woozy. It was nice, like being wrapped in a warm blanket. But when she came to and saw where she was, it wasn't so nice.

She was in a restroom stall. How long had she been here? She got to her feet and left the bathroom, pushing her way through the theater's crowded lobby, ignoring the judgmental looks cast her way by the beautiful people drinking champagne. The movie must be over.

Outside, she kicked off her patent leather pumps. In her expensive black nylons, she walked in the spitting rain down the dirty Seattle sidewalk toward home. A bright pink MARTINI BAR sign caught her attention. Even as she vowed to pass by, she found herself going inside. She headed straight for the long mahogany bar.

"What can I get for you?" asked a thin artsy-looking man.

"Tequila straight shot," she said.

She drank the shot and ordered another. The loud music comforted her. She drank the other shot. All around her, people were talking and laughing. A man in an expensive Italian suit sidled up beside her. He was tall and fit, with blond hair. Banker, probably. Too young for her, of course. He couldn't be much past thirty-five.

He turned to her. She could tell that he knew who she was, and that small recognition seduced her. "Can I buy you a drink?"

"I don't know. Can you?" Was she slurring her words?

His gaze moved from her face, down to her breasts, and then back to her face. "I'd say a drink, at the very least."

"I don't usually pick up strangers," she lied. Lately there were only strangers in her life. Everyone else, everyone who mattered, had forgotten about her.

He touched her chin, a jawline caress. "I'm Troy," he said.

She felt the crushing weight of her loneliness. When was the last time a man had wanted her? "I'm Tully Hart," she said.

"I know."

He kissed her. He tasted sweet, of liquor and of cigarettes. She wanted to lose herself in pure physical sensation. She wanted to forget everything that had gone wrong with her life.

"Kiss me again," she said, hating the pathetic pleading she heard in her voice. It was how she'd sounded as a child waiting for her mother to return. *What's wrong with me?* that little girl had asked anyone who would listen, but there had never been an answer. As he kissed her and pressed his body into hers, Tully started to cry.

September 3, 2010, 2:01 a.m.

TULLY was the last person to leave the bar. The doors banged shut behind her; the neon sign clicked off. It was past two now; the Seattle streets were empty. She made her way down the sidewalk, a little unsteady on her feet. A man had kissed her—a stranger—and she'd started to cry. Pathetic. No wonder he'd backed away.

At her condominium building, she pushed past the doorman.

In the elevator, she saw herself in the wall of mirrors. She looked terrible. Her auburn hair—in need of coloring—was a bird's nest; mascara ran like war paint down her cheeks.

The elevator doors opened, and she stepped out into the hallway. It took four tries to get her key into the lock. She was dizzy.

Somewhere between the dining room and the living room, she banged into a chrome side table and almost fell. She sank onto the thick down-filled white sofa cushion with a sigh and closed her eyes, thinking what a mess her life had become.

"Damn you, Katie Ryan," she whispered. But her best friend was gone. Dead. That was what had started all of it. Losing Kate. Tully had begun to plummet at her best friend's death, and she hadn't been able to pull out of the dive. She screamed, "I *need* you!"

She let her head fall forward. Did she fall asleep? Maybe . . .

When she opened her eyes again, she stared bleary-eyed at the pile of mail on her coffee table. Junk mail, mostly. A picture snagged her attention. She pushed the mail aside to reveal a *Star* magazine. There was a small photograph of her face in the upper right corner. Not a good picture. Beneath it a single, terrible word.

Addict.

She grabbed the magazine, opened it. There it was: her picture again. It was a small story, not even a full page.

THE REAL STORY BEHIND THE RUMORS

Aging isn't easy for any woman in the public eye, but it may be proving especially difficult for Tully Hart, the ex-star of the once-phenom talk show *The Girlfriend Hour*. Ms. Hart's goddaughter, Marah Ryan, contacted *Star* exclusively. Ms. Ryan, 20, confirms that the fifty-year-old Hart has been struggling lately with demons she's had all her life. In recent months Hart has "gained an alarming amount of weight" and been abusing drugs and alcohol, according to Ms. Ryan. . . .

"Oh, my God . . ."

Marah. The betrayal hurt so badly she couldn't breathe. She read the rest of the story, and the pain she'd been holding at bay for months, years, roared to life, sucking her to the bleakest place she'd ever been. She staggered to her feet and reached for her car keys.

She couldn't live like this anymore.

September 3, 2010, 4:16 a.m.

WHERE am I?

What happened? I am in darkness. I try to move, but I can't make my body work. I open my eyes at last. It is dark.

There is someone in here with me. Or some*thing*. It makes a banging sound, hammers falling on steel. *Bang-scrape, bang-scrape.* Pain. Excruciating. A searing agony in my head, a throbbing in my arm. Something inside me is broken. *Help me,* I try to say, but darkness swallows my feeble intent.

OPENYOUREYES.

I hear the voice, and relief overwhelms me. I am not alone.

OPENYOUREYES.

I can't. Nothing works.

SHESALIVE.

The darkness shifts around me, and pain explodes again.

ONETWOTHREELIFT.

I feel myself being pulled, lifted by cold hands. I scream in pain, but the sound is swallowed, or maybe it's only in my head.

It comes to me suddenly. I am dying.

CHAPTER TWO

September 3, 2010, 4:39 a.m.

JOHNNY Ryan woke, thinking, *Something's wrong.* He sat upright and looked around. There was nothing to see, nothing out of place.

He was in his home office, on Bainbridge Island. Once again, he'd fallen asleep working. The curse of the working-from-home single parent. There weren't enough hours in the day to get everything done, so he stole hours from the night. He still didn't sleep well in his bed, anyway.

Beside him a computer monitor revealed a frozen image of a ratty-looking street kid sitting beneath a neon sign, smoking a cigarette. Johnny hit the PLAY key. On-screen, Kevin—street name Frizz—started talking about his parents.

They don't care, the kid said with a shrug.

What makes you so sure? Johnny asked in the voice-over.

I'm here, aren't I?

Johnny knew about a parent's worry, about how a child could slip into the shadows and disappear. It was why he was here, working on a documentary about street kids. Maybe if he looked hard enough, asked enough questions, he'd find her.

He stared at the images on-screen. Whenever he saw a shape in the background, a silhouette that could be a young woman, he peered harder at the picture, thinking: *Marah?*

But none of the girls he'd seen in the last year of making this documentary was his daughter. Marah had run away from home and disappeared. He didn't even know if she was still in Seattle.

He turned off the lights in his upstairs office and walked down the dark, quiet hallway. To his right, family photographs hung along the wall. Sometimes he followed the trail of these pictures and let them pull him back to a happier time. Sometimes he let himself stand in front of his wife's picture and lose himself in the smile that had once illuminated his world. Tonight he kept moving.

He paused at his sons' room and eased the door open. It was something he did now: check obsessively on his eleven-year-old twins. Once you'd learned how bad life could go, you tried desperately to protect those who remained. They were there, asleep.

He moved on to Marah's closed door. There, he didn't slow down. It hurt too much to look in her room.

He went into his own room and closed the door behind him. Heading into the bathroom, he stripped off his shirt and tossed it in the hamper. In the bathroom mirror, he caught sight of himself. He looked . . . sad. It was in the eyes, mostly. His hair was longer than it should be, with fine strands of gray weaving through the black. With a sigh he turned on the shower and stepped in, letting the hot water pour over him. When he got out, he felt ready to take on the day. There was no point in trying to sleep. He dressed in an old Nirvana T-shirt and a pair of worn jeans. As he headed back into the hallway, the phone rang. It was the landline.

He frowned. It was 2010. In this new age only the rarest of calls came in on the old number. Only bad news came at this hour.

Marah.

He lunged for the phone and answered. "Hello?"

"Is Kathleen Ryan there?"

Damned telemarketers. "Kathleen Ryan passed away almost four years ago. You need to take her off your call list. Who is this?"

"Officer Jerry Malone, Seattle police. There's been an accident. The victim has Kathleen Ryan's name in her wallet as an emergency contact."

There was only one person in the world who would still have Katie's name as an emergency contact. What in the hell had she done now? "It's Tully Hart, right? Is it a DUI? Because if she's—"

"I don't have that information, sir."

"How bad is it?"

"I can't answer that. She's being taken to Sacred Heart right now. You'll need to speak to someone there."

Johnny hung up on the officer. He looked at his watch. If he moved quickly, he could make the five-twenty ferry and be at the hospital in fifty-five minutes. He dialed another number.

"H-hello?"

"Corrin, I'm sorry to call you so early, but it's an emergency. Can you pick up the boys and take them to school? I need to go to Sacred Heart. There's been an accident. I don't want to leave the boys alone, but I don't have time to bring them to you."

"Don't worry," she said. "I'll be there in fifteen minutes."

"Thanks. I owe you one." He hurried down the hallway and pushed open the boys' bedroom door. "Get dressed, boys. *Now*."

They sat up slowly. "Huh?" Wills said.

"I'm leaving. Corrin is going to pick you up in fifteen minutes. You're going to Tommy's house. Corrin might need to pick you up from soccer practice, too. I don't know when I'll be home."

"What's wrong?" Lucas asked. They knew about emergencies, these boys. "Is it Marah?"

Of course that would be their worry. They all worried about her. "Marah's fine. It's Tully."

"What's wrong with Tully?" Lucas asked, looking scared.

They loved Tully so much. How many times in the last year had they begged to see her? How many times had Johnny made some excuse? Guilt flared at that.

"I'll let you know what's up as soon as I can," Johnny promised. "Be ready for school when Corrin gets here, okay?"

He kissed them good-bye. He looked back at them one last time—two identical boys who needed haircuts, standing in their boxer shorts and oversized T-shirts, frowning with worry. Then he went to his car. They were eleven; they could be alone for ten minutes.

He started the engine and drove to the ferry. On board, he stayed in his car for the thirty-five-minute crossing.

At precisely six ten, he pulled up into the hospital's parking lot.

He entered the familiar hospital and strode up to the information desk. "Tallulah Hart," he said grimly. "I'm family."

"Sir, I—"

"I want an update on Tully's condition, and I want it *now*."

"Oh," the woman said. "I'll be right back."

He walked away from the reception desk and began pacing. God, he hated this place, with its all too familiar smells.

In the past four years, he'd learned how to go on without his wife, the love of his life, but it had not been easy. He'd had to stop looking back. The memories simply hurt too much.

But how could he not look back here, of all places? They'd come to this hospital for surgery and chemotherapy and radiation; they'd spent hours together here, he and Kate, promising each other that cancer was no match for their love.

When they'd finally faced the truth, they'd been in a room here.

In 2006. He'd been lying with her, holding her, trying not to notice how thin she'd become in the year of her life's fight.

Pain was a liquid fire in her body; she hurt everywhere. She took as much morphine as she'd dared, but she'd wanted to be alert so that her kids wouldn't be afraid. *I want to go home,* she'd said.

All he'd been able to think was, *She's dying.*

"My babies," she'd said quietly, and then laughed. "Well, they're not babies anymore. They're losing teeth. It's a dollar, by the way. For the tooth fairy. And always take a picture. And Marah. Tell her I understand. I was mean to my mom at sixteen, too."

"I am not ready for this conversation," he'd said, hating his weakness. He'd seen the disappointment in her gaze.

"I need Tully," she'd said then, surprising him. His wife and Tully Hart had been best friends—until a fight had torn them apart. They hadn't spoken in two years, and in those years, Kate had faced cancer. Johnny couldn't forgive Tully, not for the fight (which had been Tully's fault) or for her absence when Kate needed her most.

"No. After what she did to you?"

"I need Tully," she'd said again. "She's been my best friend since eighth grade. You have to forgive her, Johnny."

"It's not that easy. She hurt you."

"And I hurt her. Best friends fight. They lose sight of what matters. Believe me, I know what matters now, and I need her."

"What makes you think she'll come if you call?"

"She'll come." She'd made him look at her. "You need to take care of her . . . after."

"Don't say that," he'd whispered.

"She's not as strong as she pretends to be. Promise me."

TullyandKate. If not for Tully, Johnny wouldn't have met the love of his life.

From the moment Tully had walked into his office, Johnny had been mesmerized by her. She was twenty years old and full of passion and fire. She'd talked herself into a job at the small TV station he'd run then. She had been more alive and brighter than anyone he'd ever met. He'd known instantly that she would be famous.

When she'd introduced him to her best friend, Kate Mularkey, he'd barely noticed. It wasn't until later, when Katie dared to kiss him, that Johnny saw his future in a woman's eyes. He remembered the first time they'd made love—him twenty-six, her twenty-one, but only she had been naive. *Is it always like that?* she'd asked.

Love had come to him just like that, long before he'd been ready. *No,* he'd said, unable even then to lie to her. *It's not.*

After he and Kate had married, they'd watched Tully's meteoric rise in journalism from afar, but no matter how separate Kate's life became from Tully's, the two women stayed closer than sisters. They'd talked on the phone almost daily, and Tully had come to their home for most holidays. When she'd given up on the networks and New York and returned to Seattle to try her hand at her own daytime talk show, Tully—and Kate—had begged Johnny to produce it. Those had been good years. Successful years. Until cancer and Kate's death had torn everything apart.

He knew when it had begun to unravel. At Kate's funeral, almost four years ago. October of 2006. They'd been in the first row of St. Cecilia's Church, acutely aware of why they were there. Johnny sat marine-straight. He was supposed to be strong now for their children. It was a promise he'd made to her, but it was hard to keep. Sixteen-year-old Marah sat equally rigid beside him. She hadn't looked him in the eyes in hours, maybe in days. He knew he should bridge that divide, but when he looked at her, he lost his nerve.

He made the mistake of glancing to his left, where a large easel held a poster of Kate. In the picture she was a young mother, standing on the beach in front of their Bainbridge Island house, her hair windblown, her smile big and bright, her arms flung wide to welcome the three children running toward her. She had asked him to find that picture for her, one night when they lay in bed. He knew what it meant. *Not yet,* he'd murmured.

She hadn't asked him again. Even at the end, she'd been the stronger one, protecting all of them with her optimism.

How many words had she hoarded in her heart so that he wouldn't be wounded by her fear? How alone had she felt?

It had been only two days, and already he wanted a do over. He wanted to hold her again, one more time, and say, *Tell me, baby, what are you afraid of?*

Father Michael stepped up to the pulpit.

"I'm not surprised so many people are here to say good-bye to Kate. She was an important person to so many of us. You won't be surprised that she gave me strict orders for this service. She wanted me to tell you all to hold on to each other. She wanted you to take your sorrow and transform it into joy. She wanted you to remember the sound of her laughter and the love she had for her family. She wanted you to *live*." His voice broke. "That was Kathleen Mularkey Ryan. Even at the end, she was thinking of others."

Marah groaned quietly. Johnny reached for her hand. She startled at his touch, looked at him. There it was, that unfathomable grief.

Music started up. "Crazy for You." The song they'd danced to at their wedding. He closed his eyes and felt her beside him.

Finally the service ended. He and his children left the church and went into the bright sunlit day. Tully was in the parking lot, with her face tilted up. She had her arms stretched wide, and she was moving as if there were music somewhere. Dancing.

He said her name so harshly that Marah flinched beside him.

Tully turned and saw them coming. She tugged the buds out of her ears. "How was it?" she asked quietly.

He felt a surge of rage at her. Of course Tully had put herself first. It *hurt* to go to Kate's funeral, so Tully didn't. She stood in the parking lot and danced. Danced. Some best friend. Kate might be able to forgive Tully her selfishness; it wasn't so easy for Johnny.

He turned to his family. "Get in the car, everyone."

"Johnny—" Tully reached for him, but he stepped aside. He couldn't be touched now. "I couldn't go in," she said.

"Yeah. Who could?" he said bitterly. "People are coming to the house. It's what she wanted. I hope you can make it."

He heard the sharpness of her indrawn breath and knew he'd hurt her. Good, he thought. She *should* be hurting. We're *all* hurting. He herded his family into the SUV, and they drove home in silence.

Pale late-afternoon sunlight shone down on their caramel-colored Craftsman-style house. The yard was a disaster, forgotten in the year of Katie's cancer. He parked in the garage and led the way into the house, where the faint scent of illness lingered in the fabric of the drapes.

"What now, Dad?"

He knew without turning who would have asked this question. Lucas, the boy who'd cried at every goldfish's death and drawn a picture for his dying mother every day. He felt everything so keenly. *Especially Lucas,* Kate had said on her last, terrible night. *He won't know how to miss me so much. Hold him.*

Johnny turned.

Wills and Lucas stood there, standing so close their shoulders were touching. The eight-year-olds had on matching black pants and gray V-neck sweaters.

Marah came up beside her brothers. All of them looked at him.

This was his moment to speak, to offer comforting words, to give them advice they would remember. As their father, it was his job to turn the next few hours into a celebration of his wife's life.

Johnny was still trying to figure out what to say to his wounded children when the doorbell rang for the first time. He flinched at the sound.

Afterward he was vaguely aware of time passing, of people crowding around him and doors opening and closing. Of the sun setting and night pressing against the windowpanes.

Someone touched his arm.

"I'm so sorry, Johnny," he heard a woman say, and he turned. She stood beside him, dressed in black, holding a casserole dish.

He heard "better place" and walked away. He pushed through the crowd and went to the bar set up in the kitchen. At the sink his mother-in-law, Margie, put down the pitcher she'd been filling with water. She moved toward him, pausing at the bar to pour him a large Scotch and water over ice. She handed it to him.

"Where's Bud?" he asked.

"Watching TV with Sean and the boys."

Johnny nodded. His father-in-law had always been a quiet man, and the death of his only daughter had broken him. Even Margie, who had remained vital and dark-haired and laughing well past her last birthday, had aged immeasurably since the diagnosis.

"Go to your kids," Margie said.

"I should stay here and help you."

"I'm fine," she said, patting his arm. "But I'm worried about Marah. Sixteen is a tough age to lose a mother, and I think she regrets how much she and Kate fought before Kate got sick."

He took a long sip of his drink, watched the ice rattle in his glass when he was done. "I don't know what to say to them."

"Words aren't what matters." Margie led him out of the kitchen.

Even in a crowd of mourners, Tully Hart was the center of attention. In a black sheath dress that probably cost as much as some of the cars parked in the driveway, she managed to look beautiful in grief. Her shoulder-length hair was auburn, and she must have redone her makeup since the funeral. In the living room, surrounded by people, she gestured dramatically, obviously telling a story, and when she finished, everyone around her laughed.

"How can she smile?" Johnny asked Margie.

"Tully knows a thing or two about heartbreak, don't forget. I remember the first time I ever saw her. Must have been '73 or '74. I walked across the street to her house because she'd befriended Kate and I wanted to check her out. Inside that rundown old house, I met her mom, Cloud. Well, I didn't *meet* her. Cloud was lying on the sofa spread-eagled, with a mound of marijuana on her stomach. When I looked at Tully, who was maybe thirteen, I saw the kind of shame that marks you forever. Tully thinks no one can love her. Except Kate. I don't think the loss has really hit her yet, but when it does, it's going to be ugly."

Tully put a CD into the stereo and cranked the music. *"Born to be w-iiii-ld"* blared through the speakers. The people in the living room backed away. "Come on," Tully said, "who wants a straight shot?"

Johnny knew he should stop her, but every time he looked at Tully, he thought *Kate's gone,* and the wound cracked open again. Turning away, he went up to comfort his children.

Outside the twins' bedroom, he drew in a sharp breath and opened the door. The navy-blue walls—hand-painted by Kate to show clouds and stars and moons—had been covered over the years with the boys' artwork and some of their favorite movie posters. Golden T-ball and soccer trophies stood proudly on the dresser top.

His father-in-law, Bud, sat in the big chair that easily held both boys when they played video games, and Sean, Kate's younger brother, lay asleep on Wills's bed.

Marah sat on the rug in front of the TV, with Lucas beside her. Wills was in the corner, watching the movie with his arms crossed.

"Hey," Johnny said quietly, closing the door behind him.

"Dad!" Lucas lurched to his feet. Johnny scooped his son into his arms and held him tightly.

Bud got to his feet. "I'll give you some time." He went to the bed, thumped Sean on the shoulder, and said, "Wake up."

Sean came awake with a start. He looked confused until he saw Johnny. "Oh, right." He followed his dad out of the room.

Lucas slid out of Johnny's arms and stood beside him. Johnny looked at his grieving children, and they looked at him. Their reactions to their mother's death were as different as they were. Lucas, the tenderhearted, was undone by missing his mom and confused about where exactly she'd gone. His twin, Wills, was a kid who relied on athleticism and popularity. And this loss had offended and scared him. He didn't like being afraid, so he got angry instead.

And then there was beautiful sixteen-year-old Marah, for whom everything had always come easily. In the cancer year, she had become contained and quiet, as if she thought that if she made no noise, the inevitability of this day could be avoided. He knew how deeply she regretted the way she'd treated Kate before she got sick.

They all looked to him to put their world back together.

But Kate was the heart and soul of this family, the glue that held them all together. Not him. How would they heal?

Marah rose suddenly. She looked sylphlike in her grief, pale and almost ethereal, with her long black hair, black dress, and nearly translucent skin. She moved toward him.

"I'll put the boys to bed," she said, reaching out for Lucas. "Come on, rugrat. I'll read you a story."

"Way to make us feel better, Dad," Wills said, his mouth tightening. It was a dark, sadly adult expression on an eight-year-old face.

"It will get better," Johnny said, hating his weakness.

"Will it?" Wills said. "How?"

Lucas looked up at him. "Yeah, how, Dad?"

He looked at Marah.

"Sleep will help," she said, and Johnny was pathetically grateful to her. Tomorrow he'd be better. Do better. *I'm sorry, Katie.*

"Good night," he said in a thick voice, his eyes burning with tears.

Lucas looked up at him. "I love you, Daddy."

Johnny dropped slowly to his knees and opened his arms. His sons pushed into his embrace, and he held them tightly. "I love you, too." Over their heads he stared up at Marah, who appeared unmoved, her gaze unfocused. "Marah?"

She finally looked at him. "Don't bother," she said softly.

"Your mom made us promise to be strong. Together."

"Yeah," she said, her lower lip trembling just a little. "I know."

"We can do it," he said. He heard the unsteadiness of his voice.

"Yeah. Sure we can," Marah said with a sigh. Then: "Come on, boys, let's get ready for bed."

Johnny knew he should stay, comfort Marah, but he had no words to say. Instead, he took the coward's route and left the room. He went downstairs, pushed through the crowd, and went outside.

It was full on night now, and there wasn't a star in the sky. In the tree limbs overhead, mason jars hung from strands of ropey twine, their insides full of black stones and votive candles. How many nights had he and Kate sat out here beneath the tiara of candlelight?

"Hey."

Her voice surprised him. And irritated him.

"You left me dancing all by myself," Tully said. She had a blue wool blanket wrapped around her; its end dragged on the ground.

"It must be intermission," he said, not looking at her.

"What do you mean?"

He could smell tequila on her breath. "The Tully Hart center-of-attention show. It must be intermission."

"Kate asked me to make tonight fun," she said. She was shaking.

"I can't believe you didn't come to her funeral," he said. His anger swelled again. "It would have broken her heart."

"She *knew* I wouldn't come. She even—"

"And that makes it okay? Don't you think Marah would have liked to see you in there? Don't you care about your goddaughter?"

Before she could answer, he went back inside.

He knew he'd lashed out unfairly. In another time, in another world, he'd care enough to apologize. Kate would want him to, but right now he couldn't manage the effort. His wife had been gone for forty-eight hours, and already he was a worse version of himself.

CHAPTER THREE

THAT night, at four a.m., Johnny gave up on the idea of sleep. He climbed out of bed and drifted from room to room, more than once finding himself standing somewhere with no clear memory of how he'd come to be there. Somehow he ended up back in his bedroom. Her water glass was still on the nightstand. So were her reading glasses and the mittens she'd worn to bed at the end, when she'd always been cold. *You were the one for me, John Ryan. I loved you with every breath I took for two decades.* It was what she'd said to him on her last night.

He got dressed and went downstairs. As he made a pot of coffee, he tried to imagine the new version of his life. All he saw were empty spaces at the dining-room table, a carpool with the wrong driver, a breakfast made by the wrong hands.

He leaned against the counter, drinking coffee. As he poured the third cup, he felt someone touch his shoulder, and he flinched.

Margie, his mother-in-law, smiled at him tiredly. Bud came up beside his wife. Johnny poured each of them a cup of coffee.

"We need to take Sean to the airport, but after that, we can come back here and help," Margie said. "For as long as you need us."

The airport. That was the answer. He couldn't feed his kids and drive them to school and then go to work at the station.

"I'm getting us the hell out of here," he said.

"Oh?" Margie said. "Where to?"

He said the first thing that came into his head. "Kauai." Katie had loved it there. They'd always meant to take the kids.

"Runnin' away doesn't change a thing," Bud said gruffly.

"I know that, Bud. But I'm drowning here."

Margie touched Johnny's arm. "What can we do to help?"

Now that Johnny had a plan—however imperfect—he felt better. "I'll get started on reservations. Don't tell the kids. Let them sleep."

"When will you leave?"

"Hopefully today."

"You'd better call Tully. She's planning to be here at eleven."

Johnny nodded. Tully was the least of his concerns right now.

"Okay," Margie said. "I'll clean out the fridge."

"I'll stop the milk delivery and call the police," Bud said. "Just so they know to watch the house."

Johnny thanked them both and then went into his office. By six fifty he'd bought airline tickets and reserved a car and rented a house online. All he had to do now was tell the kids.

In the boys' room he went to the bunk beds and found both of his sons on the bottom bunk.

He ruffled Lucas's coarse brown hair. "Hey, Skywalker."

"I wanna be Skywalker," Wills murmured in his sleep.

Johnny smiled. "You're the Conqueror, remember?"

"No one knows who William the Conqueror is," Wills said. "He needs a video game."

Lucas sat up, looking blearily around. "Is it school time already?"

"We're not going to school today," Johnny said. "We're going to Hawaii. I'm going to teach my kids how to surf."

"You don't know how to surf," Wills said, frowning.

"He does, too. Don't you, Dad?" Lucas said.

"I will in a week," Johnny said, and they cheered, bouncing up and down on the bed. "Brush your teeth and get dressed."

The boys jumped out of bed and raced to their bathroom. He walked slowly out of the room and down the hallway.

He knocked on Marah's door and heard her exhausted "What?"

He stepped into her room. He knew it wouldn't be easy, talking his sixteen-year-old daughter into a vacation. Nothing mattered more to Marah than her friends. That would be especially true now.

She stood brushing her long, shiny black hair, dressed for school in low-rise flare-legged jeans and a T-shirt that was toddler-size. He pushed his irritation aside. "Hey," he said.

"Hey," she answered. She put down her brush. He understood now why Kate had been wounded so often by the judgment in their daughter's eyes. She had a way of cutting you with a glance.

"I'm sorry about last night," he said. He sat on her bed and waited for her to join him there. When she didn't, he felt a wave of exhaustion. She was fragile—they all were—but Marah was like Tully. Neither of them knew how to show weakness. All Marah would let herself care about was that he'd interrupted her routine.

"We're going to Hawaii for a week. We're leaving here in two hours. Kauai is—"

"What? No *way*," she screeched. "I *can't* take off from school. I have to keep my grades up. I promised Mom I'd do well."

"That's admirable, Marah. But we need some time away as a family. To figure things out. We can get your assignments."

She stomped her foot. "You know *nothing* about high school. Do you know how competitive it is out there?"

"One week will hardly throw you under the bus."

He knew there was a right way to handle this and a wrong way; he just didn't know what the right way was. He stood up. "We're going. Leaving at ten. Pack a bag."

She grabbed his arm. "Let me stay with Aunt Tully!"

He looked down at her. "Tully? As a chaperone? Uh. No."

"Grandma and Grandpa would stay here with me."

"Marah, we're going. We need to be together, the four of us."

"You're ruining my life." She went into her bathroom.

He knew better than to wait for her to change her mind. In his bedroom he grabbed his phone and dialed.

"Hello?" Tully answered, sounding as bad as he felt.

Johnny knew he should apologize for last night, but every time he thought about it, he felt a rush of anger. He said, "We're going to Kauai today."

"What?"

"We need time together now. Our flight is at two."

"That's not much time to get ready."

"Yeah." He was already worried about that. "I gotta go." She was still talking, asking something about the weather, when he hung up.

SeaTac International Airport was surprisingly crowded on this midweek October afternoon in 2006. They'd arrived early to drop off Kate's brother, Sean, who was returning home.

At the self-service kiosk, Johnny got their boarding passes and then glanced at his children, each of whom held some electronic device; Marah had just learned how to send something called a text on her new cell phone. He had no idea what a text was.

Behind them the airport's pneumatic doors whooshed opened, and Tully came running toward them wearing a sundress, ridiculously high-heeled sandals, and a floppy white hat. She was rolling a Louis Vuitton duffel behind her. She came to a breathless stop in front of them. "What's wrong? If it's the time, I did my best."

Johnny stared at her. What the hell was she doing here?

"Tully!" Marah cried out. "Thank God."

Johnny took Tully by the arm and pulled her aside. "You aren't invited, Tul. It's just the four of us. I can't believe you thought—"

"Oh." The word was spoken quietly. He could see how hurt she was. "You said 'we.' I thought you meant me, too."

He knew how often she'd been left behind in her life, abandoned by her mother, but he didn't have the strength to worry about Tully Hart right now. "Come on, kids," he said harshly, giving them only a few minutes to say good-bye to Tully. He hugged his in-laws.

"Let Tully come," Marah whined. "Please . . ."

Johnny kept moving. It was all he could think of to do.

THEY landed in Kauai at four p.m., but it felt as if they'd been traveling for days. Johnny moved down the jetway while the boys walked on ahead. He fell into step beside Marah. "Hey."

She rolled her eyes and kept walking.

Outside, the sun was shining brightly. Bougainvillea in full pink bloom crawled over the parking-area fence. Within ten minutes they were in a rented silver Mustang convertible and heading north along the only highway on the island. They stopped at a Safeway store, loaded up on groceries, and then piled back into the car.

The coastline was an endless golden sandy beach lashed by crashing blue waves and rimmed in black lava rock outcroppings.

"Uh, it's pretty here," he said to Marah, who was beside him in the front passenger seat staring at her phone. Texting.

"Yeah," Marah said without looking up.

"Marah," he said in a warning tone.

She looked over at him. "I am getting homework from Ashley. I *told* you I couldn't leave school." She glanced to her right. "Waves. Sand. Fat white people in Hawaiian shirts. Men who wear socks with their sandals. Great vacation, Dad. I totally forgot that Mom just died. Thanks." Then she went back to texting.

He gave up.

The town of Hanalei was a funky collection of wooden buildings and brightly colored signs and shave-ice stands. The house they'd rented was an old-fashioned Hawaiian cottage. He pulled into the crushed coral driveway and parked.

The boys were out of the car in an instant. Johnny carried two suitcases up the front steps and opened the door. The wooden-floored cottage was decorated in 1950s bamboo-framed furniture with thick floral cushions. A koa-wood kitchen and eating nook was on the left side of the main room, with a comfortable living room on the right side. A good-sized TV delighted the boys..

He went to the set of glass sliding doors that faced the bay. Beyond the grassy yard lay Hanalei Bay. He remembered the last time he and Kate had been here. *Take me to bed, Johnny Ryan. I'll make it worth your while. . . .*

Wills bumped into him hard. "We're hungry, Dad."

Lucas skidded up beside them. "Starving."

Of course. It was nine p.m. at home. How had he forgotten that they needed dinner? "We'll go to a bar that your mom and I love."

Lucas giggled. "We can't go in a bar, Dad."

He ruffled Lucas's hair. "Not in Washington, but here it's okay."

"That's so cool," Wills said.

Johnny heard Marah in the kitchen putting groceries away. That seemed like a good sign. He hadn't had to beg or threaten her.

It took them less than thirty minutes to put their things away, claim their rooms, and change into shorts and T-shirts; then they walked along the quiet street to a ramshackle old wooden building near the center of town. The Tahiti Nui. Kate had loved the retro Polynesian kitsch of the place.

Inside the bar, which was filled with tourists and locals, they found a small bamboo table near the "stage."

The waitress had just delivered their pizza when the band—two Hawaiians with guitars—showed up. Their first song was Israel Kamakawiwo'ole's iconic ukulele version of "Somewhere Over the Rainbow." Johnny felt Kate materialize on the bench seat beside him, felt her swaying to the music, singing quietly.

Later, as they walked home in the fading light, the boys were so tired they started fighting. Johnny was too weary to care. In the house he helped them get ready for bed and tucked them in.

Afterward he walked through the house, looking for his daughter. He found her on the lanai, sitting in a beach chair.

"We should have come here when she was alive," Marah said.

That stung. They'd meant to. How many times had they planned a trip, only to cancel for some now-forgotten reason? You think you have all the time in the world. "Maybe she's watching us."

"Yeah. Right."

"A lot of people believe in that."

"I wish I was one of them."

Johnny sighed. "Yeah. Me, too."

"You were wrong," Marah said.

"About what?"

"The view doesn't change anything."

"I needed to get away. Can you understand that?"

"Yeah, well, I needed to stay."

She got up and went back into the house. Johnny was shaken by her words. He hadn't thought of what his kids needed—not really. He'd folded their needs into his own and told himself they'd all be better off. Kate would be disappointed in him. Already. Again. And even worse, he knew his daughter was right.

It wasn't paradise he wanted to see. It was his wife's smile, and that was gone forever. This view didn't change a thing.

EVEN in paradise Johnny slept poorly, unaccustomed to being alone. Each morning, he was the first to waken. He started his day with a cup of coffee on the lanai. From there he watched daylight come to the bay. He often talked to Katie out here, saying things he wished he'd said before. As Kate lay dying, he knew that Margie had let Katie talk about what scared her—leaving her children, her pain—but Johnny had been unable to listen, even on the last day.

I'm ready, Johnny. I need you to be ready, too.

I can't be, he'd said. What he should have said was, *I will always love you.* He should have held her hand and told her it was okay.

"I'm sorry, Katie," he said to her now—too late. He strained for a sign that she'd heard. A breeze in his hair, a flower falling in his lap. Something. But there was nothing.

The island had helped the boys, he thought. They learned to body-surf and buried each other in the sand. Lucas talked about Kate often. *Mom would have loved this* became a common refrain, and it helped them all. Well, that wasn't quite right. After a week in Kauai, Johnny still had no idea what would help Marah. She did everything that was asked of her, but she was a ghost version of herself. When Kate was mentioned, Marah invariably said something like, *She's gone,* and walked away. Not once had she put a toe in the water.

He tried to imagine their life as it would be after they went home. He couldn't. Neither could he imagine going home, standing in Kate's kitchen, sleeping on one side of a bed, waiting for her kiss to waken him every morning. They all needed a fresh start. It was the only way. And not a one-week vacation.

The morning they were leaving, he made a call. "Bill," he said when his friend answered. "Are you still looking for an executive producer for *Good Morning Los Angeles*?"

September 3, 2010, 6:21 a.m.

"Mr. Ryan?"

Johnny came back to the present. When he opened his eyes, he was sitting on a hard plastic chair in the hospital waiting room.

A man stood in front of him, wearing blue scrubs. "I'm Dr. Reggie Bevan. Neurosurgeon. You're Talullah Hart's family?"

"Yes," he said after a pause. "How is she?"

"She's in critical condition. We've stabilized her enough for surgery, but—" "Code Blue, Trauma Nine" blared through the hall.

Johnny got to his feet. "Is that about her?"

"Yes," the doctor said. He turned and ran toward the elevators.

CHAPTER FOUR

WHERE am I? Darkness. I can't open my eyes.

CLEAR.

Something hits me in the chest so hard I lose control of my body. I feel myself arch up and flop back down.

NOTHINGDRBEVAN.

There is another crush of devastating pain and then . . . nothing.

It takes no effort to open my eyes now. A light appears, diffuse, almost like a distant sunrise. Then I'm up high, looking down.

Below me I see a crowd of people moving feverishly, calling out words I can't understand. There are machines in the room. And something red is spilling across the floor.

They are doctors and nurses. I am in a hospital room. They are trying to save someone's life. They are clustered around a body on a gurney. *My* body. It is my blood dripping onto the floor.

The weird thing is that I feel nothing. It is *me,* Tully Hart. I am the body bleeding out, but this is me, too; I'm floating above it all. SHESCODING.

I should care, but I don't. I turn suddenly, and the walls are gone. In the distance I see a light, and it beckons to me. I think *Go* and I am moving. I float into a world that is sharp and clear. Blue sky, green grass, a snow-white cloud. And incandescent light that is like nothing I've ever seen. It bathes me. For the first time in as long as I can remember, I feel completely at peace. Night falls around me.

When I look up, I see an array of stars. The Big Dipper. Orion's Belt. The same constellations I once studied from my yard as a girl, back when the world didn't seem big enough to hold all my dreams.

A bicycle appears, an old-fashioned banana-seated girl's bike. I climb on, pedaling . . . where? I don't know. It is the middle of a starry night, and I am speeding downhill like a kid again.

I know this place. Summer Hill. It is woven into my soul. Obviously I'm not *really* here. The real me is lying on a hospital bed.

I throw my arms open and let my speed pick up, remembering the first time I did this. We were in the eighth grade, Kate and me, and we were on these bikes, on this hill, riding into the start of a friendship that is the only true love story of my life. I forced her, of course. Threw rocks at her bedroom window and woke her up and begged her to sneak out with me.

Did I know how our lives could be changed with that one choice? No. But I knew my life needed changing. How could I not? My mother had perfected the art of leaving me, and I had spent my entire childhood pretending truth was fiction. Only with Kate had I really been honest. The only person who had ever loved me for me.

No experience was real until I told Katie about it; no day was quite right if we didn't talk. By the time we were eighteen, we were TullyandKate, impossible to separate. I was there at her wedding and at the birth of her babies, and when she took her last breath.

With my hands outstretched and memories running alongside me, I think: *This is how I should die.*

Die? Who says you get to die?

I would know that voice anywhere. I have missed it every single day for the last four years. I turn my head and see an impossible sight: Kate is on a bike beside me. We're TullyandKate again.

The next thing I know, we are sitting on the grassy bank of the Pilchuck River, just like we used to, back in the early seventies.

Hey, Tul, she says.

Happiness unfolds inside of me. I feel safer here than I have ever felt in my life. It soothes me. I have been in pain for so long.

I turn to Kate, drink in the sight of her. I have missed her so much. She is translucent almost, shimmery. When she looks at me, I see both sadness and joy in her eyes.

What happened? Kate asks quietly.

She is asking why I am here—and in the hospital. I want to tell her everything, but words dance away like fairies when I reach for them. Maybe I don't want to remember why I am here.

Talk to me, Tul.

I *want* to talk to my best friend, tell her how I screwed up. She always made everything okay. I remember when it started to go wrong. The one day that was worse than all the rest—the one day that changed everything. October of 2006. The funeral. I remember being in the middle of the St. Cecilia's parking lot . . . all alone.

Kate has given me an iPod as her good-bye gift, and a letter. I am supposed to listen to "Dancing Queen" and dance all by myself. I don't want to do it, but what choice do I have, and really, when I hear the words *"you can dance,"* for a wondrous moment the music takes me away from here. And then it is over.

I see her family coming toward me. Someone says something— what, I don't know. I answer. We pretend to be okay for each other. Johnny is angry. How could it be any other way?

"People are coming to the house," Johnny says.

The thought of it—a so-called celebration of Kate's life—makes me feel sick.

I was not good at the whole making-death-a-positive-transition thing. I should have listened to her fear, comforted her. Instead, I'd promised her that everything would be okay, that she would heal.

But I'd made another promise, too. At the end. I'd sworn to take care of her family, and I would not let her down again.

I follow Margie and Bud to their Volvo. The four miles that stretch between the Catholic church and the Ryan house seem to take forever. And then we are there.

The yard has a wild untended look to it. We park, and I get out. Kate's brother, Sean, comes up beside me. He is five years younger than Kate and me, but he is so slight and nerdy and hunched that he looks older. His green eyes are so like Katie's that I hug him.

He steps away, and I am left alone at the car, staring up at a house that has always felt like my home, too. I can't go in, but I have to.

I draw in a deep breath. If there's one thing I know how to do, it's to go on. I have perfected the art of denial, haven't I? I have always been able to ignore my pain, smile, and go on.

I join Margie in the kitchen. Together we go about the business of setting up for a party. I set up easels and place photographs on them, the pictures Kate had chosen to reflect her life. I can't look at any of them.

I hear the doorbell ring. It is time.

I move through the party, pouring wine and taking plates away. As I move, I hear snippets of conversation. People are talking about Kate, sharing memories. I don't listen; it hurts too much.

A woman comes up to me and says, "She talked about you a lot."

I smile. "We were best friends for more than thirty years."

"She was so brave during her chemo, wasn't she?"

I can't answer that. I wasn't there for her, not then. In the three decades of our friendship, there was a two-year blip when a fight escalated. I hurt Kate deeply, and I didn't apologize. It was the worst mistake of my life.

In my absence my best friend battled cancer and had a double mastectomy. I was not there for her when her hair fell out or when her test results turned bad. I will regret it for as long as I breathe.

"I was there when she shaved her head," another woman says. "She was *laughing,* calling herself GI Kate. I never saw her cry."

I can't take any more of this. Kate had asked me to keep the party going. *No one livens up a party like you, Tul. Be there for me.*

Always, girlfriend.

I break free of the women and go over to the stereo. "This is for you, Katie Scarlett," I say, and pop a CD into the stereo. When the music starts, I crank up the volume. "Who wants a straight shot?"

I see Johnny across the room. The love of her life and, sadly, the only man I've ever been able to count on. When I look at him, I see how broken he is. Maybe if you didn't know him, you wouldn't see it—the place he'd missed in his morning shave, the lines beneath his eyes. I know that he has been scrubbed bare by grief.

I've known this man for most of my life, first as my boss and then as my best friend's husband. For all the big events of both our lives, we've been together, and that's a comfort to me.

The music, our music, pours like elixir into my veins, fills me. Without thinking, I sway to the beat. I can see the way people are looking at me. Staring. As if I'm inappropriate. But the music, our music, brings her back to me in a way no spoken words ever could.

I come to a stop in front of an easel. On it is a picture of Kate and me. We are young and smiling, our arms looped around each other.

Grief pulls the legs out from underneath me; I fall to my knees. The tears I have been holding back burst out in wracking sobs. I feel a hand on my shoulder. I look up and see Margie.

"Come on," she says, helping me to my feet. I cling to her, let her help me into the laundry room, where it is quiet. We hold on to each other but say nothing. What is there to say?

And suddenly I am exhausted. I touch Margie's shoulder, noticing how thin and fragile she has become. It scares me.

I make my way back into the living room, but I know that I can't do what Kate asked of me. I can't pretend to celebrate her life. Me, who has spent a lifetime pretending to be fine-good-great, can't do that now. It is too soon.

THE next thing I know, it's morning. Before I even open my eyes it hits me. *She's gone.*

As I get out of bed, I feel a headache start. My bedroom feels foreign to me. I have hardly been here in the last seven months. In April, when I found out about Kate's cancer, I'd changed my life, walked away from everything—my TV talk show and my condominium—and dedicated my life to my best friend. Now I am home again, and it feels like a place I've never been.

My phone rings, and I stumble toward it. The caller ID says RYAN. I pick up, hearing the strain in my voice as I say, "Hello?"

"What happened to you last night?" Johnny says.

"I couldn't take it," I say, slumping onto my bed. "I tried."

"Yeah. Big surprise."

"What does *that* mean?" I sit up. "The music? It's what Kate wanted."

"Did you even talk to your goddaughter?"

"I tried," I say, stung. "She only wanted to be with her friends. And I read the boys a story before bed. But"—my voice cracks—"I couldn't stand it, Johnny. Being without her—"

"You were okay for the two years of your fight."

I draw in a sharp breath. He has never said anything like this before. In April, when Kate called and I came running to the hospital, Johnny welcomed me back into the family. "She forgave me. And believe me, I was not okay."

He sighs. "None of this matters anymore," he says after a pause. "She loved you. That's that. And we're all hurting. How are we going to make it? Every time I look at the bed or at her clothes in the closet . . ." He clears his throat. "We're going to Kauai today."

"What?"

"We need time together. Our flight is at two, on Hawaiian."

"That's not much time to get ready," I say. An image blossoms in my mind—the five of us on the beach, healing together. "It's perfect. Sunshine and—"

"Yeah. I gotta go."

He's right. We can talk later. Now I need to hurry.

I HANG up, and in twenty minutes I am packed and showered. Johnny hates it when I'm late. Tully-time, he calls it, and he's not smiling when he says it. In my closet, I find a teal-and-white silk Lilly Pulitzer dress and pair it with silver high-heeled sandals and a white straw hat. As I slip into the dress, I imagine this vacation. It is something I need desperately—this time away with the only family I have. We will grieve together, share memories, and keep Kate's spirit alive.

I am ready at eleven twenty, and I call for a Town Car.

I grab my small rolling bag and leave the condo. Downstairs a black Town Car is waiting in front of the building. "SeaTac," I say.

At SeaTac it takes me a minute to find them in the crowd, but there they are, by the Hawaiian Airlines ticket counter.

"I'm here!" I yell, waving like a game-show contestant trying to get noticed. I run toward them. Johnny stares at me in confusion.

I come to a stop. "What's wrong? If it's the time, I did my best."

"Tully!" Marah says, grinning. "Thank God."

Johnny takes me by the arm and pulls me aside.

"You aren't invited on this trip, Tul. It's just the four of us. I can't believe you thought—"

I feel as if I've been punched. The only thing I can think of to say is, "Oh. You said 'we.' I thought you meant me, too."

"You understand," he says, phrasing it as a statement.

I feel like that abandoned ten-year-old again, forgotten by my mother, wondering why I am so easy to leave behind.

The twins come up on either side of us, jubilant in their excitement, amped up on the idea of adventure.

"You comin' to Kauai with us, Aunt Tully?" Lucas says.

"We're gonna *surf*," Wills says.

"I have to work," I say, even though everyone knows that I walked away from my show.

"Yeah," Marah says. "'Cuz, like, having you come would make it fun, so natch you're not coming."

I untangle myself from the boys and go to Marah. "Cut your old man some slack. You're too young to know about true love, but they found it, and now she's gone."

"And, like, *sand* is going to help? Can I stay with you?"

I want it so badly I feel sick, and although I am notoriously self-centered, this is not about me. And Johnny is in no mood for this. "No, Marah. Not this time. You need to be with your family."

"I thought you were part of the family."

Obviously not. "Have fun" is all I can manage.

As I watch them walk away, I feel scaldingly, achingly alone.

Margie moves closer. Her soft, lined palm presses against my cheek. I smell the citrusy hand lotion she loves. "They need this," she says quietly. I know how tired she is—to her bones.

Then I hear her crying; it is a sound as soft as a feather falling. She has been strong for so long. I know there are no words, so I just pull her into my arms. Finally she lets go and steps back.

"You want to come home with us?"

I don't want to be alone, but I can't go to the house on Firefly Lane. Not yet. "I can't," I say, and I see that she understands.

At home I pace the rooms of my high-rise condominium. It has never been a home, this place. There are few personal mementos. My designer pretty much chose everything, and apparently she liked ivory. Everything is some shade of off-white.

It is beautiful in its way and looks like the home of a woman who has it all. But here I am, forty-six and alone.

My career has been my choice, over and over. As far back as I can remember, I've had dreams with a capital *D*. It began in the house on Firefly Lane, with Kate, when we were fourteen years old. It is a story I've told in a dozen interviews over the years. How Katie and I were in her house and Margie and Bud were watching the news and Margie said, "Jean Enerson is changing the world. She's one of the first women to anchor the nightly news."

And I said, "I'm going to be a reporter."

I wanted to become a woman the whole world admired. I needed success like a fish needed water. Without it who would I be? It is what I have in life—fame and money and success.

At that, I know. It is time for me to go back to work. *That's* how I will get through this grief. I will do what I've always done. I'll look strong and pretend. I'll let the adoration of strangers soothe me.

I go back into my walk-in closet and exchange my dress for a pair of black pants and a blouse. The pants are so tight I can't get them zipped. How is it that I didn't notice gaining weight? I grab a knit skirt and put it on instead. I grab my purse and head out.

It is only a handful of blocks to my studio, and today, in honor of the widening of my ass, I decide to walk. It is a gorgeous fall day in Seattle, one of those sunshine masterpieces that turn this city into one of the prettiest in the country.

I come to the large warehouse-type building that houses my production company, Firefly, Inc. The space is expensive, located in Pioneer Square, less than a block from the shores of Elliott Bay, but what do I care about cost? The show I produce makes millions.

I unlock the door and go inside. The halls are dark and empty, a stark reminder that I walked away and never looked back. As I walk toward the studio, my heartbeat speeds up. My palms turn damp.

And then I am there, standing at the red curtain that separates backstage from my world. I push the curtain aside.

The last time I was on this stage, I told my audience about Katie, how she'd been diagnosed with breast cancer, and I talked about the warning signs, and then I signed off. Now I would have to explain how it felt to sit by my best friend's bed and tell her it would be okay long past the time when that was true. Or how it felt to gather her pills and pour out the last of the water in the pitcher by her empty bed.

I can't do it. Not yet. I can't talk about Katie, and if I can't talk about her, I can't stride back into my old life, onto my stage.

For the first time in forever, I don't know who I am.

WHEN I step back out onto the street, it is raining. The weather in Seattle is like that: quicksilver.

When I get to my building, I go up to my penthouse and walk

idly into the kitchen, where mail is piled in stacks. In all my months away, I didn't check messages or open my bills. I counted on the machinery of my life—agents, managers, accountants, stockbrokers—to keep me on track.

I know I need to take charge again, but honestly, the thought of going through all this mail is daunting. Instead, I call my business manager, Frank. It's what I pay him for. The number rings repeatedly and then goes to voice mail. I don't bother to leave a message.

Mrs. Mularkey used to say that a good night's sleep could change everything. So I go into my room and crawl into bed. For the next five days, I do almost nothing except eat too much and sleep poorly. Each morning when I wake up, I think this is it; this is the day I will be able to climb out of this grief and be me again, and each night, I drink until I can't remember the sound of my best friend's voice.

And then it comes to me, on the sixth day after Kate's funeral. I need closure. That's how I will heal. I need to look this grief in the heart and say good-bye. I need to help Johnny and the kids, too.

Suddenly I know how to do it.

It is nightfall when I pull into the Ryan's driveway and park. Stars litter the charcoal sky, a faint breeze ruffles the cedar trees that line the property. I struggle to lift the four flattened cardboard moving boxes out of my Mercedes and carry them across the yard.

Inside, the house is dark and quieter than I can ever remember it being. *I can't do it.* What have I been thinking? *Closure.*

And there is more, something else. I remember our last night together, Katie's and mine. She had made her mind up; we all knew it. We had spent one last hour alone, just the two of us. *Take care of them,* she'd whispered, clutching my hand. *I've done everything for them.* At this she laughed, a breathy release of air. *They won't know how to start without me. Help them.*

And I had said, *Who will help me?*

The shame of that washes over me, tightens my stomach. *I'll always be with you,* she'd lied, and that had been the end of it. She'd asked for Johnny and the kids then.

I tighten my hold on the boxes and trudge upstairs with them. In Kate and Johnny's bedroom I pause, feeling reluctant to intrude.

Help them. What had Johnny said to me the last time we spoke? *Every time I look at the clothes in her closet . . .*

I swallow and go into their walk-in closet. Johnny's clothes are on the right side of the closet. Kate's are on the left.

I unfold one of the boxes and tape the ends and set it beside me. I grab an armful of clothes and sit down on the cold hardwood floor.

Sweaters. Cardigans, turtlenecks, V-necks. I fold each one carefully, breathing in her lingering scent—lavender and citrus.

I do okay until I come to a worn UW sweatshirt. The memory washes over me: We are in Kate's old bedroom, packing to go to college together. A couple of eighteen-year-old girls who have dreamed of this moment for years. We were going to join the same sorority and become famous journalists.

They'll want you, Kate had said. I'd known she was feeling afraid, the unpopular girl her classmates called Kootie all those years ago.

You know I won't join a sorority unless we're in it together.

That was what Kate had never understood, or at least hadn't believed: Of the two of us, I needed her more than she needed me.

I fold up the sweatshirt and set it aside. I will take it home.

For the rest of that night, I sit in my best friend's closet, listening to the soundtrack of our friendship and boxing up her life.

I go downstairs and pour myself a glass of wine. It occurs to me that I've left my lunch dishes on the counter and the takeout boxes from my dinner should really go in the garbage, but how can I think of that when the music is in me again, taking me back?

I go to the CD player and crank the volume so I can hear it upstairs. For just a moment I close my eyes and dance, and I imagine her here, hip bumping me and laughing. Then I go back to work.

I WAKE up on the floor of her closet, wearing a pair of her black sweatpants and the old UW sweatshirt. The wineglass beside me has fallen on its side. The bottle is empty. No wonder I feel terrible.

I struggle to sit up. It is my second night here, and I am almost done packing Kate's things away. Her side of the closet is empty, and there are six boxes stacked beneath the silver rod. On the floor is Kate's journal, the one she wrote in the last months of her life.

Marah will come looking for me one day, Kate had said, pressing the journal into my hands. *Be with her when she reads it.*

The music is still blaring downstairs. I'd drunk too much wine and forgotten to turn it off last night. Prince. "Purple Rain."

At least I have done *something.* This will make Johnny's life easier when he gets back. It is one difficult job he needn't do.

Downstairs the music snaps off.

Before I start to leave the closet, Johnny appears in the doorway.

"What the *hell?*" he yells at me.

I am so taken aback I just stare at him. Was it today that they were returning from Kauai?

He glances past me, sees the boxes lining the wall with labels like KATE'S SUMMER CLOTHES and GOODWILL and KATE, MISC.

I see how he is struggling for composure as his children come up behind him. I push my way into his embrace, waiting for him to hold me. When he doesn't, I step back.

"How *dare* you come into this house and go through her things and box them up as if they're garbage." His voice breaks, words vibrate. "Is that her sweater you're wearing?"

"I was trying to help."

"Help? Is it a *help* to leave empty wine bottles and food cartons on the counter? Is it a help to blast music at the edge of pain? Do you think it will *help* me to look into her empty closet?"

"Johnny—" He pushes me aside, and I almost drop the journal.

"Give me that," he says in a voice that is trip-wire tight.

I hold it to my chest. "She entrusted it to me. I'm supposed to be with Marah when she reads it. I promised Katie."

"She made a lot of mistakes when it came to you."

This is happening so fast I can't quite process it. "Did I make a mistake in cleaning out her closet? I thought you—"

"You *only* ever think about yourself, Tully."

"Dad," Marah says. "Mom wouldn't want—"

"She's gone," he says sharply. I see how the words hit him, how grief rearranges his face, and I whisper his name, not knowing what else to say. He's wrong. I had meant to help.

Johnny backs away from me. He looks at his children, who look scared now and uncertain. "We're moving," he says.

Marah goes pale. "What?"

"We're moving," Johnny says. "To Los Angeles. I've taken a new job. We need a new start. I can't live here without her."

"If this is because I tried to help—"

He laughs. It is a dry, scraping sound. "Of course you think it's about you. Did you *hear* me? I can't live in her house."

I reach for him.

He sidesteps me. "Just go, Tully."

I clutch the journal and ease past him. I hug the boys together, kissing their plump cheeks, trying to imprint their images on my soul. "You'll visit us, Aunt Tully, right?" Lucas says unevenly.

Marah grabs my arm. "Let me live with you."

"You belong with your family," I say quietly.

"This isn't a family anymore." Marah's eyes fill with tears.

I can't listen to any more. I pull my goddaughter into a desperate hug. When I leave the room, I can hardly see through my tears.

CHAPTER FIVE

"WILL you *please* stop humming?" I say to Kate. "How am I supposed to think with you making that racket?"

I am not humming.

"Okay. Quit beeping. What are you, the Road Runner?" The sound amplifies steadily. "Stop making that noise." I am starting to get a headache. A real headache. Pain sparks to life behind my eyes.

I am as quiet as the grave over here.

"Very funny. Wait. That's not you. It sounds like a car alarm."

WELOSTHER, someone says—yells, really. Who?

Beside me I hear Katie sigh. She whispers my name and then says: *Time.* It scares me. Have I used up all the time allotted to me? What happened to me? I know she knows. "Kate?"

Nothing.

Suddenly I am falling, tumbling. I can hear voices, but the words make no sense and the pain is brutalizing.

ALLCLEAR.

I feel my spirit ebbing away. I scream for help, but it's all in my head. The sound I imagine fades away, and I do the same. . . .

September 3, 2010, 6:27 a.m.

JOHNNY stood outside Trauma Nine. It had taken him five seconds to decide to follow Dr. Bevan to this room. He was a journalist, after all. He'd made a career out of going where he wasn't wanted.

As he opened the door, he was pushed aside by a woman in scrubs. He slipped behind her into the crowded room. It was swarming with people who had collected around a gurney. They were all talking at once. He couldn't see the patient.

An alarm sounded. Someone yelled, "We lost her. Charge."

A high humming sound thrummed through the room.

"All clear."

He heard a high *wrrr,* and then the body on the table arched up and thumped back down.

"She's back," someone said. A few of the nurses stepped away from the bed, and for the first time, he saw the patient. Tully.

She lay unconscious, her face battered and bloodied; a bone stuck up through the ripped flesh of her arm.

Dr. Bevan materialized beside him. "You shouldn't be here."

Johnny waved the comment away. As he stood there, shocked by the extent of her injuries, what he felt was shame. Somehow he had a part to play in this. He'd blamed Tully for something that wasn't her fault and cut her out of his life.

"We need to get her to the OR, Mr. Ryan."

"Will she live?"

"Her chances are not good," Dr. Bevan said.

"Save her," Johnny said as the gurney rolled past him.

Feeling numb, he walked out of the room and made his way down the hall and into the fourth-floor surgical waiting area. He checked in with the woman at the desk, told her he was waiting for word on Tully Hart, and took a seat.

For hours he sat in the waiting room. He hadn't called anyone yet. He was waiting for word on Tully's condition. Bud and Margie lived in Arizona now; Johnny didn't want Margie to rush to the airport unless it was absolutely necessary. He would have called Tully's mom, but he had no idea how to reach her.

And there was Marah. He didn't know if she'd even take his call.

"Mr. Ryan?"

Johnny looked up and saw the surgeon coming toward him. He stood. "How is she, Dr. Bevan?"

"She survived the surgeries. Right now the biggest concern is cerebral edema—swelling in her brain. She sustained massive head trauma. We put a shunt in to help with the swelling, but the efficacy of that is uncertain. We have lowered her body temperature and put her in a medically induced coma to help relieve the pressure, but her condition is critical. She's on a ventilator."

"May I see her?"

The doctor nodded. "Of course. Come with me." He led Johnny to the elevator and up to the ICU.

Tully lay in a narrow bed surrounded by machines. Her hair had been shaved, and a hole had been drilled into her skull. A catheter and pump were working to relieve the pressure on her brain. There were several tubes going into her—a breathing tube, a feeding tube, a tube into her head. A black screen behind the bed showed the intracranial pressure; another tracked her heartbeat. Her left arm was in a cast.

"Brain injuries are impossible to predict," Dr. Brevan said. "We don't really know the extent of her injuries yet. We hope to know more in twenty-four hours, but this is uncertain territory."

"Will she be herself when she wakes up?"

"*If* she wakes up is really the question. Her brain is functioning, although we don't know how well because of the medications we have her on. Her pupils are responsive, and that's a good sign. The coma will give her body time. But if a bleed develops . . ."

He didn't have to finish the sentence. Johnny knew.

"What happened to her?" Johnny asked.

"Car accident, but I don't have any details." Dr. Bevan turned to him. "We believe it helps to talk to comatose patients." He patted Johnny's shoulder and headed out of the room.

Johnny sat down beside the bed. He didn't know what to say to her, not now, after all that had been said—and left unsaid—between them. The one thing he knew for sure was this: If Kate were here, she'd kick his ass for how he'd unraveled after her death and how he'd treated her best friend.

He did the only thing he could think of to reach Tully. Quietly, feeling stupid but doing it anyway, he started to sing the only song that came to him, the one that had always reminded him of Tully: "Just a small-town girl, living in a lo-nely wor-ld . . ."

WHERE am I? Dead? Alive? Somewhere in between?

"Kate?"

I feel a whoosh of warmth beside me, and my relief is enormous.

"Katie," I say, turning. "Where were you?"

Gone, she says simply. *Now I'm back. Open your eyes.*

I open my eyes slowly, and it's like waking up on the face of the sun. I gasp. When my eyes adjust, I see that I am back in the hospital room with my body. Below me an operation is going on.

Look, Tully.

I don't want to. A cold dread has taken hold of me. I know what I am going to see. My body is on the table. Someone is shaving my head. I hear a sound like a buzz saw starting up, and I feel sick.

"I don't like it here," I say to Kate. "Take me somewhere."

We'll always be here, but close your eyes.

"Gladly." The sudden darkness scares me. It's weird, really, because I'm not afraid of anything.

Ha. You are more afraid of love than anybody I know. It's why you keep testing people and pushing them away. Open your eyes.

I open my eyes, and color bleeds down from the blackness above. First comes the sky, a perfect, cloudless blue, and then the cherry trees in bloom. Pink Gothic buildings sketch themselves into place, and finally the green, green grass. We are at the University of Washington. There are young men and women—kids—everywhere. Somewhere a boom box is turned on as high as it will go.

"None of this is real," I say. "Right?"

Real is relative.

Not far from where we are sitting in the grass, a pair of girls are stretched side by side; one is brunette; the other is blond. The blonde is wearing parachute pants and a T-shirt. The other girl—okay, it's me, I know it, I can remember when I wore my hair all ratted up like that, and I remember the white sweater. It had been my favorite.

I lie back, feeling the grass prickling beneath my bare arms. How many times in our four years at the UW did we do exactly this? The light around us is magical. My pain is a distant memory here.

What happened tonight? Kate asks.

"I can't remember." It's true; I can't. "Why are you here, Kate?"

You called for me, remember? I came because you need me. And to remind you.

"Of what?"

Memories are who we are, Tul. Love and memories are what last. That's why your life flashes before your eyes when you die—you're picking the memories you want. It's like packing.

"Then I am screwed. I don't remember anything, and love—"

A voice is speaking. "Will she be herself when she wakes up?"

"Hey," I say. "That's—"

Johnny. The way she says her husband's name is so full of love and pain that for a second I am speechless.

"*If* she wakes up is really the question. . . ." A male voice.

Wait. They are talking about my *death*. And the chance of something worse—a brain-damaged life.

I concentrate hard, and I am in the hospital room again.

Johnny is standing by my bed. "I'm sorry," he says to the me that can't hear. I have waited so long to hear those words from him. I can see now that he loved me. He will miss me, even after all of it.

I want to answer him, to let him know that he has reached me, that I am *here,* but nothing works. "Open your eyes," I say to my body. "Open your eyes. Tell him you're sorry, too."

And then he starts to sing. "Just a small-town girl . . ."

God, I love that man, Kate says.

Someone else walks into the room. A beefy man in a brown sport coat and blue slacks. "I'm Detective Gates," the man says.

I hear the words *car accident* and images flash through my mind—a rainy night, a concrete stanchion, my hands on the steering wheel. It almost becomes a memory.

Kate takes my hand in the darkness, and we are flying. We touch down, soft as a butterfly landing, in a pair of worn wooden chairs that face the beach. The world is dark, but candles flicker in Mason jars from the branches of an old maple tree.

Her back deck. Kate's.

I hear Kate breathing beside me. *Johnny fell apart,* she says, reminding me of where we were before: talking about my life.

"We all did." That's the sad, sorry truth of it. "You were the glue that held us all together. Without you . . ."

What happened to you after he moved to Los Angeles?

"Can't I just walk into the light and be done with all this?"

You yelled for me, remember? You said you needed me. I'm here. And this is why: You need to remember. You've heard of your life flashing before your eyes at the end? This is it. So talk.

I lean back in the chair. "After you died, Johnny and the kids moved to Los Angeles. It happened fast, that moving. I remember standing with your mom and dad in the driveway waving good-bye. After that I went home and crawled into bed. . . ."

I KNOW I need to go back to work, but the idea is overwhelming. I can't summon the strength to begin the process of starting my life over without a best friend.

Somehow I lose two weeks. I mean, I don't really *lose* them. I know where they are and where I am. I call Marah every night at eleven o'clock. I know that she can't sleep, either. I listen to her complain about her father's decision to move, and I tell her that it will be okay, but neither of us believes it. I promise to visit soon.

Finally, I can't stand it anymore. I throw the covers off, and I see myself for the first time: My hair is tangled and dirty, my eyes are glazed, and my clothes are a wrinkled mess. I look like my mother. I am ashamed that I have fallen so far so fast.

It is time to recover. I have to put all of this behind me and go on. I know how to do that. I've been doing it all my life. I call my agent, make an appointment to see him. He is in Los Angeles: I will see my agent, get a job, and surprise Johnny and the kids with a visit. Yes. Perfect. A plan.

With an appointment made, I feel better. I take a shower and style my hair with care. I notice that I am gray at the roots.

I apply makeup with a heavy hand. I'm going out into the world, after all, and there are cameras everywhere these days. I dress in the only thing that fits comfortably over my widening hips—a black-knit pencil skirt, knee-length boots, and a black silk fitted blouse.

I call my travel agent and make reservations, and all the while I am smiling, thinking I can do this—and then I open the door to my condo and feel a flash of panic. I am *afraid* to leave my house.

I don't know what is wrong with me, but I won't stand for it. I take a deep breath and plunge forward. All the way to the elevator, and down to my car, and into the driver's seat. I can feel my heart thudding in my chest.

I start the car and drive out into the busy Seattle street. A heavy rain is falling. I want to turn back, but I don't. I force myself to keep going until I am on the plane, seated in first class.

"Martini," I say to the flight attendant. The look on her face reminds me that it is not yet noon. I will be better once I am back to work. It has always been my salvation.

In Los Angeles I see a driver holding up a sign: HART. I hand him my calfskin overnight bag and follow him out to a waiting Town

Car. On the drive from LAX to Century City, I lean into the cushy seat and close my eyes, taking a moment to collect my thoughts and organize my ideas. I am ready for my comeback.

The car pulls up to the imposing white building identified only by a discreet carved sign: CREATIVE ARTISTS AGENCY.

Inside, the building is an endless stretch of white marble and glass. Everyone is dressed well, in expensive suits. The girl at the front desk doesn't recognize me. Not even when I say my name.

"Oh," she says. "Is Mr. Davison expecting you?"

"Yes," I say, trying to maintain a smile.

"Take a seat, please."

Honestly, I feel like putting this girl in her place, but I need to be careful, so I bite my tongue and take a seat in the waiting room.

Where I wait. At least twenty minutes after my appointment time, a young man in an Italian suit comes for me. Wordlessly, like a drone, he leads me up to the third floor and into a corner office.

My agent, George Davison, is seated behind a huge desk. He stands at my entrance. We hug, a little awkwardly, and I step back.

"Well. Well," he says, indicating a chair for me.

I sit down. "You look good," I say.

He glances at me. I see the way he notices my weight gain. He sees the gray in my hair. I shift uncomfortably in my seat.

"Your call surprised me," he says.

"It hasn't been that long."

"Almost eight months. I left at least a dozen messages for you. None of which were returned."

"You know what happened, George. My best friend got cancer."

"And now?"

"She died." It's the first time I've said it out loud.

"I'm sorry."

I wipe my eyes. "Yes. Well. I'm ready to go back to work now. I'd like to start taping on Monday."

"Tell me you're joking."

I don't like the way George is looking at me. "I don't know what you mean, George."

"Your show, *The Girlfriend Hour,* was number one in its time spot last year. Advertisers were clamoring to buy time."

"I am aware of that, George. That's why I'm here."

"You walked off the set, Tully. How do you think the network felt about your exit? Or your employees, all of whom were suddenly unemployed?"

"I . . . I . . ."

"That's right. You didn't think about them, did you? The network wanted to sue you."

"I had no idea—"

"Unreturned phone calls," he snaps. "I fought like a tiger to protect you. They decided not to sue—thought it would be a public relations nightmare because of the cancer card. But they pulled the show, no reruns, and replaced you."

How do I not know this? "They replaced me? With whom?"

"The *Rachael Ray* show. It's kicking ass in the ratings."

"What are you saying? I own my show, George. I produce it."

"Too bad you don't own a network. And they have the right to air reruns exclusively for now. They aren't running them, either. That's how angry they are."

I can't even process this information. I have been successful forever. "You're saying *The Girlfriend Hour* is done?"

"No, Tully. I'm saying *you're* done. Who is going to hire someone who walks away without a conversation?"

Okay, so this is bad. "I'll produce another show. On spec."

"Have you spoken to your business manager recently?"

"No. Why?"

"Do you remember donating a substantial sum to Stand Up 2 Cancer four months ago?"

"It was a gift for Kate. And it was great publicity."

"A lovely gesture, yes. Except you have no money coming in, Tully. Not since you walked. You had to pay off a lot of employee contracts when you stopped taping the show. It cost you a small fortune. And face it—saving money was never your strong point."

"Are you saying I'm broke?"

"Broke? No. You're still more than comfortable. But I've spoken to Frank. You don't have enough to bankroll production. And no one is going to want to invest in you right now."

I feel that edgy panic coming back. "So I need a job."

George became my agent almost two decades ago, when I was low man on the totem pole at the network morning show. He'd brokered every major contract of my career and helped me make millions, most of which I'd pissed away on extravagant travel and gifts. "It won't be easy. You're kryptonite, Tul."

"You're saying I can only work at the local level?"

"I'm saying you'll be *lucky* to work at the local level."

The pity and compassion in his gaze is more than I can bear. "I've worked since I was fourteen, George, and I was on air before my twenty-second birthday. No one gave me anything." My voice breaks. "I put everything into my work. Everything. I don't have kids or a husband or a family. I have . . . work."

"You should have thought about that before," he says. The gentleness of his voice takes none of the sting out of his observation.

He's right. I know the journalism business and, worse, TV. I know "out of sight, out of mind." I know you can't do what I did and come back from it. So why didn't I know it in April?

I did. I chose Kate instead. "Find me a job, George. I'm begging you." I've never begged for anything . . . except my mother's love. And that was a waste of time.

I walk quickly through the hallowed white halls. I will solve this. I will. It is a setback, but I am a survivor and always have been.

I flag down my driver and get into the back of the Town Car, grateful for the dark, quiet interior. I have a pounding headache.

"Beverly Hills, ma'am?"

Johnny and the kids. I want to go to them now. I want to spill these troubles to Johnny and have him tell me I will be all right. But I can't do it. My shame is overwhelming, and pride stops me.

I put on my sunglasses. "LAX."

When the flight is over, I walk off the plane like a zombie.

On my show, I used to tell my viewers that you could have it all in life. I told them to ask for help, to take time for yourself, know what you want. Be selfish. Be selfless.

The truth is, I have no idea how to have it all. I've never had anything except my career. With Kate and the Ryans it was enough, but now I see the void in my life.

I am shaking as I pull up in front of my building. I open the door and go into the lobby. My heart is pounding. Someone touches me.

"Ms. Hart?" It is my doorman, Stanley. "Are you okay?"

I shake my head slightly to clear it. I feel . . . buzzed somehow.

"You're crying, Ms. Hart," my doorman says tenderly.

I look up at him. My mind is blank. My heart is racing so fast I feel sick and out of breath. What is wrong with me?

It feels suddenly as if a semi has driven into my chest. I reach for Stanley, chirp "Help" as I trip and crash to the cold concrete floor.

"Ms. Hart?"

I open my eyes and discover that I'm in a hospital bed.

There's a man in a white coat standing beside me. He is tall, with black hair that is too long. His face is sharply planed, his nose a little hawklike. His skin is the color of creamed coffee. He's part Hawaiian, maybe, or Asian and African American. I see tattoos, along his wrists—tribal ones.

"I'm Dr. Grant," he says. "You're in the ER. Do you remember what happened?"

I remember all of it; amnesia would be a gift. But I don't want to talk about it, especially not with this man, who looks at me as if I'm damaged goods. "I remember," I answer.

"That's good." He glances down at my chart. "Talullah."

He has no idea who I am. That depresses me. "So when can I get out of here? My heart is doing its job now." Which reminds me: I'm forty-six years old. How could I have had a heart attack?

He puts on a pair of reading glasses. "Talullah—"

"Tully. Only my brain-damaged mother calls me Talullah."

He looks at me. "Your mother is brain-damaged?"

"It was a joke."

He is not impressed by my humor. "I see. Well, you didn't have a heart attack. A panic attack often mirrors the symptoms—"

I sit up. "Oh, no. I did *not* have a panic attack."

"Did you take any drugs prior to the panic attack?"

"I did *not* have a panic attack. And of course I didn't take drugs."

He seems not to know what to make of me. "I've taken liberty of contacting a colleague for a consult—".

Before he can finish, the door opens and Dr. Harriet Bloom walks in. She is tall and thin; severe is the word that comes to mind, until you see the softness in her eyes. She is a prominent psychiatrist and has been a guest on my show many times.

"Hello, Tully. I'm glad I was on call." Harriet smiles at me and then looks at the doctor. "So, Desmond, how is our patient?"

"Not pleased to have had a panic attack."

"Call me a car service, Harriet," I say. "I'm getting out of here."

"She's a board certified psychiatrist," Desmond says to me. "She doesn't call car services."

Harriet gives me an apologetic smile. "Des doesn't watch TV."

I am not surprised. He has that too-cool-for-school look about him. I'll bet he was a hell-raiser at some point, but middle-aged men with ponytails and tattoos are not exactly my demographic.

"I've ordered an MRI. The paramedics say she hit the ground pretty hard." He looks down at me. "Be well, Ms. Hart." The smile he gives me is irritatingly kind, and then he leaves.

"You had a panic attack," Harriet says when we are alone.

"Says Dr. Granola."

"You had a panic attack," Harriet says, more gently. She moves closer to the bed. "You've been depressed, I take it?"

I want to lie. Instead, I nod. "I'm tired," I say. "I never sleep."

"I am going to prescribe Xanax for your anxiety," Harriet says. "And I think a few therapy sessions could help."

"The Tully Hart life tour? Thanks, but no, thanks. 'Why think about what hurts' has always been my motto."

"I know about depression," she says. "Depression is nothing to be ashamed of, Tully, and it's nothing to ignore. It can get worse."

I am too exhausted to question her, and honestly, I don't want to know what she has to say. The pain in my neck is increasing.

Harriet writes two prescriptions, handing them to me. Xanax for panic attacks and Ambien for sleeping.

All of my life I have avoided narcotics. When you grow up watching your mother get high and stumble around and puke, you see the unglamorous side of drugs. I look at Harriet. "My mom—"

"I know," Harriet says. It is one of the truths that come with life in the fishbowl of fame. Everyone knows my sad story. "Your mom has an issue with substance abuse. You're right to be careful, but just follow the prescription."

"It would be nice to sleep."

"How long have you been pretending not to be in pain?"

The question hits me hard. "My best friend died last month."

"Ah," Harriet says. Just that. Then she nods and says, "Come see me, Tully. Make an appointment. I can help."

After she leaves, the truth of my circumstance climbs into the bed with me and takes up too much room.

A nice woman takes me down for an MRI, and then a gorgeous young doctor tells me that at my age, falls like mine often cause neck trauma and that the pain will diminish. He writes me a prescription for pain pills and tells me that physical therapy will help.

By the time I am wheeled back into my room, I am beyond tired. The nurse gives me Ambien. For the first time in months, I sleep through the night.

THE Xanax helps. On it I feel less anxious. By the time Dr. Granola discharges me, I have come up with a plan.

At home I immediately start making phone calls. I've been in the business for decades; surely someone needs a prime-time anchor.

An old friend, Jane Rice, is my first call. "Of course," she says. "Come in and see me."

I almost laugh. That's how relieved I feel. George was wrong.

I prepare for my interview with care. I know how important first impressions are. I go to get my hair cut and colored.

"Oh, my," Charles—my longtime hairdresser—says when I climb into his chair. "Someone has been going native."

On the day of my meeting with Jane, I dress carefully—a black suit and pale lavender blouse. I have not been in the KING TV building in years, but I immediately feel comfortable. This is my world. At the reception desk I am greeted like a heroine.

An assistant leads me up the stairs to a small office on the second floor, where Jane Rice is standing by the window, waiting for me. "Tully," she says, striding forward, her hand outstretched.

We shake hands. "Hello, Jane. Thanks for seeing me."

I take the seat she has indicated.

She sits behind her desk and scoots in close, looking at me.

And I know. Just like that. "You can't hire me." I may have been a talk-show host for the last few years, but I am still a journalist. I read people well. That's one of my skills.

She sighs. "I tried. I guess you really burned some bridges."

"Nothing?" I say quietly, hoping my voice doesn't betray my desperation. "How about a reporting job, not on camera?"

"I'm sorry, Tully. You were a hero to me," she says. "I used to watch you on CBS and dream of being like you."

Were a hero. Suddenly I feel old. I get to my feet. "Thank you, Jane," I say quietly as I leave her office.

A Xanax calms me. I know I shouldn't take it, but I need it.

AT HOME I ignore my mounting panic and get to work. I sit down at my desk and start making calls to everyone I know in the business, especially anyone for whom I have ever done a favor.

By six o'clock I am exhausted and defeated. I have called all my contacts in the top ten markets and on the major cable channels, and my agent. No one has an offer for me.

My condo suddenly feels smaller than a shoe box, and I am starting to hyperventilate again. I dress in whatever I can find—jeans that are too tight and a tunic-length sweater.

It is past six thirty when I leave my building. The streets and sidewalks are full of commuters coming home from work. I don't even know where I'm going, until I see the outdoor seating area in front of the Virginia Inn restaurant and bar.

I sidle through the outdoor tables and go inside. The smoky dark interior is exactly what I need. I order a dirty martini at the bar.

"Talullah, right?"

I glance sideways. Dr. Granola is beside me. Just my luck to run into a man who has seen me at my worst. His long hair is unbound and falls forward. Cufflike tattoos cover his forearm. "Tully," I say. "What are you doing in a place like this?"

"Collecting for the widows and orphans fund."

It figures.

He laughs. "I'm having a drink. Same as you. How are you?"

I know what he is asking, and I don't like it. "Fine. Thanks." The bartender hands me my drink. "Later, Doc." I carry my drink to a table in the back of the bar. I slump onto the hard seat.

"May I join you?"

I look up. "Would it make an impact if I said no?"

"An impact? Of course." He sits down in the chair opposite me. "I thought about calling you," he says after an awkward silence.

"And?"

"I hadn't decided. Do you date much?"

It surprises me enough that I laugh. Apparently, he's a man who says what is on his mind. "No. Do you?"

"I'm a single doctor. I get set up more often than a set of bowling pins. You want me to tell you how it works these days?"

"Fine," I say. "How does the dating game work these days?"

"At our age we all have stories. They matter more than you'd think. Sharing them and hearing them is the start of it. The way I see it, there are two ways to go: Tell your story up front and let the chips fall where they may, or stretch them out over a bunch of dinners. So here's my plan. Why don't you tell me your story and I'll tell you mine, and we'll see if this is a date or if we're ships passing in the night."

"It's not a date. I bought my drink, and I didn't shave my legs."

He smiles and leans back in his chair.

There is something about him that intrigues me, a charm I didn't see the first time. And really, what better thing do I have to do? "You first."

"My story is simple. I was born in Maine, in a farmhouse, on land that had been in my family for generations. Janie Traynor was my neighbor down the road. We fell in love somewhere around eighth grade. We went to NYU, got married, and had a beautiful daughter." His smile starts to fall, but he hikes it back up. "Drunk driver," he says. "Janie and Emily died at the scene. Since then, it's just me. I moved to Seattle, thinking a new view would help. I'm forty-three, in case you were wondering. You seem like a woman who wants details." He leans forward. "Your turn."

"I'm forty-six—I'll lead with that, although I don't like to. Unfortunately, you can get my entire life story off of Wikipedia, so there's no point in my lying. I have a degree in journalism from the UW. I worked my way up the network news ranks and became famous. I started a successful talk show, *The Girlfriend Hour.* Work has been my life, but . . . a few months ago I learned that my best friend had been diagnosed with breast cancer. I walked away from my career to be with her. Apparently, this is an unforgivable breach, and I am now a cautionary tale instead of a shining star. I have never been married and have no children, and my only living relative—my mother—calls herself Cloud. That pretty much sums her up."

"You didn't say anything about love," he says quietly.

"No, I didn't. I picked my career."

"Hmmm. Your story is sadder than mine."

He's looking at me, as if I am somehow vulnerable. I toss back the rest of my martini and get to my feet. Whatever he is going to say next, I don't want to hear. "Thanks for the dating matrix," I say. "Bye, Dr. Granola."

"Desmond," I hear him say, but I am already heading for the door.

At home I take two Ambien and crawl into bed.

September 3, 2010, 8:10 a.m.

TIME slowed to a crawl in hospitals. Johnny sat in the uncomfortable chair, tucked in close to Tully's bed.

He pulled the cell phone out of his pocket and called Margie and Bud. They lived in Arizona now, near Margie's widowed sister.

Margie answered on the third ring. "Johnny!" she said, and he could hear the smile in her voice. "How good to hear from you."

"Hey, Margie."

There was a pause, then: "What's wrong?"

"It's Tully. She's been in a car accident. She's here in Sacred Heart." He paused. "It's bad, Margie. She's in a coma—"

"We'll be on the next flight out. I'll send Bud straight to Bainbridge to be with the boys when they get home from school."

"Thanks, Margie."

"And I'll get ahold of Dorothy. Does Marah know yet?"

He sighed at the thought of calling his daughter. "No. Honestly, I have no idea if I'll be able to get hold of her. Or if she'll care."

"Call her," Margie said gently.

Johnny said good-bye. The edge his daughter lived in these days was narrow; a whisper could push her off.

Beside him a machine beeped steadily, reminding him with every chirp that it was keeping Tully alive, giving her a chance.

A chance that Dr. Bevan reported was *not good*.

Reluctantly, he made another call.

Marah.

CHAPTER SIX

September 3, 2010, 10:17 a.m.

THE Dark Magick Bookstore in Portland, Oregon, prided itself on an ambience created by dim lighting, burning incense, and black curtains. Used books stood on dusty shelves; there were sections devoted to subjects like spiritual healing, Wiccan practices, Pagan rituals, and meditation. The only problem was shoplifters. In the muddy lighting, it was tough to keep track of the merchandise.

Marah Ryan had told her boss this on several occasions, but the woman refused to be bothered with worldly concerns.

So Marah let it go. It wasn't as if she really cared. This was just another stupid job in a long line of stupid jobs she'd had since high school. The only good thing about it was that no one hassled her for the way she looked. Oh, and usually the hours were good. But this week was inventory, so she had had to come in super early.

Now, as she stood in the voodoo section counting and recording black skull candles, she toyed with the idea of quitting, but the idea of looking for work *again,* of moving on, depressed her.

Then again, everything depressed her. She wasn't supposed to look to the future; she was supposed to accept the present. That was what the shrink told her years ago, the shark-eyed woman in a plaid suit who'd lied to Marah about almost everything. Dr. Harriet Bloom.

Time heals all wounds.

Give yourself permission to grieve.

Whatever you feel is okay.

Examination was the only solace. Instead of looking away from heartache, you needed to crawl inside of it, wear it like a warm coat on a cold day. There was *peace* in loss, beauty in death, freedom in regret. She had learned that the hard way.

She finished counting the skull candles. It was time for her break.

"I'm going to lunch, Star," she called out, and walked out of the store. As the door opened, a cat's screech sounded—the store's version of a welcome bell. She stepped out into the light. Literally.

A text notice blipped on her phone. She looked down at it. Her dad had called four times in the last two hours.

Marah shoved her phone in her back pocket and started walking.

After climbing the hill, she went to the sagging old brick building with the cracked windows and lopsided stoop. Dirty sheets hung as drapes in several of the windows. Home.

She climbed four flights of stairs. On the front door of the apartment, an eviction notice hung from a nail. She ripped it away and tossed it to the floor, then opened the door. The small studio apartment was thick with smoke and smelled of marijuana. Leif was strumming his guitar, and Sabrina was smoking dope. The boy who called himself Mouse was asleep on a mound of sleeping bags. Paxton sat in the La-Z-Boy chair she'd rescued from the trash.

As usual, he was dressed all in black—skinny jeans, unlaced antique-looking boots, and a ripped Nine Inch Nails T-shirt. The pallor of his skin was emphasized by shoulder-length blue-streaked black hair and whiskey-colored eyes. Paxton looked up at her, gave her a stoned smile. He offered her a piece of paper with scribbles written across it.

"My latest," he said.

She read the poem "It is us . . . we two . . . alone in the dark, waiting, knowing . . . love is our salvation and our demise . . . no one sees us save each other."

His romanticism spoke to her damaged soul. He was the only person she'd ever met who shared her pain, and he'd shown her how to transform it, to become one with it. Each of the people in this room knew about the fine lines a knife could leave behind.

Her cell phone bleated. She reached into her pocket and pulled out the small purple Motorola Razr she'd had for years.

"My dad's calling," she said. "Again."

Paxton stared up at her. "Hey, Sabrina, pass me the bong. The princess is getting a call."

Pax was right; she had been like a princess . . . until the queen's death. Then the whole fairy tale had collapsed. The bleating stopped. Immediately a text came in. It read EMERGENCY. CALL ME.

It wasn't like she could forget the last time she'd seen her dad. December 2009. She knew he missed her and that he regretted their last conversation. How many times had he left messages begging her to come home? But he'd never claimed that there was an emergency. He'd never tried to trick her into calling.

She went into a kitchen that smelled of mildew. There, she called her dad's cell. He answered quickly. "Marah, it's Dad," he said.

"Yeah. I got that."

He sighed. "Are you ready to tell me where you are yet? Dr. Bloom says this phase—"

"It's not a phase. It's my life. What's the emergency?"

"Tully has been in a car accident," he said. "It's bad. We don't know if she's going to make it."

Marah drew in a breath. *Not Tully, too.* "Oh, my God. . . ."

"Where are you? I could come get you—"

"Portland," she said quietly.

"Oregon? I'll get you a plane ticket." There was a long pause. "There are flights every hour. I can have an open ticket waiting for you at the Alaska Counter."

"Two tickets," she said.

He paused again. "Fine. Two. What flight—"

She snapped the phone shut without saying good-bye.

Paxton strolled into the kitchen. "What's up? You look freaked."

"My godmother might be dying," she said. "I need to see her."

"After what she did?"

"Come with me. Please? I can't go alone," she said. *"Please."*

His gaze narrowed; she felt sliced by the sharpness of it.

He tucked his long hair behind one silver-beaded ear. "It's a bad idea."

"We won't stay long. Please, Pax. I'll get money from my dad."

"Sure," he said finally. "I'll go."

MARAH felt people staring at her and Pax as they walked through the small Portland airport. She liked that so-called normal people were offended by Pax's Goth look.

Marah boarded the plane, took her seat, and connected her seat belt. She stared into the window, seeing a shadowy reflection of her pale face: heavily lined brown eyes, purplish lips, and spiked pink hair. A ping sounded through the aircraft, and they were off.

She closed her eyes. She didn't want to remember the past, not ever. For years she had buried all of it—the diagnosis, the cancer, the good-byes, the funeral, and the long gray months that had followed—but it was all clawing its way to the surface.

She saw herself as she'd been then: a fifteen-year-old girl on her way to school on an ordinary day.

"You don't think you're wearing that to school?" Mom said.

"There's nothing wrong with my clothes." Marah got up from the table. "This is fashion, Mom." She let her gaze sweep her mom's outfit—cheap flannel pajamas, tired hair, out-of-date slippers—and frowned. "You should trust me on this."

"Your outfit is perfect for Pioneer Square at midnight with your pimp. Unfortunately, it's a Tuesday morning and you're a sophomore in high school. Let me be more specific: That jean skirt is so short I can see your underwear—pink with flowers—and the T-shirt clearly came from the toddler department. You are not showing your stomach at school."

Marah stomped her foot in frustration. This was what she wanted Tyler to see her in today. He would think her cool instead of young.

Mom reached for the chair in front of her and clutched it as if she were an old, old lady. With a sigh she sat down. "I don't feel good enough to fight with you today, Marah. Please."

"So don't."

"Exactly. I'm not fighting. The cool thing is that I'm your mother. That makes me the CEO of this house. Or the warden. Point is, my house, my rules. Change your clothes or face the consequences. Consequences that begin with being late for school and losing your precious new phone and go downhill from there."

"You're trying to ruin my life."

"Ah, you have uncovered my master plan. Rats."

I don't feel good enough to fight with you today.

That had been state's evidence #1. Not that Marah had cared. She'd gone on doing what she did—working it at school, being popular, making sure that everyone who was anyone wanted to be her friend. Until that first family meeting.

"I had a doctor's appointment today," Mom said. "There's nothing for you to worry about, but I'm sick."

Marah could hear the boys talking, asking stupid questions, not getting it. Lucas—the mama's boy—ran up and hugged Mom.

Dad herded the boys out of the room. As he passed Marah, he looked down at her, and there were tears in his eyes, and she felt her knees give out. There was only one reason he would cry.

She looked at her mother—the pale skin, the dark circles under her eyes. It was as if her mom had been dunked in bleach and come out as this colorless version of herself. Sick. "It's cancer, isn't it?"

"Yes."

Marah was shaking so hard she clasped her hands together. How was it she hadn't known this was possible, that your whole life could tilt sideways in a second? "You'll be fine. Right?"

"I'm going to the best doctors," Mom said. "I'll beat this thing."

Marah released her breath. "Okay, then," she said at last, feeling that terrible tightness in her chest ease up. Her mom never lied.

But she had. She'd lied and she'd died, and without her Marah's life had lost its shape.

The horrible "celebration of Mom's life" had been unbearable. October of 2006. The night of the funeral. She'd been sitting at the top of the stairs, staring down at a roomful of people in black. She knew she should go and mingle, but she couldn't stand all those pictures of her mom. It had been only two days, and already the vibrant woman in the photos was fading from memory. All Marah could picture in her mind was the colorless, dying version of her.

The doorbell rang. Her friends came through the front door, their makeup smeared by tears, their eyes wide with sorrow.

Marah had never needed them more. Ashley and Coral and Lindsey rushed up the stairs and hugged her, all of them at once, and the tears she'd been holding back burst out.

"We don't know what to say," Coral said.

"Your mom was way cool," Ashley said, and Lindsey nodded.

Marah wiped her eyes. "I wish I'd told her that."

"She totally, like, *knows*," Ash said.

"The Pavilion is showing a midnighter of *Nightmare Before Christmas*. I think we should go," Lindsey said.

Marah almost said, *My Mom would never let me.* At the thought, her eyes glazed with tears and she felt unsteady. "Let's go," she said, leading them down the stairs and through the living room. As she reached for the front door, she would have sworn she heard her mother's voice. *Come back here, young lady. You four are not going to a midnight show. Nothing good happens on this island after eleven.*

"Do you have to, like, tell your dad we're going?" Lindsey asked.

"No," Marah said softly. Her dad hadn't come looking for her once tonight, and Tully cried every time she looked at her. "No one will even notice I'm gone."

THE next morning, her dad decided they needed a vacation. Why he thought sand and surf would help, Marah had no idea. She tried to talk him out of it, but she had no vote in the things that mattered. So she went on the stupid vacation.

She hated paradise. The sunshine pissed her off, and seeing her dad's sad face made her want to cry. He tried to make contact with her, but the pain in his eyes just made it worse. She called her friends ten times a day until the vacation from hell was finally over.

When they had landed back in Seattle, Marah felt herself relaxing. She'd thought the worst was over. How wrong she'd been.

An hour later all hell had broken loose. They'd come home to find music blaring, empty food containers on the kitchen counter, and Tully in the closet with Mom's clothes all boxed up. Dad had blown a gasket and said terrible things to Tully and made her cry, but nothing he said was as bad as: "We're moving."

IN NOVEMBER of 2006, less than a month after Mom's funeral, they moved to California. The two weeks before their departure were terrible. Horrible. Marah stopped eating, stopped sleeping. All she cared about was talking to her friends.

Marah couldn't stomach the idea of locking up their home and driving away. The only slightly good news was that they weren't selling it. Someday, Dad had promised, they'd return. The big things— furniture, art, rugs—they left behind. When the day finally came to move, she'd sobbed and told her dad she hated him.

On the two-day drive to Los Angeles, Marah said nothing. Not one word. She put her headphones on and listened to music, texting one message after another to her friends.

They left green-and-blue Washington and drove south. By central California everything was brown. Stubby brown hills huddled beneath a bright sun. There wasn't a decent tree for miles. Los Angeles was worse: flat and endless. By the time they pulled up to the house Dad had rented in Beverly Hills, Marah had a headache.

"Wow," Lucas said.

"What do you think, Marah?" Dad said, turning to look at her.

It was a house that had obviously been remodeled sometime recently—an old seventies rambler that had been punched up to look modern and boxy. The yard out front was carefully manicured.

This wasn't a home. Not for the Ryans, anyway. Inside, everything was sleek and cold, with floor-to-ceiling windows and a stainless-steel kitchen and gray stone floors. The furniture was defiantly modern, with sharp edges and chrome accents.

She looked at her Dad. "Mom would have hated this."

ON HER first day at Beverly Hills High School, Marah knew that she would never fit in here. The kids were like beings from another planet. The student parking lot was filled with Porsches and BMWs. The girls were gorgeous, with expertly colored hair and purses that cost more than some cars. They clung together in well-dressed pods. No one even said hi to Marah.

For the whole day, she moved through her classes on autopilot. None of her teachers called on her or asked her questions. She sat alone at lunch. In fifth period she took a seat in the back and put her head down while the other students took a test. The loneliness she felt was epic, overwhelming. She kept thinking how much she needed her friends—and her mom—to talk to.

"Marah?"

The teacher—Ms. Appleby—had stopped at her desk. "Come see me if you need help getting up to speed. We all know how hard it is, with your mom . . ."

"Dead," Marah said flatly. If adults were going to talk to her, they might as well say the word. Ms. Appleby moved away fast.

Marah smiled grimly. It wasn't much of a defense, having to say the word, but at least it was effective.

The bell rang. The other kids jumped up and started talking. Marah didn't make eye contact with any of them. She was dressed wrong; she'd known it when she stepped onto the bus. This wasn't a school where Macy's jeans and a fitted blouse would cut it.

She skipped last period and left early. Maybe *that* would get her dad's attention. She walked all the way home, but it didn't help to be in this cold, echoey house. The boys were with Irena—the older woman Dad had hired to be a part-time nanny—and Dad was still at work. She walked through the big, impersonal house, but it wasn't until she got to her room that her resolve started to crack.

She reached for the small Shrek music box she'd packed so carefully. She'd gotten it from Tully on her twelfth birthday.

She turned the key to wind it and lifted the hinged lid. Inside was a collection of her favorite things—an agate from Kalaloch Beach, an old plastic dinosaur, a Frodo action figure, the garnet earrings Tully had bought her for her thirteenth birthday, and the pink Space Needle pocketknife she'd gotten at the Seattle Center.

She opened the knife. She pressed the blade against her left palm. A tingle moved through her. A *feeling*. She moved the blade and accidentally cut a perfect line in the middle of her hand. Blood followed the cut in a beaded line. The color of it mesmerized her.

She couldn't look away. This *hurt*, and she welcomed the honesty of that, the clarity. She watched her own blood slide down the side of her hand and plop onto her black shoe.

For the first time in months, she felt better.

IN THE weeks that followed, Marah lost weight and marked her grief in small red slices on the inside of her upper arm and at the tops of her thighs. Every time she felt overwhelmed or lost or mad at God, she cut herself. She knew she was doing something bad and sick, but she couldn't stop. Cutting allowed her to carry on.

On Christmas morning Marah woke early. Her first dreamy thought was, *It's Christmas, Mom,* and then she remembered.

Downstairs she heard the sounds of her family coming together. Footsteps thudded on the stairs; doors banged shut. Her brothers screamed for her. They were probably already running around like puppies on crack. But Mom wasn't here.

She got out of bed and went to her dresser, to the pretty Shrek box. Her hands were shaking as she opened it. There it was, her knife. She eased it open. She stuck the blade deep into the pad of her fingertip. She felt her skin slice open. Blood oozed up. The pressure that had been building in her chest disappeared.

Her cell phone rang. She found it by her bed. "Hello?"

"Hey, Marah. It's Tully. I wanted to call you before your big present-opening day started. I know how much time that takes your household, with all that opening-one-at-a-time."

Marah grabbed a sock and wrapped it around her finger.

"What's the matter?" Tully said.

"Nothing. You know . . . Christmas without her."

"Yeah. Have you made any friends yet?" Tully asked.

Marah hated this question. She didn't know how to answer. She hadn't made any friends at BHHS, but she hadn't really tried to, either.

"You don't need tons of friends, Marah. You just need one."

"TullyandKate," she said dully. The mythic friendship story.

"I'm here for you. You know that, right?"

"So help me. Tell me how to be happy."

Tully sighed. "Your mom would be better at a time like this. She believed in happy endings and life getting better. Me, I pretty much live in the life-blows-and-then-you-die school of thought."

"I don't like it here," Marah said quietly. "I miss her every day."

"Me, too."

After that, there was nothing to say. Gone was gone.

"I love you, Marah."

"What are you doing for Christmas?"

Marah heard her godmother draw in a breath. "Oh, you know."

"It's all changed," Marah said.

"Yeah," Tully said. "It's all changed, and I hate it. Especially on days like today."

That was what Marah loved about her godmother. Tully was the only one who never lied and told her it would all get better.

THE FIRST FEW MONTHS AT BEVERLY Hills High were a nightmare. Marah's grades dropped. The curriculum was difficult, but that wasn't the problem. She couldn't concentrate, and she didn't care.

She looked in her father's eyes and saw how deeply she'd disappointed him. *How can I help you?* he'd asked quietly. Before, she'd thought that was what she was waiting for—that offer—but when he said it, she felt even worse. She didn't want help. She just wanted to disappear. And she knew how to do it now. Make no waves.

After that, Marah pretended to be fine. As long as she brought her grades up and smiled at dinner, her dad looked right through her. He was too busy working. All she had to do was pretend she was on some sports team and she could be gone as much as she wanted, and no one ever asked to come to one of her games or asked her if she was okay.

By senior year she had it down to a science: She woke on time every morning. Rarely did she bother showering or washing her hair. It was too exhausting. And it wasn't like it mattered if she were clean or dirty. She'd given up hope of making friends.

Finally, it was June of 2008. Her graduation from Beverly Hills High. Everyone was downstairs, waiting for her. Grandma and Grandpa and Tully had flown in for the Big Event.

As she reached for her graduation robe, Marah felt a cold dread. She put on the robe and went to the mirror. She was pale and thin. How was it that none of the people who supposedly loved her had noticed how bad she looked? Mom would have seen how unhappy she was. That was one of the truths Marah had learned: No one knew you as well as your mom. She would give anything for one of the oh-no-you-don't-young-lady looks she used to hate.

Her dad yelled up from downstairs: "Time to go, Marah."

She walked to her dresser and stared longingly at the Shrek music box. She opened the lid. Slowly she took the knife and pulled up her sleeve and made a slice on the inside of her forearm, where it wouldn't be seen. But she cut too deep. She knew it instantly.

Blood rushed down her arm. She needed help. And not just to stop the bleeding. She was out of control somehow.

She went downstairs. In the living room blood splattered the stone floor at her feet.

"I need help," Marah said quietly.

Tully was the first to respond. She swooped forward and grabbed Marah's other wrist and dragged her into the bathroom. Dad rushed in behind them as Tully burrowed through drawers.

"What the hell happened?" her dad yelled.

"Bandages," Tully snapped, kneeling beside Marah. *"Now!"*

Dad left and was back in no time with gauze and adhesive. He stood back, looking confused and angry while Tully applied pressure to stop the bleeding and then bandaged the wound. "There," she said. "But I think she'll need stitches." Tully stepped back, allowed Dad to move in.

"Marah?" he said. "What happened?"

She was too ashamed to answer.

Tully said, "You asked for help. You mean therapy, don't you?"

Marah stared up into her godmother's warm brown gaze. "Yes."

"I don't understand," Dad said, looking from Tully to Marah.

"She did it on purpose," Tully said.

Marah could see how confused her father was. It made no sense to him that cutting herself *helped*. "How could I not know that you were hurting yourself?"

"I know someone who can help her," Tully said. "In Seattle. Remember Dr. Harriet Bloom? From my show? I bet I could get Marah in to see her on Monday."

"Seattle," Marah said. It was a lifeline being thrown to her. How often had she dreamed of going back to see her friends? But now she found that she didn't care. It was more proof that she was sick.

Dad shook his head. "I don't know. . . ."

"She did it down here, Johnny, in Los Angeles," Tully said. "Today of all days. I may not be Freud, but I can tell you this is a cry for help. Let me help her."

"You?" he said sharply.

"You're still angry with me? No, don't answer that. I don't care. I am not going to back down this time, Johnny Ryan. I promised Katie

I would take care of Marah. You obviously haven't done a great job."

"Tully." The warning in his voice was unmistakable.

"Let me take her home and get her in to see Harriet on Monday, or Tuesday at the latest. Then we can decide what comes next."

Dad looked at Marah. "Do you want to go see Dr. Bloom?"

Marah didn't care about Dr. Bloom. She didn't want anything except to be left alone. And to leave Los Angeles. "Yeah," she said.

Dad turned to Tully. "I'll come up as soon as I can."

Tully nodded.

Dad didn't look convinced. He stood up and faced Tully. "I can trust you to take care of her for a few days?"

"I'll be like a mama hen sitting on precious eggs."

"I will want a full report."

Tully nodded. "You'll have one."

CHAPTER SEVEN

MARAH didn't go to her high school graduation after all, and it was a relief. Instead, she boarded a plane with Tully and flew back to Seattle. True to her word, Tully got Marah a two-o'clock appointment with Dr. Harriet Bloom on the following Monday. Today.

Marah didn't want to get out of bed. Still, she did what was expected of her. She took a shower and washed her hair. When she put on her 7 for All Mankind jeans, she was horrified at how much weight she'd lost. She chose a heavy sweatshirt to give her slight frame a little bulk and to hide the scars on her upper arms. Then she left the bedroom and shut the door with a little click.

In no time Tully was beside her, holding her by the arm, guiding her out of the condominium. As they walked uptown, Tully talked.

Marah tried to listen, but her heart was beating so fast it deafened her to anything else. She didn't want to sit with some stranger and talk about cutting herself.

"Here we are," Tully said at last, and Marah found herself standing in front of a tall glass building. She followed Tully into the elevator and up to the doctor's office, where a serious young woman offered them seats. Marah perched on an overstuffed blue chair.

Tully sat down beside her and took her hand. "Marah?"

It was a waste of time to ignore Tully. "Uh-huh?"

"There's nothing wrong with how you feel," Tully said gently. "Sometimes missing her hurts more than I can stand, too."

No one *ever* said stuff like this anymore. "What do you do when it, you know, hurts to remember?"

"If I told you, your mom would come down from heaven and kick my ass. I'm supposed to be the responsible adult here."

"Fine," Marah said. "Don't tell me how you handle it."

Tully didn't respond for a minute. Finally, she said, "I started having panic attacks after her death, so I take Xanax. And I can't sleep anymore. And sometimes I drink too much. What do you do?"

"I cut myself," Marah said. It felt surprisingly good to admit.

"We are quite a pair," Tully said with a wan smile.

Behind them a door opened. "You must be Marah Ryan. I'm Dr. Harriet Bloom," the woman said, extending a hand.

Marah stood up reluctantly. Now she really wanted to bolt. "Hi."

Tully got to her feet. "Hi, Harriet. Thanks for agreeing to help us on such short notice. I know you had to change your schedule. You'll need some background information. I'll come in for—"

"No," the doctor said.

Tully looked nonplussed. "But—"

"This is between Marah and me. She's in good hands. I promise."

Marah didn't think so. Still, she followed the doctor into her sleek office. Windows looked out over the Sound. A desk cut the room in half; behind it was a black leather chair. Two chairs sat facing the desk, and a black sofa was pushed against the back wall.

"I suppose you want me to lie down," Marah said.

Dr. Bloom sat behind her desk. "You may sit wherever you like."

Marah flopped into the chair and stared at the plant in the corner, counting its leaves. One . . . two . . . three . . .

"Do you think there's something you'd like to talk about?" the doctor asked after at least ten minutes had passed.

Marah shrugged. "Not really." Fifty-two . . . fifty-three . . .

"How do you know Tully?"

"She's a friend of—"

"Your mother's?"

The way she said it was all wrong, clinical; the way you'd ask about a car or a vacuum, but still Marah felt her stomach tightening.

"She's gone, right?"

Marah paused. "She's in my dad's closet, actually."

"Excuse me?"

Marah smiled. Score one for the home team. "We cremated her and put her in this rosewood box. When Tully wanted to scatter her ashes, Dad wasn't ready, and when Dad was ready, Tully wasn't. So Mom's in the closet behind my dad's sweaters."

"What about when you were ready?"

Marah blinked. "What do you mean?"

"When would you like to scatter your mother's ashes?"

"No one's asked me that."

"Why do you think that is?"

Marah shrugged. She didn't like where this was going.

"Why do you think you're here, Marah?" the doctor said.

"You know why."

"I know what you did to yourself. The cutting. I know it makes you feel better when you do it."

Marah glanced at Dr. Bloom, who sat perfectly still. "But when you're done and your razor blade or knife is full of dried blood, I bet you feel worse. Ashamed, maybe, or afraid."

Marah rolled her eyes.

"Well," Dr. Bloom said. "That's all the time we have for today."

Marah shot to her feet and turned for the door. Dr. Bloom said, "I have a teen grief group meeting that might help you, Marah. Would you like to join us? It's Wednesday night."

"Whatever." Marah opened the office door.

Tully lurched to her feet. "How was it?"

Marah glanced away from Tully and saw a young man dressed in skintight, torn black jeans that disappeared into scuffed black boots with the laces falling slack. He was thin and wearing a black T-shirt that read BITE ME beneath a smoke-colored jacket. His shoulder-length hair was black, tinged here and there in streaks of magenta and green. When he looked up, Marah saw that his eyes were strange, almost golden, and heavy black guyliner accentuated the color. His skin was pale. Like maybe he was sick.

Dr. Bloom came up beside Marah. "Paxton, perhaps you'd tell Marah that our therapy group isn't such a bad little gathering."

The young man—Paxton—stood up and moved toward Marah with the kind of grace that seemed staged.

"Tully?" Dr. Bloom said. "May I speak to you for a moment?"

Marah was aware of the two older women moving away from her, whispering to each other.

"You're afraid of me," the boy said when he was close to her.

"You think I'm scared of a little black clothing?"

"Nice girls like you should stay in suburbia where it's safe. The group isn't for you."

"You don't know anything about me. But maybe you should stop playing in your mom's makeup."

His laugh surprised her. "Fire. I like that."

"Hey, Marah," Tully said. "It's time to go." She strode across the waiting room, took Marah's arm, and led her out of the room.

ALL the way home, Tully kept asking Marah if she wanted to go to Bainbridge Island to see her friends, and Marah wanted to say yes, but she didn't belong there anymore. In the year and a half of her absence, the old friendships had degraded. She had nothing in common with those girls anymore.

Tully led Marah into the elegant condo. "So. How was it?"

Marah shrugged.

Tully sat on the sofa. "Don't shut me out, Marah. I want to help."

She was tired of disappointing people. "I know." She sat down.

"I should have made your dad put you in counseling when Kate died. But we fell apart, your dad and me. I asked about you, though, and talked to you every week. You never said a thing."

"Why should you have known?"

"I know about abandonment and grief. I know about shutting down. When my gran died, I barely let myself grieve. When my mom left me—every time—I told myself it didn't hurt."

"And with Mom's death?"

"It's been harder. I'm not bouncing back well."

"Yeah. Me, either."

"Dr. Bloom thinks you should attend that teen grief therapy session Wednesday night."

"Yeah. Like that will help."

She saw how her answer wounded Tully. Marah sighed. She had too much of her own pain. She couldn't bear Tully's, too.

"Fine," Marah said. "I'll go."

Tully got up and pulled Marah into a hug.

She could handle a few therapy sessions if it would get everyone off her back. In September she'd be a college freshman at the UW and she could live however she wanted. "Thanks," she said tightly. "Now I'm going to lie down. I'm tired."

"I'll call your dad and tell him how it went. He'll be here on Thursday to meet Dr. Bloom after your next appointment."

Marah nodded and headed toward the guest bedroom. She couldn't believe she'd agreed to go to a teen grief therapy meeting.

She didn't mean to go to the closet, didn't want to, but this buzzing in her blood was making her crazy. She found the knife. She pushed her sleeve up. Dozens of scar lines crisscrossed her skin.

She touched the sharp tip of the blade to her skin, then cut. She watched her blood well and fall, like tears, into her waiting palm. Every bad emotion filled those drops of blood and fell away, left her body. *I am the only one who can hurt me. Only me.*

IN THE morning she put on a robe and wandered out of her room.

She found Tully asleep on the sofa. An empty wineglass lay on its side on the table. There was a prescription pill container near it.

"Tully?"

Tully sat up slowly. "Oh. Marah." She rubbed her eyes and shook her head as if to clear it. "What time is it?" Her speech was slow.

"Almost ten."

"Ten! Get dressed. I have a surprise planned for you."

"I don't want to be surprised."

"Of course you do. Go. Take a shower."

Marah took a shower and put on a pair of baggy jeans and an oversized T-shirt. Without bothering to dry her hair, she pulled it back in a ponytail and went out into the kitchen.

Tully was already there, dressed in a blue suit that was at least a size too small. She was taking a pill and washing it down with coffee when Marah came up beside her.

Marah eyed her. "What are you taking?"

"The pill? It's a vitamin. At my age you can't forget vitamins."

The doorbell rang. Marah was instantly suspicious.

"Come on," Tully said, herding her toward the door. "Open it."

Marah opened the door. Ashley, Lindsey, and Coral stood there. When they saw Marah, they pulled her into a group hug.

Marah felt as if she were experiencing it all from some great distance. Before she knew it, she was being swept out of the condo. They were all talking to her at once as they climbed into Coral's Honda and drove down to the ferry terminal, where a boat was waiting. They drove right on and parked.

"It's *so* cool that you're back," Lindsey said.

"Yeah. We, like, couldn't believe when Tully called. Were you going to surprise us?" Ashley asked.

"Of course she was," Coral said from the driver's seat, and launched into a long story about Tyler Britt dating some girl and getting a minor-in-possession ticket.

Marah kept a smile on her face the whole time, but what she was thinking was, *I can hardly remember my crush on Tyler Britt.*

Later, when they were out at Lytle Beach drinking Cokes and noshing on Doritos, Marah didn't know what to say. She felt oddly separate. Coral was talking about college and how glad she was that she and Ashley were going to be roommates at Western Washington University, and Lindsey was whining that she didn't want to go off to Santa Clara alone.

"Where are you going?" Coral asked Marah.

"UW," Marah said. She didn't belong here with these girls who giggled and dreamed of falling in love and starting college and thought their moms were too strict. She wasn't like them anymore.

And by the time their day was over, the awkward silences in the car attested to their understanding of this truth. They walked her up to the condo and gathered around her at the door.

"We missed you," Coral said quietly. It sounded like good-bye.

"I missed you, too," Marah said, and it was true.

When they left, Marah walked back into Tully's condo. She found Tully in the kitchen, putting dishes away.

"How was it?"

Marah heard something in Tully's voice, a slurring of words that didn't quite make sense. If she didn't know better, she'd think Tully had had a few drinks, but it was way early for that.

And really, Marah didn't care. She just wanted to climb into bed and pull the covers up over her head and go to sleep. "It was great," she said dully. "Better than great. I'm tired, though, so I'm going to take a nap." She headed for her room.

TELL me that's not what you're wearing," Tully said when Marah walked into the living room on Wednesday night wearing torn low-rise flared jeans and an oversized gray sweatshirt.

"Huh? It's teen grief therapy," Marah said. "Let's face it, if you're invited, fashion isn't your biggest problem."

Tully got to her feet and crossed the room to stand in front of Marah. "I have a lot of really great personality traits. I have a few flaws, I'll admit—gaping holes in the fabric—but mostly I am an amazing person. I know how hard it is to be human. The point is, I love you, and I'm not your mom or dad. It's not my job to see that you grow up to be a successful, well-adjusted adult. My job is to tell you stories about your mom when you're ready and to love you no matter what. I'm supposed to say what your mother would say—when I can figure out what that would be. This time it's easy." She smiled tenderly. "You're hiding, baby girl. Behind dirty hair and baggy clothes. But I see you, and it's time to come back to us."

Tully didn't give Marah time to answer. She went into her walk-in closet and came back with a white crinkly fitted blouse with a deep V-neck and lace around the collar. "You're wearing this."

Marah yanked the blouse from Tully and went into the bathroom. She didn't want Tully to see her scars. When she walked over to the mirror, Marah barely recognized herself. Her thinness was accentuated by the fitted blouse; it made her look fragile and feminine. The jeans hugged her slim hips. She felt strangely nervous as she walked back into the living room. She felt exposed.

Tully pulled the elastic band from Marah's long black hair, let it fall free. "You are gorgeous. Every boy in the meeting will be driven crazy by you. Not that we care what therapy boys think."

"I'm a therapy girl," she said quietly. "Crazy."

"You're sad, not crazy. Sad makes sense. Come on."

Marah followed Tully down to the lobby. Together they walked down First Street to the oldest part of the city. Pioneer Square. Tully came to a stop in front of a squat brick building. "Do you want me to walk you inside?"

"No. That guy with the eyeliner already thinks I'm Miss Suburbia. All I need is a chaperone."

"The guy from the waiting room? Edward Scissorhands?"

"I'm just saying it would be embarrassing."

"I get it. Okay." Tully turned to her. "You know how to get back to my place? It's eight blocks up First."

Marah nodded. Her mother would never have let her be alone in this part of town after dark.

She followed the stairs down into a musty basement. At the closed door, upon which had been tacked a notice for TEEN GRIEF GROUP, she paused. She opened the door and went inside.

It was a big room, with a long table at one end that held a coffeemaker, cups, and an array of baked treats. Seven metal chairs formed a circle in the center of the room. There were already four kids here. Marah looked at a large pimply girl with greasy hair. Beside her was a girl so thin that if she turned sideways, she'd vanish. Next to her sat a girl dressed in black, with magenta-colored hair. She slouched away from a plump boy in glasses beside her.

Dr. Bloom sat in the circle, too, wearing fitted navy pants and a gray turtleneck. As neutral as Switzerland. Marah wasn't fooled: There was nothing casual about the way Dr. Bloom looked at her.

"We're glad you could join us, Marah," Dr. Bloom said.

Marah took a seat by the heavy girl. She had barely taken her place when the door creaked open and Paxton walked in. As before, he was dressed like a vampire, in black jeans and unlaced boots and a poorly fitted black T-shirt. A tattoo of words snaked over the ridge of his collarbone and curled up his throat. Marah looked away quickly.

He sat across from Marah, next to the girl with the magenta hair. Marah waited to the count of fifty to look at him again.

He was staring at her, smiling like he thought she was hot for him. She rolled her eyes and looked away.

"Well, it's seven o'clock, so we can get started," Dr. Bloom said. "As you can see, we have a new member, Marah. Who would like to make the introductions?"

Finally, Magenta Hair said, "I'm Ricki. Dead mom. The fat chick's Denise. Her grandma has Parkinsons. Todd hasn't spoken in four months, so we don't know what his problem is. Elisa stopped eating when her dad killed himself. And Pax is here by court order. Dead sister." She looked at Marah. "What's your story?"

Marah felt everyone looking at her. "I . . . I . . ."

"Cutter," Pax said quietly. "But why?"

Marah looked up sharply.

"Paxton," Dr. Bloom said. "This is a *support* group. Life is hard. Each of you has experienced a profound loss, and you know how hard it can be to keep going."

"My mother died," Marah said evenly.

"Would you like to talk about her?" Dr. Bloom asked gently.

Marah couldn't look away from Pax's golden gaze. "No."

"Who would?" he said quietly.

"How about you, Paxton?" Dr. Bloom said. "Do you have something you'd like to share with the group?"

"Never to suffer would never to have been blessed," he said.

Dr. Bloom said, "We've talked about hiding behind other people's words. You're twenty-two. It's time to find your own voice."

"You don't want to hear what I have to say," Paxton said.

Court order. Why would the court order grief therapy?

"On the contrary, Paxton," Dr. Bloom said. "You've been coming here for months and you haven't talked about your sister once."

"And I won't," he said. "The court can order me to come, but it can't make me talk."

Dr. Bloom turned slightly toward Stick Girl. "Elisa, perhaps you'd like to tell us more about how eating went this week. . . ."

An hour later, as if by some secret alarm, the kids lurched out of their seats and rushed from the room. By the time Marah retrieved her purse and stood up, only Dr. Bloom was still there.

"I hope that wasn't too painful," the doctor said, walking over to her. "Beginnings can be difficult."

"No. Fine. I mean, yes. Thanks. It was great."

Outside, Pioneer Square was full of tourists and locals. Paxton appeared out of the darkness. "You're waiting for me," he said.

She laughed. "Yeah, because guys in makeup really rev my engines." She turned to face him. "You were waiting for me. Why?"

"You'll have to come with me to find out." He held out his hand.

She saw his pale hand and long fingers . . . and the angry red scars that ran like an equal sign across his wrist. Cut marks.

"You're scared," he said. "You're a good girl from the suburbs."

"I used to be." She felt the tightness in her chest ease up. Maybe she could become a different version of herself.

"Marah? Paxton?" Dr. Bloom walked up to them. Marah felt a strange sadness, as if a beautiful opportunity had just been lost. She smiled at the doctor. When she turned back, Paxton was gone.

"Be careful," Dr. Bloom said, following Marah's gaze across the street where Paxton stood in the shadows between two buildings.

"Is he dangerous?"

Dr. Bloom said, "I can't answer that, Marah. But I would ask this: Are you looking at him *because* you think he's dangerous? That can be risky for a girl in a vulnerable situation."

"I'm not looking at him at all," Marah said.

"No," Dr. Bloom said. "Of course you're not."

At that, Marah headed up the dark street for home.

THE next day, her dad was set to arrive. Marah couldn't stop pacing. Finally he was there, giving Marah an uncertain smile.

"Hey, Dad." She should have been happy to see him, but just seeing him made her think of her mom and all that had been lost.

"How are you?" he said, pulling her into an awkward hug.

What should she say? He wanted a lie. *I'm fine.*

"I've found someone in Los Angeles, a doctor who specializes in teens who are in trouble," Dad said. "He can see you on Monday."

Marah smiled shakily. One thing she knew now for sure: She couldn't go back to Los Angeles with him.

"I like Dr. Bloom," she said. "And the group is kind of lame, but I don't mind."

Dad frowned. "But she's in Seattle. This doctor in L.A.—"

"I want to stay here for the summer, Dad. Live with Tully. I like Dr. Bloom." She turned to Tully, who looked thunderstruck. "Can I live here for the summer?"

"Are you kidding me?" Dad said. "She's no chaperone."

Marah dug her heels in. Suddenly she was certain: This was what she wanted. "I'll be starting the UW in September anyway. This way, I'll be able to make new friends and see my old ones. Please?"

She saw the war going on within him—he wasn't ready to let her go, but he saw that she wanted this. Maybe, even, that she needed it.

"This is a bad idea," he said to Tully. "You can't even keep plants alive. And you know nothing about kids."

"She's an adult," Tully said.

"Please, Dad? *Please?*"

He sighed. It was done. He looked at her. "I've given my notice in

L.A. We'll be moving back here in September. It was going to be a surprise. We want to be here when you're at the UW."

"That's great," she said, not really caring.

He looked at Tully. "You better take good care of her, Tully."

In Dr. Bloom's office, Marah slouched in the chair. She'd been staring at the ficus plant while Dr. Bloom scribbled something.

She asked, "If you aren't going to say anything, why am I here?"

"Yours is the voice that matters, Marah. And you know you're welcome to leave."

"Tully and my dad are out there."

"And you don't want them to know you aren't committed to therapy. Why is that? You're depressed, Marah, and you're cutting yourself. It's not a bad idea for you to consider why you do it."

Marah looked up.

Dr. Bloom's gaze was steady. "I'd really like to help you, if you'll let me." She paused. "Do you want to be happy again?"

Marah wanted it so badly she felt sick. She thought about the network of scars on her thighs and arms and the way pain fascinated her. *Don't give up, baby girl.*

"Yeah," she said, and felt a tightening of anxiety in her stomach.

"That's a start," Dr. Bloom said. "And now our time is up."

Marah got to her feet and followed Dr. Bloom out of the office. In the waiting room, her dad was sitting on the sofa by Tully. At her entrance he got to his feet.

Dr. Bloom said: "Can we talk, Mr. Ryan? In my office?"

Tully said, "I'm coming in, too," and in a blink they were gone and Marah was alone in the waiting room. She looked back at the closed door. What was the doctor telling them?

"Well, well, well."

She turned slowly. Paxton leaned against the wall with his arms crossed. He was dressed all in black again.

"I've been thinking about you." He touched the back of her hand. "Do you know how to have fun, Suburb Girl?"

"Like what, Animal Sacrifice?"

The smile he gave her was slow and seductive. No one had ever stared at her so intently. "Meet me tomorrow night at midnight."

"No."

"Curfew, huh. Poor little rich girl. Okay, then. But I'll wait for you at the pergola in Pioneer Square."

She heard the door opening behind her. Her dad was saying, "Thank you, Dr. Bloom."

Marah pulled away from Paxton. He laughed quietly.

"Marah," Dad said sharply. She knew what he was seeing: his once perfect daughter talking to a young man wearing makeup and chains. "Let's go," Dad said.

CHAPTER EIGHT

THAT night, Marah lay in bed, staring at the ceiling. She had finally convinced her father to let her stay with Tully for the summer, but he had laid down a matrix of rules. Just thinking about it gave Marah a headache. She couldn't help being relieved when he left.

The next day, she and Tully acted like tourists, enjoying the beautiful summer day along the waterfront. But when night fell and Marah went to bed, she found herself thinking about Paxton.

Meet me . . . midnight . . . I'll wait for you at the pergola.

She couldn't seem to banish that promise from her mind. In his presence she felt challenged somehow, *seen;* alive.

It was crazy. *He* was crazy. Mom would hate him.

Her digital alarm clock said 11:42.

Marah sat up. She was going to meet him. When the decision settled in place, she knew it had been there all along. She eased out of bed and changed back into her clothes. She put on makeup for the first time in forever. Then she crept out of her room.

Tully's bedroom door was closed; there was a light underneath.

She dashed off a note—"Meeting Paxton in Pioneer Square"—

and put it under her pillow. Just in case the police needed somewhere to start looking. In no time she was outside walking on the sidewalk.

Pioneer Square was busy, even this late. This was the original skid row, named back in the days when giant logs slid down Yesler Street toward the water. Now it was a haven for both the homeless and those drawn to nightclubs and jazz bars—life in the dark. The pergola was a local landmark, a black ornate ironwork fixture on the corner of First and James.

She saw Paxton before he saw her. She said, "Hey."

He looked up. "You came," he said, and something made her realize how much he'd wanted her here. He hadn't been as certain of her as she'd thought.

"I'm not afraid of you," she said firmly.

"I'm afraid of you," he answered matter-of-factly.

Marah had no idea what that meant, but she remembered her mom telling her about the first time she'd kissed Dad. *He said he was afraid of me,* Mom had said. *He didn't know it, but he was already in love with me.*

Paxton reached out his hand. "You ready, Suburb Girl?"

She took his hand. "I am, Guyliner Boy."

He led her down the street and onto a city bus. When they got off, they were somewhere she'd never been before. Seattle was distant from here, a glittering diadem set against the night sky. The land in front of her rolled downhill; at its end a rusted behemoth lurked. Gas Works Park. She recognized it now. The centerpiece of this waterfront park was the old rusted gasification plant. Paxton led her into a hidden place within the structure, then pulled a cardboard box out from a hiding place and made them a place to sit.

"Have you ever had absinthe?" He pulled out enough supplies for a science experiment.

She shivered. "No. What is it?"

"Magic in a bottle."

He set out glasses and several bottles; then he performed a ritual of sorts, with spoons and sugar cubes and water. As the sugar cube melted into the liquid, the absinthe became a foamy milky green.

He handed her the glass. As she drank, the night seemed to waken. She was well into her second glass of absinthe when Paxton took hold of her hand, turned her palm up. He let his fingers move up along the flesh of her inner arm to the first silvery scar.

"Blood can be so beautiful, so cleansing."

Here was someone who understood her. "When did you start?"

"After my sister died. It was my drugs that killed her. That's why the court ordered therapy. It was that or jail."

"Your parents?"

"They divorced because of it. Neither can forgive me."

"So you didn't used to be like . . ." She nodded at his look.

"I needed a change," he said.

He gazed at her with beautiful vulnerability and touched her face. "Do you believe in love at first sight?"

"I do now," she said.

It felt desperately solemn, this moment. He'd brought her back to life. She didn't care if he was dangerous or did drugs or couldn't be trusted. This feeling, this coming alive, was worth any risk.

"Let's get high," he murmured softly. "It'll make you forget."

September 3, 2010, 1:16 p.m.

PING. "Flight attendants, please take your seats."

Marah let go of the memory and opened her eyes. Real life came back with a vengeance: It was 2010. She was flying to Seattle to see Tully, who had been in a car accident and might not make it.

"Are you all right?"

Pax.

"They don't love you, Marah. Not like I do. If they did, they would respect your choices."

She stared out the window as the plane touched down and taxied to the terminal. She saw a ghostly image of her own face in the window. Pale skin, pink hair, and black-rimmed eyes.

Paxton unhooked his seat belt and grabbed his brown paper bag out from under the seat in front of him. Marah did the same.

As she walked through the terminal, she clutched the wrinkled bag that held her possessions. Outside the terminal, Marah wished now she'd told her dad what flight they'd be on.

"Let's get a cab," Paxton said. "You just got paid, right?"

Marah hesitated. Paxton never seemed to quite grasp the truth of their finances. Her minimum-wage job didn't exactly afford them the money for luxuries like a cab ride to Seattle from SeaTac. She was the only one of the roommates who even had a job. Paxton was too creative to hold down a steady job—it cut into his poetry writing time. But when he sold his poetry, they'd be rich.

She could have said no to the cab, but lately it was too easy to make him angry. "Yeah," she said.

"Besides, Daddy will give you money," he said, and he didn't sound unhappy. It confused her. He wanted them to have nothing to do with her family. So why was it okay to take money from them?

They climbed into a cab. Marah named the hospital and then leaned back against Pax. Twenty-five minutes later the car stopped in front of the hospital. It was raining now, one of those nibbling, inconsistent September rains that came and went.

They walked into the bright lobby, and Marah came to an abrupt stop. *Sit with me during chemo, baby girl. Tell me about Tyler. . . .*

"You don't have to do this," Pax said. "It's your life, not theirs."

She reached for his hand, but he pulled away. She understood: He wanted her to know that he didn't want to be here.

On the fourth floor they walked toward the ICU. A place she knew all too well. She saw her father and grandmother in the waiting room. Dad stood slowly. Grandma Margie got to her feet, too.

Marah had to force herself to keep walking. She hadn't seen her dad in so long; she was surprised by how much older he looked.

Grandma Margie limped forward and pulled Marah into a fierce hug. "It can be hard to come home. Good for you," Grandma said. She looked thinner since the last time Marah had seen her. "Grandpa's at home, waiting for your brothers. He sends his love."

Her brothers. Marah's throat tightened at the thought of them. She hadn't realized how much she'd missed them until right now.

Dad's hair was grayer. He came closer and pulled her into a hug.

When he let go and stepped back, she knew they were both think-ing about the last time they'd been together. She and Dad and Tully.

"I can't stay long," Marah said.

"Do you have something more important to do?"

"Still judging us, I see," Pax said lazily. "Big surprise."

Dad seemed determined not to look at Pax. "I don't want to jump into this again. Do you want to see your godmother?"

"Yes," Marah said.

"Come on," Dad said. "I'll take you to her."

Marah turned to Paxton. "Will you—"

He shook his head. Of course he didn't want to go. He hated pre-tense of any kind. He couldn't pretend to care about Tully's health. That would be dishonest.

She and Dad walked down the hallway. Outside a glass-walled room in the ICU, he stopped and turned to her.

"She's in bad shape. You need to prepare yourself. The doctors have put her into a medically induced coma in hopes that her brain swelling will go down. They've shaved her head and she's bandaged up, so be ready. The doctors think she can hear us, though."

Marah nodded and reached for the door.

"Baby?"

She paused, turned.

"I'm sorry."

She stared up at him, seeing remorse in his eyes—and love—and it affected her profoundly. She couldn't think about him—and them—now. She went into the ICU room and closed the door.

Marah approached the bed. Tully didn't look faded as her mom had at the end. She looked ruined—crushed, almost—pierced by needles and hooked up to machines. Her face was bruised and cut.

Marah was responsible for this; she knew it. Her betrayal had to be part of why her godmother was here. "What's wrong with me?"

She'd never voiced this query before, not when she'd started smoking pot or sleeping with Pax, not when she ran away with Pax. Not even when she sold the story to *Star* magazine.

But she asked it now. She'd betrayed her godmother and ruined everything, broken the only hearts that mattered. Something must be wrong with her. But what?

"I know you'll never forgive me," she said, wishing now, for the first time, that she knew how to forgive herself.

I WAKEN in a darkness so complete I wonder if I am dead.

"Katie?" This time I think I make a sound.

Shhh. Relax. I need you to listen. You can hear her.

There is a break in her voice when she says *her.*

"Marah." When I say her name, lights come on. I see that I am in the hospital room again. Marah is sitting beside me. Her hair is cotton-candy pink, razor cut and unattractive as hell.

She is saying my name and trying not to cry. I love this girl, and her sadness scalds my soul. She needs me to wake up.

I concentrate hard, say, "Marah, don't cry." Nothing. My body just lies there, inert, breathing through a tube, eyes shut.

"Tully . . . I'm so sorry . . . for what I did."

The light flickers. Kate pulls away from me and floats around the bed to stand by her daughter. *Feel me, baby girl.*

Marah gasps and looks up. "M-Mom?" Then she slumps forward in defeat. "When will I learn? You're *gone.*"

"Can it be undone?" I ask Kate quietly. "Can I wake up?"

You tell me.

"I tried to help Marah, but . . . really. When have I ever been the person you want beside you in a foxhole?"

Always, Tul. You were the only one who didn't know that.

"I'm afraid to remember what happened."

I know, but it's time. Talk to me. Remember.

I scroll through memories. I think about the months after her death. The Ryans moved to Los Angeles, and we lost touch. I had lunch once a month with Margie, but I saw the sadness in her eyes, and I wasn't surprised when she told me she and Bud were moving to Arizona. And me, I applied for every broadcasting job I could find. But I was apparently unemployable. In May of 2008, a month before Marah's high school graduation and nineteen months after Kate's death, I am in the waiting room of KCPO, the TV station where I first worked for Johnny all those years ago. I am literally back where I began. I have begged for an interview with Fred Rorback, whom I've known for years. Today I am starting over. This is what I tell myself as I walk into Fred's office. He is bald now, and smiling at me in a way I don't like. There is sympathy in his eyes as he stands to greet me.

"Hi, Fred," I say, shaking his hand. "It's good of you to see me."

"Of course," he says, sitting down. On his desk is a stack of paper. He points to it. "Do you know what those are?"

"No."

"The letters you wrote me in 1977. One hundred and twelve letters from a seventeen-year-old girl, asking for a job at the ABC affiliate station. I knew you'd be someone."

"Maybe I wouldn't have been if you hadn't given me that break in '85." I never really thought about Fred after I left KLUE for New York. How hard would it have been to look back just once?

"I was sorry to hear about your show," he says.

And there we are. "I guess I screwed up," I say quietly. "I need a job, Fred. I'll do anything."

"I don't have any anchor spots open, Tully, and—"

"Anything," I say again, fisting my hands. "I need a chance, Fred. I need to prove that I'm a team player."

He smiles sadly. "You've never been a team player, Tully. That's why you are a superstar. Do you remember how much notice you gave me when you got the network job in New York? None. You came to my office, thanked me for the opportunity, and said goodbye. This is the first time I've seen you since."

I feel hopelessness well up. I refuse to let him see how deeply his words affect me, though. Pride is all I have left.

As I LEAVE Fred's office and step back out onto the Seattle sidewalk, I am consumed by a sense of failure.

I pass a Barnes & Noble bookstore. The book in the window catches my eye. I stop dead. *Of course.* I should have thought of this before. It takes several tries to call my agent.

"George," I snap when he finally answers. "Guess where I am?"

"Where?"

"At a bookstore."

"And I care . . . why?"

"Because I'm looking at Barbara Walters's memoir. If I remember correctly, she got five million. And DeGeneres scored a huge deal." This may be the best idea I've ever had. "I want a book deal."

George says nothing for so long, I prompt him again. "Well?"

He sighs. "Let me throw out a line and see if anyone bites. But let me ask you this, Tully: Are you sure about this? You've got some dark things in your past."

"I'm sure, George. Find me a deal."

How hard can it be? I am a journalist. I'll write the story of my life. It will be a best seller—inspirational and heartfelt.

By the time I get home, I am excited for the first time in forever. I change out of my suit and put on sweats and pull out my laptop. Then I curl up on my sofa and begin. I type: Second Act.

Then I scroll down, indent for the paragraph, and stare at the blank screen long enough to decide that maybe wine will help.

I pour a glass and return to the sofa. The blank screen again.

Research. Any writer has to begin with research. I know that from my days in journalism. I know about digging for a story.

And my life story is no exception. I have been the subject of several magazine articles and TV news shows, but I have carefully managed all of it. I have turned a bad childhood into a Cinderella fairy tale. How many times did I say that it had been a blessing of sorts, how often I'd been abandoned? The lack of a mother's love made me try harder. Ambition, I say, saved me.

In a memoir, for once I will have to tell the whole truth. That is what George asked me. I blithely said yes, but can I? I have to. Maybe I need to. A best-selling memoir could give me my life back.

I don't have much from my early years, but what I do have is in my storage unit downstairs in the parking garage. I haven't been in the unit for years, let alone looked into the boxes.

I am going to do it. But I can't make myself move. Instead, I stand there at my window drinking one glass of wine after another until the sky begins to darken. "Do it," I say to my own reflection. On my way out of the condo, I grab another glass of wine.

In the parking garage I find my unit, unlock the metal door, and step inside. It is about twelve-feet square. There are my skis and tennis rackets and golf clubs and my extra luggage. And two boxes. Two. The evidence of my life doesn't take up much room.

I reach for the first box. Across it is written a single word: "Firefly Lane." The second box says, "Queen Anne."

I feel a shiver of dread. These two boxes represent the two halves of my former life: my grandmother and my mother. At seventeen I'd become the executrix of my grandmother's estate. She'd left me everything—the house on Queen Anne and the rental property on Firefly Lane. Alone, headed into foster care, I packed up the house on Queen Anne and kept only these few things. The Firefly Lane box contained the few things that my mother and I collected in our brief time together. I lived with her only once, in 1974, in the house on Firefly lane, until one day when she simply disappeared.

I pull the box marked "Queen Anne" toward me. I peel the flaps back and reach inside. The first thing I find in the shadowy interior is my old scrapbook.

I run my fingertip over the white cover. Gran had given me this album on my eleventh birthday. *Your mom has problems,* Gran had said on that birthday while I sat on the floor, crying.

Is that why she doesn't love me?

I open the scrapbook and see a picture of myself at eleven, leaning over a cake to blow out the candles. Pasted on the other side is the first of hundreds of letters I'd written to my mother and never mailed. *Dear Mommy, Today is my eleventh birthday—*

"Stop it," I say to myself. This is old news, old pain. I close the scrapbook. If Katie were here, I could go through this box, pull up my pain, and examine it. Without her I don't have the strength.

I leave the storage unit, forgetting to even lock it. If I am lucky, maybe someone will steal these boxes before I go through them. I am halfway to the elevator when my cell phone rings. It is Margie.

"Hey, Tully. I'm making reservations for Saturday night in Los Angeles. What was the name of that restaurant you love?"

I smile. How had I forgotten, even for a moment? This weekend is Marah's high school graduation. I will be with the Mularkeys and the Ryans for two days. It is a gift I won't take for granted. Maybe I will even ask Johnny for help in getting a job. "Don't worry, Margie. I already made reservations for all of us. Seven o'clock at Madeo."

CHAPTER NINE

THIS weekend I am going to be my old self. I will laugh with Johnny and hold on to my goddaughter and play Xbox games with the boys. I will focus on who is left.

But when the Town Car pulls up in front of a contemporary house on an uberlandscaped lot in Beverly Hills, I feel panic tug at my resolution. *Kate would hate this house.* A Xanax calms my nerves.

I get out of the car and haul my single suitcase up the stone walkway. I open the door and step inside, calling out.

The twins come bursting down a wide stone staircase. Both have long, unruly brown hair and wide, toothy grins. I am knocked back by the exuberance of their hug.

"I *knew* she'd come," Lucas says.

Wills says, "What did you get Marah?"

"Probably a Ferrari," Johnny says, coming into the room.

I know we are both thinking of the woman who isn't here. He comes toward me. I hip-bump him because I don't know what to say. Before he can respond, I hear Margie call for me. In minutes I am surrounded by them—the boys, Johnny, Bud, and Margie. Everyone is smiling and laughing. When the twins drag their grandparents back upstairs for some game, Johnny and I are alone.

"How is Marah?" I ask.

"Fine. Doing well, I think" is what he says, but I hear more truth in his sigh. "How are you?"

This is my moment. I could tell him the truth, maybe even ask for help. I could tell him about my collapsed career and ask for advice.

I can't do it. Maybe it is his sorrow, or my pride, or a mixture of the two. All I know for sure is I don't want pity. "I'm fine," I say. "I'm writing a memoir. George tells me it is sure to be a best seller."

He nods and looks away. Later I can't help thinking about my lie to Johnny. I wonder if I am the kind of fine that Marah is.

Marah is not fine. We learn that lesson the hard way. On Saturday, when we are gathered in the living room, Marah comes down the stairs. She looks . . . ghastly is all I can think of.

"I need help," she says, and lifts her hand. She is bleeding profusely. I rush to help her, and so does Johnny. Once again we say things we shouldn't. What I know is this: Marah needs help, and I have promised to be there for her. I swear to Johnny that I will take care of her in Seattle, get her in to see Dr. Bloom.

In the end he decides to let her live with me for the summer. But he doesn't like it. Not at all. And he makes sure I know it.

IN JUNE of 2008, Marah moves into my condo on a beautiful early summer day. I feel proud; never have I fulfilled my promise to Katie more completely. It's true that I am not my best self these days. I am drinking more than I should and taking a few too many Xanax. I can no longer sleep without sleeping pills.

But all of that will fade now that I have this obligation. I help her unpack her small suitcase, and then in the evening we sit in the living room together, talking about her mother as if Kate is at the store. I know it is wrong, this pretense, but we need it, both of us.

"Are you ready for Monday?" I ask.

"My appointment with Dr. Bloom?" she says. "No, not really."

"I'll be here with you every step of the way," I promise.

The next day, while Marah is in the meeting with Dr. Bloom, I wait impatiently, pacing back and forth in front of the closed door.

"You're wearing a groove in the carpet. Take a Xanax."

A boy stands in the door, looking absurdly like the Prince of Darkness—all in black, with enough macabre jewelry to fill a store on Bourbon Street. But he is strangely handsome beneath all the Goth-ware. He is holding a book of poetry.

Before I can answer, Marah comes out of the office looking shaken. Then Dr. Bloom appears and asks me to step aside with her.

"I'll be right back," I say to Marah, and go to the doctor.

"I'll want to see her twice a week," Dr. Bloom says quietly. "At least until she starts school in the fall. And I have a teen grief support group that might help her. It meets Wednesdays. Seven p.m."

"She'll do whatever you suggest," I promise.

"Will she?"

"Of course. So how did it go?" I ask. "Did she—"

"Marah's an adult, Tully. Our sessions are private."

"Oh. What should I tell her father? He's expecting a report."

Dr. Bloom thinks and then says, "Marah is fragile, Tully. My advice would be to treat her as such. I would watch her carefully. Be there for her. She could make a bad decision in her current state."

On the way home, I ask Marah how it went with Dr. Bloom.

What she says is "Fine."

That night, I call Johnny and tell him everything. He is worried—I hear it in his voice—but I promise that I am taking care of her.

WHEN Marah goes to her first teen grief therapy meeting, I decide to work on my book. At least, I try to. But when the phone rings, I jump on it. George, my agent, is calling to tell me that he has had some interest in my book idea—no offers yet, but he thinks there's hope.

When Marah comes home from her meeting, I make us two cups of hot cocoa and we sit together in bed, just as we used to when she was little. Finally Marah says, "I can't talk about my mom to her."

I have no answer to that, and I can't insult her with a lie. I have been urged to go to therapy several times in my life. There's a river of sadness in me; it's always been there, but now it is rising, spilling over its banks. But I don't believe that words will make it back down. I believe in sucking up, in going on. Look where it has gotten me.

I put an arm around Marah and pull her close. We talk quietly about what scares her; I tell her that her mother would want her to stay in therapy. We sit there a long time, both of us thinking of the woman who brought us together and left us alone.

The next day, Johnny arrives and tries to get Marah to come home to Los Angeles, but she is firm in her resolve to stay with me.

"ARE you looking forward to the UW?" I ask Marah on a Friday afternoon. We are on my sofa, tucked together under a cream-colored cashmere throw. Johnny has gone back to Los Angeles.

"Scared, I'd say."

"Yeah, your mom was, too. But we loved it, and so will you."

"I am looking forward to my creative writing class."

"Your mom was a talented writer. If you'd read her journal—"

"No," Marah says sharply. It is what she says to me each time I broach this tender subject. Someday she will be ready.

Beside me the cell phone rings. I lean over, check the caller ID. "Hi, George," I say.

"I'm calling about your book deal. We have an offer. It's the only offer we got. And it's a good one."

When your agent starts to sell you, it's trouble. "How much?"

"Fifty thousand dollars. In advance. Against royalties."

"Oh." I know it is a lot of money in the ordinary world, but I have spent so many years in an extraordinary world that it hits me hard, this proof that I have lost so much of my fame.

"It is what it is, Tully. But it can be your comeback. Yours is a Cinderella story. Make the world yours again."

I have only one choice, and I know it. "I'll take it," I say.

THAT night, I am too wired to sleep. At eleven o'clock I give up on the pretense of it. I roam through my darkened condo. Once, I almost go to Marah's room and waken her, but I know that would be selfish. Finally, at about eleven twenty, I decide to work. I crawl back into bed and pull my computer into my lap, opening my most recent document. There it is: "Second Act." And a blue screen.

Research. That's what I need. I have to go through the boxes in my storage unit. I can't put it off any more. After pouring myself a glass of wine, I go downstairs.

I go to the "Queen Anne" box and open it. I pull the scrapbook out and place it on the floor beside me. I lean over and peer into the dark interior. The first thing I see is a stuffed rabbit.

Mathilda. She is missing one shiny black eye. This gift from my grandmother had been my best friend growing up.

I put Mathilda aside and reach in again. I pull out a small gray Magilla Gorilla T-shirt. My mom bought it for me. It's the only thing I ever remember her giving to me. I am young—maybe four or five. I am at the kitchen table when *she* comes in. A stranger.

My Talullah, she says, lurching unsteadily toward me. She smells funny. Like sweet smoke. *Did you miss your mommy?*

Upstairs a bell rings. *That's Grandpa,* I say. The next thing I know, I am in the stranger's arms and she is running out of the house.

Gran is behind us, yelling, "Stop! Dorothy—"

The woman says something about *him* and adds a bunch of words I don't understand. I remember her asking me to call her Mom. And I remember how hard the seat was in her car and how I was supposed to pee by the side of the road. I remember the smell of smoke in the car and her friends. They scared me.

I remember the brownies. I ate them, and my mom thought it was so funny when I lost my balance and started throwing up.

I remember waking up in a hospital bed, with my name, TALULLAH ROSE, pinned to my chest.

Who was that lady? I asked Gran when she came to pick me up.

Your mama, Gran said. I remember those two words as if I heard them yesterday.

I sigh and put the T-shirt back in the box. Maybe this memoir is a bad idea. I leave the storage unit, remembering to lock it this time.

"YOU don't need to walk me to all of my therapy appointments, you know," Marah says to me on a bright and sunny Monday in late June as we walk up First Street toward the public market.

"I know. I want to," I say, linking my arm through hers.

Here's what I have learned in the two weeks she has lived with me: Being responsible for a teenager is exhausting and terrifying. Every time she goes into the bathroom, I worry that she's cutting herself. I am constantly trying to do the right thing, but let's face it, what I know about motherhood wouldn't fill a Jell-O shot.

Now, in Dr. Bloom's waiting room, I open up my laptop and stare at the blank blue screen. I have to get started on this thing.

I've read a hundred memoirs in my life. They always begin in the same way: with the backstory. I need to set the stage, so to speak.

And there it is. The thing that stops me: I can't write my story without knowing my own history. And my mother's. I know almost nothing about her, and I know even less about my father. My history is this blank, yawning void. No wonder I can't write anything.

I have to talk to my mother.

At the thought, I swallow a Xanax without water. Then I slowly pick up my cell phone and call my business manager.

"Frank," I say when he answers. "This is Tully. Is my mother still cashing her monthly checks?"

"I'm glad you called. We need to talk about your finances—"

"Yeah, sure. But now I need to know about my mom. Is she still cashing her check?"

He tells me to hold and then comes back on the line. "Yes. Every month. She's living in your house in Snohomish. Has been for a few years. We sent you notice. I think she moved in when your friend was sick."

"My mom's living on Firefly Lane?" Did I know that, really?

"Yes. And now can we talk about—"

I hang up. Marah is coming out of Dr. Bloom's office.

"Dr. Bloom thinks I should get a job," Marah says.

"Yeah, sure," I say, frowning. Really, all I can think about is my mother. "That's a great idea."

ALL afternoon I pace in my apartment, trying to think clearly. My mother is living in one of the two houses I inherited from my grandmother. The house I have never been able to sell because it is across the street from the Mularkeys. This means that if I go to talk to her, I have to go back to the place where Kate and I met.

And I have to either take Marah with me or leave her alone. Neither choice seems particularly appealing.

"Tully?"

"Yes, honey?" Do I look as distracted as I feel?

"I just heard from Ashley. A bunch of my high school friends are going to Luther Burbank Beach today. Can I go?"

Relief comes in a sweet rush. It is the first time she has asked to spend time with her old friends. It is the sign I have been waiting for. "I think that's a great idea. When will you be home?"

"There's this movie afterward. A nine-o'clock show. *Wall-E*."

"So you'll be home by . . ."

"Eleven?"

That seems more than reasonable. And it gives me plenty of time. "And someone will walk you home?"

Marah laughs. "Of course."

"Okay, then. I have a business thing to do, anyway, so I'll be gone most of the day. Be safe."

Marah surprises me by hugging me tightly, and it gives me the strength I need. I am going to see my mother. I am going to ask her real questions, and I won't leave until I have some answers.

SNOHOMISH is one of those small western Washington communities that has changed with the times. Once a dairy farming community tucked in a verdant valley between the Cascade Mountain Range and the Snohomish and Pilchuck rivers, it has blossomed into yet another of Seattle's bedroom communities. But the old town still shines through in places. Every now and then an old farmhouse stands, its fenced acres thick with tall grass and grazing cattle.

And then there is Firefly Lane. On this small ribbon of asphalt, change has come slowly, if at all.

The unreliable sun is playing hide-and-seek among the wafting clouds. How long has it been since I was here? Four years?

Without even thinking, I turn into the Mularkey driveway, seeing the For Sale sign planted by the mailbox. They are renting in Arizona now; when this house sells, they'll buy something.

The house looks exactly as it always did—a pretty white farmhouse with a wraparound porch overlooking two sloped green acres. I see Kate's upstairs window, and in a blink I am fourteen again, standing here with my bike, throwing stones at her window.

I smile at the memory. The rebel and the rule follower. That's what we'd seemed like in the beginning. Kate had followed me anywhere—or so it had seemed to me then, through my girl's eyes.

What I hadn't known until too late was that I was following her, all those years ago. I am the one who can't let go.

The drive from her childhood home to mine takes less than a minute, but to me it feels like a shift from one world to another. My grandparents' old rental house looks different than I remember. The side yard is torn up; there are mounds of landscape debris piled in the middle of dirt fields. I can only imagine what I will find inside. In the thirtysome years of my adulthood, I have seen my mother a handful of times, always—only—when I have gone in search of her.

I park the car and get out. I pick my way across the torn-up landscaping, stepping over trowels and empty seed packets. The front door is wooden. I knock. There is no answer. She is probably passed out on the floor somewhere, dead drunk. I test the knob and find that the house is unlocked. I open the door cautiously and go inside, calling out "Hello" as I go.

Someone has ripped up the shag carpeting in the living room and exposed the dirty floorboards beneath. Gone is the seventies furniture. Instead, there is a single overstuffed chair positioned next to a garage-sale side table. A card table plays host to two folding chairs.

Deep inside, I know nothing will come of this meeting. I've spent each of my forty-eight years aching for a love that has never been mine. At least now I know better than to expect something different. I sit down on the rickety folding chair to wait. I wait for hours.

Finally, at just past eight o'clock in the evening, I hear the crunching of tires on gravel. My heart speeds up.

The door opens, and I see my mother for the first time in two or three years. Her skin has the wrinkled gray cast that comes with years of hardscrabble, drunken living.

"Tully," she says. It surprises me, the use of my nickname. All my life she has called me Talullah, which I hate.

"Hi, Cloud," I say, standing.

"I'm Dorothy now."

Another name change. Before I can say anything, a man comes into the house and stands beside her. He is tall and whipcord lean, with wrinkles in his tanned cheeks that look like furrows.

My mother is high, I'm pretty sure. But since I don't think I've ever seen her sober, how would I know?

"I'm so glad to see you," she says, giving me an uncertain smile.

I believe her, but I *always* believe her. Believing her is my Achilles heel. My faith is as constant as her rejection.

"This is Edgar," my mother says.

"Hi," he says, giving my mother a frown. Her dealer, probably.

"Do you have any family photographs?" I say a little impatiently. "Pictures of me as a girl, that kind of thing."

"No."

I wish it didn't hurt, but it does, and the hurt pisses me off. "You took no pictures of me as a baby?"

She shakes her head, saying nothing. There is no excuse.

"Can you tell me *anything* about my childhood or who my dad was or where I was born?"

She flinches at each word, pales.

I say, "Who are you?"

"You don't want to know," she says. "Trust me."

I am wasting my time. Whatever I need for my book, I won't find it here. I push past her and leave the house.

I get in my car and drive home. All the way back to Seattle, I replay the scene with my mother in my head, trying to glean meaning, but there is nothing there. I pull up to my building and park.

I know I should go upstairs and work on my book, but I can't do it, can't walk up into my empty apartment. I need a drink.

I call Marah—she's a good girl who answers immediately—and tell her I'm going to be home late. She tells me she's already in bed and watching a movie and not to wake her when I get home.

I go straight to the bar, where I allow myself only two dirty martinis. It is almost one o'clock in the morning when I unlock my door. All of the lights are on, and I can hear the TV.

Frowning, I walk down the hallway. As I pass Marah's bedroom door, I pause. Her light is on. I can see it beneath the closed door.

I knock gently. There is no answer, so I open the door quietly.

The room is empty. The TV is on. Marah is not here. At one o'clock in the morning. She *lied* to me.

I call her phone. There is no answer. I text: WHERE ARE YOU???

Should I call Johnny? Or the police?

It is one ten now. I am shaking as I pick up the phone. I have dialed 9-1 when I hear a key jiggling in the lock.

Marah comes in, trying to tiptoe, but even from here I can see that she is off balance, and she keeps giggling and shushing herself.

"Marah." My voice is so sharp I sound like a mother.

She turns, trips. I lead her into her bedroom. She stumbles along.

"So," I say when she collapses onto her bed. "You're drunk."

"I only had two beersh," she says.

"Uh-huh." I help her get undressed and help her into the bathroom. When she sees the toilet, she moans, "I'm gonna be shick—"

When she is done puking, I help her brush her teeth and guide her into bed. She is pale now, and as weak as a rag doll.

I crawl into bed beside her and put an arm around her. She leans against me and sighs. "I feel terrible."

"Consider this a life lesson. So what were you really drinking?"

"Abshinthe."

"Absinthe." That is not what I expected. "Girls like Ashley and Lindsey and Coral drink rum and cokes," I say, frowning. Am I really so old that I don't know what kids are drinking these days?

"I . . . uh . . . wasn't with them," she says.

This stops me. "Who were you with?"

She looks at me. "A bunch of kids from my therapy group.

They're cooler than I thought. And really, Aunt Tully, it's just drinking. Everyone does it."

That's true. And she's definitely drunk; I can smell it on her breath. Drugs would be different.

"Paxton is way cool," Marah says quietly.

"The Goth kid?"

"That's harsh." Marah sighed dreamily. "Sometimes when he talks about his sister and how much he misses her, I start to cry. And he totally gets how much I miss my mom. When I'm in a sad mood, he reads me his poetry and holds me until I feel better."

Poetry. Sorrow. Darkness. Of course Marah is drawn in. But still, Marah is young and Dr. Bloom says she's fragile. "As long as you're with a group of kids—"

"Totally," Marah says earnestly. "And we're just friends, Tully. Me and Pax, I mean. You won't tell my dad, right? I mean, he wouldn't understand me being friends with someone like Pax."

"I'm glad you're just friends. Keep it that way, okay? I guess every girl gets swept away by a brooding poet at least once in her life. I remember this weekend in Dublin, back in— Oh, wait. I can't tell you that story."

"You can tell me *anything,* Tully. You're my best friend."

She twists me around her little finger with that one. I love her so much right now it honestly hurts. But I need to take care of her.

"I won't tell your dad about Pax, because you're right: He'd freak. But I won't lie to him, so don't make me. Deal?"

"Deal."

"And Marah, if I come home to an empty house again, I'm calling your dad first and the cops second."

Her smile falls. "Okay."

IT CHANGES something in me, that late-night talk with Marah. *You're my best friend.* I know it's not quite true, that really we are surrogates for each other, both of us standing in for Kate. But Marah's love for me—and my love for her—is the lifeline I have needed. For the first time in my life, I am truly *needed.* I want to be there for

Marah in a way I've never been there for anyone. Not even Kate. The truth is that Kate didn't need me. I was the one with the need.

Now, for once, I am the strong and stable one, or I intend to be. I put my Xanax and sleeping pills away and cut back on the wine. Each morning, I get up early to make her breakfast and make the calls for dinner takeout to be delivered.

Then I go to work on my memoir. I decide to let go of the part of my story I don't know. I still care deeply, but I accept the reality. I will have to write a memoir based on what I know. So, on a gorgeous day in July, I simply begin.

> Here's the thing: When you grow up as I have, a lost girl without any real past, you latch on to the people who seem to love you. At least, that's what I did. I craved unconditional love. I needed someone to say it to me. My mother never said it. Neither did my grandmother. There was no one else.
>
> Until 1974, when I moved into the house my grandparents bought as an investment. Did I know when I moved into a run-down house with my mom that my world had just shifted? No. But from the moment I met Kathleen Scarlett Mularkey, I believed in myself because she believed in me.
>
> Maybe you're wondering why my memoir begins with my best friend. I'm starting here, at what seems to be the end, because my story is really about our friendship. Once—not long ago—I had a TV show. *The Girlfriend Hour.* I walked away from it when Katie was losing her battle with cancer.
>
> Apparently, walking away from a TV show without warning is bad. I am now unemployable. How could I have done it differently, though? I took so much from Katie and gave too little back. That was my time to be there for her.

"Aunt Tully?"

"Yeah?" I say distractedly, reading over what I've done.

"I'm leaving for work now," Marah says. She is dressed in all black, and her makeup is a little heavy. She calls it a uniform for her new job as a barista in Pioneer Square.

I glance at my watch. "It's seven thirty."

"I have the night shift. You know that."

Do I? Has she told me this before? She only got this job a week ago. "Take a cab home. You need money?"

She smiles. "I'm fine. Thanks. How's the book going?"

"Great. Thanks." She comes over and gives me a kiss. As soon as she leaves, I go back to work.

CHAPTER TEN

FOR the rest of the summer, I work seriously on my book. Unlike most memoirs, mine ignores the early years of my life and begins with my career. I start in the early days at KCPO, with Johnny and Kate, and then drift toward New York and the network. Recording the story of my ambition fuels me, reminds me that I can do anything I set my mind to. When I am not working, Marah and I act like best friends: going to movies and walking downtown and buying school supplies for the UW. She is doing so well that I have stopped worrying obsessively about her.

Until a sunny day in late August of 2008 changes everything.

On that afternoon, I am in the King County library, where I am putting together a collection of the many articles written about me over the years. I have planned on being here all day, but when I look up and see the sun shining through the windows, I make a snap decision. Enough work for the day. I pack up my laptop, and I walk down the busy Seattle sidewalk toward Pioneer Square.

The Wicked Brew is a small, trendy place. The interior smells like coffee mixed with incense and clove cigarettes.

The kid at the cash register is wearing skinny black jeans and a vintage velvet jacket over a black T-shirt "Can I help you?"

"I'm looking for Marah Ryan. She's working today."

"Dude, no one by that name works here."

"Are you new?"

"I've been here forever, dude, like half a year. No one named Marah works here. You want a latte?"

Marah has been lying to me all summer.

By the time I reach my condo, I am fuming mad. I fling open the door and call out for her.

No answer. I look at my watch. It's two twelve in the afternoon.

I go to her bedroom door, turn the knob, and go inside. Marah is in bed with that boy, Paxton. Naked. An ice-cold wave of *pissed off* overwhelms me, and I shout at him to get off of my goddaughter.

Marah pulls a pillow over her naked breasts. "Tully—"

The boy just lies there, smiling at me as if I owe him something.

"In the living room," I say. "Now. *Dressed.*"

I go to the living room and take a Xanax to calm my runaway nerves. I feel a panic attack forming. What will I tell Johnny?

Like a mama hen, Johnny. You can trust me.

Marah walks in quickly. Her brown eyes are wide with worry. I see how much makeup she has on—heavy eyeliner, purplish lipstick, pale foundation. There is no work uniform. She dresses like a Goth when she goes out. She is wearing skinny black jeans and a black mesh top over a black cami. Paxton comes out beside her. He doesn't move so much as glide forward in his tight black jeans and black Converse tennis shoes.

"Y-you remember Pax," Marah says.

"Sit down," I snap. Marah complies instantly.

Paxton moves closer to me. There's sadness in his eyes, and it is perversely seductive. Marah never had a chance with this kid. How did I not see that? It was my job to protect her, and I failed. *I failed.*

"I love her," he says quietly.

Marah gives him a desperate look, and I realize how deep this trouble runs. *Love.* I sit slowly, looking at them.

One thing I know for sure. "I have to tell your dad."

Marah gasps. "He'll make me move back to L.A."

"Tell him," Paxton says, taking Marah's hand. "He can't do a thing. She's an adult."

"An adult with no money and no job," I point out.

She pulls away from Paxton and kneels in front of me. "You said my mom fell in love with Dad the first time she saw him."

"Yes, but—"

"I love him, Tully. You're my best friend. Please understand."

I want to tell her she's wrong, that she can't love a boy who wears guyliner and tells her what she feels, but what do I know about love? All I can do is try to undo the damage. But how?

"Don't tell my dad. Please. It's not a lie," she adds. "Just don't say anything unless he asks."

It is a terrible and dangerous bargain I make. I know what will happen if Johnny finds out about this secret, and it will not bode well for me. But if I tell him, I will lose her; it's that simple.

"Fine," I say. I'll keep Marah so busy for the next three weeks she won't have time to see Paxton. "But only if you promise not to lie to me anymore."

Marah smiles in a way that makes me feel uncomfortable, and I know why. She has been lying to me all this time.

What good is her promise?

In September I am Marah's shadow. The only time we are apart is when we're sleeping, and I check on her at least once every night and I make sure she knows it. Johnny and the boys move back into the house on Bainbridge Island. He calls three nights a week and asks how she is doing—every time, I tell him she is doing well. He pretends not to be hurt that his daughter doesn't want to visit.

As my warden grip tightens, Marah pulls away from me. She has decided I am not cool anymore, that I can't be trusted.

I try to rise above all of it and to show her that I love her. In this cold-war atmosphere, my anxiety begins to grow again. I go see a new doctor and get new prescriptions. By September twenty-first I am beside myself with guilt and worry, but I am holding on.

When Johnny shows up, ready to take Marah off to college, I feel sick at the trust he has placed in me and my failure.

"I'm ready," Marah says quietly. She is wearing artfully ripped black jeans and a black long-sleeved T-shirt. Too much eyeliner and mascara accentuate her pallor and make her look tired. And scared.

I can see that Johnny is about to say the wrong thing—anything about her appearance is the wrong thing lately. Boy, do I know that.

I raise my voice to cover his. "Do you have everything?"

"I guess so," she says. Her shoulders slump, and she turns hesitant and uncertain. "I should have picked a smaller school," she says.

"You're ready," Johnny says. "Your mom said you were born ready."

Marah looks up sharply. The moment feels charged. I feel Kate's presence. I know I am not alone in this feeling, either. In silence we leave my condo and get into the car and drive north. I can almost hear Kate's off-key humming along with the radio.

"Your mom and I had so much fun here," I say as the Gothic pink spires of the university come into view. Kate had thrown herself into sorority and collegiate life. Me, I hadn't cared about anything except my future career.

I get out of the car and help Marah with her luggage. The three of us walk through the campus toward the dorms. McMahon Hall rises up, a collection of jutting gray buildings.

"It's not too late to sign you up for Rush," I say.

Marah rolls her eyes. "A sorority? Gross."

"Are you saying that you're too mature to join a sorority?"

Marah smiles for the first time all day. "No. Just too cool."

"You wish, Goth girl. If you had seen us in our parachute pants and banana clips, you'd be screamin' jealous." Even Johnny laughs.

The room—Marah's—is one of a collection of prison cell–size rooms fanned out around a bathroom. In her suite, two twin beds take up most of the space. There are also two wooden desks.

Marah sits down on the mattress nearest her. She looks so young and scared it breaks my heart. Johnny sits down beside her. He says, "We are proud of you."

"I wish I knew what she'd say to me now," Marah says.

I hear the way her voice breaks, and I sit down on her other side. "She would say that life is full of unexpected joy and to throw yourself into your college years."

The door behind us opens. We turn.

Paxton stands there, dressed in black, holding a bouquet of dark purple roses. He sees Johnny and me and he stops.

"Who the hell are you?" Johnny says, getting to his feet.

"He's my friend," Marah says.

I see it all in a kind of slow motion. Johnny's anger, and Marah's desperation, and Paxton's not-so-subtle arrogance and disdain. Marah throws herself at her dad, clinging to his arm, trying to slow him down. I step between Johnny and Paxton.

"Johnny," I say sternly. "This is Marah's day. She will remember it forever."

I can see him working to reel in his anger. Slowly he turns his back on Paxton. It is a comment, to be sure, one Paxton appreciates but Marah does not. I can see how much it costs Johnny to pretend that he doesn't mind Paxton being here.

Marah goes to stand by Paxton. They are like onyx candlesticks.

"Well," I say brightly. "Let's go out for lunch. You, too, Pax. I want to take Marah down Memory Lane. I'll show her where her mom and I used to study in Suzzallo Library—"

"No," Marah says. "I don't want to go on your memory tour."

"I . . . I don't understand. We talked about this all summer."

Marah looks at Paxton, who nods encouragingly. This is *his* opinion. "My mom's dead," Marah says, and the flatness in her voice is devastating. "It doesn't help to keep talking about her all the time."

I am dumbstruck.

Johnny moves toward her. "Marah—"

"I appreciate you guys bringing me here, but I'm stressed out enough. Can we just call it a day?"

I wonder if this hurts Johnny as much as it does me.

"Sure," Johnny says gruffly. He ignores Paxton and takes Marah in his arms. Anger flares in Paxton's bourbon-colored eyes.

This is my fault. I took her to Dr. Bloom's, where she met this obviously troubled young man, and when she told me about him, I should have protected her. And when I found out they were having sex, I should have told Johnny. I certainly would have told Kate.

In Marah's eyes I see a carefully banked irritation. She wants us gone so that she can be alone with Paxton.

"Maybe you should live with me this quarter," I say. I hear Paxton make a sound of contempt, and I want to smack him.

Marah barely smiles. "I'm ready to be on my own."

I pull her into a hug that lasts half as long as I would like.

"Keep in touch," Johnny says. Then he takes my arm and pulls me away. I stumble along beside him, blinded by tears.

The next thing I know, Johnny and I are at a bar on the Ave.

"That was brutal," he says when our drinks finally arrive. "When the hell did she make friends with that loser?"

I feel sick to my stomach. "Group therapy."

"Great. Money well spent." Johnny sighs. "I wish Katie were here. She'd know how to handle this."

"If Kate were here, there'd be nothing to handle."

Johnny nods and orders us both another drink.

CHRISTMAS of 2008 surprises me.

It has been three months since Marah moved into her dorm, and in that short time, life has changed. I have been writing regularly. It energizes me, gives me something to do in the long and empty hours of the day and night. I have become a hermit of sorts. I rarely leave my condo. Everything can be delivered, and really, I don't know what to do with myself in the world these days. So I write.

Until Margie calls me one rainy day in late December.

"Hey," she says, "what time are you getting over here Friday?"

"Over here?" I ask.

"To Bainbridge Island. Johnny and the twins are home, so we're having Christmas here. We can't have the girlfriend hour without you."

And there it is. The thing I have been waiting for without even knowing it.

IT IS a new beginning, that Christmas on Bainbridge Island; at least, it seems like one. We are all together again for the first time in so long—Bud and Margie come up from Arizona, Johnny and the twins have moved back home. Even Marah comes home for a week. We all pretend not to notice how thin and sullen she is.

When we separate, we promise to stay in closer touch, to get together more often. Johnny hugs me tightly, and in the embrace I remember who we used to be to each other. Friends.

For the next few months I am almost my old self. I write almost every day; I make progress, and it helps anchor me. I call Marah every Monday; it's true that she often doesn't pick up my call, and if I nag, she hangs up. And yet I find a way to be okay with that. I believe our fake conversations will grow real over time. Soon I'm sure she will see Paxton for who he really is. But when her freshman year ends and he's still by her side, I begin to worry more.

In May of that year—2009—Lucas calls and invites me to his last baseball game of the season. I meet Johnny at the ballpark and sit with him in the stands. As long as we don't mention Kate, we can laugh together again. For the rest of the summer and into that autumn, I visit often.

By the winter of 2009, I feel almost like my old self. I have even come up with a plan to bring Marah home from school early to decorate for the holidays.

"ARE you ready?" Johnny says when I open the door to my condo. I can see that he is impatient, excited.

"I was born ready. You know that." I follow him down to his car.

On this cold mid-December evening a few snowflakes begin to fall, but it lends a festive air. We talk about Marah on the way—her falling grades and our hope that she will do better in this sophomore year than she did in her freshman.

The University of Washington's sprawling Gothic campus seems smaller in this weather. McMahon Hall is quiet. At Marah's room we pause and look at each other. "Should we yell surprise?" I ask.

"It'll be obvious when she opens the door." Johnny knocks.

We hear footsteps, and the door suddenly opens. Paxton is standing there, wearing boxer shorts and combat boots, holding a bong. The look in his eyes is glassy and blank. "Whoa . . ." he says.

Johnny pushes Paxton so hard the kid stumbles and falls. The place reeks of marijuana.

Marah is in bed, wearing only a bra and panties. "Wha' the hell are you doin' here?" she says. She is obviously high.

Johnny grabs Paxton and throws him sideways, then pins him to the wall. "You raped her," Johnny says. His voice is terrifying.

Marah climbs out of bed, falls to the floor. "Dad, don't . . ."

"Ask *her* if I raped your daughter," Paxton says, nodding at me.

Johnny looks at me. I open my mouth, but nothing comes out.

"What?" Johnny yells at me. "What do you know about this?"

"She knew we were sleeping together," Paxton says with a small smile. He is tearing us apart; he knows it and enjoys it.

Johnny's gaze turns cold. "What? How *dare* you not tell me?"

I am almost too scared to answer. "She made me promise."

"Kate would not forgive you for this." He knows exactly how these words strip me bare. He spins to face his daughter.

She is on her feet now. She pulls on a pair of jeans. "I'm sick of pretending to be who you want me to be," Marah says. Tears fill her eyes. "I'm quitting school and getting the hell out of here. I need my own life." She is shaking as she puts on her shoes.

"This would break your mom's heart," Johnny says, looking as angry and scared as I've ever seen him.

Marah stares at him. "She's dead."

"Come on, Marah," Paxton says. "Let's get the hell out of here."

"Don't go," I whisper. "Please. He'll ruin you."

Marah turns unsteadily. "You said every girl needed a poet once in her life. I thought *you'd* understand."

"He'll ruin you," I say. "That's what I should have told you."

"Yeah," Marah says, her face tightening. "Tell me all about love, Tully. 'Cuz you know so much about it."

"She doesn't, but I do," Johnny says to Marah. "And so do you. Your mom wouldn't want you anywhere near this kid. You come home with me *now*. Or—"

"Or what? Don't come home at all?" Marah snaps back. She turns to Paxton, says, "Get me out of here."

"Fine. Go," Johnny snaps.

When I hear the door shut, I turn to Johnny. "Johnny, please—"

"Don't. You knew she was sleeping with that kid . . ." His voice cracks. "This is YOUR fault. Stay the hell away from my family."

OH, TULLY.

Over the faint whir of the ventilator and the beep of the heart monitor, I hear the disappointment in Katie's voice. I forget where my body is—or try to—and live in the memory of where we are supposed to be. The Quad at the UW. Good times.

You let them both walk away?

"I ruined everything," I say. "I missed having you to talk to."

I'm here now. Talk to me. Tell me what happened after Marah ran away and Johnny said he didn't want to see you anymore. Do you remember?

I remember. December of 2009 was the beginning of the end.

After that horrible scene, I run out of the dorms. It is a snowy mess outside. I go hail a cab and get into the backseat.

At home I go straight to the bathroom and take two Xanax, but the pills don't stop me from falling apart. Not this time. What had I been thinking, to say those things to Marah, to hide the truth from Johnny? He's right. This is my fault.

For the next two weeks the weather matches my mood. Gray, swollen skies cry with me. I know I am depressed, but the strange thing is that I find it comforting. Now, alone in my apartment, I revel in my pain. I don't even pretend to work on my book. The sleeping pills I take at night leave me feeling fuzzy in the morning, and even with them in my system, I toss and turn at night.

Until Christmas Eve. Thirteen days after the fight at Marah's dorm room. On that morning, I wake up with a plan.

I stumble out of bed and make my way to the bathroom. I fumble with the Xanax container and take two. I need two because I'm going out, and just the idea of it sends me into a panic.

I gather the presents I bought weeks ago. Before. I ignore my rising panic, open the door, and step out into the hallway.

Today is Christmas Eve. A day of family and forgiveness.

The elevator ride to the parking garage is a test of my will. It feels heroic to make it to my car, to start the engine.

Outside, the streets of Seattle are dusted white with snow. Holiday decorations fill the windows on either side of the street. It is four o'clock on Christmas Eve. I drive onto the ferry and park, deciding to stay in my car for the crossing.

I am going to apologize. I will throw myself to my knees if I have to, beg Johnny to forgive me. I want this so much. Need it. The loneliness is unbearable, as is the guilt.

On Bainbridge Island, I drive slowly off of the ferry. The nearer I get to their driveway, the looser my hold on panic becomes. I turn into the driveway and stop. I take another Xanax.

I see a white Ford sedan in the driveway. That must be Bud and Margie's rental car. Through the falling snow, I see the Christmas lights strung along the eaves and the golden glow of the windows. Inside, the tree is lit up; shadowy people are gathered around it.

I turn off my lights and imagine it. I will knock on the door, and Johnny will answer. *I am so sorry,* I will say. *Forgive me.*

No. He will not forgive me. Why should he? His daughter is gone. She has run away with a dangerous young man because of me. Johnny will leave me standing there with my presents.

I can't do it, can't reach out and be smacked down again. I back out of the driveway, go back down to the ferry. In less than an hour I am downtown again. The roads are icy, and I slow down.

Then suddenly I am sobbing even as my heart is racing and a hot flash sweeps through me in pins and needless. I try to wipe my eyes and to calm down, but I can't. How many Xanax did I take?

This is the thing on my mind when the red lights flash behind me. I put on my turn signal and pull off to the side of the road. The police cruiser pulls up behind me. That damn red light stills.

The officer comes to my window and taps on the glass. Smiling too brightly, I hit the button and the window slides downward. "Hello, Officer," I say, waiting for recognition. *Oh, Ms. Hart. My wife-sister-daughter-mother loves your show.*

"License and registration, please," he says.

Oh. Right. Those days are over.

I fish my license out of my wallet and retrieve the registration documents from my visor. I can see that my hand is trembling.

He shines a flashlight onto my license, then turns the light on me. "Have you been drinking, Ms. Hart?"

"No," I say, and I think it's true. Isn't it?

"Step out of the vehicle, please."

I get out of my car and stand on the side of the road.

"Walk forty feet on this line, Ms. Hart. Heel to toe."

I can't keep my balance. I keep taking too big a step. I can't think straight, and I wish I hadn't taken those last two Xanax.

"Okay. You can stop. Stand here, in front of me. Tilt your head back and spread your arms and touch your nose with one finger."

I fling my arms out and immediately lose my balance and stumble sideways. He catches me before I fall off the sidewalk.

He shoves a Breathalyzer at me and says, "Blow."

"No," I say quietly, staring up at him. "I'm not drunk. I have panic attacks. I have a prescription—"

He pulls my arms together and puts me in handcuffs. Handcuffs!

He maneuvers me back to his cruiser. He reads me my rights and tells me I'm under arrest and forces me into the backseat.

At the police station he leads me into the building. A woman takes me into a room and searches me. They take all my belongings and then book and fingerprint me. Then they take my picture.

CHRISTMAS Eve in a jail cell. A new low.

I sit on the bench in some holding area. It is eleven o'clock when the woman comes to the cell door and unlocks it. "We've impounded your car. You can go if someone will pick you up."

"Can I take a cab?"

"Sorry, no. We haven't got your tox report back yet. We can't simply release you. There must be someone you can call."

I realize that this whole thing has just gotten worse. I will sit in jail overnight before I will call Margie on Christmas Eve and ask her to bail me out of jail.

I can only think of one person to call, and I don't know why his name comes to me. "Desmond Grant," I say. "He's an emergency-room doctor at Sacred Heart. I have his number in my purse."

The woman nods. "Come on, then."

We walk to a roomful of empty desks. The woman hands me my purse. I dig through it and find both the phone number and my phone. I punch in the number and wait.

"Hello?"

"Desmond?" I am already regretting this call.

"Tully?" he says, and I hear the surprise in his voice.

I don't want to say anything.

"Tully?" he says again, sounding concerned. "Are you okay?"

"I'm in the King County jail," I say softly. "DUI. But I didn't drink anything. They won't let me leave unless someone will be responsible for me. I know it's Christmas Eve and—"

"I'll be right there," he says.

"Thanks." I clear my throat and hang up.

I sit in a chair by the wall, ignoring the stream of drunks and hookers and street kids who are brought in every few minutes.

Finally the door opens and I see Desmond walk in; snow swirls in behind him. I stand, unsteady, feeling stupid and ashamed.

He crosses the room toward me. "Are you okay?"

"I've been better. I'm sorry to call you so late. And on Christmas Eve. And for this." Shame tightens my throat.

"My shift ends in ten minutes anyway. Where can I take you?"

"Home," I say. All I want is to be in my own bed.

He takes me by the arm and leads me out to his car. I tell him the address, and we drive the few blocks to my building in silence.

He pulls up in front of the building, turns to me.

I see the question in his gaze. The truth is that I don't want to invite him up, but how can I turn him away *now,* after he came for me? "Would you like to come up for a drink?"

His gaze is questioning, unnerving. "Okay," he says at last.

I open my car door and get out so fast I almost fall. The doorman steadies me. "Thanks," I mutter. Without waiting for Desmond, I walk across the lobby and press the up button at the elevator. In more silence we ride up together.

At my condo I open the door and let him inside. He follows me to the living room, with its view of the city. "Wine?" I ask.

"How about some coffee for both of us."

I go into the kitchen and make coffee. Then I excuse myself. In the bathroom I am appalled by my appearance—hair flattened and frizzied by the snow, face pale and tired, no makeup. I open the medicine cabinet, find my Xanax, and take one. Then I return to the living room. He has found my CD player and put on Christmas music.

"I'm surprised you called me," he says.

The answer to that is so pathetic, I remain quiet. I sit on my sofa. The full impact of this night is hitting me now. The Xanax isn't working fast enough. I feel panic coming on.

"Look, Desmond, I'm really tired. Thanks for coming, though."

I see him set his cup down on the coffee table and turn slowly toward me. He takes me by the hand and pulls me to my feet. The way he looks at me makes it hard to breathe. He *sees* me somehow. "You're like the Lady of Shalott, Tully, watching the world from the safety of your high-rise tower. You've done it all, succeeded beyond most people's wildest dreams. So why don't you have anyone to call on Christmas Eve or anywhere to be?"

"Leave," I say tiredly. I hate him for his question, for exposing my loneliness and my fear and for acting like I could do something differently. "Please." All I want to do is crawl into bed and sleep.

CHAPTER ELEVEN

BY JUNE of 2010, I know I am in trouble. Depression descends like a bell jar around me. I feel detached from everything and everyone.

I am deciding—again—to quit drinking, when my cell phone rings. I see the caller ID, and I dive for the phone. "Margie!"

"Hello, Tully."

I sink down to the sofa, realizing how much I needed to hear from a friend. "It's so good to hear from you!"

"I'm in the city. I thought I'd drop by. I'll be there in ten minutes."

I really am a mess. I will talk to Margie—my almost-mom. Maybe she can help me. "I'd love that."

I disconnect the call. Then I put on makeup and dress in jeans and a short-sleeved top. I am pathetically eager to see someone who loves me, to be welcomed and wanted.

The doorbell rings, and I run for it, opening the door.

There stands my mother, looking thin and ragged. She is dressed like a refugee from a seventies commune: baggy pants, Birkenstock sandals, and an embroidered Mexican tunic top. I am so bewildered by the sight of her that I don't know what to say.

"Margie sent me," she says. "But it was my idea. I wanted to see you. I knew you wouldn't open the door for me."

"Why are you here?"

She walks past me. In the living room she turns, and in a hesitant voice she says, "You have a drug or alcohol problem."

For a second my mind goes black. I think, *I've been caught.* I shake my head. "No," I say. "My medications are *prescribed.* You make it sound like I'm a drug addict." I laugh at the idea of that.

I cannot remember a time she held or kissed me or told me she loved me. But now she's going to call me an addict and *help* me.

"I've been through rehab," she says in a timid voice. "I think—"

"You have no right to say anything to me," I yell at her.

"Tully," my mother says. "Margie says your voice has been slurred the last few times she's talked to you. I saw your mug shot on TV. I know what you're going through."

"Go away," I say, my voice breaking.

"Why did you come to see me in Snohomish?"

"I'm writing a book about my life."

"You had questions."

I laugh. "Yeah. A lot of good it did me."

"Tully, maybe—"

"No maybes. Not from you. Not again. I can't take it." I grab her by the arm, shove her out into the hall, and slam the door shut. Then I go to my bedroom and climb into bed, pulling the covers over my head.

She is wrong. I don't have a problem. So what if I need Xanax to keep the panic attacks at bay and Ambien to sleep? So what if I like a few glasses of wine at night? I can stop whenever I want to.

It's *her* fault I'm in pain. My mother. She and Margie have betrayed me. That is the cruelest part of all.

September 3, 2010, 2:10 p.m.

IN THE hospital conference room the police detective stood with a small notepad reviewing his notes.

Johnny glanced around the quiet room. Most of the chairs were empty, pushed in close to the table. Beside him Margie was trying her best to sit tall and straight, but this had been a long vigil. He'd called her early this morning; she and Bud had been on a plane from Arizona by nine fifteen. Now Bud was at Johnny's, waiting for the boys to come home from school. Marah was in with Tully.

The detective cleared his throat. "The toxicology report won't be in for a while, but a search of Ms. Hart's residence revealed several prescription drugs—Vicodin, Xanax, and Ambien. We haven't found any witnesses to the accident yet, but our estimate is that she was driving in excess of fifty miles per hour on Columbia Street, heading toward the waterfront. She hit a concrete stanchion. She was not wearing her seat belt, and ironically, that may have saved her life. She went through the windshield and was exceptionally lucky not to hit the stanchion when she was thrown from the car."

"Were there skid marks?" Johnny asked. He heard Margie draw in a breath. Skid marks before a collision meant that the driver had tried to stop. No skid marks meant something else.

The detective looked at Johnny. "I don't know."

Johnny nodded. "Thanks, Detective."

After the detective left, Margie turned to Johnny. He saw the tears in her eyes and regretted his question. His mother-in-law had already suffered so much. "I'm sorry, Margie."

"Do you think she drove into it on purpose?"

The question stripped Johnny of his strength. He couldn't help thinking about the last time he'd been with Tully—and Marah.

He looked at Margie. "You've seen her more recently than I have. What do you think?"

Margie sighed. "I think she felt very alone in the last year."

Johnny got to his feet and mumbled an excuse about needing to use the bathroom and left the room.

In the hallway he saw a door and a sign: CHAPEL. He opened the door. The first thing he noticed was the quiet. The second was the girl seated in the front pew. All he could see was a tuft of pink hair. He moved forward slowly. "May I join you?"

Marah looked up sharply. "Like I could stop you."

"Do you want to stop me?" he asked quietly. He had so many mistakes with her, he didn't want to add to the pile by pushing her too hard when she'd come here to be alone.

She stared at him a long time and then slowly shook her head.

He sat down. "Does praying help you?"

"Not so far." Tears filled her eyes. "It's my fault that she's here."

"It's not your fault, baby. It was a car accident."

"It's your fault, too," Marah said, sounding miserable.

Johnny knew what his daughter meant. They'd let Tully down.

"We cut her out of our lives. I can't *stand* this," Marah cried. She bolted to her feet and headed for the door.

"Marah!" he yelled, getting up. "Don't hurt yourself."

"Too late," she said, and left the room.

Feeling every one of his fifty-five years, Johnny went back out to the waiting room, where he found Margie. He sat down beside her.

"I tried calling Dorothy again," she said. "No answer."

"Will she get the note you had Bud put on her door?"

"Sooner or later," she said quietly. "I hope it's sooner."

September 3, 2010, 2:59 p.m.

ON THIS cool September afternoon, leaves were falling all over the town of Snohomish. As Dorothy Hart stood in her stall at the farmer's market, she saw a bustle of color and activity. The market sprang up every Friday from noon to five: white tent roofs rose above it all, like ice-cream peaks; beneath them was a dazzling array of fruits and nuts, berries, herbs, vegetables, crafts, and honey.

Dorothy had a long, low table set up, dotted with boxes that held this week's crop: apples, raspberries, baskets full of herbs, beans, tomatoes, broccoli, carrots, and summer squash.

At two thirty she was almost out of everything. She packed up her boxes and carried them across the aisle to the Cascade Farms stall. The owner, a big wild-haired man, gave her a smile. "Looks like a good day for you, Dorothy."

"Really good, Owen. Thanks again for letting me use part of your booth. The raspberries were gone in a nanosecond."

She handed him the stack of boxes. He put them in the back of his pickup truck. He would drop them off at her house later.

She was sixty-nine years old, with long gray hair, skin that looked like ten miles of dry riverbed, and eyes that held all the sorrow she'd experienced in her life. She walked back to her stall, retied the bandanna across her forehead, and climbed onto the rusted bike that was her only mode of transportation.

One day at a time. The guiding tenet of this new life of hers. In the past six years, she'd turned her life around, pared down and stripped away until only what mattered remained. She grew and sold her organic produce, and she ate only fruits, nuts, vegetables, and grains. She was not pretty anymore, and she was as thin and stringy as her beans, but none of that bothered her.

She pedaled to Main Street, then parked her bike outside the pharmacy. Inside, she strode directly to the prescription counter.

"Hey, Dorothy," the pharmacist said.

"Hey, Scott."

He handed her the medication that had made such a difference in her life. "Thanks." She paid for her pills and headed out. She climbed onto her bicycle and pedaled the three miles home.

At her driveway on Firefly Lane, she wheeled left and hung on tightly as the old bike rattled down toward the house.

There was a note pinned to her front door. Frowning, she got off her bike. When was the last time someone had left her a note?

*Tully is in Sacred Heart hospital. Johnny says to hurry. Cab
fare under mat. 426 E.*
    M

Dorothy lifted up the doormat. A white envelope lay on the cement beneath. Inside was a one-hundred-dollar bill.

Dorothy hurried through the rambler that had once belonged to her parents and now was owned by her daughter—the same house a much younger Dorothy had once lived in with a fourteen-year-old Tully. The only place they'd ever lived together.

Dorothy took her pill. In the kitchen she opened the phone book, looked up the number, and called a cab. When the cab horn honked out front, she grabbed her purse and ran out.

She stared at her farm as the cab pulled out of the driveway. More than four years ago this place had saved her. She often thought that her tears had been the moisture that made her vegetables grow. She was grateful for the prescription drugs. The veil they provided was a softening of the world around her. Enough so that her emotions— her unreliable and dangerous moods—were calmed. Without them she knew she could spiral downward, into the darkness that had been home for most of her life.

Memories clamored at her, pushing, demanding, until she couldn't hear the cabbie breathing or the traffic zipping past them.

Time unspooled and wrapped around her, and she had no will to resist. She gave in, and for a split second the world went still.

Then she heard a dog barking, a chain snapping taut, and she knew where she was, *when* she was: 2005. November. She was sixty-four years old, a woman who called herself Cloud. She lived in a trailer off a logging road near Eatonville. The sweet, cloying smell of marijuana engulfed her. She was high, but not high enough.

Maybe a drink would help. In the kitchen she glanced dully around, noticing the stack of dirty dishes. She should do those before Truc got home. He hated it when she didn't clean up.

She opened the fridge. A fifth of Vodka lay in the rack on the door. She was reaching for it when she heard a diesel engine. Shoot.

Outside, the dogs were barking, snarling. She could hear them leaping toward him, straining their collars, snapping against long coils of chain.

She went to the door and opened it. There was his big red logging truck, parked by the woodpile. Truc climbed out of the cab. He was a big man, with straggly brown hair. His eyes were small and black.

"H-hey, Truc," she said, snapping open a beer for him. "I didn't think you'd be home until Tuesday."

He came in, and she knew he'd been drinking. He took the beer. "It's Tuesday," he growled. He finished the beer. He reached out and pulled her into his big arms and held her tightly. "I missed you," he whispered, and she wondered where he'd been since his shift ended. At the Lucky Spot, probably, drinking boilermakers.

He was touchy lately, and getting touchier all the time. She never knew what would set him off. "I missed you, too," she said.

The place reeked of pot, she realized. And garbage, maybe.

"Cloud," he said so quietly that the hair on the back of her neck stood up. What had she done or not done? Cleaning. She'd forgotten to clean. She was unable to even think of an excuse.

"You know I hate a mess like this. With all I give you—"

She felt her nose crumple beneath his fist. Blood sprayed everywhere, and she stood there, bleeding down her shirt.

She woke to the sound of heavy breathing. Her mouth was dry, and everything hurt. She'd woken up in this condition more times than she could count. She was in bed, with Truc sprawled beside her. It was still dark out. Night. She inched out of bed and winced as she put her weight on her left ankle. Sprained in one of her falls.

She limped to the bathroom and saw herself in the mirror. Her hair was matted with blood. Her eye was swollen shut, and the bruising around it was purple, brown, and yellow. Her nose was flattened, and dried blood caked her chin and cheeks.

She dressed in what she could find. She had to get away from

Truc before he killed her. She had thought this before, but in the end he always found her. But she wasn't young anymore.

She went to the bedside table and fumbled through his wallet, where she found three twenties. She reached down for her important belongings—the ragged macaroni-and-bead necklace and an old black-and-white photograph. She limped out of the room, kept going, and didn't look back.

Outside, it was dark in the woods, and the pain of each step reverberated up through her body as she walked. But she didn't stop or slow down until she got to the bus station in Eatonville.

She climbed onto the bus when it arrived, ignoring the bus driver's judgmental look. Two and a half hours later she got off the bus in downtown Seattle. Pioneer Square, to be exact. It was where you could disappear. She knew all about being invisible. But as she moved in this place that should have welcomed her with its dark corners, her headache intensified. She hurt so much she couldn't think straight. The next thing she knew, she was falling.

CLOUD came awake in stages. First came the realization of her pain, then of her breathing, then that she smelled clean. That told her where she was. Hospital. She'd been in enough of them to recognize the sights and smells and sounds. She remembered the night before in staccato images—a red flashing light, being lifted onto a gurney. Doctors and nurses buzzing around her, asking who had beaten her up. She'd closed her eyes and ignored them.

There was someone in the room with her. "Hello, Dorothy," said a plump black woman. "I'm Dr. Karen Moody. I've got your medical records. And I've spoken to the police. It all tells quite a story."

Cloud stared at her, saying nothing.

"The number of broken bones is certainly not normal. And I saw the cigarette burns on your collarbone. I'm guessing there are more." The doctor closed the chart. "And I'm guessing you self-medicate to forget."

"Is that your way of calling me a drunk and a stoner? If it is, you're right. I'm both. Have been for decades."

The doctor stared down at her. Then she reached into her pocket and pulled out a card. "Take this, Dorothy. I work at a rehab facility. If you're ready to change your life, I'd like to help you."

Cloud took the card and watched the woman walk out of the room and shut the door behind her.

Cloud pushed the covers back and got out of bed. Limping to the closet, she opened the door and saw a brown paper bag. Inside lay the clothes she'd been wearing. At the bottom lay her necklace. Well, it was just a few bits of dried macaroni and a single bead strung on a ragged strand of string. Cloud picked it up.

Happy birthday. I made this for you. . . . Ten-year-old Tully had held it out as if it were the Hope diamond.

What would have happened if Cloud had said, *It's perfect. I love it. I love you,* all those years ago? At that, she thought: *I need a drink.* She opened the door of her hospital room. Moving cautiously down the hallway, she made her way to an exit.

The dark night swallowed her. She began walking. Limping. Soon it was dawn. When rain began to fall, she climbed into the stoop of a vacant-looking building and sat down.

How many times in her life had she slept in a place just like this? And this was a better choice than others she'd made. Men like Truc. They were all the same. Fists and booze and anger.

She dug through her pocket for money she'd taken from Truc's wallet. But what she pulled out was a business card: DR. KAREN MOODY, OCCIDENTAL REHAB. Written across the bottom was: WHEN YOU'RE READY TO MAKE A CHANGE.

Cloud had heard these words a thousand times. But now, as she sat on the stoop, the word *change* filled her with longing.

Occidental. The street was less than a block away.

She was so tired of this life. She hauled herself to an unsteady stand. She limped out into the rain and kept going.

The rehab center was housed in a small flat-roofed brick building that dated back to Seattle's gritty pioneer beginning. She took a deep breath and reached for the door handle. It was locked.

She sat down on the concrete stoop, this time unprotected by an overhang. Rain drenched her. Her headache came back, but she didn't move. She sat there until a sound roused her. She looked up and saw Dr. Moody beneath an umbrella.

"I'll fail," Cloud said dully, shivering hard.

Dr. Moody came up the steps. "Let's go inside where it's dry."

"I guess dry is the point."

Dr. Moody laughed. "A sense of humor. Good. You'll need it."

CLOUD Hart went into rehab, and forty-five days later Dorothy Hart emerged. Now she stood in her small room and packed up her belongings: a macaroni necklace and a creased photograph with the date OCTOBER 1962 stamped on its scalloped white edge.

They had seemed like nothing when she walked into this building, these two small personal items. But now she understood their value. They were her treasures; somehow she'd held on to them. Dr. Moody claimed that it was the Real Dorothy who'd kept them, the healthy part of her who had been strong enough to survive it all.

Dorothy didn't know about that. Honestly, she tried never to think about the girl she'd once been. Sobriety didn't make it easier to look back. The opposite was true, in fact. Now she lived her life in moments. Every dry second was a triumph.

It had begun like all of her Hail Mary passes at normalcy—with a feeling of relief. Nothing was more comforting in the beginning than relinquishing control. Then the shaking started. Her craziness had been epic—throwing chairs, screaming to be let go.

She'd ended up in a detox ward for seventy-two of the longest hours of her life. And then, miraculously, she'd fallen asleep and wakened in another world, washed ashore. Disorientated, still shaking, weak as a newborn puppy. Dry.

She sat in the group therapy sessions like a ghost. She remembered when it had changed for her. It had been in group, about three weeks after her detox. She'd been listening to Gilda complain about the time she'd been raped at a fraternity party, crying hard, and Dr. Moody had looked right at Cloud.

"How does that make you feel, Cloud?"

A memory floated up. *He's smoking. The red tip is terrible.*

"I used to be Dorothy" was how she'd answered.

"You can be her again," Dr. Moody had said.

"I'm Dorothy," she'd said slowly, "and I'm an addict. . . ."

That had been the beginning, maybe the only real one ever. From then on, recovery had been her addiction, honesty her drug of choice. She talked and talked and talked. But even with her new sober-zealotry, she never named her daughter or talked about her youth. Some pains ran too deep for sharing with strangers.

"Are you ready to leave us?"

She heard Dr. Moody's kind voice, and Dorothy turned.

Dr. Moody stood in the doorway. In her jeans and ethnic-embroidered top, she looked like exactly who she was—a woman who gave all her time and energy to helping others. Dorothy wished she had money to give to this woman who had saved her.

"I think I'm ready, but I don't feel like I am. What if—"

"One day at a time," Dr. Moody said.

"One day at a time," Dorothy said, nodding. She could do it that way, she hoped. Break her life into bite-size pieces.

Dr. Moody held out a small envelope. "This is for you."

Dorothy stared at the picture of tomatoes on it. "Tomato seeds."

"For your organic garden."

In the past weeks this "plan" had come to Dorothy. But could she do it? Could she really move back into her parents' old investment property on Firefly Lane and grow things? She'd never successfully cared for anything. She'd never succeeded, period.

"You can do this, Dorothy. Will you contact your daughter?"

Dorothy released a heavy sigh. A parade of memories sidled into the room. All the times "Cloud" had abandoned Tully. "Not yet."

"When?"

"When I believe."

"In what?"

All Dorothy could do was change and atone and hope that some-day she would be strong enough to face her daughter and apologize.

"In me," she said at last, and Dr. Moody nodded.

ONE DAY AT A TIME. DOROTHY started slowly. She wrote to her daughter's business manager and told him she was moving into her parents' old rental house on Firefly Lane. It had been vacant for years. Each day when she went to the mailbox, she thought: *She'll answer.* But in January of 2006, the first year of her sober life, she heard a businesslike *I'll forward your monthly allowance to 17 Firefly Lane* from the manager and not a word from her daughter.

She pushed herself hard. She rose at dawn and worked in the field until nightfall. In the evenings she rode her bike into town and attended meetings. *Hi, I'm Dorothy, and I'm an addict.* As odd as it sounded, the roteness of it all soothed her. The strangers became friends. She'd met Myron there, and through Myron, Peggy, and through Peggy, Edgar and the organic farming community.

By June of 2006, she had cleared a quarter of an acre and roto-tilled a small patch of earth. She was kneeling in the dirt, tilling with a gardening trowel, when she heard someone call out. She put down her trowel and stood up.

A small, older woman was crossing the street, coming toward the gate. She was dressed in jeans and a white sweatshirt that read WORLD'S BEST GRANDMA. Her black hair framed a round apple-cheeked face with a pointed chin.

"Oh," the woman said, stopping abruptly. "It's you."

Dorothy was about to say, *I don't know you,* when a memory struck. *I'm lying on the sofa with a mound of weed on my stomach, high as a kite. I try to smile at the do-gooder who has just walked into the house, but I am so high, all I can do is laugh and swear. Talullah is bright red with embarrassment.*

"You're Oven-Mitt Girl's mom," Dorothy said quietly. "From across the street."

"Margie Mularkey. And yes, to my daughter's horror, I sent her here with a hot casserole in about 1974. You were . . . indisposed."

"High. And probably drunk."

Margie nodded. "I came to see what was going on. I didn't know you'd moved in. The house has been empty for a long time. I should have noticed, but we've had a tough year. Been gone a lot."

"I could keep an eye on the place for you. Collect your mail."

"That would be nice. I'd appreciate it. There's a milk box on the porch. Maybe you could put the mail in there."

"I could do that."

Margie glanced away. She was looking down the road. "The girls used to sneak out at night and ride their bikes on this road. They thought I didn't know." At that, Margie crumpled to the ground.

Dorothy rushed to the woman and helped her to the patio and into a dirty chair. "I, uh, haven't cleaned the outdoor furniture yet."

Margie laughed dully. "It's July. Summer just started." She reached into her pocket and pulled out a pack of cigarettes.

Dorothy sat cross-legged on the weed-choked cement patio, watching a tear slip down the woman's round cheek.

"Don't mind me," Margie said. "I've been holding this in too long. Katie, my daughter, has cancer."

Dorothy had no idea what people said at a time like this.

"Thank you," Margie said into the silence.

"What for?"

"Not saying 'She'll be fine' or, worse, 'I'm sorry.' "

"Bad stuff happens," Dorothy said.

"Yeah. I didn't used to know that."

"How's Tully?"

"She's with Katie. I think she'd like it if you went to see her."

"I've hurt her a few times too many. Don't want to do it again."

"Yes," Margie said. "She's always been more fragile than she seems." They sat there a little longer, saying nothing. Finally, Margie stood. "Well, I have to get back."

Dorothy nodded. She walked Margie up to Firefly Lane. As Margie started across the street, Dorothy said, "Margie? I'll bet she knows how much you love her. Your Katie. That would mean a lot."

Margie nodded and wiped her eyes. "Thanks, Cloud."

"I'm Dorothy now."

Margie smiled tiredly. "Dorothy, I hope you don't mind me saying this: Time passes. Trust me. Strong girls suddenly get sick. Don't wait too long to see your daughter."

CHAPTER TWELVE

IN OCTOBER of 2006, rain fell from swollen clouds day after day, turning Dorothy's carefully tilled fields into a black and muddy mess. Still, she went out every day to care for this ground that had become the whole of her focus. She was busy planting when a floral delivery van turned into the driveway across the street.

The house was empty now, she knew. The Mularkeys were either at the hospital or Kate's house every day. Dorothy had picked up their mail and placed it in the silver milk-delivery box. Several times she'd found the box empty, so she knew Bud and Margie were home occasionally, but she'd not seen either of them in the past month.

She put down her trowel and walked toward the driveway. Another delivery truck chugged down the Mularkeys' driveway.

Two flower deliveries in thirty minutes. She walked to the white farmhouse's welcoming front porch and couldn't help thinking that *this* was the house that came closest to home for her daughter.

The porch was full of flower arrangements. Dorothy plucked the envelope from a bouquet near her and opened it.

> We are so sorry for your loss.
> Kate will be missed.
> Love, the Goldstein family

This would break Tully's heart, pure and simple. Dorothy might not know much about her daughter, but she knew this: Kate was the ground beneath her daughter's feet. What could she do to help?

Maybe this terrible moment would be the time to show Tully that she had changed. She hurried back to her house. It took less than thirty minutes to find out the funeral plans. It would be held in a few days at the Catholic church on Bainbridge Island.

Dorothy rode her bike into town and had her hair cut. Then she went to one of the small local boutiques on First Street and purchased a pair of simple black pants and a matching turtleneck.

On the day of the funeral, she dressed carefully in her new clothes. She climbed onto her bike and rode into town.

Downtown, she splurged on a chai tea latte and waited impatiently for the bus. When the bus pulled up, she got on. She could do this. She could go to her daughter and help her. At last.

The bus pulled up to the ferry terminal and came to a wheezing stop. Dorothy disembarked and boarded the ferry for Bainbridge.

The island was pretty in a well-tended way, with quaint shops and quiet streets. She moved with the steady stream of locals and tourists, off the boat, up the terminal, and out into the sunshine.

The distance to the church was farther than she'd thought, so she arrived late. The service had already begun. The doors were closed. She wasn't about to go into that church alone. She found a bench beneath a maple tree at the edge of the parking lot and sat.

When she looked up again, Tully stood alone in front of the church. Dorothy got to her feet and started to move forward, but then she stopped. Mourners poured out of the church. Several of them collected around Tully. Kate's family.

She'd been an idiot to think that her presence would help. Her daughter *had* people who cared about her, and about whom she cared. She'd come all this way, following a beam of light that couldn't be grasped.

September 3, 2010, 4:57 p.m.
"LADY? Lady? Are you getting out?"

Dorothy came back to the present with a start. She was in the cab, parked in front of the hospital's emergency entrance. She fumbled with the money and paid the cabbie.

Then she walked to the front door and into the austere lobby. At the reception desk she stopped, cleared her throat. "I'm Doro—Cloud Hart," she said quietly. The old name pinched like a bad bra, but it was how Tully knew her. "Tully's mother."

The woman at the desk nodded and gave her the room number. Dorothy headed for the elevator and rode it to the fourth floor.

Margie sat in the waiting room. Her grandsons were playing cards on the floor. At Dorothy's arrival, Margie stood. Beside her was that good-looking man who'd been Kate's husband. He saw Margie stand; then he slowly got to his feet, too.

Margie came forward, her hands outstretched. "I'm glad you got my note. I didn't have time to go looking for you."

"Thank you," Dorothy said. "How is she?"

"Our girl is a fighter," Margie said.

Our girl. As if she and Margie were both mothers to Tully.

"You remember Johnny," Margie said. "Katie's husband and Tully's friend."

"We met years ago," Dorothy said. It wasn't a good memory.

"You've never done anything but hurt her," he said softly.

"I know."

"If you hurt her now, it's me you'll be dealing with. Got that?"

Dorothy didn't look away. "Thank you."

He frowned. "For what?"

"Loving her."

He looked surprised by that.

Margie took Dorothy's arm and led her into an ICU enclave with glass-walled rooms that fanned out behind a central nurses station desk. There, Margie went to speak with the woman at the desk.

"Okay," Margie said when she returned. "That's her room right there. Go talk to her, Dorothy. The doctors think it helps."

Dorothy nodded. Her hand was shaking as she opened the door. Inside, the bed was hidden behind a privacy curtain. She pushed it aside. Tully lay there, surrounded by machines. A clear plastic tube invaded her mouth. Her face was scraped and bruised. She was bald, and a plastic tube went into her head. One arm was in a cast.

Dorothy pulled a chair up to the bed and sat down. She knew what Tully would want to hear. It was what her daughter had come to Snohomish for, what she'd asked for in a thousand ways over the years. The truth. Dorothy's story. Their story.

She could do this. At last. She *could*. This was what her daughter needed from her. She drew in a deep breath.

"When I was a kid, California was beautiful. Citrus groves instead of freeways. Oil derricks pumping up and down on the hillsides. I remember when they built Disneyland," she said.

"We were Ukrainian. Did you know that? As a girl, I . . . thought it meant 'ugly'—Ukrainian—and it might as well have. It was the first of the secrets I learned to keep. Fitting in. This is what mattered to my parents in the plastic, shiny world of the fifties. In the fifties, girls were like dolls. We were expected to be perfect, with nothing on our minds except pleasing our parents, getting good grades, and marrying the right boy.

We lived in one of the first cul-de-sacs in Orange County. Rancho Flamingo, it was called, a horseshoe plan of ranch-style houses set on identical lots. Every house had sliding doors that led out to a patio, and if you had *really* made it, you had a swimming pool.

I was an awkward girl, with frizzy hair and thick eyebrows. Mom told me to just stay quiet and be a good girl. I did. I kept quiet. By junior high I was an outcast, or maybe just invisible. And then it got worse. In the summer, I began to change physically. I started my period, and my breasts developed, and I lost layers of baby fat. The first time I showed up at a pool party in an Annette Funicello two-piece, my father hauled me into the house and pushed me into a corner and told me I looked like a tramp.

I knew he wanted something from me, but I didn't understand.

HE CAME into my room one night when I was fifteen. He was drunk and smelled like cigarettes, and he hurt me. Afterward he said it was my fault for dressing like a tramp. I believed him. He was my dad. I was used to believing him.

I tried to tell my mom—more than once—but she avoided me now, snapped at me for the smallest things. She couldn't stand the sight of me. After that, I tried to disappear completely. I buttoned my sweaters to my throat and wore no makeup at all.

My life went like that for years. My dad got drunker and angrier and meaner, and I got quieter and more depressed and hopeless, but I thought I was okay. Until one day in class when a boy pointed at me and laughed and everyone joined in. Or I thought they did. I started screaming and crying and pulling at my hair. The classroom went deathly silent. The teacher sent me to the principal's office.

Appearances. That's what mattered to my parents. They didn't care *why* I'd cried in class or pulled out my own hair, just that I'd done it in public.

THEY said the hospital was for my own good.

You're a bad girl, Dorothy. Everyone has problems. Why are you so selfish? Of course your father loves you. Why would you say such terrible things?

The hospital—they called it a sanatorium—was in another city. When we got to the place, it looked like a prison on a hill.

Inside, everyone wore white and looked grim. I think that's when I noticed the bars on the windows.

The doctor's name was Corduroy. Or Velvet. Some fabric.

Sit down, Miss Hart.

I turned to my mom and begged to be taken home. I couldn't make her understand how sorry I was and how scared, and I started screaming and crying.

I heard my mother scream, MAKE HER STOP DOING THAT.

When I woke up, I was in a bed with my wrists and ankles strapped down. A nurse wheeled a machine into the room, up to the bed. Someone smeared cold goo into my temples. Dr. Seersucker came in next. He leaned over me and fit metal plates to either side of my head. He clamped the strap around my head. Then he jammed something in my mouth, and I gagged.

The jolt is impossible to describe. I know now it was a bolt of electricity burning through me. When it finally let me go, I sagged onto the bed lifelessly, feeling as close to dead as I could imagine.

I had no idea what I'd done that was terrible enough to warrant this punishment, and I wanted someone to hold me and love me and tell me it would be okay.

You might think I am stupid because you've seen me high so much of the time, but I'm smart. It took no time for me to learn where I'd screwed up. I hadn't known the cost of changing lanes.

Be good. Be quiet. Do as you're told. Answer direct questions with answers; never say you don't know; never say your father hurts you. Don't tell them that your mother knows what's happening to you and doesn't care. Oh, no. And never say you're sorry.

Dorothy Jean? Never had my mother's voice sounded so sweet.

Mommy, I said. *Can I come home now? I'll be good.*

The doctors say you can. I hope they're right. I can't believe you belong with . . . these people.

I followed my mother out to her big blue Chrysler and slid into the leather seat. She immediately lit up a cigarette, and as she moved the car into gear, ash sprayed down onto the seat. That's how I knew she was upset. My mother didn't believe in mess.

Once we were home, I got out of the car. I went inside and stepped into the brightness of our living room. My father stood by the fireplace, dressed in his Frank Sinatra suit, holding a martini in one hand and a lit Camel cigarette in the other. *So you're back.*

The doctors say she's fine, Winston, my mother said.

I remember setting the table for dinner that night, trying to grasp what I was supposed to be. I turned slowly to look at my mother, who was in the kitchen stirring something. She wore cat's-eye black horn-rimmed glasses and a charcoal-gray sweater set. There was not an ounce of softness in her.

Mom? I said quietly, coming up beside her.

She cocked her head just enough to look at me. *When life gives you lemons, Dorothy Jean, you make lemonade.*

But he—

Enough, she snapped. *You have to forget. Forget all of it and you'll learn to smile again in no time. As I have.* Her eyes pleaded with me. *Please, Dorothy. Your father won't put up with this.*

I couldn't tell if she wanted to help me and didn't know how, or if she didn't care. I did know that if I told the truth again, or showed pain, my father would send me away and she would let him do it.

That night, he woke me up, of course. While I was away, his anger had spread. I had humiliated him with my "lies."

I told him I was sorry—a terrible mistake. He burned me with a cigarette and told me to keep my mouth shut. I just stared at him. It made him even angrier, my silence. But it was all I had. I'd learned my lesson, remember. I couldn't stop him from hurting me, but when he looked at me that night, he saw something new, too. *Girls have babies, you know,* I whispered softly. *Proof.*

He backed away and slammed the door shut. It was the last time he came to my bed, but not the last time he hurt me. All I had to do was look at him and he hit me.

School was worse when I got back from the sanitorium, too. I survived it, though. I kept my head down. I was damaged goods. There was an odd comfort in it. I no longer had to pretend at all.

My mother couldn't stand the new me, with my baggy clothes and untended hair and sleepy eyes. But by the spring of my junior year, I started noticing the other kids, the ones I hadn't seen before, the ones who lived on the wrong side of the tracks. One day they were invisible like me, and the next day they were everywhere, dressing like James Dean in *Rebel Without a Cause,* rolling packs of cigarettes in their T-shirt sleeves.

Hoods, we called them at first, and then greasers. It was supposed to be an insult, but they only laughed.

I remember being in home ec, listening to Mrs. Peabody drone on about the importance of a stocked cupboard for a housewife. When the bell rang, I walked woodenly to my locker. I felt someone come up behind me. The hallway went quiet. I turned.

He was tall and broad-shouldered, with curly black hair. His skin was dark, and he had strong white teeth and a square jaw. He wore a white T-shirt and faded jeans. A black leather jacket hung negligently from one hand. He lit his cigarette, right there in the hallway.

Principal Moro came bustling down the hallway, pushing through the crowd, telling everyone to get to his or her classroom.

The boy touched my chin. *I'm Rafe Montoya,* he said.

Dorothy Jean was all I could get out.

You don't look crazy to me, Dorothy, he said. *Are you?*

It was the first time someone had asked, and my first thought was to lie. Then I saw how he was looking at me, and I said, *Maybe.*

The smile he gave me was sadder than anything I'd seen in a long while. *That just means you're paying attention, Dorothy.*

I knew one thing for sure: Good girls from Rancho Flamingo did not talk to boys with dark skin named Montoya. But from the second I saw him, I couldn't think about anything else.

Rafael Montoya changed the course of my life when he said those words to me. *It just means you're paying attention.*

I wanted to be a bad girl suddenly. The good-girl thing had been such a disaster. Now I agonized over my hair, straining to make it look like the popular girls. I plucked my brows until they were perfect arches above my eyes. I wore one pretty Peter Pan–collared dress after another. Everyone noticed the change. I hovered in the hallways, looking for him. It was as if I took myself apart and re-organized the pieces in the image of what I imagined he would want.

I can't remember now how long it went on, me waiting and hoping. Weeks, maybe longer. Then one day I was standing by my locker when I heard him say, *I've been looking for you.*

I turned around. *You looked for me?*

And you looked for me. Admit it.

He slowly lifted his arm and used one finger to tuck the hair behind my ear. At his touch, I felt this . . . flare of longing. It was as if for the first time, someone saw me. I wanted his touch, and wanting it terrified me. All I'd known of sex was pain and degradation.

I knew it was dangerous to be excited by this boy. But when he touched my chin and made me look at him, it was already too late.

Be with me, he said. *Don't care about what they think.*

Can we keep it quiet? I asked.

I could tell my question hurt him, and I hated that. It wasn't until later, when he took me to bed and taught me about love and passion and sex that I told him all of it, every sordid detail of my ugly life. He held me and told me he'd never let anyone hurt me again. We kept our relationship hidden until the day I realized I was pregnant.

CHAPTER THIRTEEN

PEOPLE think high school girls didn't get pregnant in my day, but we did. The difference was that girls disappeared. They were simply gone one day—off to visit an elderly aunt or an ill cousin—and back sometime later; thinner, usually, and quieter.

I loved Rafe—thoroughly, utterly. I didn't know then that love was fragile and that your future could turn on a dime. One night in late May of my junior year, my father came home and informed my mother and me that he'd been promoted and that we were moving to Seattle. *July first,* Dad said.

I had to tell Rafe everything. As scared as I was to tell him, I was excited, too. Maybe even a little proud. We had made this, created a child out of our love, and wasn't that what I'd been raised to do?

A baby, he said, and suddenly I was imagining you: ten fingers, ten toes, a mop of black hair. In an instant I fashioned a dream life for the three of us, but then he was quiet, and my doubt set in.

I can go away, I said into the silence. *To . . . wherever girls go.*

No. This is our baby, he said fiercely. *We'll be a family.*

I had never loved anyone as much as I loved him then.

That afternoon we started to plan. I knew I couldn't tell my parents. If they could lock me away and give away my child, I knew they'd do it. And I didn't think twice about quitting school. I was no scholar. I wanted to be a wife and mother.

We would leave right after his graduation from high school, less than a month away. He was alone, essentially, too. His mother had died at his birth; he'd come to Southern California with an uncle, after his father deserted the family. They were migrant workers. Rafe wanted something more for himself, and we were naive enough to think we could find it together.

On the date we'd chosen for our escape, I was crazy nervous. At dinner I couldn't get a word out. *What's wrong with her, Ma?* my dad said, frowning at me through the blue smoke of his cigarette.

I washed and dried the dishes, making sure everything was done to my father's exacting standards. By then my parents had moved into the living room. *I have a lot of homework to do tonight,* I said, standing at the edge of the room. *And . . . I have cramps.*

Dorothy Jean! my mother snapped. But my father understood. He hated to be anywhere near me when I was "unclean."

Behind my closed door, I waited for them to turn off the lights, my packed suitcase under the bed. At nine fifteen I heard them turn off the TV and lock up. I positioned pillows and stuffed animals in my bed and pulled the covers over them. I opened my door and crept through the hallway. At the back door I paused. Then I saw the head-lights waiting at the end of the cul-de-sac, and I ran toward my future.

IT WASN'T until we burned through the first tank of gas that the fear set in. How would we live, *really?* I was seventeen years old and pregnant, with no high school diploma and no job skills. Rafe was barely eighteen, with no family or money to fall back on.

The money we had took us only as far as northern California. Rafe did the only thing he knew. He worked on one farm after an-other, picking whatever was in season. We lived in tents or shacks or cabins. I remember always being tired and broke and dusty and lonely. He wouldn't let me work in my condition. Instead, I stayed in whatever hovel we'd found and tried to make it homey. We meant to get married. We were happy. I remember that. I loved your father. Even when we both started to change, I hung on.

The day you were born—in a tent in a field in Salinas, by the way—I felt overwhelmed by love. We named you Talullah because we knew you would be extraordinary, and Rose because your pink skin was the softest thing I'd ever touched. I did love you. I *do.*

But something happened to me when you were born. I started having nightmares about my father. Nowadays someone would tell a young mother about postpartum depression, but not back then. I would wake in the night, screaming. Rafe couldn't understand.

One night, when he was crazed with worry, we started fighting. Our first real fight. He stormed out, and in his absence I fell apart. I knew I'd been bad, that I'd lost him, that he'd never really loved me—how could he? When he finally came home, you were naked and screaming and I just sat there, dazed, staring at you. He called me crazy, and I . . . snapped. I slapped him in the face as hard as I could.

It was awful. The police were called. They put handcuffs on Rafe and took him away and made me give them my driver's license. That was 1962, remember. I was nineteen years old—an adult, a mother—but they called my father.

I sat in a stinky dirty cell in the jail for hours. Long enough for Rafe to be fingerprinted and booked for assault and for my parents to drive down from Seattle. Some sour-faced woman from social services took you away from me. I sat there, weighed down by a despair so bleak I couldn't breathe. I was crazy. I knew that now.

In the morning I tried to tell the police I'd lied about Rafe hitting me, but they didn't care. They kept me locked up "for my own safety" until my father came for me.

THE hospital they sent me to the second time was much worse than the first. I was there for two years.

I left the hospital a different person. My memory was shaky—time leapt away from me sometimes. What I remembered was love. It was the slimmest of strands, my memories, but they kept me alive in there. *He loves me. I'm not alone.* And there was you.

I kept an image of you in my mind through all of it—your pink cheeks and chocolate-brown eyes—Rafe's eyes—and the way you launched forward when you were trying to crawl. When they let me out, my mother stood waiting for me. *Are you better now?*

I am. How's Talullah?

We've told everyone she's our niece. They know we went to court to get custody, so don't say anything.

You took her away from me?

Your father was right. You have no business raising a child.

My father was all I said, but it was enough.

Don't start that again. She led me out of the hospital and down the steps and into a new sky-blue Chevrolet Impala. All I could think about was saving you from that terrible house where *he* lived, but I knew I would have to be smart. I don't remember a single word passing between us until we pulled into the garage.

It helped you, didn't it? my mom said, and I saw a glimmer of worry in her eyes. *They told us you needed help.*

I knew I could never tell her the truth. *I'm better,* I said dully.

But when I walked in that new house, full of the furniture of my youth and smelling of my dad's Old Spice aftershave and Camel cigarettes, I felt so sick I ran to the kitchen sink and threw up.

WHEN I first saw you again, I started to cry.

Dorothy, don't upset her, my mother said. *She doesn't know you.*

She wouldn't let me touch you. My mother was sure my poison would infect you somehow, and how could I disagree?

You seemed happy with her, and she smiled around you, even laughed. I couldn't remember ever making her as happy as you did. You had your own room and toys, and she rocked you to sleep. That first night home, I stood in the doorway of your room and watched her sing to you, and I felt anger so sharp I felt faint.

I felt my father come up behind me. He put a hand on my hip and whispered, *She's going to be a looker. Your little wetback.*

I spun around. *Don't you even* look *at my daughter.*

He smiled. *I'll do what I want. Don't you know that by now?*

I screamed in rage and pushed him away from me. His eyes widened as he lost his balance and tumbled down the hardwood stairs. When he was still, I went down to stand beside him. Blood seeped out from the back of his head.

What have you done? my mother screamed. She had you in her arms; you were sleeping. Even her cries didn't waken you.

He's dead, I said.

Oh, my Lord. Winston! My mother ran back into the room, and I could hear her calling the police. I ran up after her, caught her as she was hanging up. She turned. *I'll get you help,* she said.

Help. I knew what that meant. Electroshock and ice baths and barred windows and medications. *Give her to me,* I pleaded.

She's not safe with you. My mother's arms tightened around you. I saw how she was fighting for you, and it hurt me so much.

Why didn't you fight him for me? You know what he did to me.

She shook her head. Then very quietly: *I'll protect her.*

I heard the sirens coming. If they found me here, they'd arrest me. I was a murderer now. My own mother had called the police.

I'll be back for her, I promised. *I'll find Rafe, and we'll be back.*

I ran out of my parents' house. I couldn't feel anything but happy about his death. I had saved you from him, at least. I wanted to save you from my mother, too, but really, how could I care for you alone? We needed Rafe to make us a family.

I walked down to First Avenue and stuck out my thumb. When a VW bus pulled over, the driver asked me where I was going.

Salinas, I said. It was all I could think of. The last place I'd seen him. I climbed aboard and stared out the window and listened to the music coming from his scratchy radio. "Blowin' in the Wind."

"You get high?" the driver asked me, and I thought, *Why not?*

THEY say pot isn't addictive. It was for me. Once I smoked my first joint, I couldn't stop. I needed the calm it gave me. That was when I started to live like a vampire, up all night, high all the time. But in every town I went through, I asked about Rafe.

I drifted that way for months, until I made it to Los Angeles. Alone, I hitchhiked out to Rancho Flamingo and saw the house I'd grown up in. Then I made my way to Rafe's old house.

I didn't expect to find him there, and I wasn't wrong. Still, someone answered the door. His uncle. I knew the moment I saw him. He had Rafe's dark eyes—your eyes, Tully—and the wavy hair.

I'm Dorothy Hart, I said.

I know who you are. You got him put in jail.

What could I say to that? *Would you tell me where he is?*

He looked at me for so long I started to feel sick. Then he made a little "follow me" motion and went into the shadow-filled house.

At a small fireplace, the old man turned to me. *He loved you.*

How could I tell this man my shame—that I'd been chained like an animal for years? That I would have cut off my arm to get free. *I love him, too. I know he thinks I ran away, but—*

Then it sank in.

Loved you. *Loved.* I didn't want to hear what he would say next.

He looked for you. Very long. Vietnam, he said at last.

That's when I noticed the flag folded into a small triangle and framed in wood sitting on the mantel. *He knew you would come looking for him. He tell me give you this.*

The old man reached behind the flag and pulled out a small piece of ordinary notebook paper. It had been folded into a small square.

Querida, he'd written, and my heart stopped at that. I swore I heard his voice. *I love you and will always love you. When I come back, I will find you and Talullah and we will begin again. Wait for me, querida, as I wait for you.*

I looked at the old man and saw my pain reflected in his eyes. I clutched the note. I stumbled out of his house and walked until it got dark, and even then I kept walking.

THAT was the start of me losing time again. Days, weeks. Now I know it was because I was doing so many drugs. I was desperate to turn on and tune out. When I looked back—finally, when I got sober—I thought, *Of course.* It was the early sixties, I was barely an adult; I'd been molested and abused, and I thought it was my fault. No wonder I lost myself so completely to drugs.

Then one night I dreamed about my father. In my nightmare he was alive and coming for you. Once the nightmare descended into my life, nothing could get rid of it. Finally I couldn't stand it anymore. I told this guy—Pooh Bear, we called him—to take me home. The next thing I knew, there were five of us in an old VW bus, banging our way north. We made pot brownies in a cast-iron skillet over an open fire and dropped acid.

And then one day I woke up, still high, and found that we were parked in front of my mother's house. The bus was half on the street and half on the sidewalk. I don't think any of us remember parking. I jumped out of the van and went into the house.

You were right there at the table, playing with a spoon, when I opened the door and went in. Somewhere upstairs a bell tinkled. *That's Grandpa,* you said, and I felt rage explode inside of me. How could he be alive? And what had he done to you?

I went up the stairs, screaming for my mother.

She was in her bedroom, with my father, who looked like a cadaver in a twin bed. His face was slack. *He's alive?* I screamed.

I wanted to tell my mother I was taking you, but I couldn't think straight. I ran downstairs and scooped you into my arms.

My mother ran down behind me. *He's paralyzed, Dorothy Jean. I told the police he had a stroke. I swear. You're safe. You can stay.*

I had you in my arms. I imagined redemption for myself, a new beginning for us. So I took you. And nearly killed you by letting you eat a brownie filled with marijuana. It wasn't even my idea to take you to the hospital when you started flipping out. It was Pooh Bear's. I carried you to the emergency room and ran.

It wasn't until later, when you were asleep, that I snuck in and pinned your name on your shirt with my mother's phone number. It was all I could think of to do. I got it finally: I didn't deserve you.

I kissed you before I left.

I bet you don't remember any of this. I hope you don't.

September 3, 2010, 6:15 p.m.

Beeeeep . . .

The noise sliced through Dorothy's memories, brought her back to the present. She had been so deep in her story that it took her a moment to clear her head. She lurched to her feet.

"Help!" she screamed. "Someone get in here! Please. I think her heart is stopping. Please! Now! Someone save my daughter!"

THE brightness around me is gorgeous, like lying inside of a star. Beside me I hear Katie breathing. "She's there . . . here," I said, awed by the very idea that my mother would come to see me.

I am listening to her voice, trying to make sense of her words. There's something about a picture, and a word—*querida*—that doesn't make sense. None of it makes sense, actually.

Then I hear something else. A beep. An alarm goes off, blaring.

"Katie?" I look sideways and see that I am alone. What's wrong?

I will myself to see where I really am. And suddenly I'm back in my body. I'm in a bed with metal railings. I see my mother beside me. She is screaming something about her daughter—me. Nurses and doctors rush in and push her aside.

Pain explodes in my chest. Then the green line goes flat.

September 3, 2010, 6:26 p.m.

"SHE'S dead. Why are we still here?"

Marah turned to Paxton. He sat on the floor in the waiting room with his long legs stretched out. Beside him lay a heap of food wrappers—cookies, cakes, potato chips, candy bars; he'd bought whatever was for sale in the vending machine. He kept sending Marah to her dad for more money. She frowned at him.

"Why are you looking at me like that? On TV, when someone flatlines, it's over. Your dad texted you ten minutes ago that her heart stopped. Then the doctor wanted a meeting. She's toast."

All at once she *saw* him. It was like having the house lights go up on a decrepit theater that had looked magical in the dark. She scrambled to her feet and started to run. She skidded into Tully's ICU room just as Dr. Bevan was saying, "We've stabilized her again. Her brain activity is good, but of course, we can't know anything for sure until she wakes up." He paused. "If she wakes up."

Marah pressed back against the wall. Her father and grandmother were standing by the doctor. Dorothy stood off by herself.

"We've begun warming her body temperature, and we're bringing her out of the coma, but that's a slow process. Tomorrow we'll assess her progress. We'll take her off the ventilator and see."

"Will she die when you take her off the machine?" Marah asked, surprising herself by speaking aloud. Everyone looked at her.

"Come here," Dad said. She moved cautiously toward him.

They'd been at odds for so long it felt weird going to him for comfort, but when she sidled in close, all the bad years fell away.

"The truth is that we don't know," Dr. Bevan said. "Brain injuries are impossible to predict. She may wake up and breathe on her own, or she may breathe on her own and not wake up. Or she may not be able to breathe on her own. When she's off the medications and her body temperature is back to normal, we'll be able to assess her brain activity better." He closed the chart.

Marah looked at her dad. "I want to get her iPod—the one Mom made for her. Maybe if she hears her music . . ." She couldn't finish.

"There's my girl," he said. "The songs meant so much to both of them. Will the doorman let you into her apartment?"

"I still have a key. I'll take Pax to her house and get the iPod. Then . . . we could come back to the house. If that's okay."

"Okay? We moved back to Bainbridge for you, Marah. I've kept the light on every night since you left."

An hour later Marah and Pax were in a cab.

"What are we, *servants?*" Paxton sat slumped beside her.

She didn't answer. A moment later he said, "How much money did the old man give you? Can we stop for a hamburger?"

Marah didn't look at him. They both knew full well that her dad had given her enough money for a burger and that Paxton would spend every cent she'd been given.

The cab stopped in front of Tully's building, and Marah paid the cabbie. She led Pax through the lobby and into the elevator. On the top floor they exited the elevator and went to Tully's condo. Marah unlocked the door and made her way down the hall.

"I'm hungry," Paxton said, already bored. "Is that Red Robin still down the block? A cheeseburger would be good."

Marah was happy to give him enough money to get rid of him.

When he was gone, she walked past the coffee table, where piles of mail lay. On top lay the newest *Star* magazine, its pages open to the story. Marah's legs almost gave out. Tully had been reading the magazine last night before she got in her car. Here was the proof.

She looked away from the evidence of her betrayal and kept walking. The iPod station in the living room was empty, so Marah went to Tully's bedroom and looked around. Guilt swirled around her.

He'll ruin you. That's the last thing Tully had said to her on that terrible December night in her dorm room when Marah had chosen Paxton over everyone else who loved her. Had it really only been nine months ago? It felt like a lifetime.

It seemed so romantic at first, all that "us against them." Marah quit college and moved into the apartment Paxton shared with six other kids. It was a fifth-floor walk-up in a vermin-infested building in Pioneer Square. She didn't mind that Paxton had no money and no job. His poetry would make them rich someday. Besides, Marah had money. She'd saved all of her high school graduation-gift money in a savings account. During college, her dad had given her enough money that she'd never needed to crack into her savings.

It wasn't until recently—the summer of 2010—that the money in Marah's account ran out and everything began to change. Paxton decided that marijuana was "lame" and that meth and heroin were "where it's at." Money seemed to disappear from Marah's wallet; she was never one hundred percent sure, not enough to accuse him.

She'd worked from the start. Paxton couldn't hold down a job, because he needed nights to slam poetry in the clubs and days to work on his verses. She'd been happy to be his muse.

A few months ago, in June, Paxton had come home from a club one night late, high, and told her that Seattle was "over." They packed up the next day and followed one of Paxton's new friends to Portland, where they'd moved into a dirty apartment with five other kids. She'd gotten her job at Dark Magick within the week.

It wasn't until ten days ago that Marah really understood the precariousness of their life together. She'd come home to an eviction notice nailed onto the door of their apartment.

Marah walked around in a fog; fear had set in like an iceberg. She didn't want to be homeless. There was no one she could talk to about her fear, either. Until she remembered: *My job is to love you.*

How many times had Tully offered to help her? *I don't judge peo-*

ple. I know how hard it is to be human. She knew where she had to go.

The next day, without telling Paxton, she called in sick to work, took her last few precious dollars, and bought a bus ticket to Seattle.

She arrived at Tully's apartment and stood outside the door trying to work up the nerve to knock. When she finally did, there was no answer. Marah pulled out the spare key. Unlocking the door, she went inside. Music was playing in the living room. "Tully?"

Tully came out of the bedroom. "Marah," she said. She seemed weird. Shaky and pale. She kept blinking as if she couldn't focus.

She's high. Marah had seen it enough in the past two years.

Marah knew instantly that Tully wouldn't help her. Not this Tully, who couldn't even stand up straight. Still, she tried. She begged; she pleaded; she asked for money.

Tully said pretty things, but in the end the answer was no.

Marah wanted to cry, she was so disappointed. "My mom said I could count on you. When she was dying, she said you'd help me and love me no matter what."

"I'm trying to, Marah. I want to help you—"

"As long as I do what you want. Paxton was right." Marah said the last words in a jangle of pain. She ran out of the condominium. It wasn't until she was in the bus station that she knew how to solve her problem. Beside her was one of those celebrity magazines. It was open to a story about Lindsay Lohan, who'd been pulled over driving a Maserati while she was on probation. The headline read STAR OUT OF CONTROL ONLY DAYS AFTER LEAVING REHAB.

She picked up the magazine, called the hotline number, and said, *I'm Marah Ryan, Tully Hart's goddaughter. How much would you pay for a story about her?* Even as she asked, she felt sick. Some things, some choices, you just knew were wrong.

"Marah? Check this out."

She heard her name as if from far away. She came to slowly, remembering where she was: standing in Tully's closet.

Marah saw Paxton holding a half-eaten hamburger in one hand while he pawed through Tully's jewelry box with the other.

"Check it out." He held up a single diamond stud earring nearly the size of a pencil eraser. It flashed colored light, even in the dark closet.

"Put it back, Paxton," she said tiredly.

He gave her his best smile. "Oh, come on. Your godmother wouldn't even notice if this went missing. Think of it, Marah. We could go to San Francisco, like we've been dreaming of. You know how stuck I've been in my poetry. It's because of our money and how we don't have any. How can I be creative when you're gone all day, working?" He moved toward her. "This could be our future, Mar." The intensity in his eyes scared her just a little.

For the first time, she noticed the selfishness in his gaze.

He took the silver-and-black skull earring out of his earlobe and put Tully's diamond in its place. "Let's go."

He was so sure of her, so certain she would fold her will into his own. And why wouldn't he be? That was what she'd done from the beginning. In Dr. Bloom's office she'd seen a gorgeous, troubled poet who'd promised her a way through her pain. He'd told her it was okay to cut herself; it was beautiful. Then she'd followed him into the underbelly of the world and let its darkness conceal her.

"Why do you love me, Pax?"

"You're my muse. You know that." He gave her a lazy smile.

"But you hardly write anymore."

She saw the anger flash. "What do you know about it?"

And there went her heart, tearing free, falling. She couldn't help thinking about the love she'd grown up around. The way her parents loved each other and their kids. She took a step forward, feeling strangely as if she were both breaking free and growing up at the same time. She suddenly ached for the life she once had.

Paxton loved her most when she was broken and cutting herself. What kind of love was that? She knew how wounded he had been by his sister's death and his parents' abandonment. There was more to him than the poet or the Goth or even the thief. Or, someday, there could be more. But he wasn't enough for her now.

"I loved you," she said.

"And I love you." He took her hand and led her out of the condo. Marah wondered if love—or the end of it—would always hurt like this. "I forgot something," she said at the front door, tugging free, coming to a stop. "Meet me at the elevator."

"Sure." He walked over to the elevator, pushed the button.

Marah backed into the condo and then locked the door.

He came running back for her, banging on the door, screaming and shouting. Tears stung her eyes until he yelled, "Screw you, then, you fake bitch," and stomped away.

MARAH found the iPod and packed it in a shopping bag with its portable docking station. She found her mom's journal, too, and packed that in the bag. For someday.

Then she left the condo and went down to the ferry terminal. Boarding the next boat, she took a seat and pulled out the iPod. She put the buds in her ears and hit PLAY. Elton John sang to her. *"Goodbye, yellow brick ro-ad. . . ."* Of course.

She turned her head and stared out at the black Sound, watching the tiny golden lights of Bainbridge Island appear. When the ferry docked, she put the iPod back in the box and walked out to the terminal, where she caught a bus and rode it out to her road.

She saw her house for the first time in more than a year. The cedar shingles, stained the color of caramel, looked dark on this cool night. On the porch she paused, expecting for a second to hear her mother's voice. *Hey, baby girl, how was your day?*

She opened the door and went inside. The house welcomed her in the way it had since she'd first come home from kindergarten. She heard a door whack open upstairs.

"She's here! Move it or lose it, Skywalker!"

Her brothers careened out of their upstairs bedroom and came thundering down the stairs in tandem. They were both dressed in football sweats and wore skater-boy haircuts and silver braces.

When she'd last seen them, they'd been *boys;* now they were almost twelve, but they hugged her with the fierceness of little boys who'd missed their big sister. And she had missed them, too.

"Where's Paxton?" Wills asked when they finally let her go.

"Gone," she said quietly. "It's just me."

"Excellent," Wills said.

"We missed you, Mar," Lucas said earnestly.

She pulled them into another hug.

"How's Tully?" Lucas said when he drew back. "Did you see her? Dad says we can go tomorrow. She'll be awake, right?"

Marah didn't know what to say, so she gave a shrug. "Sure."

"Cool," Wills said.

Within moments they were thundering up the stairs again, calling dibs on something.

Marah picked up the shopping bag and climbed the stairs to her old room, opening the door slowly. Inside, nothing had changed. Her camp pictures were still on the dresser; her yearbooks were stacked alongside her Harry Potter books. She tossed the bag onto the bed and walked over to her desk. She picked up her old, tattered, often-read copy of *The Hobbit*. The book Mom had given her.

I don't think you're quite ready for The Hobbit *yet, but someday soon, maybe in a few years, something will happen to hurt your feelings again. Maybe you'll feel alone with your sadness, not ready to share it with me or Daddy, and if that happens, you'll remember this book in your nightstand. You can read it then, let it take you away. It really helped me when I was thirteen.*

"I love you, Mommy," Marah had said. Her mom had laughed and said, "I hope you remember that when you're a teenager."

Marah felt a surge of loss so keen it brought tears to her eyes and thought: *She knew me.*

CHAPTER FOURTEEN

I AM back in my make-believe world, with my best friend beside me. I am lying in grass, staring up at a starlit sky. "Katie, how can it be raining?" I feel the soft drops against my cheek, and for no reason that makes sense, I feel sad. Something is wrong.

It's not raining. It's your mother. She's crying. Look.

Were my eyes closed? I open them slowly. Light appears suddenly, and I see where I am. The hospital room. Of course. It is the other places that are mirages. This is real.

My mother is beside the bed, smaller and thinner than I remember. She is still dressed for another era—flower power and Woodstock. But none of that is what matters. She is crying. For me.

I don't know how to believe in her, but I don't know how to let go, either. She's my mother. It means something that she's here.

"I've never seen you in pain," she says to my body. Her voice is almost a whisper. "I never saw you scrape your knees or fall off a bike." Tears are falling from her eyes.

"I'll tell you everything. How I became Cloud, how I tried to be good enough for you and failed. How I survived all those bad years. I'll tell you everything you want to know, but I can't do any of it if you don't wake up." She leans over the bed, looks down at me. "I'm so proud of you," my mother says.

She doesn't wipe her tears away. They fall onto my face. "I love you, Tully." On this, her voice breaks. "Maybe you don't care, and maybe I'm too late, but I love you."

I have waited my whole life to hear those words from my mother.

Tul?

I turn to Kate, see her glowing face and her beautiful green eyes. In them I see my whole life. That's what your best friend is: a mirror. I know why she is here suddenly and what I have to do.

It's time, she says, and I understand at last. I have to make a choice, but first I have to remember. I know instinctively that it will hurt. "Will you stay with me?"

Forever, if I could.

It is time, at last, to face why my body is here, broken and hooked up to machines in this white room.

"Okay," I say, gathering my courage. "It starts with Marah." How long ago did she come to visit me? A week? Ten days? It's late August of 2010, well after my mother's so-called intervention.

I have been . . . trying to write my memoir, but it isn't working.

How long has it been since I left my condo? I can't open the door. I *hate* this weakness, but my will is gone.

Each morning, I make a vow to myself: I will stop taking Xanax, and I will leave my home and venture out into the world. I will look for Marah. Or a job. Or a life.

Today is no different. I wake late and realize instantly that I must have taken too many sleeping pills last night. I get up. *Today* I change my life. I will start with a shower. The hot water makes me feel worse. I relive too much: Johnny's anger, Kate's death, Marah's running away. I dress slowly, in sweats. I am shaky and headachy. Eating will help. And one Xanax.

As I am pouring a cup of coffee, my cell phone rings. I answer it quickly. "Yes?"

"Tully? It's George. I've gotten you a ticket to an advance screening of *The American,* with George Clooney. I'll e-mail you the details. It's a charitable event at a theater on Capital Hill. The network guys will be there. This is your chance to wow them. September second. Seven p.m. Don't be late, and look good."

"Thanks, George," I say, smiling for the first time in days.

I feel hope stir inside of me. Then it hits me: I have to leave my condo and go out in public. I start to panic.

No. I can do this. I can. I take another Xanax. I head back to my closet to pick out some clothes for the event. I will need . . .

"Tully?"

Am I imagining Marah's voice? I am unsteady on my feet as I make my way through the condo, toward a voice I don't really believe is even there.

But she is there, in my living room. She is dressed in black, with her hair spiked and pink. She looks dangerously thin.

She is going to give me another chance. "Marah," I say, loving her so much it hurts. "I'm so glad you're back. Are you okay?"

"I'm fine." She looks . . . not scared, exactly, but uncomfortable. "I need . . ."

I move toward her, a little off balance. Does she notice?

"I need money."

My little fairy tale collapses. She doesn't want *me,* isn't here for my help. She wants money; then she'll leave again. What would Johnny say if he found out I gave her money and let her go?

I take hold of her wrist and push her sleeve up. Her forearm is pale and crisscrossed with a web of scars, some silvery and old, some new. My heart breaks for her. I can see that she is hurting. I will never let her down again. I will be the godmother Kate wanted me to be. "If you're okay, why are you still hurting yourself?" I try to ask it gently, but I am shaking. "I want to help you, you know I do—"

"Are you going to give me money or not?"

"What's it for?"

"None of your business."

The words hurt me as deeply as she obviously intended. "Look at me," I say, wanting desperately to make her understand how dangerous her choices are. "I've screwed up my life, Marah. I don't have any family; no husband and no kids. The one thing I did have—my career—I lost. Don't end up like me. Alone. You have a family that loves you. Go home. Johnny will help you."

"I have Pax."

"Some men are worse than being alone, Marah."

"Like you would know. Will you help me or not?"

Even in my precarious state, I know I can't do what she is asking. I want to, but I have learned. "I'll give you a place to live and set you up with Dr. Bloom, but I won't make the same mistake again. I won't go behind your dad's back and give you money so you can live with that weirdo who doesn't care that you cut yourself."

After that, we say terrible things to each other. This girl I love as much as my own life gives me a look that could shatter wood. Then she leaves, slamming the door behind her.

THE day of the movie premiere sneaks up on me. On the evening of September second, I am moving listlessly from room to room when my cell phone bleats out an appointment alert. *Movie. Harvard Exit. Eight p.m. Network brass.* I look at the time. It is 7:03.

I will go. I *must* go. This is my opportunity. I will dress up, look good, and retake my place in the spotlight. This is America, after all, the land of the second chances, especially for celebrities. People will understand. Who doesn't have anxieties these days?

I am a little panicked, but a Xanax will help, so I take two. I have to be perfect. And I can be. I go into my closet. I am too overweight to make a fashion statement, so I pluck an old standby off the rack: a vintage black jersey Valentino sheath and patterned black hose. It now fits me like a sausage casing, but it's the best I can do.

I can't do much with my hair beyond pulling it back into a sleek ponytail. Huge gold-and-black pearl earrings draw the attention away from my sallow face (I hope). I put on makeup and still I look tired. Old. Trying not to think about that, I slip into an expensive pair of bright pink patent leather pumps and grab an evening bag.

I am reaching for my doorknob when panic hits, but I push through it. I open the door, step out into the hallway.

The doorman hails a Town Car, and I collapse in the backseat. I close my eyes and survive this panic one second at a time, but when the car pulls up in front of the theater, I feel light-headed.

I climb out. It feels as if I am wading through mud as I approach the red carpet. It is raining, I notice. When did that start?

My hands are shaking now. I tilt my chin and force myself to walk the red carpet. A few flashbulbs go off—then they see it is me and the photographers turn away. I make my way into the theater and collapse into one of the velvet seats.

The house light dims; the movie begins. I try to pay attention, but I can't do it. Anxiety is a living, breathing entity inside of me. I need to get out of here, just for a second.

I find a sign for the restroom and follow it. I stumbled into a stall and sink down onto the closed seat, kicking the door shut. I slump back, trying to calm down, and close my eyes. *Relax, Tully. Relax.*

The next thing I know, I am waking up. How long have I been here, passed out in a toilet stall in a movie theater?

Downstairs I see the way people look at me. They step out of my way, as if I am carrying a contagious disease. My DUI mug shot is what they are seeing when they look at me. And suddenly I know:

I can't do it. I can't meet the network brass and plead my case and get my job back. It's too late. I elbow my way through the crowd, muttering apologies I don't mean.

SOMETIME later a man tries to pick me up in a bar. I almost let him. I remember him looking at me, smiling, saying something that made me ache with longing—not for him, of course. For my lost life. I hear myself begging him to kiss me, and I cry when he does, because it felt so good and not nearly good enough.

After the bar closes, I walk home. My condo is dark when I get there. I turn on all the lights as I totter past, ricocheting off the walls and tables as I go. I slump onto my sofa and close my eyes.

When I open my eyes again, I see the pile of mail on my coffee table. I am about to look away when a pictures catches my attention. My picture. There, beneath the bills and junk mail, is a *Star* magazine with my mug shot in the upper left corner. Beneath it is a single, terrible word: *Addict*.

THE REAL STORY BEHIND THE RUMORS

Aging isn't easy for any woman in the public eye, but it may be proving especially difficult for Tully Hart, the ex-star of the once phenom talk show *The Girlfriend Hour.* Ms. Hart's god-daughter, Marah Ryan, contacted *Star* exclusively. Ms. Ryan, 20, confirms that the fifty-year-old Hart has been struggling lately with demons that she's had all her life. In recent months she has "gained an alarming amount of weight" and been abusing drugs and alcohol, according to Ms. Ryan. Tully Hart once appeared to have it all, but the aging talk-show host, who has openly spoken of her difficult childhood, appears to be crumbling under the pressure of her recent failures. Most drug addicts . . .

I let the magazine slide to the floor. The pain I have been holding at bay for months, years, roars to life, sucks me into the bleakest, loneliest place I've ever been.

I stumble out of the living room and leave my condo, grabbing my car keys as I go. I don't know where I'm going. Just out. Away. My heart can't hold this loss. I don't want to be strong anymore. I want to be . . . gone.

As I careen through the underground parking lot, I fish the Xanax out of my evening bag and swallow two. I get into my car, rev the engine, and drive away. I turn onto First Street without even looking to my left. Tears and rain blur my view. And there it is: a hulking concrete stanchion that supports the aging viaduct.

I see that huge black post and I think: *End it*. End it.

The simplicity of it takes my breath away. I don't have to be in pain anymore. All it would take is a turn of the wheel.

"OH, MY God." I turn to Kate. "I tried to turn at the last second to avoid hitting the stanchion."

I know. Look.

I see that we are in the hospital room again. There are people around my bed. I'm hovering above it all, looking down on them.

I see Johnny with his arms crossed tightly. Margie is crying quietly, a handkerchief held to her mouth, and my mother looks devastated. The twins are there, standing close together.

In the silence that falls between us, I hear strains of a song coming from the iPod on the bedside table; the volume is so low I can barely hear it. *"Hello Darkness my old friend . . ."*

And then I hear voices. They are talking about my body, about me, about taking me off life support. They are here, my friends and family, to watch me die.

Or breathe, Kate says. Then: *It's time. Do you want to go back?*

I get it. Everything has been leading up to this moment.

I see Marah walk into the hospital room. She stands by Johnny, who puts an arm around her.

She needs you, Kate says to me. *And so do my boys.*

I made her a promise to be there for her children, and I failed.

They love me. I can see that. I do want to undo what I've done and have a chance to be another version of myself. A better version.

And I love them. How was it that I have believed I was incapable of love, all these years, when I feel it so deeply? I turn to say this to Kate, and she smiles at me, my best friend.

Say good-bye to me, she says quietly. *I'll always be with you, Tul. I'm in your memories.*

I know she's right. Maybe I've known it all along. She is gone. I lost her a long time ago, but I didn't know how to let go. But I have to, for both of our sakes. "Ah, Katie . . ." I say.

See? she says. *You're saying good-bye.*

She moves toward me, and I feel a brush of skin against mine. *Slip out the back, Jack,* she says. *Make a new plan, Stan.*

The music. Always the music.

"I love you," I say quietly, and finally it is enough. Love is what lasts. I understand that now. "Good-bye."

At that, just the single word, I am plunged back into the darkness.

I CAN see myself, I think, from a distance. I am in pain. A headache blinds me, it hurts so much.

I have to get to my feet . . . walk . . . but I am tired. So tired. Still, I try. I get up. Each step sends pain ringing up my spine, but I keep walking, trudging forward without thinking. Suddenly there is a hill above me, growing fast, reaching upward. I can't make it.

From far away I hear: "Wake up, Tully, please—"

"I can't do it, Katie." I almost ask her why. But I know why.

Faith. It is something I have never had.

"Come back, Tully."

I follow the line of my goddaughter's voice. In this black world it shimmers like gossamer, just beyond my reach. I reach for it, follow it. Then I take a deep, painful breath and try to stand.

September 4, 2010, 11:21 a.m.

"ARE you ready?" Dr. Bevan asked.

Marah didn't want this. It was better to keep her godmother plugged in, breathing. What if she died?

They were all here: Dad, Grandma and Grandpa, the twins, and Tully's weird mom. Dad had spoken to Marah and the boys this morning on the ferry, explained to them what this all meant. They had raised Tully's body temperature and taken her off the heavy meds. Now they were going to unplug her from the ventilator. Hopefully she would wake up and breathe on her own.

Dr. Bevan put Tully's chart in a sleeve at the end of the bed. A nurse came in and removed the breathing tube from Tully's mouth.

Tully took a rattling, phlegmy breath and released it. Beneath the white cotton blanket, her chest rose and fell, rose and fell.

"Tallulah," Dr. Bevan said. He pried open her eyelids and shone a beam of light in her eyes. Her pupils reacted. "Can you hear me?"

"Don't call her that," Dorothy said. "She hates that name."

"Come on, Tully," Marah said. Nothing happened.

Finally Dr. Bevan said, "Well. Time will tell, I guess. Brain injuries are tricky. We'll monitor her closely over the next few hours. Her brain activity is normal, and her pupils are reactive. And she's breathing on her own. Those are very good signs."

"So we wait," Dad said.

Dr. Bevan nodded. "We wait."

Dad reached out and held Marah's hand. His hand was a lifeline suddenly. How had she forgotten that, how her dad could hold her steady? He'd always been able to, even back in the old days.

Dad said, "I'm going to take the boys and your grandpa out for lunch. You hungry?"

Marah shook her head.

"Dorothy and I are going for some coffee," Grandma said, moving toward Marah. "You want to come with us?"

"I'll stay with her," Marah said.

After everyone left, she stood at her godmother's bedside. In almost all of her best childhood memories, Tully was there.

"Tully?" Marah said. "Please hear me. It's Marah, and I'm so sorry for what I did. I want you to wake up and yell at me. Please."

September 12, 2010, 10:17 a.m.

"I'M SORRY," Dr. Bevan said.

Dorothy wondered if the man knew how often he'd said these

words in the past week. Dr. Bevan was sorry that Tully hadn't wakened from her coma. He still handed out hope as if it were a bit of hard candy he kept in his pocket for emergencies, but the hope in his eyes had begun to dim. He'd ordered a tracheotomy to maintain something called efficient aeration of the lungs; a nasogastric feeding tube had been inserted into her nostril and taped in place.

Tully looked as if she were sleeping. Each of the last eight days, Dorothy had thought: *Today. Today Tully will wake up.*

Now Dr. Bevan had called them here for a meeting.

Dorothy stood in the corner. Johnny stood with his arms crossed at his chest and his sons standing close. Margie looked smaller, hunched. And Bud had hardly taken off his sunglasses. But it was Marah who looked the worst. She was the walking wounded.

"It's time," Dr. Bevan said, "to talk about the future. Tully has been primarily unresponsive for eight days. She has recovered adequately from her acute injuries and shows no substantial evidence of brain injury, but the evidence of cognitive awareness fails to meet the medical criteria for intensive ongoing rehabilitation. This means that although there have been some reports of her opening her eyes or—once—coughing, we believe it's time to consider custodial care. A hospital is no longer the place for her."

Dorothy swallowed hard. "Can . . . I take care of her at home?"

A frown tugged at the doctor's mouth. "It's a complicated, difficult job, caring for a comatose patient. And single caretakers often find themselves overwhelmed."

Johnny moved in to stand beside Dorothy. "I could come every other weekend to help out."

"Me, too," Marah said, moving to Dorothy's other side.

The twins stepped forward together. "Us, too."

Dorothy was surprised by the swell of emotion that filled her. She had never stood up for her daughter before, and no one had ever stood up for her.

"There's a local company that specializes in care of comatose patients at home. It can be prohibitively expensive, but if money is not the issue, you could engage their services. A registered nurse could come to the house every day, or every other day, to change Tully's catheter and check her corneas for ulceration and run some tests, but even so, it will take a lot of work, Ms. Hart."

"I'll take care of her," Dorothy said.

"I'll research the insurance and take care of all the financial and medical arrangements," Johnny said. "We can reassess later if we need to. I'll talk to her business manager this week. Her condo is worth several million. We can sell it if we need to, but my guess is that she has the maximum insurance coverage."

Marge held Dorothy's hand. "The house in Snohomish hasn't sold yet. Bud and I could move back to help you."

"You are amazing," Dorothy said quietly. "But if you're there, it will be too easy for me to let you be her mother. I need to be the person who is responsible. I hope you understand."

Margie's look said it all. "I'm only a phone call away."

Dorothy released a heavy sigh. There. It was done. For the first time in her life, she was going to be Tully's mother.

September 12, 2010, 6:17 p.m.

JOHNNY had spent most of the day with Tully's business manager, Frank, going over her finances. Now he sat alone in his car on the ferry, with a stack of her financial records in the seat beside him.

He'd had no idea how her life had unraveled since Kate's death. He'd imagined her retirement from TV had been her choice, that the "book deal" had been lucrative. He would have found the truth easily—if he'd cared enough to look. He hadn't.

When they docked, he drove over the bumpy metal ramp and onto the smooth asphalt of the road.

At the end of his driveway, the house was drenched in late afternoon light. September was a good month in the Northwest.

He pulled into the dark garage and sat there a minute collecting his thoughts. When he felt strong again, he went into the house.

As he stepped inside, the boys came running down the stairs. In the past few years, they'd become a trio, he and the twins. And yet he could see fissures forming in their relationship. Both of them had begun to keep secrets. They answered ordinary questions evasively. "Who was that on the phone?" was a good example. "No one." "Oh, so you're talking to no one?" Like that.

"Hey, Dad," Wills said, jumping down the last three steps. Lucas was a second behind.

How he loved these boys. And he'd let them down in a million ways without Kate to guide him. Alone, he hadn't been as good a parent as his sons—or Marah—deserved. Would they forgive him?

Johnny said, "We're going out to clean Dorothy's house tomorrow and paint. Get ready for Tully to go home. I know how much you'll want to help."

"She and Mom liked blue," Wills said. "That would be a good color for her room."

Lucas took a step forward, looked up at Johnny. "It's not your fault, Dad," he said quietly. "Tully, I mean."

"You're so much like your mom," Johnny said.

"And Wills is like you," Lucas said. The family myth. And true.

Johnny smiled. Maybe that's how they would make it in the future, by keeping Kate alive in small ways while they moved on. He was ready, at last, to do that. "Where's your sister?"

"Gee, Dad. Guess," Wills said.

"In her room?"

He moved past them and went up the stairs. Although he paused at Marah's closed door, he neither knocked nor said anything. He was trying to give her space. In the hospital he'd seen how deep her pain ran, and he'd learned a good lesson in the past few years: Listening mattered as much as talking. He wouldn't fail her again.

He went into his room, tossed the pile of paperwork on his bed, and then took a long, hot shower. There was a knock on his door. He dressed quickly in jeans and a T-shirt and called out, "Come in."

The door opened. Marah stood there. "Can I talk to you?"

"Of course."

She glanced away. "Not here." Turning, she walked downstairs.

Out on the deck she sat down in her mother's favorite Adirondack chair. Above them the sprawling branches of the maple tree were plush with autumn. Scarlet, tangerine, and lemon-yellow leaves lay scattered across the deck. Johnny sat down beside Marah.

"I sold a story to *Star* magazine," she said. "I told them Tully was a drug addict and an alcoholic. They paid me eight hundred and fifty dollars. It came out last week. I . . . saw it on Tully's coffee table at home. She read it before she got in the car."

Johnny thought: *Help me, Katie.* Then he said, "That's what you meant when you said this was your fault."

The anguish in her eyes was heart-wrenching. "It is my fault."

"We fell apart without your mom," Johnny said. "And that's on me. It hurt too much to be around Tully, so I walked away. Hell, I ran away. You aren't the only one who hurt her."

"That doesn't help much," she said miserably.

He said quietly, "I've thought about that day in your dorm room a thousand times. I would do anything to have a do-over and to tell you that I love you no matter what choice you make and that you can always count on me to love you."

"I needed that," she said, wiping her eyes.

"I would tell Tully I'm sorry, too. I was wrong to blame her."

Marah nodded but said nothing.

Johnny thought of all the mistakes he'd made with this girl, the times he'd walked away when he should have stayed, the times he'd remained silent when he should have spoken. All the wrong turns a single father makes when he's in over his head. "Can you forgive me?"

She gazed at him steadily. "I love you, Dad," she said.

"I love you, too, Munchkin."

Marah's smile was weak and a little sad. "What about Tully? She probably thinks—"

"What would you say to her right now?"

"I'd tell her how much I love her, but I won't get a chance."

"You'll get a chance. You can tell her when she wakes up."

"I have a little trouble believing in miracles these days."

"Your mom would hate to hear that. She would tell you that everything works out the way it's supposed to and don't give up hope until you have to and—"

"Certainly not then," Marah said, her voice an echo of his. "I want to see Dr. Bloom again, if that's okay."

Thank you, Katie. "I'll make an appointment."

CHAPTER FIFTEEN

September 14, 2010, 9:13 a.m.

ON THE day before Tully was to be brought home, the Ryans and Mularkeys descended on the house on Firefly Lane.

The back bedroom—Tully's at fourteen and now again, at fifty—had been scrubbed and painted sky blue. The hospital bed had been delivered and set up. From her bed, Tully would be able to look through the window across the field to her once-best-friend's house. In the middle of it all, a nurse showed up from the coma-care company and talked to Dorothy for two hours about Tully's care.

Now Dorothy was in the hospital again, walking down the corridor to her daughter's room. She opened the door and went inside.

There was a man sitting by her daughter's bed, reading. At Dorothy's entrance, he looked up. He was probably not more than forty-five, and there was an exotic multicultural look to him. His hair was drawn back into a ponytail.

"I'm sorry," he said, rising. "I'm Desmond Grant, an ER doc."

"Dorothy. I'm her mother. You visit her often?"

"I try to come in either before or after my shifts." He smiled. "I hear she's going home today."

"Yes. In about an hour."

"It was nice to meet you." He headed for the door.

"Desmond? Seventeen Firefly Lane in Snohomish. That's where we'll be. If you want to finish reading her that book."

"Thanks, Dorothy. I'd like that."

She watched him leave and then walked over to the bed. In the eleven days since the accident, Tully's facial bruising had gone from a plum color to a rotten banana brown. The tiny lacerations had scabbed over. Her full lips were cracked and dry.

Dorothy reached into her pocket, pulling out a small jar of bee cream. She glazed the soft mixture across Tully's lips. "That will make them feel better. How did you sleep last night? . . . Me? Not so good," she went on, as if they were conversing. "I was nervous about your homecoming. I don't want to let you down. Oh. You don't think I will? I'm glad of that."

The door opened, and Dr. Bevan and Johnny came into the room, along with several nurses and two paramedics.

After that, everything moved quickly. Tully was transported from the bed to a gurney, disconnected from the IV and machines, and wheeled away. At the front desk, Dorothy signed a bunch of paperwork, collected some discharge papers and care-procedure brochures and a set of notes from Dr. Bevan. By the time she was in Johnny's car following the ambulance, she felt sick with worry.

At home they pulled up behind the ambulance and parked.

Dorothy hustled ahead to open the front door and turn on the lights and lead the paramedics to Tully's bedroom, where the Ryan kids had tacked up a huge WELCOME HOME TULLY poster.

All too quickly, Tully was in bed and the ambulance was gone.

"Do you want me to stay?" Johnny asked.

Dorothy had been so lost in her own thoughts that his voice surprised her. "Oh. No. But thank you."

"Marah will be here Thursday. She's bringing food. And I'll be here for the weekend with the boys. Margie and Bud gave us the keys to the house across the street."

Today was Monday.

"And Margie wanted me to remind you that she's only a few hours away. If you need help, she'll be on the next flight."

Dorothy forced a smile. "I can do this," she said. They walked to the door. There, Johnny paused and looked down at her.

"I wonder if you know how much this would mean to her."

"I know how much it means to me. How often do second chances come around?" Dorothy walked him outside and watched him drive away. Then she went back inside to stand by Tully's bedside.

An hour later the nurse showed up. For the next three hours, Dorothy learned step by step what to do to care for her daughter. By the end of the visit, she had a notebook full of notations and reminders. "You're ready," the nurse said at last as night fell outside.

Dorothy swallowed hard. "I don't know."

The nurse smiled gently. "Just go through your list. You'll be fine. And don't forget. She can probably hear you. So talk, sing, tell jokes. Anything."

That night, Dorothy slipped quietly into the bedroom and lit a gardenia-scented candle and turned on the bedside lamp.

She hit the bed's controls and elevated it to an exact angle of thirty-five degrees, paused, and then lowered it. Then she raised it again. "I'm supposed to elevate and lower your head for fifteen minutes every two hours." When she was done with that, Dorothy gently peeled back the blankets and began massaging Tully's hands and forearms. All the while, she talked.

Afterward she had no idea what she'd even said. She just knew that when she touched her daughter's feet, smoothing lotion onto the dry, cracked skin, she started to cry.

Two weeks after Tully left the hospital, Marah had her first meeting with Dr. Bloom. As she walked through the empty waiting room, she couldn't help imagining Paxton there, with his sad and soulful eyes, and the black hair that continually fell across his face.

"Marah," Dr. Bloom said with a smile. "It's good to see you."

"Thanks." Marah sat down in the chair facing the desk.

Dr. Bloom said, "What would you like to talk about today?"

There were so many choices, so many mistakes to work through. Marah said, "I miss my mom, and Tully's in a coma, and I've screwed up my life so badly I just want to crawl in a hole and hide."

"You've done that already," Dr. Bloom said. Had her voice always been that gentle? "With Paxton. And here you are."

Marah felt a shock of recognition at the words. Bloom was right.

It had all been a way of hiding—the pink hair, the drugs, the sex. But she had loved Paxton. That, at least, had been real.

"What were you hiding from?"

"Then? Missing my mom."

"There is pain you can't outrun, Marah. Maybe you know that now. Some pains you have to look in the eye. You will always miss her. I know that from experience. There will be days when the missing will be so sharp it takes your breath away. But there will be good days, too. Months and years of them. You'll be searching for her all your life. You'll find her, too. I promise you that."

"She would hate how I treated Tully," she said softly.

"I think you'd be amazed at how easily a mother forgives. And a godmother, too. The question is, Can you forgive yourself?"

Marah looked up, her eyes stinging with tears. "I need to."

"Okay, then. That's where we will start."

It helped, Marah learned, all that looking back, all that talking about her mom and Tully and guilt and forgiveness. Sometimes she lay in bed at night trying to imagine her mother talking to her.

Because that's what she missed most: her mother's voice. And through it all, she knew there was a place she could find her mother's voice when she was strong enough. But she needed Tully to be with her. That was the promise Marah had made to Mom.

For weeks afterward, Dorothy fell into bed at night exhausted and woke tired. The to-do care list was never far from her grasp. It took her more than a month to stop being afraid.

By late November she had begun to leave her to-do list behind. The nurse, Nora, came by four times a week. Only last week she'd said, "Why, Dot, I couldn't do better myself. Honest!"

As Christmas Day 2010 dawned crisp and clear over the town of Snohomish, she finally felt at peace, or as at peace as a woman with a daughter in a coma could feel. She woke early and set about readying the house to feel like a holiday home. There were no ornaments in the back storage closet, of course. But in that closet, she stumbled across the two cardboard boxes full of Tully's mementos.

When Johnny had delivered the boxes, along with Tully's clothes and photos, Dorothy thought they seemed sacrosanct—for Tully's eyes alone—but now she wondered if the contents could help Tully. She picked up the box marked "Queen Anne" and carried it to Tully's bedroom. Tully lay still, her eyes closed, her breathing even.

"I brought up your things," she said to Tully. "I thought maybe, for Christmas, I could talk to you about what's in here."

Tully didn't move. A fuzz of graying mahogany hair had begun to grow back in, giving her a new chicklike appearance. The bruises and lacerations had healed.

Dorothy pulled up the chair and sat down. She opened the box. The first thing she pulled out was a small Magilla Gorilla T-shirt; at its touch, she felt slammed by a memory.

Mommy, can I have a brownie?

Sure. A little pot never hurt anyone. Clem, pass me the brownies.

And then: *Dot, your kid is flopping all over. . . .*

She realized how long she'd been silent. "Oh. Sorry. You probably think I left, but I'm still here." She set the shirt aside.

The next thing she pulled out was a photo album. On the first page, there was a photograph of a skinny girl blowing out a candle. On the opposite page was a letter. She began reading it aloud.

"Dear Mommy, Today is my 11th birthday.

"How are you? I am fine. I bet you're on your way to see me because you miss me as much as I miss you.

"Love, your daughter, Tully"

In bed Tully made a sound. Her eyes fluttered open. Dorothy rose quickly. "Tully? Can you hear me?"

Tully closed her eyes again. Dorothy stood there a long time, waiting for more. It wasn't unusual, Tully opening her eyes. "I'll keep reading," Dorothy said, sitting down again, turning the page.

There were hundreds of letters, written at first in a wobbly child's hand, and then, as the years went on, in a more confident young woman's handwriting. Dorothy read them all.

She longed to stop reading—each word of each letter was like a stab to the heart—but she couldn't stop. Here was her child's life, all laid out in letters. She read through her tears.

In about 1972 the letters stopped.

Dorothy turned the last page. There, taped to the back page, she found a small blue envelope that was addressed to "Dorothy Jean."

She caught her breath. Only one person called her Dorothy Jean.

Slowly she opened the envelope, saying in a nervous voice, "There's a letter here from my mom. Did you know it was here?"

She pulled out a single sheet of stationery, as thin as parchment.

> Dear Dorothy Jean,
>
> I always thought you'd come home. For years I prayed. I begged God to send you back to me. I told Him that if He granted me just one more chance, I would not be blind again.
>
> But neither God nor you listened to an old woman's prayers. I can't say as I blame either one of you.
>
> Sorry. It is so small. Five letters and I was never strong enough to say it. I never tried to stop your father. I was afraid. We both know how he liked his lit cigarettes, didn't we? I am dying now, fading despite my best intentions to wait for you. I was better for Tully. I want you to know that.
>
> But I am sorry. I want you to know that.
>
> If only we could try again. If only.

Dorothy stared down at the words. She'd always thought of herself as the only victim of that house. Maybe there had been two of them. Three if you counted Tully, who had certainly been ruined by her grandfather's evil—not directly, perhaps, but ruined just the same. Three generations of women broken by a single man.

She looked at her daughter. "No more secrets," she whispered. She would tell Tully everything, including the regret in her mother's letter. That would be her Christmas gift to her daughter. Then Dorothy would write her entire story so that Tully would have it for her memoir. Maybe then, someday, they could heal.

"Would you like that, Tully?" she asked, praying for an answer.

Beside her, Tully breathed evenly, in and out.

THAT YEAR WINTER SEEMED TO last forever. Gray days followed one another like dirty sheets on a line.

By June, locals had forgotten all about the dismal winter. In July, when the farmer's markets started up again, there were complaints about how hot it had grown.

Like the flowers in her yard, Marah had spent the long months gathering strength. Now, though, it was time to look forward.

"Are you sure you want to do this alone?" her dad asked.

"Yeah," she said. She had things to say to Tully—things she'd held back, waiting for a miracle—but it had been almost a year, and Marah was preparing now to go off to college.

"I promised Mom something, and I have to keep that promise."

He kissed her. "I'm proud of you. Have I told you that lately?"

She smiled. "Every day since I got rid of the pink hair."

He walked her to the car, parked in the driveway. "Drive safely."

It was a sentence that meant a lot more to her these days. Nodding, she climbed into the driver's seat and started the car.

It was a gorgeous late summer day. On the island, tourists thronged onto and off the ferry. Traffic was bumper to bumper, and Marah followed the crowd north. In Snohomish she turned off the highway and went to Firefly Lane.

She sat in the driveway for a moment, staring at the bag beside her. Finally she picked it up and went to the front door.

The air smelled fresh and crisp. She could see that Dorothy's vegetable garden was teeming with tomatoes, green beans, broccoli.

The door opened before she knocked. Dorothy stood there. "Marah! I know she's been waiting for you," she said. It was what Dorothy had said to her every Thursday for months. "She opened her eyes twice this week. That's a good sign, I think. Don't you?"

"Sure," Marah said in a tight voice. She *had* thought that a few months ago, back when it started to happen. She'd called for Dorothy and waited, leaning forward, saying, *Come on, Tully, come back. . . .*

She lifted the gray bag. "I brought her something to read."

"Great! Great! I could use some time in the garden."

Marah went down the hallway to Tully's room. Sunlight poured through the window, making the blue walls shimmer like seawater.

Tully lay in her hospital bed, angled up, her eyes closed. On the bedside table was a worn paperback copy of *Anna Karenina* that Desmond had been reading to Tully for months.

"Hey," Marah said. "I'm going off to college. I know I've been talking about it for months. Loyola Marymount. In Los Angeles. Ironic, right? I think a smaller school will be good for me." She wrung her hands together. This wasn't what she'd come for.

For months she'd believed in a miracle. Now, though, it was time to say good-bye. And something else.

The ache in her chest was getting bigger. She reached for the chair by the bed and sat down, scooting close. "I'm the reason you crashed your car, aren't I? Because I sold that story to the magazine. I wish we could start over, you and me. I miss you so much."

She reached down for the gray bag on the floor beside her. She pulled out her most prized possession. Her mother's journal. *Katie's Story* was written in Tully's bold, scrawling handwriting.

Marah stared down at those two words. How was it possible that she was still afraid to read what was written on these pages? "I promised her I'd read this with you when I was ready. I'm not really ready, and you're not really you, but I'm leaving and Dr. Bloom tells me it's time. And she's right. It is time."

Marah said quietly, "Here goes," and started to read aloud.

> Panic always comes to me in the same way. First I get a knot in the pit of my stomach, then a fluttery breathlessness. But what causes my fear is different every day. It could be a kiss from my husband or the look of sadness in his eyes. Sometimes I know he's already grieving for me. Worse yet is Marah's acceptance of everything I say. I would give anything for one of our old knock-down drag-out fights. Marah, those fights were real life. You were struggling to break free of being my daughter but unsure of how to be yourself, while I was afraid to let you go. It's the circle of love. I only wish I'd recognized it then. I know you regret some of the things you said to me, as I regret my own

words. None of that matters. I love you, and I know you love me.

But I want to go deeper than that. It starts in 1960 in a small farming town up north, in a clapboard house on a hill. When it gets good, though, is 1974, when the coolest girl in the world moved in to the house across the street. . . .

Marah lost herself in the story of a lonely fourteen-year-old girl who got made fun of on the bus and lived through her favorite fictional characters.

They called me Kootie and laughed at my clothes, and I never said a word, just hugged my schoolbooks closer to my chest. Frodo was my best friend that year, and Gandalf and Sam and Aragon. I imagined myself on some mythical quest.

Marah could picture it: an unpopular girl who met another lonely girl; the start of a friendship that changed both of their lives.

When I met your father, it was magic. Sometimes, if you're lucky, you can look into a pair of eyes and see your whole future. I wish that kind of love for you kids—don't accept anything less. When I held my babies and looked into their murky eyes, I found my life's work. I was born to be a mother, and I loved every second of it. You and your brothers, Marah, taught me everything there was to know about love, and it breaks my heart to leave you.

The journal kept going, winding and turning and bending through the years of her mother's life.

Here's what you need to know, Marah. I know losing me will wound you deeply. You'll remember our arguments.

Forget them, baby girl. That was just you being you and me being me. Remember the rest of it—the hugs, the kisses, the sand castles we made, the cupcakes we decorated, the stories we told each other. Remember how I loved you. Let everything else go. Just remember how we loved each other.

Love. Family. Laughter. That's what I remember.

Marah pictured her mother down to the minutest detail—her blond hair that never seemed to fall right, her green eyes that looked right into your soul, the way she knew when a slammed door was an invitation and when it wasn't, the way she laughed, the way she whispered, "Always, baby girl," just before a kiss good night.

"Oh, my God, Tully. . . . I remember her. . . ."

I FEEL my heart beating. But there is something prodding me, unsettling the beat of my heart. I open my eyes, but there is nothing.

"Tully."

That's me. Or it was me. I become aware of tiny bits of light. Words. The starlight points are words, floating down to me.

". . . the sand castles we made . . ."

I draw in a sharp breath of discovery. *Marah.*

It is her voice I hear, but the words are Kate's. Her journal. I read it so many times over the years, I have memorized it.

Someone takes my hand. *You can hear her,* Kate says.

I turn, and there she is, bathed in gorgeous, impossible light. I see her inside the glow—her green eyes, her blond hair, her wide smile.

Through the dark I hear: "Oh, my God, Tully. I remember her."

Just like that, I remember *me*. The life I lived, the lessons I didn't learn, the way I failed the people I loved. I remember watching them gather around my bedside. I want them back. I want me back.

I stare at Katie and see it in her eyes: our past. There's more, too: longing. I see the love she has for us—me, Johnny, her children, her parents—and how that love is shiny with both hope and loss.

What do you want, Tully?

Marah's words fall around us, glimmering, landing on my skin like kisses. "I want another chance," I say, and as I say it, the power of my choice pulses through me, gives strength to my tired limbs.

I came to say good-bye. I need to move on, Tul. So do you. I need you to say good-bye to me and smile. That's all I need.

"I'm afraid."

Fly away.

"But—"

I'm gone, Tul. But I'll always be with you. Go. . . .

"I'll never forget us."

I know that. Now go. Live. . . . It's such a gift. And tell my boys—

"I know," I say quietly. She has given me messages. I will tell Lucas that his mother comes to him at night and whispers in his ear and watches over his sleep, that she is happy and wants the same for him. I'll tell Wills it's okay to be sad and to stop fighting to fill that empty space where his mom used to be. *I'm not gone*—that was her message. *Just away.*

Turning away from her is the hardest thing I've ever done. Instantly I am cold, and my body feels heavy. There is a huge hill in front of me. I have to get to the top, where the world is, but I am so tired. I climb slowly. Each step fights me.

I am not going to make it.

No. I *will* make it. I imagine Katie beside me, just like the old days, pushing our bikes up Summer Hill with only moonlight to guide us. I surge forward, and suddenly I am cresting the hill.

Light is everywhere now. I blink.

"I did it, Katie," I whisper. There is someone beside me.

Marah. She looks like she used to, beautiful and healthy. "Tully?" she says cautiously, as if I am a spirit or an illusion.

My girl is back. "Marah" takes me forever to say.

I try to smile, but I am so weak. Is that my mother's face? It can't be. Maybe I imagine it. The next thing I know, I'm asleep again.

CHAPTER SIXTEEN

DOROTHY sat in the waiting room, hands clasped in her lap. They were all here now—Johnny and his twin sons, Marah, Margie and Bud. It had been three days since Tully opened her eyes and tried to speak. They had immediately moved her back to the hospital.

It had seemed like a miracle at first, but now she wasn't so sure.

Dr. Bevan assured them that Tully was truly waking; he told them that it often took time to become fully conscious after so long. He warned that there would probably be some lasting effects.

Dorothy had prayed for this moment. Her prayer was always the same: *Please, God, let her wake up.* What if Tully woke up and wanted nothing to do with her?

"You're humming again," Margie said gently.

"I'm afraid."

"Of course you are. You're a mother. Fear is the job description."

"What if she doesn't want anything to do with me when she wakes up?"

Margie's smile was sad. "She always wanted something to do with you, Dorothy. I remember the first time she asked me what was wrong with her, why you didn't love her. It broke my heart. I told her that sometimes life didn't work out the way you expected but that you never gave up hope. She was seventeen then. Your mother had just died, and she was afraid of where she would live. We took her in, gave her a place to live. That very first night, when she was in bed in Katie's room, I sat down beside her and told her good night. She looked up at me and said, 'She'll miss me someday,' and I said, 'How could she not?' and Tully said, 'I'll wait.' And she did, Dorothy. She waited for you in a thousand different ways."

Dorothy wished she were the kind of woman who could believe a thing like that.

TIME passed for Tully in blurry images—a white car, a moving bed, a TV tucked up in the corner of a white room, voices that were a distant drone. Now there was only one voice. Sounds came at her, breaking apart, forming . . . words.

"Hello, Tully."

She blinked slowly and opened her eyes. There was a man standing beside her. A man in a white coat.

"I'm Dr. Bevan. You're in Sacred Heart Hospital. You were in a car accident and sustained a serious head trauma. Your left arm was broken, as was your left ankle. Both bones healed nicely."

Car accident? "How . . . long?" She would sleep for a minute. She heard something. She opened her eyes.

"Hey."

Johnny. He was here, beside her. Behind him stood Margie and Marah and . . . Cloud? What was her mother doing here?

"You're back," Johnny said. "We thought we'd lost you."

She was desperate to tell him. "Johnny . . . I . . ." *Saw her.* What did that mean? Saw who?

"Don't worry, Tul," he said. "We have time now."

She closed her eyes and drifted back to sleep.

Johnny was still there when she woke up again. So was Margie. It felt different, this waking; she knew it instantly.

Margie saw her open her eyes. "There you are."

"Hey," Tully croaked. It took concentration to find that simple word. She could tell that her speech was slow, a little slurry.

"How long . . . here?" She knew there were more words that belonged in her question, but she couldn't grab hold of them.

"You got here six days ago," Johnny said evenly. He drew in a breath. "Your accident was on September third, 2010."

Margie said, "Today is August twenty-seventh, 2011."

"You were in a coma for almost a year," Johnny said.

She closed her eyes, feeling a little flutter of panic. She couldn't remember anything about a car accident or being in a coma, or—

Hey, Tul.

Suddenly it was there in the darkness with her, a beautiful memory. Two women on bikes, riding, their arms outstretched and . . . starlight . . . Katie beside her saying, *Who says you get to die?*

It couldn't be real. She'd imagined it. That had to be the answer.

"They had me on some big drugs, I guess, right?" Tully said.

"Yes," Margie said. "To save your life."

So that was it. In a drugged-out half-dead state, she'd imagined her best friend. It was hardly a surprise.

"You have some therapy to do," Margie said. "Dr. Bevan doesn't think it will be long before you're ready to live at home by yourself."

"Home," Tully said quietly, wondering exactly where that was.

IN HER DREAM SHE WAS IN AN Adirondack chair by the beach and Katie was beside her. But it wasn't the gray pebbled shore of Bainbridge Island, nor was it the choppy blue waters of the bay.

Where are we? her dream self asked, and as she waited for an answer, light spilled across the turquoise water, illuminated everything until it was so bright Tully couldn't see.

When someone hip-bumps you or tells you that it's not all about you or when our music plays, listen and you'll hear me in all of it.

Tully woke with a start.

Katie.

The memory of being in the light bowled her over. She'd been with Katie somewhere—over there. She'd held her hand, heard her say, *I'll always be with you. Whenever you hear our music or laugh so hard you cry, I'll be there. When you close your eyes at night and remember, I'll be there. Always.*

It was real. Somehow. Impossibly. It wasn't drugs or her brain injury or wishful thinking. It was real.

THE next day was an endless series of medical tests: Tully was poked and prodded and zapped and x-rayed. It surprised her—and everyone else—how quickly she was improving.

"Are you ready?" Johnny said when she'd been discharged.

"Where is everyone?"

"Preparing for your homecoming. Are you ready?"

She sat in a wheelchair, wearing a helmet in case of a fall.

"Yeah." She had trouble finding words, so she kept it simple.

"How many of your fans are out there?"

She gave a sigh. "No fans for me."

He turned her wheelchair toward the window. "Look closely."

Down in front of the hospital's entrance was a crowd of people in the parking lot. There were at least three dozen of them. "I don't see . . ." she started, and then she saw the signs.

WE ♥ U TULLY ♥!
UR GIRLFRIENDS NEVER GAVE UP!

"Your recovery is big news. Fans and reporters started gathering as soon as word leaked. They love you, Tul."

She didn't know what to say to that. Johnny grabbed the chair's rubberized handles and wheeled her out of the room.

In the lobby he stopped and set the brake. "I won't be long. I'll just send your fans and the reporters on their way."

As Johnny came forward, cameras pointed at him.

"I know you have all been apprised of Tully Hart's miraculous recovery. The doctors here at Sacred Heart, especially Dr. Reginald Bevan, gave Tully exceptional care, and I know she'd want me to thank them for her. I know she'd want me to thank her fans, too."

"Where is she?" someone yelled.

Johnny held up a hand. "I'm sure you can all understand that Tully is focused on her recovery right now. She—"

A gasp went through the crowd.

Tully sat just outside the hospital doors. She was out of breath, and the chair was cockeyed, no doubt because she was too weak to roll herself steadily forward. He went to her.

"Are you sure?" he asked her.

"Abso . . . lutely. Let's do it."

He wheeled her forward; the crowd quieted.

She smiled uneasily at them, said, "I've looked better."

The roar of approval almost knocked Johnny back.

"Thank you," she said when the crowd finally quieted down.

"When will you go back on air?" one of the reporters yelled.

She looked out across the crowd and then at Johnny. He knew how desperately she had always needed to be *someone*. Hell, she'd given up everything to be loved by strangers.

She drew in a deep breath and said, "No more." She wanted to explain herself, to say that she was done with fame, that she didn't need it anymore, but it was just too hard.

The crowd erupted in noise; questions were hurled at Tully.

She turned to Johnny. "I've never been more proud of you," he said, too softly for anyone to hear.

"For quitting?"

He touched her face. "For never quitting." He took control of the wheelchair and steered her back into the hospital lobby.

In no time they were in the car and heading north on I-5.

She was supposed to be going home. "Wrong way."

"Are you in the driver's seat?" Johnny asked. He didn't glance at her, but she could tell he was smiling. "No. You're not. I know you've recently suffered a brain injury, but I'm sure you remember that the driver drives the car and the passenger enjoys the view."

"Where . . . we going?"

"Snohomish."

For the first time, Tully thought about her yearlong coma. How come no one had told her where she'd been all that time? "Have Bud and Margie been taking care of me?"

He exited the highway toward Snohomish. "You've been staying at your house in Snohomish. With your mother."

"My *mother?*"

His gaze softened. "There have been more than a few miracles in all of this."

Tully didn't know what to say. And yet, a memory teased her. Katie saying, *Listen. It's your mother.*

Johnny pulled up to the house on Firefly Lane and stopped, turning toward Tully. "I don't know how to tell you how sorry I am."

The tenderness she felt for this man was so sharp it was almost pain. How could she make him understand what she'd learned in that darkness—and in the light?

"I saw her," she said quietly. "Katie. Call me crazy or brain damaged or drugged. Whatever. I saw her, and she told me to tell you 'You did fine, and there's nothing for the kids to forgive you for.'"

He frowned.

"She thought you'd been kicking your ass about not being strong enough for her. You wish you'd let her tell you she was afraid. She said, 'Tell him he was all I ever needed and he said everything I needed to hear.'"

Tully reached over and held his hand. "I'll forgive you for breaking my heart if you forgive me, too. For all of it."

He nodded slowly. "I missed you, Tul."

"Yeah, Johnny boy. I missed you, too."

MARAH threw herself into the decorations for Tully's homecoming, but even as she talked to her grandparents and teased with her brothers, she felt as if she were walking on eggshells. She wanted Tully's forgiveness so desperately, but she didn't deserve it. The only other person who looked uncomfortable with the upcoming celebration was Dorothy. While everyone had busied themselves with decorating, Dorothy had said something about needing supplies at the nursery. She'd been gone for hours.

At Tully's homecoming, everyone cheered and clapped and welcomed her back to the house .

"I *knew* you'd be okay," Lucas told Tully. "I prayed every night."

"*I* prayed every night, too," Wills said, not to be outdone.

Tully looked exhausted sitting there, her head cocked in a strange way; the clunky silver helmet made her look almost childlike. "I know . . . two boys . . . who have a birthday coming up. I missed a year. Buy *two* presents now." Tully had to work really hard to say all that, and when she was done, she was out of breath.

"Probably Ferraris," Dad said.

Grandma laughed, and sent the boys to the kitchen for the cake.

Marah made it through the party. Fortunately for her, Tully tired easily and said her good nights at about eight o'clock.

"Roll me to bed?" Tully said, taking hold of her hand, squeezing.

"Sure." Marah wheeled her godmother down the hallway toward the back bedroom. There she maneuvered Tully into the room, where there was a hospital bed, flowers everywhere, and pictures on the tables. An IV stand stood beside the bed.

"This is where I've been," Tully said. "For a year. . . ."

"Yes."

Marah helped her into the bathroom, where Tully brushed her teeth and slipped into a nightgown. Then she got back into the wheelchair and Marah maneuvered her to the bed. There, she helped Tully to her feet.

Tully faced her. In one look, Marah saw all of it: *My job is to love you . . . the fight . . . You're my best friend . . .* and the lies.

"I missed you," Tully said.

Marah burst into tears. Suddenly she was crying for all of it—for the loss of her mom and for finding her in the journal, for the way she'd betrayed Tully, and all the wounds she'd inflicted on people who loved her. Tully brought her hands up slowly, cupped Marah's cheek in her palms. "Your voice brought me back."

"The *Star* article—"

"Old news. Here, help me into bed. I'm exhausted."

Marah wiped her eyes and helped Tully into bed. Then she climbed up into bed beside her, just like in the old days.

Tully was quiet for a long moment before she said: "It's true, all that going-into-the-light/your-life-flashing-before-your-eyes stuff. When I was in the coma, I . . . left my body. I could see your dad in the hospital room with me. It was like I was looking down on this woman who looked just like me but wasn't me. And I couldn't take it, so I turned, and there was this . . . light, and I followed it, and the next thing I knew, I was on my bike on Summer Hill, riding in the dark. With your mom beside me."

Marah drew in a sharp breath, clamped a hand over her mouth.

"She's with us, Marah. She will *always* be watching over you and loving you."

"I want to believe that."

"It's a choice." Tully smiled. "She's glad you ditched the pink hair, by the way. I was supposed to tell you that. And there was one more thing. . . ." She frowned, trying to remember. "She said, 'All things come to an end, even this story.' Does that make sense?"

"It's from *The Hobbit,*" Marah said.

"The kid's book? That's weird."

Marah smiled. She didn't think it was weird at all.

"I'M DOROTHY, and I'm an addict."

"Hi, Dorothy!"

She stood in the middle of the ragtag circle of people who had come to tonight's Narcotics Anonymous meeting. She needed this tonight, of all nights.

At the close of the meeting, she left the church and got onto her bicycle. She rode along the main street, then headed out of town.

At her place, she veered down onto the driveway and came to a stop. Balancing her bike against the side of the house, she went to the front door and turned the knob. Inside, a few lights had been left on, but mostly it was quiet.

She closed the door behind her. Everywhere she looked, she saw evidence of the party she'd missed—the banner, the stack of brightly colored napkins on the counter, the wineglasses drying by the sink. What a coward she was.

She found herself heading toward the back door, going out onto the deck. She smelled cigarette smoke.

"You were waiting for me?" she said quietly.

Margie said, "Of course. I knew how hard this would be for you. But you've been hiding long enough. Do you remember what I told you about motherhood?"

Dorothy sat down. "You told me a lot of things."

"When you're a mom, you learn about fear. You're always afraid. Always." She turned. "The irony is they need us to be strong. I was strong for my Katie," Margie said.

Dorothy heard the way her friend's voice broke on that, and she got up from her chair and pulled Margie up into her arms. She felt how thin the woman was.

When Margie drew back, her eyes were wet with tears. "You helped me get through it, you know that, right? All those times you let me sit over here and smoke my cigarettes while you planted your seeds and pulled up your weeds."

"I didn't say anything."

"You were there for me, Dorothy. Like you were there for Tully." She tried to smile, then said, "Go see your daughter."

TULLY woke from a deep sleep, disoriented. She sat up quickly.

"Tully, are you okay?"

She blinked slowly and remembered where she was. In her old bedroom, in the house on Firefly Lane.

Her mother sat in a chair against the wall. She was wearing white socks and Birkenstock sandals. And the tattered remnant of that macaroni necklace Tully had made for her in Bible camp.

Dorothy turned on the bedside light. "I . . . was worried. Your first night here and all. I hope you don't mind that I'm here."

"Hey, Cloud," Tully said.

"I'm Dorothy now," her mother said. She moved toward the bed. "I picked the name Cloud at a commune in the early seventies. A lot of bad ideas seemed good back then."

"I'm told you took care of me."

"It was nothing."

"A year of caring for a woman in a coma? That's not nothing."

Her mother reached into her pocket and pulled out a small gold token. A triangle was stamped onto the coin; on the left side of the triangle was the word SOBRIETY in black, on the right side was the word ANNIVERSARY. Inside the triangle was the Roman numeral V. "Remember that night you saw me in the hospital, back in '05?"

Tully remembered every time she'd ever seen her mother. "Yes."

"That was rock bottom for me. I went into rehab not long after that. You paid for it, by the way, so thanks for that."

"And you stayed sober?"

"Yes."

Tully was afraid to believe in the unexpected hope that unfurled at her mother's confession. And she was afraid not to. "That's why you came to my condo and tried to help me."

"As interventions go, it was pretty lame." She smiled crookedly. "I took care of you to make up for all the times I didn't."

"I heard your voice," Tully said. *I'm so proud of you. I never told you that, did I?* "You stood by my bed and told me a story."

Her mother looked startled and then a little sad. "I should have told it to you years ago."

"You said you were proud of me."

She reached out and touched Tully's cheek with a mother's tenderness. "How could I not be proud of you? I always loved you, Tully. It was my own life I was running from." Slowly she reached into the nightstand drawer and pulled out a photograph. "Maybe this will be our beginning." She handed the picture to Tully.

It was about the size of a playing card, with white scalloped edges that were bent and mangled. It was a photograph of a young man, sitting on a porch step. His hair was long and black. His cowboy boots had seen better days, and his hands were dark with grime.

But his smile was wide and white and should have been too big for his angular face but wasn't. His eyes were as black as night. Beside him a brown-haired baby lay sleeping in a baggy diaper. The man's hand lay possessively on the infant's small, bare back.

"You and your father," her mother said softly.

"My father? You said you didn't know who—"

"I lied. I fell in love with him in high school."

Tully looked back down at the picture, barely able to breathe. She had never seen a hint of her own features in a relative's face. But here was her *dad,* and she looked like him. "I have his smile."

"Yes. And you laugh just like he did."

Tully felt something deep inside of her click into place.

"He loved you," her mother said. "And me, too."

Tully heard the break in her mother's voice.

"Rafael Benecio Montoya—Rafe."

Tully couldn't hold on to the emotion swelling inside her heart. This changed *everything,* changed her. She had a father. A dad. And he *loved* her. "Can I—"

"Rafe died in Vietnam."

Tully didn't realize that she'd even constructed a dreamscape, but she felt it fall to pieces around her. "Oh."

"I'll tell you all about him, though," her mother said. "How he used to sing songs to you in Spanish and throw you into the air to hear you laugh. He picked your name because it was Choctaw, and he said that made you a *real* American. That's why I always called you Tallulah. To remember him."

Tully looked up into her mother's watery eyes and saw love and loss and heartache. And hope, too. The whole of their lives. "I've waited so long."

Dorothy gently touched Tully's cheek. "I know," she said softly.

It was the touch Tully had waited for all of her life.

In her dreams, Tully is sitting in one of the Adirondack chairs on my deck. I am beside her, of course; we are as we used to be: young and laughing. Always talking. In the branches of that old maple tree, several Mason jars hang from lengths of twine; in them votive candles burn brightly over our heads.

I know that sometimes, when Tully sits in her chair out here, she thinks about me. She remembers the two of us flying down Summer Hill on bikes, our arms outflung.

Here, in her dreams, we will be friends forever, together. Here there will be no cancer, no growing old, no lost chances, no arguments. I'm always with you, I say to her in her sleep, and she knows it's true.

I turn, just a sideways glance, and I am somewhere else, some when else. Inside my house on Bainbridge Island. My family is gathered together, laughing over some joke. Marah is home from college for winter break; she has made the kind of friend that lasts through a lifetime. My father is healthy. Johnny has begun to smile again—soon he will find himself falling in love. He will fight it . . . and he will give in. And my beautiful sons are becoming men before my very eyes. Wills still goes through life in fifth gear, loud and booming and defiant, while Lucas slips along behind, barely noticed in a crowd until you see his smile. But it is Lucas I hear at night, Lucas who talks to me in his sleep, afraid that he will forget me. The way I miss them all is sometimes unbearable. But they are going to be fine. I know it, and now they do, too.

Soon my mom will be with me, although she doesn't know it yet.

I look away for an instant, and I am back on Firefly Lane. It is morning. Tully limps out into the kitchen and has tea with her mother, and they work in the garden, and I can see how strong she is growing. No more wheelchair for her. Not even a cane now.

Time passes. How much?

In her world, maybe days. Weeks . . .

And suddenly there is a man in the orchard, talking to Dorothy.

Tully moves toward him. Her steps are slow, and her balance is still a little tenuous. She passes her mother and goes to the man.

"Des," Tully says. She reaches out for him, and he takes her hand in his. When they touch, I glimpse their future—beach with a pair of wooden chairs set near the tideline . . . a table set for some holiday dinner, with my family and hers gathered around it . . . an aging house with a wraparound porch that overlooks the sea. I see all of this in the time it takes my best friend's heart to take a single beat.

I know in that moment she will be okay. Life will go on for her as it must, but she will always remember us—two girls who'd taken a chance on each other a lifetime ago and become best friends.

I move closer to her; I know she feels me. At last, I whisper in her ear. She hears me, or maybe she only thinks she knows what I would say now. It doesn't matter.

It is time for me to let go.

Not of TullyandKate. We will always be a part of each other.

But I have to move on, as she has.

When I look back one last time, from far, far away, she is smiling.

Share Your Thoughts!

Communicate with us directly to chat about the stories and tell us what you liked or disliked. We want to keep giving you the kinds of books you want to read, and this is one way to make that happen. So let us know what you think. Share your thoughts with us at **SelectEditions@gmail.com**.

Second Time Around

KRISTIN Hannah has published twenty novels, but *Fly Away,* which continues the story of *Firefly Lane* (2008), is her first sequel. *Firefly Lane* explored the teenage friendship of Kate and Tully, following them into adulthood and ending with the death of Kate from breast cancer. *Fly Away* deals with the aftermath of Kate's death, and its profound affect on both Tully and Kate's family.

So why a sequel? "The book was so personal to me," explains Hannah, referring to *Firefly Lane.* "I ended up very invested in the characters, and I always knew there was more. I guess I always knew I would come back to it. I didn't think it would be five years later, but it took me a while to find the story." For those five years, Hannah found herself haunted by Tully and Kate. "I couldn't quite let them go, even when I went on to write other novels."

Hannah was careful to make *Fly Away* a novel that could stand on its own and not be dependent on its predecessor. That process, however, was a challenge. When she first decided to tackle the sequel, she found she had too many options. Which characters should she focus on? She wrote multiple drafts, but nothing seemed to work. "I felt lost in the forest of too many choices," she said.

Finally she figured out what was wrong: She was missing Kate. Kate was the character who held everyone together in the first book, so Hannah realized she needed to be the anchor in the sequel as well. However, there was a problem. She'd killed off Kate in *Firefly Lane*.

Being a spiritual person, Hannah chose to take a risk. "I asked my readers to accompany me on an extraordinary journey . . . even if it was a little unorthodox," she says. Once she made this decision, *Fly Away* quickly fell into place, and the writing flowed.

Because *Firefly Lane* had been so popular, Hannah felt a lot of pressure not to let her fans down. "I have been blown away by your support of Kate and Tully and the world of *Firefly Lane*," she told her readers on her blog. "I thought of you all the time while writing this book. It was so important to me that I not disappoint you."

Both books have a special spot in her heart. Much of *Firefly Lane* came from her own history, in part because Hannah's mother died of breast cancer. "It took me a long time to find the strength to go back and look at that topic." But as she wrote, Hannah found it actually made her feel closer to her mother. ◼

Vital Stats

BORN: September 1960; Southern California
RESIDENCES: Washington State and Hawaii
FAMILY: Husband; one son
FAVORITE BOOK: *To Kill A Mockingbird* by Harper Lee
WRITES HER BOOKS: Longhand
FAVORITE VACATION PLACE: Botswana or Hawaii
WEBSITE: KristinHannah.com

ACKNOWLEDGMENTS

Pages 4 and 147: © John Taylor. Pages 4 and 293: Bill
Miles. Pages 5 and 395: © Hachette UK Ltd. Pages 5 and
575: Charles Bush.

The original editions of the books in this volume are published and copyrighted as follows:

THE SILVER STAR, published at $26.00 by Scribner, a division of Simon & Schuster, Inc.
© 2013 by Jeannette Walls

POLITICAL SUICIDE, published at $27.99 by St. Martin's Press, LLC
© 2013 by Michael Palmer

A STREET CAT NAMED BOB, published at $24.99 by Thomas Dunne Books,
an imprint of St. Martin's Press, LLC
© 2012 by James Bowen and Garry Jenkins

FLY AWAY, published at $27.99 by St. Martin's Press, LLC
© 2013 by Kristin Hannah

The volumes in this series are issued every two to three months.
The typical volume contains four outstanding books in condensed form.
None of the selections in any volume has appeared in *Reader's Digest* itself.
Any reader may receive this service by writing
The Reader's Digest Association, Inc.,
44 South Broadway, White Plains, NY 10601
or by calling 1-800-481-1454.
In Canada write to:
The Reader's Digest Association (Canada) Ltd.,
1125 Stanley Street, Montreal, Quebec H3B 5H5
or call 1-800-465-0780.

Some of the titles in this volume are also available in a large-print format.
For information about Select Editions Large Type call 1-800-877-5293.

Visit us on the Web at:
rd.com
readersdigest.ca (in Canada)